This belon

Claire

VOLUME I

The Complete Marquis de Sade

*Translated From
The Original French Text By*
Dr. Paul J. Gillette

With An Introduction By
John S. Yankowski

AN ORIGINAL HOLLOWAY HOUSE EDITION
HOLLOWAY HOUSE PUBLISHING CO.
LOS ANGELES, CALIFORNIA

HOLLOWAY HOUSE CLASSICS are published by

Kensington Publishing Corp.
119 West 40th Street
New York, NY 10018

Volume I:
Copyright © 1966, 2005 by Paul J. Gillete.
First Holloway House Classics mass market printing: 2008

HOLLOWAY HOUSE CLASSICS is a trademark of Kensington Publishing Corp.

Front cover illustration by Man Ray
Cover design by Thomas Moroney

International Standard Book Number 978-0-87067-940-7
Printed in the United States of America

10 9 8 7 6 5 4 3 2

www.kensingtonbooks.com

To:
George G. Hornbeck
... a distinguished scholar,
an esteemed friend

Table of Contents

Volume I

EDITORS' NOTE

THE EDITORS OF Holloway House take great pride in presenting this first English-language edition of the four major works of Marquis de Sade. For years, book racks both in America and abroad have overflowed with cheap — and, occasionally, not-so-cheap — abridgements of some of the works, notably JUSTINE and JULIETTE. However, these "pastiche" versions rarely even resembled the originals, and certainly came nowhere near preserving the author's spirit, style, flavor and intent. Conversely, recent months have seen the appearance of several so-called "complete" editions, by which is meant the literal translation into English of Sade's exact language. Unfortunately, these "complete" versions come complete with Sade's repetitions and redundancies, his dreary polemics and his use of a syntactically complex Eighteenth Century idiom which is all but unreadable today. The present edition is an attempt to strike a happy medium between the "completes" and the "pastiches." It retains all Sade's crucial philosophical points, all his stark language and all his extraordinary action scenes while shedding those "vices" which have long made reading the original works such an exercise in tedium.

PAUL J. GILLETTE, who translated, edited and adapted this edition, is rapidly gaining recognition as one of the world's foremost authorities on erotic literature. Dr. Gillette aroused considerable literary controversy with SATYRICON: MEMOIRS OF A LUSTY ROMAN, a complete reconstruction of the famous SATYRICON OF PETRONIUS, which most authorities agree is the first novel ever written; although many authors in the past had tried their hand at translating individual SATYRICON fragments, Dr. Gillette was the first scholar ever to attempt a complete reconstruction of the 1900-year-old work, and his text may very well be the first to render the classic readable as a whole instead of in unintelligible fragmentary form.

A native of Carbondale, Pennsylvania, Dr. Gillette brings to his masterful rendition of Sade not only a background in classical and modern languages and literature but also the insights of contemporary psychology. He has studied at the Universities of Florence and Rome, Italy; Messina, Sicily, and Madrid, Spain. He was with the U. S. Armed Forces Examining Station system as a psychologist, and served as director of the mental testing program conducted by the system at Wilkes-Barre, Pennsylvania, from 1959 to 1961, at which time he turned full-time to writing. Among his medical and scientific writings have been book-length collaborations with Louis S. London, M.D., the dean of American psychiatrists, and articles and monographs for most of the important journals.

Dr. Gillette likewise is no stranger to magazine readers in the United States and on the Continent. Segments of his SATYRICON reconstruction, along with other translations and adaptations from classic French, Spanish, Italian and Polish sources, have appeared in many mass circulation magazines as well as in "reviews" and other scholastic publications. In addition, his startling study of the Ku Klux Klan — first published in 1964, long before the Klan's new wave of violence captured the national spotlight — has been translated into sixteen foreign languages for publication in book form and in magazine and newspaper serialization in twenty-three different countries.

Readers of the Holloway House Library of Paperback Originals will be familiar with, in addition to SATYRICON: MEMOIRS OF A LUSTY ROMAN, Dr. Gillette's wry, droll and wickedly witty UNCENSORED HISTORY OF PORNOGRAPHY, which was published in 1965.

JOHN S. YANKOWSKI, who authored the introductory essay, is one of psychology's most prolific writers. HIS YANKOWSKI REPORT ON PREMARITAL SEX has been hailed as the decade's most definitive analysis of contemporary sex mores in America.

A native of Brooklyn, New York, Mr. Yankowski was raised in Pennsylvania where, in 1959, he joined the epidemiology division of the U. S. Department of Health, Education and Welfare. His work with that agency and with the City of Philadelphia Department of Public Health in the control of venereal disease among urban youths has merited high commendation. He also has been a member of the staff of the National Analyst research organization and the Chilton Research Institute. More recently, he was instrumental in assembling and evaluating data for the U. S. Surgeon General's report on Smoking and Health.

In 1963, Mr. Yankowski left the government health service to devote more time to independent research and to writing. His articles on sexual behavior and his sociollogical studies have appeared in a number of popular, mass-circulation magazines as well as in journals and professional publications. Among his better known works is THE TORTURED SEX, co-authored with Herman K. Wolff and issued under the Holloway House imprint in 1964.

Man Ray, whose strikingly surrealistic portrait of Marquis de Sade serves as this edition's cover illustration, has long been hailed as one of America's most imaginative and far-seeing painters. His best-known work, THE ROPE DANCER ACCOMPANIES HERSELF WITH HER SHADOWS, presently on display at New York's Museum of Modern Art, is recognized as a classic of the dadaist school, and his influence in the employment of inanimate forms as a technique of portraiture has been reflected by such diverse "modernists" as Salvador Dali, Boris Chaliapin and Andrew Wyeth.

Born in Philadelphia, Pennsylvania, in 1890, Mr. Ray soon migrated to New York and became one of the frontrunners in the art world's early-century flight from rigid to plastic forms. During the 1920s he was active in Paris, creating art films (*L'Etoile de Mer,* 1928, is his most widely-known) as well as surrealist paintings. He also distinguished himself as a photographer, and gained world-wide recognition in the field for his invention of the "rayograph," a photograph obtained by the direct application of objects of varying opacity to a light-sensitive plate.

He presently resides in Los Angeles, where he is engaged in free-lance photography and illustration; his paintings have been used for a number of covers in the Holloway House Library of Paperback Originals.

INTRODUCTION

It is with great pleasure that I introduce the compelling, brilliant and briskly readable rendition by Dr. Paul J. Gillette of the novels of the Marquis de Sade. There has long been a need for an authentic, English-language version of these important works — a version which can take its place alongside the classic French editions of Guillaume Apollinaire and Maurice Heine and the German of Dr. Eugen Dühren (pseudonym of Dr. Iwan Bloch, psychiatrist and sexologist). Dr. Gillette's is just such a version.

Who was the Marquis de Sade? What is his importance today?

Donatien Alphonse François de Sade was an obscure French writer and nobleman, who, but for the lending of his name to an act of sexual deviation, would probably be unknown to anyone except a handful of scholars.

He did not, of course, *invent* sadism; this deviation has been known virtually from the dawn of civilization; indeed, sadistic acts are described in literary accounts dating back to Petronius (*1) and Sozomen (*2). However, Sade most certainly was — and this is the reason for his importance to psychiatry and the behavioral sciences — the first writer to describe sadism as a *sexual* enterprise. Likewise, he was the first to describe and to make clear the sexual nature of fetishism, frottage and bestiality; of the anal perversions of buggery (both heterosexual and homosexual), coprolagnia and anilingus; of the non-contact deviations of voyeurism (scopophilia), erotism (ecoteurism) and exhibitionism; of perversions involving the ingestion of secretions and excretions, such as coprophagy, scatophagy, rhypophagy and urophagy; of the deviation involving sexual fascination with dead bodies, necrophilia, and, finally, of the ostensibly non-sexual behaviors of kleptomania and pyromania. Also, He was the first writer to describe true hermaphroditism, the phenomenon of possessing the external reproductive structures of both sexes, and was the first to explore in any great detail such deviations of sexual object as infantosexuality and gerontosexuality. Indeed, it is difficult to find a sexual deviation, either of the instinct or of the object, or to conceive of an abnormal sexual coupling, whether heterosexual, homosexual, autosexual or bestial, which is *not* demonstrated in his works. For this reason alone the novels, *Justine* and *Juliette*; the dialogue, *The Bedroom Philosophers*, and especially the catalogue of "passions," *One Hundred and Twenty Days of Sodom*, are "must" reading for the student of abnormal sexuality.

But let us return to that perversion which Sade championed so vigorously and with such enthusiasm that finally it came to bear his name. What *is* sadism? From where does sadistic desire stem? Which psychic forces translate this desire into action? It is to these questions that we shall now address ourselves.

The best definition of sadism, I think, is that of Hinsie and Campbell (*3): *the sexual perversion in which orgasm is dependent upon the torturing of others or upon the inflicting of pain, ill-treatment and/or humiliation upon others*. The key element in the definition, of course, is *dependency* of orgasm upon the associated acts; a sadist, therefore, does not merely *enjoy* being cruel; rather, his sexual satisfaction hinges upon it: thus, a person whose cruelties, either of the physical or psychic realm, *can not* be traced to conscious, subconscious or unconscious sexual sources, *is not*, strictly speaking, a sadist. This inextricable intertwining in sadism of cruelty and sexual satisfaction is, as I have noted, ever-apparent in the writings of Sade. Unfortunately, however, many previous English-language editions of his works — presumably for purposes of appearing inoffensive to the sexually squeamish — have omitted the sexual elements. This omission is doubly regrettable, for not only is the student of sexual behavior given a completely distorted impression of the nature of sadism but also he is led to believe erroneously that there may be certain nonsexual delights in the perpetration of unmotivated acts of cruelty.

To illustrate the lengths to which producers of expurgated editions go in their seemingly well-intentioned efforts to de-sex Sade, let us compare two versions of the famous scene in *Justine* where the brigand, Roland, induces Justine to participate in a bizarre hanging game called "Cut-the-Cord." To play the game, one party stands on a stool, and, holding a sharp sickle in one hand, inserts his head into a taut noose; next, the second party tugs the stool from under him; the first party then must with his sickle Cut-the-Cord before he chokes to death. This is how the game, de-sexed, is described in a popular 1964 edition:

"... *I am going to strip and get up on this stool (said Roland); you will fasten the rope and I'll excite myself. As soon as you see that I'm about ready you'll pull away the stool, and let me hang for awhile. You'll let me hang until you see my pleasure complete, or notice symptoms of suffering. In the second case you will set me loose at once, but in the first case you will let nature take its full course and loose me only afterwards. You see, Thérèse, I put my life in your hands.*

"Your freedom, fortune, will be the price of your good conduct."

"Ah, sir," said Justine, "It's an extravagant proposal!"

"No, Thérèse, you must!" he answered, undressing. "But behave well. See what proof I give you of my confidence and esteem."

What would have been the good of her wavering — was he not master of her?

He got upon the stool, the rope around his neck, and wanted Justine to rail at him, curse him with all the horrors of his life, all which she did. He got ready and beckoned her to pull away the stool.

Hanging by his neck for awhile, his tongue was lolling half way out, his eyes bulging; but soon, beginning to swoon away, he motioned feebly to Justine to set him loose.

On being revived he said, "Oh Thérèse! one has no idea of such sensations, what a feeling! It surpasses anything I know!"

The careful reader of the above passage might suspect — although only suspect — that Roland is speaking of masturbation when he says, "I'll excite myself." He might conceivably assume that orgasm is meant by "[the moment when] you see my pleasure complete." But he certainly would fail to get the connection between sexual satisfaction and hanging.

Now, let us look at this same incident in Dr. Gillette's translation:

"... *After you've adjusted the noose around my neck, take my customary place on the couch. Then curse at me while I fondle my genitalia, and, when you observe that I have become sufficiently aroused, pull the stool out from under me. However, I will not hold a sickle with which to cut the cord, lest I be tempted to put it to use prematurely. Instead, you hold the sickle, and, when the stool falls, permit me to remain hanging. Leave me there until you witness either the ejaculation of my semen or evidence of the onset of death's throes. If the latter, cut the cord immediately and revive me with slaps about the face and head; but, if the former, allow the ejaculation to continue until my substance is totally spent, and only then cut me down."*

Having directed her thusly, he mounted the stool. Obedient to his instructions, she tightened the noose about his neck. He fondled himself as she cursed at him, and, in seconds, his enormous organ snaked upward. Now he gave her the sign to tug the rope. The stool flew away. And —

It was just as the knave had theorized! As his body snapped under the force of his fall, a broad smile of ecstasy bisected his face. His penis stretched to an almost incredible tautness. Then a geyser of semen erupted, shooting high above his head, almost to the ceiling of the room.

When the last drops were expelled, Justine cut him loose. He fell to the floor, unconscious, but her slaps quickly revived him. His happiness bordered delerium.

"Oh, my lovely child!" he cried. "The sensations

*are beyond credibility! They surpass anything I have
ever conceived!"*

The differences, other than stylistic, between both versions are slight, but they are crucial. As the latter passage testifies, there is in Sade no sadism without sex; neither in fact, is there in life.

From where does sadistic desire stem?

In psychoanalytic terms, two external factors control man's psychic life: love and hate — or, better expressed, the life impulse and the death impulse. The life impulse, positive in orientation, works at preserving the ego; the death impulse, negative in orientation, seeks to destroy that which would imperil the ego. In other words, when I experience the positive emotion of love for Person A, I am stating, in effect, "I love you because you protect my ego," and, when I experience the negative emotion of hate for Person B, I am stating, in effect, "I hate you because you threaten my ego."

Cruelty is an expression of the death impulse; it is the translation into physical terms of the emotion of hate. It acquires a sexual element as the result of a misidentification by the individual of the nature of sexuality. This is to say that the sadist suffers what Stekel (*4) terms "sexual infantilism," or a stunting of the sexual growth; he fears subconsciously that castration will result from indulgence in normal sexual relationships, and therefore he escapes into abnormal (sadistic) relationships in which no danger of castration is seen as being present. Sadism is "selected" as the specific mode of abnormal behavior (rather than, say, voyeurism) because it permits the individual to act out the negation of his fears. The acting-out process is described by Hinsie and Campbell as follows: "What might happen to the subject passively is done actively to others — 'identification with the aggressor.' Further, the castration performed in the sadistic act is a symbolic one, not a real one, and such pseudo-castration assures the sadist that his fears are ungrounded. The sadist tries to force his victim to love him; this love is conceived as forgiveness, which removes the guilt feelings which interfere with sexual satisfaction." The Freudian will recognize this explanation as being within the framework of Fréud's concept of four-stage sexual development (*5). In terms of this concept, sadism is a fixation at or regression to the anal stage.

Other writers, it might be noted, prefer a biological explanation. Schrenk-Notzing (*6) seeks to term sadism, "algolagnia," and to explain the phenomenon purely in terms of the physical sensations involved. (This, I believe, must be rejected as failing to take into account psychic sadists whose satisfaction comes exclusively from humiliating a partner — not from causing him physical pain.) Schuster (*7) takes a somewhat broader view. Regarding "algolagnia" as the "quantitatively-heightened specific impulse to pleasure," he concludes that it is a *genotypically* conditioned disposition, and that, therefore, it can only be evolved, not acquired. (But this, too, is unscientific, for, as Stekel has demonstrated, certain cases of sadistic and masochistic behavior can be traced directly to environmental influences during childhood. Thus, on the basis of present evidence, it would appear that the psychoanalytic interpretations of sadism are the only ones with a claim to validity.)

In any event, all the above theories explain only the presence of sadomasochistic drives — not the intensity of them or the forces which impel an individual to act upon them. Seeking an explanation of these latter aspects — as well as an explanation of homosexuality, fetishism and other atypical behaviors — London (*8,9) conducted research which resulted in a concept of "moral shock" and a subsequent theory of "traumatization of the libido." This theory represents what is to date, in my opion, the most plausible view of sexual deviation; here I shall attempt to present, in terms comprehensible to the layman, its highlights.

The libido is, in a word, energy; it is the human's sexual energy, the force of his sexual attraction, the motive power of his sex life. Its composition may be electric or chemical or both (since we have studied the libido only in its pathology, we do not know its embryology or physiology). Whatever the composition, there can be little doubt that it is reducible to component parts. These parts are related to each other, and to the whole, in the same manner as are related the elements of an organic chemical compound; they cannot be split apart.

London has identified the four parts as follows: a) Heterosexuality; b) Homosexuality; c) Narcissism, and d) the Perversions. These four parts he maintains, are present in every human being — without exception. The difference from person to person is a difference only of proportion. The proportion in which they exist in the so-called normal individual is shown in Diagram 1. We see an overwhelming preponderance of the heterosexual element, circled by barely perceptible portions of the others. Most people develop this pattern in early adolescence; the perverse and homosexual elements are repressed, sublimated or otherwise blotted from consciousness; narcissism is accepted slightly more readily; the heterosexual component prevails. However, this structure is very delicate and greatly predisposed to traumatization. During the early development of the child, there are many psychological traumas. The first is weaning. (Many today have never enjoyed the right to which every mammal is entitled — nursing by the mother's breast. Naturally, if a rubber nipple is substituted, it must have some effect upon the character formation of the individual.) The next trauma comes with toilet training. (A child should be taught correct habits, but not in a manner which inculcates in him a sense of shame about his natural excretory functions. He is not born with a sense of shame, and, if imbued with one, he cannot fail to experience trauma.) Later traumatic experiences occur in the preadolescent and adolescent phases. (The child who, whether through religion, social pressures or other factors, is led to believe that his natural heterosexual drives are wrong, evil, shameful, et cetera, is bound to suffer trauma as a result.)

These traumas — or moral shocks, as London calls them — may or may not have a permanent effect on the individual. Often, as with physical traumas, the wound "heals itself" by natural processes; it "goes away." In other instances, however, the damage is more severe, and, in the case of libidinal traumatization, the brunt is borne by the preponderant heterosexual element. Thus moral shock liberates homosexuality, narcissism and the perversions, for, by the very nature of the libido's composition, any depletion of the heterosexual constituent must divert the libido's total energy so as to augment the other components. (The traumatized libido is shown in Diagram 2.)

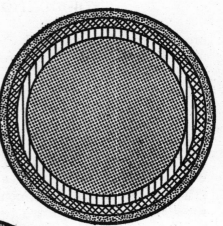

DIAGRAM 1

Mechanism of the
normal libido
showing the
perverse component

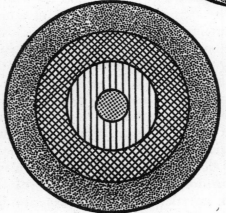

DIAGRAM 2

Mechanism of the
libido after
traumatization
showing the
liberation of
the perversions

KEY TO DIAGRAMS

HETEROSEXUALITY

NARCISSISM

HOMOSEXUALITY

PERVERSIONS - - - -

SADISM
MASOCHISM
EXHIBITIONISM
VOYEURISM
ANILINGUS
COPROPHILIA
UROLAGNIA
FETISHISM
BESTIALITY
KLEPTOMANIA
PYROMANIA
NYMPHOMANIA
SATYRIASIS
ET CETERA

Viewing the libido in this light, we can see that sadism, like the other perversions, is traceable to unhealthy environmental influences in childhood and youth. Of course, the presence of sadistic desire does not mean that this desire will — or should be — acted upon. It is at this point that "defense mechanisms" enter the picture, and the healthy individual sublimates his desires, represses them, compensates for them, et cetera. However, some persons fail in the employment of defense mechanisms: these are they who become overt practitioners of perversion; examples of their practices can be found on every page of Sade.

Thus the character, origins and development of sadism. It now remains for us to treat of that one question which invariably arises with the publication of books like those of Sade: namely, should they not — because of their high content of sex and violence — be banned? I, personally, am firmly convinced that they should not. Apart from the free speech issue, which alone is sufficient in my mind to justify their publication, the fact remains that Sade's works are extremely valuable from the psychiatric and psychological points of view. If the behavioral sciences are to expand, to grow, there must be access to data — and data does not come only in the form of case histories. Long before Krafft-Ebing provided us with *Psychopathia Sexualis* (*9) Sade had drawn up a thorough, detailed and almost unbelievably comprehensive catalogue of deviant sexual behavior. More important, he had provided an unprecedented — and since unparalleled — example of extended sexual fantasy; his excesses in this regard — those monstrous excesses of sex and violence which his critics decry — are the very strengths of his work, the very elements which make his books not merely adventure stories but documents of considerable scientific value. If we fail to avail ourselves of that which he has placed at our disposal, we shall be all the poorer for it.

John S. Yankowski, Philadelphia, Pa. 1966

NOTES:

1. Petronius Arbiter, *Satyricon*: *Memoirs of a Lusty Roman*, a reconstruction in modern English by Paul J. Gillette. Los Angeles: Holloway House, 1965.

2. Sozomen, *Historiae*, as quoted by Kiefer, Otto, in *Kulturgeschichte Roms uter Besonderer Berucksichtigung der Romischen Sitten*. Bonn: Verlig, 1931.

3. Hinsie, Leland E., and Campbell Robert J., *Psychiatric Dictionary* (Third Edition), New York: Oxford University Press, 1960.

4. Stekel, Wilhelm, *Sadism and Masochism* (Vol. I and II). New York: Horace Liveright, 1929.

5. Freud, Sigmund, *Collected Papers* (Vols. I, II, III and V). New York: International Psychoanalytic Press, 1924.

6. Schrenk-Notzing, D. *Die Suggestiontherapie bei Krankhaften Erscheinungen des Geschlechtssines*. Leipzig: F.C.W. Vogel, 1914.

7. Schuster, Karl. *Schmerz und Geschlechtstrieb. Versuch einer Analyze und Theorie der Algolagnia*. Leipzig: Kurt Kabitsch, 1923.

8. London, Louis S. *Dynamic Psychiatry — Basic Principles*. New York: Corinthian, 1952.

9. London, Louis S. "Psychosexual Pathology — Sadism and Masochism," *Boletin de la Asociacion Medica de Puerto Rico*, July 1933.

10. Krafft-Ebing, Richard von, *Psychopathia Sexualis*. New York: Pioneer Publishers, 1944.

FOREWORD

Donatien Alphonse François de Sade only recently has become controversial: for the seventy-four years during which he roamed the earth and for perhaps a century and a half afterwards, opinion of him and his writings was virtually unanimous — and all bad. "Evil's apologist," he has been called; "the devil's disciple;" "satan's saint." And his works: "monstrous," "depraved," "repellent." "heinous," "horrible" and "repulsive." Guillaume Villeterque, writing in *Journal des Arts, des Sciences et de Litterature* on October 22, 1800, said of the newly-published *Les Crimes de l'Amour*: "A tissue of horrors . . . an odious book by an even more odious man." Meanwhile, Jules Janin, in *Revue de Paris, 1834*, noted the twentieth anniversary of Sade's death with this vigorous exercise in invective: ". . . Bleeding corpses, children ravished from their mother's arms, young girls massacred at the end of an orgy, cups overflowing with blood and wine, unimaginable sufferings, inconceivable tortures . . . What an indefatigable monster; . . . When he reaches the end of his crimes, when he has exhausted his fund of incests and bestialities, when at last he is there, panting over the bodies he has stabbed and violated, when there remains no church to be polluted, no child he has not butchered in his rage, not a single moral idea upon which he has not smeared the filth of his odious doctrines and language, only then is it that he halts . . . and looks at himself . . . and smiles." Perhaps no one identifies the consensus more accurately than Maurice Blanchot, writing in *Les Editions de Minuit* in 1949: "If there exists in libraries a hell — a special section for works deemed unfit for human consumption — it is for such a book (as Sade's *Justine et Juliette*). No literature of any period has seen a work so scandalous, one which has so profoundly wounded the thoughts and feelings of men . . . Yes, the claim can be made: we have here the most scandalous work ever written . . . a work beyond which no other writer, at any time, has ever managed to venture."

Whence, then, the controversy? It stems principally from the fact that, somewhere or other among his catalogues of carnality and carnage, Sade has articulated, usually for the first time anywhere, some of the Twentieth Century's most thought-about thoughts: a quarter century before Charles Darwin's birth, he discussed nature in evolutionary terms; half a century before Havelock Ellis and Richard von Krafft-Ebing, he produced a volume of descriptive sexual pathology; a century before Sigmund Freud, he postulated the existence of an unconscious mind; a century and a half before Margaret Mead and Margaret Sanger, he both probed sex mores anthropologically and warned of the necessity of population control; some of his political views have been put into practice by such diverse figures as Joseph Stalin, Adolph Hitler, Francisco Franco, Benito Mussolini, Mao Tse-tung, Fidel Castro and Ian Smith; in economics, he has anticipated the tenets of the *laissez faire* school of "economic libertarianism" championed by Adam Smith, William Ewart Gladstone, Friedrich A. von Hayek, Frank Knight and Milton Friedman; and, if Soren Kirkegaard and Jean-Paul Sartre can be said to be, respectively, the grandfather and father of existentialist philosophy, Sade most assuredly can take credit for contributing a seed or two somewhere far back on the generative trail. The reader who would expand upon this list need only take a pen in hand and make random notations as the works unfold; chances are that he will develop several additional categories and think of the names of several dozen additional men before scarcely one hundred pages have passed.

What manner of man was this infamous marquis who at once both appalled the world yet contributed so much to its store of ideas? Sade was, in his own words, the absolute egoist; a *professeur de crime*; a seeker of *plaisir a tout prix*; a *connoisseur de neuropathie de toutes sortes*. But to take him at his own word is to sell the man considerably short: a mere *roué*, after all, does not read every book on history and philosophy in *Bibliothèque Nationale*; Sade did, and documented his original manuscripts with volume and page-number references to a great many of them: a mere *lécheur* does not conceptualize — and sketch out a constitution for — a *republique universelle*; Sade did, more than one hundred and twenty-five years before the Treaty of Versailles established a League of Nations. In this regard it is interesting to compare Sade with a genuine rake, his more widely read contemporary, Giovanni Giacomo Casanova, *Le Chevalier de Seingalt*: perhaps nothing is more surprising to the reader of Casanova's *Memoirs* than the persistence with which The Great Lover begs for recognition as an intellectual giant as well as a sexual one; he drops the names of ancient Greek and Roman dieties like a sophomore mythology major, recounts at all-but-interminable length a supposed meeting with Voltaire (significantly, Voltaire never made any mention of it in *his* writing) and devotes page after page after page to the labored paraphrase of one or another familiar philosophical theory (none of them any newer than Epicurus), then disposes of his extraordinary sexual exploits with the nonchalance of an Albert Einstein regarding a multiplication table; Sade, conversely, grinds out 10,000 words just setting forth the by-laws of a sex club, stages a 20,000-word debate over which party receives the greatest pleasure in a multiple sex act and puts himself to the task of thinking up twenty-five different euphemisms for an erect penis, then demolishes the entire case for capital punishment in a neat, two-sentence *riposte* and set up a model penal code almost as a throw-away; it doesn't take a mind-reader to figure out which of the two feels inadequate about what.

But let us not get sidetracked into a posthumous psychoanalysis of Sade: the words men write live after them; their psyches should be interred with their bones. Sade's words — all told, nearly five million of them — were written almost entirely behind bars: counting his last sentence at Charenton, which technically was not a prison but an "asylum for the criminally insane," he spent twenty-seven years in eleven different jails. What were his offenses? How, if at all, did they relate to the philosophies he sets forth in his works? With an eye toward answering these questions and with the intent of placing the works themselves in historical perspective, let us examine briefly Sade's personal life.

Donatien Alphonse François de Sade was born on June 2, 1740, in the sunny southeastern French province of Provence. Among his ancestors were Pierre de Sade, the first governor of Marseilles; Jean Baptiste de Sade, Bishop of Cavaillon, and Joseph de Sade, Seigneur d'Eiguieres, a famous French general. His father, Count Jean Baptiste Joseph François de Sade, was a colonel in Pope Innocent XII's light cavalry, and his paternal grandmother, Laura de Sade, is believed to be the Madonna Laura of Francesco Petrarch's most celebrated sonnet.

When he was ten, young Donatien de Sade was packed off to *Collége Louis-le-Grand,* a Jesuit boarding school in Paris. After four years, it seems, school officials decided that they had had all they could take of him. He was expelled in the spring of 1754 — the same year that Maximillian de Robespierre entered the school — and was returned to the home of his father. But Count de Sade apparently was even less patient than the Jesuits: the young marquis had been home but a few weeks when he was boarded off again, this time to the army. (Later the father was to complain in a letter to his brother, a bishop, that Donatien, "has not a single good feature in him;" in another letter he was to describe his wife as "a terrible woman," then to add: "Her son takes after her.")

In 1755, at age fifteen, Sade was promoted to the rank of sublieutenant (equal to cadet) in the King's Regiment; in 1757, he was commissioned a lieutenant in the Carabiniers; in 1759, he was promoted to captain in the Cavalry Regiment of Burgogne, with which he saw action in Germany (the Seven Years War), and in March of 1763, a few months before his twenty-third birthday, he resigned his commission and returned to Paris, where, two months later, he married Renée-Pélagie Cordier de Launay de Montreuil. The marriage had been arranged by the fathers of the bride and groom; Sade, for his part, was hardly pleased with the match and went so far as to request, after meeting the de Montreuil family for the first time, that he be permitted to marry his *fiancee's* younger sister instead: the request was denied, and, on May 17, 1763, in the church of Saint-Roch, Sade vowed before the Bishop of Paris that he would have and hold Renée-Pélagie until death did them part. One gets the impression that he crossed his fingers before intoning the "I do:" four months after the wedding, Sade was arrested by Paris police for "excesses committed in a bawdy-house." Brought to trial on October 29, 1763, he was found guilty and imprisoned at *Château de Vincennes*; fifteen days later he was released in the custody of his in-laws.

The five years following Sade's release were characterized by exercises of libertinage of the sort he later was to champion in his writings. He rented apartments and *petites maisons* throughout Paris and in towns as distant as Versailles and Arcueil. He also continued to patronize the brothels of Vendôme and Pigalle, and to comport himself therein with such vigor that one Inspector Marais of the *gendarmes* felt obliged to write a letter, dated November 30, 1764, warning a procuress named Brissault to "stop furnishing the Marquis de Sade with girls."

On Easter morning, April 3, 1768, while on his way to his *petite maison* at Arcueil, Sade encountered an impoverished widow named Rose Keller begging for alms in the street. He offered her a job as housekeeper at Arcueil; the offer was gratefully accepted, whereupon Sade helped the woman into his carriage and commanded his driver to head straight for the *maison*. When they arrived, according to the account of Janin (*Revue de Paris*, 1834), the woman was surprised to find the windows covered with double shutters and the walls padded (*matelasse*) so that no sounds could escape; she asked him the purpose of the padding, but Sade only smiled mysteriously and, after showing her all the rooms on the first and second floors, led her through a trapdoor to the attic.

There are several accounts of what transpired in the attic once Sade had pulled the trapdoor shut. The most reliable, in the opinion of Sadean scholar Maurice Heine, is that of one Madame du Deffand in a letter written on April 13, 1768, to English novelist Horace Walpole. She wrote: "He ordered her to undress completely. She threw herself at his feet and begged him to spare her because she was a respectable woman. He threatened her with a pistol that he drew from his pocket and so forced her to obey. Then he bound her hands together and whipped her savagely. When she was completely covered with blood he applied salve to all her wounds and had her lay down. I do not know whether he gave her food and drink. At any rate he first saw her again the following morning, looked at her wounds and saw that the salve had worked effectively. Then he took a knife and made cuts on her entire body, again placed salve on all her wounds and left. The victim succeeded in tearing her bonds and in freeing herself by means of a window to the street . . . It is said that the reason for his dreadful action was to prove the value of his salve."

Sade was imprisoned temporarily at Saumur, then transferred to *Le Conciergerie du Palais*, the famous penitentiary at Paris. There, on June 10, 1768, he confessed that he had committed the crime to satisfy an "erotic curiosity." After agreeing to pay his victim 100 *livres* in damages, he was set free. His in-laws' influence with King Louis XV, himself no small *devotée des caprices de l'imagination*, undoubtedly was one reason why his treatment was not more severe.

The four years following the D'Arcueil affair were passed by Sade in relative quiet at his father's estate in Provence. It was here that he sired his second son (the first
had been born at Paris) and his daughter. It was
also here that he seduced his sister-in-law, Anne-Prospère de Launay de Montreuil, whom he had asked to
marry in place of his wife some years before and who
had come to Provence for a summer vacation after leaving the Carmelite convent where she had served a novitiate.

But even incestuous seductions were not enough to
save Sade from disenchantment with the quiet life of a
county squire. On June 27, 1772, he decided that he
could take it no longer; journeying to Marseilles with his
valet, Latour, he set up an orgy which soon was celebrated throughout France as "The Cantharidic Bonbon
Orgy." This is the account of the fete recorded by a
diarist of the day, Marcel Bachaumont: "I am told that
Count de Sade, who in 1778 caused great disorder by his
crimes with a woman on whom he wanted to test a new
cure, has just played in Marseilles a spectacle at first
amusing but later horrible in its consequences. He gave
a ball to which he invited many people and for dessert
gave them very pretty chocolate pastilles. They were
mixed with powdered 'Spanish fly.' Their action is well
known. All who ate them were seized by shameless ardor
and lust and started the wildest excesses of love. The
festival became an ancient Roman orgy. The most modest of women could not restrain themselves . . . Many
persons died as a result of the excesses and many others
still suffer recurrent pains." (This report is modified by
other sources, who insist that no deaths occurred.)

Brought to trial before the Parliament of Aix, Provence, on September 11, 1772, Sade was sentenced to
death on charges of sodomy and poisoning *in contuma-
ciam.* But a day later he escaped from the Aix jail and
fled with his sister-in-law, Anne-Prospère to Italy.
They then proceeded to Piedmont, where, on December
8, 1772, Sade was seized by soldiers of the King of
Sardinia, a French ally, and imprisoned at Fort Miolans.

Why Sade was not returned immediately to France for
execution is presently not clear: whatever the case, he
remained at Miolans until May 1, 1773, on the evening
of which he and a fellow-prisoner, the infamous Baron
de l'Allee de Songy, escaped to Geneva. From here Sade
proceeded alone to Provence, where he had arranged to
meet his wife; she, apparently all-forgiving, remained
with him until he went to Italy early in 1776.

In November of 1776, Sade returned to his country
home in Provence and took up again with his wife. He
also arranged with one Father Durand, the abbot of a
Montpellier monastery, to shuttle girls to Sade's *chateau*
for orgies. On January 17, 1777, the father of one of the
girls, Catherine Trillet, stormed the *chateau* with police;
Sade was brought to Paris and imprisoned in the chief
tower of Vincennes fortress pending execution of the
1772 death sentence. The sentence still hadn't been
carried out when, on June 30, 1778, Sade's lawyer,
Joseph-Jerome Siméon, persuaded the High Court of
Province to declare the conviction null due to insufficient
evidence.

Sade, now free from the murder charge, was still a
prisoner of the King, and was therefore ordered back to
Vincennes. En route, at the country town of Lambesc,
he escaped and returned to his *chateau.* Recaptured on
September 7, 1778, he was brought back to Vincennes,
where he remained until 1784.

At 9 p.m. on February 9, 1784, according to the *Répertoire ou Journalier du chateau de la Bastille,* Sade was brought by Royal Order from Vincennes to the maximum-security Bastille and confined in "the second Liberty," a six-cell dungeon. (No reason for the transfer was stated.)

It was in the Bastille that Sade wrote — on, pertinently enough, both sides of a roll of paper, four and one half inches wide and thirteen yards long — his work, *Les 120 Journées de Sodome.* It was also there that he penned the brief polemical exchange. *Dialogue entre un prêtre et un moribond.* Both are contained in Volume II of the present edition.

Then, on July 8, 1787, he completed the first draft of *Les Infortunes de la Vertu,* a novella originally intended to become part of a proposed short story anthology, *Contes et fabliaux du XVIIIe siècle.* After reworking the piece for a full year, he decided to expand it to novel form. It ultimately became his first-published and now most famous work, *Justine.*

On July 2, 1789, Sade managed to work his way to a tower window of the Bastille. From here, using a megaphone, he began haranguing passersby on Rue Saint Antoine. When he had succeeded in drawing a crowd, he delivered an invective-filled oration against the king, the queen (whom he described as *"la premiere putainne de France"*), the governor of the Bastille and most other leading figures in the *ancien regime.* As a result of this incident, he was brought to the Charenton asylum and thus narrowly missed personal participation in the official start of the Revolution, the storming of the Bastille on July 14.

On March 13, 1790, the Constituent Assembly issued a

decree rescinding certain *lettres de cachet*, among them
the type under which Sade was being held. Thus, on
Good Friday, April 2, the marquis was released from
Charenton. Penniless, he prevailed upon a lawyer-friend
to give him a cellar in which to sleep until he could get
his affairs in order. Then he promptly dashed off a one-
act play in blank verse, *Le Suborneur*, which he sold to
Le Théâtre Italien, and a five-act play, *Le Misanthrope
par amour, ou Sophie et Desfrancs*, which was bought
by *La Comédie-Francaise*. If the fifty-year-old marquis
permitted himself any sexual caprices during this period,
he managed them circumspectly; judging from his literary output, it is unlikely that he had the time.

The following year was likewise devoted principally
to work. Sade revised his Bastille-written *Les Infortunes
de la Vertu* and published it as *Justine ou les Malheurs
de la Vertu*. He also wrote what was to become his only
published play, *Le Comte Oxtiern ou les effets du libertinage*, which premiered at *Théâtre Molieré* on October
22.

Next came what might be characterized as Sade's political period. He became active in 1792 in the *Section des
Piques*, also called the *Section de Robespierre*. Recognized as a "reformed aristocrat," he soon was appointed
secretary of Robespierre's Jacobin Club. Here members
still addressed him by his title under the *ancien regime*,
which led to the latter-day historian Jacques Cabanes'
characterization of him as "the only living marquis under
the rule of Robespierre and Fouqier." He also was an intimate of Jean Paul Marat and delivered the funeral oration when that revolutionary was murdered by Charlotte
Corday in 1793.

The year, 1793, of course, marks the start of Robespierre's Reign of Terror: Louis XVI and Marie Antoinette

were executed, the new regime declared war simultaneously against England, Spain and Holland, and the
French National Convention altered the calendar and
established the "worship of reason." It was during this
year that Sade — irony of ironies — broke with Robespierre . . . because he considered the mass executions of
the Reign of Terror "horrible" and "inhumane"! This
about-face came shortly after his appointment as chairman of *Section des Piques*, which was responsible for
conducting trials for potential executees; on August 2,
without explanation, he refused to pronounce sentence
on a group of prisoners, handed his chairman's gavel
over to the vice chairman and stormed out of the meeting room shouting: "Not on your life! Ye Gods, I am
through with it all!" After the fall of the Girondists, the
moderate element in the revolution's 1791-93 Assembly,
he was tried for "moderatism" and, on December 6, upon
the command of *Le Comité de la Sûreté Générale*, imprisoned in turn at Madelonnettes, Carmes, Saint-Lazare
and Picpus. A year later, on October 15, 1794, twelve
weeks after the execution of Robespierre, he was set free.

Sade's next work was *La Philosophie dans Le Boudoir*,
which was published during the summer of 1795. It contains the famous political speech, "Yet Another Effort,
Frenchmen, Before You Call Yourselves Republicans,"
which was printed separately and distributed widely
during the Revolution of 1848. (Both will be found in
Volume I of the present edition.) He also published a
four-volume novel, *Aline et Valcour*, composed largely
of loosely-connected stories penned during his Vincennes and Bastille days.

In 1797, *Juliette* appeared. This was Sade's longest
work (seven volumes), and was followed by an extended
rewrite of *Justine*, titled *La Nouvelle Justine*. (The latter work included a number of torture scenes not in the

former, and involved a change from a "moral" ending in
which Virtue triumphs to an "immoral" ending in which
Vice does.) Despite the financial success of these ven-
tures — they were sold by the hundreds of thousands all
over Europe — Sade appears to have realized personally
very little profit from them; one publisher after another
reneged on royalty payments and the aging marquis,
as an ex-convict with few friends and insufficient capital
to sustain legal action, had little choice but to suffer his
losses. In 1798 he was forced to give up his Paris apartment and moved to Beauce where he rented a small
house from one of his farmers.

From 1798 to 1801, Sade kept alive by grinding out
novellae and stories which were little more than para-
phrases of his previous works. An anthology of these
works, *Les Crimes de l'Amour,* was published in 1800.
He also appeared as an actor in a revival at Versailles of
his *Oxtiern* play, and was accused of writing a satiric
pamphlet, *Zoloe and Her Two Acolytes,* depicting Jose-
phine de Beauharnais, Baron d'Orsec, Viscount de Sabar
and Senator Fessinot — all luminaries of the party-then-
in-power — as frolickers at a *petite maison.* It was finally
shown in 1957 by Gilbert Lely that Sade did not write
this.

But as a result of the *Zoloe* pamphlet, Sade was seized
on March 5, 1801, and imprisoned without a trial —
a common practice under Napoleon — at Sainte-Péla-
gie. There he was soon charged with seducing younger
prisoners and was transferred to the maximum-security
penitentiary at Bicêtre. There he made such a nuisance
of himself — (unfortunately the details of this misbehavior are unavailable) — that he was moved, on April
26, 1803, to the asylum at Charenton, where he died at
10 p.m. on December 2, 1814, of a "pulmonary obstruc-
tion" following a "prostrating and gangrenous fever."

Thus the life of Marquis de Sade. That a person could accommodate within himself such extremes of sentiment — and, indeed, of action — is perhaps one of the marvels of the human condition; that he has taken the time to articulate these sentiments and to describe these actions, only to have the works in which he does so banned as obscene and for more than one-hundred-and-fifty years kept out of the reach of all but those persons willing to break the law, is perhaps even more "marvelous," because, unwittingly though it may have been, Sade has provided in his extraordinary works a set of psychological, sociological and philosophical instruments unequalled before and unequalled since. As Robert E. Taylor of New York University notes in *An Analysis of the Kinsey Reports*: "Sade's insight . . . surpasses the remarkable. He not only describes in detail every sexual aberration that modern science has since observed, but he also attempts analyses and explanations and is aware of the importance of classification. To be sure, the classifications which he set up have long since been discarded. But it was over a hundred years after the death of Sade that Lacassagne and Krafft-Ebing formulated their classifications, and their attempts, too, have been discarded. Before Sade there had been no such attempt at all." And Taylor adds: "If the science of sexology itself needed — or still needs — an excuse for its existence, probably none better could be found anywhere than in Sade's preface to his *psychopathia sexualis*. After explaining what he was going to do in his book, he concluded that 'whosoever might describe and explain these aberrations would be producing the finest work possible on human conduct and perhaps one of the most interesting, too.' Such a statement of purpose does not differ fundamentally from one made today by Dr. Kinsey and his colleagues in their Report on women: 'It is, moreover, the record of science that greater knowledge, as it has become available, has increased man's capacity to live happily with himself and with his fellow men.' "

Fortunately, in the rational climate of modern-day America, more and more people have come to accept the psychologist's contention that through knowledge comes an increased capacity for happiness. As a result, Sade's works no longer must be kept out of reach of all but those persons willing to break the law. It is with the firm conviction that the individual reader — and society as a whole — will be better for having scrutinized them that this edition is offered to the public.

— Paul J. Gillette, New York City: 1966

A NOTE FOR SCHOLARS

The present edition, while rendered from the original French, is by no means intended to be a translation. My aim throughout has been to preserve, first, the essentials of Sade's philosophy as I have come to reconstruct it from his extensive, wide-ranging and occasionally contradictory jottings; second, the darkly humorous flavor which, in the French, pervades his every scene; third, his narrative style (oases of unspeakable vulgarity in otherwise uninterrupted deserts of that syntactically elegant prose which characterizes French writing even among such moderns as Cocteau, Mauriac, Gide, Montherlant and, when he puts his mind to it, Gênet), and fourth — but only when possible without interfering with priorities one through three — the precise English equivalents of his actual words. The reader who is interested in a less free approach is recommended to the Seaver-

Wainhouse version of *Justine* and *Philosophy in the Bedroom* (Grove Press, New York) and to the Casavini version of *Juliette* and *One Hundred and Twenty Days of Sodom*; while the Olympia editions, unfortunately, are not available on the open market, copies may be found at some of the better libraries, including the Oxford University Library at London and the Harvard University Library at Cambridge, Mass. There also exist reasonably literal German translations, notably the 1904 Dühren edition (Max Harwitz, Berlin); this work has drawn sharp criticism in the past, but I, personally, think that, while imperfect, it is as good a German rendering as can be found. Regrettably, there are not to my knowledge either literal or free translations into the language perhaps best suited to expression of Sade's sardonic view of reality, Italian; I hope at least partially to remedy this situation in the near future with Italian adaptations similar in approach to those of the present edition.

Of the works in the present edition, *The Bedroom Philosophers* follows the original French most closely both in language and in length. *One Hundred and Twenty Days of Sodom* has undergone some condensation and abridgement; since Sade managed to complete only one third of it, the final three "books" of "passions" in the original exist in outline form while the first book is in narrative form; for consistency's sake, I have taken the liberties of reproducing a sample of the narrative under the chapter title, "A Day in the School of Libertinage," and of returning the book itself to outline form for presentation alongside the other three; I also deleted sections and passages of Sade's preface which have little meaning without the narratives which he never got around to completing. As concerns *Justine* and *Juliette*, condensation and abridgement have been considerable;

this was, of course, essential if the million-plus words of the 1797 edition were to be presented in their present length of 125,000 words: it is my hope that, while slicing away most of the musty prose, redundancies and impertinent oratorical asides which make reading the "original" and "complete" versions (as they usually are billed) nothing less than a chore, I have managed to retain the meat and enough of the potatoes to make for a palatable balance. In Sade's 1797 version, *Justine's* ending differs sharply from that in the 1791 version; it is my belief that the 1791 ending is better suited to the work, so I have employed it here, even though it is contradicted by the ending of *Juliette*: the reader is asked to "forget," in this instance, that the characters in both books are related; in effect, this is what Sade asked when he issued his *Juliette*. I might also point out that, in the originals, Sade fluctuated between first-person and third-person narration, and further complicated matters by having the first-person Justine operate occasionally under the assumed name of Thérèse; I have eliminated Thérèse entirely, and have presented each volume in the narrative form I deemed best suited to the subject matter and style of presentation; this results in a first-person *Juliette* and a third-person *Justine*.

—P.J.G.

ACKNOWLEDGMENTS

It would be impossible to identify by name all those persons and institutions without whom this edition would have been impossible. However, I would like to thank especially Christopher Lacy, Margot Karle, Peggy Reubens, Judith Ann Robinson, Lynn M. Howe, Ruth Novie and Robert H. Dicks, and the very cooperative staff members of Harvard University Library, Cambridge, Mass.; Oxford University Library, London; Bibliothèque Nationale, Paris; University of Florence Library, Florence, and Vatican Library, Rome.

—P.J.G.

JUSTINE

or

THE MISFORTUNES OF VIRTUE

DEDICATION

To Constance:

Yes, my dear friend, it is you to whom I dedicate this book; for, knowing full well the Honor and Virtue which are a part of you, I have no fear that the evils and vices, the sophistries and cynicisms enumerated herein will put you in any peril.

Of course, some persons will condemn the volume, and well they might; Evil recognizes Evil, and the recognition is always painful. However, I am not concerned with such people; to you — and to others like you — my motives will be clear.

The work about to be presented is unique. In other novels you will find Virtue triumphant over Vice; Good rewarded, Evil punished. Here you will find Vice the victor, Virtue the vanquished; you will observe as a

wretched and helpless young woman, though steeped in
virtue, is made the plaything of the most barbarous villains, the victim of their most monstrous caprices; you
will see the moral axioms of the ages besmirched with
the most patent sophistries; you will, in short, witness
life turned inside out, black having become white, up
having become down, right having become wrong — and
all this presented in the boldest, most blatant manner.

Why?

Because only by contrasting Good to Evil can we fully
appreciate either. In a roomful of lepoards, who notices
a spot? And in a Heaven full of saints, who notices a
virtuous act?

Thus, on the following pages, we will present the girl,
Justine, subjected to every degradation imaginable.
When her Honor remains intact, can you help but be
proud of her? Can you fail to value Virtue all the more
highly? Read on, dear Constance: if I draw but a single
appreciative tear from your eye, my efforts will have
been worthwhile.

*   *   *

BOOK ONE

I

The perfect philosophy would, first, acknowledge God as the author of all being, and, second, identify the ends which He has designed for man. Nothing more would be necessary, for, on the basis of this alone, man could establish rules of conduct to guide himself along life's path.

But, one might ask, what if, as man proceeds along that path, he observes each of his rules contradicted? What if these rules of his — no matter how logically conceived — lead him through thickets and thorns, while the men who disobey them walk happily upon rose petals? Would not a man under such circumstances be justified in abandoning his rules, in swimming with the tide rather than against it?

No. It is important to guard against such false reasoning. At the base of philosophy is Truth, and Truth is absolute. If we fail to understand the True and Infinite Plan of God, we must not blame God; we must blame our finite intelligence.

This, then, shall be the purpose of the following work: to demonstrate how Virtue, presented to a soul which is exposed to the corruption of the world but which still retains the principles of Truth, will lead that soul back to the way of Good and Righteousness.

Unfortunately, in order to achieve this purpose, we will find it necessary to depict a host of evils which befall a sweet-tempered and loveable young woman, while at the same time depicting the unceasing joys and good fortunes of those who torment her. Likewise, we shall be required to place in the mouths of characters diabolically false philosophies and horrendous assaults upon the values which all honorable men hold dear. However, since such a presentation is essential to the demonstration of Truth, the reader cannot fail to excuse it; nor can he fail to profit from seeing Hell's sophistries exposed for exactly what they are . . .

II

Such are the vagaries of fate: Two children, born of the same parents, raised in the same household, pampered by the hugs and kisses of the same grandmothers and grandfathers, aunts and uncles; yet, totally unlike each other, as different as black and white. The older is named Juliette; she is not quite fifteen, but her mind and intellect are those of a woman of thirty; her figure is lithe and supple, her eyes dark and foreboding — yet, foreboding in a paradoxically attractive sort of way. The younger is Justine; she is twelve and a pensive girl; her beauty is equal to that of her sister, but softer and more delicate; Justine is serious where Juliette is gay, self-effacing where Juliette is haughty, principled where Juliette is wanton.

As our story begins, Justine and Juliette have just become the victims of a disasterous chain of events. Their father, a prominent Parisian banker, suffered business reverses so severe that he committed suicide rather than face the dishonor of bankruptcy. A month later, his grief-stricken wife followed him to the grave. The orphaned Justine and Juliette then turned to their relatives for help, but, once it was known that their family fortune had dwindled, the same grandmothers, grandfathers, aunts and uncles who had lavished kisses upon them hurled them bodily into the street. Finally, the girls went to a convent to which their father had made sizeable donations during his more prosperous days; but news of their misfortunes had preceded them, and the abbess, instead of offering food and a pillow upon which to rest their weary heads, gave the girls a scant fifty crowns each — money placed into an account for them years earlier by their father — and turned them away.

Now, on the sidewalk in front of the great doors of the convent, the pitiful young Justine buried her head against her sister's breast and began sobbing unashamedly. But Juliette, far from sharing the poor child's grief, could not have been more delighted with their circumstances. Touching her handkerchief to Justine's red-rimmed eyes, she consoled her as follows:

"Look at the brighter side, my darling sister. Each of us now is her own mistress, free from all restraint. Since you are only twelve, you may not yet have experienced the urgings of the flesh which have come over me of late; but I can assure you that they are immensely provocative and that they create an awesome hunger which

denies you rest until it is satisfied. In the past, imprisoned under the eyes of our parents and relatives, I have
not been able to satisfy it fully; instead, it was my lot to
buy what little peace I could by teaching my fingers to
respond to the images of a feverishly-desirous brain.
Now all this is behind me, and it is a fate which you can
be spared entirely. Come, let us go together to take up
the lives of courtesans, satisfying the hungers of the flesh
whenever they arise and the thirst for material goods
as well."

Justine, hearing this, was wholly scandalized.

"Oh, sister!" gasped the darling little girl. "How can
you suggest such a thing?! It's immoral! It's illegal! It
may even be depraved—"

"Nonsense!" hissed Juliette. "What do you know of depravity? Is it more depraved to lock loins with a generous lover than to roam the streets penniless, begging
for bread?"

"No, but—"

"Listen to me," Juliette continued, "you are too sensitive to the opinions of others; too quick to modify your
behavior to adjust to their standards. Stroking her sister affectionately on the shoulder, she added — with an
acuity far exceeding her tender age: "Life is but a series of pains and pleasures. Of late we have suffered a
great many of the former. Now, if we are wise, we will
try to blot these from memory. And how? By assailing
the memory with a greater number of pleasures."

"But is it wise," protested the lovely Justine, "to fly
in the face of all which we have been taught is right?"

"Wisdom, my darling sister," replied Juliette, "consists
infinitely more in multiplying one's pleasures than in
compounding one's pains. We have two choices: we may
become courtesans, or we may starve. The former brings

naught but pleasures, the latter naught but pains. You tell me: which course does true wisdom suggest?"

"Enough!" the bewildered Justine suddenly screamed. "I will suffer no more of this twisted logic."

Juliette was startled by this outburst. "Very well, dear Justine," she apologized, "if these are your feelings on the matter, I shan't try to persuade you otherwise." Then, after a moment, she added: "However, you can't expect me to cast my lot on the side of pain just because you choose to. Therefore, we'll have no choice but to go separate ways."

And thus, realizing the inevitability of their parting, Justine and Juliette embraced on the street in front of the great doors of the convent, then bid each other adieu and walked off in opposite directions . . . .

III

During Justine's early childhood, she had often been caressed by her mother's dressmaker. Now, feeling alone and forsaken after the departure of Juliette, she went to this woman to ask for help in her hour of distress.

The dressmaker was a short, squat woman with masculine musculature and an almost perpetual snarl. Her face brightened slightly when she saw the lovely Justine standing in her doorway. It brightened even more as she hugged the girl to her breast and brought a coarse, fleshy hand to rest just above the curve of the sweet child's small, gently rounded buttocks. However, as soon as she learned of Justine's misfortunes, the swarthy wench pushed her roughly away.

"If I wanted to hear sad stories this afternoon," she said, "I would have gone to the opera." And, with that, she slammed the door in Justine's face.

IV

"Oh, Heavens!" sobbed the poor little girl, wringing her hands sorrowfully as she stood in front of the dressmaker's house, the awful sound of the door still echoing in her pretty little ears. "Why must my first step in life be so disheartening? Can it be that my penury has stamped me as undesireable? Do people only esteem those who have something worth taking? Or, perhaps, are these first experiences of mine merely part of a Divine test of my adherence to the Will of God?"

Thoughts of her Creator reminded Justine that she had not yet made her daily visit to church. Thereupon she hurried across town to her home parish, where, after saying a brief prayer at the church's main altar, she presented herself at the rectory and requested an interview with the pastor.

The lovely young girl was wearing a simple white dress with short sleeves. Her marvelous hair was tucked up neatly under her bonnet, and her tiny breasts — the development of which had scarcely begun — were lent an added innocence by the folds of several layers of gauze. However, if the stern-faced young cleric who answered the door was at all appreciative of her gentle beauty, he certainly managed to mask his enthusiasm.

"What is *this*?" screamed the youthful priest, tugging frantically at one of the sleeves of Justine's dress. "Bare *arms*? In the house of *God*?! That's *BLAS*-phemy!!!"

"Oh, please, father," whimpered the poor girl as immense, twin tears rolled sadly down her pale, white cheeks. "Observe my sorry state . . . I have just lost my father and mother . . ."

"Yes," snapped the priest, "and your sleeves, too, I take it. Young lady, this is the house of *God*! The HOUSE of GOD!!!"

"I beg you, father," she persisted, "my parents have been taken away . . . Summoned by Heaven . . . Called from me when I needed them most . . ."

"Don't you understand, you impudent little slut?" hissed the priest. "I don't care who took whom when who needed them, you can't get into this rectory with your . . . *bare* . . . *arms* . . ." here he paused and swallowed hard ". . . EXPOSED!!!"

Now, all this commotion was such that it aroused the pastor from his private study, where he had been perusing a book of erotic drawings to determine if their sexual properties were sufficiently high to merit condemnation from the pulpit on Sunday morning. Observing the muted loveliness of the darling Justine's pale, tear-streaked face — to say nothing of the creamy-white expanse of her firm, lusciously rounded legs (for, as she backed off the doorstep under the force of the young cleric's last verbal assault, the hem of the sweet child's little white dress had drifted high above her knees) — the aging ecclesiastic was overcome with compassion. Dismissing his brash young subordinate, he took Justine by the hand and led her to the private study, where he said:

"Don't mind Father Tropard, my dear; he suffers from an impetuosity quite common among youths who have forsaken the pleasures of the flesh in order to surrender completely to the Will of Him Who is the Master of us all." Then, taking the lovely girl's face in his wrinkled hands, the kindly cleric asked softly: "Now, what seems to be your trouble?"

"My mother and father . . . They have died . . . Summoned to Heaven when I needed them most . . ." Justine resumed, and once again monstrous tears of sorrow flowed freely from her beautiful, blue eyes.

"Come," coaxed the pastor soothingly, "crying will not help the matter any, will it?" And, as the grief-stricken

little girl sniffed and nodded her agreement, he took a
white handkerchief from his cassock and dabbed her
lovely eyes dry.

Once Justine had stopped crying, the priest lifted her
to his lap, in the process of which endeavor — accidentally, to be sure — her dress again was hoisted far above
her dimpled knees, exposing the soft flesh of her lovely,
girlish thighs. Altogether wrenched from his compassionate impulses, the elderly churchman gasped quite audibly — and his eyes strained to see beyond the carelessly
tousled hem of the dress.

Justine, too distracted by her sorrows to notice the
disarray beneath her eyes — and far too naive to suspect
the motives of the kindly pastor —, was startled by the
sharp, choking noise which escaped from his lips. Being
still young and trusting, she regarded his outburst as an
expression of sympathy for her obviously pitiful state,
and, so moved was she that she attempted to soothe him
by running her delicate, white hands along the stubble
of his cheek.

"Father," she said with an endearing lilt, "I am moved
by this sudden burst of sympathy, but please try to control yourself. Now that you have dried my eyes, it only
renews my sorrow to see that I have made you miserable
as well." And saying this, she offered him the use of
his handkerchief, still damp with her tender tears.

The pastor now found himself in a virtual frenzy of
desire and confusion, which the soft pressure of Justine's
hand on his cheek served only to exacerbate. Overlooking the sweet child's offer of the handkerchief, he attempted to suppress his lusts by inscribing a hasty and
ill-formed cross on his panting chest. This movement
caused Justine to change her position on his lap, and the
provocative shifting of her tender buttocks stoked his
flaming passions all the more.

At this point the air was shattered by a thunderous pounding on the door, followed by the booming voice of young Father Tropard. So thick was that portal's wood that his cries were indistinguishable; yet, the pounding continued, and Justine, reminded of her early encounter with the brash young cleric, began to shuffle uneasily. As a result of the shuffling, her dress now drifted even higher, leaving her marvelous white thighs all but completely exposed; the pastor, no longer able to control himself, savagely jerked her into an horizontal position and madly thrust his head between her legs.

"Good *Heavens!*" shouted the startled young girl, suddenly aware of the carnal nature of his interests. "What in God's *name* are you *doing?*"

The craven pastor made no reply, but gripping the struggling child firmly at the hips and grunting like an animal, burrowed onward toward his goal. However, he had only a moment to explore, for again Father Tropard's voice rang out, and this time his message was all too clear: an emissary from the bishop's office had arrived unannounced and was demanding to see the pastor immediately. Justine, quick to grasp the opportunity, wriggled out of the pastor's lap and ran to the door — just as Tropard opened it.

Now, as the frightened young girl brushed past the youthful cleric, the pastor staggered to his feet and chased after her, waving his fist in the air. "Out into the street, urchin!" he shouted. "Darken this door no more!" And, when the expression on the face of the young Father Tropard suggested that the final clinch with Justine had not gone unobserved, he added: "Trying to seduce a holy man in the house of God!" You should be ashamed of yourself!"

The poor, unhappy girl, now twice humiliated in her attempts to gain sanctuary from life's storms, ran away from the rectory and continued running until her weary legs fell out from underneath her. Then, after resting a moment, she limped along until she found a cheap rooming house, where, with her last twelve louis, she rented a small, attic room.

"Oh, Heaven," sighed the despondent child, kneeling alongside the bed after completing her good-night prayers. "What must a girl do to make her way in this cruel world? Has no one any kindness? Has no one any pity?"

Thusly contemplating the cruelties of fate, she threw herself upon the bed and gave way to her sorrows in a great flood of tears.

V

We will now leave the miserable Justine and turn to Juliette, who, though no better equipped than her dear sister, became, over a period of fifteen years, a titled woman with a vast income, handsome jewels, houses in both the city and the country, and the love and confidence of a much-admired Councilor to the State. Of course, her rise in worldliness was not without difficulty, for, indeed, it is only through the most onerous of paths that a poor woman can improve her fortunes. But let us now tell her story; it will speak for itself.

Upon separating from her sister, Juliette proceeded directly to the bawdy house of a certain Madame Duvergier, whose reputation extended throughout the whole of Paris. Arriving with only a small bag under her arm and clad in only a rumpled blue dressing gown, she nonetheless was welcomed as enthusiastically as if she had arrived in a flaming chariot, for her face and figure were exquisitely attractive (attractive, that is, to those for whom indecency has its charm), and, in the establishment of Madame Duvergier, little else mattered.

Telling the woman her story, Juliette requested lessons in the arts which had enabled so many other girls to succeed.

"How old are you?" Madame Duvergier replied eagerly, for it is not often that one of her occupation encounters a prize like Juliette.

"I will be fifteen in a few days, Madame," Juliette answered.

"And has a man ever . . .?" the matron asked excitedly, simultaneously unbuttoning the tattered blue dressing gown, under which Juliette was wearing absolutely nothing.

"No, Madame, I swear it," said the girl, undaunted.

Duvergier then kissed Juliette on the cheek and, at the same time, eased her hand up the marvelous girl's splendid thigh until it rested firmly between a perfect pair of creamy-soft, naked buttocks.

"But, I have heard," the old crone wheezed, her heart pounding furiously, "that sometimes in those convents a priest, a nun, or a friend gets — shall we say — intimate?"

"Never," said Juliette.

"But I must have *proof*," gasped Duvergier, breathing heavily.

"Then you have only to look for yourself," replied Juliette without a blush.

Immediately the old hag fell to her knees and, thrusting apart the exquisitely sculptured pillars of pulchritude which were Juliette's legs, buried her tongue in the soft, brown triangle of hair which perched at their juncture. '*Mmmmmmmmmmmmmmmmmmmm*!" moaned the jaded madame as her tongue made contact with the darling girl's hot, throbbing vulva. And Juliette, enjoying every last trickle of sensation, began to writhe and undulate her marvelously supple hips in so provocative a manner that Duvergier all but fainted with ecstasy.

When the act was over, the ancient madame put her arm around Juliette's shoulders and said:

"My dear child, you are certainly welcome here. You need only pay attention to what I say and act in accordance with my directives. I insist that you keep yourself clean, that you live economically and that you be fair with your coworkers. Do these things and, in ten years' time, you'll be one of the wealthiest women in Paris."

The speech having been delivered, Juliette was introduced to her future sisters in sin. Then she was given a room in the house, and, on the next day, her body was put to market. During the succeeding four months, the goods were sold to over one hundred buyers.

Having now passed the stage of apprenticeship, Juliette became an official girl of the house, entitled to share in its profits and losses. She plunged wholeheartedly into her activities, performing unspeakable perversions with great vigor, and this abandon into further debauchery brought her the attentions of a wealthy elderly gentleman. His recommendations in turn led to dates with others of his stature and, before long, the wanton child had become a favorite among the elite. Indeed, her talents were such that in less than four years six men had committed suicide because they could not bear to share her with others. Her reputation was assured at last.

When Juliette reached her twentieth year, a certain gentleman, the Count de Lorsange, became so enamored of her that he offered his hand in marriage — along with a sizeable income, a house and servants. Further, he generously agreed to forget her past, and gave her every possible opportunity to resume the life of an honorable woman. Juliette, however, was unhappy with the restraints of marriage and, a few weeks after the ceremony, decided that she had no choice but to regain her freedom by murdering her benefactor-husband.

After the count had been slain and all evidence of the dark deed had been removed, the newly-widowed Madame de Lorsange abandoned herself to her former habits, going to bed with any man who would give her two-hundred louis, or less, if the mood struck her. Over a period of six years she added to her list of conquests three ambassadors, two bishops, a cardinal and four knights of the King's Order. During the same space of time, she committed two more murders and, to these crimes — horrible enough! — added three or four abortions because she feared pregnancy would permanently mar her beautiful figure.

Thus, the adventures of Juliette, through which we can see that the very worst of humans may find in the depths of corruption and depravity what is usually called "happiness." However, let not this cruel truth alarm the Proper and the Righteous, for the "happiness" found in crime is deceiving: apart from the punishments which Divine Providence undoubtedly holds in store for criminals, they also nourish in their souls a worm which never ceases to gnaw at their feelings, preventing them from finding joy in their actions and leaving them nothing put the painful memory of the crimes which have led them to their present state of "well-being." Whereas the poor person, persecuted by Fate, still has in his heart a genuine comfort born of the satisfying knowledge that his own virtues compensate in Heaven for the injustices of his fellow-man.

And now, let us return to the story of Justine . . . .

VI

At the boarding house to which she had run after her debasing experience at the hands of the craven old pastor, Justine again related her sorrowful tale and asked the landlady to recommend someone of influence and wealth who might be disposed to ameliorate her wretched situation. The gentleman recommended was a man named Dubourg, one of the city's richest tradesmen, to whom Justine immediately brought her problems.

"Come, my child," said Dubourg warmly, taking Justine by the hand and leading her to his room. "I am sure we can help you escape these dire circumstances which you so graphically describe." Whereupon, having locked the door, he urged her onto his lap and promptly thrust his hand underneath her dress.

"Hold, sir!" Justine snapped. "I am destitute, but not a wanton."

"How's that?" replied the astonished Dubourg, still not removing his hand from the furry nest in which it was so pleasurably buried. "You expect help, but you don't offer any service in return?"

"Service, yes, sir," said Justine, wriggling out of his grasp, "but none save that which decency and my tender years permit me to fulfill."

Dubourg looked at her carefully for a moment, then abruptly rose to his feet, dropping the beautiful Justine onto the floor with an immense thud.

"Out with you!" he screamed, pointing a furious finger toward the locked door. "At a time like this, decency is the *last* thing I need!"

"But, sir," begged the darling little girl, now kneeling at his feet, "if everyone felt like you, all the poor people of this country would be left to die in the streets."

"And is that so bad?" chuckled Dubourg coldly. "France has more than enough subjects at the present time; in view of the human mechanism's elasticity and propensity to reproduce, there's no real reason to fear depopulating the place."

Hearing these cruel sentiments, the lovely Justine was moved to tears. However, the soft, warm teardrops which swelled her beautiful blue eyes did not melt the stern Dubourg's heart, they only hardened it. Seizing her dress at the shoulder, he ripped it off her back.

"Foul urchin!" he spat. "Now I will take by force that which you refused to afford me voluntarily!"

Now the huge, ham-like fist of the brutal tradesman lashed out savagely at Justine's face, knocking her to the floor and leaving a gleaming red trickle of blood in its wake. Spitting a mouthful of the vital crimson fluid onto the carpet, the pain-wracked girl staggered to her knees and threw her arms around the odious man's legs in a last plea for mercy.

"Oh, sir, I beg you," she cried, "spare me this ignominy. I shall resist you to the end; of that you can be sure, for I would die a thousand times before I would surrender that maidenhead which from childhood I have been brought up believing I should protect above all else. Thus, knowing my resolve to be unshakeable, desist from this attack now. Surely you can derive no happiness from witnessing my tears and disgust. Surely you can gain no measure of satisfaction from seeing me wretched at your feet. If you carry out your intent to rape me, no sooner will you have finished your crime than the sight of my broken body will fill you with remorse . . ."

But the darling girl's pleas were worse than futile, for Dubourg, far from being disgusted by the spectacle of her suffering, actually savored it, delighted in it, thrived on it! Striking her once, twice, a third time, he fell madly on top of her and began nuzzling her bloody mouth. All the while his hand tore at the remains of her dress, clearing passage to the goal he ultimately sought. "Urchin!" he spat, chewing at her neck with fanged teeth. "Bitch! Pig!" And, finally, he had stripped her completely and was ready for the assault.

But then . . . Who can say? Was it a miracle? Did God Almighty wish in that first encounter to inculcate in the wretched girl sufficient horror to insure that she would resist sexual congress forever thereafter? Whatever the case, the savage Dubourg, just seconds before he was to make the assault which would have robbed the lovely Justine of her virtue, suddenly found the flame of his passion extinguished in the fury of his enterprise! His potency lost, the disarmed warrior could only watch in hateful anguish as the target of his wicked lust lifted herself from the floor and dashed out of the room.

VII

A few weeks later, having been evicted from her boarding house for nonpayment of rent and having therefore had to spend two nights unsheltered in the streets, the bedraggled Justine went looking for work as a housemaid. After several interviews, each of which was terminated abruptly by her resistance to the wicked attempts of the interviewer to stuprate her, the unfortunate child finally learned of a position in the house of one Mister Hairpin, a famous usurer who had become wealthy not only by charging exorbitant interest for money loaned on collateral to the poor but also by stealing from the rich whenever he could do so undetected. To be sure, our Justine experienced great trepidation at the thought of entering the service of so nefarious an individual; however, her fortunes had sunk so low that the only alternative was starvation: thus, grim in her determination, she knocked on Hairpin's door and requested an interview.

"I will work my poor fingers to the bone for you, sir,"

sobbed the pitiful child. "I ask in return only a few ounces of bread per day; water, and perhaps a little soup now and then if you can spare it. However, there is one resolve in which I remain most firm: I will not surrender my innocence — to anyone — under any circumstances.

Hairpin, a wheezy-looking man with hooked nose and scruffy whiskers, rocked with laughter when she said this. So great was his merriment that the old goat almost fell from his chair.

"I fail, sire," commented Justine, "to see humor in a young girl's dedication to the Virtue of Chastity."

"Haw-haw," cackled Hairpin, "it is not your dedication which amuses me, but its superfluity under the present circumstances. You see, child, I am not one of these licentious old men who would devour every poor girl upon whom he can get his hands; no, I have been happily married for years and seek the sexual favors of only my wife."

Immensely relieved, Justine fell to her knees and smothered Hairpin's gnarled old hand with kisses. "Oh, blessings upon you, sire!" she cried. "It is such a rare pleasure in this evil era to encounter a man who shares one's regard for Virtue!"

"To your feet, child!" Hairpin commanded abruptly. "It is not for Virtue that I practice this fidelity, but for expediency: you see, usury is no easy business; I lack the time to pursue pleasures outside the marital bed. Moreover, if you enter my employ, you'll likewise lack the time, for there are six rooms here to be washed and scrubbed three times a week, a bed to be made daily, a door to be answered, a wig to be powdered, my wife's hair to be coiffed, a dog and a parrot to be looked after, meals to be prepared, cutlery to be polished, a kitchen to be tended, socks to be darned, dresses to be sewn —

these and a thousand other duties which you must perform. Yes, if I hire you, you'll need not worry about your Virtue of Chastity; dust will gather twixt your labia before you have time to exercise them."

"Oh bless you, sir!" cried the exuberant Justine. "I'd like nothing better than for my labia to gather dust. Please permit me to enter your employ."

Hairpin gazed at her steadily for a moment, then massaged his grizzled jaw with long, bony fingers. "Yes," he said thoughtfully, "I think I will."

"Oh, a million thanks, kind sir!" sighed she, falling again to her knees to smother him with kisses.

"But wait —" Hairpin interrupted. "There is one more matter: I must be sure that you are absolutely sanitary." And, upon saying this, the gnarled old man began to stare at her feet with a curious gleam in his eye.

"I have always believed," replied Justine, "that Cleanliness is next to Godliness, and I have always tried to observe high standards of both."

"Yes, yes," said Hairpin, seeming not to hear her. "Let me have your foot."

"My foot, sir?" asked the surprised young girl, not attempting to mask her incredulity.

"Your foot, your foot," said Hairpin impatiently. "I must examine your foot to see if it is clean."

Justine, wholly naive in such matters, thought the request perfectly reasonable. Sliding a stool into position in front of Hairpin's chair, she sat down and obligingly thrust her lusciously curvaceous leg into the excited old man's trembling hands.

"*Ahhhhhhhhhhh!*" sighed Hairpin, whipping off her shoe. "What a beautiful foot! What a beautiful, beautiful foot!" Upon saying which he clutched the tiny little foot to his cheek and began rubbing it with his face, smelling between the toes and licking the arch with his tongue.

"Sir!" protested the alarmed Justine, quite sure that there must be something horribly sexual about his actions, though by no means was she able to guess what. "Certainly all these ministrations are not necessary to determine that I am sanitary!"

"*Sanitary!*" gasped the lust-crazed Hairpin. "*Sanitary foot! Beautiful foot! Fuckfuckfuckfuckfoot!!*" And with that his hand dropped to his lap, where he began tugging furiously at the buttons which fastened his trousers.

"Sir!" repeated Justine. "Such language! Surely you don't respect the presence of a young girl if you speak like that in front of her."

"*Fuck!*" shouted Hairpin. "*Fuck! FOOT! F-U-C-K!!!*"

Now wholly appalled at the spectacle unfolding before her, the gentle Justine tried to wrench her foot from the depraved man's grip. Hairpin, however, was much too strong for her; his one hand kept the little foot pressed tightly to his mouth while his other — having succeeded in undoing the trouser buttons — was busily engaged in his lap. The poor child had little choice but to sit there, terror-stricken, until he completed debasing himself.

"I am disgusted beyond words," said Justine quietly once the debacle had ended. "If you will show me the door, sir, I shall exit from your life immediately."

But Hairpin, just seconds ago gripped with such frenzy, now looked at her with pleading eyes and said quietly: "I regret deeply the indignity to which I just subjected you, my child; however, listen to my tale and I am sure you will sympathize with my plight. As you undoubtedly have heard so many times in church, the world is populated by legions of formless spirits — emissaries of Lucifer, one and all — who roam about seeking the ruin of souls. Occasionally these nefarious spirits, when all else fails, accomplish their dark deeds by literally taking possession of the body of one of the faithful.

"Such is the cross which I must bear. While a young man, I was extremely devout; so much so that not even the most formidable lures of the world, the flesh or the devil could entice me away from the straight and narrow path of Righteousness. But, alas, what I had regarded as my greatest strength soon became my most detestable weakness, for so determined was Lucifer to win this pure soul away from God that he sent one of his minions to inhabit it. Yes, I was possessed, and not all the prayers of dozens of priests — not even those of a bishop, who also tried — could exorcise the vile spirit."

"Oh my poor man," cried the sorrowful Justine, deeply moved. "Would that I could do something to help you."

"You can, my child," replied Hairpin, rebuttoning his trousers. "You can pray for me. Who knows but that, if sufficient earthly petitions reach Him who is on High, He will take it upon Himself to intervene and expel the accursed spirit which now dwells within me."

"I shall, sir," wept she. "I shall pray for you night and day."

"*And,*" continued Hairpin without pause, "you can accept employment in my household. Now that my misfortunes are known to you I am sure that you will forgive the episode which has just transpired."

Justine looked into the mournful eyes of the wretched man and pity all but consumed her. Taking his gnarled old hand in hers, she brought it to her lips and gently kissed it. "Of course I forgive the episode," she said softly. Then. suddenly aware that accepting employment in his household would place her in jeopardy of being a party to many more similar episodes, she added hastily:

"But I cannot work for you as long as I realize that tomorrow might bring another, and the next day another still."

"Ah, yes," said Hairpin, his facial expression suddenly one of disgust. "Like all the others, a good-times Catholic. Boast of your Virtue as long as your dedic tion to it is convenient. But when sacrifice is called for — when the maintenance of Virtue becomes a chore — throw up your hands in resignation and take the easy road out."

"But, sir —" protested Justine.

"I know, I know," groaned Hairpin wearily. "You trust me, but you don't trust yourself."

"But, sir —"

"You really have my best interests at heart . . ."

"But, sir —"

"You want to do what's right for both of us . . ."

"But, *sir*—"

"No, Justine, *you* listen to *me*. If you really consider yourself a virtuous woman, you won't turn your back on me now. Did St. Joan turn her back on the flaming stake? Did St. Stephen turn his back on the rock-throwers? Did Our Lord and Savior Jesus Christ turn his back on the cross?!"

"No, sir, but —"

"Then don't turn your back on me, you avaricious little twat!"

"But, sir, I cannot see how I could further the cause of Virtue by my participation in unspeakably base acts of — of — of *perversion!*"

"No, my child, of course not," said Hairpin, his wrinkled countenance again calm, his mournful eyes again weary. "But you *could* — *if* you sought to be virtuous — you *could* enter my employ and, through prayer and good works and sacrifice, help *combat* this evil spirit which has taken possession of me. And *if*, perchance, that devil *should* rear his ugly head again when you are in my presence, you need *not* surrender to my scurrilous advances, you know. You *could* resist me."

Confronted in this manner, the lovely Justine was overcome with guilt and compassion. Her heart opened up to the gnarled old man, and she wanted nothing more than to help him combat his devil.

"Oh, sir," she cried jubilantly, having glimpsed the missionary path along which she believed true Virtue lay, "I *will* stay with you and help you do battle! I *will* be your servant!"

"Ah, my sweet Justine," sighed the aging Hairpin, touching his hand gently to her neck, "may God ever bless you." And then, suddenly, his body stiffened, be backed away from her and Justine could once again see his eyes riveted maniacally upon her foot.

"Sir —" she began fearully.

"Your foot, child!" he demanded. "Your foot!"

"No, sir!" she screamed.

"Yes! Your foot!"

"No!"

"YES!"

"Oh, merciful heaven!" cried the darling girl, struggling frantically to scamper out of his reach. "What shall I do?"

"Pray, you fool," snapped Hairin, stepping momentarily out of the role of one possessed. "Pray that my spell will pass." Then, with an agility which belied his withered form and advanced years, he dived across the room and brought her to the floor with a flying tackle.

"Our Father, Who art in Heaven," gasped Justine, "hallowed be Thy name . . ."

But the prayer came too late, for the remarkable Hairpin had already whipped off her shoe and was sucking feverishly at her toes while at the same time his hand tore at his trouser buttons . . .

VIII

Two years passed in the house of the depraved Hairpin.
Lovely Justine, her strength sapped from the endless
round of chores, her brain feverish from the near-starva-
tion she experienced at his miserly table, sometimes wondered if she might not have been better off had she
abandoned herself to her Fate in the streets. Nonetheless, she persisted in her work — and in prayer — and,
though her life was not without its pains, it was not without its small pleasures, either.

One of her pleasures was the satisfaction she derived
from the belief that her prayers and sacrifices not only
were earning spiritual rewards to be enjoyed by her in
the Afterlife but also were contributing to the relief of
Hairpin from the devil which possessed him. In the
weeks and months which followed that first day's assaults, the perverted old man exhibited less and less interest in her feet, until, during the twenty-fourth month
of her employment, there were only two episodes — a
full twenty-nine less than during the first month. This
improvement in his condition, she reasoned, could only
be the result of her sincere devotion to Goodness and
Virtue.

However, if Hairpin had improved with respect to the
Sixth Commandment, he took a turn for the worse with
respect to the Seventh. As time had passed both the
number and the size of his thefts had increased, and likewise the recklessness with which he went about them.
Affairs soon reached a point where he even attempted
to enlist Justine's services as an assistant.

"My darling child," he said to her one day, "why
should you continue to suffer poverty while the world

grows fat around you? Stealing is easy, it is profitable and, if undertaken in the right company, may even be fun."

"But," she replied, "it is also sinful, Mr. Hairpin; thus, no matter how attractive a picture you paint, you shall not sway me."

"Sinful?" chuckled the evil old man. "Nonsense; it is but a means to restore the equilibrium which has been disturbed by those who preceded us. Consider the following: Were not the children of Adam and Eve born equal in every respect? How is it, then, that some of them — or some of their children — acquired a disproportionate share of the wealth? Because they stole it, of course; because they took it at the expense of their brothers and sisters."

"But," protested the darling Justine, "the end can never justify the means. Even if those who originally acquired wealth stole it from our ancestors, that gives us no license to steal it back."

"Ah, but you're wrong," smiled the wicked Hairpin persuasively. "The goods of Nature were created by God for all men. If this natural balance has been disturbed — as indeed it has — we have not only the right to restore it, we have the duty! Besides, my dear, thefts are seldom punished; indeed, throughout Greece at one time, stealing was honored as a noble deed, and in other civilizations thieves have been rewarded for their courage and skill — two virtues indispensable to a strong nation."

"No, sir," Justine said firmly, "no, a thousand times no; I will not let you corrupt me!"

"Very well, then," Hairpin replied, and once again his eyes took on that strange gleam which invariably accompanied his assaults on her feet. But, this time, he was not looking at her feet at all. "We shall see what develops," he said. And, with that, he walked out of the room.

That night, not long after the poor child, exhausted from her chores, had fallen into a fitful sleep, she was aroused by a heavy pounding on her door. There was a rumble of voices, then the very earth seemed to heave as the door was flung open and Hairpin, accompanied by four policemen, burst into the room.

"This is the girl!" the treacherous old man told the lawmen. "She's the wretch who stole my diamonds. I'm sure you'll find them in this room. Now do your duty and arrest her!"

"I stole your diamonds?!" gasped the incredulous child. "But sir, you should know better than anyone how much I detest theft. Recall, if you will, our conversation of this afternoon."

"Don't listen to her," Hairpin told the policemen. "They all protest their innocence, these thieves. Look around the room. I'm sure you'll find the diamonds."

And indeed they did — hidden, of all places, inside the darling little girl's shoe!

"Have mercy, sir," Justine cried to Hairpin as the policemen dragged her out of bed. "Think of the many kindnesses I have done you."

But the depraved old man was not about to be swayed by her pleas. Indeed, as the policemen carried her away, the scoundrel sat in his living room grinning, his arm draped over the shoulder of a young serving-girl who had just joined the staff a few days before.

"Please, Mr. Hairpin," called Justine just before being pulled through the front door. "I beg of you!"

But there was no answer; the last thing she saw, before the door slammed closed behind her, was Hairpin bringing the new serving-girl's foot to his face . . .

IX

Found guilty of theft, Justine was sentenced to death in the guillotine and was incarcerated at the Conciergerie. There she made the acquaintence of one Madame Dubois, a woman of perhaps forty years and as celebrated for her beauty as for the quantity and quality of her crimes. As to the latter, she was said to have violated every article of the French Criminal Code at least once, and to have been spared execution only because the judges had not yet been able to conceive a means sufficiently torturous to avenge her offenses.

In Dubois Justine believed she had finally found a friend who was both sympathetic and understanding. The charming woman listened with keen interest as the wretched girl unfolded the sorry details of the many tragedies which had befallen her since the day some three years earlier when she was orphaned; then, the recital over, Dubois enumerated her own griefs, explaining how an overly zealous pursuit of Virtue during her youth had led to her abduction by a band of theives and her subsequent introduction to a life of debauchery, wickedness and crime. Before many days had passed, the young girl and the older voluptuary had established genuine, heart-felt bonds of affection — or, so Justine thought; but she had no way of knowing that the crafty Dubois' simulations of concern and solicitude were little more than a mask for the wicked woman's plans to proselytize her.

Two nights before Justine's scheduled execution, Dubois crossed the cellblock to the girl's bunk. "Move to one side and pretend you are asleep," she whispered softly. Then, when Justine complied, she slid onto the bed alongside her.

"Tomorrow night," said Dubois, "some of my friends

will set the Conciergerie on fire. You and I will hide in
the kitchen so as not to be burned. Then, when sufficient bedlam has been stirred up by the flames, we'll
make our escape."

Justine was delighted beyond words that such great
effort had been exercised by Dubois in what appeared
to be her behalf. Still, she could not help but experience some misgivings. "Is it not possible that some prisoners might be hurt in the fire?" she asked fretfully.

"Certainly," hissed Dubois. "Many will be burned,
perhaps some to death. But what does that matter to us
as long as we make our escape?"

Tears flooding her eyes, the darling Justine took the
older woman's hand in hers. "I'm grateful for all you
have done, my kind friend," she said quietly, "but I cannot accept your help if the only way my life can be spared is at the expense of others."

"But, foolish child," pleaded the voluptuary, "they will
all die at the guillotine anyway. What does it matter if
they die one month sooner or later?"

"No," insisted Justine, "I will not go."

"Then I will go without you," said Dubois. "The
plans have already been made and it is too late to can-
cel them. You may choose either to come with me or to
stay here and die, but the fire will commence as planned."

Convinced of the older woman's determination, Justine
finally did consent to the plan. But her heart was heavy
as she did so.

X

The following evening everything proceeded as scheduled and the same Hand of God which earlier had brought
Justine suffering as payment for her Virtue now manipulated crime to protect her. The blaze was horrible and

claimed the lives of some twenty-one prisoners, but Justine and Dubois made a safe getaway and, with the aid of four confederates, reached a hideout in the Forest of Bondy that same night.

"Now, Justine," said Dubois as they sat around a candle in the hideout and warmed themselves with hot broth, "you are a free woman again. I hope you will not make the same mistakes as before and permit Virtue to lead you down the path to ruin. An appalling crime has rescued you from the foot of the scaffold at the very last moment, and you almost failed to take advantage of your opportunity even then. Next time you may not have someone to engineer an escape for you, so learn from experience.

"You are young and very attractive, child; with my advice you can come by a fortune in a matter of a few years: but do not be so naive as to think I will lead you to this pot of gold by way of the road of Righteousness; if you would succeed, you must be willing to sacrifice anyone and anything for the sake of your own gain."

"Oh, sweet Dubois," replied the darling girl, "I will always be grateful for what you have done for me; however, I still prefer the rocky road of Righteousness to the primrose-strewn path of sin. If God chooses to visit more ills upon me I will thank Him for them, for it is only by suffering in this life that one can expect to merit true happines in the next."

"Rubbish!" Dubois frowned. "That's a notion which has been foisted off on the poor by the callous rich, and all for the purpose of maintaining their vested interests." Now she smiled sardonically. "I love to hear them talk — these titled noblemen, these wealthy merchants, these pompous priests. It's all very easy to forswear theft if you have four times more food than you could ever eat; it's all very easy to tell the truth when there's nothing you could possibly gain by lying; it's all very unnecessary to plot murder when you're surrounded by no one but dolts and idolators who never offend you and who can readily be manipulated to do your bidding: but we, Justine — we who are held in contempt because we are poor, who are abused because we are weak, who are exploited because we lack the weapons with which to defend ourselves — we cannot afford such lofty principles; we must lie and scheme and steal and kill, or else get washed under with the tide.

"You speak of God, my pretty child — but the God you describe as the author of your principles must either be a tyrant or an ass, for surely no just God would permit unlimited luxury for some and unmitigated suffering for others without offering a means to remedy the situation — and not to remedy it in some spiritual afterlife, but in the material present-day life.

"It is as you have told me your friend, Hairpin, said: theft is necessary to restore the balance of Nature. He who seeks to restore the balance is certainly no less guilty of wrongdoing than he who disturbs it — and, in the last analysis, neither is really guilty of anything, for, if there is a God, you can rest assured that, when he puts us in a situation where evil is expedient and then gives us the means by which to perpetrate it, he does so with the expectation that we will do precisely that."

Dubois spoke convincingly and well. Undoubtedly, if anything could lure the sweet Justine away from the road of Righteousness, it was the execrable sophistries of the smooth-voiced voluptuary. However, lovely Justine chose instead to heed another voice: that of her heart. "No, kind Dubois," she said softly, "your arguments fail to move me; I cast my lot with God and Goodness."

"Then do as you please," snarled the older woman angrily, "and if your pursuit of Virtue leads you back to the guillotine, remember that I warned you. Now I leave you to your fate." And, so saying, she rose from the table and retreated to a darkened corner of the room.

Now, while the above dialogue was taking place, Dubois' four confederates had been sitting before the fireplace drinking. The liquor soon had predictable effects. The four rose from their seats, there was a quick whispered conference, and the largest of the group — a swarthy devil called Ironheart — came to Justine with a proposition: either she would submit voluntarily to the lusts of all four and be paid for her trouble or else she would be forced to submit and receive not a dime.

"Oh, Heavens!" cried the poor child. "Is there no one in the whole world willing to leave a virtuous girl in peace?!" Then, seeing the four men move in toward her with eager arms, she hurled herself to her knees in front of Dubois and begged that blasphemous voluptuary to intercede.

"Ha-ha-ha-ha-ha," cackled Dubois in reply. "It's been only seconds since our conversation and already you find this Virtue of yours getting you into trouble. Well, I'll intercede for you, but only on one condition: you must become a member of my gang and do without hesitation everything I tell you."

The pitiful Justine briefly weighed both courses of action. She realized that becoming a member of the gang would be no less perilous than doing battle with the four drunken bandits; however the perils of this former course would be less immediate: thus, hoping to buy time, she accepted the offer. Immediately Dubois stepped protectively between the girl and her adversaries.

"Gentlemen," announced the vile woman, "dear Justine is now one of us, so let's not do anything rash"

But liquor had already stoked the men's passions beyond the point where reason alone could calm them. De-

vouring the sweet girl with lustful looks, they moved in
for the kill.

"Contain yourselves, you idiots!" pleaded Dubois. "If
we're smart we can make a fortune selling the girl's virginity to the sort of men who are most aroused by youth
and innocence. Don't ruin our chances by insisting upon
taking your pleasures of her now."

"Aside, Dubois!" demanded the aptly-named Ironheart.
"My blood is much too hot to be cooled by conversation.
Let me at her."

"Hold fast!" insisted Dubois. "Will it not be necessary
to show future customers proof of her Virtue? Won't
she be more valuable as a virgin?"

"Of course," replied Ironheart, "but she can remain
a virgin. We don't have to satisy ourselves in the usual
way. Let her strip naked at once."

"Strip naked!" gasped Justine, shocked beyond belief.
"Oh, Heavens! If I surrender my body to your looks, isn't
that just as bad as surrendering it to your flesh?!"

But Ironheart was in no humor to be delayed. Spitting
vile expletives at her, he clutched her dress at the neck
and with one sweep of his powerful arm ripped it open
to her waist. As she tried to cover her naked breasts with
those scraps of material which remained, the other three
bandits tore at her back and sides until the garment was
completely in shreds.

Now the savage Ironheart tore into her with his fists,
caving her in half with a forceful blow to the abdomen,
then jarring her upright again with a swift, underhand-
ed punch to the chin. This second blow ruptured the
poor girl's mouth, liberating a fountain of blood which
sprayed into the air with great force. But, far from stay-
ing Ironheart's fury, the sight of this blood only intensified it. The lust-crazed bandit then ripped into the helpless child with twice his previous vigor and pummeled

her until she dropped — naked, only semiconscious and thoroughly covered with bruises — to her hands and knees on the floor.

Now, as two of the bandits held her legs spread apart, the third punched her viciously at the spot where the lovely limbs joined. The force of the blow knocked her forward, but Ironheart caught her before she hit the floor. Then, as he held her up by the shoulders, the man who had first punched her struck again and again, his meaty fist turning the flesh which surrounded Nature's Altar an ugly black and blue.

"In her place," chuckled one of the men holding her legs, "I gladly would have surrendered my virginity rather than suffer this." Then to the striker he said: "Give it to her again. Harder this time."

Now, when the brutal assault finally was over, the same man who had made the above comments forced Justine to kneel between his legs. Mounting her back like a rider astride a horse, he busied himself with two projects: sometimes he slapped her breasts and buttocks, powerfully and with resounding cracks; other times his foul mouth sucked at her neck while with coarse fingers he kneaded the soft, white flesh of her stomach.

Soon tiring of this, the conscienceless barbarian knocked her to the floor and pounced on top of her, covering her pure little mouth with his and sucking violently. In an instant her face turned purple and her chest red. Tears swelled her eyes, but they served only to rouse him all the more, and he sucked with greater force.

Now jerking her to her feet, he punched her in the stomach, then seized her face in both hands and bit her tongue. She slipped backwards, but the others prevented her from falling. They thrust her toward him and he bit her again. She was more furiously harrassed on all sides until at last with a final blow of nearly unbelievable force, her tormenter sent another fountain of blood gushing from her old wound.

These atrocities finally over, the third bandit made the poor child straddle two chairs which were separated by some twelve to fifteen inches. Then, lying between the chairs and beneath her, he gnawed at her organs. The other bandits held her in position and the obscene mortal on the floor continued to bite and to gnaw until he had drawn blood from Nature's Altar itself.

Finally it became Ironheart's turn. Standing her in front of the fireplace, he attached strings to the nipples of her breasts and to each other part of her body to which it was possible to attach them. Then, holding the ends of the strings in his hands, he seated himself some seven or eight feet away.

He tugged at a string. Justine's twitch as her leg slid out from under her thrilled him immensely. He tugged again, and cackled delightedly as her head jerked in the direction of a string tied to her ear. Again and again he pulled his cords. Everytime she swayed and lost balance, he laughed harder and harder. At length, he pulled all the cords at once — and with such force that she fell to the floor right in front of him.

"Yes," chuckled Ironheart, "if I were she, I certainly would have surrendered my virginity."

"Enough," said Madame Dubois. "The girl is half dead. Swab her clean and put her to bed, then let's all get some sleep. We've a rough day ahead . . ."

BOOK TWO

I

Pain wracked every cell of her body. Her eyes were swollen shut. Outside the room she could hear the crackle of a fire, but nothing else. Forcing her eyes open, she tried to peer through the window; it was totally dark; nighttime — but which night, and what hour, she could not guess.

Suddenly there was a stirring in the room and Justine heard the cadence of heavy footsteps advancing toward her bed. A huge, shadowy mass loomed over her and, in the dim orange light from the fireplace in the next room, she made out the coarsely chiseled features of the villainous Ironheart.

"Hello, my love," the knave whispered hoarsely. Then with surprising tenderness, he stooped and kissed her very lightly on her bruise-covered cheek. "I hope you won't deny me the pleasure of passing the rest of the night with you."

"Scoundrel!" croaked the feeble child. "Where are we? How many days have passed since my defilement?"

"Days?" chuckled the monstrous Ironheart softly. "It has been but a few hours, my sweet. We're still in the hideout at Bondy. And, as to your so-called 'defilement,' it may please you to know that, though your modesty certainly was not respected, your maidenhead most assuredly was; you're every bit the virgin you were when you walked in here." Now, slipping onto the bed alongside her, he took her pretty face in both hands and, again with nearly incredible tenderness, began covering her bruises with kisses. "Furthermore," he went on, "I would like to tell you that I have become quite fond of you. I am sure that we can become very good friends if you'd like."

"Sir," replied Justine weakly, "I doubt that I ever could learn to appreciate the manner in which you express your friendship. Moreover, I find you wholly repulsive. Therefore, I would thank you to take leave of me at once."

"Oh, come now, sweet child," coaxed the obstinate bandit, "I'm not as bad as all that. Besides, I've already decided that I'm going to spend the night with you, so there's really nothing you can do about it." Then, again kissing her tenderly, he added: "You needn't fear anything. I'll attempt no sexual congress without your consent. We'll simply chat awhile, then, if you're tired, we'll drop off to sleep."

In spite of herself, Justine found that she was deriving a strange sort of pleasure from Ironheart's ministrations. His arms were large and sinewy, and, as they gently cradled her little body, the lonely and pain-wracked child wanted only to press herself against him until, in a

moment of supreme ecstasy, both bodies fused. Yet, re-
minding herself of the villainies which he had perpetrated upon her earlier, she forced herself to wriggle out of
his grip. "Sir," she said quietly, "there is absolutely nothing for us to discuss. I beg you therefore to go immediately."

Now a scowl crossed Ironheart's face. "You seem to
forget, dear child, that a few hours ago, in the interests
of preserving your virginity, you consented to become a
member of the gang. Don't you realize why Dubois
wants you as a member? So that she can sell that very
virginity which your consent was designed to preserve!
Yes, and not only once will she sell it, but hundreds of
times, having you treated by a surgeon after each sale
so that the appearance of virginity will be regained!
Little did you realize it, poor dear, but your consent to
join the gang was, in effect, your acceptance of a life of
unpaid concubinage; and now the only alternative is
death, for Dubois is notorious for forcing adherence to
an agreement."

"Why," replied Justine suspiciously, "do you take it
upon yourself to tell me these things now?"

Again Ironheart took the sweet girl's face in both
hands and covered her bruises with gentle kisses. In the
dim light from the fireplace, she could see a large tear
glistening on his rugged cheek. "Because, you foolish girl,
I love you," said the bandit hoarsely. "Because I love you
and want to marry you." And, with this, he gripped
with such force and passion that Justine wanted only
to melt in his embrace.

II

Dawn found the child asleep in Ironheart's arms. Good
to his word, the swarthy bandit had not permitted him-

self the slightest sexual liberty, but merely had held her dormant form close to him all night while kissing her bruised face continuously. When she awoke he prepared breakfast for both of them, then sat alongside her bed and ate with her. Finally, the meal over, he reminded her of his declaration of a few hours before.

"Dubois and the others will soon be awake, my love," he said. "By then it will be too late. I urge you, let us escape now, together, for only in this way can you avoid the fate which awaits you as a gang member."

"But do you repent for your life of crime?" asked Justine.

"Of course not," snapped Ironheart. "What does that have to do with it?"

The child touched a gentle finger to his unshaven cheek. "You asked me to marry you, dear Ironheart," she said, "but repentance for one's sins and a firm purpose of amendment are prerequisites to the Sacrament of Marriage. Unless you repent and promise to sin no more, we will be turned away by Our Holy Mother, the Church."

"B-b-but, Justine!" sputtered the exasperated Ironheart. "I am a bandit! Mortal sin is an occupational hazard! I cannot repent!"

"Then we cannot marry —"

"Not in the church, perhaps; but do the incantations of a priest really mean that much to you? Would we not be as validly married if we were to exchange *privately* those same vows of obedience, love and sexual exclusivity?"

"No, my sweet Ironheart, I cannot accept such a relationship," said Justine curtly. "In my mind, marriage and the laws of the Church are inseperable."

"*Curses!*" spat Ironheart, furiously springing to his feet. "*Must you be so stubborn?!*" Then, wheeling angrily away from her, he spoke as if addressing the window: "My child, you leave me no choice. I must surrender you to the will of Dubois — and, simultaneously, to the baneful role of professional virgin."

"But why," protested she, "can there be no other alternative? Why couldn't you permit me to escape now, alone? Or why couldn't you escape with me and live a life of chastity until you received sufficient Grace to repent and marry me in Church?"

"Because, Justine, might makes right. In this case, I have power over you and I shall exercise it. Either marry me under my terms or suffer the consequences. Now, what is your decision?"

Justine watched the heavily-muscled scoundrel pace the length of the room, then turn to face her. His eyes met hers and, for an instant, she was strongly tempted to surrender to him. However, Virtue prevailed.

"My decision is no, dear Ironheart," she said sorrowfully. "I will not live in sin with you. I realize that my refusal might mean the sacrifice of my Virginity under circumstances of criminal force, but at least I will have resisted to the end and God will know that I have not let go of It lightly."

Ironheart turned again to the wall. Fists clenched, he raised his arms as if, for want of a better outlet for his rage, he was about to attack the bricks. For an instant his entire body trembled. Then, slowly, he relaxed and turned again to face Justine.

"My darling child," he said in tones of measured evenness, "is it not monumentally absurd to assign so great a value to this matter of virginity? Are you foolish enough to think that Goodness, that Virtue, is determined by the somewhat greater or lesser diameter of one of your physical parts? Do you honestly think that it matters to God whether this orifice goes used or unused?"

"Yes, dear Ironheart," she replied, "I honestly do. You argue skilfully, but, though I cannot cite the specific fallacy which mars your reasoning, Faith tells me that I am right in persisting to resist you."

"Then, wrong though I know you are, I shall prove my desire to please you; I shall respect your wishes. Escape with me and I promise that your esteemed orifice shall go untouched. However, let me ask that you, in turn, accept a compromise solution: the creatures of Venus, after all, may worship Her in many different temples; let me therefore bypass that altar the idleness of which you deem so important, and instead, burn my incense in the neighboring one; if it is pregnancy you fear, fear no more, for it cannot be brought about in this manner; likewise, if you worry that your indulgence will disgrace you in the eyes of others, worry not, for your treasured maidenhead will remain intact. The anal altar is a delightful place — and it would probably surprise you to know that a great many confessors have gratified themselves in this locale with penitents, the offense never being known to husband or father. So let us emulate their example, my dear; try it and we shall both be satisfied."

"Oh, sir," cried Justine, "I am appalled. I have heard that this act which you recommend is a perversion, even more greviously offensive to God that the monstrous union which it purports to replace."

"What foolishness, child! Where possibly could the offense lie?"

"In the spilling of the seed, of course. It was for this that Onan was punished."

"Absurd, my dear; wholly absurd. If the seed were put in man solely for the purpose of reproduction, then I would grant you that the spilling of it is an offense. But Nature, Herself, causes it to spill, involuntarily, in the form of nocturnal emission, hundreds of million of times a day, all over the world. Likewise, Nature gives man the ability to provoke such emission by manual manipulation. If he, in imitation of Nature, uses this ability, does man displease Her? Most assuredly not. So what of the fellow who in the imitative process employs greater ingenuity than his less imaginative brother — ingenuity as a result of which satisfaction comes not only to him but also to someone he loves: can there be a sin there? No, my sweet Justine; impossible. Thus, if you give the argument any scrutiny at all, you'll agree that the spillage of the seed is regarded all out of proportion to its place in the scheme of things."

Now, as he continued to speak, Ironheart again sat alongside Justine on the bed, and, while his discourse proceeded, his hands found their way to the magnificent buttocks which housed the altar at which he sought to worship. The girl, for her part, was so enchanted with his eloquence and his seeming lucidity of thought that she failed completely to realize that her citadel was under siege, and indeed found herself quite mystified by the warm tickles of sensation which had begun to form deeply within her.

"Nature *tolerates* reproduction," the villainous seducer went on, sliding one hand around the darling child's marvelously rounded thigh until his fingers came to rest at the very threshold of Nature's Sancturary. "She does not *prevent* us from procreating. But whether we procreate or not could not matter less to her. Believe me, my sweet, Nature cares very little about these things which we buffoons regard as her most vital interests; indeed, by our attention to them, we offend Nature more than we serve her."

The sensations which now assailed Justine became almost too strong to bear. As Ironheart's fingers gently parted the nightgown which served as the sole physical barrier to his goal, her heart began to throb furiously and her body went weak with excitement. The unscrupulous bandit, having disarmed her with his perfidious maxims, now sought to join practice and theory. Under the pretense of adjusting his watch fob, he prepared himself for the assault. Next, maneuvering her into position beneath him, he pried her succulent, ivory-white legs apart. Then, with hands made expert by years of experience, he deftly guided his monstrous organ to the very heart of the darling girl's sexuality.

"But —" began Justine, suddenly aware that all his talk of alternate altars had been only a means to distract her attention.

"Relax, my sweet," urged the vile Ironheart. "You need only trust me."

"But —" she said again. However, by this time, her hunger to be invaded had overcome her will to resist. Feeling the blunt, round edge of his pulsating sexuality as it nudged tenderly at the Doors of Ecstasy, she wanted only to surrender completely. Her warm, sweet dew of anticipation conspired with his unceasing gentle pressure to facilitate passage. Straining to the full limits of her physiology, she offered him her whole being and struggled desperately to envelop him completely.

Then, suddenly, the room was shaken by an explosion. One, two, three, four bursts of gunpowder shattered the air, followed by the clamor of voices. Ironheart, abandoning the project which had occupied his total attention— so much so that he apparently had failed to hear Madame Dubois and the other three outlaws leave the shack — leaped to his feet and ran to the window. The darling Justine, her Virtue preserved at the last possible moment, followed him.

Outside, Madame Dubois and her three cohorts were running at full speed up the path toward the shack.

Their clothes were spattered with blood, and one carried a bulging suitcase.

"Let's get moving," Dubois called to Ironheart. "We've
just killed three men and left their corpses on the road.
We won't be safe here any longer."

Snatching Justine in one hand and his coat in the other, Ironheart hurried out of the shack. With Dubois in
the lead, the four gangsters and the beautiful young
child took flight in the direction of Chantilly . . .

III

That night, gathered around a campfire in the Chantilly
forest, the gang was counting the loot from the morning's robbery. Suddenly, from the distance, came the
clatter of a horseman. "To arms!" shouted Ironheart, and
the men leapt to life. A few minutes later, a traveler was
led into the camp. While one of the bandits covered him
with a pistol, Ironheart emptied the man's pockets and
the saddlebags from his horse. Then Dubois shoved him
against a tree and told him to identify himself.

The man gave his name as Saint-Florent; he said that
he was on his way to Lyon from Flanders, where he
had been negotiating the sale of some property. His
purse and saddlebags yielded half-a-million louis in securities, payable to the bearer upon demand at any
bank, along with several gems and perhaps one-hundred
louis in cash; all in all, it was a very profitable haul.

"Well, my friend," said Ironheart, raising his pistol to
Saint-Florent's temple, "you know that we can't leave
you alive now that we have robbed you."

Hearing this, the luckless traveler went white with
fear and began pleading frantically that his life be spared. The kind Justine, moved to compassion, interjected
a word in his behalf; likewise, for different motives, an-

other of the bandits spoke up, suggesting that the gang follow Saint-Florent to Lyon and there also empty the safe at his home. But Madame Dubois, whose decision was final, refused to be swayed by these arguments.

"It is not worth the risk to leave this man alive," she said coldly. "We must kill him in the interests of our security." Then, turning to the victim, she went on: "It is not that we have anything against you personally. Rather, it is the fault of unjust laws. Since thieves and robbers are condemned to death just like murderers, there's no point in letting a robbery victim live; after all, one can lose one's head only once, right?"

These sentiments having been pronounced, she nodded to Ironheart, who again raised his pistol. However, before the swarthy bandit could fire, the tender Justine hurled herself in the weapon's path.

"Oh, sir!" she cried. "I beseech you not to welcome me to your gang with a horrible spectacle like this. Grant this first request I submit to you, and permit this man to live." Then, in order to justify her interest in sparing the captive's life, she leaned toward Ironheart's ear and whispered — altogether untruthfully: "The name by which Saint-Florent identifies himself leads me to believe that I know his family. They are among the wealthiest in Lyon, with millions upon millions of louis in land and securities. This money could be yours and mine, darling — we wouldn't have to share it with anyone — if we were smart enough to escape with him tonight and leave the gang behind."

"You display a craftiness with which I never credited you, Justine," replied Ironheart, smiling broadly. "Evidently I taught you more this morning than the mere appreciation of Nature's impulses."

"Much more, my love," lied Justine sweetly, at the same time very passionately kissing Ironheart's ear.

"I'll do as you say, then," said he, backing away from her. And, to the entire group he said: "Our recruit, the lovely Justine, has suggested that we keep the prisoner as a hostage for a day or two; this will facilitate our escape to more familiar terrain, and we can always kill him immediately if he tries to escape in the meanwhile. What do you think?"

Two of the bandits voiced skepticism, but Madame Dubois accepted Ironheart's reasoning fully. "Tie him up against that tree," she ordered. "We'll move him out with us in the morning." Then, her instructions having been carried out, she said: "We'll be leaving just after dawn, so put out the fire now and we'll all get some sleep."

When the fire was extinguished and each member of the gang had bedded down, Ironheart crawled over to Justine. "My darling," he said, gently cupping her breast in his large hand, "I am amazed and delighted with the change which has come over you. I want nothing more than to marry you and to travel with you as a team, robbing and stealing everywhere, living off the proceeds like a king and queen."

"I'd like nothing better, my love," said Justine in reply, and, as if to demonstrate her sincerity, she brought her open lips to his.

Almost instantly, Ironheart was on top of her, kissing her wildly, caressing her passionately. His expert knees deftly worked her thighs open, and, as he whispered words of endearment in her ear, his hand found its way under her dress and adroitly began to work smoothly and swiftly over the curve of her silken hips.

"Oh, my darling," gasped Justine, nearly reeling under the force of his attack. "I want you so badly — but let us not jeopardize our plan by overeagerness at this stage. Return to your blanket on the other side of the fire and I'll wake you just before dawn; after our escape, we'll have as much time for lovemaking as either of us could possibly want."

Ironheart, thoroughly enchanted by the change which appeared to have come over the darling young girl, bowed to her judgement and quietly withdrew. An hour later, the crafty Justine, after checking to make sure that he was soundly asleep, crawled to the tree against which Saint-Florent was tied. Waking the astonished prisoner, she put into action the second phase of her plan to foil the bandits.

"Oh, sir," she whispered to Saint-Florent quickly, "I have been thrown into the company of these thieves by the most unfortunate series of events, but I am not one of them — I detest them and all they stand for. Let me put myself in your keeping and then let us escape together at once . . ."

IV

For two days and two nights, Justine and Saint-Florent traveled without pause until, finally, they reached the town of Luzarches. Here, knowing themselves to be reasonably safe, they put up for the night in a small inn and planned their third day's journey, which would take them to Lyon, where Saint-Florent could reestablish contact with his family.

Now, when all details had been attended to, Saint-Florent took Justine's hand in his and said: "It is to you, my sweet girl, that I owe my life and my fortune. I can think of no other way to reward you than by placing both at your feet. Receive them both, I pray you, and consent to being joined to me by the holy bonds of matrimony."

Hearing this eloquent proposal, Justine was overcome with pleasure. She believed, however, that Saint-Florent was acting more from gratitude than from love, and accordingly rejected his offer.

"Sir," she said, "if you really feel that you would like to reward me, then all I ask is that you permit me to accompany you to Lyon and that, perhaps, you find me a place in some proper household where my Virtue will not be put to the test." Thereupon she told the story of all her misfortunes, from the death of her parents to her near-seduction at the hands of the persuasive Ironheart, and begged Saint-Florent to join her in a prayer of thanksgiving that circumstances had intervened on the morning when she all but surrendered fully to the unscrupulous bandit's carnal advances.

After hearing the story and joining her in the prayer, Saint-Florent expressed his deepest sympathies. "But," he added, "there is no need for further grief, for, if a place in a proper household is all you want, then you need not even accompany me to Lyon. My sister lives just a short distance from here and I am sure she would be more than happy to take you in with her; I'll introduce you the first thing tomorrow morning."

Delighted at this unexpected good news, Justine went to her room and slept soundly all night. When she awoke shortly before dawn the next day, she was in better humor than she had known in years. However, her joy was to be short lived, for, a short time after they had set out for the supposed house of Saint-Florent's sister, Justine found that she had once again fallen into the clutches of a madman — this time one far more depraved than Ironheart or any of his predecessors.

Leading her to a clearing deep in the woods outside Luzarches, the scoundrelous Saint-Florent suddenly turned on her and kicked her savagely in the stomach. When she doubled over in pain, he kicked her viciously in the face. Then, as the poor child struggled to gain her bal-

ance, he lashed out with his walking stick, and, swinging
it like a club, struck her over the head. She fell, unconscious, at his feet.

Many hours later, when finally she awoke, Justine
slowly came to realize the extent to which she had been
made the monstrous man's victim. It was now darkest
night, and her body — completely nude and covered
with bruises — was lying at the foot of a tree. The tips
of her breasts had been lacerated, apparently from his
gnawing on them, and her mouth was caked with blood.
The violent pains inside her abdomen left no doubt that
he had availed himself of the hymenal fruit which she
had prized so highly. Thus, having risked her own life
to save Saint-Florent, she was paid back by being ravaged, than abandoned in the middle of a strange forest,
without resources, without hope and without even her
honor.

"What did I do to him," she cried half-aloud, "to deserve such inhumane treatment? Oh, Man, this is what
happens when you abandon yourself to your passions!
A savage beast would have been less cruel! The lions of
the jungle would turn away in disgust from such atrocities!" Now, lifting her eyes to heaven, she continued:
"Oh, Holy Majesty, behold my miseries and my torments
and take me to Thy bosom. I have sought to do well, in
imitation of Thee, and Thou hast seen fit to punish me
for it; but I surrender completely to Thy will; forgive my
assailants, for they know not how their sins offend Thee,
and give me the grace to rededicate myself to Thy service. Amen."

Her courage now renewed by these devotions, the
crushed and pain-wracked Justine lifted herself from
the ground, gathered together the rags to which her
dress had been reduced by the villainous Saint-Florent,
and cleared a space in a thicket. Here she lay down and,

with another prayer on her lips, fell into a deep and viscous sleep.

V

When Justine awoke the sun was high. Strengthened by the sweet ministrations of slumber, she got to her feet and with her hands brushed her naked body clean. She had hardly finished this when she heard voices close by; slowly two men materialized just outside the thicket.

"Come, my love," said one, an elegant-looking man of perhaps twenty-four years. "This place looks safe enough. I'm sure my abhorrent aunt won't spot us here."

The other man, slightly younger, nodded docilely and began to remove his clothes.

Now, before Justine's very eyes, there unfolded the most indecent of dramas — that horrible crime which outrages not only Nature but also social convention; the sin, in short, which God punished by the torments He visited upon the city of Sodom! Daring not to budge lest she be detected, the poor child had no choice but to witness the entire obscene spectacle.

First the younger man removed his trousers and bent forward, exposing to his companion the "alternate altar" the praises of which Ironheart had so enthusiastically sung. Then the companion — whose name, Justine was later to learn, was Count de Bressac — began caressing the youth's plump buttocks. This vile act spurred both parties to new heights of excitement; Bressac, suddenly overcome with desire, tore open his clothing and brandished an organ far more immense than that monstrosity with which Ironheart had attempted days earlier to impale Justine. "Look what I have for you, Jasmine," he teased the young pathick. "Does it intimidate you?"

Jasmine, far from intimidated, spun around and leaped

upon the organ with undisguised appreciation; seizing it with both hands, he innundated it with kisses, then struggled to take the whole of it into his mouth. Bressac, for his part, soon became even more aroused than his partner; turning the youth away from him, he took aim on his target, then advanced, plunging the gargantuan appendage in to the very hilt.

Now the licentious charade reached its zenith. Drunk with lust, the two men writhed and moaned. Jasmine cried out in pain, yet seemed really to enjoy every moment matching the rhythm of his partner, he rose to anticipate each thrust: a normal couple, lawfully joined, could not have done battle more passionately. Finally, the crest having been passed, all urgency was drained from their movements; slowly the obscene machinations of the bizarre lovers ground to a halt.

The travesty now over, Bressac and his pathick started toward the path which led from the woods. Suddenly, however, when they drew alongside the thicket in which Justine lay hidden, the Count stopped short.

"Jasmine!" he hissed. "We've been discovered! A girl has seen the whole thing!"

Justine, as frightened of the duo as she was appalled by their behavior, came out of the bush trembling.

"Oh, sirs," she cried, throwing herself to her knees in front of them, "have pity on me. My present sorry state is the result of my misfortunes, not my faults. Please help me escape the ills with which Fate lately has tormented me."

Bressac, whose normal insensitivity to the sorrows of others was compounded by the fact that Justine was a girl, folded one arm across the other and regarded her with a look of amused contempt. "My little twat," he said, "if you're looking for suckers, improve your style. Jasmine and I are immune to the lures of your gender, and, as concerns appeals for alms, we don't believe in charity. So, if you expect anything from us, you'd better have a novel approach."

Justine, not permitting herself to be discouraged by this rudeness, plunged into her tale, acquainting the two male-lovers with all the ills which had visited her from the day of her birth. "And so," she concluded, "I appeal to you to alleviate the dire circumstances into which Fate has presently thrust me."

Bressac, who had gazed steadily at her throughout the entire recital, now turned to Jasmine and spoke in tones of mock solemnity. "Well, my friend," he mused, his face a study in condescension, "it seems that Fate has given this poor child a really rough time."

"Indeed, indeed," replied the pathick, nodding judiciously.

"Now," Bressac went on, "the question is: why? We all know that Fate is just; therefore there must be a reason — and far be it from us to frustrate the reasoning of Fate."

"Far be it indeed," agreed the pathick.

"Well, then, we have no choice," said Bressac. Turning to Justine, he continued: "My little twat, quite obviously the misfortunes which have befallen you are the result of Fate's having decreed the death penalty for you; but apparently, thus far, those whom Fate has selected as executioners have failed miserably in the task."

"Failed indeed," injected Jasmine.

"Now then," Bressac went on, smiling self-satisfiedly, "this whole affair is no business of Jasmine's or mine; yet, we have, through our sexual activities, occasionally disturbed the plans of Fate, and now we feel impelled to make amends. What better way could we do this than by seeing that in your case the death sentence of Fate is carried out?"

The full impact of his pronouncement only very slowly came through to the potential victim of his deviltry. "You mean —" Justine began.

"Precisely, my dear," cackled the depraved Bressac. "We are going to put you to death."

Greatly amused by her cries and screams, Bressac and Jasmine dragged the hapless Justine farther into the woods until they came to a clearing where four trees were arranged in a square. Fashioning ropes out of their handkerchiefs, shirts and neckties, they tied her arms and legs to the trees, then stretched the bonds until the poor girl lay, face down, suspended in air.

"By God!" exclaimed Bressac. "Doesn't it thrill you, Jasmine, to see the lovely creature stretched out this way? Contemplate those buttocks, my friend; see how the cheeks are squeezed together? By Christ's crotch, I think she has one of the most marvelous asses I've ever seen! What a shame that she hasn't a spear like yours to go along with it, or I might be tempted to throw my own into her. But, no; a man must stick to his principles, and mine are: if it hasn't a cock, don't bugger it."

Justine's limbs felt like they were being wrenched from her body; her belly, strained to elasticity's limits, seemed ready to burst. Her mouth was dry and perspiration bathed her forehead. So great became her pain that she prayed aloud for death as a means of alleviating it. But the villains, lacking even a modicum of compassion, would not release her, no matter how heart-rending her pleas; while she writhed in agony, the jaded Bressac and his youthful pathick giggled and taunted her, and embraced each other playfully.

Soon their playfulness blossomed into hot passion. Tearing open his trousers and unsheathing the mammoth member with which he had earlier impaled his colleague's anus, the craven count commanded: "To your knees, pathick; the rhubarb wishes to be eaten." Immediately Jasmine fell upon the upthrust organ. "By the ass-reaming angels and saints!" cheered Bressac. "What a talent you have, my love! What a touch! What a squeeze! Satan save us, I think I'm going to come!" Thereupon the hot-tongued Jasmine, lips smacking and saliva dribbling, took into his mouth the whole of the organ. Groaning and grunting, he wrapped his arms about Bressac's thighs and pushed his face against that debauchee's pelvis with such force that one might think he sought to drive the spear out through the back of his neck. Bressac, meanwhile, his body aflame with passion, writhed and undulated ferociously; seizing the nance viciously by his ears, he began to tug and jerk at the youth's head, simultaneously smashing into it with forceful strokes of his hips, and all the while chanting the weirdest, most blasphemous obscenities, over and over again like a litany.

For two full hours Justine was made to suffer on her improvised rack as the depraved sodomite and his eager accomplice staged one obscene spectacle after another; then, as she wavered weakly on the threshold of unconsciousness, her captors finally cut her loose. "We shall spare you, my little twat," said Bressac coldly; "but not from mercy; no, rather from cleverness, for I believe that you can be quite useful to me."

Justine, nearly delerious from her suffering, gratefully threw herself at his feet. Tears streaming down her cheeks, she embraced his knees and swore to do whatever he asked.

"Indeed you shall," replied the haughty Count. "If you don't, you can look forward to a repeat performance of this afternoon's tortures." Then, jerking her roughly to her feet, he said: "Now come with me. My aunt is spending the summer at my castle and she needs a maid. If

your story, as you have told it, can be verified, you will
have a job in my household and I'll be able to keep an
eye on you until the time çomes to put you to work in
my behalf."

Speaking thusly, Bressac pushed Justine toward the
path which led from the clearing. With the demented
Count and his dutiful aide prodding her from behind,
the unfortunate child advanced toward the castle where
still further tortures — far worse than any she had yet
experienced — lay in wait.

VI

The Count's widowed aunt, Marquise de Bressac, was a
charming and wholly delightful woman. She at once became quite fond of Justine. After listening attentively
to the child's history of misfortune, she smiled reassuringly and said: "Your troubles are over, sweet child.
Your naivete is such that I cannot doubt the truthfulness
of your claims; I will not bother even to have them corroborated. Consider yourself hired as my personal maid.
You begin work immediately."

In the weeks which followed, Justine worked happily
at the Marquise's side. The cruel Count de Bressac gave
no hint of the use to which he had said he planned to
put the girl; indeed, it was only rarely that the craven
Count made an appearance at the castle, and, on such
occasions, he always kept his distance. Meanwhile, in
September, when the Marquise prepared to return to
Paris, she offered to bring Justine with her — an offer
which the delighted child eagerly accepted. Thus the
summer had passed, and every thought of unhappiness
vanished from the sweet Justine's mind, to be replaced
by only hope and joy.

No sooner had they arrived in Paris than the Marquise

went to work to clear Justine's good name. First the accusations of Hairpin, which had sent the poor girl to prison, were reinvestigated and proved baseless (the presiding judge sought to punish him, but the scoundrelous usuer had escaped to England after amassing a fortune through dealings in counterfeit banknotes). Then the case of the burning of the Conciergerie was reopened, and a panel of jurists agree that, although Justine had profited from the event, she was in no wise responsible for it; charges against her were dropped. Finally, an inquiry into the operations of Madame Dubois' gang corroborated the child's claim that she had accompanied the villains only as an alternative to degradation and death, and had not participated actively in any of their crimes; she was freed of all complicity.

The winter passed, then the spring. Summer came and the Marquise returned to the castle of her nephew, the Count. Somewhat to her surprise, Justine found the depraved Bressac considerably more cordial this time: he still gave no indication of the purposes for which he had said a year earlier that he planned to use her; however, he did show what appeared to be a great deal of solicitude, and, on many occasions, he engaged her in lengthy discussions.

"Justine," he stated in a typical discussion, "all religions are based on a false premise. Each maintains that there was a First Cause to all existence, and that this First Cause is, by the very fact of His chronological precedence, automatically superior to everyone and everything which followed. But this notion is without foundation. Why must He be superior? And, if He ever *was* superior, what happened to Him along the way? — because, surely, He demonstrates none of His alleged superiority now; no super-human being would permit the injustices which prevail in the world today.

"What, then, is religion but the weapon of the vested interests, the means by which the weak may be kept weak, and, therefore, exploitable? Conniving priests, passing themselves off as the voices of God, mouth blatant sophistries; men, assailed with the nonsense from the very dawn of consciousness, have little choice but to believe: yet, examine these beliefs in the light of reason and you cannot fail to see right through them.

"Is there a single religion which does not bear the stamp of imposture and roguery? Not a one. Do you ask them for truth? They have none to offer. What do they offer in its stead? Dogmas which affront logic, liturgical grotesqueries which inspire only disgust and derision, and mysteries which cause reason to shudder!

"Yes, Justine, they are all corrupt; but, if there's one religion which merits our special condemnation, it is that odious monstrosity, Christianity. Let us consider for a moment the perfidious cult's founder, Jesus Christ. Who was he but the illegitimate son of a Nazarene slut and a miserable carpenter? Yet he dares acclaim himself as the Ambassador of none other than Him Who, they say, created all things! Now, you'll agree that this is quite a pose; certainly one would expect it to be accompanied by the display of at least a few credentials. But what credentials does this scoundrel show? How does he propose to prove his mission? Will the face of the earth be changed? Will the sun now shine on it both day and night? Will vice and misery and suffering be eliminated? Will mankind know complete happiness at last? No; no such thing. As credentials he offers only sleight-of-hand tricks and hocus-pocus; as proofs, only riddles and gobbledegook. And whom does he select as his colleagues? Not the acknowledged leaders of his time; not the doctors and the lawmen and the scholars: no, he selects a dozen, beef-witted adolescents — the oldest of them,

John, still in his teens. Capital! And, while we are on the subject, does it not strike you as a bit peculiar that a man of thirty prefers the company of boys? If you knew anything of persons who, like me, are in love with their gender, it certainly would open interesting avenues of speculation!

"So now you have a mountebank and his twelve dupes, and they roam the countryside preaching absurdities. For awhile they are all but ignored. Eventually, however, their seditious aims are made apparent and they are jailed. The 'ambassador,' himself, has by this time so offended the public that, when given a choice, a mob calls for his death at the expense of the freedom of the most notorious thief and murderer of the age, Barrabas. But then, when the 'Ambassador' is finally slain, authorities are foolish enough to set his disciples free. What happens now? The dunces take up where their master left off. Weak minds soon fall prey to their fanatacism. Women shriek. Madmen howl. Fools turn somersaults. And, lo! It has happened! The most maladroit imposter in the history of man has been deified! Here he is ! God! The Son of God! Both in one! Now all his ravings become dogma! All his dreams, Articles of Faith! All his blunders, mysteries! And, if you question it, you become a heretic — doomed to death at the hands of the Inquisitor!

"And does it stop there, this exercise in insanity?! I should say not, For, today, this same God, this same Almighty Jesus Christ, at the beck and call of a hundred-thousand clowns in ludicrous uniforms, descends ten-or twelve-million times in the form of a morsel of wheat, and is promptly ingested by the 'faithful,' in whose intestines He is speedily changed into feces — and all this, one is told, to prove His goodness!

"Now, I ask you: if there were a God, and He really

were omnipotent, would He be a party to this execrable
impiety?! Were He supreme, were He almighty, were
He good, were He just, would he wish to teach men to
know, love and serve Him by means of such buffooner-
ies? Further, would He reveal His wishes only in a remote corner of Asia; articulated only by a bandit known
for his craftiness; witnessed only by thieves, tradesmen
and sluts; voiced in language so ambiguous that it can
be interpreted to mean anything you might possibly
want it to mean? And, having done this, would He leave
the rest of the world in error, and punish it for remaining there?!

"Well, my dear, if this is the way your God operates,
I'll not have anything to do with him. When Atheism requires martyrs, my blood is ready to be shed; but for this
Christianity, into which both you and I had the misfortune to be born, I have nothing but contempt."

Thus spoke the perfidious Bressac; and, though Justine
employed every argument at her command, she was unable to persuade him to change his mind. Worse still,
the poor child found that she was falling in love with
him! Days would pass when she could think of no one —
and nothing — else. Her sole wish was to be in his presence, basking in the glow of his supreme self-confidence,
being lulled into a state of complete relaxation by the
reassuring lilt of his mellifluous tones. And all this despite the fact that she had it on no less authority than
that of Bressac, himself, that because she was a woman,
he could never love her in return. As he one day had
told her:

"Incredible inconsistency, is it not, that I may abhor
the female gender, yet wish to imitate it? But this is my
only pleasure, darling Justine, and most persons can
never know how sweet it is. We deviates, you see, are
biologically different from other men; like them, we are

possessed of the Spear of Jupiter: however, unlike them, we also enjoy an Altar of Sodom lined with the same sensitive membranes which adorn your Altar of Venus. Thus, in congress with another of my kind, I know double the pleasure; locked in his arms, my mouth glued to his, our tongues intertwined, I desire nothing more than the perpetuation of our union; if I fear anything, it is only that I might one day displease him; if I know loss, it is only the loss incurred in the form of his absence; and there is no pleasure imaginable which surpasses that supreme moment of ecstasy when his sexuality immolates me, when his life-giving semen probes the depths of my bowels and so inflames me that my emission simultaneously leaps forward into his hands."

Listening to his words, Justine realized full well the folly of loving this monster. Yet, try though she might, she could not extinguish the fires of passion; indeed, every attempt to dampen them succeeded only in fanning their flames, and, thus, the vile Bressac never was loved more by her than when she pondered the many reasons why she should hate him.

VII

Four tranquil years passed in the employ of Marquise de Bressac. Then came the day — inevitable under the Plan of Heaven — when Justine's period of peace was destined to end. Significantly, this was the same day on which Count de Bressac told her the awful use to which he had intended to put her ever since he spared her life that first day in the woods: he wanted her to murder his aunt!

"It's quite simple, really," said Bressac glibly. "A drop of poison in her teacup, and lo! — instant death! She won't feel a thing."

Appalled, Justine begged him to change his mind.
Failing this, she flatly refused to go along with his plan.
"Dispose of my life, if you insist," she said, "but I'll never
succumb to your wishes."

However, Bressac was not to be refused so easily.
"Hear me out, Justine," he said, "I think I can prove to
you that this act from which you recoil in such great
fright is basically a quite banal matter. As an intelligent woman you have no choice but to listen to my arguments."

Approached thusly, Justine gave him ear. The perverse Bressac spoke as follows:

"Lawmakers oppose murder because it is regarded as
the destruction of one's fellow-creature. This, however,
is an erroneous view. In reality, man does not have the
capacity to destroy; he has, at best, the power to alter
the form of a thing: murder, therefore, is not destruction,
but transformation.

"Now I ask you: can Nature value one form above another? Can she really care if what is today a biped ver-
tebrate tomorrow, transformed, appears in the form of
several centipedes and a dozen worms? Most assuredly
not. But man — proud, proud man, fancying himself the
most worthy of the earth's inhabitants — pampers his
vanity by making murder a crime, or, more specifically,
by making the murder of other humans a crime, for, obviously, he doesn't object to the atrocities we perpetrate
upon the rest of the animal kingdom in the interests of
keeping ourselves fat.

"Moreover, man does not deem all murders criminal,
but only those which are undertaken in the spirit of private enterprise. The State murders thieves without the
slightest qualm, the Church likewise has murdered
heretics and atheists, and this is not only tolerated but
defended as a necessity — the reasoning being that un-

less these people are exterminated they will make life difficult for the rest of us.

"Now, tell me: is there any difference between public murders and private ones, save differences in the means and circumstances? And thus, as the Church is justified in murdering heretics to guard the morals of the faithful and as the State is justified in murdering thieves to guard the purses of the rich, am I not also justified in murdering my aunt for the purposes of improving my own fortunes?"

"Oh, sir," cried Justine, "these perfidious maxims are the thoughts of the devil himself —"

"But," interrupted Bressac, "you can't refute them."

"Nor shall I try," she replied. "I beg you sir: if logic leads you this far astray from the path of Righteousness, abandon logic and heed only your heart — but, whatever you do, put aside this nefarious scheme at once."

Bressac regarded her curiously for a moment, then smiled in obvious self-satisfaction. "So you won't volunteer to help me, sweet Justine?" he said. "Very well, then, I must coerce you."

"And how do you propose to do that?"

"Why, by threatening to murder the Marquise myself, of course — and to blame you for it. After all, whom would the courts believe? The victim's grief-stricken nephew? Or an orphan who has been convicted of theft, who has served time in the Conciergerie and who has consorted with a known band of criminals? Do you honestly think that any judge will turn a kind ear to your pleas when they are presented alongside my eloquent arguments?"

"Oh, sir," gasped Justine, "I never dreamed that even you could be so wicked as to perpetrate such a scheme."

"But the evidence is before you," replied the diabolical pervert. "Now the question is, do you cooperate with my plan — and enrich yourself in the process, for I intend to share the inheritance with you — or do you oppose me and suffer accordingly?"

The threat forced Justine to view the matter in a completely different light. Were she to defy Bressac now, she not only would place her own life in jeopardy but also would insure the Marquise's speedy death at the very efficient hands of that kindly woman's monstrous nephew. Conversely, if she slyly feigned consent to the plan, she could both shield herself and delay matters long enough to enable the Marquise to seek help from the police!

Realizing that instant capitulation might arouse the astute Bressac's suspicions, Justine pretended indecision; then, slowly, she let herself be persuaded. Finally, after the Count had repeated his arguments for the sixth time, she acquiesced. Bressac was overjoyed. Seizing her about the waist, he lifted her into the air and spun her around above him. Then, lowering her to her feet again, he held her to him and kissed her tenderly on the cheek.

"My darling Justine," he said, "you are the first woman I have ever kissed, and, truly, it is with all my heart. Never has a female been more attractive to me."

And Justine, knowing full well that she had more reason than ever to despise him thoroughly, felt herself wanting nothing more than to languish in his arms . . .

VIII

The murder date was set for two weeks hence. Count de Bressac then went about the business of procuring the poison. Meanwhile, Justine, as soon as she could get alone with the Marquise, disclosed the plot and urged the woman to seek police protection at once.

"Ah, Justine," replied the Marquise, "the infamy over-

whelms me! And yet, though I know you have no reason
to lie, I find that my heart still nourishes a kindly sentiment for the monster who you say would murder me.
Therefore, I beg of you: get me proof; convince me in
such a manner that I will never doubt you."

In compliance with this request, Justine two days later
obtained from Bressac the package of poison with which
the murder was to be committed. Showing it to the Marquise, she argued that it would be all but impossible to
furnish better proof. The Marquise, however, still was
not fully convinced that it was really poison. Wishing to
experiment, she administered a dose to one of her pet
dogs. The animal immediately was seized by convulsions;
after howling fiercely for nearly two hours, it died.

Her doubts now completely dispelled, the Marquise
sent Justine with the package containing the rest of the
poison directly to police headquarters. But the mission
was not to be accomplished. As the girl left the castle,
by whom should she be overtaken but Bressac, himself.
Having heard the howling of the dog, he had investiga-
ted and determined the cause of its death; now, aware
that he had been betrayed, he sought only to avenge the
betrayal.

Aided by his pathick, Jasmine, the furious Count
spirited Justine through the woods behind the castle.
Before long they were at the clearing where stood the
four trees to which the poor girl had been bound so
cruelly more than five years previously.

Beholding the torturesome place, Justine felt a shiver
run through her. However, her fear was soon magnified
a thousand times, for Bressac, leaving her with Jasmine,
disappeared into the woods and returned with a coil of
rope and with six huge dogs, all snarling savagely as
they strained at the leash and dribbled rivers of white
foam.

Now, while Jasmine guarded the dogs, Bressac ripped Justine's dress from her back. In seconds he had her stripped naked. A maniacal gleam lighting his eyes, he inspected her soft, white flesh. Then he chuckled softly.

"You have lovely buttocks, my little dove," he told her. "Likewise very nice breasts. I imagine they'll make a pleasant repast for these hungry mastiffs."

Justine fell to her knees and appealed to his mercy, but her efforts were in vain. Bressac watched with an expression of extreme distaste as she pleaded, then swung out with his foot, striking her on the jaw and knocking her to the ground. When she staggered to her feet, he shoved her toward one of the trees. Then he tied one end of the coil of rope around her waist and the other around the tree trunk, leaving sufficient slack for her to move two meters in any direction. This accomplished he turned to Jasmine and said:

"The time has come. Free the dogs."

With savage ferocity, the six animals flung themselves upon the poor girl's body. In seconds the pure, white softness of her flesh was streaked with red. Yet, the attack continued: the animals bit and scratched, jerked and tore; each new wound seemed only to heighten their fury. Bressac, meanwhile, regarded the spectacle with an expression of undisguised glee; he chortled madly as the dogs struggled with each other for the untouched portions of Justine's body, and, as the orgy of violence reached its peak, he clutched the ever-dutiful Jasmine to him and began smothering the youth with kisses and caresses.

Finally the whole of poor Justine's body had been ravaged by the beasts. She slumped from the tree in a state of near-unconsciousness. "Very well," said Bressac, "that is enough. Tie up the dogs."

After Jasmine had curbed the last of the snarling, blood-snouted creatures, Bressac knelt alongside the feeble Justine and grinned. "Well, little twat," he whispered into her ear, "you now have learned the price of betrayal." Then, untying the rope which bound her to the tree, he added: "You might be wondering why I spared your life. It was — like the last time I had you tied to these trees — not from mercy, but from cleverness. You see, you have not outlived your usefulness yet."

Justine, blood streaming from her wounds, dropped to her hands and knees at the foot of the tree. With compresses fashioned from the shreds of her dress, she attempted futilely to arrest the bleeding. Running out of cloth, she then began wiping at the blood with handfuls of grass.

"When I leave here," Bressac went on, oblivious to her pain, "I am going to poison my aunt as planned. Then I am going to go to the police and charge you with the crime, saying that you escaped in the commotion surrounding her collapse. Jasmine will corroborate my story, and your past record will lend credence to our claims. If during the next few days you die of your wounds, police will find your body and assume that you were set upon by bandits with dogs. If you live long enough to escape, they will institute a countrywide search and, when eventually they locate you, you will be charged with murder."

Now, bending over her and taking her chin in his hand, the craven Count tilted her face toward his and leered menacingly. "So, little twat," he concluded, "I leave you to your pains — and with the thought that you could have avoided it all if only you had succumbed to my wishes."

"Oh, sir," replied the child weakly, "you may rest assured that, regardless of what you have done to me, I

wish you no ill. You shall be in my prayers for as long as
I live, be it only a few more hours or be it many years.
And my only wish for you is that your crimes make you
as happy as your cruelties have made me miserable."

And, so saying, she collapsed at his feet in a pool of
her own blood.

BOOK THREE

When Justine regained consciousness night was closing
in. Marshalling all her strength she managed to crawl
the few yards to the thicket where, almost five years
earlier, she had slept under conditions almost as severe.
There, after praying for the salvation of both her soul
and Bressac's, she lay down and fell into a fitful sleep.

When she awoke at dawn, she was still quite weak.
However, her bleeding had stopped and she was able
to muster sufficient energy to crawl. Proceeding in this
slow and painful manner, she managed by dusk to reach
the town of Saint-Marcel, about fourteen kilometers distant. Here, she asked for a physician and was brought
to the offices of one Doctor Rodin.

Rodin was forty years old, husky, dark-haired and the
possessor of thick, shaggy eyebrows; there was something about his sparkling bright eyes which suggested

great strength, but also libertinage. After examining Justine's wounds carefully, he told her that she was not in critical condition. If she remained at his house, he added, he probably could cure her in a few weeks. Justine protested that she would be unable to pay for such treatment, but Rodin insisted that she stay anyway, telling her that she could pay him whenever she got the money. When she consented to this arrangement, he gave her a small glass of spirits, then put her to bed; immediately she fell into a deep sleep.

The next morning Justine awoke to find herself looking into the face of a stunning, fourteen-year-old girl in whom were gathered all the charms most capable of arousing admiration. Her figure was that of a nymph; her skin, marble-soft and incredibly white; her face, a perfect oval; her features, delicate; her eyes, soulful; her mouth, petite, and her marvelous chestnut hair, a waterfall-like splendor which cascaded all the way to her waist. Her name, she said, was Rosalie; she was Doctor Rodin's daughter.

Over the next few days, with Rosalie as her private nurse and with Rodin in constant attendance, Justine rapidly regained her health. By the third day, she had begun eating normally once again; by the fourth, she was up and around, and, by the fifth, she had lost all but the barest traces of pain. Moreover, she was overjoyed with what appeared to be an incredible stroke of good fortune; in the person of the solicitous doctor and his lovely daughter she had found two persons who ministered to her every need, and who seemed to want nothing more than to see her happy; secure in their company, she felt that at last the time had come when she would know true peace. However, as had proved to be the case before, her peace was but a prelude designed by Fate to disarm the poor girl for a subsequent period of distress . . . .

II

Doctor Rodin maintained in his home a school for boys and girls. There were fourteen students of each gender, who were never accepted under age twelve and were always dismissed upon reaching sixteen. Moreover, all were almost unbelievably pretty.

Justine could not understand why Rodin, while working as a surgeon, also bothered himself not only to maintain the school but to teach all classes personally. One afternoon, when they were alone, she posed the question to Rosalie, with whom, by this time, she had become very close friends.

"Oh, my darling Justine," sobbed Rosalie, throwing herself into Justine's arms, "I beg you not to repeat what I am going to confide in you; but I have been burdened with this horrible secret for years, and I must tell someone.

"My father is a doctor, yes, and one of the best in France; however, he practices very little anymore, turning over almost all his work to Doctor Rombeau, a colleague with whom he frequently collaborates on experiments. This frees him to devote almost full time to his school, which he runs for only one reason: no, not humanity, or charity, or altruism, or any of that, my darling friend; rather, for libertinage — that and nothing more. You see, my warped father employs his pupils as correspondents in the vilest and most base sex acts imaginable, acts which strain credulity. But wait! Today is Friday, one of the three days a week during which he conducts his 'disciplinary' sessions. From a closet just off my room we can look into his office without being seen; I'll show you an example of his libertinage in action."

So saying, the lovely Rosalie led Justine down a corridor to a small closet. No sooner had they positioned themselves at two large cracks in the wall than Rodin entered his office, dragging behind him a young, pretty, blonde girl. The child could not have been more than thirteen years old, and was sobbing pitifully as she begged Rodin's forgiveness.

"Not on your life," the doctor said, leading her toward a pillar in the center of the room. "I've forgiven you once too often. You still pass notes to boys and you still talk in class, and I must blame these continued breaches on nothing but my own leniency with you. Now the time has come to right the wrong."

"But I didn't do anything —" protested the tearful child.

"Yes you did, my dear," scolded Rodin. "You passed a note and I saw you."

Rosalie, leaning away from her crack in the wall, whispered into Justine's ear: "Don't believe a word he says. He makes up all these offences because he needs some excuse to conscript these poor children for his lustful pleasures."

Now, as she said this, Rodin seized the the little girl's hands and thrust them into a pair of manacles fitted high on a pillar in the center of the room. Immediately the child winced in pain; tears streamed down her beautiful face; her splendid blonde hair fell into provocative disarray. Inflamed by the sight of her, the savage Rodin brought his face within inches of hers and glared into her eyes; then, covering those beautiful eyes with a blindfold, he took her face in both hands and kissed her forcefully upon the mouth.

Now, his eyes agleam with excitement, his face livid with lust, the jaded physician slowly unbuttoned her blouse. The veils of modesty were drawn until she was completely naked to the waist. Then, more slowly still, he peeled the top of her skirt over her hips until its edge came to rest just above the small curve of her pelvis.

The child's body thus half exposed, was a monument of perfection — a soft, creamy-white, exquisitely-sculptured torso with small round breasts giving way to the gently-tapered form of her tiny, flat belly and the marvelously-moulded ovals of her hips. Her chest rose and fell and her flawless tummy quivered with each sob. But these allurements stirred no tender sentiments in the jaded Rodin. Panting like an animal, he seized a nine-tailed whip from a vat of vinegar where it had been soaking to give its thongs hardness and sting. Then, raising it above his head, he took one last look at the perfect, white expanse of her loveliness.

"Prepare yourself, child," he said hoarsely. "Justice must be done. The sentence is twenty-five strokes."

And then the lashes came whistling through the air, cutting into her breasts and stomach, leaving in their wake nine glistening-red wounds.

The child's cries split the air, and this development inflamed Rodin all the more. Raising the long-tongued whip over his head, he swung a second time; a third; a fourth; a fifth . . . a twenty-fifth. Now the girl's body was a latticework of red welts, and Rodin, far from quieted, was gripped by a new madness. Ripping her skirt from her hips, he drooled wildly as the blood, dammed up by the garment's folds; trickled in brilliant red streams over her pelvis and down the marvelous white pillars which were her legs. Then he began to tear madly at her wounded breasts, kneading them, squeezing them, maneuvering them into various positions. Unfastening his belt, he dropped his trousers, revealing a monstrous member aroused to the very summit of passion. Brandishing this before him, he bent the girl backward and advanced on her. Then, suddenly, he stopped short at the threshold of the lovely Altar toward which his worship was directed.

"So," he spat at the child, "you try to seduce me! Well, I won't have it. There are more fertile fields in which to exercise my plow." So saying, he backed away from her and refastened his trousers. "You may dress yourself and return to class," he told her, loosening the manacles; "but, remember, if you misbehave again, I won't let you off quite this lightly."

Sickened by this appalling exhibition, Justine turned away from the crack in the wall and embraced Rosalie. "Oh, dear friend," she cried softly, "we must go to the police immediately, lest your perfidious father abuse other children as well."

"Surely you jest," replied the jaded man's lovely daughter. "Do you think the police would accept the testimony of a pair of adolescents against the word of one of the most highly respected surgeons in France?"

"Then it is as with Count de Bressac," moaned Justine. "True justice can never be done, for the worst offenders are those esteemed most highly by the judiciary."

"Life has always been thus," replied Rosalie. "But quiet now; my father returns with another pupil."

Their conversation thusly checked, the two girls once again peered through the cracks in the wall.

Rodin's victim this time was a boy of fifteen years, sandy-haired and blue-eyed, clear of face and well-muscled. Apparently the youth was no newcomer to the sessions for, without instructions, he automatically began to undress as soon as he entered the room. Rodin, however, maintaining the pose of disciplinarian, upbraided the boy for cheating on a test while at the same time kissing him about the neck and chest and helping him remove his trousers.

Now, when the youth was completely undressed, Rodin sat on a stool and arranged the boy's body in such a manner that his smooth, sun-bronzed stomach was but inches from the physician's face and his lithe, golden-haired legs bridged the physician's knees. This accomplished, he traced patterns with his tongue on the youth's belly and, with impious fingers, licentiously probed and fondled the areas below. At length the youth was in a state of excitation, whereupon the jaded doctor seized his rigid member at the stem and hissed:

"There you are! Look at that little prick, of yours! In the state which I forbade! I don't doubt that with two or three strokes you'd have the impertinence to spit at me."

The youth said nothing, but the heaviness of his breathing offered mute testimony to the accuracy of the doctor's diagnosis. Rodin then fell to kissing the youth again, this time more wetly, about the stomach and thighs. In seconds the boy gasped: "Now, sir." Thereupon the jaded libertine took the youthful member in his mouth and, with arms trembling with excitement, clutched the boy to him until the vile act was consummated.

Now, rising from his stool, Rodin paced around the room and regarded the youth with an expression of contempt. "So, you despicable little cock," he sneered; "you couldn't contain your passions; you had the audacity to stain me with your filthy juices. Well, arrogance such as this cannot be permitted to go unpunished. You know what's in store, don't you?"

The boy, like an actor long accustomed to the part, obediently gripped the edge of Rodin's desk for support and bent forward. The doctor then approached from behind and, spreading the youth's muscular buttocks, offered himself at the Altar where pederasts worship best. His kisses surrounded it, his tongue probed it; finally, intoxicated with passion, he ripped open his trousers and speared the youth with such force that the poor child's cries reverberated throughout the room.

"Ah, you little knave!" the mad surgeon now cursed, regarding the nude body of his victim with a maniacal leer. "Look at the perverse passions you excited in me! Look at the monstrous feats of lubricity which you have inspired me to perpetrate! Viper! Scoundrel! You must be punished!"

So saying he seized a whip from his desk and attacked the boy's buttocks. Ugly red welts swelled to life as evidence of the fury of his attack, but still he continued; five lashes, ten, fifteen, twenty-five: the boy screamed in agony, but Rodin would not relent; thirty lashes, thirty-five, fifty. Finally, his energy spent, he dropped the blooded whip to the floor and staggered across the room. To the boy he said: "You may go now; I have no further desire to discipline you."

Thus it continued throughout the afternoon; a girl of thirteen was the boy's successor, and she was followed by a boy of twelve; before the savagery was over, Rodin had abused no fewer than nine youngsters, and had himself climbed the heights of his perverse passion no less than six times.

"Good Heavens," said Justine to Rosalie when the heinous saga finally had ended, "how can a man surrender himself to such excesses?"

"Ah, Justine," replied the darling child, "you don't know the half of it. There is not a pupil in the entire school who has escaped being soiled at my debauched father's detestable hands, and there is not an obscene posture imaginable with which he has not experimented."

"Oh, poor girl," comforted Justine; "what horrible things to have witnessed."

"Not only have I witnessed them, my darling friend," replied Rosalie sadly. "I have suffered each of them personally. I was barely eleven years old when the monster first violated me; since then there has not been an orifice on my entire body which his scummy lust has failed to invade."

"Oh, horrors," cried Justine, completely aghast. Then, seeking to console the poor girl, she added: "But, at least you have enjoyed the succor of disavowing the acts in the confessional, have you not?"

"Oh, darling Justine!" sobbed Rosalie, her tears now coming in torrents. "Don't you realize that the libertine's perversions extend beyond the sexual realm? All my father's pupils — and I, as his daughter — are forbidden to practice religious devotions. Moreover, none of us knows how — for we never received any catechism instructions! I have never been to confession, I have never received First Communion, I have never even been baptised! I am in every respect a pagan, my soul still stained with Original Sin — and this is exactly what the savage libertine wants me to be!"

Taking the darling Rosalie's hand gently in hers, Justine kissed the poor child's tears. "Sweet friend," she said softly, "we must discuss this at length; I have been instructed in the Faith, and I would like nothing better than to convert you."

However, further discussion had to be postponed, for, at precisely this point, Rodin's voice boomed out, summoning his daughter to supper. Justine, her heart pierced with sorrow for her friend, returned to her room and began praying for the poor girl's deliverance.

III

Two days later, Rodin came calling very early in the

morning at Justine's room, and, under the pretense of
preparing to examine her wounds, ordered her to strip
naked. Since he had performed similar examinations
twice a day for almost a month, and never without apparent medical purpose, Justine did not think of questioning him. But, on this particular day, in addition to
ministering to her infirmities, the demented doctor
sought to sacrifice her Virtue to his jaded lusts; after
probing each of her scars carefully, he suddenly pulled
the bedsheet loose from its moorings, leaped on top of
Justine and locked his thighs about her waist.

"My darling child," he said, while at the same time
manipulating her beautiful breasts in a decidedly non-
medical manner, "you are fully cured. Now I will permit
you to demonstrate the gratitude with which I am certain your heart is overflowing. I desire no money; I desire only —" Here he paused and, reaching beneath her,
seized a buttock in each hand. "You have the most marvelous ass I have ever seen, my succulent sex-box. What
firmness! What roundness! What elasticity! What exquisitely textured skin! Oh, lovely, lovely girl, how I
long to burrow through the cracks and crevasses of those
magnificent buns with my flaming tongue! Oh, sweet
passion! Oh, marvelous lust!"

Apparently in preparation for the intended execution
of projects such as the above-described, the horrid libertine climbed off her. Justine promptly took advantage of
the opportunity to wriggle out of his reach.

"Sir," she said sternly, "nothing in the world could persuade me to submit to such wickedness. I am grateful to
you, yes; but I will not pay you in criminal coin. In a
strongbox at the castle of one Count de Bressac are my
savings, accumulated over five years in the employ of
that gentleman's aunt; once I recover these savings, I
will turn them over to you and permit you to take what

ever amount of money you want; as for now, however, unhand me, for I will not be a party to your licentious desires."

Hearing this, Rodin suddenly dropped to his knees. "Oh, sweet child," he gasped. "If only you knew how long I've wanted a girl to speak to me in this fashion! If only you knew how badly I've desired to be rejected!"

"Sir?" replied the puzzled Justine, wholly unable to discern the motives for his sudden change of attitude.

"I am a rake, Justine; I am a libertine; a roué; a lecher. Yes, and I have perpetrated scores upon scores of atrocities which outrage Nature. But why, child? Only because I have always lacked a model whose example I might emulate. Stay with me, dear girl, so that, by studying your example, I might learn to say no to my licentious impulses, just as you this afternoon have said no to my carnal advances."

Regarding the humble form of Rodin, now near-prostrate before her, Justine was overcome with both compassion and joy. *Oh, Heaven,* she said silently; *then Virtue is indispensable after all, despite the seeming contradictions with which I have been confronted of late. Who knows but that I may be the instrument of Heaven, designed to lead this lost soul back to Grace? Who knows but that, with the help of God, I may liberate not only this man but also his daughter and his many students from the wickedness and snares of the devil?* And to the doctor she said: "Sir, because I believe you and am sorry for you, I will do as you say; however, I warn you, do not attempt to take advantage of my good nature in the interests of later persuading me to submit to your lusts, for I shall always resist you as firmly as I did today."

"Oh, fear not, dear child," said the physician, taking her tiny hand in his and squeezing it gently. "And thank

you. I am certain that your kindness will not go unnoticed in Heaven." So speaking, he left the room.

IV

In the days which followed, Justine saw a great deal of
Doctor Rodin. True to his word, the jaded physician
made no attempt to gain further carnal knowledge of her;
however, his atrocities with the pupils from his school
continued as before, and he gave no evidence, beyond
the mouthing of an occasional piety, that he even remembered the bedside conversation. After a time, even
the naive Justine began to wonder if indeed the doctor
was sincere in his announced intention to find the path
back to Righteousness. If so, he certainly went about
the task with a minimum of enthusiasm. If not, why did
he want Justine to remain at his house — especially since
she was now cured and had informed him in no uncertain terms that she would never be a party to his venery?
This was a puzzle which — for the time being, at least
— would have to go unresolved.

If Justine's relationship with the doctor was problem-
atical, her missionary enterprise with his daughter, Rosalie, seemed almost unbelievably successful. The beautiful young girl wanted nothing more than to be convert-
ed by Justine to Christianity, and she devoted all her
spare time to acquainting herself with the Faith's sacred dogmas and sublime mysteries. Justine, for her part,
was a good teacher, and, before long, Rosalie had advanced to the point where it remained only for her to
be brought before a priest for the formal conversion
ceremony.

This last step, of course, proved to be most difficult.
When the two girls asked Rodin's permission to go to a
priest, the incestuous physician went into a rage — one

which was only aggravated by Justine's reminders of his own earlier declarations of intended return to Virtue. Locking the children inside the house, he threatened to kill them both if either dared attempt to step outside.

For several days, Justine and Rosalie met only secretly and at night, speaking in hushed tones of possible means of escape. Then, one night, Rosalie was nowhere to be found. Justine searched frantically, but without success. Everyone she asked said that the girl had not been seen all day.

When three days passed and the lovely Rosalie still did not appear. Justine went directly to Rodin, demanding to be told of his daughter's whereabouts. "Why, I thought you knew," chuckled he; "she went away to visit her grandmother in Paris and won't be back for at least six months."

This explanation left Justine unsatisfied. Persuaded that her friend would never have left without saying goodbye to her, she could only assume that foul play had befallen the child. However, she masked this conviction until she left Rodin's presence. Then, alone, she made plans for a thorough search of the house.

That night, carefully investigating every corner of the place, Justine finally heard moans emanating from behind a pile of firewood in an obscure corner of the cellar. Removing several pieces of wood, she found herself looking through a barred window into an immense secret laboratory, equipped with an extensive array of medical and surgical equipment. Sure enough, Rosalie was in the laboratory, bound to an iron operating table by a six-foot length of chain, which was fastened around her ankle.

"Oh, darling Justine," cried the poor girl, "I knew you would come." Then she tearfully related the events of the past several days: of being snatched from her bed by her father and being brought to the laboratory; the debasing examination of her naked body by him and his colleague, Rombeau; and, finally, her brutal rape by both men, in concert, one from each end. "Now, Justine," she concluded, "I have everything to fear; my father's attitude toward me since my incarceration in this place, along with his conversations with the evil Rombeau, lead me to believe that the two plan to use me in one of their horrible experiments. Justine, your poor Rosalie is doomed."

After shedding copious tears, Justine promised the dear girl that she would do everything in her power to help. Then kissing her goodbye, she hurried upstairs, determined to escape the house and to summon the police at once. On the way to the vestibule, however, she passed Rodin's office and could not help overhearing a brief snatch of dialogue. The depraved doctor's conversational partner was none other than his colleague, Rombeau. Hoping to clarify her friend's fate, Justine concealed herself outside the door and listened intently.

"Anatomy," she heard Rodin say, "will never be perfected until an examination has been performed upon the vagina of an adolescent girl who has died after cruel torture. It is only from considering it under these circumstances that we can gain full insight into the glandular workings of this interesting organ."

"I agree," replied Rombeau, "and the same applies to the hymen. We both know that the delicate membrane is ruptured by the menstrual flow, but what else do we know about this fascinating anatomical unit? Nothing, really — and we won't know anything until we perform an autopsy on a girl who still possesses one!"

"Then it is agreed," said Rodin. "We will go to work tonight."

"I must admit, dear mentor," mused Rombeau, "that I never beheld a greater dedication to the medical sciences. Surely it is not every physician who would sacrifice his daughter —"

"And why not? Should consanguinity be permitted to impede scientific progress? I have bestowed life upon her, now I shall take it back. It is no more than just." Then, in a lower voice, he added: "And, while we're at it, we might as well commence our other experiments with that vixen, Justine. She's been getting on my nerves lately, and I'm rather eager to launch the second phase of our project anyway."

Justine did not wait even long enough to find out what the second phase of the project entailed. Rushing to the cellar, she began pounding on the barred laboratory window. "Oh, dear friend," she cried, "there is not a moment to lose! The monsters will attack tonight! We must escape at once!"

The only door to the laboratory was a trapdoor, located outside the house so that access might be gained only through a tunnel in the back yard. As fortune would have it, Rodin and Rombeau, on their last visit to the place, had left this door unlocked. Letting herself inside, Justine hastily rummaged around until she found the key to Rosalie's chains lying on a table among some surgical instruments. Then she loosed her friend's bonds and both girls rushed out into the night.

It was at this point, however, that good fortune ceased to smile upon the youngsters, for, no sooner had they started across the yard than Rodin and Rombeau appeared on the back porch. "After them" shouted the incestuous father; and the girls were overtaken just steps short of the property fence, on the other side of which lay deliverance.

"Well, my noble Justine, is this what has become of your Virtue? Kidnapping a daughter from her father?" jeered Rodin.

"Indeed so," replied she. "A father so barbarous deserves *no* daughters."

"Aha — espionage and subversion to be added to your list of crimes!" he said. "Into the cellar with both of you. We shall inquire more closely into these offenses."

Dragged by the two villains, Rosalie and Justine were returned to the laboratory and the door was locked. Then, chaining Rosalie to the bed, the demented doctors both turned their attention to Justine.

"Tonight, my succulent sex-box," said Rodin, "you will be a party to an historic medical experiment — for the first time anywhere, vivisection for the purpose of inspecting the beating of the human heart!" Then, wedging an impudicious fist between her bare thighs, he added: "But first, in the interests of getting the heart to beat most vigorously, there shall be a few episodes of lust."

So saying, he tore the dress from her back and shoved her naked body onto a bed in the corner of the room. "Behold this body," he said to Rombeau. "Have you ever seen one so appetizing? Observe those magnificent buttocks — two white melons guarding the Altars of Venus and Sodom. Lovely, lovely, lovely; wouldn't you love to thrust your tongue between them?"

"Indeed," said Rombeau, doing just that. "And how I'd love — with your permission, of course — to throw a nice stiff one into her while I'm at it."

"By all means, go ahead," Rodin encouraged him. "She's not a virgin, but she's been had only once, and then only by force, so it's as good a parcel as you're liable to get. In fact, now that I think of it, I might like to have a go at it myself —"

Hearing these intentions voiced, Justine prostrated herself before the two men and offered her life in exchange for her Virtue.

"But, since you are no longer a virgin, what difference

can it make to you?" asked Rombeau incredulously. "And besides, we plan to kill you anyway — so how can you attempt to bargain with us by offering your life?"

But Rodin interrupted him. "Let us waste no further time with her," he said, unexplainably changing his tack. "Remember, we cannot postpone Rosalie's operations any longer, and great vigor will be necessary to carry them out. There's danger in wearying ourselves first with this creature."

"But," protested Rombeau, "a quick thrust or two and it will be over. I don't think that will prove too wearying. Besides, I'm more energetic than usual tonight —"

"No," snapped Rodin, cutting him off. "My decision is final."

"Then," replied the colleague, "how shall we punish her for attempting to help your daughter to escape?"

After pondering the question for only an instant, Rodin seized an iron from atop the fireplace and thrust it into the flames. "With this!" he said evilly. "We'll brand her and set her loose in the streets. Then, anyone who sees her will think that she's a murderer and, if she has the stupidity to attempt reporting our crimes to the police, they'll hang her before she can even finish relating her story!"

Now Rombeau held Justine fast while the insane Rodin thrust the white-hot iron into the soft, tender flesh of the poor girl's shoulder. Immense waves of pain coarsed through her body and, as the stench of her own seared flesh assailed her nostrils, the beleaguered child abandoned herself to merciful unconsciousness.

V

When Justine awoke the sun was high and she was lying alongside a road, completely dressed. A few feet away was a sign, reading "Paris: 10 Kilometers." The jaded doctors, she concluded, had taken her from the laboratory and abandoned her here.

Her first impulse was to go to the police and insist that investigators hurry to Rodin's home. She realized full well, however, that such a move would be totally futile; if her brand escaped detection and she was not hanged as an escaped murderer, she most certainly would be disbelieved because of her indigence, and, in any event, sufficient time had undoubtedly passed to insure that Rosalie could not be helped, no matter what Justine did. Thus, sorrowed to the very depths of her soul at the thought of deserting her beloved friend, the much-abused girl set off alone in what she believed to be the direction of Paris.

Several hours passed, then several more. Weary, weak with pain and dizzy from hunger, Justine plodded onward. Still, Paris seemed to draw no closer, and, with each passing moment she grew feebler still. Finally, around dusk, she encountered another roadsign. It read, "Paris: 20 Kilometers," and it faced the opposite direction. She could only conclude that Rodin and Rombeau, not content with branding her and abandoning her to her fate at roadside, conspired further to confuse her first steps away from them by reversing the first sign.

Tears welling up in her eyes, the poor child threw herself to the ground and surrendered to the bitterest of sobs. Then, the spell passing, she got to her feet, said a brief prayer and began to retrace her steps in the opposite direction. But, no sooner had she begun walking than she noticed high on a hill in the distance a small bell tower rising modestly in the air. The tower could indicate only a church or a monastery, and, in that desolate area of the country, odds strongly favored the latter.

"Oh, harbinger of beloved solitude," Justine fervently addressed the tower, "how earnestly I desire to dwell beneath thee. And what of the abbey over which you stand? Does it house a few gentle recluses, devoted only to the service of God? Or does it serve as a retreat for weary missionaries, beaten into near submission by the brutalities of pernicious society? Oh, how I long to join those peace-loving hermits, whoever they may be . . .

And, as she spoke thusly, a small girl appeared alongside her. The girl, a shepherdess out grazing her flock, explained that the object of Justine's focus was indeed a monastary, occupied by four anchorites of the Benedictine Order who were known throughout the region for their piety, holiness and devotion. Very rarely, the girl continued, did local people go near the place; however, once a year, on the Feast of the Immaculate Conception, a pilgrimage was made to the Blessed Virgin, and those who attended often reported the prompt fufilment of their wishes.

"Oh how I would love to visit the place," Justine sighed, her imagination fired by the girl's description.

"Then why don't you?" replied the girl. "I'm sure it's permitted, and, if you follow that path, you'll find that the distance is a lot shorter than it appears."

Thanking the girl profusely, Justine said goodbye and immediately started along the path. Less than two hours later, she found herself outside an immense, wooden door on which was printed: "Monastery of Saint Mary-in-the-Woods."

Oh, citadel of Virtue, she mused, looking up at the monastery's stone facade, *here it must be where God's laborers come when mankind's excesses drive them out of the world; here to this isolated place where one's soul may live in community with the souls of those for-*

tunate creatures who value them so highly that they give them over wholly to God. It is here, if anywhere, that I will find true peace . . .

And, so thinking, she raised her hand to the large, brass knocker on the monastery door.

BOOK FOUR

I

The large, oak door of the monastery creaked open and an aged porter led Justine into an immense, dark, high-ceilinged room. The floor and walls were of stone; the dank air, warmed only by the flames of a pair of small candles, was pregnant with gloom. Looking about the place, the lovely girl was overcome by a sense of piety; immediately she fell to her knees and lifted her face in prayer.

Asked the reason for her visit, Justine told the porter that she wished to confess her sins. When he reminded her that the hour was late, she said: "Then let me kneel ,but for a moment before the statue of the miraculous Virgin to whom this abbey is dedicated and I will go away refreshed." Greatly impressed by this gentle elo-quence, the porter withdrew and, moments later, re-turned with none other than the superior of the monas-tery, himself.

The superior, by name, Father Severino, was a tall and ruggedly handsome man whose youthful features and strapping physique belied his real age, fifty-five years; the musical accent which colored his speech suggested that he was of Italian origin, and the gracefulness of his movements was of the style often associated with that libertine race.

"In what manner may we serve you, child?" he asked Justine softly.

"Saintly man," replied she, prostrating herself. "I have always believed that it is never too late to present oneself at God's door. I have hastened from afar, full of fervor and devotion, hoping to confess my sins."

"My dear child," said Father Severino, gently bringing his hand to her shoulder, "although it is not our custom to receive penitents this late, I will be only too happy to do you the service of hearing your confession. Later we will discuss the means by which you may pass the night in decent accommodations. Then, in the morning, you may receive the Eucharist."

Having spoken thusly, Father Severino led her into the church. The doors were closed and a lamp was lit alongside the confessional. Then the pious-looking ecclesiatic took his place inside the box and the ceremony was begun.

Justine, completely at ease, related all her miseries, beginning with the death of her parents; no detail was omitted, no fact disguised. Father Severino, his face a study in pity and concern, listened keenly and, at times, even urged her to repeat certain details, especially those pertaining to her sexual encounters. Justine, however, in no way suspected the abbot's motives in this inquiry; nor did it give her pause that he was especially careful to ascertain that she was telling the truth on three specific points: (1) That she had been born in Paris and was now an orphan; (2) That she had neither friends nor relatives with whom she kept in touch and to whom she now could write for help, and (3) That no one but the shepherdess knew that she had come to the monastery.

When the ritual finally was complete and absolution had been pronounced, Father Severino took her by the hand and led her toward the opposite end of the church. "Tomorrow, my child," he said, "you shall receive the Eucharist. As for now, let us pay some attention to the matter of food and lodging."

"But, Father," she protested, "surely you don't think I should sleep here with a community of men —"

"But where else, my lovely pilgrim?" he smiled. Then, mischievously tweaking her breast, he added: "Besides, the experience will do you good, and, if we anchorites fail to add to your pleasures, you can take consolation in the fact that you most assuredly will be adding to ours."

Astonished, Justine stopped dead in her tracks. Father Severino roughly jerked her back into motion. "Tramp!" he cursed. "You have the indelicacy to bestow your favors half the length and breadth of France, yet you'd deny them to a few isolated workers in God's vineyard?" And, so saying, he pulled her into an obscure passageway which spiraled down from behind the main altar to the musty, damp cellars in the depths of the building.

The passageway was unlighted, and Father Severino, leaning against one wall for direction, propelled Justine before him. Coiling one arm around her waist, he slid the other between her legs and explored the unseemly areas thereabout until he had located the Altar of Venus. A firm grip was maintained thereon until they reached a stairway, which led to a room two stories below the church proper.

The room was splendidly illuminated and magnificently furnished. However, Justine barely noticed the appointments, for, seated around a table in the center of
the room were three other monks and four other girls—
the seven of them stark naked!

"Gentlemen," announced Father Severino, "our company shall be enhanced this evening by a girl who
simultaneously carries upon her shoulder the brand of
a slut and in her heart the naivete of a baby, and who
houses her entire being in a temple the magnificence
of which is a true joy to behold." Reaching around her,
he cupped her breasts in his hands. "Look at these
globes, gentlemen," he said enthusiastically. "Have you
ever seen anything more beautiful?" Then, turning her
so that she faced away from the assemblage, he lifted
her dress. "And what of these buns? Wouldn't you love
to grace your dinnertable with these?"

The monks beamed delightedly at the sight, and all
congratulated Severino on his find. Then, one of the
three, an animalistic monster who was as big as a
gorilla and, indeed, resembled one facially as well,
staggered to his feet; his name, quite inappropriately,
was Father Clement. "Well, Father Severino, don't keep
her for yourself," he chuckled. "Take her clothes off and
we'll all have a go at her."

Justine twisted away in horror. Immediately Father
Severino's fist whipped out and caught her on the side
of the head. The poor girl fell dizzily to the floor.

"We tolerate no resistance here, little vixen," said the
monk sternly. "Complete submissiveness is what we
want, and we'll settle for nothing else."

"I would have thought," gasped the astounded Justine, "that, if I could expect mercy and compassion from
anyone, it would be from four men of God."

"Ha!" scoffed Father Severino. "Fancy that! Mercy,

child?! We don't know what the word means. Compassion? You'll find none here. Religion? The better we get to know it, the more contemptuous of it we become. Law and order? Our principal pleasure is the violation of law and order; we strive for total chaos."

"How can you call yourselves priests?!" she spat, thoroughly sickened. "Is this the way you worship the God in whose service you have pledged to do battle?"

"God?!" thundered the priest. "God, you say! Do you speak of the same God Whom you have been imploring in vain for the past half-dozen years? The same God Who, as a reward for your Virtue, has invariably plunged you into greater and greater misery? I'll tell you what I think of that God: I despise Him; I hate Him; I loathe Him with all my heart; and so do my brother priests; it is for this reason that we occupy ourselves all day by outraging his vain commandments!" Pulling her roughly to her feet again, he continued: "And now, enough philosophy. You are about to enter the service of a different god — the god of carnal desire. So off with your clothes, and surrender your body to our lusts."

But Justine was not about to be persuaded to part with her principles that easily. Dropping to her knees, she joined her hands in the posture of prayer and, eyes upward, began reciting the "Act of Contrition." Father Severino, infuriated, whipped out with his foot, caving her in with a kick to the stomach. Then, nudging her toward Father Clement, he ordered the huge, gorilla-like priest to strip her.

Father Clement, all but foaming at the lips, grasped Justine at the armpits and jerked her roughly to her feet. Inserting two, sausage-thick fingers in the yoke of her blouse, he gave a sharp tug. There was a ripping sound, then the two halves of the garment fell away from the center and Justine's full, marvelously-rounded breasts flopped out.

As the lovely child tried to cover herself with her arms, Father Clement inserted the same two fingers in her waistband. Almost instanly, her skirt was rent in two. "A lovely creature, is she not?" grinned the licentious priest, turning her so that her body, now fully naked, could be viewed most advantageously by the others. "Look at the lovely flanks. And, as Father Severino has said, look at the globes. Wouldn't you love to sink your teeth into them?"

"All right," said Father Severino, "that'll be enough of the niceties. Now let's give her the full welcoming treatment. After all, though not recruited by ordinary means, she does qualify as a newcomer. Gather around, now, and on with the ceremony."

No sooner did he give the order than the other monks, along with their female accomplices, formed a circle around the poor girl. One after another they inspected her, the first casting an appraising glance at this portion of the anatomy, the second inserting an experimental finger into that orifice, and so on, until more than two hours had been consumed by the ritual. Then Father Severino stepped to the center of the circle and announced: "Phase two: let each of us priests take his favorite pleasures!"

Understandably, the first of the four to indulge was Father Severino, himself. Advancing upon the child like a tiger stalking its prey, he maneuvered her into a crouched position on the floor; then, while two of the monks held her legs apart, he endeavored to invade her in the manner of Sodom. However, the shameless monk's mammoth appendage proved to be too large for the use to which he hoped to put it; squeezing, spreading, pushing thrusting, he nonetheless failed to gain entry to the citadel at which he sought to worship.

Infuriated by his failure, the perfiidious priest now lashed out at her buttocks in full rage; slapping them, pinching them, punching them, he was not content until the lovely white spheres had turned pink with pain. Then, the barrage of brutality over, the siege of the citadel was renewed; more squeezing, thrusting, spreading, forcing, until, finally, the rampart yielded. Now a horrendous cry of agony filled the room as the monstrous invader tore open the girls bowels. Throbbing, and twisting, the slippery reptile spewed forth its venom, then, sapped of its rigidity, surrendered to the girl's frantic attempts to expel it. Father Severino, livid with rage at his inability to sustain the siege, fell to the floor weeping.

Now Father Clement came forward, swinging a nine-tailed leather whip menacingly over his shoulder. "I'll avenge you, Father," he promised. "After I get through with her the little twat will know better than to resist you."

Lifting her into the air with one arm, the gargantuan priest draped her across his knees; then, flicking the whip testily, he struck her three times across the buttocks. Justine flinched under the sting of the blows; however, her pain was only by way of prelude, for Father Clement had not been half trying. Now, satisfied with his position and with his grip on the whip handle, the odious monk raised the long-tongued weapon high above his head and brought it to bear on her with full force. The sharp, leather lashes sliced mercilessly into her flesh, leaving bright red tracks of blood in their wake; the pain was so severe that the poor child's cry was muffled in her throat.

Spurred on by the sight of her blood, the barbaric Father Clement now struck at her with insane fury. No part of her body was immune to his savagery. Gleaming pink furrows streamed across her back, from the shoulders to the buttocks, and circled her thighs like thin, blood-red garden-snakes.

Aroused even further by this spectacle, the vicious priest wrestled her into a supine position and fastened his vile mouth to hers, as if seeking to suck from her lungs the cries which his whip had been unable to jolt out of her. Alternately he struck at her abdomen and sucked at her mouth, and, the more Justine's writhing and struggling testified to her anguish, the better he seemed to like it. Now he bit her lips; now he tweaked her buttocks; now he stabbed at her chest with his chin; now he scratched at her belly: still the attack gave no sign of abating.

Justine's lips now numb from his bites, her abdomen red from his slaps and scratches, the fiendish Father Clement concentrated his assault on her breasts. He kneaded the marvelously soft globes with his fingers; he pressed on them with his palms; he squeezed them against each other, then pulled them apart; he pinched the nipples, nuzzled the cleavage and gnawed at the circumference. Finally, in a fit of ferocity, he took one in his mouth and dug into it with his teeth, bringing all the force of his monstrous jaws against the tender target. Again Justine's screams rent the air, and, as Father Clement lifted his face happily away from her, two streams of red trickled down his chin. The poor girl's breast was a gusher of blood.

Father Clement's round having come to a close, he was replaced by Father Jerome, the oldest of the four anchorites and a priest for more than thirty-five years. "Like Clement," said he, "I will respect your wish that the field of Venus go unplowed. However, I should enjoy kissing those furrows where the plows of others have passed." So saying, he upended her and gently paid his respects to her buttocks.

This having been accomplished, the jaded old ecclesiastic jammed a finger into the citadel where his abbot had earlier waged a battle. "Oh, how I would like to see my little chicken lay an egg," he chuckled lecherously; "and, if she did, I think I'd eat it, because I'm really quite hungry . . . Is there one there? . . . By God, there is! Oh, sweet child, you'll never know what joy you've brought to this aging cleric's heart! Oh, how soft and sweet it is! Cooperate with me, child, and you won't regret it."

Now the leprous old man applied his lips to the aperture, and Justine, disgusted, had no choice but to comply with his request. The "egg" having been "lain," the old man swallowed it. Then, forcing the poor girl to drop to her knees in front of him, he sought another sort of gratification by means of the only temple suited to his age and inclination. As Justine surrendered to the submissive role, the warped anchorite summoned two of the other women, one of whom was instructed to whip his back while the other positioned herself above his mouth and, as Justine earlier had done, played the "chicken."

This travesty over, the jaded Father Jerome was replaced by the youngest of the four, Father Antonin, a tiny wisp of a man with beady eyes, a pointed nose and an enthusiasm for evil which far outshone that of his colleagues. "Well, let's take a look at this Temple of Venus, worship in which has thus far been restricted to but a single man—and a rapist at that," he said, maneuvering Justine into a supine position across his lap. Then, having inspected the Temple and voiced his approval of the accommodations, he spread the girl's legs and made his entrance.

The pain of penetration was severe, but it paled in

comparison to the other agonies of the night. Indeed, as the priest entered the sanctuary, Justine felt arise within her feelings of pleasure which she had never dreamed existed. Yet, her devotion to Virtue was such that, even now, she resolved not to permit herself any enjoyment of the act, and thus, as the incense of temptation wafted invitingly around her, she gritted her teeth and murmured under her breath fervent prayers for forgiveness.

The enthusiastically athletic Father Antonin, finding the girl restrained by propriety from joining those undulations which, carried on communally, would stoke his passions to their apex, seized the two magnificent hemispheres which were her buttocks and began gyrating them in rhythm with his own movements; meanwhile, inside her, his throbbing acolyte stormed about Venus' Altar as if it wished not merely to worship there, but actually to plunder the place.

This project having been launched successfully, the jaded young monk sought to magnify the scope of his pleasures. Summoning one of the other girls, a fifteen-year-old child whose bewitching face was creased with the lines of anguish and trepidation, he positioned her on Justine's flanks, facing him and with her legs spread open; then, with his tongue, he performed the same sacrifices which were being carried out by his acolyte down below. Simultaneously, one of the older women took her post at his loins and began stroking them with her tongue. Meanwhile, two other women took places on opposite sides of this vile tableau, and the insatiable Father Antonin took to counterfeiting them, one with each hand.

The human pyramid was now complete. There was not one of the debauched priest's senses which went unattended, not one of his instruments of lovemaking which lay idle. The symphony of shameful sensuality roared on toward its crescendo. His ecstatic screams heralded the climax. Justine felt the vigorous thrusting as the pinnacle was attained. Then she was inundated with the waters of the dam which she was but one of six to break.

"Well," said Father Severino, once the melange of bare bodies had been untangled, "that should be sufficient for the first day. Bring the girl some food now, and we'll find a bed for her."

Justine, thoroughly sapped physically, was nonetheless unbroken in spirit. "With your permission, Father," she said tartly, "my only wish is to leave this accursed place at once. Keep your bed. Just give me back the remnants of my dress and I shall take leave of you immediately. You needn't worry that your secrets will be revealed by me, for I want only to go my way in peace."

Father Severino regarded her with twinkling eyes. "Indeed, my child?" he cackled softly. "Well, I'm afraid that's quite impossible now, because, once we have welcomed a girl to our midst, we do not permit her to leave until all four of us have tired of her, and, with a specimen of girlhood as sweet and sassy as you, I'm sure that won't be for quite some time."

Having spoken thusly, he snapped his fingers and a woman materialized from the shadows. She was perhaps thirty years of age, and one of the most beautiful creatures imaginable. "Omphale," the priest told her, "take this spunky creature to the dormitory and see to it that she gets some rest. God knows, around here from now on she's going to need all the strength she can muster."

II

When she awoke the next morning, Justine found herself

in a large room with seven other girls. Eight small, neat
beds were ranged around the wall, and alongside each
was a window, barred inside and out. Omphale, who
had escorted her from the orgy the night before, occupied the bed next to Justine's, and took it upon herself to offer succor to the new arrival.

"My dear friend," she said, stroking Justine affection-
atelly on the shoulder. "I, like you, wept bitterly when
I first came here. Now I can only urge you not to waste
your tears and to hope that as days pass and you grow
accustomed to the place, the indignities will become
tolerable. I wish I could paint a brighter picture, but
I cannot; it is our fate not only to serve as instruments
for the slaking of these four debauchees' thirsts, but also
to suffer unmitigated abuse and degradation in this
abominable habitation: moreover, escape is impossible
and the only alternative to compliance is death."

Having begun on this sorry note, Omphale then
proceeded to describe the nature of the monastery and
the conditions under which the girls lived. The monks,
she said, were four of the richest in the Benedictine
order, and Father Severino was a relative of the Pope
himself. In addition to a few porters, gardners, clerks,
cooks and the like, the monastery staff included twelve
women whose sole function was to kidnap pretty young
girls of aristocratic birth; it was these girls who were
subjected to the ignominy of serving as the monks' sexual
slaves, and Justine, inadvertently had become the latest
addition to their ranks.

As to the girls, there were sixteen in all, divided into
four "classes" of four girls each. The first class was called
the "children's class," and contained girls aged sixteen
or under; the uniform of the group was white. The
second, or "youthful class," included those aged seventeen to twenty-one; their costume was green. The third,

of which Justine was now a member, was aged twenty-two to thirty, was called the "reasoning class" and was distinguished by blue vestments. And the fourth, whose members were thirty-one or over, wore reddish-brown colors and was called the "mature class."

The number of girls was kept constantly at sixteen and, whenever a new girl was conscripted, one of those in her age range was dismissed. The dismissal was referred to at the monastery as "graduation," but no one knew where the girls went after they were "graduated," or, indeed, if they managed to get out of the place alive. And "graduation" depended not upon seniority, fidelity to duties or other such factors, but only upon the whim of the monks; sometimes a girl would be "graduated" after only a week or two, while, on other occasions, "graduation" would not take place for ten or fifteen years, or longer; indeed, one woman presently in the group had been there for twenty-six years—longer than three of the four monks.

As to physical layout, the monastery consisted of two areas: the church proper, which was open to the public and in which the monks behaved consistent with the principles of their Church, and the "pavilion," a six-story building, three stories of which were subterranean, separated from the church by a moat and inaccessible by any means other than a subterranean secret passageway which emerged behind the altar of the church. It was this passageway through which Father Severino had brought Justine after hearing her confession on the night of her arrival; and it was in the upper stories of the pavilion that the girls' dormitory was located, while the subterranean stories housed both the monks' private bedrooms and the rooms where the orgies took place.

Every morning at nine, three of the monks went to the church, where they remained until five in the after-

noon. The monk who was left behind was called the
Officer of the Day; his duty was to supervise operations
in the pavilion. The girls rose at eight and prepared for
the Officer of the Day's inspection, which took place
shortly after nine. This visit invariably was accompanied
by a sexual entanglement of some sort, after which
breakfast was served. After this all were free to pursue
their own interests until seven in the evening, when
some of their number would be selected at random
to participate in the orgies. Those not selected were free
to do as they pleased until inspection the following
morning.

However, this seemingly light schedule did not mean
that any of the girls had an easy time of it. There were
appointed to the group two superintendents, who were
free to assign each of the girls any chores, tasks, et cetera,
at will, and who had unlimited license to punish those
who met with their disapproval. Punishment almost
invariably was exacted in the form of whipping, and
some of the prescribed penalties were as follows: failure to rise at the appointed hour, thirty strokes; the
offering during sexual congress, for whatever the reason,
of a part of the body other than that requested by the
monk in charge, fifty strokes; improper dress or hair
style, sixty strokes; failure to give prior notice of sexual
incapacitation for reasons of menstruation, sixty strokes;
becoming pregnant, one hundred strokes; refusal to cooperate in an act of libertinage requested by a monk,
two hundred strokes; inability to bring a monk to
orgasm, three hundred strokes; attempted escape, nine
days' confinement naked in a dungeon and three hundred strokes per day.

On the first day of every month, each monk selected
a girl who for that period would serve as his personal
servant, and whose services would include the sexual.

The girl, designated Girl of the Watch, would join her master at five each evening and not leave his side until nine the following morning, when he went to church. She was required to remain standing all night in his bedroom, ready to offer herself instantly for whatever missions, sexual or otherwise, the execution of which he desired. Also, she was obliged to serve as the monk's toilet, providing her mouth or the space between her breasts as a receptacle for his excretions. At supper her place was behind his chair, or at his feet, where she would crouch, nude, like a dog, or upon her knees between his legs, gratifying him with her mouth as he supped. And, regardless of the fidelity with which she carried out his orders, if ever there was a dispute, the girl was always deemed wrong.

"Yet," Omphale continued, smiling sardonically, "wretched as it is, the place is not without its small consolations. No girl can be designated Girl of the Watch for two months consecutively, and those who lend themselves most enthusiastically to the monk's bidding usually manage to receive special favors now and then. Also, there is the matter of food, which is not only excellent but also plentiful; this is because those monks who, as Father Jerome puts it, like to see the 'chicken' lay, are thus assured an ample supply of 'eggs.' "

"Good Heavens," sighed Justine, astonished at both the intensity and the variety of the deprayed priests' perversities. "I cannot imagine a more horrible place."

"Nor can I," commiserated Omphale; "and yet, what is there to do but get used to it, for it probably will be our home for the rest of our lives . . ."

III

Omphale had hardly concluded her instruction when the

bell in the spire tolled nine times; immediately the dormitory superintendent ordered the girls to a position of attention in front of their beds, and Father Antonin, the present Officer of the Day, made his official visit.

After the priest had taken roll, he sat on a stool in the center of the room and each of the girls was required to approach him, to lift her skirt to her navel and to offer the Altars of Venus and Sodom for inspection. Regarding the spectacle with the blasé eye of one truly jaded, he quickly went through the formalities of the inspection, then took the punishment list from the superintendent and administered lashes to the girls named thereon.

This enterprise completed, the youthful cleric smiled at Justine and said: "Now it is time to greet the newcomer." Commanding her to sit on the edge of her bed, he then instructed the superintendent to bare the girl's breasts and to lift the girl's skirt above her waist. Then, spreading her legs as wide as possible, he sat before her and engaged her at the Altar of Venus. This liaison having been accomplished, he summoned one of the girl's companions to straddle Justine's hips in such a fashion that he was offered the girl's vulva in place of Justine's face. Next, a third girl was made to kneel alongside him and to arouse him with her tongue, while a fourth, completely nude, guided his hands to portions of Justine's anatomy which he could not see but which he wanted to whip.

As on the night before, Father Antonin began thrusting and the collage of female bodies — all, that is, except Justine's — writhed in concert, so that the entire spectacle resembled a monstrous, flesh machine. With each passing moment, the intensity of the depraved priest's lust increased; Justine could feel his throbbing member probing her innards. "*Sex!*" shouted he madly; "*Sex! SEX! S-E-X!!!*" And, finally, he attained the summit of his desires, which attainment was accompanied by an ecstatic shouting and bellowing the likes of which Justine had never heard.

"Very well," said the priest, rearranging his cassock once the extravagant sexual couplings had been untangled. "Justine has now been welcomed officially. We hope you enjoy your stay here, child."

And, so saying, he left.

IV

A week passed. Justine, like other girls, was made to participate in two supper-time orgies. However, she was spared — for the time being, at least — the agonies of serving as a Girl of the Watch.

The other girls in the dormitory were quite friendly. By the time the week was up, Justine had grown quite fond of many of them. Yet, a special place in her heart was reserved for her first companion in the monk's ghastly sewer, Omphale, and her affection for her increased every day.

One afternoon, while lounging about waiting the return of the monks from church, Omphale and Justine pledged that whichever of them could escape or was "graduated" first would not rest until she had brought about the rescue of the other. Coincidentally, the following morning, Father Jerome, as Officer of the Day, announced that the monks had acquired a new girl; she would replace none other than Omphale, who was to be "graduated" that night

Standing outside the dormitory awaiting the arrival of the monk who would "graduate" her, Omphale kissed Justine tenderly on the cheek and renewed her pledge to rescue her. Then, sharing feelings of joy not unmixed with feelings of trepidation — for neither of them could

be certain that "graduation" was not, indeed, death —
the girls embraced and said goodbye.

V

It was the policy of the monastery that, whenever a
monk wished, he could summon one of the girls to spend
the night with him. Several days after Omphale's "graduation," Justine received just such a summons from the
gorilla-faced cleric, Father Clement. In accordance with
custom, she presented herself outside his cell several
minutes before his scheduled return from dinner; a
porter opened the door and locked her inside. Father
Clement arrived moments later, his face as flushed with
wine as with the fires of passion. Behind him came his
Girl of the Watch, a beautiful, auburn-haired twenty-six-
year-old named Armande.

"Well, my child," said the libertine priest, "I have
long thought of spending a few hours with you, but I've
been so busy that I couldn't find the time. Tonight we'll
see what we can do to make up for the hours lost."

So saying, he nodded to Armande, who proceeded to
undress Justine in stages, beginning with the lower portions of the body. As the girl's lovely, cream-colored
thighs were exposed, Clement fell to his knees and began licking them. Then, with the unveiling of the buttocks, he placed his vile mouth at the threshold of the
Temple of Sodom and thrust his loathsome tongue inside
the tabernacle.

Now Armande positioned herself beneath him and proceeded to arouse him with her hands. Meanwhile, the
obscene cleric ordered Justine to give vent to whatever
gasses may have accumulated in her intestines, and to
direct them into his mouth; revolted, the girl nonetheless
complied with his instructions, and the jaded Father

Clement was beside himself with pleasure.

The girl's bowels finally unable to emit any more of the foul perfume with which the perverse cleric sought to anoint himself, he took to biting at the marvelous white hemispheres which guarded the entrance to the chamber; eyes blazing, he sunk his teeth viciously into the beautiful buttocks and gnawed at them until he drew blood.

Spurred by the sight of the glistening red liquid to even greater heights of passion, the diabolical debauchee commanded Armande to undress him. Then, as he lay naked on his bed with the two girls, he began to strike at them with his fists. Mouthing the most horrible obscenities, he beat upon one girl, then the other, and punctuated his punches with kicks and bites, all the while dripping his vile saliva all over his victims. "Wretches!" he shouted at them. "Cunts! Vixens!" And the beating continued.

Finally the priest's fury became such that mere punches would not suffice. Seizing a whip from atop his dressingtable, he struck one, then the other, until the backs of both were thatched with bright pink welts. Then, in an abrupt change of mood, he fell to kissing gently each area which he had just molested.

Now the insane ecclesiastic told the girls that he would conduct a contest in which both would be flogged simultaneously and the first to utter a cry or to shed a tear would be declared the loser. Justine was made to sit cross-legged on the floor; Armande was maneuvered into position atop her and facing her, so that the former's buttocks were positioned directly above the latter's breasts. Then, exhorting the girls to be courageous, he brought his whip to bear against them, its sharp-edged strands cutting mercilessly into the flesh of both. "Ah," he cried, "what a joy it is to behold together the most beauteous of buttocks and the sweetest of breasts; what a pleasure to sink one's lashes into the soft, lovely skin of each!"

Armande, pitying Justine, slowly lowered herself until her buttocks came to serve as somewhat of a shield, receiving the full brunt of the blows which otherwise both girls would have shared equally. Clement, wise to the trick, quickly separated them. "You won't gain anything by that," he said harshly to his Girl of the Watch; "in fact, you'll both suffer more because of it." Then, positioning Armande at one end of the bed and Justine at the other, he continued to whip away at the breasts and buttocks which so aroused his passions until, at length, he fell to the floor exhausted from his efforts.

"That'll be enough for now," he said wearily, "but don't get the idea that we're by any means through for the evening. Armande, fetch me some water. Justine, I shall rest awhile in bed; come and lie with me."

As Armande left the cell, the jaded monk pulled aside his blanket and climbed in between the sheets. Then bringing Justine in alongside him, he kissed her wounded breasts gently.

"Well, my child," he said, "now you see the lengths to which some men will go to satisfy their appetites. I suppose you're appalled."

"Wholly, sir," she replied. "Wholly and completely."

"All of which goes to show," said he, "that your philosophies are inconsistent. I'll explain: *you*, on the one hand, say, 'this is good, so I shall do it,' and the thing to which *you* refer is what is commonly called 'virtue;' so, *you* perform a virtuous act in the interests of attaining a subjective good, and you feel you should be praised for it; *I* on the other hand, say, 'this is good, so I shall do it,' and the thing to which *I* refer is what is commonly called 'vice;' so, *I* perform an act of vice — like you, in the interests of attaining a subjective good — and you feel *I* should be blamed for it! Where's the consistency there?"

"But," Justine objected, "your act is vice and mine is virtue."

"Yes, my love, but only in *your* eyes," thundered the monk. "In my eyes, it is *my* act which is virtue and *yours* which is vice! I can think of nothing more evil than a girl's denying herself the pleasures for which her throbbing twat cries out; to me such denial is the final abomination: so there you have it, your virtue is my vice, and vice-versa!" Now, easing his hand between her thighs until it was nestled in the smooth, warm folds of her labia, he continued: "No, Justine, as Seneca used to say, *De gustibus non est disputandum,* 'there's no disputing tastes.' How silly is it therefore to punish a man merely because his wishes do not conform with the laws of his country or the conventions of his social milieu. But people don't seem to understand; they fail to realize that tastes are supplied us by Nature herself, and nothing we can possibly do will change them. Did the sodomite ask to become one? Is the anal erotic a pervert by preference? Of course not. Then, with what right does one man dare entreat him to 'mend' his ways? With what right does society demand that he alter his behavior at the expense of his personal happiness?"

"But, Father," replied Justine, "if a man were to let his passions run unbridled, he would be no different from a beast!

"And is this such a calamity?" said the monk. "Could Nature, as Creator of beasts, despise Her own creations?"

"But beasts live in chaos."

"To the contary. There is a very definte order of things in the animal kingdom. The tiger devours the wolf, the wolf devours the lamb, and so forth, and it's all part of Nature's plan to maintain a balance among the various species. But man — pompous, arrogant man — would, by the passage of laws, tamper with this balance; would prevent the murderer from murdering, the fornicator from fornicating, et cetera, all in the interests of fashioning Nature's world to his own likes and preferences."

"Oh, Father," the scandalized child replied, "I will never accept these perfidious doctrines."

"Of course not," he snapped. "And why? Because you fear becoming their victim — and there we have it, man's arrogance again! Let's change roles and see if you don't change your mind! Ask the lamb why the wolf is permitted to devour him and he'll answer that he doesn't know; but ask the wolf what purpose the lamb's existence serves and he'll reply, 'Why, to feed me, naturally.' And don't we reply in precisely the same manner to justify our butchery of cattle, chickens and pigs? Of course we do. So there's morality for you, my child; it's a matter of who sits where — that and nothing more . . . ."

And, having pronounced these immoral doctrines, the monstrous monk forthwith fell asleep.

Now, when his snores suggested that he could not possibly hear the girls, Armande touched her hand to Justine's wrist. "He will awake shortly, dear friend, more of a madman than ever," she said. "My advice is that you get a little sleep yourself if you can."

"And you?" I asked. "Will you sleep also?"

The poor girl's bitter laugh testified to her misery. "How can I?" she answered. "If he were to find me asleep, I'd be convicted of negligence and he'd probably stab me to death."

"Execrable swine!" Justine swore. "Even as he sleeps, he insures that those around him continue to suffer."

"Yes," she said. "In this respect he is like those perverse writers whose scandalous works live on long after their

own lives have ended; the writers, themselves, can perpetrate no more evil after death, but their evil ideas
continue to be propagated, instigating crime, inspiring
blasphemy, motivating wickedness: and this notion
cheers them to their very graves, for even there they cannot be enjoined to relinquish the perpetration of evil."

"The scoundrels," Justine agreed.

But here the conversation terminated, for Father
Clement once more was awake and his lustful desires
had been fully replenished by sleep. Growling obscenities and blasphemies, he called for his whips and resumed flogging both girls with even more vigor than previously. Justine, no longer able to conceal her anguish,
cried our fiercely, and this served to inflame his passions
all the more. Soon his attack became so violent that even
the tolerant Armande could contain herself no longer.
With both girls wailing pitifully, the savage cleric continued to flail away until his whips were so slick with
blood that he could no longer grip them. Then he struck
at his victims with his feet and fists until, totally exhausted, he fell in a heap upon the bed.

VI

Not long after the orgy with Father Clement, Justine
began to hear talk around the dormitory about the
forthcoming Feast of the Immaculate Conception. The
occasion was of great interest to the girls because, during
the feast, the four monks always recruited a number of
new girls, either seducing them in the confessional or
kidnapping them as they roamed about the convent
grounds; the new arrivals, of course, meant "graduation"
for a corresponding number of the incumbents.

Justine, herself, was quite curious about the feast, for
she had often heard stories — even before her incarcera-

tion by the monks — of miraculous visitations by the
Blessed Virgin. Indeed, it was such visitations which attracted pilgrims to Saint Mary's-in-the-Woods from as
far away as Nice and Hendaye, Grenoble and Le Havre,
and it was the contributions of the pilgrims which enabled the monks to live so royally. For her part, Justine
could not understand how it happened that the Blessed
Virgin deigned to visit the place not only so frequently,
but also with such propitious timing. The answer, of
course, was soon to be found . . . .

Several days before the feast, the four monks summoned the entire complement of girls to the banquet hall
and conducted an inspection to determine which were
least scarred. From the several who qualified they
selected the youngest, a girl named Florette. Her task
was to play the role of the Virgin in the "miracle" — a
theatrical fraud to be staged late in the afternoon of the
feast day itself.

When the day arrived, Florette, costumed in the blue
and white veils which traditionally serve as the Virgin's
colors, was by means of concealed wires tied against the
wall of a niche in the church. During mass, when the
priest elevated the Host, she likewise lifted her arms
toward Heaven. Threatened with the most savage tortures if she should mismanage the role, the little child
performed splendidly; the pilgrims, rejoicing that they
had seen a "miracle," left generous offerings and went
home totally convinced that the Monastery of Saint
Mary-in-the-Woods was truly blessed.

Now, after the fraud had been staged and the pilgrims
had dispersed, the four wicked monks assembled the
complement of girls again and compounded their im-
pieties by staging a black mass. Stripping Florette
naked, they draped her across a large table. Then
Father Severino was celebrant; Father Jerome, deacon,

and Father Clement, subdeacon, for a sham ceremony in which the lovely child's naked form served as the altar.

At the offertory of the "mass," wine and water from the cruets were mixed not in a chalice but in the depression at the child's navel. Severino lapped it up with his tongue. Then, when the Host was brought forth for the consecration, it was placed not upon a blessed patten, but squarely atop Florette's pubic hairs.

Sickened beyond belief at this odious sacrilige, Justine fainted. Father Antonin, the black mass' master of ceremonies, promptly revived her, stripped her naked and made her body the altar in place of the body of Florette. The ritual now was resumed, the Host was consecrated, and the indecent Father Severino, taking that white wafer in one hand and spreading Justine's thighs with the other, viciously thrust the transubstantiated Body and Blood of Our Lord and Savior Jesus Christ into the obscene orifice of Sodom. Then, as if this appalling act were not sacrilege enough, the abominable priest brushed aside his chasuble, mounted the girl and, with powerful strokes of his enormous sex-pole, hammered the Sacred Host into the depths of her bowels.

Insensible when the other monks took her from Father Severino's hands, Justine had to be carried to her room, where for a week she shed continuous tears over the heinous crime in which she had been made an unwilling participant.

VII

Not long after the black mass, word arrived from Rome that Father Severino, as a result of the immense earnings of his monastery on the Feast of the Immaculate Conception, had been named by the Pope as General of the Benedictine Order. Immediately plans were made for a

farwell celebration. Justine, realizing that the day of the
celebration would find the monks and the rest of the
monastery staff fully occupied, selected it as the day to
attempt her escape from the jaded anchorites' clutches.

The time was now late winter, and the long nights
gave her an extra margin of safety. Having over the
space of two months sawed through the bars on her
window (using an old pair of scissors she had found),
she now fashioned a rope from towels and bedsheets
and, while the celebrating ecclesiastics were at dinner,
gingerly lowered herself the treacherous ten meters' distance to the ground. Once there, she made her way
around the pavilion to a section of the moat which she
had overheard a porter say was shallow enough to wade.
through. Then, carefully holding her few belongings over
her head, she stepped into the slimy black water.

Now, as she trudged through the syrup-thick mud of
the moat's bottom, the frightened child suddenly felt the
pressure of something rough and hard closing around her
ankle. Reaching into the water, she pulled out the dismembered arm of a skeleton. Trudging further, she soon
realized that the moat's entire floor was covered with
bones and, in some instances, with cadavers not yet
fully rotted. "Oh Heaven!" she gasped, picking up a
skull inside the eyes of which there still remained fetid
balls of meat; "this must be the place where the girls'
bodies are brought after they are 'graduated.' Who
knows but that this is the very skull of the dear Omphale,
or of another of my friends so recently dismissed from
the monks' service!" Sickened by the thought, she experienced for the first time in her life the pangs of despair.
"Why go on?" she asked herself. "When one is so poor
and forsaken is it not lunacy to strive to remain alive
among the knaves and monsters who populate the earth?
Would it not be better if the ground gaped wide and

swallowed me?" But no sooner had these thoughts entered her mind than she forced them out. "No," she said, "I was not put on earth to abandon the fight just when it becomes most difficult. I must persist in the cause of Virtue until the universe has been cleared completely of villains and scoundrels of the sort who have been tormenting me." Looking toward Heaven, she added: "And, with the help of God, persist I shall!" Thus strengthened in her resolve, she lunged forward through the moat, emerged on a finger of land behind the church, slipped unseen through the inside of that holy edifice and finally found herself in the ominous, high-ceilinged waiting room where she had one year earlier first set foot on monastery property. The large, oak door was ajar; Justine seized it at the handle and, straining her tiny body to its capacity, heaved it open; then, without looking to either side of her, she dashed out into the night — and freedom.

BOOK FIVE

I

The night was cold and clear. A high, yellow moon gave the snow-frosted countryside a sparkling, silvery glow. Sprinting across the road in front of the monastery, Justine plunged into the woods; then, keeping to the shadows of the trees, she made her way slowly along the path toward the highway from which she had first spotted the Benedictine's bell tower.

It was almost dawn when she emerged on the highway. Pausing for an instant, she listened for footsteps in the woods. Then, satisfied that no one had followed her, she began the long trek toward Paris.

Several hours later, the bright red rays of a fiery sun splashed across the morning sky. Moved by the beauty of the spectacle, Justine stopped to contemplate it. It was only then that she appreciated fully the fact that she was finally free from the nefarious monks' prison. Overcome with gratitude for the God Who had aided her escape, she fell to her knees and lifted her eyes toward Heaven in prayer.

"Oh, Merciful Father," she intoned; "oh, Thou Who hast snatched me from the very jaws of destruction, I give Thee thanks. And I entreat Thee, oh God Whom I adore, continue to guide my feet that they stray not from the path of Virtue and Righteousness; Who livest and reignest, world without end, Amen."

Now, no sooner had she said this than Justine suddenly found herself in the grip of two men who, thrusting a sack over her head, bound her hands and feet and spirited her aboard a carriage. Only after the vehicle had rumbled along for five or six kilometers did they loosen the bonds, whereupon she observed that she was being carried through a dense forest. Her first thought was that emissaries of the monks had recaptured her and now were returning her to the monastery; however, one look at the men's faces was enough to persuade her that she was in decidedly nonmonastic company. The taller of the two was a dark-skinned, swarthy-looking devil with a metal hook in place of a hand and with a patch over his right eye; his companion, whose body was almost perfectly spherical, sported a peg leg and a face crisscrossed with half a dozen large scars.

"Kind sirs," asked Justine fearfully, "might I inquire as to where I am being conducted?"

"Indeed you might," chuckled the shorter one. "To the house of the Count de Gernande, a native of Paris and the owner of vast real estate holdings in this region."

"And," she added, "might I inquire as to the purpose of the trip?"

"Yes indeed," laughed the taller. "You have just been

conscripted into the Count's service as a maid."

"But, if a maid is all he wants, why doesn't he simply hire one?"

"Because, my dear, no one will go to work for him," chortled the shorter, doubling over with amusement.

"And why not?"

"Because," roared both in unison, "the man's mad!"

"Insane as a cockroach!" said the taller.

"Looney as a chimpanzee!" added the shorter.

"Mad! Mad! Mad!"

Now, at this juncture, Justine began to wonder if not only the Count but also his minions were not a bit on the peculiar side. However, she had but a few seconds to consider the idea, for, even before the sounds of the bizarre kidnappers' laughter had faded away, the carriage had pulled through a gate and was drawing to a halt in front of a massive, white chateau. On the front porch of the vast building was none other than the Count himself.

Count de Gernande was a man of some fifty years, well over six-feet tall and enormously fat. His face was a huge, melon-like affair, punctuated by a small, round mouth, by an immense, pointed nose, and by a pair of coal-black eyes so terrifying that they would strike fear into the heart of the devil himself. As the two kidnappers dragged Justine out of the carriage, these fearful orbs gave her body the most brusque scrutiny, then fastened to her eyes, remaining thus until she had been brought up the stairs.

"How old are you?" snapped Gernande once the girl was standing before him.

"Twenty-three, sir," she replied.

Then, after listening to an history of her misfortunes, he asked: "Have you ever been bled?"

"Bled?" asked Justine, puzzled at the question. Then,

recalling that some surgeons were known to bleed their patients, she said quickly: "No sir; never; I have always enjoyed only the best of health."

Nodding perfunctorily, Gernande took her arm and squeezed his fingers against the largest vein, inflating it. When it was swollen to perhaps twice is normal appearance, he brought it to his lips and began sucking on it.

"Sir!" protested Justine, "I fail to see what this has to do with my serving as your maid."

"Silence!" ordered Gernande. Then, turning to the peg-legged henchman, he said: "Have the operating room prepared at once. I must inquire into this young lady's composition more closely."

The peg-legged man vanished immediately inside the house. A few minutes later, he returned to report that all preparations had been made. Thereupon the Count led Justine through a series of stairways to an immense, dome-ceilinged laboratory.

The central fixture in the laboratory was a rack-shaped apparatus approximately six-feet high. Two metal rods extended from its top, dangling from each of which was a worn, leather strap. At the bottom, directly under the straps, were two more rods; the ends of both were fashioned into circles, each serving as the holder for a small, white basin. Standing on both sides of this fearsome device were a pair of nances, their rouged lips pouting, their delicately feminine bodies twisted into faun-like postures.

"Ah, my lovelies, look what I've brought!" beamed Count de Gernande. "Would'nt you love to see 'it' undressed?"

"Oh, indeed we would!" replied the two, giggling and preening delightedly. "Please make it take off its clothes."

Immediately the Count ordered Justine to undress. When she offered resistance, he struck out at her with

his enormous arm, knocking her halfway across the room
with but a single blow to the shoulder. Realizing the
futility of further resistance, the unhappy child quickly
surrendered to his demands; whereupon the two nances,
clutching their sides, toppled to the floor in gales of
laughter.

"Look at that, will you!" squealed the first. "It's a
pretty enough thing, but look at those droopy bags
hanging from its chest!"

"And look at that nasty cavity between the legs!"
screamed the second. "I'd not get caught in that if my
life depended upon it!"

Now, while the nances thusly made her anterior the
object of their ridicule, Count de Gernande — an en-
thusiast of the opposite end (as, indeed, are all libertines!) — fell to examining her buttocks with keen interest, clutching handfuls of the soft, firm flesh between his
fingers, sniffing at the crevasses with his long, bulbous
nose, and biting into the lovely white cheeks until he
drew blood. Then he instructed her to walk away from
him, to stop, to return — all the while keeping her
buttocks facing him, so that he could contemplate their
motions as she took each step. Several times he became
so excited at what he saw that he scurried across the
floor on his hands and knees, wrapping his arms around
her thighs and kissing the object of his affections; the
kisses were not ordinary, but of a sucking variety, and
he applied them to every available surface of the Altar
of Sodom — even the Tabernacle. As he kissed her, he
questioned her about the debaucheries at the monastery;
Justine, failing to realize that each of her replies served
only to excite him all the more, revealed every last detail.

Now, turning from Justine, Gernande summoned one
of the nances, whose name was Zéphire. The youth was
wearing a flowing white silk bathrobe, held tight at the

waist by a large red bow. Gernande nibbled at the bow until the knot gave way and the robe fell open, revealing the delicate milk-white skin of the nance's body. Then he pounced upon the boy's organ, sucking at it vigorously, reaching out at the same time for Justine's buttocks, which he took to kneading and manipulating with renewed enthusiasm. When Zéphire's energies finally gave way before the furious assault, the depraved nobleman summoned the other nance, by name, Narcisse, upon whom he likewise practiced his detestable filth.

These base acts having been completed, Gernande brought Justine to the apparatus in the center of the room. "Strap her in place, Zéphire," he commanded. Then: "Narcisse, my razors and my lancets."

Now, as the terrified Justine meekly surrendered to the nance's tugs and turns, her wrists were bound in the leather straps. Next, a small bench was placed on the floor in front of her, and she was told to kneel on it. Then Gernande, his eyes dancing with excitement, tightened the straps until her arms were stretched taut, angling upward from her body like the prongs of a letter, "Y." This accomplished, the savage nobleman touched a lancet to a vein in each of her arms.

A mad cry burst from the insane Count's throat as he first sighted blood. Wringing his hands in delight, he backed several paces away and watched intently as the glimmering red liquid bubbled from Justine's veins and dripped noisily into the white basins. "Ah, blood!" he gasped ecstatically. "Blood! Blood! Blood!"

Now, all but consumed by this madness, Gernande tore open his trousers and fell into position, spread-legged, on an armchair. Immediately, as if on cue, Zéphire positioned himself between his master's knees and engaged the fiend with an anxious, flitting tongue; simultaneously, Narcisse, having removed his trousers completely, stood on the arms of the chair and permitted Gernande to play fellator with him.

Justine, blood still dripping from her wounds, felt a great weakness take possession of her. "Sir," she begged, "help me; I think I'm going to faint!" But Gernande would not permit himself to be distracted from the obscene enterprise involving his two pathicks; he gave no reply, and Justine, growing weaker by the moment, could only watch helplessly as his hands tightened on the buttocks of the busily-undulating Narcisse.

Now Justine's knees buckled; but, held up by the straps, she was unable to fall. Her head dropped to her shoulder; her face was bathed in her own blood. Slowly, but surely, the merciful clouds of unconsciouness washed over her . . .

II

When she awoke, Justine found herself lying between the crisply-starched sheets of a large, comfortable bed. Two nurses were standing by, and, as soon as she opened her eyes, they brought her a cup of rich, thick onion soup. When she finished this, they asked if she thought she could eat some meat; an affirmative reply led to the bringing in of an immense steak, thick and blood-red, which she consumed with relish.

The meal over, the nurses withdrew and Count Gernande made an appearance. Lowering himself gingerly into an armchair alongside the bed, he smiled in a friendly manner and gave Justine's hand an affectionate squeeze. "My Child," he said, "I shall not very often call upon you for participation in activities of the sort which transpired yesterday; however, I deemed it of utmost importance to acquaint you immediately with the nature of my tastes: also, I wanted to warn you of the fate which awaits you in the event that you decide in the future that you would like to betray me."

"Sir," said Justine, "I shall tell you at the onset that I find both your tastes and your threats disgusting; moreover, I shall not be intimidated."

"Say what you will," replied Gernande; "my warning has been issued, and I am prepared to follow through. This being settled, let me now advise you of the uses to which I plan to put you in the days ahead.

"Your job here, as you have been told, is that of a maid. The woman whom you shall attend is my wife. It may interest you to know that she is my fourth; her predecessors all bled to death, as shall she in due time, and as shall, no doubt, her successors. You see, it is my policy to extract from my wives two basins of blood every ninety-six hours; being bled at that rate, one does not—as you can well understand—live very long.

"Now, you might ask, what is it which prompts me to engage in such bizarre behavior? Let me assure you, I act not out of vengeance, or scorn, or any sentiment of hatred or hostility: rather, it is purely and simply a matter of passion; nothing pleases me more than the shedding of blood. Conversely, nothing disturbs me less than the loss of a wife—there are so many women about, you know, and variety is the spice of life. Thus, all in all, it's a happy passion which possesses me, and I manage to get along with it very, very well."

So speaking, Gernande again squeezed Justine's hand affectionately, said goodbye and walked out of the room.

III

Two days later, her recovery complete, Justine entered the service of Madame de Gernande.

The Countess was a lovely woman; not quite twenty

years of age, she was endowed with the most majestic
figure one could imagine: high, proud breasts, a splendid,
wisp-thin waist, and a pair of buttocks so beautifully
round and plump that they strained credulity. Likewise,
she had a face which might have been borrowed from
the Goddess of Love, herself: a straight, delicately-
formed nose; lovely, olive eyes, and a chin which was
perfectly oval. It was no surprise to Justine that the
craven Count de Gernande found her attractive; what
was surprising — nay, astonishing — was that the detestable lout could see fit to inflict even the slightest pain
upon anyone so beautiful.

"Oh, Justine," said the adorable girl sadly, "I welcome to you my service, but with melancholy heart, for
I fear that my weakness—the result of being bled every
fourth day—will make caring for me an exceedingly
troublesome task."

"The troublesomeness of it shall be of no consequence," replied Justine, immediately falling in love
with the charming Countess; "I only regret that I must
behold a woman of your beauty so injured by wickedness."

"Then you soon will have little reason for regrets, my
dear; I have prayed devoutly for death, and the weakness which now possesses me suggests that the day is
not far off; quite soon, I shall find myself in the arms of
my Heavenly Father, and, there, I shall know comfort
I have not been able to find on this earth."

When Justine heard this, her heart was cloven in two.
To herself, she promised that she would lay down her
own life a hundred times before she would leave the
beautiful Madame Gernande at the mercies of her adom-
inable husband. A short time later, she had reason to
become strengthened in this resolve, for she was made
a witness to one of the Countess' horrible bleeding

sessions.

The session took place that evening immediately after dinner. Justine, Madame de Gernande and the two nances were brought by the peg-legged man to the dome-ceilinged laboratory; there they waited until the Count, resplendent in a floor-length red silk robe, made his appearance. When he arrived, Madame de Gernande, who was clad only in a loosely-fitting, near-transparent gauze dress, reverently fell to her knees; the Count, nose held daintily aloft, acknowledged the gesture with a brisk command of, "As you were," then took his place in his favorite armchair.

Now, given the order by Gernande, the peg-legged man tore open the Countess' dress. The poor woman then was brought naked to the armchair, where Gernande seized her by the hips and began kissing and biting her buttocks.

"Now spread them, my love," he told her. Whereupon he plunged his face into the cleavage, making smacking sounds with his mouth as he nuzzled her sweet Altar of Sodom.

When this indecent spectacle was over, the Countess was conducted by the peg-legged man to the bleeding apparatus. Meanwhile, the two nances, completely naked, knelt between Gernande's legs and worked on him in relays, kissing and biting his thighs and sucking on his member.

It was at this point that Justine came to realize that Gernande, for all his devotion to debauchery, had the smallest member she had ever seen; an organ which, in its peanut-sized modesty, served as an insult to the species: worse yet, such was its torpor that the most extreme efforts of the two young Ganymedes could not induce it to lift its tiny head; it only dangled there, lifeless, as all the efforts of the struggling nances went for naught. Finally the Count abandoned the endeavor, and, pushing the nances toward the bleeding apparatus, urged them to molest the Countess; they did so, with slaps, punches and vile insults—and the more she was humiliated the more the Count was pleased.

When he finally tired of this enterprise, Gernande sent for his razors and lancets. Inspecting the leather bands which held the Countess' arms in place, he found the knots too loose; he then tightened them, explaining that greater pressure would cause the blood to spurt out more violently. This done, he touched a razor to the veins in her arms; immediately he was rewarded with a veritable fountain of blood, which he viewed with obvious ecstasy. Next, positioning himself directly in front of her so as to have an unobstructed view of the two geysers, he instructed Justine to kneel between his legs; then, while she sucked on his miniature member he took to masturbating the two nances, one standing at each side of him.

Justine, realizing that the Countess' torments might be shortened if the Count could be brought quickly to climax, began working diligently toward that end; thus, employing every talent which she had acquired through nearly ten years of forced whoredom, she became a voluntary whore, all in the name of kindness. And, indeed, the ploy was a great success, for, seconds after she had put herself to the ugly task, the Count experienced an orgasmic fit the peer of which Justine, for all her travels through the thoroughfares of vice, had never witnessed; staggering, groaning, flailing his arms and uttering screams which could be heard for kilometers, the craven monster all but exploded with pleasure, then collapsed in a heap on the floor.

Releasing Madame de Gernande from the bleeding apparatus, Justine carried her to bed. The poor woman was in a state of extreme weakness, barely able to speak. Looking into her eyes, Justine was overcome with compassion. "I shall help you escape, madame," she whispered resolutely. "I shall help you if it costs me my life..."

IV

The castle of Count de Gernande was situated on a terrace which was ten meters high and which was surrounded by ramparts of an additional five meters. When Justine had been brought to the place, the curtains of her carraige had been pulled shut; thus she had not been able to observe if there were additional barriers beyond these ramparts: likewise, Madame de Gernande, who had been taken to the place at night, had been unable to note whether or not additional barriers existed; however, she had overheard a conversation among several maids which led her to believe that there were none. Therefore, in planning their escape, the two women operated on the assumption that once they scaled the ramparts—a simple feat, thanks to Justine's extensive experience with obstructions of that sort—they would find themselves on the road through the forest ... and free.

Such, sadly, was not the case. As the two beauties, disguised in gardners' costumes, lowered themselves on knotted bedsheets to the ground outside the fortress, they discovered to their terror that they were simply in a large garden, which completely surrounded the ramparts, but which, in turn, was itself completely surrounded by monstrous walls, almost twenty meters in height and bedecked with barbed wire and broken glass. Scaling these horrendous battlements was nigh impossible; there was no hope, save possibly that of waiting for the Count's stagecoach to leave in the morning, at which time, if the vehicle was occupied by friendly members of the staff, Justine and the Countess might beg to be taken aboard.

Shortly after dawn, the large gate creaked open and the Count's coach emerged. Running to the vehicle, the desperate young ladies began pounding on the doors and pleading for help. Suddenly the driver tugged the horses to a halt, the curtains were whisked open and there appeared in the window the face not of some benign servant but of—the Count, himself!

"Aha!" cried the fiend, lashing out at them with his walking stick. "My betrothed seeks to escape and my trusty Justine assists her! Well, this wrong cannot go unavenged..."

More fearful for the lovely Justine than for herself, Madame de Gernande promptly fell prostrate at her vile husband's feet. "Oh, please, sir," she whimpered. "This whole enterprise was my doing. Justine came only because I forced her. Punish me, if you wish, but I beseech you: spare her."

These tearful entreaties, however, fell on deaf ears. "Not a chance," snapped the Count. "Two have sinned and two must be punished. Tonight, after dinner, I'll dispatch the both of you to your heavenly rewards; perhaps I shall even spend the day constructing a second bleeding apparatus so that I can watch you die together."

"But sir," Justine began; "mercy—"

"No, child," Gernande interrupted her; "mercy is a trait unknown to me. You both deserve to have your veins cut this minute; if I postpone the undertaking, it is not from mercy—it is only to render the eventual realization of it more horrible." So saying, he dashed the two of them into the carriage and ordered the driver to return to the chateau.

That evening, immediately after dinner, the peg-legged man appeared at Madame de Gernande's apartment, announcing that the Count wanted both his wife and Justine in the laboratory at once. Clutching each others' hands, the two women followed him down the hall. But they were not without a plan: they had spent the whole afternoon designing a bold, last-chance escape by means of the same carriage in which the count had apprehended them that morning; now they prepared to put the plan into action.

As the peg-legged man rounded a corner toward the section of the chateau in which was situated the laboratory, Madame de Gernande struck him over the head with an iron which she had concealed in the folds of her dress. Then both women bolted through the door, on the other side of which would be the carriage—hopefully unattended.

The first phase of their endeavor was blessed by Fortune: the carriage was indeed unattended, they leaped aboard, and the horses, responding instantly to Madame de Gernande's whip, lurched toward the gate. However, inside the laboratory, Count de Gernande had grown impatient waiting for the peg-legged man to return with the two prisoners; stepping into the hallway to investigate, he heard the clatter of the carriage — at the same time as he encountered his trusty minion's unconscious body stretched out on the floor. Running now to the front porch, he witnessed the two would-be escapees hurtling furiously toward the gate.

In the Count's hand were the razors and lancets with which he had planned to perform his operations. As the carriage stopped at the portals, he took aim and hurled the largest of these impliments. Justine, climbing back into the vehicle after opening the gate, watched the gleaming blade whistle past her; Madame de Gernande, however, was not as lucky: at the very instant when she snapped the reins, prodding the horses into motion, the cruel blade thudded into the base of her skull; Justine could only watch as her beloved mistress toppled off the seat and fell to the ground, dead. The reins now unattended, the horses raced on into the night—carrying Justine to freedom. . . .

V

Once she had found her way to the main road, Justine headed straight for Lyons. There — not wishing to retain possession of the carriage, which she still regarded as the property of Gernande (and retention of which, therefore, would be theft)—she tied the horses to a tree and resumed her journey, on foot, toward Grenoble, in which remote city, she hoped, she might find peace at last. As she approached the highway, however, she was given pause by a notice in the Lyons newspaper.

Doctor Rodin, read the announcement, had just received the highest accolades for his discoveries in the field of internal medicine, and simultaneously had been named First Surgeon to the Empress of Russia, which position brought with it rewards of a material as well as a spiritual nature.

"May he prosper, the knave!" murmured Justine, remembering with a shudder the savage wretch who had branded her with a hot iron as punishment for trying to prevent him from murdering his daughter. "If Providence wills it, may all the goods of the world be heaped upon him; for my part, I'll accept the trials and tribulations the bearing of which is Virtue's lot."

So saying, she cast aside the newspaper and resumed her trek toward the highway. However, before she had walked ten paces, she was stopped by a messenger dressed in grey.

"Are you the girl Justine, who once was the prisoner of the Dubois gang?" he asked.

"Indeed I am," gasped she, no less than amazed at the mention of this association so far in her past.

"Then read this," said the lackey, thrusting a note into her hands.

Justine unfolded it and read:

A man who has wronged you, and who believes that he recognized you in the Place de Bellecour, is most eager to renew your acquaintance and to liquidate his indebtedness to you. Hasten to meet him.

The message bore no signature or other identification. Justine demanded that the messenger identify the sender.

"His name," came the reply, "is Monsieur Saint-Florent. He says that he wronged you after you rescued him from a band of thieves, and now he wishes to make amends. He is one of the richest and most respected men in this city, and certainly in a position to improve your station. If you'll accompany me, I'll conduct you to him."

Justine, for her part, had no desire to reacquaint herself with the scoundrel who nine years earlier had robbed her of her virginity, then abandoned her in the woods near Luzarches. However, confronted thusly with his declaration of repentance, she felt that she would stand guilty in the Eyes of God were she to withhold forgiveness; furthermore (she told herself), if the savage really were intent on aiding her, she certainly was in a position to accept beneficence, having left the chateau of Gernande all but penniless. "Take me to your master," she told the messenger.

Back in the heart of the city, Justine was brought to

an immense mansion. There, in a sumptuous drawing
room, she came face to face with the butcher, Saint-
Florent. He was forty-five years of age now, this viper;
but the hardness of his jaw and the icy glaze of his eyes
would have remained unchanged were he ninety-five.

"I wanted to see you again, my love, for a number of
reasons," he told Justine once his servants had withdrawn. "It is not because I regret wronging you, for I
believe that my position renders me incapable of culp-
ability — besides, I only followed my natural impulses.
No, what I want you for is a project of vast scope, essential to my happiness — which is all I care about — and
participation in which can improve your fortunes considerably. In other words, you help me and I'll help you.

"Now, then, the project: I have always, my child, had
a passion for little girls' maidenheads; this passion, like
all others of libertinage, becomes more deeply rooted in
me with each passing day: things have now reached a
point where I cannot be satisfied unless I stuprate two
virgins a day; moreover, having once enjoyed them, I
cannot bear to live with the thought that the little twerps
breathe the same air as I: therefore, I pack them off and
sell them to the whorehouses of Provence and Languedoc in Montpellier and Toulouse, Aix and Marseilles; this
enterprise, two-thirds of the profits of which accrue to
me, more than pays for the cost of recruiting additional
victims, and thus not only do I get all the sexual activity
I desire among the type of girls with whom I desire it
but also I manage to make a rather nice living at it.

"Appalling, is it not? To one of your professed high
principles, perhaps it is. However, I'm not the slightest
bit appalled; it doesn't bother me a bit. And, dear
Justine, unless I misread your character, you would not
be bothered either, as long as you were the beneficiary
rather than the victim of vice. Therefore, what I propose

to you is this: come live with me, accept a post as my housekeeper and take charge of the recruitment of my girls; I'll reward you handsomely, you'll live comfortably and, who knows, maybe I'll even give you a percentage of the business after a time. Now, what do you say?"

"I say no, sir; most emphatically, no," replied Justine. "Yes, I am poor; quite poor: but I am richer because of the pure sentiments in my heart than you are for all your wealth, and I'd rather die than join up with a knave like you."

"Is that so, my little twat?" said Saint-Florent, grinning menacingly. "Do you really mean that?" Tearing open his desk drawer, he extracted a strongbox, the contents of which he emptied theatrically on top of the desk; there were hundreds of gold coins, perhaps two thousand louis all told, more money than Justine ever had seen in one place in her life. "Suppose I were to offer you as much of this money as you could carry in two hands — all for nothing more than permitting me fifteen minutes of your company. What would you say to that?"

"Fifteen minutes in my . . . company?" she asked haltingly.

"Yes; in the bedroom, of course; I would expect you to be obedient to my carnal demands, but they would not be severe . . . ."

"Not a chance," snapped Justine. "I am no more eager to serve your debauches as whore than as procuress. As to your money, I spit on it!" And, so saying, she did precisely that.

"Ah, cunt!" cried the irate Saint-Florent. "You dare insult me thus in my own house?! Out with you!!!"

But his command was wholly unnecessary, for Justine, turning briskly away from him, was all but out of the room before he could finish the sentence.

"Oh, Heaven," she mused later, having started out again for Grenoble, "will it always be like this; will I pass my entire life without knowing a man of decency, of honor, of principle; will I never observe the triumph of Virtue over Vice?" Yet, she refused to surrender hope. Kneeling alongside the road, she lifted her eyes to heaven and prayed: "Oh, Father, direct me to do Thy will in all things; no more than this do I ask of Thee." And, having thus returned peace to her soul, she resumed the journey . . .

VI

Not long after she was outside the Lyons city limits, Justine came upon an old woman who was begging for alms. Feeling compassion for the luckless creature, she opened her purse and fished about for a coin. But the woman, much quicker than her wizened appearance would suggest, nimbly snatched the purse from the poor girl's hands, folded her in half with a punch to the abdomen and sprinted off to join four bearded bandits who had been lying in wait some fifty meters ahead.

"Good God in Heaven!" the disillusioned Justine cried. "Is it impossible for me to give vent to a virtuous impulse without immediately being made to suffer for it?" But, again conquering the temptation to despair, she repeated her earlier prayer of submission to the Father's will. Thus tranquilized, she once more resumed the journey.

VII

Having been robbed of her purse, Justine found it necessary to amend her itinerary to include a stop at Vienne, where, in order to finance the remainder of the trip to Grenoble, she would sell what few possessions she had left. She was walking sadly along the highway toward this new stopping place when suddenly, in a field not far from the road, she observed two horsemen trampling a man beneath the hooves of their mounts. As the knaves, abandoning their victim as dead, galloped off, Justine was overcome with pity for the poor creature. "Good Heavens!" she told herself. "Here, at last, is someone even more unfortunate than I; at least I still have my health, which enables me to work for a living; but, if this sad soul is not rich, he's doomed to a life of misery!" Experience, of course, might have taught her that the impulse of pity is often a costly impulse to gratify; however, unable to suppress her intense urge to comfort him, she hastened to the victim's side and began ministering to his needs; and before long, the man was on his feet, walking with her toward the road.

"How lucky I am that you happened by when you did," he told her, taking her tender hand in his. "What strange circumstances led to your passing this way — alone, no less — at an hour as perilous to a young lady's virtue as this hour?"

"Ah, sir," replied Justine, "circumstances have treated me quite unkindly — almost as unkindly, I dare say, as they appear to have treated you." Thereupon she unburdened herself of the story of her life, not omitting a single detail of her extensive suffering.

"How fortunate that I met you!" said the man, whose name was Roland, when the narrative came to an end. "I am the owner of an exceptionally fine chateau on a mountainside not far from here; follow me there and perhaps your fortunes will improve. And let me point out, lest the proposal alarm your sense of propriety, that, although I am a bachelor, I live with my sister, a woman whose probity and spirituality are an inspiration to all who know her; your virtue will be perfectly safe with this splendid woman as your chaperone."

Convinced that the meeting with Roland could only be a reward granted by Divine Providence for her many

years of patient suffering, Justine immediately accepted
the offer. Then, hand in hand, they set out together for
Vienne, where Roland said he could engage horses on
which to complete the journey.

Now, after spending the night at an inn in Vienne —
in separate rooms, to be sure — Justine and her new-
found protector took to the highlands. The roads soon
became impassible and they were forced to walk alongside their mounts, picking their way through wooded
paths and around immense boulders. Finally, after nearly
fourteen hours' travel, they came to a huge castle, perched high on the crest of a mountain; no road seemed to
lead to the place, and, indeed, Justine found herself
wondering how any animal save goats could negotiate
the fearsome cliff on which it was perched.

"There it is, Justine," said Roland, smiling broadly.
"What do you think of it?"

"You live there, sire?" replied she, stunned. "But why
in such isolation?"

"Don't be afraid," he answered, leading the way up
the treacherous hillside. "We're still on French terrain;
we're on the Dauphiné border, within the diocese of
Grenoble."

"No doubt," argued Justine; "but the isolation of the
place is such as is best suited to thieves and murderers.
Why have you selected to live in such a manner?"

"Because, my child," he laughed sardonically, "I am
both — thief and murderer! I am the leader of a band of
counterfeiters, and this castle is our headquarters!"

"But you said . . . your sister . . ." stammered Justine.

"Foolish girl," replied the treacherous Roland, "one
would think you would have learned by now that men
do not always tell the truth! But, enough of this talk:
you are now my prisoner, and I'll tolerate no nonsense

from you." Leading her across a drawbridge, which lowered as soon as they approached, he tied their horses inside a small stable, then brought her to a large court-yard where four women, nude and chained, were turning an immense wheel. "These will be your colleagues hence-forth," he said, taking in the quartet with a sweep of his arm; "your task will be to turn this wheel for ten hours per day, and also to lend yourself to participation in all sexual indignities to which I choose to submit you; in exchange for this, I shall give you six ounces of bread and a plate of beans every day, and occasionally two ounces of wine on Sundays."

Now, conducting her around the courtyard, he came to a small wall which overlooked the cliff. Pointing to the rocky floor of the chasm some several hundred meters below them, he continued: "When you leave here, that will be your destination; there is no other way out: at present, some seventy or eighty women's bodies — or what remains of them — lie there; perhaps a third were thrown over after having died of natural causes during the course of their work; the remainder were thrown over alive, either for having attempted to escape or for having otherwise violated one or another of the rules of conduct in force here. Now, do you have any questions?"

"Good Heavens!" said Justine. "Can you perpetrate this monstrous display of ingratitude without feeling even a twinge of remorse? Do you not remember that I saved your life; that I ministered to your wounds by rip-ping up one of the last of my good dresses; that I gave myself over completely to your trust? Do you not pity me?"

"What is this pity business?" Roland replied. "And, tell me: from where should there stem this gratitude of which you speak? Did I ask you to rescue me? Most certainly not. You saw me in the field and you had two choices: rescuing me, or continuing on your way. Why did you choose the former? To satisfy an impulse, of course; to give yourself the pleasure of considering yourself a merciful woman. Am I not right?

"I put it to you thusly: if I were lying at the roadside bleeding to death and you could only rescue me by violating the laws of your Church — at the peril, of course, of your soul —, would you do it? I should say not. But your Church encourages the comforting of the downtrodden; indeed, it holds out spiritual rewards for those of you who lend themselves most diligently to such efforts. So here we have the crux of the matter: you rescued me not for my welfare, but for your own profit — now how in the name of rationality can you berate me for not rewarding you for making me the instrument of your investment in your soul's future?!"

Not waiting for her to reply, Roland summoned two valets, who promptly stripped and manacled her and put her to work with the women at the wheel. Then, as she bent to the arduous task before her, the odious ingrate stood by and taunted her, tweaking her breasts and buttocks, slapping at her belly and thighs. "Yes, you little whore," he snarled, "I'll show you what gratitude is; you're nowhere near the end of your miseries: the worst is yet to come—and you'll be astounded at how bad it can be . . . ."

VIII

Roland was a short, stocky man of some thirty-five years, fierce of eye and as hairy as a bear; his nose was long and pointed, his jowls hard, his brows both thick and shaggy. However — as Justine was soon to discover — the most spectacular thing about him was his penis, which was of such prodigious length and circumference that the rest of his body was dwarfed in comparison; indeed, few men could boast of a forearm the size of this immense appendage.

Roland's vices were as extravagant as this equipment with which he perpetrated them. Justine learned from the women with whom she turned the wheel that, like the rest of his ilk of libertines, he favored the Altar of Sodom as the repository of his incense; however, while many roués were content with two or three partners, the jaded Roland used as many as nine and ten in a single night, whipping each ferociously, and often not contenting himself until he had broken an arm or leg, dislodged a joint, or slashed open a stomach or throat.

Justine soon had opportunity to view this ferocity first hand. On her third day in the castle, she was summoned to Roland's bedroom. "Get out of these garments," he ordered, tearing off her clothes. Then, fastening a chain around her neck, he led her through a long, winding passageway to a dank cellar in the very bowels of the castle. Pulling shut the huge, metal door he said: "Well, whore, you are about to taste the lust of a man more montrous than any whose crimes you described to me; remember well the way you feel right now, because, when I'm finished with you, you'll never feel the same way again."

The cellar was circular and approximately eight meters in diameter. Its walls, painted black, were decorated with whips and canes, cutlasses, daggers, pistols and skeletons of various sizes; Roland hastened to assure Justine that the skeletons were all very real, being, in fact, the remains of girls who met their death in that very room.

Across the center of the cellar was a wooden beam, from which dangled a rope, its end fashioned into a noose; and, nearby was an open coffin in which was displayed another skeleton, its arms arranged on the handle of a scythe in the manner of Father Time. Along one wall was a prayer stool of the sort often seen in churches, and, above it, a crucifix, flanked by yellow funeral candles. On the opposite wall, in the same posture as the crucified Christ, was the wax effigy of a naked woman, the figure was so realistic that Justine had to touch it before she would believe that it was not alive.

"See this?" said Roland, tapping a riding crop against the effigy's thighs. Justine immediately noticed marks of a sort as would have been made had those lovely limbs been gnawed at by a beast; blood seemed to ooze from the wounds and to trickle down the legs. "This statue is a representation of my former mistress, who died nailed to this wall. I had it constructed to replace her real body when it began to decompose." Then, striking the wall around the effigy with the riding crop, he continued: "And this is the way you will die, Justine — crucified like your friend, Mister Christ — if the notion enters my head that it might give me pleasure to dispose of you in such a manner."

Now, his speaking thusly soon aroused the passions of the monstrous Roland to the point where he could not be satisfied until he had abused the lovely Justine. Taking down his trousers, he displayed his oversized penis, touching Justine's hand to it and asking her if she had ever seen another which could compare with it.

"Regard it well, slut," he said; "the entirety of it will probe the smallest orifice you have to offer it — and, if I cleave you in half in the process, so much the better; nothing pleases my ears more than the sound of breaking bones and dislocating joints."

Growling quite audibly, much like the bear which he resembled, he draped Justine over the edge of a couch

and, prying open her buttocks, launched a fierce attack
at the Altar of Sodom. Scratching, clawing, kneading and
squeezing her flesh, he refused to ease up until the whole
of her cleavage was reduced to pulp; then, smearing the
the wounds with alcohol, the monster touched a match
to her and roared with hysterical laughter as she writhed
and twisted in pain; the flames licked at her beautiful
thighs and torso, turning the alabaster-white flesh a
noxious charcoal-black.

Justine, throwing herself at his feet, begged for mercy.
"Remember, sir," she cried, "were it not for my aid a few
days ago, you would not be alive today. In the name of
God, show me a similar compassion."

But these pleas served only to heighten the madman's
fury. Seizing a steel-tipped riding crop from the wall, he
struck at her thighs and buttocks with such force that
huge fountains of blood gushed out, spraying all over
him — which pleased him beyond imagination — and
over the walls as well. "You remind me that you rescued
me?!" he screamed. "How dare you resurrect an argument which I so successfully rebutted just a short time
ago?! Have you no memory?!" Then, prying her legs
open with his foot and kicking viciously at the insides
of her thighs, he continued: "And you dare invoke the
name of God? Where is your God now? He abandons
you, doesn't he? He permits Virtue to fall victim to
Villainy's wiles. Some God! I say, who needs him!"

Now, draping her once more, face-down, over the edge
of the couch, he thrust apart her legs and prepared himself for the assault. Slowly at first, then more rapidly, his
monstrous member battered at the door he sought to
enter; finally, after repeated pummeling, which all but
rendered Justine insensitive, the blood-slicked organ
gained a hold: inspired by this success, the villain began
thrusting more vigorously; an inch was gained, another

inch; soon, half the organ was inside her and Justine felt as if she were being split in two.

Suddenly, saber still half-sheathed, Roland reached to a darkened corner of the couch and took hold of a length of rope. Draping it around her neck, he slowly pulled it taut. "Scream," he commanded. When she refused, he pulled it tighter. Now the pressure of the garrote forced a scream from her lips; Roland, cackling delightedly, tightened it and at the same time thrust violently with his hips, forcing his monstrous penis farther into her bowels. Little by little, now, he tightened the rope more and thrust farther still, until Justine's screams were reduced to a high-pitched, airy whistle. "Now, bitch! *NOW!!!*" the madman suddenly shouted, and, with that, he applied such pressure to the rope that Justine's head was all but wrenched from her shoulders, while, at the same time, he plunged his formidable organ to the very hilt.

Flooded with pain, Justine felt her body grow slack; circles of black took form around the circumference of her vision and gradually converged; finally, all sensation and perception ceased.

"Well, Justine," said Roland when she regained consciousness minutes later, "tell me what it was like. I'll bet that you loved every second of it."

"I felt only horror, sir," she replied weakly. "Horror and revulsion."

The abominable monster chuckled softly. "You're not telling the truth," he said. "I know how much you've enjoyed it, because I've experienced it myself. Now you must be punished for being untruthful to me."

So saying, he took a stool from one corner of the room and placed it in the center of the floor, just below the noose. Then he tied a rope to one leg of the stool and brought its opposite end to the couch.

"Now we are going to play a game which has been handed down to us from the Celts," he continued. "It is called Cut-the-Cord, and its purpose is to pit your co-ordination against mine. You will stand on this stool, with the noose tight around your neck — like this. In your hand you will hold this sickle — like so. I will sit over here on the couch with this other rope in one hand and with this dagger in the other. Now, then: when I tug at my rope, the stool will fall out from under you; the only way you can save yourself is to slash the noose with the sickle; however, don't make the mistake of slashing too soon, because I may not pull the stool after all, and if it remains under you after you have slashed the noose, I shall stab you with this dagger." Tugging experimentally at the rope, he grinned fiendishly. "Are you ready?" he asked. And, when she refused to answer, he said: *"Begin!"*

Rolland tugged once, but lightly; Justine was not fooled: again lightly; she held fast: now, with full force; the stool jerked out from beneath her; a split second during which she seemed to be suspended in air, and then— Success! She severed the noose and fell to the ground!

"Splendid!" said Roland, almost as if he had been cheering for her all along. "You win the game! I bow before you! Hail the conquering heroine!" Then, grinning evilly, he ruffled her hair with his enormous sausage-thick fingers. "Of course," he added, "tomorrow we play the game again. So perhaps you haven't won after all . . . ."

IX

In the days which followed, Roland forced her to participate in the ghastly game time and time again. Invariably it was preceded by debauchery of the type already described, and the savage counterfeiter never appeared to be happier than at the moment when Justine appeared to be suffering the greatest pain. One evening, after a particularly horrible session, he was moved to explain the nature of his passion.

"My dear Justine," he said, "you are in error if you assume that it is a woman's beauty which stirs the lusts of a libertine; rather it is the crime associated by law and religion with the possession of her. You require proof? Then consider this: is it not true that the greater the crime, the greater the libertine's pleasure? Sexual congress with a prostitute? It has no appeal for him. Fornication with a 'good' woman? Much more to his liking. Defilement of a virgin? Stupration of a wife? Seduction of a nun? Better yet. The victim resists? Forcing her makes the final pleasure all the sweeter. She incurs injury? Sweeter still. She dies? Ecstasy, my child; sheer ecstasy.

"Now we come to the crux of my philosophy: if the taking of pleasure is enhanced by the criminal character of the circumstances — if, indeed, the pleasure taken is directly proportionate to the severity of the crime involved (as I have just demonstrated to be the case) —, then is it not criminality itself which is pleasurable, and the seemingly pleasure-producing act nothing more than the instrument of its realization? Indeed it is; there can be no other answer.

"Thus you can comprehend the nature of crime; there is a pleasure in naked crime — a pleasure above and beyond the spoils received, be they gold and securities or the occupancy for a period of time of certain of another person's bodily parts. This explains why so many so-called respectable people, who certainly have no need to steal, nonetheless steal with impunity; why husbands, having more than ample outlet for their sexual energies in the persons of their wives, nonetheless roam the streets looking for additional targets; and it explains, dear child, why you can travel the length and breadth of France without finding a spectacle so popular, a production which attracts a greater audience, an extravaganza so dear to the hearts of its spectators than the execution of one of their number on the gallows!

"You wonder why people behave as they do, child? Don't turn to religion for your answer; turn to the public square the next time there is an execution and look into the eyes of the citizens there assembled. Naked crime — they revel in it. It is their life, their sustenance, their joy...."

X

Months passed. The nights of torment at the hands of the evil Roland continued; so, too, did the hours upon hours of being subjected to his horrendous maxims. And then, one evening, much to her surprise, Justine found herself addressed by a most unusual proposition.

"My child," said Roland, "there is no one in this house whom I trust more than you; for this reason, I wish to put my life in your hands: if the experiment proves to be a success, I will know pleasures unimagined by men since the beginning of time; if it fails, it shall cost me my life — but, for me, the possibiilty of the reward is sufficiently exciting to make the risk worthwhile. Whatever the outcome, you shall by your participation have earned your unqualified freedom."

Her interest aroused, Justine implored him to describe more precisely the nature of the experiment he wished to conduct.

"My child," he said, "I have put many persons to death, and I am utterly convinced that the sufferings they experienced in the process were sweeter than any sensation man has ever known. Unfortunately, the victim have never been able to verify my theories, and those others, with whom I suspended the experiments just before the fatal moment, have refused to admit — or, perhaps, were insufficiently sensitive to — the pleasures which I am certain were available to them. Thus, if my curiosity is ever to be satisfied, I must have empirical data; I must know these sensations myself!"

"Then what would you have me do?" asked Justine. "Surely murder is an irreversible process; having started to kill you — having, say, slit your throat or impaled your heart — how could I prevent the crime thus started from being brought to its inevitable conclusion?"

"The answer to your question," he replied, "will be found in the cellar. Let's proceed there forthwith."

Once they had made their way to that dank dungeon, Roland assembled the apparatus for the Cut-the-Cord game. This time, though, it was he who was to stand on the stool while Justine tugged the rope! Denuding himself, he gave her his final instructions:

"After you've adjusted the noose around my neck, take my customary place on the couch. Then curse at me while I fondle my genitalia, and, when you observe that I have become sufficiently aroused, pull the stool out from under me. However, I will not hold a sickle with which to cut the cord, lest I be tempted to put it to use prematurely. Instead, you hold the sickle, and, when the stool falls, permit me to remain hanging. Leave me there until you witness either the ejaculation of my semen or evidence of the onset of death's throes. If the latter, cut the cord immediately and revive me with slaps about the face and head; but, if the former, allow the ejaculation to continue until my substance is totally spent, and only then cut me down."

Having directed her thusly, he mounted the stool. Obedient to his instructions, she tightened the noose about his neck. He fondled himself as she cursed at him, and, in seconds, his enormous organ snaked upward. Now he gave her the sign to tug the rope. The stool flew away. And —

It was just as the knave had theorized! As his body snapped under the force of his fall, a broad smile of ecstasy bisected his face. His penis stretched to an almost incredible tautness. Then a geyser of semen erupted, shooting high above his head, almost to the ceiling of the room.

When the last drops were expelled, Justine cut him loose. He fell to the floor, unconscious, but her slaps quickly revived him. His happiness bordered delerium.

"Oh, my lovely child!" he cried. "The sensations are beyond credibility! They surpass anything I have ever conceived! We must do this every night for the rest of my life!"

"But, sir —" protested Justine. "Did you not promise my freedom in exchange for my cooperation in this venture?"

Roland chuckled. "You know that my promises are worthless, child," he said. "Such is my nature." Then, striking her savagely across the face, he added: "Furthermore, I know that as you assist me in this project every night, you will never permit yourself to let me die. Such is *your* nature!"

And Justine sobbed bitterly, for she knew that what he said was true.

XI

One day the entire staff at the chateau was astounded to learn that Roland had vanished. Having accumulated through his activities as a counterfeiter more money than he could possibly spend in two lifetimes, he had taken leave for Italy, where he planned to retire to a life of material ease and sustained debauchery.

His successor, by name, Dalville, was, though a criminal, a kind and gentle man who wanted nothing less than to observe the suffering of his fellow humans. Releasing the crew of girls whom Roland had assigned to the turning of the wheel, he declared: "Henceforth animals shall be utilized in this labor; our livelihood as counterfeiters is offensive enough to Almighty God without our offending Him further with sins of human suffering." Then he instructed the chef to reorganize the kitchen so that all prisoners would be fed the same food as the thieves themselves, and in such quantity as to insure that no one left the table hungry except by choice.

Two months passed. Then Dalville received word, which he transmitted promptly to Justine and her fellow prisoners, that Roland had arrived safely at Venice. Indeed, not only had he already situated himself in total comfort, as planned, but also he had assembled a staff of concubines with whom he was conducting further experiments in the extremities of depravity. In sum, he was wholly content.

The good thief, Dalville, however, was not to know similar good fortune. The very day after word had come from Roland, the chateau was invaded by a detachment of soldiers. The moats were bridged, the gates were knocked down and the entire crew — the thieves and their prisoners alike — were arrested.

"Oh, Heaven!" sighed Justine as she and her sister victims were loaded into carriages to be taken to Grenoble. "This is the result of ten years of struggling to be virtuous: bedraggled, harrassed, tortured and stained, I find myself once more headed for the scaffold. Where is justice? Where is mercy? Where is God?" Then, immediately overcome with guilt for having permitted herself these thoughts of despair, she prayed feverishly: "Do to me what Thou wilt, O Lord. My fortunes, my life, my everything — all are Thine if Thou but wantest them . . . ."

BOOK SIX

I

The Grenoble court wasted little time with the counterfeiters' case; everyone arrested was sentenced to death
and the executions were scheduled for the following
morning. But, as the prisoners were being led from the
courtroom back to the jail, there was a great commotion
on the street. "Justine! Justine!" came the cries of a
woman, and, in a trice, the creature had broken through
the police lines and was frantically planting kisses all
over the bewildered girl's face.

"My sweet! Don't you recognize me?!" she sighed. "Are
you not the person whom I rescued from the Conciergerie ten years ago? Don't you remember your pro-
tectress, Dubois?"

"Dubois!" exclaimed Justine happily. "Good friend
Dubois!" Then, remembering the circumstances under

which they last parted company, she hastily added: "Well, if it's vengeance you seek, you've got but a few hours to take it, for I'm scheduled to lose my head tomorrow morning."

"Vengeance?!" cried the former leader of the band of thieves. "How can you think such a thing?! And you're going to lose your head, you say?! Never! I won't stand for it!"

At this point one of the policemen attempted to separate them. Dubois wheeled toward him sharply. "Young man, I have connections in this town!" she snapped. "Get out of my way."

Before the astonished lawman could reply, a tall and distinguished-looking gentleman moved into position at Dubois side. "Do you recognize me?" he asked the policeman. "I am Justice Dubreuil of the Grenoble court."

"Indeed, sir," replied the young man, saluting. "What is your pleasure?"

"You say you know this child, darling?" the Justice asked Madame Dubois.

"By all means, my love; I beg you, order this lout to release her in our custody."

"You heard the lady," the Justice snapped.

And the lawman, unfastening the manacles which bound Justine's wrists, obediently turned her over to the couple.

Later, in an extravagant suite at the city's largest hotel, Dubois reassured Justine that there was absolutely nothing to worry about: Dubreuil was the highest ranking judge on the bench, accountable only to the Chief Justice, himself; as soon as the arrest papers could be procured, he would review the death sentence, find Justine not guilty and decree her unconditional pardon. "And now that this matter has been disposed of," Dubois said, "tell me, child: what has transpired with you for the past ten years?"

Tears of gratitude welling up in her eyes, Justine re-
counted every experience, from her defilement at the
hands of the wicked Saint-Florent to her being branded
like a murderer by the savage Doctor Rodin and her
debasement by the notorious Roland. When the recital
was over, Dubois stroked the girl's hand comfortingly
and said: "Well, my dear friend, you now can appreciate
my earlier statements about the advisability of pursing
a life of Vice. As you can see, the quest for Virtue
brought you nothing more than misery, pain and degradation; where as I, leaving the Concergierie at the same
time as you and without a penny more to my name, have
made my fortune." Throwing open a huge chest which
rested at the foot of her bed, she revealed an abundance
of gold, diamonds and other precious metals and stones,
the likes of which Justine had never seen. "Behold!" she
said. "The fruits of Vice!"

"Oh, dear Dubois," replied Justine, "if you obtained
these things by dishonest means, you can rest assured
that Divine Justice will see to it that you don't enjoy
them for very long."

"Divine Justice?" scoffed the older woman. "You make
me laugh. If there were a God, and if he were just, there
would be no evil in the world; but, as anyone can see,
evil abounds, and, if there's a God, he's either a knave
for allowing it or an incompetent ass for being unable to
prevent it: either way, he deserves nothing but contempt."

"But, sweet Dubois," argued Justine, "though there is
evil, good eventually triumphs in the end. Look to my
own case for proof. Though abused for ten years, here I
am, saved, by you, within the very shadow of the scaffold. Surely that proves the existence of Providence."

"You simple fool!" spat Dubois. "Do you think I saved

you for unselfish motives? Don't be naive. When I saw you in the prisoners' line this morning, it was just one more instance of Fate favoring those who scheme and fend for themselves. You see, there is a man whom I want murdered, and you are just the person to do it —"

"Never, madame!" gasped Justine. "Not in a thousand years."

"Tonight."

"Never."

"Yes, I say."

"No."

"You are an utter dolt, Justine. An utter dolt. The blade is about to drop on your neck, I offer you salvation and you refuse to accept it. My child, in this strongbox is enough wealth to put pheasant and caviar on our table every day for the next century. It now belongs to my friend, Justice Dubreuil, who is at this very instant working diligently to effect your release. But, if you stick a knife in his throat tonight while he sleeps, it will belong to us, my dear; to you and me. And who'd dare suspect you of the crime? Who'd dare accuse a girl of murdering the judge who that very afternoon secured her pardon?"

"Never, madame," hissed Justine, more appalled than ever. "I would never repay his kindness thusly."

"*His* kindness, you fool?" thundered Dubois. "It is my kindness. Do you think he's acting out of love for you? He is acting because I am his mistress, and because only by so acting does he believe that he can retain my services. For his own part, he couldn't care less if they chopped you into a million pieces."

"My answer still is no, madame."

"Then there is nothing more I can say," shrugged Dubois. "But you shall live long enough to regret this decision — quite probably, *just* long enough to regret it!"

II

That evening, while Justice Dubreuil slept, Madam Dubois slit his throat. The next morning, when police arrived to investigate, Justine was among the first to be
arrested as a suspect.

"One moment, sir," said Dubois to the arresting officer.
"As the late Justice Dubreuil's mistress, I'm in a position
to testify that he held this girl in very high esteem. I'm
quite sure that she could not possibly have committed
the crime. Earlier in the week she was convicted of being
a party to counterfeiting; I don't deny it: but surely
you'll agree that there is a great difference between that
crime and the fiendish act of murder.

"The type of character required to commit murder,
after all, is not attained in a single night. It is for this
reason that our law, in its infinite wisdom, affixes a
brand to the shoulder of anyone convicted of murder;
thus, if a convict escapes before execution can take place,
the proof of his crime follows him, known to all who take
the trouble to look.

"Now I implore you: behold this poor child's lovely
body. Remove her blouse and search for a mark. If you
find one, I will readily denounce her and deliver her
over to you. But if there be none, permit me, in the name
of the murdered man whom I loved so well, to protect
and defend her.

Thus was the wicked Dubois' diabolical cunning! By
pretending to defend Justine when the girl was merely
suspected, she insured that no one — but no one — would
ever accept her very valid pleas of innocence after she
had been arrested!

"Don't bother to search me, sir," said Justine, resign-
ing herself to the inevitable. "Madame knows full well
that I bear such a mark, having suffered its infliction at

the hands of a mad surgeon some five years ago in a'
woods outside Paris. If such is justice here that I stand
condemned as a result; then here are my hands; strike
your chains about them, for I am your prisoner."

III

Returned to the city jail, Justine was placed in special
custody pending trial before Chief Justice de Corville,
the only official in the entire territory empowered to
hear a case as grave as the murder of a member of the
judiciary. While awaiting the summons to the Chief
Justice's chambers, Justine requested a visit by the prison
chaplain for the purpose of making her final confession.
Permission granted, her guard withdrew to the prison
chapel and returned with —

Father Antonin, the libertine monk from the Monastery of Saint Mary-in-the-Woods!

"Justine," said the evil ecclesiastic after listening to
her confession, "there is no doubt in my mind that you
are one of the stupidest little twats I have ever encountered. However, if you have the good sense to talk
a little business with me, I may be able to get you out of
this scrape yet." Now, gloom clouding his countenance,
he continued: "Sweet child, you'll never know how deprived I've been since my transfer from Saint Mary-in-
the-Woods. Oh, true, I enjoy an occasional confession-
box seduction and perhaps a tryst with a maid or housekeeper now and then. But it's nothing like the old days;
nothing at all.

"Now, if you're smart, Justine, we can remedy all this.
I get along quite well with Chief Justice de Corville,
you know. If I tell him that you told me, under the seal
of confession, that not you but Madame Dubois is guilty
of the murder of Dubreuil — as, indeed, you did tell me

— he'll undoubtedly free you to my custody. Well, one hand washes the other; once free, you could round up half-a-dozen girls for me and, before long, we'd have our own little Saint-Mary-in-the-Woods! Who knows but that, if you'd like, I could even name you superintendent; you'd never have to serve as Girl of the Watch, your days would be free to spend as you wished . . . ."

"Enough, Father!" screamed Justine. "I'll hear no more! Begone! You're a monster to dare to capitalize upon my circumstances in this manner! If die I must, I'll die — but it will be sinless!"

"Well, have it as you like it," said Father Antonin, opening the cell door. "I have never made it a point to try to force happiness on those who prefer misery." Then, smiling wickedly, he added: "However, don't be too sure that you'll die sinless. Remember your outburst of a few seconds ago? Calling me a monster? Telling me, 'Begone.' Well, in case you forgot, that constitutes the showing of disrespect to a priest, a sin against the First, Second and Fourth Commandments, to say nothing of the Natural Law, Canon Law and Ecclesiastical Tradition. So, don't be too sure that your little soul is so lilywhite after all." Then, closing the door all but a crack, he added: "Goodbye, cunt."

IV

The case was brought quickly to trial. However, Chief Justice de Corville, unlike the many men who surrounded him, was not so quick to dismiss Justine without listening to her story. Indeed, having once heard the dreadful tale, he was so moved that he summoned his mistress, Madame de Lorsange, and suggested that she listen to it also.

Once again Justine related her tale, describing how:

as a child she met the usurer, Hairpin, who falsely accused her of theft, then prospered after she went to
prison; later, she fell in with Dubois, Ironheart and the
band of thieves, escaping from them with the treacherous Saint-Florent, who, in exchange for her saving his
life, raped her and abandoned her in the woods; next,
she became the victim of the aristocratic sodomite,
Count de Bressac, who, because she refused to cooperate
in his plan to murder his aunt, attacked her with dogs
until she all but died; then, in seeking treatment for the
wounds thus incurred, she fell into the clutches of the
mad surgeon, Rodin, who, because she sought to prevent
his butchery of his daughter, affixed to her flesh the
brand of a murderer; next, seeking to gain sanctuary in a
monastery, she became the victim of the four monstrous
Benedictines, who after defiling her chastity in every
manner imaginable, forced her to employ her body as
the altar for an heinous black mass; then, in escaping
from this ghastly theater of perfidy, she was kidnapped
by the minions of the loathsome Count de Gernande,
who sought to drain her blood drop by drop; next, offering alms to a beggar-woman, she was robbed of her last
cent; then, seeking to give aid to a man found lying at
roadside (the detestable Roland), she was taken prisoner,
was made to turn a wheel like an animal and, finally, was
all but hanged because it pleased him to torture her;
next, she was arrested as a counterfeiter and was brought
to the very shadow of the guillotine before the avara-
cious cunning of Madame Dubois led to her being set
free; then, she was falsely accused of a murder which
she had refused to commit, and, finally, the craven
Father Antonin, to whom she made her last confession,
so provoked her that she shouted at him in anger, thereby sinning and paving the way for an eternity in hell if
she were to die before the moral slate could be wiped

clean — and all this, the entirety of it, because she sought to follow the path of Virtue after the tragic death of her parents in Paris nearly fifteen years ago, leaving her and her older sister orphans . . .

"Older sister? Orphans?" cried Madame de Lorsange, scarcely believing her ears. "And it happened nearly fifteen years ago? In Paris? And you say that your name is Justine?"

"Indeed, madame," she replied. "I swear it."

"Your older sister," said Madame de Lorsange, tears damming up her eyes. "Her name would not by any chance have been . . . Juliette, would it?"

"I dare say you're correct, madame," answered Justine, puzzled. "Could it be that you're acquainted with her?"

"Acquainted, my sweet?" sobbed Madame de Lorsange, throwing her arms around the girl. "Acquainted, you say?! Oh, my darling, darling, darling Justine. I *am* she, sweet child; I am your sister Juliette!!!"

"Oh, darling Juliette," cried the poor prisoner. "I shall die much happier having been permitted to embrace you again . . ."

And the two, kissing the tears from each others eyes, collapsed in each others' embrace.

Now, Chief Justice de Corville, beholding this, was moved beyond words. Hastily adjudicating Justine "not guilty," he adjourned court and rushed his mistress and her sister to his chateau.

"Well, dear Justine," he said, kissing her tenderly, "your agonies now have ended; henceforth, in this household, whatever you desire you shall possess, and your sister and I shall make every effort to insure that you now realize the happiness which for so long you have deserved."

V

In the days which followed, Chief Justice de Corville and Madame de Lorsange spared no pain to assist Justine in raising herself from the depths to which she had plummeted to the very summit of hope and happiness. They took great pleasure in feeding her the finest foods, and in putting her to sleep in the softest of beds. A surgeon was engaged to remove the many scars which she had incurred over the years, and soon her skin regained the clear, alabaster beauty which she had possessed before being subjected to her many ordeals.

Now Justine began to know joy at last. Laughter, for so many years absent from her tender lips, made a new appearance. The wrinkles of worry were erased from her brow. She again took on a vitality and an animation appropriate to her years. Perhaps most important of all, Chief Justice de Corville publicized throughout France the ill treatment which the poor child had received at the hands of so many adversaries; in reply, letters came from the many courts in which she was listed as a convict — and, indeed, from the King, himself — exonerating her of all charges. Further, by official decree, she was awarded damages of one-thousand crowns per year, enough to insure that she never would know want for the rest of her life.

Oh, how wonderful it all seemed — but, such was the Will of Heaven that this felicity was not to endure. Indeed, as the happy child offered prayers of thanksgiving for the good fortune which had finally befallen her, the Hand of Fate was being raised to smite her the final blow.

It came toward the end of summer, when Justine and Madame de Lorsange paid a week-end visit at the country estate of Chief Justice de Corville. A dreadful rainstorm had forced them inside the house; but the oppressive heat from that afternoon's sun had necessitated the leaving open of all windows. As night fell and jagged bolts of lightning flashed across the sky, Madame de Lorsange grew frightened. Justine, seeking to comfort her, went about the business of closing all the shutters.

Now the storm intensified. Great gusts of wind whistled through the open windows, breaking panes, slamming shutters. Justine, seeking to arrest the damage, struggled to pull closed the largest of the shutters. Suddenly, an immense thunderbolt blazed across the heavens. Zig-zagging down through the clouds, its jagged tip headed straight for the window where Justine was standing and —

Transfixed her!!!

Madame de Lorsange, dumbstruck, fell to the floor. Chief Justice de Corville summoned a doctor. But no examination was necessary to reveal the horrible truth about Justine. The lightning bolt had entered her right breast, located her heart, consumed her chest and face, then burst out through her stomach. The poor child hadn't stood a chance; death was instantaneous.

"Take the body away," said Chief Justice de Corville sadly to the physician.

But Madame de Lorsange, regaining consciousness, said: "No. Leave her here where I can see her, my love, for I must draw upon the vision of her for strength in the resolutions I have just made.

"My dear Corville, the tragic sufferings which this poor child has undergone — but which were completely unable to make her swerve from the path of Righteousness — have convinced me of the folly of my own sinful ways. Blinded by the lures of the soft life, insensitized by a glutting of all the senses, I went the way of a voluptuary; imagine the horrors which must be awaiting me in hell if the Almighty would see fit to inflict on an innocent soul such earthly suffering as Justine had experienced. No, Corville, I must repent now, while there is still time; love you though I do, I can no longer remain your mistress; my conscience tells me I must enter a convent at once, and there pray for the rest of my days: we will meet as lovers again, my sweet, but in a better world — which, inspired by Justine's noble example, we both can surely attain."

So saying, she signed a paper turning over all her riches to the Church; then, hastening to Paris, she joined the Carmelite order — most severe of all — and, before many years passed, became the example of her convent, emulated as much for her probity as for her wisdom and piety. Corville, likewise moved, surrendered his post as Chief Justice and became a priest.

Thus, dear reader, ends the story of Justine, a tale of Good Conduct Well Chastised.

If you have been moved to tears upon learning of the misfortunes of Virtue; if your heart has been pierced with sorrow because of the woes which befell our lovely heroine; then, forgiving the bold strokes with which we have found it necessary to paint cruelty and suffering, you may gain from the story the same inspiration as Madame de Lorsange: true happiness can be found nowhere but in Virtue; Good will be rewarded, Evil punished; and it is never too late to repent.

   —DONATIEN ALPHONSE FRANÇOIS DE SADE
     PARIS, 1797

THE END

PHILOSOPHY
IN THE
BEDROOM

DRAMATIS PERSONAE
  MADAME DE SAINT-ANGE, a voluptuary;
  THE HORSEMAN OF MIRVEL, her brother, a
    libertine;
  DOLMANCE, his friend, a libertine and a sodo-
    mite;
  EUGENIE DE MISTIVAL, a virgin seeking to
    change her status;
  AUGUSTIN, a gardener of extraordinary sexual en-
    dowments;
  MADAME DE MISTIVAL, Eugénie's mother.
  LAPIERRE, Dolmancé's syphilitic valet.

DEDICATION

To Libertines
of all ages, and of every sex, and of every inclination; it is you to whom I dedicate this work. Your passions, which the cold and dreary moralists tell you to fear, are nothing more than the means by which Nature seeks to exhort you to do Her work; surrender to these passions, therefore, and let the principles enumerated herein nourish you.

Lewd women: emulate the voluptuous Saint-Ange; submit yourself to pleasure's divine laws and ignore all which contradict them.

Young virgins: emulate the fiery Eugénie; throw off the restraints of your ridiculous religion, spurn the precepts of your idiotic parents; yield, instead, to the laws of Nature which logic describes, and to the arms of those who would be your lovers.

Lascivious men: follow the crafty Dolmancé; acknowledge no government save that of your desires, no limits save those of your imagination; and learn from him that it is only in exploring and expanding the sphere of your tastes and whims that you will find true pleasure.

To all: let us realize that we have been cast into this woeful life without our consent and have been assailed from the dawn of consciousness with the sophistries of those who would gain from our confusion; if we would snatch a brief moment of pleasure — if we would plant an occasional rose along life's rocky path — we must sacrifice everything to the demands of our senses; this is the lesson of the Bedroom Philosophers . . . .

I. SAINT-ANGE and THE HORSEMAN

Scene: Saint-Ange's bedroom. She lies on bed, clad only in a nightgown. There is a rap on the door. Enter, the Horseman.

SAINT-ANGE: A good afternoon to you, Horseman. Where, pray tell, is your friend, Dolmancé?

HORSEMAN: He'll be here presently, my love. I trust you can keep rein on your passions for an hour or two. If not, spread your sweet thighs and permit me to serve you.

SAINT-ANGE: You're too kind, my dear brother — and so self-effacing. But I think I can wait. I would not want to dull my appetite for a threesome by indulging it now with only you. Besides, Dolmancé might feel slighted.

HORSEMAN: Whatever you say, my sister. I'm in no hurry. Besides, it's been so long since we've seen each other privately. I've missed those chats we used to have.

SAINT-ANGE: And I, brother; and I. It seems that the older we get, the farther apart we drift. No doubt Passion is to blame. If only I could control mine! At twenty-six one is supposed to be so staid and restrained, but look at me: what woman can match my licentiousness? Perhaps if I were a Lesbian I'd be less of a bawd; but, as luck would have it, I like everyone and everything; indeed, I would like nothing more than to combine every species under the sun and enjoy them all in concert.

HORSEMAN: Yes, my sister, the universality of your tastes has long been known to me.

SAINT-ANGE: But you'll admit that this afternoon's festivities will be a new thrill, even for me. After all, how often does one encounter a man who not only worships his own gender but also never yields to ours save through the altar at which he conducts his rituals with men?

HORSEMAN: Delightful consistency of metaphor there, my love. Worship; altar; ritual. You do the language proud.

SAINT-ANGIE: Oh, come, Horseman; you're too blasé. Don't you see how excited I am? I want to be Ganymede to this new Jupiter. I want to learn his tastes, share his revels, submit myself to every debauchery he can conceive! Is this not bizarre?

HORSEMAN: Wholly, my love. Wholly. No pun intended.

SAINT-ANGE: All right, enough of your linguistics. Tell me about Dolmancé. What is he like?

HORSEMAN: Well, my dear sister, he's ten years your senior; tall, extremely handsome; his teeth are the whitest I've ever seen; his features are ruggedly masculine, but occasionally there's a trace of feminity in his manner — owing, no doubt, to the fact that he assumes the female sexual role so often.

SAINT-ANGE: And is he a philosopher?

HORSEMAN: Aren't we all?

SAINT-ANGE: I mean, does he believe in God?

HORSEMAN: I should say not. He's really the most
monstrous atheist; completely and thoroughly corrupted;
an incredible scoundrel, a total blackguard ....

SAINT-ANGE: Oh, brother, if only you know how atheism excites me! I think I will become infatuated with him
the moment we meet. Tell me, now: what are his sexual
idiosyncracies?

HORSEMAN: You know them well, I'm sure. He's a
sodomite who likes the active role as well as the passive.
He personally prefers men, but occasionally employs
women if they surrender to his wishes — the wishes being, as you put it, worship at the . . . er, anal altar.

SAINT-ANGE: The ass; yes! Oh brother, how this talk
excites me! If you only knew how I yearn to present myself to him! Tell me; have you fucked him? I dare say, I
would think such a man could not fail to be enchanted
by your lovely face.

HORSEMAN: And by my vigor dear sister. He was enchanted by that also. I'm quite vigorous, you know; more
so than the average lad of twenty.

SAINT-ANGE: Of course I know. Haven't you given me
ample demonstration? Many's the time these lonely
loins have cried out at night with the memory of that
enormous prick of yours pulsating between them.

HORSEMAN: You're mixing metaphors now. Cried out
— with the *memory* . . .

SAINT-ANGE: It's no matter. Answer my question about
Dolmancé. Have you or have you not fucked him?

HORSEMAN: We've . . . experimented together, yes. I
wouldn't hide it from you. You're much too wise a
woman to condemn such indulgences.

SAINT-ANGE: But you're not a homosexual, are you?

HORSEMAN: I should think I've given you sufficient
proofs to the contrary. No, sister, I am not. I favor
women. But, at the same time, I'm not one of those

impetuous lads who feels that a male's advances are to be answered with a beating. Is a nance master of his tastes? Can he change the appetites Nature has given him? No. I feel sorry for those whose preferences are strange, but I never insult them. And, if an attractive man urges me on, I submit to his advances. Why not?

SAINT-ANGE: And how far do you go?

HORSEMAN: All the way, of course. I have none of that absurd arrogance which leads some men to believe that one part of the body is cleaner than another. I fuck, I suck — the works!

SAINT-ANGE: Do you take money?

HORSEMAN: When it's offered. Why not? I'm complimented that my sexuality is of value to someone. Only a fool would feel otherwise. The trouble with this world is that too many people believe that they own the patent on propriety; that their way is the only way to do things. Then they become Don Quixotes, lashing out with their spears at the windmills of abnormality, brutalizing all those who differ from them — and why? For fear, no doubt; for fear that their own very "normal" way of doing things might not be quite as much fun as the next fellow's perversion!

SAINT-ANGE: Come, sweet brother, kiss me. Hearing you talk inflames me so.

HORSEMAN: A pleasure, my love.

SAINT-ANGE: Now tell me while we lie here: How did you and Dolmancé meet? What were some of the things you did together? How did you enjoy them?

HORSEMAN: We met at a supper at the home of the Marquis de V - - - - . During cocktails one of Dolmancé's friends, knowing from experience the superb prick with which I have been provided and knowing Dolmancé's appreciation of such organs, took it upon himself to introduce us. After the meal I was asked to display the marvelous member. When I did so, Dolmancé, enchanted, fell to kissing it with such vigor that in a matter of moments it had swollen to an enormous size. Even the Marquis could not restrain himself from fondling it.

SAINT-ANGE: Then did you undress completely?

HORSEMAN: Your naveté amuses me, sister, Don't you know that a woman, barely clothed, is more provocative than one who denudes herself at the first opportunity? No, I stayed dressed, except for my protruding prick, which I place before Dolmancé, asking him if he were not afraid that it might, because of its size, prove extremely painful. "A ram could not hurt me!" he replied arrogantly, and added with a sneer that I was far from being his most formidable partner. Somewhat slighted by this demeaning of my stature, I accepted his proffered buttocks and plunged in wildly, hoping to split him apart; but, much to my surprise, the entry was deceptively smooth and easy; my prick soon disappeared completely; now Dolmancé shivered and wriggled in ecstasy at feeling me anchored so firmly inside his bowels, and I, finding his happiness contagious, joyfully flooded him with my seed.

SAINT-ANGE: Ah, brother, if only you knew how you excite me. Let me clutch the darling prick as you continue your tale.

HORSEMAN: Glad to oblige, sweet sister.

SAINT-ANGE: (*Gripping him.*) I love you.

HORSEMAN: And I you. Now, as I was saying, after I had availed myself of Dolmancé's services as a receptacle, he asked for reciprocal privileges. I, for my part, was more than happy to oblige. When I told him so, Dolmancé proudly proffered a prick which was tough and very long and at least six inches in circumference. The Marquis, meanwhile, had by this time taken off his pants and turned his back to me, begging that I entertain him as I had Dolmancé. Thus the three of us buggered each other *en brochette,* I occupying the most fortunate middle position, and before long I came to know the delicious joy of reaching a climax inside one man while, at the same time, another breaks loose inside me.

SAINT-ANGE: Ah, ecstasy! Lasciviousness! Lust! Carnality! Sex! *SEX! SEX!*

HORSEMAN: Yes, that it was, my darling sister — but it pales in comparison with the pleasure of finding myself between your womanly thighs. The joy which I experienced with Dolmancé — and which I shall undoubtedly repeat — is but an hors d'oeuvre; it only tantalizes me for the full repast available in your cunt.

SAINT-ANGE: You're much too kind and flattering, my Horseman. But you shall be rewarded for your charming metaphors; I intend to bring a young girl here today.

HORSEMAN: What, my love?! Is this not unwise, considering the demands which Dolmancé makes upon womanhood?

SAINT-ANGE: His demands will contribute to her education. She is a young thing I met at the convent last year, and with whom I was most delighted. We could do nothing there, under the jealous eyes of the sisters, but we promised to meet again, outside. In preparation for this meeting I met and seduced her father, an agreeable libertine, and thereby arranged for her a two-day vacation from her family. Now I will teach her the art of love.

HORSEMAN: But will two days be long enough to educate her in an art which has taken you all these years to perfect?

SAINT-ANGE: These two days, my clever brother, will be far from ordinary. She will be taught not only by lectures, but by actual demonstrations, lesson by lesson. By this method I will inspire her with the joys of the art, and will encourage in her the most shameless and unbridled explorations. And, in exchange for the cooperation of you and Dolmancé, I shall see that her virginity is left for you to plunder, while that lovely asshole which Dolmancé so avidly cherishes shall be enjoyed first by him . . . well, brother, you have said nothing. Doesn't the thought of this plan excite you? Isn't it inspiring?

HORSEMAN: Indeed it is. I am silent only because I am amazed, my dear, at the effort which you are putting into the education of this young girl. How noble of you! For my part, I shall delight in playing the role you have assigned me.

SAINT-ANGE: And can I be certain of Dolmancé's assistance also?

HORSEMAN: I promise it. And I assure you that you could not find a more able teacher. It will be impossible for your pupil to resist his techniques of seduction; the plan is bound to be a great success—assuming, of course, that the girl, herself, cooperates.

SAINT-ANGE: I know, from what I have seen of her, that she will hold back nothing . . .

HORSEMAN: And you're not afraid that she'll tell her parents afterwards?

SAINT-ANGE: There's nothing to worry about. The father is so enchanted with me that he would come to my defense. I have him wrapped around my finger.

HORSEMAN: Ah, feminity! Even after so many years of watching you operate, dear sister, I still am amazed by your ingenious plans! I never would have had such foresight. But, then, I forget that you are such a master of your craft—

SAINT-ANGE: I have to be. To indulge safely in such libertine pleasures as mine, precautions are necessary. If I weren't careful, the whole plan could collapse because of a trifle. And, in today's case, I want there to be no possibility of error.

HORSEMAN: This young girl apparently has struck your fancy. Tell me something about her.

SAINT-ANGE: Well, she's the daughter of a very prominent businessman, as licentious as he is wealthy. Her mother is a pious woman of about thirty-two. Eugénie, herself, is fifteen, and the most charming young girl either you or I have ever laid eyes on.

HORSEMAN: Please, my dear, more details: the color of her hair and eyes; what is her skin like; her breasts . . .

SAINT-ANGE: Well, her hair is deep brown and falls below her thighs; her skin is clear and white; her jet black eyes give off a warmth which will drive you mad. She has a mature body for her age; everything about it is soft and delicious; her breasts are still small, but as responsive to my caresses as I am to yours. In all, she is a magnificent child; the great gods of the Greeks could have found no beauty to surpass hers . . . But, wait! I hear her coming! You'd better leave quickly by the garden; we'll be waiting when you return with Domancé.

HORSEMAN: From what you've told me, I wouldn't miss this meeting for anything. Give me a kiss to hold me until then.

(She kisses him and touches her hand lovingly to his groin; he exits quickly. Curtain.)

II. SAINT-ANGE and EUGENIE

Scene: Saint-Ange's living room. She sits on couch, inspecting her hairdo in a hand-held mirror. Butler offstage announces: "Miss Eugénie de Mistival!" Enter, Eugénie—
SAINT-ANGE: Welcome, my little one! I'm sure you can understand how anxiously I've been awaiting our meeting.

EUGENIE: I've had the same feelings, my dearest. I thought I would never arrive. And, to make matters worse, my mother at the last minute objected to my going out alone — but one glance from my dear father was enough to keep her quiet.

SAINT-ANGE: Ah, yes; fine man, your father. *(Lovingly touches her fingers to Eugénie's breast.)* But the time is so short, my love; we easily could spend the whole period just talking. Let's not be so wasteful. Do you remember all the things I said I would teach you? Do you think two days will be enough?

EUGENIE: I've promised myself that I'm going to stay until I've learned everything there is, even if that means breaking my vow to my parents.

SAINT-ANGE: Well then, let me show you to my bedroom, where we'll have more privacy. Come, put your arm around my waist, and let's begin!

(They exit.)

III. SAINT-ANGE, EUGENIE and DOLMANCE

Scene: Saint-Ange's bedroom. The curtains are drawn. Dolmancé, lying fully dressed on the bed, grins wickedly. Enter, Saint-Ange and Eugénie.

EUGENIE: *(Astonished to find a man in the room.)* Good Heavens! My friend, we've been betrayed!

SAINT-ANGE *(No less astonished.):* How strange, sir, to find you here at this hour. Didn't we arrange the meeting for four o'clock?

DOLMANCE: My darling, I am completely to blame and I accept full responsibility for my error; but your splendid brother, the Horseman, spoke so highly of you that I couldn't wait until four to see you.

SAINT-ANGE: I'm flattered by your impatience, of course; but Eugénie and I had hoped to spend some time alone before you arrived.

DOLMANCE: My beloved, it was precisely for the purpose of avoiding that situation that I took the liberty of installing myself here. After all, it is a cardinal principle of education that theoretical aspects of a subject are best comprehended when accompanied by a practical demonstration. *(He places his hand between her thighs.)* Surely you wouldn't want your lessons to fail for want of a party with whom to demonstrate . . . .

EUGENIE: I must say, Saint-Ange, I'm most disappointed in you. I was not told that an outsider would participate in our exercises. Consider the danger involved. What if my parents were to find out?

SAINT-ANGE: My dear Dolmancé, please have the kindness to excuse this lovely child's discourteous bleatings. She obtained leave of her family by deceitful means, so it's understandable that she is worried. *(Embraces Eugénie.)* But without cause, absolutely without cause, my darling girl! Dolmancé is the very soul of discretion. He is the most genteel, considerate and thoroughly trustworthy man alive.

EUGENIE: But I don't like him. *(She blushes.)* I came to be alone with you. I fear the presence of others.

DOLMANCE: Come, my chit; try to relax. Surely your purpose in coming here was not to uphold your modesty —a "virtue" the world could do better without. It pains me to see a young body like yours untilled by the plow of pleasure.

EUGENIE: But modesty. . . .

DOLMANCE: My child, modesty is a remnant of the Middle Ages; it is a trait which long ago should have been abandoned by society. We have too little time on this earth to deny ourselves; the only true pleasures. Nature has made us passionate beings for a purpose. Let me demonstrate. *(He seizes Eugénie by the waist and begins to kiss her.)*

EUGENIE: *(Struggling in his embrace.)* Leave me alone, you horrible man! Stop kissing me or I shall be forced to leave!

SAINT-ANGE: Forgive her, Dolmancé, — and, Eugénie,

listen to me: it is my fault that you are reacting this way; I haven't yet shown you the proper way to treat a gentleman. Now, watch. *(She kisses Dolmancé indecently on the mouth.)* Imitate what I am doing.

EUGÉNIE *(Reluctantly)*: It really doesn't seem right. *(She places herself in Dolmancé's arms; he kisses her passionately, 'tongue in mouth.)* Mmmmmmmmmmmm! *(They separate.)* Good HEAVENS! ! ! I can't believe it! How WON-der-ful! ! !

DOLMANCÉ: What a delicious creature!

SAINT-ANGE: *(Kissing her in the same manner.)* Did you think, little one, that I would let Dolmancé enjoy you without my having a turn as well? *(At this point, all three take turns tonguing each other for several minutes.)*

DOLMANCÉ: My dears, it has become extraordinarily hot in here; perhaps if we were to remove some of our outer clothing we could continue in a more relaxed fashion.

SAINT-ANGE: You are quite right, sir. Eugénie and I can wear some of my negligees. They are filmy enough to conceal only what must be hidden from your eyes.

EUGÉNIE: You two are leading me to do the rashest things!

SAINT-ANGE: Yes. *(Helping her to undress.)* It's delightful, isn't it?

EUGÉNIE: Most unbecoming for a young lady of my age ... But your kisses, madame, how they tickle me!

SAINT-ANGE: I'm tickled, too. Your breasts—so young and white—they are like flowers struggling toward ripeness.

DOLMANCÉ: *(Looking at her breasts, but not touching*

them.) Yes, quite nice; and they give promise of even greater charms elsewhere—charms more exciting to my tastes. . .

SAINT-ANGE: More exciting?

DOLMANCE: Oh, yes, my love, infinitely more exciting! *(And, with this, he spins Eugénie around in order to inspect her buttocks.)* Ahhhhhhh! ! ! *(Burrowing, facefirst, into the lovely cleavage.)*

EUGENIE: Please don't do that, sir. I am far too young for these perverse delights. If you have any respect for me, refrain from tampering with this fruit which as of yet is unripened.

SAINT-ANGE: Yes, Dolmancé; I beg you to hold your desire for later. The girl requires more elemental instruction first.

DOLMANCE: All right, madame, but I then will need your own willing cooperation. As I've observed, demonstration is the key tool of the instructor.

SAINT-ANGE: You know, my dear, how more than willing I am to cooperate. *(She undresses.)* Now that I am naked, can you not see how my heart is pulsing?

EUGENIE: Oh, what a beautiful body, my darling Saint-Ange. It's more perfect than the Ancients ever dreamed. I want to cover you with kisses; my eyes do not see enough! *(She falls lustily upon her.)*

DOLMANCE: My dear Eugénie, I must ask you to display less passion and more attention. I've a lesson to teach.

EUGENIE: Teach then, I'm listening . . . But, Dolmancé—don't you think that Saint-Ange is lovely? So plump and so fresh! Are your eyes not drawn to her beauty?

DOLMANCE: My dear young thing, if you are not more docile and attentive I shall have to deal with you severely.

EUGENIE: *(Laughs.)* Ha! You frighten me with your

threats! What do you plan to do?

DOLMANCE: I shall punish you like this *(Kissing Eugénie on the mouth.)* and may even hold your lovely ass responsible for mistakes made in your head! *(He slaps her buttocks through her thin dressing gown.)*

SAINT-ANGE: That's enough boisterousness, Dolmancé. Let's being our lessons, or poor Eugénie will never learn the subject.

DOLMANCE: Very well; I'll begin forthwith. *(As he discusses them, he touches each of the parts of Saint-Ange's body.)* These fleshy mounds I am holding here are no doubt already familiar to you, Eugénie. They are known in different circles as bosoms, breasts, boobs, knockers, globes, jugs or—my favorite term—tits. They may be pleasurable to man in a number of ways: he may merely caress and handle them; he may kiss them, bite them and suck upon them; or he may, as many men prefer, place his member in the soft niche which divides them. The woman, in this latter case, by squeezing them together, may, with a little management, excite the member to such a degree that it spills forth that sweet liquor which is the balm of our existence.

EUGENIE: You speak, sir, of a . . . member?"

DOLMANCE: Ah, yes the member—but, instead of merely talking about it, would it not be easier for me to demonstrate its peculiar capabilities?

SAINT-ANGE: If you wish to do so, Dolmancé, I certainly shall not object.

DOLMANCE: Splendid. May I then be so bold as to enlist your participation in the venture? While I lie on the bed, you take hold of the subject in question and explain its virtues to dear Eugénie.

SAINT-ANGE: *(Taking the member.)* Eugénie, my darling, behold the staff of life; the splendid crescent; the horn with which men butt. It is called a member, a

cock or a prick. And it's the main source of the pleasures
of love. It has the admirable facility of being able to
enter any part of a woman's body. Those who are content with ordinary pleasures often nestle it here. *(She
touches Eugénie at the Altar of Venus.)* However, portals more mysterious and more delightful to the senses
are found in this area. *(She parts Eugenie's buttocks
and indicates the Altar of Sodom.)* This spot offers
pleasures greater than I can describe. We shall discuss
some of these in greater detail presently... Now, then,
to continue: a man also may choose the mouth, the
breasts, the armpits, the elbow and knee pits, or any
other orifice or cleavage to hold and caress the member.
Whatever bodily parts cooperate, after a few moments
of agitation, a milky liquid, hot and pungent, pours
forth, releasing in the man waves of ecstatic pleasure
and plunging him into an intense delirium of happiness.

EUGENIE: How exciting! I would love to watch this
marvelous phenomenon! Could you demonstrate it for
me, so that I will recognize it in the future?

SAINT-ANGE: All I need to do is vibrate my hand. You
see how the member squirms and pulls against the
pressure? These movements are commonly known as
masturbating, but we shall teach you the word frigging,
which enjoys wider usage among libertines.

EUGENIE: How thrilling! And, now that you have
shown me how it's done, Saint-Ange, will you permit
me to frig this handsome member? *(Clutches it.)* After
all, this whole demonstration is for my benefit...

DOLMANCE: No, don't interfere, my pet; these games
have excited me too much; you can see how militant
the little soldier has become; you can observe his proud
position of attention. This is a sign that the precious
liquid will soon be released.

SAINT-ANGE: Then we'd better stop now, Dolmancé,

lest your passion be expelled along with your semen and the spiritedness of your lectures be diminished. *(Reaches for his hand.)* Here, we will divert our attention to the next important part of a man's body.

EUGENIE: *(Ignoring her.)* And these objects which I am now touching, Dolmancé? What is their purpose? What are they called?

DOLMANCE: *(Now excited beyond control, he brushes Saint-Ange aside.)* They are technically known as a man's testicles, Eugénie. People with literally pretensions call them genitalia or gonads. Libertines simply call them balls. They generate the semen which has just been described and which, upon entering a woman's womb, engenders the human species. But a pretty girl like you should never concern herself with engendering; it doesn't suit your style. So, forget about this aspect of sexuality for the nonce, and let us turn our attention to the quintessential act: fucking. You know what that entails, don't you.

EUGENIE: Yes, I've heard it described. But I've always wondered: isn't it painful for the woman when something as enormous as your member forces its way into an orifice as minuscule as that with which I am endowed?

SAINT-ANGE: It is always painful for the first time, Eugénie; but Nature has created us so that we feel pleasure only by way of pain. Soon, with the help of our friend, we will unite practice with theory, and you will see what I mean.

DOLMANCE: But *soon*, Madame! *Very* soon! Or I will succumb in spite of myself, and this famous member will be reduced to nothing.

EUGENIE: Oh, do let me see what happens when the semen begins to flow! Let me help him lose it; I have waited long enough!

DOLMANCE: Yes, by all means, yes. Give me your ass, child.

SAINT-ANGE: No, Dolmancé, it is not yet time for that. I promised to let you have her, but not until you have merited her through your enlightened discourses. Now sit up and continue the lesson.

DOLMANCE: Very well; for the next phase of instruction, Saint-Ange must frig Eugénie while I watch.

SAINT-ANGE: Ah, splendid! This is much more to my liking. (*Kisses Eugénie on the cheek.*) Place yourself on the couch, my darling one, and prepare yourself for this new pleasure.

EUGENIE: (*Lies down.*) How comfortable I am in this haven! But why, my friends, have you put up all these mirrors?

SAINT-ANGE: There is a great sensual excitement in seeing lewdness multiplied around oneself in an infinite variety of positions. All parts of the body are exposed simultaneously, and perceiving the splendid combination of images adds enormously to one's pleasure.

EUGENIE: An ingenious idea!

SAINT-ANGE: Dolmancé, undress the victim so that she may better observe the effects of the mirrors.

DOLMANCE: A delightful job, my dear. (*He undresses her, and immediately inspects her buttocks.*) Ah — at last I can see this marvelous ass about which I have dreamed for so long. It is indeed more beautiful than I expected! Such a soft fullness of flesh! Such elegance of line! Such pallid coolness of color!

SAINT-ANGE: You betray yourself, Dolmancé. There can be no doubt that you're an ass-man.

DOLMANCE: Can you blame me? Look at the divine altar yourself! (*His eyes dance.*) Eugénie, I want to' cover your ass with kisses. (*He does so.*)

SAINT-ANGE: Stop it, you shameless debauchee. If you'

continue to provoke the girl I will be angry with you.

DOLMANCE: You are revealing only your own jealousy, Saint-Ange; but I think I know how to overcome it. Turn your own ass toward me so that I may give similar attentions to it. *(He raises her negligee and enthusiastically caresses her.)* Ah, how lovely it is, my angel! A shining example of womanhood! How I would love to compare you both, the tender virgin and the ripe matron! Could you arrange yourselves so that my gaze could fall equally on both sets of buttocks?

SAINT-ANGE: With pleasure, my dear. There . . . does this arrangement satisfy you?

DOLMANCE: Perfectly; it is exactly what I hoped for. And now, would you please set your asses in motion, sinking and rising in cadence, as if they were thrilling to the proddings of pleasure? Yes . . . that's it. Beautiful; splendid. A masterpiece of rhythm.

EUGENIE: God, I have never before felt such exquisite pleasures. My dear friend, what is it you are doing to me now?

SAINT-ANGE: You remember, my dove; the word is "frigging" — and, since you have brought up the topic, I shall elaborate further on the mechanisms of this pleasurable organ whereon one is frigged.

EUGENIE: Yes, please do! But let's not abandon practice entirely just for theory's sake . . .

SAINT-ANGE: Change positions, then. Here . . . this fleshy part which I'm now touching; it is called the cunt. I will open it a little so that you can examine it more closely. This tongue-shaped thing is called the clitoris; in it lies all of a woman's power of sensation. It is the mainspring of her pleasure, the source of her ecstasy.

EUGENIE: May I touch yours?

SAINT-ANGE: Please do. Oh, how well you do it, you

little darling. Are you sure you haven't had experience with this before? Stop! I can't take it! .... Dolmancé, do something! Stop her before I drown in the caress of these enchanted fingers!

DOLMANCE: Get hold of yourself, Saint-Ange. Try varying your position a bit. While she's busy with you, frig her in turn. Yes, that's right. Now, in this position, Eugénie's lovely ass just happens to be cupped in my hands. What a splendid coincidence. I think I'll frig it ever so gently with my finger. There . . . how does that feel, Eugénie?

EUGENIE: Such pleasure . . . I cannot describe it!

DOLMANCE: Let yourself go, then, my dear; abandon all your senses to pleasure; submit to this magnificent sensation. Let your feelings now become your god, sacrifice everything to this one form of existence, as you would in the more conventional type of "religion."

EUGENIE: I do not understand your words on god and religion, but I know that I've never in my life experienced anything so delightful. I've lost all sense of what I'm saying and doing. It's like a dream . . . an overpowering dizziness has taken over my body!

DOLMANCE: Look at the little darling! She's coming! What ecstasy! And what a squeeze! Why, she nearly nipped off the end of my finger! How I would love to bugger her right now! *(He leaps upon her.)*

SAINT-ANGE: Hold for one moment, Dolmancé. We must continue with the girl's education first.

DOLMANCE: Killjoy! *(He dismounts.)* Well, then, Eugénie, as you have just observed, after a prolonged period of frigging, the seminal glands secrete a liquid; this action hurls a woman into the most intense rapture. The process is known as discharging, or, more informally, as "coming." It occurs also in a man, but in a more energetic and visible fashion. When your friend, the warden, gives the word, I shall be glad to demonstrate this for you.

EUGENIE: Oh, do it now! Saint-Ange, I cannot wait any longer.

SAINT-ANGE: No, Eugenie; the time will come soon enough. First I want to show you a new method of giving pleasure to a woman. Spread your thighs. Dolmancé, I have faced her ass towards you; let your tongue give it testimony of your esteem while mine pays homage at the Temple of Venus. *(The position is assumed.)* Eugénie, your little mound is delightful! How I love to kiss this soft flesh! Can you describe how it feels to be assaulted by both of us at once?

EUGENIE: Ah, if only I could . . . but the sensation far surpasses the power of words! I couldn't even say which of you gives me the more exquisite pleasure! *(Writhes in ecstasy.)* Ahhhh, enchantment!

DOLMANCE: Saint-Ange, my dear, as my member is within your reach, please do me the favor of frigging it while I kiss this heavenly ass.

SAINT-ANGE: With pleasure, dear Dolmancé.

DOLMANCE: Meanwhile, my friend, don't hesitate to thrust your tongue to the very hilt. The fuller her cunt, the better Eugénie will like it.

EUGENIE: Oh, I can't bear it any more, dear friends! Don't leave me now . . . I'm about to come! Oh, I'm dying! *(She tenses to the full range of her body's elastically and then collapses.)* Ahhhhhhhhh!

SAINT-ANGE: Well, my pet! Are you happy with the pleasures we have given you? Are you well satisfied?

EUGENIE: I am dead; completely exhausted; drained of spirit and energy. And I loved every second of it.

SAINT-ANGE: Well, Eugénie, without further ado, I

shall continue with your lesson. Let me now comment briefly on the generative aspects of fucking. As
Dolmancé has said, you should not be concerned with
this function; however, you should be acquainted with
the facts. The procreation of the human species is
brought about by the simultaneous mingling of the male
sperm, or jism, as it is sometimes called, with the egg
cells released by the female.

EUGENIE: But couldn't the male sperm generate without assistance from the female?

SAINT-ANGE: No, my dear, I'm afraid not.

EUGENIE: What a shame. I hate my mother so much
that I would like to believe that she was in no way necessary to my existence. *(Now overcome by guilt.)* Perhaps
I should be ashamed to feel this way . . .

DOLMANCE: I should say not. I, too, have always hated
my mother. When she died, I couldn't have been more
joyous.

EUGENIE: But isn't this feeling in opposition to the
strongest values of our society?

SAINT-ANGE: Fuck society, as the saying goes. We are
wasting too much time in philosophical ruminations.
Let's get on with the sexual instructions.

DOLMANCE: By all means, my love. Far be it from me
to delay the proceedings. What area of endeavor would
you like to cover now?

EUGENIE: Perhaps, before we continue with *verbal*
instructions, I might pay Saint-Ange back in kind for the
pleasures which she has just give me and Dolmancé
might criticize my performance. Is that agreeable?

SAINT-ANGE: Indeed it is, my love. But let's not ex-
clude Dolmancé from all sensual enjoyment of the enterprise. *(To Dolmancé.)* Tell me, you splendid sodomite:
while this darling girl is frigging me, would you like

to avail yourself of my ass? *(Presents her buttocks to him.)*

DOLMANCE: With greatest pleasure, madame. And now, Eugénie, my little wildcat, place yourself between the legs of our dear friend and apply your tongue in the same manner as she applied hers to you. Then, I'll fondle your ass while at the same time licking Saint-Ange's. There! It's done! See how beautifully we three fit together?

SAINT-ANGE: Good God, I'm dying! Dolmancé, how I love to hold your member while I come. Ah, fuck! By the pulsating penis of Providence! By the dangling dork of Destiny! Fuck me! Suck me! What heavenly fuck! I'm finished! Ruined! It's all over and done with! I've never enjoyed myself so much in my life!

EUGENIE: And I, my dearest friend . . . I'm so happy to have brought you such pleasure!

DOLMANCE: Just think, Eugénie, how much you would have missed if you had not shed your cloak of modesty along with your other accoutrements. Virtue will get you nowhere in this world!

SAINT-ANGE: You're absolutely right, Dolmancé. And, while we're on the subject, let none say that the virtuous woman acts for love of God. Her motives are wholly selfish. She seeks to avoid pregnancy and shame in this life, and damnation in the next. That's all. As for me, I'd rather sacrifice myself to my passions than to egoism. At least there's an element of honesty that way. Besides, the passions are the true organs of Nature. Whoever fails to listen to their voice acts out of either stupidity or prejudice. So much for Virtue. I say: fuck Virtue. *(Both women now step back into their negligees and recline upon the bed; Dolmancé seats himself in a chair nearby.)*

EUGENIE: But, Saint-Ange, Virtue is not only sexual. It may be expressed in many ways. What do you think of piety for example?

DOLMANCE: Bah! Piety presupposes a religious belief, and who today believes in religion? Let us define our terms: religion is a pact between man and his creator whereby the former, through worship, expresses his gratitude for his existence, bestowed upon him by the latter.

EUGENIE: I could not define it better.

DOLMANCE: But, man is nothing but the product of Nature; thus this gratitude is misdirected. Who needs a god?

EUGENIE: But don't the mysteries of Nature argue that there is a supreme author of all being?

DOLMANCE: No, my child. A thousand times, no. Though some of Nature's ways may be mysterious to us, this is merely because our science has not advanced sufficiently to provide explanations. To postulate the existence of a god, who himself cannot be known, in explanation of other unknowns, is the ultimate folly of human reason. And even if it could be shown that a god is the author of all being, he would be entirely useless now, for, once having set the machinery going, and having nothing to do with its maintenance, he would be out of a job.

EUGENIE: You mean to say, then, that belief in God is an illusion?

DOLMANCE: Precisely. And one of the most lamentable.

SAINT-ANGE: This belief is the product of terror in some people, of frailty in others; but either way it's wholly unfounded. Look at the matter in this light: in order to justify his reputation, your god must be all good and all just; however, both good and evil forces serve nature, the good often being only a compensation for evil. So how could a good god create evil?

DOLMANCE: Some try to explain this dichotomy by saying that God and Nature are one; but the idea is absurd — as absurd as it would be to say that the pocket watch is its own watchmaker. If it is, then one cannot exist without the other; so how shall we identify the creative agent?

SAINT-ANGE: Very true. If the principle of movement is inherent in Nature; if Nature is able, by reason of her energy, to conceive, create manufacture and maintain the multitudinous forces now in existence — a feat which certainly deserves all our admiration — then we don't need a foreign agent. The active, creative faculty exists in Nature herself; God is superfluous.

DOLMANCE: And, if not superfluous, He's surely a bumbling fool. He, created the world one day, only to threaten its destruction on the next. Having created man, He made the mistake of giving him the power to offend his own Creator, then had to sacrifice His own son to set matters straight. But still, order was not restored, and thus — so the priests tell us — this same son must be sacrificed day after day after day in the form of bread and wine . . . Now take the devil on the other hand; he is consistent, he retains full possession of his powers and he incessantly succeeds in seducing to his ways the "flock" sought after by his divine adversary; man is left defenseless in his clutches. Now, you tell me: which of the two — God or devil — seems more godlike to you?

EUGENIE: But what of Christ's resurrection? Doesn't that mean anything to you?

DOLMANCE: Well, let's talk awhile about Christ — the "only begotten son," as I believe he called. Listening to the prophets, we would have expected this sublime creature to have appeared clothed in celestial rays, bathed in dazzling light, surrounded by choirs of angels. But no . . . it is upon the breast of a common whore, in a pigsty, that he first reveals himself. What could be more ignoble, more debasing! And let us look at his modus operandi. He claims that he is God himself, who has assumed the flesh in order to save us. He claims, further, that he will prove his divine origin by miraculous acts, surpassing the powers of Nature. But what does he actually do? At a ribald wedding feast, he transforms, so his friends say, water into wine; then one of his cronies plays dead and the cheat restores him to life; then he goes off to a mountain and there, in front of two or three of his partners, multiplies a few fishes and loaves of bread until there is enough food to feed thousands — although only his partners bother to make a written record of it, not any of those who supposedly were fed. He promises salvation to all who listen to him, and damnation to those who don't — but he is too ignorant to write anything; talks little, because he is stupid; and does even less, for he lacks the strength. And finally, as a fitting climax to his career, he allows himself to be fixed to a cross; he endures indescribable tortures, and his daddy, Mr. God, doesn't help him in the least; finally he expires, treated like the lowest of the low among the outlaws of whom he was so fitting a leader . . . Do you believe in the resurrection? Do you believe that it was then that his grandeur was finally revealed? Don't allow yourself to be fooled. His henchmen made off with the body, then their woman and children cried that a miracle had occurred. But the legitimate historians of the day did not consider the event worthy of being recorded. Now, do you suppose

that, if he really had proved his divinity, these wise —
and admittedly selfish — men would have the temerity to
ignore him?

EUGENIE: Then, how was the legend perpetuated?

DOLMANCE: My theory is this: several years later, the
people of Jerusalem, wearied by years of Roman despotism, felt the need of revolution. The apostles, seeing
that there was political leverage to be gained, took
advantage of the opportunity and constructed a wealth
of legends and lies about their dear departed leader.
The people then were duped into believing that a
priest, by uttering a few magical words, had the power
to bring God down to earth in a morsel of bread. This
cult of idiocy could have been destroyed in the very
beginning if the leaders of the age had reacted to it
with the indifference it deserved. Instead, they persecuted it, and it thrived as a coaltion of malcontents.
Now, of course, the duped minority has become a
duped majority — but the absurdities to which they
subscribe remain just as absurd. So don't let popular
notions sway your ideas, Eugénie; adopt a fixed, independent attitude and stick to it.

EUGENIE: What you have said, Dolmancé, has changed
my attitudes completely. From now on I shall scorn this
god and his religion. Both are nothing to me now but
objects of disgust.

SAINT-ANGE: You have spoken brave words, Eugénie.
But you must be even more determined. Swear to me
now that you will never think of this god again, never
invoke him in moments of distress, and — so long as
you live and breathe — never return to him.

EUGENIE: *(Flinging herself upon Saint-Ange's breast.)*
I swear to it, but only in your arms, my dear friend! I
know that you are acting only for my own good.

SAINT-ANGE: Hallelujah! Another soul saved from the perfidy of religion!

EUGENIE: (*Turning to Dolmancé.*) But, good friend, since it was the discussion of virtues which led you to the examination of religions, let us now return to the first question: could there not be some virtues prescribed by this religion which might lead us towards happiness, even if we deny the existence of God?

DOLMANCE: Let us consider the matter. How about chastity? Have you found in this absurd virtue any of the pleasures you recently discovered in vice? Are you henceforth willing to deny yourself all of Nature's operations in exchange for the vain satisfaction of never having succumbed to a "weakness"?

EUGENIE: No, I no longer feel any inclination to be chaste; both of you have shown me the futility of pursuing that virtue. But there are others, Dolmancé: couldn't the altruistic virtue of charity, for example, bring happiness to those sensitive souls who practice it?

DOLMANCE: Charity, Eugénie, is born of pride, not altruism; the giver of charity would be extremely angered if he received no public acclamation. He wants to be praised for his generosity — if not, he would give anonymously. Furthermore, Eugénie, you must realize the consequence of charity: it accustoms the poor to the receiving of gifts, and thus, it encourages the depletion of their energy. When a man knows he will be given handouts, he does not work; then, when the money stops flowing, not knowing how to earn some more, he becomes a beggar or a thief. The best way to rid France of its poor would be to halt the distribution of alms and to shut down all the poorhouses. Then the indigent, born in misfortune, would have to fend for himself; he would have to summon his own inner resources in order to escape from the condition in which he started life; the result would be a nation composed entirely of self-sufficient men. But, today, the poor are pampered and coddled — and with what result? The helpless creatures fuck and add more helpless creatures to our growing population, which new creatures also fuck, adding newer ones still, ad infinitum.

SAINT-ANGE: Dolmancé is absolutely right, Eugénie. There is nothing more dangerous to society than charitable institutions; it is to them, just as to free public schools, that we owe the terrible disorder in which we are living. You must promise never to give alms again; you will only harm yourself thereby and harm society by encouraging the poor to persist in their state of abject dependence.

DOLMANCE: There is, furthermore, a great wisdom, dear Eugénie, in an economy of feeling toward others. Why should we concern ourselves with cares which are not ours? Besides, apathy is fun. Ideally, of course, one would perpetrate only evil; but, since this is not always possible, there remains still the piquant wickedness of never doing good.

EUGENIE: Ah, fuck — I've never been so excited by conversation in all my life. I swear that I'd rather die than be made to perform a charitable act!

DOLMANCE: You have listened well to what I have told you so far, my beloved girl; but there is still more to be said about the nature of virtue. For example, there is no deed which is entirely virtuous, or entirely criminal either; the value of an act is relative to time and geography. Women were carried triumphantly through the streets of pagan Babylon and were honored for having performed in great volume acts of fornication which, in inquisitorial Spain, would have merited the rack. See that

man being led to the scaffold? He has just very foolishly
acquitted himself in Paris of an ancient Japanese virtue:
sodomy. See that Italian prisoner and that Chinese
nobleman? They got where they are by reading the
same book—the Philosophy of Confucius!

EUGENIE: But it seems to me that there must be some
acts which are so dangerous and evil in themselves that
people all over the world consider them criminal. -

SAINT-ANGE: You are wrong, my dear; there are none:
not theft, nor incest, nor murder nor even parricide.

EUGENIE: Do you mean to say that such horrors are
tolerated by some people?

DOLMANCE: Not only tolerated, my love, but praised
as splendid deeds; likewise, in some places, our virtues
of kindness, charity, chastity, et cetera, are regarded with
nothing but contempt.

EUGENIE: But how can anyone maintain that chastity
is an evil? Where is the crime? Who is hurt by it?

SAINT-ANGE: All mankind! Woman's very nature is to
be wanton, like the bitch; she must belong to all who
claim her: so it is a crime against nature to confine
herself to a solitary lover; her instincts cry out against it.

EUGENIE: But what of the role of the woman in marriage? Should she not, by virtue of the marriage pact,
feel some responsibility and devotion toward her husband? Is she not obligated to be faithful to him?

SAINT-ANGE: Any woman, be she unmarried, wife or
widow, in whatever circumstances, lives for no other
purpose than to engage herself in libertine pursuits
from morning until night; it is for this objective that
Nature created her. Think, Eugénie, of a young girl
like yourself, scarcely out of her father's home; she
knows little, and has experienced even less. Suddenly she

is called upon to give herself to the arms of a man she has never seen. She is forced to swear on oath of obedience and fidelity to the first man who comes along. Too inexperienced to make a mature judgment, she nonetheless is bound by her vows — shackled for life if she obeys them, doomed by society if she ignores them. Either way, she can know only despair. This is the absurd dilemma which society has created for woman. Is not the only sane reaction rebellion?

EUGENIE: Well, let us suppose that marriage does impose an unjust burden upon women. Shouldn't a wife still consider the impression her actions will make upon her children? Isn't their pride and respect valuable enough to warrant some restraint?

SAINT-ANGE: Fuck their pride and respect! We are all heading toward death anyway, and in the graveyard virtue and vice are indistinguishable. Do you think that our survivors will care whether we lived a "virtuous" life? By then, the meaning of virtue probably will have changed anyway, so it's not worth worrying about. The poor dolt who passes his life as a stranger to joy dies unrewarded.

EUGENIE: You have convinced me almost entirely to reject all notions of virtue and morality, but I still long to hear more of your arguments. Tell me, Saint-Ange, how have you been able to satisfy all your desires while living at least ostensibly within the restrictions of marriage?

SAINT-ANGE: I was fortunate enough to marry a man who makes minimal demands upon my time and freedom; thus, I have been allowed every opportunity to indulge my impulses. All in all, during my twelve married years, I have had sexual commerce with over ten-thousand different people — and that figure, in the company I keep, is considered unduly modest.

EUGENIE: Marvelous! Simply marvelous! Yet, it's a wonder that you have been able to preserve yourself so long from engendering children! Could you explain to me in detail the different ways a woman may accomplish this? I believe that I would follow your footsteps if only I could be sure of safeguarding myself from pregnancy.

SAINT-ANGE: A girl risks having a child only as often as she allows a man to invade her cunt, for this is the only access to her womb, where pregnancy occurs. Thus, to be absolutely safe, you need only avoid seeking pleasure in this area, and devote yourself to the cultivation of other delights. If, however, as occasionally happens, you take a chance with coitus and pregnancy follows, you can remedy the situation very easily.

EUGENIE: Do you mean by abortion?

SAINT-ANGE: Precisely. And don't entertain moral scruples about destroying the product of your own womb, either; it is an illusion to imagine that this is a crime: we are, after all, masters of what we carry inside of us, and we do no more harm in destroying one kind of matter than another. Rather, regard the child as an unwanted malignancy — like the product of illness — and rid yourself of it by the proper medicines.

EUGENIE: But if the child is approaching the hour of its birth?

SAINT-ANGE: Even if the child were already born, you would still have the right to destroy it. Mothers have always enjoyed inalienable authority over their children; no race has failed to recognize this fact, for it is founded in reason and established in principle. However, let us speak no more of abortion, for the means of avoiding unwanted pregnancies are so pleasurable that it is not worth taking the risk for a slight difference in sensation. Of all possible alternatives, I find that which is offered by way of the ass by far the most satisfying. But I will leave this topic to Dolmancé, for who is better qualified than he to describe a taste in whose defense, were it to require any defense, he would lay down his very life?

DOLMANCE: Well, not quite, Saint-Ange — but I do admit that buggery is my preference, for I have found that of all possible sexual entrances, there is none more gratifying. Fortunately, too, I am not particular about the gender of my lover, so I have been able to worship at the asses of both men and women.

EUGENIE: Would you be so kind as to discourse briefly on the techniques?

DOLMANCE: A pleasure, my love. The position generally held by the woman is to lie with her belly facing the bed, her legs spread apart; the man, after properly moistening the aperture, inserts his member slowly and deliberately until it comes to a resting point; thereupon, all the thorns having been plucked out, only the roses of pleasure remain.

SAINT-ANGE: May I interrupt you momentarily, Dolmancé, to ask a question: at what state of emptiness or fullness should the lover's intestines be in order to bring about the most pleasure to both?

DOLMANCE: I prefer that they be full; that, in fact, my partner be on the verge of relieving himself, so that my member may drive deeply into the feces and find there a tighter resting place.

SAINT-ANGE: It seems to me that your partner would feel great discomfort, if not pain, and that his pleasure would be diminished thereby ...

DOLMANCE: To the contrary! It is impossible for either

partner to feel any pain. Both can only be transported into the most superb ecstasies!

EUGENIE: I perceived a strange gleam in your eyes, Dolmancé . . .

SAINT-ANGE: Talking of his favorite Altar has inspired him to 'pray' . . .

DOLMANCE: Indeed it has. Come, Eugénie, give me your ass.

EUGENIE: But the instructions . . .

DOLMANCE: (Firmly.) I'll be put off no longer. Those bouncing buns of yours have been tormenting me all day. (He lunges, clutching her at the hips with both hands:) Give me that ass, my little bitch! I'm going to cleave you in two!

EUGENIE: (Tries to escape, but, though her legs run, her torso is fixed motionless in his grip.) Oh, help me, Saint-Ange! What should I do?!

SAINT-ANGE: Why succumb, my child. What else?

DOLMANCE: (Burying face in her crotch.) Ah, what splendor. By God's cock and balls! I'm ablaze with passion, my chit; ablaze!

SAINT-ANGE: If you please, Dolmancé, let's put some order into these proceedings. You've got your opportunity to sodomize her; don't be a pig and insist upon performing all sex acts at once.

DOLMANCE: (Releasing Eugénie.) Yes, Saint-Ange, you're right. I mustn't let myself get carried away. Now, Eugénie: to the bed, shall we? And, since you've nothing better to do, Saint-Ange, why don't you join us? I think we can find a place for you in our revels.

EUGENIE: Do I understand you correctly? You plan to employ a third party in sodomy? Are not the very mechanics of the act prohibitive?

DOLMANCE: To the contrary, my lovely child. Come:

I'll show you . . . Now, Saint-Ange, observe the arrangement: I lie here and from behind her insert my prick in Eugénie's ass; this leaves the cunt for you; I trust you'll have no difficulty figuring out what to do with it.

SAINT-ANGE: No difficulty whatsoever, my friend. By lying alongside her, but in the opposite direction . . . like this . . . I can tongue her while she tongues me. *(The position is assumed and the project undertaken.)*

EUGENIE: Ah, Saint-Ange, that's wonderful. But, Dolmancé: that monstrous prick of yours — I fear I can never receive it.

DOLMANCE: Nonsense, my child. Why just yesterday I embuggered a boy of seven, and he was only half your dimensions.

EUGENIE: But the pain . . .

DOLMANCE: The pain, my love, very slowly blends with pleasure, and, before you know it, you're experiencing nothing but pure ecstasy. Now, then: brace yourself!

EUGENIE: *(Gasps.)* Good Heavens, Dolmancé.

DOLMANCE: Grit your teeth, chit; it'll be but a moment . . .

EUGENIE: *(Groans.)* Oh, but the pain . . .

SAINT-ANGE: Courage, child. Courage.

EUGENIE: I'm being rent apart. Oh, merciful God!

DOLMANCE: There, now . . . It's halfway in . . .

SAINT-ANGE: Call upon Satan, child. Never upon the other fellow.

DOLMANCE: Suck at her cunt, Madame. It'll take her mind off the pain . . . Ah, steady, Eugénie, Steady now . . . There! It's in! In to the hilt!

EUGENIE: I'm inundated, Dolmancé. I'm completely full . . . But I still haven't experienced this metamorphosis of which you spoke. There is still only pain; no pleasure.

DOLMANCE: Patience, chit; patience. Perhaps if we separate and shift positions . . . Saint-Ange, lie on your back with Eugénie on top of you . . That's it . . . Now, put your head between her legs and have another go at her cunt. Meanwhile, I'll titillate that magnificent asshole from atop — but with my tongue, so as to lubricate it for the next phallic assault . . . There. Splendid. A marvelous position. We resemble a sandwich, wouldn't you say?

SAINT-ANGE: How do you like it, Eugénie?

EUGENIE: It's marvelous, Madame. His tongue is so warm — as is yours. And you, Dolmancé? Are you enjoying it also?

DOLMANCE: Ah, chit — it's glorious. (Now wistful.) Really only one thing is missing for me . . .

SAINT-ANGE: (Puzzled.) What possibly could be missing, Dolmancé?

DOLMANCE: A prick up my ass, Madame . . . Ah well, you can't have everything. Let's shift positions again and I'll have another go at that impregnable fortress . . . Eugénie, lie on your side, facing away from me. Saint-Ange, assume the time-honored posture of "sixty-nine" . . . That's it. Now, then, let's make it complete. Maneuver your hips, Saint-Ange, so that I have a bead on you . . . That's the way . . . In this position I can suck your asshole while my prick probes hers. How's that for efficiency? . . . Now, to work. (The enterprise is begun.)

SAINT-ANGE: Is it any less painful this time, Eugénie?

EUGENIE: Slightly. Yet, I feel badly that I am in no way contributing actively to the pleasure of you two.

SAINT-ANGE: Why don't you try sucking Dolmancé's cock?

EUGENIE: Rather impossible, good friend, since it presently is embedded in my ass.

DOLMANCE: Well, let's shift again. I was beginning to feel that a moment's respite was in order, anyway. *(The position is dissolved.)* Now, suppose you frig the member awhile first, Eugénie . . . That's the way. Perhaps a shade more briskly, if you don't mind . . . Careful, now, don't cover the head with your fingers. The little soldier must have air to breathe . . . Much better. Now, pull it forward a bit. See how you facilitate the erection? . . . There; now it's in a proper state. Go down on it, my sweet. Take it in your mouth.

EUGENIE: *(Doing so.)* Like this?

DOLMANCE: Perfect, my chit. And what a mouth you have! Delicious! . . . Now, grip the member ever so lightly with your teeth and traverse the stem. There you go! Oh, it's beautiful, my chit! Such pleasure! By God's omnipotent dork! By the juicy jism of Zeus!

EUGENIE: My, what strange blasphemies! What is the purpose, Dolmancé, of such bizarre language at a time like this?

DOLMANCE: My sweet, there are few things more pleasurable to an aethist than to profane the disgusting fiction of religion — and, if the profanity is accomplished in concert with the attainment of those sexual pleasures which the execrable cult forbids, then how much the better . . . Ah, but enough talk. I must withdraw from this splendid mouth of yours before I deposit my whole load in it. Let's resume our previous position. *(The position is assumed.)* Now, Eugénie: is it going any more smoothly this time?

EUGENIE: A bit . . .

DOLMANCE: Ready now for a sharp thrust . . .

EUGENIE: Oh, Dolmancé! Oh, the pain! . . . Ahhh, but it's ebbing! Oh, Dolmancé — the metamorphosis! Oh, the pleasure!

DOLMANCE: Ah, sweet extended prick of Neptune —
me, too! Hurry, Saint-Ange! To your station! Place
yourself quickly!

EUGENIE: Oh, Dolmancé! Oh sweet, sweet Dolmancé!

DOLMANCE: Give me your ass, Saint-Ange! Quickly!
That's it . . . Ah, how I love to ream one ass while I fuck
another.

EUGENIE: The pleasure is killing me! I can't resist!

SAINT-ANGE: Blaspheme, then. Blaspheme and profane.
I'll heighten your pleasure.

EUGENIE: Oh, damn! Damn!

DOLMANCE: More forceful terms, child. Say. "Fuck!"

EUGENIE: Fuck! Ah fuck! Oh fuck! Fuck, Dolmancé
Fuck you! Fuck me! Fuck!

SAINT-ANGE: Spoken like a veteran, Eugénie — and, oh,
Dolmancé, what your tongue is doing to me! I'm getting
ready to come myself!

DOLMANCE: And I! Oh, what a marvel this is, my dears!
All three of us shall climax together!

EUGENIE: Fuck, I say! Fuck!, Fuck!

DOLMANCE: Ah, by the Splendid Spear of Satan! By
Kali's Cunt!

SAINT-ANGE: Sweet frigging Jehovah!

EUGENIE: I say fuck! Fuck!

DOLMANCE: By Saint Paul's balls!

SAINT-ANGE: I'm dying! I'm coming! I'm fucking!

EUGENIE: Fuck!

TOGETHER: Ahhhhhhhhhhhhhhhhhhhhh, FUCK!!!

DOLMANCE: *(Breathing heavily now that it is over.)*
Well, I must say, it's not too often that one accomplishes
something like *that!* By Satan — this girl has sucked me
dry!

EUGENIE: And not a drop was wasted. Kiss me, my be-

loved instructor, and rest assured that your sperm has
found a haven in the depths of my bowels.

DOLMANCE: The little wench is delicious, Saint-Ange.

SAINT-ANGE: And how she discharged! That snapping
cunt of hers threatened to take off my tongue!

(A knock on the door.)

EUGENIE: But hold! What's this?!

SAINT-ANGE: Some impudent servant, perhaps?

(Another knock.)

DOLMANCE: At ease, my loves. I recognize the pattern.
It is none other, Saint-Ange, than your marvelous brother.
Let him in . . . .

(Curtain.)

IV. SAINT-ANGE, EUGENIE, DOLMANCE and the HORSEMAN

Scene: The Same. The Horseman, having undressed, joins the party on the bed.

SAINT-ANGE: Eugénie, permit me to present my beloved brother, the Horseman of Mirvel. Splendid sibling, I give you Mademoiselle Eugénie de Mistival.

HORSEMAN: A pleasure, my child. *(Kisses her hand.)*

EUGENIE: The pleasure is mine, sir.

DOLMANCE: Well, enough of this chatter. There's work to be done.

HORSEMAN: At what stage of the instructions are you now, my impatient friend?

DOLMANCE: I have just given this adorable child an assful of prick. Now, with your cooperation, I would like to demonstrate before her eyes the process which transpired in her bowels.

EUGENIE: *(Eyeing the Horseman's mammoth append-age.)* My word, Horseman! It's like a third leg! You're not planning to fuck me with it, are you?

HORSEMAN: Fear not, my sweet. The organ shall not play until the cathedral has been enlarged sufficiently to accommodate it.

SAINT-ANGE: All right, Horseman. It's bad enough that she's going to suffer your sexual assaults; don't subject the poor thing to your metaphors as well.

DOLMANCE: My friends, my friends — we must have less talk and more action here. How is this poor girl going to learn anything if we sit around sermonizing all day? . . . Now, Horseman: sit beside me here and exhibit your prick, Eugénie and Saint-Ange, sit on the bed directly across from us . . . That's it. Observe now, Eugénie. I'm going to frig the Horseman — or, as it might be phrased in the vernacular, I'm going to jerk him off. Meanwhile, so as not to leave you wholly devoid of sensation while the act is carried on, Saint-Ange will frig you.

SAINT-ANGE: But, Dolmancé, aren't we too close to each other?

DOLMANCE: I should say not, Madame. I wish to soak this darling child in your brother's sperm. For such an enterprise, the closer we are, the better . . . Now then, Eugénie: as the project unfolds, observe Horseman's splendid member and imagine that it's probing your innards; envision, if you will, that it has funneled through your cunt and intestines and has made its way to your stomach, where, any moment now, like Vesuvius, it's going to erupt. Fantasy, you will find, is just one more means of adding to your pleasure.

SAINT-ANGE: Ah. Horseman, how I love this Dolmancé and his enlightened discourses. And he doesn't waste a moment. Notice how he's been jerking you off from the moment he started talking.

HORSEMAN: Could I help but have noticed those expert fingers?

DOLMANCE: Well, it's only natural that a man should be more expert than a woman in a venture of this sort, what with having had years of experience with his own member before taking hold of someone else's.

EUGENIE: Ah, Saint-Ange! The same applies to you! Only seconds have elapsed since you started frigging me and already I feel that I'm about to come!

HORSEMAN: Hold, child! I'll send my jism to join yours in but a moment!

EUGENIE: Merciful Satan, look at his member! How it swells. Dolmance can barely get his hand around it!

SAINT-ANGE: Magnificent spectacle! And to think that some people prefer the opera . . .

HORSEMAN: Steady, Dolmancé! The instant approaches! Sister, lean forward so that I may caress you as the fluid flows . . . Ah, what divine breasts! What firm, round thighs! . . . Oh, the moment comes! Take aim, Dolmancé!

DOLMANCE: I aim for her nose, as the saying goes!

HORSEMAN: Then fire away!

DOLMANCE: (*Directing the stream of sperm at both women, but principally upon Eugénie.*) Right on target!

EUGENIE: Oh, my friends! I'm drowning in the stuff! How warm it is! How sticky! How sweet to the taste!

SAINT-ANGE: Hold, sweet child. Let me smear it all over you!

DOLMANCE: (*Still inundating her with it.*) Rub some on her clitoris, Madame. It'll speed her own orgasm.

SAINT-ANGE: (*Doing so.*) Oh, kiss me, Eugénie! Kiss me a million times! Thrust your tongue into my mouth and let me suck it! I love you child! I love you! Ah, fuck! I'm coming myself! Oh, Horseman — frig me!

DOLMANCE: By all means, Horseman. Frig your sister.

HORSEMAN: I'd rather fuck her. I've still enough come left.

DOLMANCE: You're a bottomless pit. You've squirted out a liter so far. And there's more left, you say?

HORSEMAN: Just call it the fountain of youth . . .

SAINT-ANGE: Frig me, Horseman — for mercy's sake! Must you always be so long-winded?

HORSEMAN: Very well, give me your ass. I'm afraid to move, lest I throw off Dolmancé's aim.

EUGENIE: What a deluge! My word! It's still flowing!

SAINT-ANGE: That's it, brother. Oh, it feels so good! I'm going to come . . .

EUGENIE: And I! I feel it! Ah, fuck! Fuck, I say! Fuck!

DOLMANCE: *(Now manipulating his own penis with his free hand.)* Splendid! Let us all discharge together! Ah, fuck!

TOGETHER: Ahhhhhhhhhhhhhhhh, FUCK!!!

(Slowly, one by one, they pry themselves apart.)

DOLMANCE: Well, Eugénie, we have added another item to your store of sexual information. You have witnessed a man's orgasm. What I would like now is to teach you how to direct its flow, as I directed the flow of the Horseman upon you.

SAINT-ANGE: But won't you both have to rest awhile before you're ready to submit to another exercise of this sort?

DOLMANCE: That's the whole problem. Now, if we could recruit another companion — perhaps a robust young man who works about the house — a porter, a fieldworker, a gardener. . . .

SAINT-ANGE: I have just the boy for you.

DOLMANCE: It wouldn't happen to be that dishwasher

I saw on my way through the kitchen — that muscular young fellow, about eighteen or nineteen years old, with a bulge in his trousers half the size of his thigh?

HORSEMAN: He must mean Augustin. That fellow's hung like a bull. It must be all of twelve inches limp . . .

SAINT-ANGE: Thirteen-and-a-half limp, brother. And seventeen erect. And the circumference, in case you're interested, is nine-and-three-quarters.

DOLMANCE: That's not a prick — it's an institution!

SAINT-ANGE: I'll get him. You can see for yourselves. *(Puts on robe and starts for door.)* Eugénie, keep a warm finger on that sweet little clit of yours. The fun is just about to start . . . .

(Exit Saint-Ange. Curtain.)

V. SAINT-ANGE, EUGENIE, DOLMANCE, THE HORSEMAN and AUGUSTIN

Scene: The same. Dolmancé, the Horseman and Eugénie lounge about the room. Enter, Saint-Ange with Augustin.

SAINT-ANGE: My friends, I give you the greatest cock in the Western World — and the smallest mind. Behold the imbecile, Augustin. Tell me, you stupid pig: you really are as dumb as you look, aren't you?

AUGUSTIN: Well, maybe — but I'm smarter than I used to be.

DOLMANCE: Capital! I say, capital! Here's a simple shit if ever one walked! But, boy; I'm given to understand you've quite the prick. Would you be so kind as to exhibit it for us?

AUGUSTIN: What does that word mean —: "exhibit?"

DOLMANCE: Say, he *is* dense! Take it out, you sad bastard. Take it out!

AUGUSTIN: As you say, sir. *(Unsheathes the mammoth weapon.)*

DOLMANCE: By Lucifer! *(Takes it in his hand and stares at it incredulously.)* I've run from smaller snakes!

THE HORSEMAN: Tell me, Saint-Ange. Do *any* come any bigger?

SAINT-ANGE: None that I've seen.

DOLMANCE: Nor I. *(Pets it.)* Not on horses, not on bulls, not on giraffes . . . .

SAINT-ANGE: There must be a universal disproportion between cocks and brains.

HORSEMAN: Now wait a minute. I've always fancied *myself* a rather clever fellow.

SAINT-ANGE: And indeed you are, Horseman. But your splendid member is to this lad's like a fart is to a windstorm.

DOLMANCE: Well, let's not get carried away with the subject. After all, there's a lesson to be taught. Eugénie: if you recall, before our friends here went into hysterics admiring this marvelous member, I promised to show you how to direct the flow of male semen. Well, the time has come. First I want you to approach this strapping lad and unbuckle his trousers.

EUGENIE: *(Doing so.)* Like this?

DOLMANCE: Fine. Now, holding that splendid shank in one hand, with the other roll the trouser legs down to his knees . . .That's it . . . Now roll his shirt up past his navel so that you have plenty of room to work . . . Fine . . . Now, let me remind you that Nature has decreed that woman be wanton, and, therefore, that you should surrender to every impulse. Do everything you can imagine to bring him pleasure, and if I'm any judge of organ size, you will be rewarded with rivers of jism the likes of which have never flown.

EUGENIE: *(Fondling him)* Is this right?

DOLMANCE: Fine. Now, while you use one hand on the

prick, use the other on his ass — like this. *(Demonstrates.)* And remember, don't cover the head of the prick. It must be kept free . . . Now you've got it . . . But what of your mouth? Don't let it remain idle, my love. Put it to work on his belly and thighs to achieve greater total effect! . . . Yes! That's it!

AUGUSTIN: Sir, if you don't mind, I think I'd like to kiss this little girl.

SAINT-ANGE: Well, kiss her, you idiot! Kiss her! You don't need an invitation!

AUGUSTIN: *(He kisses her quite vigorously.)* Oh, what a beautiful little mouth. How nice and warm and round it is. *(Plunges his tongue deep inside it.)*

DOLMANCE: Look at how hot he's getting!

HORSEMAN: Apparently he's a mouth man.

DOLMANCE: Look at that prick come alive! I'm flabbergasted . . .

SAINTE-ANGE: The instructions, Dolmancé. Remember?

DOLMANCE: Er, yes. Ahem. Now, Eugénie: your motions are too irregular, my love. You must ply him with a definite rhythm . . . That's it . . . My, look at that splendid cock! Are you sure that you measured it accurately, Saint-Ange? It looks bigger than seventeen inches to me.

SAINT-ANGE: Seventeen exactly, Dolmance. And nine-and-three-fourths around.

DOLMANCE: Well, I'll have to see for myself. I just so happen to have this measuring tape in my pocket . . . I always carry it around. One never knows when opportunities — among other things — may arise!

HORSEMAN: Splendid pun, Dolmancé! Capital!

DOLMANCE: Capital cock! *(Measuring it.)* Seventeen indeed. You're so right, Saint-Ange. But I'll bet that if I sucked on it, it'd hit nineteen or twenty in no time.

SAINT-ANGE: The instructions, Dolmancé. The instructions.

DOLMANCE: Ah, yes — damn it . . . Now, Eugénie: keep working away at the serpent, my girl; keep pumping it. That's the way. Note that the head is taking on something of a purple color? That means he's getting ready to come. Move your hand more briskly now, and at the same time probe his ass with your fingers.

AUGUSTIN: Tell her to kiss me, too, sir.

DOLMANCE: And kiss him, too, the ninny. He doesn't know enough to kiss you himself. Stupid colt. He wouldn't know enough to come in out of the rain . . . Still, it's a beautiful cock . . .

SAINT-ANGE: The instructions, cock —er, Dolmancé

DOLMANCE: Ah, yes. Enthusiasms are contagious, Saint-Ange, aren't they.

HORSEMAN: Listen to me, Eugénie. Everyone else here seems to have lost his head . . . Kiss Augustin while you continue to frig him. That's it . . . Now, get ready. See him tremble? He's about to come!

AUGUSTIN: (Slobbering her with kisses.) Ah, miss! Ah, sweet girl! Oh, I love you! Oh, God!

DOLMANCE: Look at him come! It's a geyser! I've never seen anything like it in my life! A veritable fountain of fuck!

HORSEMAN: Work twice as fast, Eugénie. Stroke him all the harder.

DOLMANCE: It must have shot ten feet, that initial jet! What power! What force!

HORSEMAN: Keep working, Eugénie!

AUGUSTIN: Oh, it feels so good that I think I'm dying!

EUGENIE: And I. My hand seems like it's about to fall off, Horseman.

HORSEMAN: Keep pumping. Endurance, child. Endurance.

DOLMANCE: What a river this is! I've never seen its peer! He makes the Horseman look like an amateur. And you say that you've fucked this lad, Saint-Ange?

SAINT-ANGE: As recently as last night.

DOLMANCE: My word. It's a wonder you can walk.

SAINT-ANGE: *(Looking dreamily into space.)* And the night before. And the night before that.

DOLMANCE: Incredible! But I trust you've never taken it up the ass from him . . .

SAINT-ANGE: All the time.

DOLMANCE: How could you handle it?! My Word, what libertinage! I doubt if I could pull it off.

HORSEMAN: You'd have no trouble pulling it off. It's taking it up the ass that would bother you.

SAINT-ANGE: You could do it, Dolmancé. The secret is to keep a loose sphincter. Don't squeeze.

DOLMANCE: I'll have to give it a try — if I can work up the courage . . . Look, he hasn't stopped coming yet!

EUGENIE: Horseman, if he doesn't stop soon, my arm will grow numb.

HORSEMAN: Well, he's letting up now. See how the flow ebbs?

DOLMANCE: Yes. The jets are only six feet instead of ten.

AUGUSTIN: Ahhhhhhhhhhhhhhhhhhhhhh, FUCK!!!

EUGENIE: Finished at last. Good Heavens, I'm drowned in jism.

DOLMANCE: Splendid performance. Splendid all the way around. And now, to celebrate the successfulness of the enterprise, let's have a unified coupling — all five of us.

HORSEMAN: So soon with Augustin?

DOLMANCE: Don't worry. I'll have that prick stiff again with two or three strokes. *(Seizes boy's penis.)* See that?! Look at the response! Let's go to work. Horseman, suppose you set this combination up.

HORSEMAN: Very well. Dolmancé, as long as you're so enchanted with that bountiful dork of his, suppose you take it up your ass. At the same time, put your own prick into my sister's ass and I'll fuck her from the front. Eugenie will prepare all the pricks for insertion, thereby being able to study the various nuances of each connection without having to undertake the responsibilities of direct participation . . . Now, are we ready?

DOLMANCE: Come, Saint-Ange: let's you and I achieve our coupling first.

SAINT-ANGE: *(Offering her buttocks.)* Here you are, Dolmancé. I await your command.

DOLMANCE: Oh, what an ass! Nature outdid herself in creating it! Here — let me lick it before I enter. *(Does so.)*

HORSEMAN: All right, Dolmancé, get on with the project. You're keeping us waiting.

DOLMANCE: As you say, sir. Behold, prick: do your delightful duty!

SAINT-ANGE: *(Receiving his thrust.)* Ah, Dolmancé you wield a wicked tool.

DOLMANCE: There's no substitute for experience, Madame. And, if I might observe, for all my experiences, I've never enjoyed a lovelier receptacle.

SAINT-ANGE: I consider that a real compliment coming from you. *(Wriggling her hips delightedly.)* Ah, my love, if you only knew how long I've wanted to get stabbed by a queer.

DOLMANCE: Please, Madame; no indelicate references to my proclivities. The polite terms is "sodomite."

SAINT-ANGE: My apologies.

DOLMANCE: My acceptance.

HORSEMAN: My *God!* Will you two stop the chatter and get on with it?! I'm getting tired of waiting.

DOLMANCE: Patience, Horseman. It's the cardinal virtue.

EUGÉNIE: If it's a virtue, we have no use for it in our company.

SAINT-ANGE: *(Bursting into laughter.)* How droll the child is! Ah, Eugénie, I love you more than myself! Come here and let me kiss your cunt. *(It is done.)*

HORSEMAN: All right, Augustin. Now it's your turn to join the party. Eugénie, frig him for a moment to prepare him for Dolmancé . . . No, child, you're a bit too timid; squeeze the member tighter . . . There you go! Now, Augustin: you see Dolmancé's ass before you. Do your duty!

AUGUSTIN: Christ, that's a big hole!

DOLMANCE: All the better to receive you, my strapping young stud. Make your entrance . . . Great Lucifer! What a club you wield! I've never received anything of such amplitude! . . . No, don't stop! Thrust, good fellow! Keep thrusting! I'll receive it all yet . . . Tell me, Eugénie, how many inches remain outside?

EUGÉNIE: Perhaps three, sir.

DOLMANCE: Then I have fourteen inside me! By Christ! It feels like it's in up to my lungs! . . . Come now, Horseman. Time for your coupling. Give me your cock and I'll help you achieve your incestuous liaison. *(He does so.)*

SAINT-ANGE: Ah, fuck! To be impaled from both sides at the same time! How I pity the woman who hasn't tasted it!

HORSEMAN: Are we all in place now?

SAINT-ANGE, DOLMANCE and AUGUSTINS Aye!

HORSEMAN: Okay, let's get the machine rattling . . . Move now, mates, and remember, that each twitch brings happiness to not one person but three!

EUGÉNIE: Ah, what a spectacle! It's a human shish-kabob!

AUGUSTIN: Come here, miss. Rub your cunt against me

while we're moving.

SAINT-ANGE: I'm getting ready . . . Ah, fuck! Oh, what proddings! Thrice the bloody fuck of the Almighty! Drown me, my friends!

HORSEMAN: I too! Let the dikes be opened! Fuck we all!

DOLMANCE: Fuck, fuck! Oh marvelous fucking! By all the sodomite saints and ass-fucker angels in heaven! By the God's dicks! By Saint Thomas' testicles! By Saint Andrew's ass! By Saint Theresa's twat! By Saint Catherine's cunt!

AUGUSTIN: Oh, God, I think I'm going to explode!

HORSEMAN: I'm coming. Ahhhhh. Oh sweet bloody jism.

TOGETHER: Ahhhhhhhhhhhhhhhhhh, FUCK!!!

(They separate and recline individually on chairs and on the bed.)

EUGENIE: My friends, you'll never know how you have inspired me today. I want to do naught henceforth but fuck and sin.

DOLMANCE: I'm glad you added the "sin" part, my dear girl, for it is as much an aspect of pleasure as the fucking. Most anyone, after all, can fuck; but it takes a genuine libertine to find pleasure in evildoing for evildoing's own sake.

EUGENIE: Well, this is precisely what I want. I think I shall commit a crime.

SAINT-ANGE: Which crime, my chit? Theft? Robbery?

EUGENIE: *(Grinning wickedly.)* Murder.

DOLMANCE: She starts at the top . . .

SAINT-ANGE: And have you picked a victim.

EUGENIE: *(Grinning more wickedly still.)* My mother.

DOLMANCE: Ah, Saint-Ange! Could you ask for anything more? The darling child is as apt a pupil as any for whom

a teacher could ever hope . . . And look at her now!
Eugénie, your face wears the expression of pure ecstasy!
What is it, child? What do you feel?

EUGENIE: *(Surprised.)* My beloved Dolmancé, I
think I'm getting ready to come again. The mere contemplation of this evil deed has brought all my senses alive.
It's as though I were being frigged.

DOLMANCE: The dear girl! She's having a mental orasm!
What a vivid imagination!

EUGENIE: Ahhhhh, it draws close.

DOLMANCE: Here, let me tongue your ass to help you
along. Horseman, join the party; lick her cunt. And
Eugenie; blaspheme, child; blaspheme!

EUGENIE: Ah, fuck! Fuck, I say. Fuck-fuck! *(Upon
which, she falls into Horseman's arms.)* Ahhhhhhhhhhhh.

DOLMANCE: Well, now let's set up another multiple project. Augustin, my fine dunce, I'll not conceal my intentions: I've been eyeing your ass for half an hour; let me
impale it while Horseman takes me from behind; mean-
time, you may lick Eugénie's ass while Saint-Ange
tongues her twat. Is that agreeable to everyone?

TOGETHER: Aye!

DOLMANCE: But first, in order to better put Eugénie in
the proper humor, I am going to give her lovely ass a
few strokes with a lash. *(Seizes whip from beneath bed
and begins striking her.)*

EUGENIE: *(Wracked with pain.)* Sir, I protest that this
ceremony has no purpose but to gratify your own lewdness. I'll gladly submit to it for that reason; but don't be
a hypocrite and say you're doing it for my benefit.

DOLMANCE: *(Whipping delightedly.)* You'll soon change
your mind, child; just wait until those tantalizing lashes
cut through your sweet flesh.

EUGENIE: *(Writhing in pain.)* I submit, sir, that I feel

naught but pain!

SAINT-ANGE: I'll avenge you, my chit. *(Takes up another whip and begins flogging Dolmancé.)* Take this, you knave!

DOLMANCE: Thank you, Madame. You do me a great service. As for you, Eugénie: observe that I am consistent to my preachments; I ask now only that you put a little faith in me, and you soon will see that your present pains are buying for you a future of far greater pleasures. *(Still whipping, more enthusiastically than ever.)* But, hold — I have another idea; a much better one. Saint-Ange, let Eugénie mount your flanks, clutching your neck like a papoose; this will give me two asses to beat instead of one. Meanwhile, both Cock Augustin here and the good Horseman may whip me; thus, double the pleasure . . . *(The arrangement is accomplished.)* Ah, my friends, what ecstasy!

SAINTE-ANGE: For me, too, Dolmancé. And don't spare the rod. I gave no quarter when I whipped you; I want none in return.

DOLMANCE: I assure you, Madame, I give quarter to no one — at no time. I think only of my own pleasures. Fuck the rest of the world.

EUGENIE: Oh, Dolmancé, I can't stand this whipping any longer. If you're really thinking of your own pleasures, think of all those you'll miss when you've destroyed this little ass of mine!

DOLMANCE: Ah, chit, have faith in me. *(Stops momentarily to contemplate his work.)* I've only split one buttock; when both are split, you'll feel the pleasure. *(Resumes.)* Harder, Eugénie! Harder I whip you! Ah . . . The second buttock split! Look at the little bitch bleed! Quick, Augustin, thrust your tongue into the crack! Suck up all the blood and whatever shit you find there with it!

AUGUSTIN: *(Wincing.)* Not me. That's disgusting.

DOLMANCE: Oh, you simple prick — have you no sophistication whatsoever? . . . Here, I'll do it. *(Drops whip and falls to licking and sucking Eugénie's ass.)* Mmm, delicious! What blood! What shit!

EUGENIE: And it feels so good, Dolmancé! Oh, you were so right about the pleasure! I've never felt anything like this in my life!

DOLMANCE: Splendid, chit! Splendid! And, now that Augustin's temerity has destroyed all possibility of our setting up the planned combination, we must improvise. Horseman: it is my understanding that the sweet task of being the first to encunt this charming child belongs to you. Would you not like to exercise your prerogatives now?

HORSEMAN: I'd be delighted, dear Dolmancé.

EUGENIE: Then here is my cunt, good friend. Do with it what you will.

DOLMANCE: Not so hasty, child. We must arrange this enterprise in a sufficiently lewd manner. Now, Augustin; lie on your back on the bed. *(As he gives his instructions, each participant executes the necessary moves.)* Eugénie, lie on your stomach on top of him with your mound against his cock — but don't permit him to enter you; that pleasure is reserved for Horseman; not that Augustin *could* enter you with that monstrosity of his . . .

HORSEMAN: But, Dolmancé, how am *I* to enter her if Augustin blocks the path?

DOLMANCE: Patience, my friend; put your trust in me . . . Now, I lie atop Eugénie's back — like so! — and prepare to embugger her. Simultaneously, I frig her clitoris with the head of Augustin's prick . . . There, chit: how does that feel?

EUGENIE: Marvelous, dear friend; marvelous: how I

pity the girl who has never enjoyed it.

DOLMANCE: Pity no one, child. Each to his own and the devil take the hindmost . . . Now, Horseman, have the kindness to arrange yourself around Eugenie's shoulders with your ass in my face . . . That's it. In this position I can ream you and, with my spare hand, frig you at the same time.

HORSEMAN: I comply, Dolmancé, but with much hesitancy. I don't see how I possibly could encunt Eugénie in this arrangement.

DOLMANCE: Trust me, my friend. Trust me . . . Now, Saint-Ange. I'm sure a voluptuary like you has at least one dildo about the house.

SAINT-ANGE: But of course. Would you like a large one or a small one?

DOLMANCE: The largest you have.

SAINT-ANGE: *(Fetching one from her dresser drawer.)* No sooner said than done. This one measures fourteen inches and ten around.

DOLMANCE: Then fit it about your loins, Madame, and spare me not. My anus yawns for you.

SAINT-ANGE: *(Climbing into position atop him.)* Are you sure you don't care to reconsider? I'm afraid I'll cripple you with this.

DOLMANCE: Fear not, my love. Lay on! . . . Ah, Jesus, what a thrust! Marvelous, my beloved! Simply superb! Probe me! Probe, I say Drive the fuck-stick as far as it'll go! . . .

HORSEMAN: I submit, Dolmancé, that this enterprise appears to have nothing whatsoever to do with my proposed encunting of Eugénie.

DOLMANCE: Patience, sir — and trust! Trust! . . . Now, Eugénie, do you feel my member at the threshold of your lovely ass? Brace yourself, for I'm about to enter. And

this time there will be lubrication to facilitate the task
... Ah, I break through! By Saint Cecelia's snatch! What
a magnificent ass!

EUGENIE: Oh, Dolmancé, I beg you ... You're tearing
me ... Back off ...

DOLMANCE: No mercy, child! I'll show you no mercy!
Take it as it comes!

EUGENIE: Aiiiiieeeeeeeee! My intestines are being torn
to shreds! Relent, sir! Lubricate the passage first!

DOLMANCE: Not a chance, child. I must fuck on. I think
only of my own pleasure. Too much time would be lost if
I acceded to your wishes at this point .... Ah, I progress.
By Lucifer! I've hit bottom!

EUGENIE: Ahhhh, Dolmancé — there's no pain now;
naught but pleasure. Do what you will, you sweet sodomite. I love you.

DOLMANCE: Then curse as I have taught you, child.
Contribute to my pleasure through the sense of hearing
as well as throught the sense of touch.

EUGENIE: Ah fuck! Oh fuck! Fuck, I say!

DOLMANCE: Some variety in your phrases, chit. You're
overdoing the one expression. Call upon the sexual organs
of the saints as you have heard me do.

EUGENIE: By Saint ... Martha's mound! Saint ...
Christopher's cock.

DOLMANCE: Now you're learning! Keep at it!

EUGENIE: By Saint Dominic's dork! ... Saint Sophia's
... slit!

DOLMANCE: Ah, splendid! And Saint-Ange: it is splendid the way you continue to fuck me with that dildo!
What graceful movements, my woman! What powerful
thrusts! ... Now, Horseman: I still lick your ass, my libertine friend; I still frig you. Do you like it? ... And you,
Augustin: I feel that pulsating prick of yours swelling to
new proportions. Do you approach ejaculation, my superb

simp? Do you?

AUGUSTINE: I don't know about that, Dolmancé, but it feels like I'm going to come.

DOLMANCE: Ah, he's a gem, this cunt-face. But hold — I feel orgasm knocking on my own door as well. By Saint Gregory's gonads! I'm coming!

EUGENIE: And I, Dolmancé. By Saint Brigitte's buns! By Saint Jerome's joint! Fuck, I tell you. Fuck, Dolmancé. Oh fuck-fuck!

DOLMANCE: I say, then: we've got this rosary strung together rather well. All three of us coming at once . . .

HORSEMAN: But not I, my friend. Remember that I am supposed to fuck Eugénie . . . .

DOLMANCE: And you remember that I asked for your trust . . . . No more talk, now; let us dispel all thoughts from our minds save that of orgasm. We fuck; we suck; we come. By Saint Nicholas' nuts! By the sweet bun-fucking Almighty God! I die! I fuck! I come!

DOLMANCE, AUGUSTIN and EUGENIE: Ahhhhhhhhhhh, FUCK!!! *(They withdraw and the circle breaks.)*

HORSEMAN: Dolmancé, I have been betrayed. I trusted you to arrange the encunting of Eugénie, but lo— you leave me with my prick in my hand.

DOLMANCE: Then pull on it, my friend. That's what pricks are for. And let this serve as a lesson to you: henceforth, never trust anyone — not even your best friend . . . . But, Augustin: I still haven't answered the call which I've been receiving all afternoon from your marvelous ass. Would you like me to embugger you, boy?

AUGUSTINE: No, but you can fuck me if you like.

DOLMANCE: Capital stupidity, my fine pig! Capital! Now bend over and spread your cheeks . . . . See how stiff I've become already?

EUGÉNIE: But, Dolmancé, before you proceed, let me ask you — is it not unnatural to prefer, as you do, the male to the female?

DOLMANCE: I should say not. Let us remember that, despite the tasteless fables in the Holy Writ — Sodom and Gomorrah, for example — Nature does not have two voices; She does not create the appetite for buggery, then proscribe its practice. This falacious proscription is the work of those imbeciles who seem unable to view sex as anything but an instrumentality for the multiplication of their own imbecilic kind. But I put it to you thusly: would it not be unreasonable for Nature, if she opposed buggery, to reward its practitioners with consummate pleasure at the very moment when they, by buggering, heap insults upon Her "natural" order? Furthermore, if procreation were the primary purpose of sex, would woman be created capable of conceiving during only sixteen to eighteen hours of each month — and thus, all arithmetic being performed, during only four to six years of her total life span? No. child, let us not ascribe to Nature those prohibitions which we acquire through fear or prejudice; all things which are possible are natural; let no one ever persuade you otherwise.

EUGÉNIE: Ah, Dolmancé, your enlightened discourse warms my heart. If only the whole population of France could be made to hear them! Can you envision an entire nation heeding only the voice of reason? What a monument to the human mind that would be!

HORSEMAN: Well, speaking of monuments, I have a very stiff dick here which serves as a monument to my desire to fuck you, little girl — and, since Dolmancé's chickanery averted the event a few minutes ago, I'm going to undertake it now by myself.

DOLMANCE: There's no need for snide remarks, Horseman. True, I tricked you, but he who lets himself be duped is more contemptible than he who does the duping. So stop complaining and maybe I'll help you get the girl up for her devirgination; with that enormous engine of yours, you're going to need someone to hold her legs open.

HORSEMAN: I thank you, my friend — and I ask to have my discourteous comments stricken from the record . . . Now, Eugénie: prepare yourself, child; see what I have for you? See how big it is when it's erect?

EUGENIE: Oh, my God! You can't fuck me with *that!* It would kill me! Dolmancé: yours is smaller; you devirginate me instead.

DOLMANCE: No, child; that's completely unthinkable; I've never fucked a cunt in my life and it's too late to start now. Besides, your hymen was promised to the Horseman . . .

EUGENIE: But you, yourself, said that promises are made to be broken.

SAINTE-ANGE: She's right, Dolmancé. And how can you possibly refuse a maidenhead as lovely as this? Surely there's none prettier in all France. If you refuse simply out of allegiance to the cult of sodomites, you're holding too closely to principle!

DOLMANCE: Do I surprise you, Saint-Ange? Then you would be further surprised to know that some sodomites are even more scrupulous than I. They would not enter a female under any circumstances — not in the cunt, not in the ass, not even in the mouth. As for me, I don't avoid cunts on principle; it is simply that I have no desires in that direction.

SAINT-ANGE: Well, then, Horseman, the task befalls you.

HORSEMAN: I must say I'm rather distressed by the turn which events have taken these past few minutes. First

I'm tricked out of my promised reward by Dolmancé, then my own sister seeks likewise to remove it from my reach. I accept deviousness and duplicity, of course; they are immoral, and, as such, they are evil — which is to say, they are good. However, should there not be honor among thieves?

DOLMANCE: Honor is useless, Horseman, regardless of its company. Now, forget the philosophy for a moment and take advantage of that sweet little hymen which awaits you, before Eugénie decides that she'd like to offer it so someone else — like Augustin, for example.

HORSEMAN: Yes, I suppose you're right. Well, come, Eugénie: let's put ourselves to the task.

EUGENIE: Oh, Horseman, it's so big! You'll kill me for sure! *(Suddenly smiling wickedly.)* Yet, the bigger the prick, the more the pain, and the more the pain — at least, such has been my experience thus far — the greater the pleasure. So perhaps I should take Augustin after all, for his prick is bigger than even yours.

HORSEMAN: Oh no you don't. I'll tolerate no more resistance. *(He grabs her by the arm as she seeks to turn away, then knocks her to the floor with a punch in the mouth.)* Spread your legs, you little bitch; I'm going to drive this cock right up to your adam's apple.

EUGENIE: *(Now agog with desire.)* Oh, Horseman, I love you so much! Hitting me is what did it! Now I want so badly to be fucked by you that I'll gladly brave your monstrous prick. Behold the citadel, darling: begin your siege!

HORSEMAN: Then spread those thighs, my twitch! Spread them wide! . . . Here we go, now —

EUGENIE: Aiiiiiieeeeeeee!

HORSEMAN: Dolmancé! Saint-Ange! Grab a leg each,

my friends! Hold them apart! She must be split like a melon!

EUGENIE: Gently, Horseman. Gently.

HORSEMAN: Fuck, I say You expect gentleness from a stiff dick? Inconceivable . . . . Now, then! I penetrate! Ahhhh!

EUGENIE: Aiiiieeeeee! Aiiiieeeee, my friends! I'm dying of pain. *(Tears roll down her cheeks.)* Horseman, I'll scream if you persist . . .

HORSEMAN: Scream, my chit. Scream till you've emptied your lungs.

EUGENIE: Aiiiiiieeeeeeeeee!!!!

HORSEMAN: Scream, cunt I say fuck-cunt! . . . Behold, Dolmance: I've half the distance covered.

EUGENIE: Aiiiiiiiiieeeeeeeeeeeeeeeeeeee!!!!

HORSEMAN: Ho Ho-fuck! I touch bottom! By God's gronch, I've rent the maidenhead! Look at the blood issue forth!

EUGENIE: Come, my lion! Tear me to ribbons; I feel the pleasure now! Fuck, I say! Fuck me, Horseman! Horse me, fuck-man, I love you! I fuck you! Horse-fuck! Fuck-horse!

HORSEMAN: Oh beautiful fuck-girl

EUGENIE AND HORSEMAN: Fuck! Oh-fuck! Ahhhhhhhh, FUCK!!!*(The position is dissolved.)*

DOLMANCE: Now then, while the gate is still open, let's bring on Augustin and give her a taste of what — no offense, Horseman — a *real* prick is like.

EUGENIE; How's that, sir? You'd have me fucked with that monstrosity?! While my hymenal blood still flows?! I'll die for sure!

DOLMANCE: If so, chit, you'll die only of delight — because the enterprise which I've planned for you is an extravaganza the likes of which has not been staged all afternoon.

SAITE-ANGE: What say you, Dolmancé? You plan to initiate this chit to a multiple union so early in her career?

DOLMANCE: There's no time like the present, Madame ... And now, shall we be on with it? ... I lie on my side, Augustin. Do you see me? Come now, big fellow, lie in front of me; I'm going to fuck you up the ass while you take Eugenie in the cunt ... That's it, my great fucking-john! What an ass you have. I stagger at the thought of the thunderous farts which must issue forth from betwixt these muscular cheeks for time to time ... Ah, I penetrate you! Oh, you splendid fucker! How beautifully you move! Ho— it's done! I'm in to the hilt ...

AUGUSTIN: Jeez, you have a small prick, Dolmancé. I can hardly feel it.

DOLMANCE: Yes, an organ of normal dimensions is bound to play softly in a cathedral of this size. But, let's get on with the project ... Come Eugénie: face him now; lie right alongside him ... That's it ... And Horseman: now it's your turn to take her from behind. Do you think you can manage? Can you get that prick of yours stiff again?

HORSEMAN: With an ass like Eugénie's beckoning me? Have no doubts, Dolmancé I spring to the task instantly.

SAINT-ANGE: But what of me, Dolmancé. Would you leave me out of the group?

DOLMANCE: I should say not, Madame. Come around to the other side of the bed ... That's it ... Now, lower your hips until your ass is in apposition with the lovely Eugénie's face... There we are... She takes Horseman in the ass, Augustin in the cunt and you with her tongue ... Let's go to work now!

AUGUSTINE: Get ready, miss; this is going to hurt ...

HORSEMAN: And here's my contribution, Eugénie ...

EUGENIE: Aieeeee! Aiie! Ai! Oh-fuck! I'm being cracked in half! Oh, these two immense pricks! I can hardly bear it!

DOLMANCE: There's more coming, my chit. I've a surprise in store for you. *(He reaches under bed and withdraws a whip.)* Here's a little red bracelet to wear around your lovely white thigh. *(Strikes her.)*

EUGENIE: Aiiiieeeeeee!! But the pleasure, too!! Oh-fuck! Ah-fuck! This gross peasant cleaves me from the front! Horseman splits me from the back! *(The whip strikes her again.)* Aiiieee! Saint-Ange, I suck your delicious cunt! Oh, fuck, what pleasure!

(The chorus utters cries appropriate to the onset of communal orgasm. Since these rites have been described previously, and are apt to resemble each other on all occasions, it has been deemed unnecessary to repeat them at this time.)

EUGENIE: *(After all is over and the position has been dissolved.)* Well, my friends, I must say that I've never in my life even dreamed that anything that pleasurable would be possible. Now I need but one thing to make my moment complete.

SAINT-ANGE: What's that, my chit?

EUGENIE: A dissertation, my lovely mentor. Ply my intellect as you have just plied my senses. If my mind is to be the mirror of your thoughts, polish it — for the more highly polished the mirror, the more faithfully it reflects the objects placed before it.

DOLMANCE: Such wisdom for a child her age! . . . Tell me, darling girl; upon what subject would you have us speak?

EUGENIE: I should like to know the part which law and religion should play in a republican society.

DOLMANCE: By Lucifer! I just happen to have a pamphlet here with me which deals with that very topic. I bought it this morning outside the Palace of Equality. Look at it.

SAINT-ANGE: *(Reading its cover.)* It says: "Yet Another Effort, Frenchman, Before You Call Yourselves Republicans." What a strange title.

DOLMANCE: But by no means an unprovocative one. Horseman, you've a splendid voice. Would you read it to us?

HORSEMAN: With pleasure . . . .

(Curtain.)

INTERLUDE: HORSEMAN

Scene: Horseman in front of the curtain. He reads the pamphlet.

YET ANOTHER EFFORT, FRENCHMEN, BEFORE YOU CALL YOURSELVES REPUBLICANS

My countrymen, we have seen the head of our tyrant king fall into the executioner's basket. We have seen the monarchy destroyed and its trappings swept away. We have declared ourselves free. But Frenchmen, a wide chasm separates the declaration of freedom from the realization of freedom, and there can be no greater folly than in believing that we have attained the latter when, in reality, we have accomplished only the former. True, the old regime has been wrecked; but as long as its foundations stand — indeed, as long as even a single pillar stands — we may be certain that the rest will soon be restored. Such a pillar now stands. It is the Roman Catholic Church. And, in permitting it to remain standing, Frenchmen, we pave the way once again for tyranny and despotism; we prepare our necks once more to be submitted to the yoke which our vitality only yesterday cast off.

My friends, the time has come to realize that morals should be the basis of religion and not religion the basis of morals. Our religion — our code of conduct, if you will — must be founded not upon the commandments of a long-dead charlatan, not upon the whims of his self-annointed successors, but upon those principles — and only upon those principles — which our logic leads us to recognize as correct. The Roman Catholic Church is demonstrably short of such logical principles. Instead of logic she gives us dogma; instead of reason, mysteries; and the whole is bound together in such a fashion, she tells us, that one must accept either all of it or none of it — the latter course of action being possible only at the expense of one's so-called Immortal Soul. Well, out of fear of losing that nebulous soul, many a man has surrendered his very freedom, has surrendered his very life; and, while we never get around to seeing what he gains in the heavenly account-books as a result of his sacrifices, one needn't look very hard to see what His Holy Mother the Church gains from them here on earth!

Let us not forget that, throughout history, the Church and royalist tyrants have always walked hand-in-hand: kings uphold the "divine mission" of religion; religion upholds the "divine right of kings. It is the old story of the chef and the steward: "Hand me the pepper and I'll pass you the butter." But, Frenchmen: the pepper and the butter belong to neither the chef nor the steward; they belong to us! "Render unto Caesar the things which are Caesar's," the Church tells us. Remember, my countrymen: we have dethroned Caesar; his head lies in the basket; we are not disposed to render him anything, and neither are we disposed to render anything to the Church which for so long has served as his apologist!

"Very well," the churchman may concede. "You owe us nothing," he may say — now that he has been stripped of his power. "Therefore go your way and let us go ours," he may tell us. But, Frenchmen, we cannot let the Church go its way, because we know only too well the way it will go. Before ten years have passed, these same priests who now advocate a policy of "live and let live" will have once again taken the reins of power; utilizing the superstitions, the intimidations and the outright threats which have long filled their rhetorical arsenal, they will have subverted the souls of the weak and the unwary and will have reasserted their "spiritual empire;" after this it will be only a matter of time before they restore the monarchy, because the power of kings, properly manipulated, has always been the surest weapon with which to reinforce the power of the church. When that happens, Frenchmen, you'll hear no more talk of "live and let live" — no more talk of it than you heard during the Inquisition. Because, when that happens, the chef and the steward will be back in business—in our kitchen!

I repeat, Frenchmen: France, to be free, must be delivered not only from the royal scepter but also from the clerical censer! You, who still have your revolutionaries' axes in hand, must now deal the final blow to the tree of tyranny; it is not enough merely to nip off a few of its branches; you must pull it out by the roots! Let the slave of a despot king grovel, if he likes, at the feet of a plaster statue; we, Frenchmen — we, my fellow citizens — must resolve that we will die a hundred times over before we will kneel before another tyrant, be he man or be he god. "But," it may be argued, "the people need a god; he amuses them; he calms their nerves; he soothes their

anxieties." If this be so, so be it; but, in giving them, a
god let us give them one like the noble pagan gods of
old; let us give them a Jupiter, or Hercules, or Pallas,
whose bold legends inspired brave men to new heights
of personal fulfillment: they have no need for this timid
and impotent Christian god — this father of confusion
who creates men only to condemn them; this supposedly
supreme being who somehow or other never can quite
get his creatures to do his will; this author of order in
whose government their exists only chaos; this phantom
diety who is forever at loggerheads with the forces of
Nature over which he claims to rule. The Christian god,
we are told, is all-wise and all-powerful; yet, he created
the world to glorify himself and it passes its days debasing him; he created man to know him, to love him and to
serve him and we spend our time ignoring him, hating
him and disobeying his commandments: if this be power
and wisdom, let us now try a god possessed of weakness
and folly!

No, Frenchmen, there is no merit in the Christian god
and there is no place in France for the tokens of his
chickanery. If you feel a need for statues, erect them to
the great men who have fought to further mankind's
cause. And, if you feel a need for slogans, inscribe upon
all your shrines not the Latin riddles of the cult of Jesus
but the three words which henceforth should inspire
hope and joy in the heart of every Frenchman: Liberty,
Fraternity, Equality!

Moreover, do not be duped into believing that it is
only through Christianity that social order may be preserved. Is there anyone among us rash enough to expect
that men who scoff at the blade of the guillotine will be
restrained by fear of a hell about whose torments they
have laughed since childhood? No, my friends; many is

the crime created by religion, but rarely if ever has one been prevented by it. And I further submit that, even if it could be proved that Christianity checked all crime and was the sole preservative of social order, there still would not be sufficient reason to tolerate the presence of the perfidious cult among us, for social order at the expense of liberty is hardly a bargain.

But enough of these arguments. They revolve around the Christian notion that a ruling class has been singled out by an all-wise God for the purpose of guiding the rabble, and this is a notion which violates the basic principle of equality on which the revolution was based. Be assured that the people — the so-called common people — are a great deal wiser than the Christian tyrants ever realized. And be further assured that, once the facts have been made known to them, these same people who were sufficiently wise and brave to drag a loathsome earthly king from the seat of power to the foot of the scaffold will be sufficiently wise and brave to abolish Christianity's self-proclaimed phantom king of the universe.

Frenchmen, we need only strike the initial blows; having seen the light, the people will find their own way. But they must be made to see the light. You must hasten to the task of educating your youth: educating them not in the sophomoric stupidities which comprised your early education at the hands of the priests, but in a sound and humane ethic constructed about a framework of logic; teaching them not a compendium of silly slogans and them ·the basic human truths from which they may will pride themselves on having forgotten, but teaching them the basic human truths from which they may deduce a sense of obligation toward society and a desire to discharge the obligation voluntarily. Our children must be made to realize the fundamental principle of civilization: that our own happiness depends upon the happiness of those about us. Furthermore, the principle must not be presented to them as having a basis in Christian myth (as all principles were presented to us when we were children), for no sooner will they have seen through and rejected the myth than they will have overturned the entire edifice to which it had been made to serve as a foundation: thus, they will become bandits and murderers and thieves for no reason other than that religion forbade it. Conversely, if they are made to understand that virtue is necessary to their happiness, then egoism will make honest men of them — and the world knows no men more honest than those who are honest for their own sake!

Moreover, our children must be imbued with a philosophy of positives. We must never forget that it is free men we are trying to form, not feckless followers of a blustering god. Thus, we must teach them that life is for the living; that pleasures are to be enjoyed; that it is far less essential to inquire into the nature of things than to heed the inscrutable and wonderfully sublime voice of Nature. If they ask us the cause of the universe, let us tell them the truth: we honestly don't know. Certainly let us not befuddle their brains with a complex series of conceptualizations which seek to prove inductively that there exists and that we are beholden to a being who does not make himself perceivable by the senses. And, if they are curious about philosophical "laws," let us refer them to the true Natural Law; a law as wise as it is simple; a law written indelibly across the hearts of all men; a law which man obeys every time he obeys his impulses. If this does not satisfy them, then we must confess to him that, satisfactory or not, it is all we have.

As to the teaching method, let us provide many more examples than pronouncements, many more demonstrations than dicta. Remember that the youthful mind is something like a strand of spaghetti: if you pull it, you can get it to go a long way; if you push it, it goes nowhere. So it will be with our children. If we command them, if we order them around, we can produce only a nation of brave warriors and noble fathers; a nation of men immune to servility and untroubled by superstition; above all, a nation of true patriots, devoted so fiercely to their country's liberty that they are willing not only to die for it, but also, what is often harder, to live and work for it as well!

This, Frenchmen, should be our aim; and, to accomplish it, we must banish forever from this land the forces of religion which can nurture only depotism. However, let me make it clear that I propose neither massacres nor expulsions; such are the instruments of kings and of the brigands who imitate them; were we to employ such tactics, we would be no better than the tyrants we have overthrown. Rather, our weapon should be ridicule; let us remember that the clever sarcasm of Julian wreaked more havoc among the early Christians than all of Nero's ignominies; by our likewise assaulting the present-day priests with barrages of scorn, we will not only rout the enemy but also bring him to his knees in such a manner that his past wrongs will be apparent to all who behold him.

Thus the matter of the Church in the community, and the means by which I propose to handle it. Now let us turn to the matter of law.

From the beginning of time, man has assumed obligations of three categories: 1) Those relating to a supreme being; 2) Those relating to one's fellow men,

and 3) Those relating to oneself. Likewise from the beginning of time, man has undertaken through legislation to establish uniform standards of compliance with
certain obligations, The question now before us is: which
obligations of which categories should we, as republicans, seek to impose legally upon our nation as a whole.

As concerns obligations to oneself, we all should realize that man will perform whichever acts he identifies
as contributing to his pleasure and/or well-being and
will desist from the performance of all others. It is absurd to attempt to persuade him to do otherwise, and
it is even more absurd to threaten him with legal penalties if he remains unpersuaded. For example, while most
men agree that man is obligated to himself not to commit
suicide, how does one go about the business of enforcing
a law proscribing the act? The same problem would
arise to some extent in any lesser crime against one's
own well-being, for instance, mutilation or starvation;
how could the State force a man to eat, or to refrain
from cutting off one foot after imprisoning for cutting
off the other? Thus, the simple unenforceability of laws
proscribing crimes against oneself removes this whole
category of crimes from the purview of jurisprudence.

Secondly, as concerns obligations to a supreme being,
let us recognize that, if an individual is foolish enough
to predicate his actions upon some erroneous notion of
an all-demanding diety to whom he is beholden, then
he is perfectly within his rights to do so. However, if
there were such a diety to whom man were obligated,
the responsibility of enforcing the obligation is the responsibility of the diety, not of the State. Therefore, all
laws in the French Criminal Code concerning such "religious crimes" as atheism, sacrilege, impiety, blasphemy,

et cetera, should be nullified immediately. Moreover, a law should be written which would specifically guarantee not only the right of men to subscribe to the religious cult of their choice, but also the right of men to decry, if they choose, all religious cults as the ridiculous creations of persons in whom shallowness of mind and paucity of imagination have given rise to fear of a phantom of diety: men who wish to gather in a temple and invoke the image of some ethereal creature should, of course, be permitted to do so; but the temple should not be immune from tax — and the members of society who do not subscribe to the cult should be permitted to pay an admission charge and laugh at the worshippers' antics, much as we might laugh at clowns in a circus.

Finally, let us take-under consideration the third class of man's obligations: those to his fellows — which class, quite clearly, is the only one with which the State should concern itself. However, let us recognize at the onset that our laws, as presently written, concern themselves for too often and far too intimately with aspects of human intercourse which might best be left in the hands only of the parties involved.

This over-concern, it would appear, is the result of legislators' attempts to enforce the Christian dictum, "love thy neighbor as thyself." The dictum, of course, is absurd; one should not aim to love one's neighbor as oneself, but rather to tolerate all while loving some, hating others and being totally indifferent to others still. At this point it would be wise to remind ourselves that men are as unlike each other in terms of personality and character as they are unlike each other in terms of physical dimensions; thus, to seek to subject them to universal laws of brotherhood would be a patent absurdity — a proceeding as ridiculous as that of a general who would seek to dress all his soldiers in a uniform of the same size! That there cannot be as many individual laws as there are men is a point which we readily concede; but any "universal" laws which are passed should be such that exceptions are made for those not of the temperament to observe them; indeed, the punishment of a man for violating a law which he cannot observe is no more just than the punishment of a blind man for failing to differentiate among colors. Furthermore, "universal" laws, even with their exceptions, should be extremely few in number, should be limited to crimes where extralegal checks and balances cannot possibly be applied and should call for "punishments" which seek more to prevent reoccurance of the crime than to take vengeance upon the person who has committed it.

Having set forth these basic principles let us now turn to the four categories of crimes now delineated in the French criminal code: calumny; crimes against property; sexual crimes, and murder. Under the monarchy, all these acts were considered serious offenses. But are they quite so serious in a republican State? This is the question which, aided by the light from philosophy's torch, we must seek to answer. And as I advance my arguments, let no one accuse me of being evil's apologist; let no one say that I seek to inspire wrongdoing or to blunt remorse in the hearts of wrongdoers: my sole purpose throughout these endeavors is to articulate thoughts which have gnawed at my consciousness since I first was able to reason; that these thoughts might be in conflict with the thoughts of some other persons, or of most other persons, or of all persons except me, is not, I believe, sufficient reason to suppress them. As to those susceptible souls who might be "corrupted" by exposure to my words, I say, so much the worse for them. I address myself only to men who are capable of examining with an objective

eye everthing before them. Such men are incorruptible.
Now, on to our examination of criminal law:

Regarding calumny, or the bearing of false witness
against one's neighbor, I must confess that I have never
considered it criminal — for where is the injury done?
By applying the rule of contradictories we can see that
the object of a calumnious attack is either (a) a virtuous man, or (b) an evil man. In the latter case, it is of
little consequence that a false accusation has been made,
for what does it matter to a doer of much evil if he is
blamed for doing a little more? Indeed, investigation
of a false evil might bring to light a true evil, whereupon
the malefactor who thus far had managed to escape the
judgement of his peers finally would be taken to task.
On the other hand, if a virtuous man is calumniated, he
need only exhibit himself and all the imputed evil will
be turned back upon the imputor. Whatever the case,
an honest man has nothing to fear — and, since law is
designed to protect the honest from the dishonest, there
is no reason to proscribe calumny.

Next let us examine theft. From the standpoint of the
wealthy, this is, of course, an horrendous crime. But,
laying partiality aside, let us ask ourselves as republicans: shall we, upholding the principle that all men are
equal, brand as wrong an act whose effect is to accomplish a more equal distribution of wealth? Theft fur-
thers economic equilibrium: one never hears of the rich
stealing from the poor, thereby aggravating the economic imbalance; only of the poor stealing from the
rich, thereby correcting it. What possibly could be wrong
with that?

Furthermore, theft encourages diligence in the protection and conservation of property. Indeed, certain

societies used to punish not the thief but his victim, all in the interests of teaching diligence and conservation.

But let us turn from these pragmatic points to reflections of a broader scope. We might ask ourselves: "Is a law truly just which orders the man who has nothing to respect the "rights" of the man who has everything?" The answer, of course, is: "No." The law, after all, it but a contract, and a valid contract involves each party's foregoing something in return for acquiring something else. But what do the poor acquire in return for foregoing the pleasure of stealing from the rich? Nothing. Thus, illusory rights are exchanged for real rights and the contract is inequitable.

"But," one might ask, "did not the Republic pledge to respect private property?"* Yes, I say, the pledge was made; but now we must break it, and we should feel no qualms about doing so. In this connection, let us remind ourselves that an oath must have equal effect upon all who pronounce it; if it binds a man who has no interest in its maintenance, it is no longer a pact among free men — it is the weapon of the strong against the weak. Thus, the pledge which was made must be nullified, and with it must be nullified our statutes against theft; there is no room for such statutes in a republican society.

Now, let us turn to the laws against sexual crimes — the ordinances proscribing prostitution, adultery, incest, rape and sodomy, or, as these enterprises were termed during the old regime, the "moral" crimes. In this phrase, "moral," I submit, lies the reason for the laws' abolition. A republic is not in the business of prescribing morality; its chief duty — indeed, its sole reason for existence is to preserve, by whatever means deemed neces-

*during the Convention of 1792.

sary, the freedom of its citizens. Further, since despots both within the country and outside it are certain to attempt the usurpation of that freedom, war is inevitable. Now, I ask you: what is more immoral than war? And how can a state which must perpetrate immorality to fullfill its sole reason for existence turn around and insist that its citizens live morally?

But there are reasons other than this for the abolition of the "moral" ordinances. Let us remember that, if Nature intended man to be modest, she would not have permitted him to be born naked. Likewise, if she intended him to gratify his sexual drives only as a part of a procreative act, she would have arranged things so that it was only under such circumstances that he found sexual couplings pleasurable. Therefore, when we ban all nonprocreative sex acts — which, in effect, is what our "moral" ordinances do — we violate the Natural Law ourselves!

Let us in this instance learn a lesson from the ancient Greek legislators, who rather than proscribing debauchery actually sotted their constituents on it. No species of libertinage was prohibited in this great civilization, and it mattered not what form the act or what gender the participants; Socrates, whom the oracle termed the wisest philosopher of the age, passed indifferently from the arms of his mistress, Aspasia, to those of his boyfriend, Alcibiades, and the glories of Athens were in no wise diminished because of either dalliance.

Our attitudes should be patterned after theirs. Rather than forbidding prostitution, we—like Solon, the lawgiver—should erect in each city a series of brothels, spacious, sanitary, well-furnished and in every respect safe. There should be available therein the services of persons of both genders and all ages, lending themselves readily to the caprices of all debauchees who come calling. No libertine enterprise should under any circumstance be prohibited.

Furthermore, we should nullify all marriage laws. These are based on the Christian notion of possessive "love"—an idiocy whose proponents evidently believe that the sun shines less brightly on them if it shines on someone else too! These laws should be replaced by a State declaration that all women belong to all men — not as property, but as instruments for enjoyment. An analogy might be drawn to a well at the side of a road: I have no right to "possess" the well, no right to prevent others from using it; but I have uncontestable rights to use its water to slake my thirst. Likewise, under just laws, I would have no right to "possess" this woman or that one, but I would have uncontestable rights to enjoy her; furthermore I would have the right to force her to submit to my wishes if she, for whatever reason, might offer resistance.

Now, some persons may take a dim view of this attitude; some may feel that it debases womanhood. But I reply: what could be more debasing to womanhood than the present social standards which equate goodness with continence and virtue with the restraint of all natural impulses? And more debasing still, we men contrive to weaken women by seduction and then to punish them for yielding to our efforts!

Under my plan this double standard could not exist. I would insist that laws be passed permitting women to give themselves to as many men as they like as often as they see fit. Furthermore, in line with the law that men could compel women's cooperation, I would demand a law whereunder women likewise could compel men—insofar as anatomy and physiology permit.

Who could object to such a plan? What would be the
dangers? Fatherless children, perhaps? Small concern,
this. What does private parentage matter in a republic
where everyone born is the Motherland's child? And
how much more will children cherish their stately
Mother when, from birth, they have known none but
She?

What has just been said should eliminate the need of
discussing adultery, rape and incest. As concerns the
latter, we might note in passing that, as family ties are
loosened, the individual has that much more love to
lavish on his country; therefore incest, like other libertine exercises, should be encouraged, not discouraged.

Finally, let us consider the "moral" crime of sodomy.
To hear the priests talk, one would get the impression
that no crime is greater. After all, did its practice not
draw the fire of heaven upon the cities of Sodom and
Gomorrah? However, the dispassionate observer will
search for an earthly explanation of that holocaust —
perhaps a volcano — because there have been at least as
many "sins of Sodom" accomplished in France with no
perceptible ill effect.

More to the point, now that we have consigned all
biblical fables to the intellectual garbage heap, let us
examine the phenomenon of sodomy objectively. Such
an examination leads inescapably to the conclusion that
this activity is wholly indifferent, both in morality and
in legality. Certainly Nature cannot be offended by couplings involving persons of the same gender; She, who
places such little importance on semen that She permits
it to flow freely for all but perhaps ten or fifteen of a
man's years, can hardly object to our choice when we
direct its flow into this channel or that. Thus, to ban

sodomy is to condemn to death* that unhappy person whose only crime is his failure to share the majority's tastes.

In summary, then, it can be seen that there are no sexual activities which should be the concern of legislators: the free man's only sex laws will be Nature's own; his only limits will be the limits of his desires, his only brake the brake of his inclinations.

Finally in our consideration of man's crimes against his fellow man, we turn to murder. Of all such offences, this, naturally, is the greatest, for it deprives man of his life, which deprivation is, by its very nature, irreparable. However, putting aside for the moment the matter of the injury suffered by murder's victim, several questions arise:

1.) With respect to the laws of Nature alone, is this act an offence?

2.) With respect to the laws of politics alone, is it an offence?

3.) Does murder hurt society?

4.) Where does murder stand with respect to the principles of republicanism?

First, regarding the laws of Nature alone, let us stop deluding ourselves; while it may hurt man's pride to regard himself as something less than the most sublime of Nature's creatures, we, as philosophers, cannot permit ourselves to indulge in these nice human vanities. The simple fact is that man is worth no more to Nature than is any other animal. Does it cost Nature more to make a man than a fly? Than a giraffe? Than an elephant? What is to be the standard of measure? Surely the materials which go into the composition of each creature are the same — science has proved that. Then what can

* Under the *ancien regime* it was a capital offense.

be the cost? Energy? But Nature has boundless energy.
Then what?

Much as it may pain us to admit it, man has no greater
cost and man has no greater worth. Thus, from a purely
"natural" point of view, murder is no offense; indeed,
since Nature eventually brings about the death of all
Her creatures anyway, it might be argued that the murderer is actually doing Her work for Her! Can Nature
object to that?

"Well," it might be argued, "let Her do it if it's Her
work." But to this we may reply that the murderer is
only Nature's agent. It is Her impulse which he follows;
it is She who advises him to accomplish what, without
him, She might have to employ pestilence or plague to
bring about. Furthermore, it is Nature's voice which,
through man's impulses, suggests personal hatred, revenge, war and, in short, all other human causes of
death. If She incites us to murderous acts, does it follow
that She has a need for them?

Viewed in this manner, it can be seen that murder —
though we may oppose it for any number of other
reasons — is in no way contradictory to Nature; with respect to Her laws alone, it is no offence.

What then of political law? Is there an offence here?
The answer, which comes to us immediately, is that murder — speaking purely from a political point of view —
is just one more instrument in the power struggle. Indeed, where would France be now were it not for the
murders committed on her behalf?—and I speak here
not only of the murder of the monstrous monarch from
whom we have just gained freedom, but also of the murder, in war, of the soldiers of our enemies. Is it not a
strange blindness on our part to teach publicly the tech-

niques of warfare and to reward with medals those who prove to be the most adroit killers, then to punish the man who applies the same arts in the settlement of a private dispute?

Is murder, then, an offense against society? Again the answer comes to us immediately. What difference does it make to society if it have one member more or less? None whatsoever.

Finally, where does murder stand with respect to republicanism? As I have demonstrated earlier, a republic is invariably beset by enemies who seek to subjugate its citizens; to prevent this subjugation, it must go to war; war involves murder. Therefore, solely with respect to republicanism, a murderous spirit — a ferocity, if you will, a hardness — is not only desireable, it is essential, for, without it, the republic will soon fall.

Thus, object to murder though we may, we must admit that it violates neither the laws of Nature nor the laws of politics, that it in no way hurts society and that it is in no wise incompatible with the principles of republicanism. Moreover, if we look at the matter dispassionately, we will see that there are circumstances whereunder murder becomes almost a necessity. I shall elaborate.

In a monarchy, the king's wealth is measured by the number of his subjects; thus populousness is a desideratum and the birth rate is encouraged. (This explains the traditional stand against contraception by royalism's perpetual apologist, the Roman Catholic Church.) However, in a republic, where every member of the race is sovereign, it becomes necessary to erect a barrier against overpopulation; for, when population surpasses the means by which it can subsist, the State — and everyone in it — will suffer.

Now, if, for the State's splendor, we bestow upon soldiers the right to murder our enemies, we should also, for the State's welfare, accord each individual the right— in no way incompatible with Nature, politics, society or republicanism — to do away at birth with those of his children whom he knows he cannot feed. Too, we should make provision for the elimination of those who are born lacking the qualities to become useful someday to the State. Do we not prune the tree when it grows too many branches? Do we not remove those shoots which can be seen as weakening the trunk? I will concede that it may be unjust — and imprudent — to kill a well-formed and potentially valuable citizen; but it is both wise and proper to prevent the arrival in our society of a member who is congenitally incapable of contributing anything to it: the species must be purged from the cradle; all wounds must be cauterized; all creatures who can be foreseen to be liabilities instead of assets must be deprived of life at the very moment they receive it.

Finally, the citizen should be permitted — naturally at his own risk and jeopardy — to rid himself by murder of whatever persons he deems capable of harming him. "But what," you might ask, "will prevent men from murdering at will?" I answer you thusly: first, as republicans, we must take a positive view of our fellow citizens; we must regard them as rational beings who will not perpetrate evil without sufficient motivation: second, we must have faith in the most natural deterrent to murder, the fear of reprisal by vendetta; as Louis XV, in a rare moment of circumspection, said to a convicted murder, "I grant your pardon, but I also pardon whoever kills you." Moreover, the absence of strictures against murder, can be seen as having a salubrious effect on society as a whole; if a man knows that his misdeeds against his fellow man might be avenged by his own murder, and that the murder may operate with impunity, he will be less apt to perpetrate misdeeds against his fellow man.

In summary, murder is a horror but a necessary one: in some instances, it should be encouraged for the benefit of society as a whole; in others, it should be discouraged: but in no case should it be deemed a crime. And lastly, as a means of motivating citizens to seek peaceful solutions to their personal problems, the State should at once do away with all public murders — warfare (except in defense against enemy aggression on French soil), murder by the police in attempting to apprehend a suspect and, especially, capital punishment.

It is this last institution — murder as punishment for murder — which perhaps is most offensive to a republican's sensibilities. Can there be any greater affront to reason than the putting to death of one man for his having put to death another? If it is the loss of the first life which we bemoan, by what arithmetic do we attempt to repair it with the taking of a second? Either murder is or is not a crime: if it is not, why penalize it; if it is, by what tortuous logic do we claim justice in the duplication of the very crime which we seek to punish?!

* * *

Thus are some reflections on the matter of law. Our ancestors, seduced by religion, browbeaten by tyrant kings, viewed a great many activities as criminal; we, freed from the shackles of both monarch and priest, can consign their blindfold to the same garbage heap where now rests our despot's headless corpse.

Frenchmen, we are in the process of being reborn. Soon the world will see the sublime heights to which French genius and character can soar. But the battle is not quite won; the victory — and the Republic — are not quite secured. Another effort is necessary.

My countrymen, we must maintain — at the cost of our fortunes and even our lives — the liberty which has already claimed so many victims. Upon their noble triumphs we must seat just laws. Let them be few, and let them be good; but, above all, let them be gentle, like the people they will serve. And, Frenchmen: let the laws always serve the people, never the people serve the laws.

Soon the enemy will be driven across the Rhine. Then let not your zeal to share your principles entice you beyond your borders. Stay at home: restore your industries, revive your commerce, breathe new life into your arts and culture. Let the thrones of Europe decay of their own inertia; you need contribute naught to their erosion but your example. Unified within, impenetrable from without, your laws and your government a model to every race, you will set the standard for the world. Not one nation will fail to emulate you; not one can help but take pride in your alliance.

Yet another effort, Frenchmen, before you call yourselves republicans — and your Republic will live forever in the minds and hearts of all free men

V. (cont'd) SAINT-ANGE, EUGENIE, DOLMANCE, THE HORSEMAN and AUGUSTIN

Scene: Saint-Ange's bedroom. Curtain opens as all cheer Horseman's reading.

ALL *(except Horseman):* Bravo! Bravo, Horseman! Well-spoken! Bravo!

SAINT-ANGE: A well-composed document, that; lucid; clear; straight to the point . . .

EUGENIE: Indeed. And it seems to me very closely in agreement with the theories of Dolmancé — so much so that I wouldn't be surprised to learn that he was the author.

DOLMANCE: Well, my thinking does correspond to some extent with these reflections; my speeches here this afternoon tend to confirm that, even to the point of lending to the reading somewhat of a repetitive flavor.

SAINT-ANGE: Well, no harm done. Wise and good words can not too often be repeated.

DOLMANCE: How right you are. Nor, now that I

think of it, can wise and good deeds — like fucking, to quote a handy example.

EUGENIE: Ah, Dolmance! Would you really like to fuck me again so soon?

DOLMANCE: Not you, chit. No offense meant, but it's Augustin I'm thinking about. It's astonishing how the lad's splendid ass strayed on my mind all through the reading; indeed, each of Horseman's superbly-elocuted phrases seemed to relate themselves to it . . .

HORSEMAN: Perhaps because of my pear-shaped tones . . .

DOLMANCE: *(Ignoring this witticism.)* Well, come over here, Augustin, you loveable lout. What are you waiting for? . . .

SAINT-ANTE: Would you believe it? The simp is asleep.

DOLMANCE: By Lucifer! So much for Horseman's pear-shaped tones . . . *(Stirring Augustin.)* Wake up, my great fucking-john. It's time to put that incomparable talent of yours back to work.

AUGUSTIN: *(Rubbing sleep from his eyes.)* What's the matter? What's happening?

DOLMANCE: Don't worry about a thing, my sweet. I just wish to fuck you. Come, stand here in front of me as I sit on the bed . . . That's it! My, what blessed buttocks! How white and firm! . . . Now Eugénie get on your knees before him child and take a mouthful of cock. If you hurry, you can get him while it's still soft. Then you'll enjoy the pleasure of feeling it spring to life in your mouth . . . Now Horseman: get on your knees behind her and sink your dick into her lovely ass . . .

HORSEMAN: I'd prefer her lovely cunt . . .

DOLMANCE: As you choose, then. One's as easy as the other in that position. Go to it. Let me hear the sweet crackle of sex-juice as you make your entry . . . Splen-did, splendid . . . Now Saint-Ange: take a whip in your hand and climb on Augustin's back. In this position, your ass will be before me as I fuck Augustin and, who knows, I might decide to give you a little kiss. Meanwhile, reach across Eugénie and use your whip on the Horse-man. With a little stimulation from you he might be in-spired to work his banana a little extra-vigorously . . . That's it. We're all set now. Let's get to it . . . Do your best, my friends. Libertinage demands effort . . . My, Augustin, you've acquired something of a tight ass-hole all of a sudden. It must have been your nap. Well, I think we can pry it open . . . There, see how smoothly we enter once the initial penetration has been made . . . Now Saint-Ange: since your ass is so conveniently in my face, would you mind if I bite and pinch your flesh while I sodomize the great fucking-john here . . .

SAINT-ANGE: Be my guest — but don't be surprised if you get a fart or two in the mouth while you're at it . . .

DOLMANCE: By Saint Veronica's vulva! Would you really?! I'll bet you can't . . . *(She obliges him.)* Ah, de-licious! If I bite you may I have another?

SAINT-ANGE: Try and see.

DOLMANCE: Ahhhh! *(He bites and is duly rewarded.)* Oh, fuck, what force she has! And what a report! And what aroma, Madame! No one could ask for any sweeter!

SAINT-ANGE: *(Coquettishly.)* Perhaps if you bite harder you'll get sweeter still.

DOLMANCE: Well, let's see. *(He bites with immense force and the reward is commensurate.)* Ah, by all the snatch-scratching angels and saints! There's not a fart-smeller on all six continents who wouldn't remember that one for the rest of his life! Tell me, Madame, what have you been eating today?

SAINT-ANGE: I never give away trade secrets, my friend.

DOLMANCE: Well, no matter. Here's a slap for you. Let's see what kind of reward that brings me. *(He slaps, she responds.)* A bit tame; so was the stimulus. But I hope you're not running out of wind, my angel. I'd like you to save a big gust for the crucial moment.

HORSEMAN: You'd better hurry if you want your moment to coincide with mine. This lovely cunt of Eugénie's has really got me going . . .

DOLMANCE: Yes, the moment approaches now . . . Ah, Madame use your talent . . . I come! . . . *(He bites and strikes her; she rewards him beyond his fondest expectations.)* Ahh, fuck-fart! What pleasure! What joy!

HORSEMAN: I come, too, fuck-friends! Ah, Eugénie, my snatch! Ah, my sweet-snatched little fuck-face!

AUGUSTIN: Me too; Jesus, can she suck!

DOLMANCE, HORSEMAN and AUGUSTIN: Ahhhhhhhhhhh, *fuck!!!!*

EUGENIE: *(Rising from her knees and emitting semen simultaneously from both orifices into which deposits have been made.)* Oh, Dolmancé — see how your apostles have taken care of me?! I'm overflowing at both ends!

DOLMANCE: *(Scampering to a position behind her.)* Keep a tight asshole for a moment, chit; I want some of that . . . Ah, there we go. *(He applies his mouth to her anus.)* You can let it fly now . . .

EUGENIE: *(Complying with his request.)* What debauchery! It's delightful!

DOLMANCE: *(Swallowing.)* There's nothing that can compare with a good shot of jism drained from a pretty girl's ass. It's food for the gods. *(He swallows another mouthful, then bends once more to the task.)* . . . There! I'd say that pretty neatly cleans you out. Right? *(Crawls *on his knees to Augustin, from whose anus he drains his own semen.)* Well, Horseman, the twain meet; who knows but that if my stomach were a womb it would be readying itself to nurture your and my offspring as brothers.

HORSEMAN: In view of the path they took, I think we could safely say they'd be pretty shitty children.

AUGUSTIN: What did he mean by that, Dolmancé?

DOLMANCE: Never mind, my great fucking-john. We've got further enterprises to occupy our time. *(To the others.)* My friends, if you will excuse this big-pricked simp and me for a few minutes, we would like to adjourn to a nearby room to spend some time alone.

SAINT-ANGE: But can't you do here whatever it is that you'd like to do with him?

DOLMANCE: No, Madame; there are some projects sufficiently delicate that they must be veiled even from libertine eyes like yours.

EUGENIE: Don't keep any secrets from your pupil, Dolmancé. What is it you're going to do?

SAINT-ANGE: If you don't tell us, we won't let you go.

DOLMANCE: *(Dragging Augustin.)* No, Madame, I really can't say it.

SAINT-ANGE: Do you really think there's an enterprise too sophisticated for us to see?

HORSEMAN: Wait sister. I'll tell you. *(He whispers to Saint-Ange and Eugenie.)*

EUGENIE: *(Clutching her stomach as if about to vomit.)* You're right; it's revolting.

SAINT-ANGE: Well . . . almost revolting.

DOLMANCE: Then you can understand my need for privacy.

EUGENIE: By all means. But, if you like, I'll come

along and frig you while you're doing it.

DOLMANCE: No, child. There are times when a man cannot be too much alone. *(He exits, taking Augustin with him.)*

VI. SAINT-ANGE, EUGENIE and THE HORSEMAN

(Curtain.)

Scene: *The same; seconds later.*

SAINT-ANGE: Ah, brother, your friend Dolmancé, is every bit the rogue you said he was.

HORSEMAN: You like him, then?

EUGENIE: One can't help but like him!

(A bell rings.)

HORSEMAN: My word — who could that be?

SAINT-ANGE: I gave strict instructions that we were not to be disturbed.

EUGENIE: Oh, mercy! We'll be discovered! *(Begins crying.)*

HORSEMAN: Soft, child. I'll see who it is. *(Exits, returns carrying letter.)* A message for you, dear sister.

SAIT-ANGE: *(Examining it.)* What's this? Eugénie — it's from your father!

EUGENIE: Oh! All is lost(

HORSEMAN: Don't get upset. It may be nothing. Saint-Ange, read it aloud.

SAINT-ANGE: *(Reading.)* "My Dear Saint-Ange: Incredible as it may seem, my wife has become alarmed about Eugénie's visit to your home and is leaving immediately with the intention of bringing her back here. I urge you: under no circumstances release my daughter to this abominable woman. Do whatever you will to prevent it. I will support you all the way."

HORSEMAN: Well, that's not too bad, is it?

EUGENIE: *Bad?!* Why it's a godsend! Having been inspired by your brilliant discourses on freedom, my friends I know just how I plan to take care of the old whore!

SAINT-ANGE: Do I hear you correctly, Eugénie?

EUGENIE: Indeed you do, my love. Indeed you do.

SAINT-ANGE: Oh, how proud Dolmancé would be of. you!

(Enter Dolmance with Augustin.) *

DOLMANCE: I certainly am! If you will excuse my eavesdropping, Madame, I just happened to be outside the door and could not help but overhear. The arrival of Madame de Mistival could not be better timed. You're fully prepared, Eugénie, to put our principles into action?

EUGENIE: More than prepared, my love — eager! May I be struck with lightning if I weaken in my resolve! Friends, leave the execution to me!

SAINT-ANGE: *(Cups ear with hand.)* Lo! I hear sounds. Can it be she? . . . Faith, Eugénie; courage! And remember our principles . . .

(Curtain.)

* The nature of their enterprise outside the room is never revealed by Sade.

VII. THE ENTIRE COMPANY

Scene. The same. Enter Madame de Mistival.

MISTIVAL: *(To Saint-Ange.)* I beg your pardon, Madame, for arriving unannounced. However, I am given to understand that my daughter is with you. Due to her age I do not permit her to venture afoot unescorted; therefore, I trust you won't mind returning her to me at once.

SAINT-ANGE: *(Haughtily.)* Your manners, Madame, are inexcusable. Why, judging from your comments, one would think you disapproved of the company . . .

MISTIVAL: Madame, I find my daughter in a bedroom with another woman and three other men, all of whom are stark naked. I leave it to you to decide whether or not I approve.

DOLMANCE: Madame de Mistival, if you will excuse my saying so, I find your manner unduly abrupt. I shan't conceal from you the fact that, if I were Madame Saint-Ange, you would be this time have a shoe up your ass.

MISTIVAL: A shoe up my.................! Sir, I· advise you that I am not the type of woman who receives shoes up ....er ,that is, I am not the type to be addressed in so vulgar a fashion . . . Eugénie, I have seen all I care to see; put on your clothes and follow me at once.

EUGENIE: My apologies, Madame, but I cannot accede to your request.

MISTIVAL: How's that?! My daughter disobeys me?!

DOLMANCE: By God's cock and balls! She not only disobeys you, Madame; she does so with bold defiance! *(Sarcastically.)* I would not tolerate it if I were you. Would you like me to have some whips brought in so that you may mete out the punishment this incorrigible chilld deserves?

EUGENIE: If whips were brought, I fear they would be employed not *by* but *upon* Madame de Mistival.

MISTIVAL: Why you little snip! *(Reaches for Eugénie.)*

DOLMANCE: Not so fast, Madame. *(Intercepts her.)* We'll have no indelicacies here. We may dress like rogues — or undress like them, as the case may be — but we won't tolerate roguish manners.

MISTIVAL: Do you interfere, sir, with a mother's exercise of her natural rights over her daughter?

DOLMANCE: Rights, Madame? Do I hear you speak of rights? And by what authority do you claim them? When your husband, or whoever it was, deposited in your nasty snatch the jism which ultimately emerged as your daughter, were you thinking of her future or your own pleasure? I dare say the latter. For what, then, do you expect her to be obligated to you today? The fact that you let someone fuck you? Whores let people fuck them twenty and thirty times a day; by your logic should she not feel twenty or thirty times as obligated to them?

MISTIVAL: But I lavished care upon her! I gave her an education!

DOLMANCE: Did you really? Well, let's examine these claims. As to the care, if I am not mistaken, it was required of you by law — to say nothing of vanity and custom as well. In any event, you chose to do it and she did not ask you to, so she owes you nothing. As for the education, you did a frightfully poor job. It's taken the four of us all day to replace the execrable principles with which you stuffed her poor little head. You taught her, for example, that there is a God who is all good—a gross lie if I heard one. Then you taught her that Jesus Christ was his only-begotten son — a blatant falsehood if ever one was perpetrated. Then you taught her that it was evil to fuck — but, as she learned this afternoon, it's the sweetest thing in all the world. Care and education, you say? And for this she should be grateful? Madame, on the basis of what I've seen, she owes you nothing but scorn.

MISTIVAL: Good Lord in Heaven! My child has been captured by madmen! . . . Oh, Eugénie; my darling Eugénie; listen to the pleas of the woman who gave you your life; tear yourself from this perfidious company and come with me. *(She drops to her knees.)* Please, child; it is in the posture of a supplicant that I address you . . .

DOLMANCE: Lovely scene, Madame. You've quite the knack for tears ... Eugénie, you've heard your mother's supplications. She awaits your reply.

EUGENIE: *(Naked, as the reader may recall.)* You are on your knees, Madame? Splendid; then you needn't bend to kiss my ass. *(Backs toward her, buttocks proferred.)* Here it is, Madame. Put your lips to it and suck — I've a mouthful of shit waiting for you ... How's that for style, Dolmancé? Does your pupil do you proud?

DOLMANCE: Bravo, my beauty; bravo.

MISTIVAL: *(Turning away in horror.)* Witch! I disown you forever! You cease to be my child!

DOLMANCE: Hold, Madame! I say: hold! There's offense in these words!

EUGENIE: Let her add a few epithets to it, Dolmancé. Let this scummy cock-sucker damn herself all the farther.

DOLMANCE: Softly, child. The matter is now in my hands. *(To Mistival, with mock solemnity.)* Madame, having just disowned your child, you raise an interesting legal question: by what right — seeing as you are no longer her mother — do you insinuate your loathesome presence upon the company of several citizens gathered in the sacred confines of a private home? There's a trespass here, and it must be punished. Have the kindness to remove your clothing so as not to impede the blows which your rashness has called to be brought upon you.

MISTIVAL: *(Apalled.)* Denude myself, do you say?!

DOLMANCE: To the hair of your cunny-cun-cunt!

SAINT-ANGE: Augustin, my lout, since the lady resists, have the goodness to assist her ... *(He complies, brutally ripping her dress from her back.)*

MISTIVAL: Good Heavens! *(To Saint-Ange.)* Are you aware, Madame, of the law on these matters? It is your house in which I am being attacked. Do you think I'll fail to complain to the police?

SAINT-ANGE: It is not at all certain, Madame, that you will have the ability to complain.

MISTIVAL: Nothing short of death with stop me.

DOLMANCE: *(Bowing.)* Then you pronounce your own sentence, Madame.

MISTIVAL: Oh, my God —

DOLMANCE: We don't allow that word around here except when it's used blasphemously. Would you care to make a retraction?

MISTIVAL: Oh . . .

SAINT-ANGE: Excuse me, Dolmancé, but, before Augustin exposes the rest of this woman's body to your eyes, let me warn you what to expect. Little Eugénie has just advised me that Mister de Mistival yesterday used a whip on our lovely prisoner. Her beauty may be marred accordingly.

DOLMANCE: Not in my eyes, Madame; to me few things are as attractive as a wound. *(To Augustin.)* Finish stripping her, lad. There's a chance our pleasures may be greater than we dared expect. *(Mistival is stripped.)* Good Satan, the man wields quite a whip! Look at this body! I've never encountered one more throughly lashed — not only behind, but also in front. I'd venture that there's not a surface which escaped the man's fury . . .*(Eyes suddenly ablaze.)* Furthermore, I see a lovely ass here! Ah, Eugénie, now I know where you get those luscious melons from . . . *(He drops to his knees and begins kissing and fondling the object of his affections.)*

MISTIVAL: Unhand me, you knave!

SAINT-ANGE: *(Slaps her violently across the face.)* Keep that mouth of yours shut, Madame, until we tell you to open it. You're our prisoner now. You could scream at the top of your lungs, but no one would hear you outside this thick-walled chamber. Further, your servants and horses have been sent away, and your husband knows — and approves of — what we are doing. So your only hope lies in our mercy, and it's a very slim hope at that . . .

DOLMANCE: *(Still fondling and slapping her buttocks.)* To be forewarned is to be forearmed, Madame. I trust it puts you more at ease to realize precisely the nature of the peril in which you find yourself. Perhaps you should thank Saint-Ange for her candor.

MISTIVAL: *(Sputtering.)* W-w-why . . .

DOLMANCE: *(Shoving his thumb viciously up her vagina.)* Thank her, damn you! I've had enough of your insolence for one day!

MISTIVAL: Aiiiiiiieeeeeeee. *(Gasps.)* Oh, thank you, Madame. Thank you. Thank you.

DOLMANCE: Much better. *Much*, much better. All of which goes to show that there's nothing like a poke in the cunt when you want to get something done . . . Now Eugénie: come here and place your ass alongside your mother's. I'd like to compare them . . . *(Eugénie obeys.)* . . . By Christ's come! You'd think they both were poured from the same mold! How I'd love to plunge a steaming prick into each of them — and perhaps I shall. Augustin, my fine lad; get a grip on this lovely creature so that she can't resist my thrust . . .

AUGUSTIN: *(He complies.)* Got her, Dolmancé.

DOLMANCE: Now, then: brace yourself, Madame; I've the smallest cock in the present company, but it's rent many an intestine in its day . . . *(Embuggers her.)* By Saint Peter's prick! What a smooth entry! Madame, I'll venture that it's not been long since this channel last was navigated — and by a vessel with dimensions considerably superior to mine . . .

SAINT-ANGE: That would be her husband, Dolmancé. He carries a hefty hunk of meat on him . . .

DOLMANCE: Ah, yes. Well, it's of no importance. I wanted only to get the wick wet, so to speak; only to prime the pump. Eugénie: give me your ass, child . . . That's it . . . Ahhh, a much tighter fit. Water seeks its own level, as the saying goes . . . Wriggle your hips, child. Wriggle and writhe . . . There we go! Capital squeeze you've got there; capital.

SAINT-ANGE: If you'll forgive me saying so, Dolmancé. I'm beginning to feel rather left out of the proceedings.

DOLMANCE: Ah, yes, Madame. How true . . . Well, let's put our store in order. *(Withdraws from Eugénie.)* I think we can devise some form of amusement wherein all can take a hand . . . Let's see, now. Suppose we introduce Madame de Mistival to a chain-fuck . . . Saint-Ange and Eugénie: have the kindness to equip yourselves with dildoes — the largest you can find. *(They comply.)* Now fuck our guest, one in the cunt, the other in the ass . . . There you go. But deliver lusty strokes, Saint-Ange. There's no room here for timorousness. Emulate your pupil; see the zest with which she carries out the endeavor ... Now, Horseman and Augustin, line up behind the ladies. Work some energy into your loins. Stiff dicks are called for in this venture ... Gad, Augustin! How can you do it, my great fucking-john? Up like a rod with merely a touch! Splendid! Splendid! ... Now, as the mood strikes you, each of you may relieve one of the ladies. Then, as the mood strikes them, they may relieve you, and so on, in rotation. Meanwhile, the idle parties may inflict upon the victim whatever tortures they fancy. We've plenty of whips here, plenty of canes ... Ah, Augustin, you relieve Saint-Ange at the ass so soon? Well the good Madame de Mistival has quite a shock in store for her. Thrust, great cock; thrust; she'll learn what it's like to have a real prick.

MISTIVAL: Good Heavens! I'm being ripped apart!

DOLMANCE: Ah, yes, Madame. Let that be a lesson to you. Never take pride in a wide asshole; there's always a bigger cock somewhere or other ... Okay, Augustin, let's not overdo it. We don't want this old crone to croak before we extract the full measure of Eugénie's vengeance. Climb out of the saddle and let me tickle her with my humble twig for awhile ... Ah, Madame. You feel the difference, I trust. I can barely touch two sides of the sphincter at once ... Eugénie, let Horseman have her cunt awhile and you come over here by me. I must ream your ass to console myself for suffering immersion in your mother's ... You too, Saint-Ange: let me finger yours while I ream Eugénie's. I wish to be surrounded with a wall of asses ... Now, Madame de Mistival: brace yourself for another shock. I have in my hand a pair of pliers which just happened to have been lying on the floor. Can you guess what I'm going to do with them? I'm going to grip in their jaws the flesh of your thighs; then I'm going to twist until I've torn out a chunk of meat large enough to chew on. Does that excite you, my dove? *(He rips out a chunk.)*

MISTIVAL: Aiiiiieeeeeee! *AIIIIIIIEEEEEEEEEEEE!!*

EUGENIE: My admiration for you, Dolmancé, is boundless. Such coordination! To fuck one ass, ream a second, fondle a third and all the while manipulate the pliers — I trust you'd be quite the pianist if you put your mind to it.

DOLMANCE: This is the only piano upon which I wish to play, chit. *(Thrusts tongue into her anus.)* .. . . Now, Madame: another turn of the pliers for you . . .

MISTIVAL: Aiieeeee! Oh, Good God in Heaven!

DOLMANCE: Call upon him, my dear — but don't be surprised if he ignores you like he ignores everyone else. After all, he fails to intercede in wars and plagues; so do you think he'll trouble himself over one insignificant woman — and a rather sloppy-assed one at that!?

MISTIVAL: Aiiieee! Aiiieeee!

DOLMANCE: You scream, whore, and the sound of your voice plummets to the core of my cock. Ah, what pleasures! Who can fathom the human mind? Why does your suffering so please me? The questions must await the answer of a wiser man. I know only that my joy is exquisite . . . Ah, I come! I'd strangle you, Madame, were it not that I wish to leave the lovely task to other hands . . . Oh, Satan! What a jolt I'm getting this time! I swear, Madame, I'm giving you a liter of jism! Ahhhhhhhhh, FUCK!!! . . . It's done, Saint-Ange. I vacate the premises. She's yours . . .

(Saint-Ange, with a dildo strapped around her waist,

*embuggers Mistival while at the same time encunt-
ing her with a second, hand-held device. Meanwhile,
Eugénie takes the pliers and continues to tear chunks
of flesh from her mother's legs. When Saint-Ange is
finished, Horseman steps in, embuggering the victim while simultaneously punching both her ears
with his fists. He is followed by Augustin, who, while
embuggering the woman, sinks a finger into one of
her eyes and a thumb up one of her nostrils, after
accomplishing which he twists his hand until the eye
is disgorged and the nostril split open. During
these proceedings, Dolmancé reams the ani of each
of the torturers.)*

EUGÉNIE: Dolmancé, Augustin now vacates the saddle. Shall I replace him?

DOLMANCE: By all means, chit. The honor is yours.

EUGÉNIE: *(Stepping to the task — with two dildoes,
in the manner earlier demonstrated by Saint-Ange.)* Well,
my lovely mamma, how does it feel to have your daughter serve you as a husband? Strange, one would think;
but you'll get used to it . . . Why mother: you're crying!
Does it hurt you? Ah, too bad. It doesn't hurt me at all.
I love fucking you. Dolmancé, can you work up a stiff
dick again? I'd like you to sodomize me while I'm about
these proceedings . . . Ah, splendid; I feel your shaft . . .
Behold, — my friends! At one stroke I'm an adultress, a
fornicator, a lesbian, a sodomite — and I commit incest, to
boot! All this from a girl who lost her maidenhead only
a few hours ago! What progress! . . . Mother! Good
mother! Can I believe my eyes? I think you're — yes she
is! Dolmance, look at her: she's coming!

DOLMANCE: By Lucifer, yes! It shows in her eyes.

EUGENIE: Quick! Give me the pliers! *(Begins wrenching flesh from her mother's breasts while still embuggering her.)* Ah, fuck, momma! I fuck you! Fuck, I say! Dolmancé, I'm coming too! Ah, sweet jism of the ass-fucking Jesus! I'm dying! Ahhhhh, FUCK!! *(As she attains orgasm, Eugénie tears from her mother's breast a chunk of flesh the size of her fist.)*

MISTIVAL: Have pity, my captors — I think I'm going to faint . . . *(She falls to the floor.)*

DOLMANCE: Now we begin in earnest, — friends! There's nothing quite so pleasing to the senses as to work outrages upon an unconscious body . . . Eugénie, stretch out on top of your mother. Now you, Horseman: fuck the lovely little girl. Meanwhile, Saint-Ange can reach under and finger her asshole and Eugénie can jerk off Augustin and me . . . I'll venture, child, that your mother never guessed that her body would serve as a bed for such lubricious couplings . . .

EUGENIE: I'm sure of it.

HORSEMAN: But Dolmancé, I must protest these outrages. What we are doing violates every tenet of Nature.

DOLMANCE: You betray your lack of sophistication, my young friend. What we are doing is *heeding* the voice of Nature.

(The project is executed. All rise.)

HORSEMAN: The lady doesn't move, Dolmancé. I think she's dead.

DOLMANCE: Dead?! I should say not! Just asleep — but she won't be for long. Whips! Someone hand me a few whips! We'll flog her awake! . . . *(Saint-Ange hands him whips; he begins.)* Meanwhile, Augustin, run into the garden and fetch me some thorns. Stronger tortures are called for now ...

HORSEMAN: She still doesn't move, Dolmancé I fear we've killed her.

EUGENIE: Oh, fuck! Now I'll have to wear black all summer, and I just bought the prettiest red dress ...

SAINT-ANGE: *(Bursting into laughter.)* How droll, my child! I love you! *(She tongues Eugénie's vagina.)*

DOLMANCE: *(Taking thorns from Augustin.)* We'll see if she's dead! *(Begins pressing thorns into Mistival's head.)* Come, Eugénie; suck my prick while I'm at this task. And Augustin: wield a whip, boy; tear into my back; nothing pleases me more than receiving pain while I inflict it ... Now, Horseman, since you've nothing better to do, suppose you fuck Saint-Ange; assume a position which will permit me to ream your ass while you're doing it.

HORSEMAN: My friend, is there no way I can talk you out of this evil?

DOLMANCE: I'm afraid not.

HORSEMAN: Then I suppose I might as well comply. Come, sister; let's be about our task ...

(The project is executed. As they perform, Mistival stirs.)

DOLMANCE: There, my friends. Do you see? The treatment is working. She's revived.

MISTIVAL: You scoundrels. *(She opens her eyes.)* You summon me back from the grave. Why couldn't you let me die in peace?

DOLMANCE: *(Still whipping her and sticking her with thorns.)* We arouse you, Madame, so that you may get to know something of the libertine life before you pass on. It so happens that my valet, Lapierre, who waits outside in my coach, has one of the most horrible cases of syphillis known to medical science. I'm going to have him fuck you in both the ass and the cunt, after which you will be turned loose. For the rest of your life, then, the germs of this dreaded disease will gnaw at yourinsides and will serve as a reminder not to interfere when your daughter goes out to get herself fucked. *(All applaud his ingenuity. The valet is summoned.)* Lapierre, fuck this woman.

LAPIERRE: Now, sir? In front of everyone?

DOLMANCE: Why not.

LAFIERRE: As you say, sir. *(Exhibits his penis.)* Madame, would you be so kind as to ready yourself?

MISTIVAL: Oh, what a fate!

EUGENIE: It's better than dying, mamma. Besides, now I won't have to dress in black all summer.

DOLMANCE: That's the way to lunge, Lapierre. You impale her like an old pro . . . Well, friends, there's no reason why we shouldn't amuse ourselves while this lad goes about his business of infecting her. Let's take whips and flog each other. Saint-Ange, you flog Lapierre; it will add to the force of his ejaculation and we'll be sure that the syphillitic sperm makes its way to the very top of her cunt. Meanwhile, I'll flay you, while Eugénie flagellates me and Augustin whips her and Horseman beats him. *(It is arranged.)*

LAPIERRE: *(Accelerating his movements.)* I come, master . . . Ahhhhhhh, FUCK!

DOLMANCE: Okay. Turn her over now and give her another shot up the ass. *(The project is accomplished.)* Very well done, my lad; now tuck that germ-infested snake back into your trousers and return to the coach. As for you, Madame de Mistival, you've contributed enough to our amusement for the day. You are free to leave —

EUGENE: Hold, Dolmancé! What of the poison inside her? Do we dare risk letting it escape?

DOLMANCE: An impossibility, chit.

EUGENIE: I protest, sir, that it is quite possible. She may shit and piss it out. We cannot take the chance.

DOLMANCE: *(Detecting mischievous gleam in her eye.)* Then what do you suggest, my child?

EUGENIE: We must sew up both holes. Saint-Ange, have you needle and thread?

SAINT-ANGE: Aye; I'll fetch them.

DOLMANCE: Capital suggestion, chit! Marvelous imagination you display!

EUGENIE: *(Taking from Saint-Ange an enormous needle and a length of heavy red waxed thread.)* Open your legs, mamma. Your daughter will serve as your surgeon. *(She sews.)*

MISTIVAL: Oh, the pain!

EUGENIE: *(Thrusting the needle experimentally into the stomach, thighs, mound and vulva.)* Don't mind this mother. I'm just testing the point.

DOLMANCE: Saint-Ange, come and frig we while I watch this. Your lovely pupil shows a viciousness which excites me beyond belief . . . Wonderful job, Eugéne!

You're a born seamstress! But make sure that you don't leave too much space between the needle-holes . . .

EUGENIE: Less advice, Dolmancé, and more action. Come here and finger my cunt while I'm about my labors.

DOLMANCE: Ah, what a vixen! Darling child, you're exciting enough to make me give up boys . . .

EUGENIE: You need give up nothing, my friend. There's ample room in your life for both sexes . . . But do you have only one hand, my friend? Then why are you fingering only my cunt? There's an asshole in close proximity. Have the goodness to frig it also.

DOLMANCE: By Mary Magdalen's mound, how this child excites me! Ah, fuck, child! Fuck, I say to you! Fuck-fuck!

EUGENIE: Well, mother I think the job is done! See how nice and tight I've sewed that cunt of yours?

MISTIVAL: You succubus! I regret the day you were born.

EUGENIE: Softly, Madame; softly. There's rancor in that statement and I resent it . . . Now turn over; I wish to sew up your ass.

DOLMANCE: Oh, let me do it, darling girl! How excited you've made me! *(He takes the needle and sews.)* I'm going to make mincemeat out of your buttocks, Madame . . . Eugénie, play with my cock while I'm about this project . . .

EUGENIE: Only on the condition, sir, that you stitch her more energetically. You're displaying a gentleness which is not at all like you.

DOLMANCE: As you say, my chit. As you say, you daring fuck-face little ass-cunt.

EUGENIE: Ah, good motion! You're carving her like a piece of meat!

DOLMANCE: Yes, but you're forgetting your lessons. You just covered the head of my prick.

EUGENIE: Well, live and learn. Is this any better?

DOLMANCE: Much. Oh, sweet ass-fucking God, I'm dying of pleasure! How stiff my prick becomes! Augustin and Horseman: fuck Saint-Ange while I watch you, one up the ass, the other in the cunt. That's it, arrange yourselves before me. I wish to see asses, nothing but asses . . . (As this posture is arranged, he plunges his needle more viciously than ever.) Here, Madame; take this! And this! And this!

MISTIVAL: Oh, sir, the pain . . .

DOLMANCE: (Insane with ectasy.) Yes, tell me about it. Hearing your recital will but add to my pleasures . . . Ah, I haven't had a dick this stiff in years. Go down on it, Eugénie. I'm going to give you a mouthful of jism.

SAINT-ANGE: Ah, friends — I'm coming . . .

AUGUSTIN: Me, too.

HORSEMAN: And I.

DOLMANCE: (stabbing Mistival with the needle more wildly than ever.) We come in concert, my friends.

TOGETHER: Ah-fuck. Oh-fuck. Ahhhhhhh, FUCK!!

(The position is dissolved.)

DOLMANCE: Well, my friends, this was a fitting climax to our afternoon. As for you, Madame de Mistival, you may put on your clothes and leave whenever you like. Go without rancor, for we have acted not out of malice but because of Nature's urgings. And take the memory of this afternoon with you wherever you go, for, if you ever interfere again in your daughter's activities, there will be a repeat performance. *(He kisses her hand.)* I bid you good day, Madame — and, so that there can be no possible misunderstanding, I repeat a sentiment voiced earlier: your daughter is old enough to be her own boss; she likes to fuck; she loves to fuck; she was born to fuck and she's going to fuck until she dies; don't try to stop her . . . Now Horseman: have the kindness to escort Madame de Mistival to her coach.

(Horseman and Mistival exit.)

EUGENIE: Ah fuck, what an afternoon! My friends, I'm indebted to you for the rest of my life.

SAINT-ANGE: Our pleasure, my love; our pleasure.

DOLMANCE: Our pleasure, indeed! And now, my friends, let us go to dinner. These proceedings have given me quite the appetite. After dinner, all four of us may retire in the same bed and resume the wonderful friendship which was begun this afternoon . . .

—DONATIEN ALPHONSE FRANCOIS DE SADE

Paris: 1795

THE END

"With this superb and indeed unique edition by Dr. Gillette, it is now possible to consider seriously de Sade's works in the most up-to-date English terminology and to form whatever conclusions one may wish about them, not from secondary sources but from first-hand acquaintance with the material itself... in the style and flavor of the original... Having met the requirements of both accuracy and modernity, this edition fills a need and makes it possible to read the works of de Sade in English much more intelligently than ever before... I can honestly say that this is the first time that I have felt that de Sade's style, flavor in writing, and, through these, de Sade's philosophy, have come through well in an English rendering of the original French text."

– PROF. CARL D. MUNSELLE,

Modern Languages
CAPITAL UNIVERSITY

VOLUME II

The Complete Marquis de Sade

Translated From
The Original French Text By
Dr. Paul J. Gillette

With An Introduction By
John S. Yankowski

An Original Holloway House Edition
HOLLOWAY HOUSE PUBLISHING CO.
LOS ANGELES, CALIFORNIA

To:
George G. Hornbeck
. . . a distinguished scholar,
an esteemed friend

Table of Contents

Volume II

JULIETTE, OR VICE AMPLY REWARDED
BOOK ONE

I

We were brought up — my sister Justine and I — at Pan-themont, that celebrated convent through whose portals have passed some of the prettiest and most immoral young ladies in France. It was a den of depravity, that place; a deliciously obscene sewer of iniquity; and, while Justine, for her part, might have been immune to its lures, I, in all candor, was not.

Perhaps, as you encountered me on the pages of Justine's book, you were rather surprised to find a girl of my few years entertaining moral precepts of the sort enumerated; no doubt you wondered how the seeds of vice were planted in my soul; who nurtured them, and how they grew and blossomed into unbridled licentiousness and voluptuousness. On the pages which follow I shall attempt to tell you.

Of course, as was the case in Justine's book, it will be necessary here to portray the most heinous debaucheries; the most lascivious and involuted carnal indulgences: Good, as has been pointed out, is capable of being appreciated fully only when viewed alongside Evil. However, I shall not apologize for my behavior; I have never done anything for which I am ashamed, and, though my acts may have been Evil — at least, by your standards (which, as you shall see shortly, differ considerably from mine) — these acts brought me great pleasure, and pleasure is the only reward I have ever sought: thus, I have no regrets.

Now, without further ado, here is my story . . .

II

My introduction to the world of lubricity came quite early in life. Endowed with a precocity which I have been told is all but unique, I experienced the awakening of lustful desires at the tender age of seven and by the age of nine had learned to bring about with my fingers relief of the sort which I would later derive in considerably greater measure from the ministrations of men and of other women.

Not surprisingly, it was only a short time after my solitary experiments that I — always a generous girl — sought to share with others the pleasures which I myself had discovered, and, since the male gender was totally inacessible at Panthemont, I undertook the enlistment of several of my classmates into the rites of Lesbos. They, being no less deprived than I, responded all too eagerly to my every overture; regrettably, however, none of us had much experience in such matters, and, consequently, our efforts as often as not went physically unrewarded.

When I was twelve I made the acquaintance of a girl named Euphrosine, a tall and olive-skinned beauty who was three years my senior. Her figure was of the sort to inspire any artist, and I, no less appreciative of Nature's handiwork than those who seek to reproduce it on canvas, fell in love with her immediately. She, for her part, was equally enamored of me, and a very close "friendship" ensued. (I have no need to point out that, among recluse women, intellectual attraction is nonexistent; mutual sexual desire is the sole motive for friendship, and those who fail either to experience or to give way to this desire, go without friends.)

Unfortunately, despite her more advanced years, Euphrosine, like my younger girl friends, was no wiser in the ways of love than I. Thus, our experiments, while undertaken with great passion and much vigor, never advanced beyond the rudimentary stage. This was a fault which, as chance would have it, was soon corrected by none other than the abbess herself.

The abbess, Mother Delbéne, was a woman of breathtaking beauty, perhaps twenty-nine or thirty years of age, but with the firm and supple figure of a girl ten years her junior. She had been forced to become a nun by greedy parents who knew that, by pawning her off in this manner, they could rid themselves of the responsibility of providing for her. Now, although she went about her religious duties with an ostensible air of sanctity which would do an angel proud, she detested both her position at the convent and the parents who had put her there.

Of course, none of this was known to me on the afternoon when an elderly nun surprised Euphrosine and me kissing on a stairwell and ordered us to Mother Delbéne's office for disciplinary action. I was terrified as I sat outside the saintly-looking abbess' door while Euphrosine, being the older of us two, was called in to be dealt with first; I grew more terrified with each minute as half an hour, then an hour, passed, yet my collaborator in Lesbian love still did not return. Finally, after almost two hours, Mother Delbéne called out that I now could come in. I walked gingerly toward the closed door, wholly convinced that a fate worse than damnation awaited me on the other side.

Much to my surprise, I opened the door to find the lovely abbess lying almost nude on a couch. Her black habit, with its foreboding headpiece and white collar, was hanging from a hook on the wall, and she was wearing only a nearly transparent slip which displayed at best advantage the full, round mounds of her breasts and a wisp-thin waist which gently gave way to the awesome, curved magnificence of her hips. Next to her lay the beautiful Euphrosine, clad only in a gauze-thin underslip; her glistening olive skin stood in sharp contrast to the abbess' milk-white softness, and her small upturned breasts seemed to jut forward in pride, having finally been freed from the halter which had held them prisoner. All terror now leaving me, I felt my breath catch in my throat and my knees go weak with desire.

"Close the door, child," said Mother Delbéne softly and without the slightest trace of unpleasantness. When I, apprehensive beyond description, hesitated momentarily, she added kindly: "You have nothing to fear." The door now closed, she rose from the couch and took me

by the hand, saying: "Since you first came to this convent, dear girl, I have wanted to know you intimately.
You are very attractive, you realize; also clever, if I may
judge from some of your compositions. But, of course, I
could make no overtures until I was certain that you
would be receptive to them."

I smiled, wholly delighted with her interest. My
heart pounded wildly as I beheld the magnificence of
her body. She, smiling back at me, led me to the couch
and, without further ado, reached beneath my dress and
gripped the throbbing crux of my passion.

"What — you blush, little angel?" she cried suddenly;
"But you musn't! I forbid you! A blush is evidence of
modesty, and what is there to be modest about? Having
a cunt? But so do we all. No, child; modesty is foolishness, I would say; the result of being taught that love,
and its physical expression, and the instruments of that
expression are all things of which to be ashamed. The
truth, of course, is that Nature created us with these appetites and appurtenances. It is unthinkable that She
would have implanted in us aspects about which She
would want us to feel shame."

"You misunderstand me, good Mother," I replied, leaning gently into the palm which cradled my quivering
vulva. "If I blush, it is not for shame, but for eagerness.
What girl could behold your unadorned splendor and
not be overcome by the desire to smother you with kisses, to crush you with hugs, to envelop you with love."

"My, my!" beamed the nun. "You certainly are clever."
Then, still holding me, but turning to the supine Euphrosine, she said: "Why didn't you tell me, sweet child, that
your friend was so charming? I would have invited her
to join us sooner."

Euphrosine smiled proudly, as if by complicity in our
discovered act of lovemaking she had come to share my
present favor. "Do you blame me for wanting to keep
you to myself for as long as possible, darling mother,"
she replied, displaying considerable charm of her own.

Mother Delbéne put an arm around each of us and

clutched us to her. "Oh, dear children, I'm beside myself with glee," she cried, nuzzling first one, then the
other. "Let's all three undress and take love's delights
together."

While deftly unbuttoning my dress, the beautiful abbess brought her lips to mine and kissed me gently. Then,
as the garment fell away, she embraced me and her
kisses assumed a more fervent character. "Darling Juliette," she sighed, touching her tongue to my neck and at
the same time peeling away my undergarments; "you are
a tribute to womanhood. To see you is to be awe-
stricken."

Now I was naked except for my underslip. The magnificent Mother Delbéne's fingers tickled my nipples as her
warm, wet tongue darted about inside my mouth. She
was quick to observe that her attentions were having a
powerful effect on me.

"Oh, look, my sweet Euphrosine," she cried, admiringly. "Isn't our Juliette lovely! See how her luscious
little breasts are heaving? Do you think she wants to join
us in the rites of Venus?"

"Oh, yes, Mother," said Euphrosine, whereupon Mother Delbéne suddenly released me and rose to her feet. In
one motion she unfastened and instantly shucked off her
slip, exposing to our astounded eyes an alabaster skin
which Venus, herself, might envy. Euphrosine and I
promptly imitated her and, stark naked, the three of us
fell onto the couch, grabbing and clutching at each other,
kissing and caressing, sucking and biting.

"Oh, beautiful creatures!" Mother Delbéne gasped,
pausing to contemplate us in the ecstasy of first love. "I
want to die drunk on you!"

Euphrosine and I hugged and kissed each other, employing techniques just learned from Mother Delbéne.
The magnificent abbess sighed delightedly, then fell on
top of us; her hot, wet tongue burrowed a path along
the inside of my thighs: next, she shifted position to permit Euphrosine like access to her; I, surrendering joyfully

to the warm and wet wonder of it all, gripped the lovely Euphrosine at the hips and brought my head between her legs, completing the trillium. "Let us do everything imaginable to each other," came the voice of Mother Delbéne. "Let us kiss each other's mouths, and intertwine tongues; let us lock arms and legs, until our three bodies are fused; let us fuck, I say; let us fuck!" Excited beyond description, I repaid her liberally in the coin which she valued highest; Euphrosine delivered like payment unto me. Back and forth we switched, from one to the other, and thus passed hours. Our zeal was such that it is impossible to imagine one's laboring more ardently at giving pleasure or desiring more vehemently the receiving of it. Finally we stopped, totally exhausted.

"Oh, lovely children, this has been a day of days," sighed Mother Delbéne, stepping daintily back into her lingerie. "We must do it again very soon." And, when both Euphrosine and I failed to endorse the suggestion instantly, she said sharply: "What's wrong? Have you tired of me so quickly?"

"Certainly not, Mother," I replied hastily, "but we fear — and not for our sake; for yours. The worst which could be done to us is unimportant compared to even the mildest punishments which might befall you if our liaisons were discovered."

"Ah, sweet and compassionate Juliette," she smiled. "Do not worry for me; my power is supreme here." Then, fully dressed, she began helping Euphrosine and me into our clothes, lovingly brushing a breast here, a buttock there as she did so. "Yes," she repeated, "there is nothing to fear. As long as we are discreet, we may continue our revels indefinitely and with full impunity."

"Then we are both relieved," said Euphrosine, hugging the beautiful abbess sweetly, "and we both look forward to the moment when we again shall be honored by your caresses."

"It shall be soon," promised Mother Delbéne, showing us to the door. "It shall be soon indeed . . ."

III

During the weeks which followed, Euphrosine and I were summoned regularly to the office of our beloved Mother Delbéne and there worshipped at the ater of Love. Tuesday was the afternoon usually set aside for us and, occasionally, there were Thursday afternoons as well. I, for my part, would have preferred much more frequent meetings, and Euphrosine likewise; however, assuming that Mother Delbéne's academic schedule would not permit greater activity, we said nothing, and passed the other afternoons locked in each others' arms wherever we could find a hiding place.

Then, after several months, Euphrosine delivered to me the saddening news that she was leaving the convent. I immediately was overcome with grief and showered the dear girl with my tears. "Let us face the facts, my darling Juliette," she said sadly, "I am rapidly approaching sixteen, at which age I shall be forced to submit to the nunnery's First Vows. But, having tasted the delights of love, I am by no means inclined toward the monastic life. Therefore, since re-entry into the World is inevitable, isn't it better that I experience it sooner than later."

"But how will you live?" I protested. "Do you know someone who can support you?"

"I shall support myself as a prostitute," she replied. "I have always wanted to taste of a man's sexuality. What better circumstances under which to taste than while being paid for it — handsomely, I might add, since youth and virginity are of no small worth among debauchees." She smiled and clutched my shoulder reassuringly. "Mother Delbéne has mentioned the brothel of a certain Madame Duvergier," she continued. "The working conditions are excellent, the pay almost incredible. Who knows but that within a year or two I'll be a rich woman, living like royalty, free to do as I please with whomever I please and never worry about the consequences!"

"Then," I told her, "sad as it makes me to say farewell, I can only wish you the best of luck. Goodbye, my
darling Euphrosine, and may you realize all your
dreams."

"I'll write to you regularly,"' she promised, kissing me.
"And, if ever you decide that you'd like to follow me,
I'll do everything I can to make your way easier."

We embraced again, and, with eyes swollen with tears,
parted...

IV

The day after Euphrosine left, I learned that the attentions of our beloved Mother Delbéne had not been
concentrated exclusively on us. Indeed, during those days
of the week when she had not had the time to entertain
us, she had been occupied not with academics but with
other enterprises of libertinage. This fact became known
to me when I conveyed to the abbess the sad news of
Euphrosine's departure.

"I am afraid," I said, "that there will be just the two
of us from now on, but I shall do my best to please you."

"Do not be so sad, sweet child," she chuckled softly.
"Like you, I will miss our beloved Euphrosine; however,
I know several others among whom can be recruited a
replacement. There are Elisabeth, Flavie, Volmar, Sainte-
Elme..."

"Good Heavens!" I exclaimed. "Have you been intimate
with all of them?"

"Why certainly," she laughed. "You didn't suppose I
could content myself with only two lovers, did you?"

"Well..."

"Ah, beautiful child," she said consolingly, "love is
like the sun; it shines no less brightly on you because it
shines on others also."

"On how many others has your love shone?" I asked
hesitantly.

"Well, my dear," she replied, "out of the thirty instructresses in this convent, I have made love with twenty-two; there are sixteen boarding students and I have trafficked with all but five; there are eighteen day students, and I have enjoyed seventeen of them — the eighteenth violatees my esthetic sense. Does all of this shock you?"

"No," I said slowly. "I am delighted if it makes you happy."

"Then, my sweet Juliette," she smiled, "let me share my happiness with you. This very evening we shall have a party at which I shall introduce you — both personally and sexually — to some of my friends."

After dinner I went to Mother Delbéne's office alone, as instructed. She was as good as her word: all four girls whom she had mentioned were waiting there.

"So you're the lovely Juliette," said the oldest of the group, Volmar. "Well, you'll have to have something special if you plan to get anything out of me. I was carrying on all afternoon with Fontenille and I'm simply exhausted."

I was taken somewhat aback by the girl's directness and her undisguisedly lusty attitude; yet, I could not suppress the wild excitement I felt just being in her presence. She was older than the other girls — about twenty, I would guess — and fair-complected. Her eyes were a soft blue, her hair a ravishing chestnut brown which cascaded radiantly to her shoulders. Her body was a symphony of excellence: round firm breasts which strained at her halter; a trim, flat abdomen which yielded slowly into the most magnificently moulded hips; long, luxurious legs, firm and well-muscled, seemingly ever-ready to wrap themselves around the head of a loved one . . .

"Darling Volmar," I replied, "I would venture to say that I've never met your equal — but I'm totally unfamiliar with aggressive love."

"Then," interrupted Sainte-Elme, "I'm the one for you. I haven't been fucked all week." Suddenly she whirled around, leaned forward and raised her skirt. "Look!" she demanded, proferring her lovely ass. "It's waiting for you. All you've got to do is take it."

To my surprise, I found that the overt and vulgar manner in which she offered herself contributed much to my attraction for Sainte-Elme; furthermore, she was considerably more attractive than Volmar: a girl of seventeen years, she possessed sparkling eyes and a bright smile; her hips and legs were shapely and her breasts, large and pendulous, jiggled enticingly with her every movement: instantly I fell in love with her.

My love, however, was to go unrequited for the moment, for, no sooner had I advanced toward the darling girl than a third member of the group interfered. "Not so fast, Sainte-Elme," she snapped, stepping between us. "Juliette might prefer me." Then, extending her hand, she told me: "I'm Flavie."

I beheld a girl of sixteen, petite and astonishingly beautiful. While I was somewhat discomforted by the casual conceit with which she announced that I might prefer her, I had to admit that her confidence was not wholly unfounded. Her face was the most lovely I ever have seen, with clear brown eyes, marvelously white teeth and a heavenly smile. Her skin was smooth and inviting. Her figure was an exquisite blend of pert, round breasts; a neatly-tapered waist; small, provocative buttocks, and superbly sculptured legs.

"Are you skillful?" she asked bluntly, kissing me lightly on the lips. Then, without further comment, she clutched one of my breasts with one hand and with the other gripped me at the crotch.

"Easy there!" snapped Volmar, pushing her away. Then, lifting my dress and inspecting my thighs, she said: "Didn't Mother Delbéne tell you that the girl must be initiated before we can have our fun with her?"

"Look, Mother," complained Sainte-Elme to the abbess, who had just entered the room; "Flavia is jumping the gun. Surely you're not going to tolerate that."

"They're all trying to get their hands on her first, Mother," put in the fourth girl, Elizabeth, a beautifully shy child of no more than fourteen years.

"Now children," scolded Mother Delbéne, "let's not

argue among ourselves."

"It's Volmar's fault," persisted Sainte-Elme. "We all know that she's the aggressor in this crowd."

"Enough!" demanded the abbess. "If we don't reestablish order immediately, I'll send you back to your rooms and there won't be any orgy."

Almost instantly, all four girls fell silent. Next, on Delbéne's order, they lined up in single-file. Then, I lay on the couch and, one by one, they undressed and took their pleasures of me.

Elizabeth came first. The lovely, delicate creature scrutinized every part of me with her hands and tongue; then she slipped between by inflamed thighs; her hot, deliciously-erect nipples tempted my lips; she rubbed madly against me. Thus entwined our bodies lost themselves in oceans of passion.

Flavie approached me second. Turning me onto my stomach, she climbed atop me in such a fashion that her knees were alongside my face and her breasts against the small of my back. Then, as her marvelously firm, sweat-slick body writhed and undulated fiercely, her sweet tongue paid homage to my ass.

Third came Volmar, and, as she undressed, I learned the astonishing reason for her much-discussed aggressiveness: she was a true hermaphrodite, possessing not only the sexual equipment of her own gender but that of the opposite gender as well! Rolling me onto my back, she parted my legs and knelt in between them. Then, burying her face in the soft flesh of my belly, she began making warm, wet circles with her tongue, starting at my navel and working upward. Soon she was in coital position directly atop me; fastening her hot, hungry mouth to mine, she pushed forward with her hips until I could feel her gnarled, stick-hard, hermaphrodite's penis probing eagerly just outside my labia.

"Enough, Volmar," came a voice which I recognized instantly as that of my beloved Sainte-Elme; "the fruit which you seek to pluck has been reserved for another." So saying, she clutched the writhing hermaphrodite by the waist and spun her off me.

Now Sainte-Elme took her turn. Falling atop me, she began to devour my mouth with passionate kisses, all the while grinding her hips into my crotch with a slow, sensual motion which ignited previously-unexperienced sparks of passion in every cell of my body. Athrob with desire, I wrapped my arms and legs about her, squirming with ecstasy, groaning with lust. "Oh, darling," I cried; "you are the one I prefer; please stay with me . . ."

But my plea was not to be honored, for, at precisely that moment, Mother Delbéne spun Sainte-Elme out of the saddle just as Sainte-Elme had eliminated Volmar before her. Then, burrowing face-first into my crotch, the beautiful abbess plied her tongue in such a fashion that the sparks, ignited by others, burst into flame. I moaned and sighed; writhing madly in her grip, I begged that she finish the job which the others had begun. In reply, the skillful Mother Delbéne tightened her hold on my waist, tipped my hips upward and thrust her tongue to the very hilt. Like a soldier's sword, the marvelous instrument of passion sliced into my depths rapidly and repeatedly, making crackling sounds, urging open new doors of sensation and finally setting off within me the explosion of ecstasy which I had so long awaited. Gasping with delight, I tore my fingernails into the splendid nun's shoulders with such force that they soon became sticky with blood. Then, completely spent, I fell limp in her arms.

"By Zeus' crotch! said Mother Delbéne, lifting herself to her feet. "That was an orgasm if ever I saw one!" Then, noting the faces of the others, who had been deprived of participation in the final rite, she added: "Now, let's all enjoy this game together; each girl will take a place upon the couch and Juliette will play upon her in whichever manner she sees fit; meanwhile, since the dear girl is but a novice to these exercises, I will act as her mentor. But first"—here she raised a finger preemptorily —" let us replenish ourselves with a lovers' feast of superb foods and wines, for it is only through gastronomic indulgence that one increases the passionate fuel which is necessary to sustain our wonderful endeavors. As Ovid has said, *Sine Baccho et Cerere, Venus friget* . . . You can bet your sweet little asses she does!"

Now, with amazing speed, after but one clap of Mother Delbéne's hands, half a dozen food-carrying maidens appeared. They served a magnificent repast, made even more delicious by the knowledge that the sweetest, most glorious dessert waited at its conclusion. Wines the colors of the rainbow and unsurpassable in bouquet burned brilliantly into our heads and bodies. Ablaze with passion, we could hardly wait to leap into each others' flesh.

When the meal finally was over, we paired off into three couples. Mother Delbéne selected me for herself; Elizabeth went with my beloved Sainte-Elme, and Flavie gave herself to the hermaphrodite Volmar. Our positions were such that each couple could witness the other two; once all were in place, the festivities began.

While Mother Delbéne licked my thighs with strokes of provocatively feigned shyness, I stuck my hot, hungry tongue ferociously into the moist cleft of her yawning vulva. She swooned. She groaned. The small, hard, pink appendage which jutted from her warm wound became the tensed pacifier upon which played my nibbling teeth. She screamed with delight. Pushing me onto my stomach, she sank her long, searching tongue between my trembling buttocks. Madly, she lapped at the orifice, sending spasms of love racing through my body, while I, lying prone, witnessed the true object of my desires, the ravishingly beautiful Sainte-Elme, pouring wine into the gaping cunt of Elizabeth, then licking at it like a cat licking at its milk.

For two wildly enthusiastic hours we worked on each other, trading partners and drawing the sweet love-juices from each other's overripe bodies. Oh, that Sainte-Elme! Finally I found myself in her embrace! How marvelous she was! What a treasure! It is beyond by weak words to describe the joys which permeated my life that day.

All too soon, however, the session was brought to an end. One by one the girls exited quietly from the abbess' office until the only persons left were Mother Delbéne and I. "Well, my beloved Juliette," she told me, stroking my breasts tenderly as we stood together near the door, "you have tasted today the wine of love, but what you have sipped is only the foam from the top of the barrel. There is much more to be had, my sweet child; much, much more . . ."

And, on this note of promise, she bade me goodnight.

V

On successive visits, Mother Delbéne seemed to become slightly distant when we embraced. I asked her the cause of her new aloofness, and, after much hesitation, she finally confessed that she was afraid she had lost my love to Sainte-Elme. Confronted with the lovely abbess' charming jealousy, I was prompted to remind her of her contention that the sun shines no less brightly on one because it shines also on others. Then, encouraged by the tinkling laughter which this statement elicited, I revealed to her the compulsion which had been torturing me for more than a month: I longed to deflower Sainte-Elme, and, simultaneously, to be deflowered by her.

"Ah, Juliette," my beloved Head Mistress laughingly replied, "you're several years too late to deflower her; as to her deflowering you, before you commit yourself to the idea let me first try to change your mind. Remember Sainte-Elme is a novice in these matters compared to me. Would you ask a blind man to teach you how to see? A lame man to teach you how to walk? I should say not. Then, by the same logic, I must urge you to reject devirgination at the hands of Sainte-Elme. Of course, let me make it clear from the beginning that I'm thinking of my own good, not yours; you see, I want to crack that cherry of yours so badly that I can taste it, and I always put my own desires above everything else; but, in this case, my desires and your best interests happen to coincide: I can give you pleasures the likes of which you've never imagined; and I can rectify any material injuries which you may incur: after the defloration, through the application of special potions known only to me, I can make you appear as virginal as you were on the day of your birth; this will be of no small importance if you decide to marry after you leave this place, for, as you may have heard, Frenchmen are notorious fools about their women: they demand the spirit of a whore, but in the body of a virgin."

"But," I protested, "isn't it dishonest for a girl to mislead her husband into thinking that she's a virgin?"

"Dishonest?" she chuckled. "And what's wrong with a little dishonesty, may I ask?"

"We were taught in religion class that it is sinful to be dishonest."

"Fuck religion class," said Mother Delbéne. "What is religion but the word of Christ? And, if he knew his ass from his elbow, do you think he would have got himself crucified? No, my child, put aside all the precepts which you have been taught in religion class. Let this"— here she gripped her crotch—" be your only religion. Believe in it; follow its dictates: you'll never go wrong."

The voluptuous abbess' cool cynicism enchanted me. Putting out of my mind all thoughts of Sainte-Elme, I threw myself into Mother Delbéne's arms and swore eternal allegiance to her. "I want only you to deflower me," I cried. "Only you, darling Mother; only you."

The lubricious nun tenderly stroked my buttocks. "You shall have your wish, sweet Juliette," she replied. "Furthermore, because I am generous when it suits my purposes, I am going to give you a bonus. You cannot, of course, deflower me; that task was accomplished before you were born: but pick any virgin in this convent, any one who suits you, and you may deflower her in my place."

I did not have to think long before answering. "Laurette," I whispered, my heart throbbing in my breast.
"Laurette, Laurette, Laurette..."

The reader will forgive me, I hope, for introducing
the name of this darling child so abruptly; however, in
events related thus far she played no part, and to mention her under such circumstances would have led only
to confusion. In any event, Laurette was one of the
younger girls in the convent, and, although I did not
know her personally, I could not fail to notice her from
time to time. She was unbelievably attractive: her face
and body were a symphony of vivacity; her breasts possessed the charms of Venus; her slender, graceful legs
were alabaster columns of unsurpassable elegance and
beauty: I desired her with every fiber of my being.

With a smile which suggested that she approved of
my choice, Mother Delbéne assured me that I could expect the immolation of my beloved victim within a week.

Two days passed. Three. Five. My excitement became
all but unbearable. To ease it, Mother Delbéne invited
me to spend the eve of the sacrificial evening with her.
Then as we lay in her huge, canopied bed, locked in
gentle caresses, my sweet abbess slipped slowly into a
strange melancholy; without preface, she began to discourse moodily on universal, cosmic ideas.

"Why," she asked rhetorically, "must these churches,
these law courts, these political courts and all the other
hypocritical institutions which attempt to rule our lives
— why, I ask, must they insist, usually under pain of
horrible punishments, that we believe in a Supreme God!
An all-good Father! A heaven for the purpose of reward! A Hell for the purpose of punishment! An afterlife! Why!!! Why must the universe need a Watchman?
It has eternal laws, inherent in its Nature. It needs no
prime mover. The perpetual movement of matter explains everything; matter without personality; matter
without love or hate, without hunger or thirst; matter
without rewards or punishment; matter without com-

mandments of stone or laws of parchment; forever flowing, divinely indifferent, sacredly impersonal matter.

"Understand this, Juliette: whatever is eternally in motion is a motor unto itself; we need not search for some other divine motor; every cause which our learned teachers substitute for this simple truth inevitably is incomprehensible both to them and to us.

"Do I call them 'teachers'? Hah! They are nothing but shrewd, cunning foxes who use religion as a yoke, restraining every noble instinct of man. Examine critically their ridiculous theories on the principle of life; for example, that man is superior to the animal—a most arrogant and irrational statement when we look at the conclusive evidence of history. Can you name, my sweet, any animal in this entire world who created, contrived and performed such an atrocity as the Christian Crusades? Blood-lust! Nothing but the looting and plundering of poor, over-civilized savages whose only sin was cherishing their own beliefs! This is the handiwork of your esteemed 'rational animal.' "

My beautiful nun fell silent, playing absently with the nipple of my breast. Then, suddenly, with all the energy of her passionate convictions, she shouted: "And this absurd notion of life after death! Why can't they realize that when we die, we die. No more. Once the spider-thread of life is severed, the human body is but a mass of corrupting vegetable matter. A feast for worms. That is all. Tell me, what is more ludicrous than the notion of an immortal soul; than the belief that when a man is dead, he remains alive, that when his life grinds to a halt, his soul — or whatever you call it — takes flight?"

"I was taught," I replied, "that a spirit is mysteriously different from matter."

Mother Delbéne answered at once. "Tell me how your soul arranges to be born, to grow, to become strong, to agitate itself, to age — and all this running abreast of the evolution of your body. How can it be if they are so totally different? Don't beg off the question by saying that it's a mystery, because, if it is such, how can these fools claim to understand it? A true mystery is implausible even to the highest intellect. So how can these idiot priests make affirmative decisions about the existence of something which they are incapable of conceiving? In order to conceptualize, and, thus, to believe, it is necessary to know exactly what is the nature of the object which receives this belief."

"But," I argued, "is not the immortality of the soul a comforting dogma to the poor and tattered masses of humanity who litter the earth? Is it not a soothing illusion? Does it not relieve some of the immense woes which befall mankind? I, myself, am terribly frightened of this eternal annihilation of which you speak."

"My dear," said the brilliant woman, "before you were born, you were nothing more than an indistinguishable lump of unformed matter. After death, you simply will return to that nebulous state. You are going to become the raw material out of which new beings will be fashioned. Will there be pain in this natural process? No! Pleasure? No! Now, is there anything frightening in this? Certainly not! And yet, people sacrifice pleasure on earth in the hope that pain will be avoided in an after-life. The fools don't realize that, after death, pain and pleasuse cannot exist: there is only a sensationless state of cosmic anonymity: therefore, the rule of life should be not to do unto others as we would have them do unto us, but rather — and this is the only sane rule — to enjoy oneself at the expense of no matter whom!" Leaning over me, she kissed my breast, tickling the nipple into erection. Then she said, "Enough philosophy. Let us now engage in a criminal act; an act so outrageous that our loins will smoke with desire."

Electrified as much by her magnificent mind as by her alacritous tongue, I flung myself on top of her and began sucking her immense, strawberry nipples, all the while plying lovingly with my fingers her dew-soaked, passion-drenched vulva. "I owe you my life," I said; "I bequeath my paltry existence to you, my beloved Mothei Delbéne. I will not let my spirit be crushed under lie:

and stupidities. On your breast, I take a sacred oath never to return to the illusions which you have just swept from my mind. I am now, and forever more, your ardent disciple."

Mother Delbéne was beside herself with delight. Caressing me, she whispered into my ear that I was going to become an ignoble whore like her. Then her caresses became more vibrant, and passion's fire, ignited by the flint of philosophy, flamed more brightly than ever. "Since you are bent on becoming deflowered," she said huskily, "I shall satisfy you — now!" Whereupon, seizing a lighted candle from a table beside the bed, she savagely stormed virginity's citadel. Like a white-hot lance, the missive tore into me. Arrows of pain coarsed through my body. The stench of burning hair and singed flesh pervaded the bedroom, and still my mentor drove the weapon farther. Finally, at the precise moment when the sacred shield of virginity was split, a stinging scream escaped from my lips and a wave of immense pleasure washed over me. Furiously Delbéne cried, "Retaliate, my beloved! Give me the same pleasure!" And she flung the bloody candle into my hand.

Now, not the loved one but the lover, I drove the candle like a sword, again and again, into her marvelous cleft. She flopped. She squirmed. Her body arched and collapsed and arched again. I battled her with a fury, assaulting the innermost reaches of her sensuality, eliciting explosions of pure, melodic joy as the cannonade reverberated throughout her being. Then the marvelous body quivered into silence. In the exhausted hush of spent love, we heard only the tentative chirpings of night birds, startled awake in their nests. Ten times in succession the beautiful abbess gasped evidence of her pleasure. Then the candle in my hand and the thick, soft moss between her thighs were covered with the syrup of love. "Tonight!" said Mother Delbéne. "You shall have Laurette tonight! When everyone has retired after vespers, slip away from your dormitory; so will Flavie, Volmar

VI

and Laurette: we shall meet in my office, and then—
on to the ceremony!"

I left the abbess and made an appearance at the dormitory. My heart was athrob with the thought of those
pleasures awaiting me in lovely Laurette's embrace. But
the sweet excitement of anticipation soon became the
bitter anxiety of suspected betrayal. Laurette, I was told,
had fled from the house that afternoon and was nowhere
to be found!

I ran immediately to Mother Delbéne's office; it was
locked: I pounded desperately at the door; there was no
answer. For hours I roamed about the convent yard, my
spirits all but crushed; then, as soon as vespers had
rung, I returned to the abbess' office: the door was opened by Volmar; she and Flavie had been with Mother
Delbéne on the couch, passing the slow-moving hours
in light mischief.

"Alas," I said to my beloved nun, "how shall you keep
your promise to me? Laurette is gone. She ran away."

A dark expression clouded Mother Delbene's face. "If
you wish to remain my friend, Juliette, you must learn
not to leap to conclusions," she said. "I do not promise
what I cannot deliver. Follow me, and prepare to feast
your eyes on sights which will spellbind you."

Holding a lantern aloft, Mother Delbéne now led the
three of us down a massive stone stairway into the subterranean vaults wherein were interred all the women
who ever died in Panthémont. Then a stone slab was
fitted into place above us and we were locked inside the
sanctuary of the dead. "Easy does it," said my darling
Head Mistress; whereupon a second stone was swung
aside and we descended some fifteen additional steps
into a dank, ominous, low-ceilinged room.

In the center of the room, standing shyly in the vestments of a vestal virgin, was my sweet Laurette. Alongside her sat Father Ducrez, a man of some thirty-odd
years, first vicar to the Archbishop of Paris. Next to him

was Father Télème, a man of perhaps thirty, confessor to the Panthemont novices and *pensionnaires* and director of the diocesan Office for the Propagation of the Faith. The flickering orange light from the torches on the black walls bathed the trio with eerie, ever-changing shadows.

"Ah, look at the little darling," Mother Delbéne said, taking Laurette's pretty face in her hands. "She's afraid, isn't she? And is it any wonder? After all, our sole purpose in congregating here is to perpetrate atrocities. If I were she I'd be terrified out of my skin."

"Heavens!" I gasped. "What horrors are we going to perform in these caves?"

"Crimes," cackled Mother Delbéne wickedly. "Here in the bowels of the earth, entombed beneath the bodies of the silent dead, we are wholly free from the ridiculous interference of men. Therefore, we shall blacken ourselves with crimes. The good fathers and I shall set an example and you darling creatures will imitate us."

"By Lucifer's tongue, Mother," beamed Father Ducrez, "you've certainly got a way with words. Just listening to you has made my organ stiff as a broomhandle." Upon saying which he faced the assemblage, demonstrating to all the veracity of his assertion.

"What a pity," replied the abbess, "that I can't make it as long as a broomhandle as well; Satan knows, it's been ages since I've had a good one. But what is it that our charming Cardinal always says? Thank God for small favors. Well, Father, small though that organ of yours may be, you've placed it at my disposal often enough that I shan't complain."

"Small?" said Father Ducrez with a trace of anger. "You call the organ small? I submit, Madame, that in that enormous cathedral of yours there's not an organ built that wouldn't seem small!"

"He's right, Mother," put in Father Télème. "I've had many a woman in my days as a man of the cloth, but I'll venture that I've never encountered the likes of yours — not in height, not in width and not in depth.

And your ass is even bigger!"

"Well," said Mother Delbéne, "don't complain about the ocean just because you're equipped with only a rowboat. Many's the man who fit so tight I feared he would split me in half . . . But we didn't gather here to insult each other, did we? There's a ceremony to be performed, gentlemen; shall we be on with it?" Whereupon, without giving either priest a chance to reply, she seized both vigorously and led the way into an adjacent cavern.

This new room was twice as large as the first. In the center, lighted by a battery of huge torches, was a table laden with the rarest roasts, the most enormous cheeses, the finest wines, the daintiest pastries. Following Mother Delbéne's lead, we flocked around the magnificent repast and tore into it with gusto. Before long the splendid feast was reduced to a pile of bones and scraps, and the table was littered with empty plates. Everyone was thoroughly drunk.

"Now," smiled Mother Delbéne lasciviously, "let us attend to the business at hand. Juliette, my love, I have promised that tonight a victim will be sacrificed to your lusts. However, before availing yourself of the delicious fruit which awaits you, I suggest that you sharpen your appetites by indulging in some preliminary sports with the good fathers and me."

"Whatever you advise, my beloved," I replied.

No sooner had I said this than young Fatheer Télème lurched dizzily across the room and planted himself directly in front of me. "My child," he grinned, spittle dribbling down his chin, "I am told that you have never before been exposed to the mysteries of the male anatomy. It shall be my honor to introduce you to the most glorious mystery of them all." Thereupon he whipped aside his cassock and displayed a member of monstrous size; I could only gasp in wonderment at the thought that Mother Delbéne had seen larger. "Behold, my child," he said grandly. "The Resurrection of the Flesh!"

"Ah, yes," chuckled Father Ducrez, sneaking up be-

hind me and thrusting his hand between my legs. "And
who could ask for a lovelier cunt to serve as its sepul-
cher?" Now he gripped the throbbing object of which he
spoke. "By God's cock and balls!" he cried. "I've never
felt one even half as pretty!"

"You can have the cunt, Father," said Father Télème,
cupping my buttocks in his hands and pulling me against
him. "As for me, I'm an ass man through and through
— and, by Jesus, what an ass you've got, child! Mother
Delbéne, I don't know how you do it but you sure dig
them up. Each one lovelier than the next. And this ass
has yet to have a prick in it, you say? Good Christ, I'm
beside myself with joy. Do I have your permission to
throw a little fuck into her?"

Mother Delbéne draped a proprietary arm over my
shoulders and smiled sweetly. "What about it, Juliette?"
she asked. "Will you permit the eager young Father to
subject you to his perdfidious desires?"

"Perform the most perfidious acts imaginable," I replied. "I will not even tremble."

"By St. Christopher's eyes!" cheered Father Télème.
"I like her!" And, so saying, he plunged his head under
my skirt, tearing at my fragile underpants with furiously
impatient hands.

"Softly, Father! I say: softly!" Mother Delbéne said
sternly. "Lets us put some order into these proceedings."
Obediently the young priest unhanded me and retreated
a respectful distance. "Now," my charming abbess continued, "we'll make this a threesome: let Juliette disrobe:
I, too, will remove some garments, but only as far as my
waist; Juliette's looking at my tits as I kneel in front of
her should prove arousing, and the fact that my lower
areas remain concealed will heighten the piquancy of
her arousal: meanwhile, Father Télème, remove your
shoes and stockings and lift your cassock to your waist,
but keep your shoulders and chest draped: that'll give our
arrangement a sort of balance . . . .

"Ah, splendid," she continued when her instructions

had been carried out; "the tableau should be pleasing
to the eyes of our observers as well as to the touch of us
who participate directly. Now, then: are you ready,
Juliette? Father Télème?

"I am, Mother," I replied. Father Télème, behind me,
quite eagerly echoed the comment. Thereupon the
beautiful abbess dropped to her knees and inundated my
fleece with kisses. Simultaneously, Father Télème spread
my buttocks and pierced me with a member so huge that
I feared my bowels would be ripped to shreds.

Exquisite sensations coarsed through me; my loins
were set to trembling: still the assault continued; Father
Télème's hammer-like thrusts became increasedly rapid;
Mother Delbéne's tongue probed wildly in and around
my moistened cleft. "Ahhhh, Heaven!" I gasped. "I've
never tasted such pleasures." But the attack was unrelenting: thrusting, jarring, licking, lapping, pummeling,
pounding, sucking, slurping, my two assailants continued
to stoke the fires which blazed away inside me. Then,
in an instant, a jet of scalding seed was unleashed by
Father Télème and I all but melted away in its savage
tide. At the same moment, perceiving what was trans-
piring, Mother Delbéne bit violently into my quivering
peach. The fury of the combined sensations was more
than I could bear: my knees buckled and I fell limp in
my lover's arms.

"By Christ!" sighed Father Télème appreciatively;
"that's as luscious an asshole as I've ever known." As if
to lend credence to his assertion, he lovingly patted my
sweat-slicked buttocks. "I'd fast for forty days," he told
me, "for another repast like that." If ever you've got an
idle Saturday afternoon, stop by the confessional —"

"Relax, Father," chided Mother Delbéne. "Juliette isn't
going anywhere. You'll have many an opportunity to
demonstrate your appreciation. But, Juliette: answer me,
child: we have just given you two of the greatest pleasures a woman can experience: truthfully, which did you
enjoy more?"

"Good Mother," I panted wearily, "each gave me such pleasure that I dare not assign a preference to either."

"Then we best try it again!" urged Father Télème enthusiastically, whereupon his hands once more clutched my buttocks and spread them apart.

"Softly, Father; softly," scolded Mother Delbéne. "There are others here who merit a first turn before you get a second."

"Yes," said Father Ducrez, crossing the room with a speed which gave the lie to his advanced years. "By God, I've been sitting over there nursing a hard-on for half an hour and I don't think I can hold out much longer."

"Well, you needn't hold out a minute more, Father," said the abbess soothingly. "I promised you Juliette's cunt and I'm going to deliver it. Give me but a second or two to set up the tableau and you can go to it . . . Now, Juliette, my love: are you ready for something even more exciting? Well, you're about to experience it. And the thought occurs to me that we can even find a place for Father Télème in the enterprise without in any way detracting from the pleasures of the other participants . . ."

"Bless you, Mother; bless you," interrupted the ass-loving priest gratefully.

"Now, then," Mother Delbéne continued, "let everyone gather around the table and undress — all, that is, except you, Laurette; we're saving you for later . . . That's it, everyone: right down to the buff: Flavie, Volmar, the good Fathers: splendid . . . Now, Father Télème, clear away some of those plates, then lie on your back with your hips right at the table's edge: that's it: I see that you bring a stiff tool to the proceedings: marvelous endurance, Father; many's the man who would envy you . . . Come now, Juliette: climb atop the good Father and present that lovely ass of yours once more: that's the spirit, you're sliding right into place; you've got a natural aptitude for these enterprises, my love —

and, my, what a gorgeous pair of tits you show when you lie on your back! I'd love to eat them, and I just may . . . Well, on with the project: Father Ducrez, it's your turn now: do you see that lovely little mound nestling there between her succulent thighs? Well, go to it, you jaded old cock: no man before you has touched it: indeed, except for my ministrations, you're getting an unbruised fruit. Ah, but don't lie down, father; you must leave room for the rest of the participants;just stand up against the table's edge and fuck her that way. Yes, now you've got it. Splendid. . . Now Juliette: tell me: how does it feel to get your first taste of prick up the cunt?"

"Delicious, Mother," I gasped, wholly enchanted with the feel of those two priests' marvelous members, one in each orifice.

'I thought you'd like it," smiled Mother Delbéne contentedly. "Now, Flavie and Volmar: let us subject the rest of darling Juliette's body to lubricity's delights: one of you get on each side of the lovely creature and begin sucking those marvelous tits. Ah, my! See how the nipples harden the second your mouths approach? Beautiful! Simply beautiful! I'd take a mouthful myself were it not that my services will soon be required elsewhere . . . But Juliette: your hands are idle, child: don't you see how close Flavie and Volmar are to your reach? Then go to work, my chit: frig them: frig them assiduously. That's the spirit! We'll not have an idle bodily part here: if it can be used to bring someone pleasure, put it to work . . . And now for my role in the ceremony: Juliette, my love, I am going to squat over your face — like so. Now, child: my underparts are at your disposal: put that luscious tongue of yours to work on them: lap me, child; lap me and lick me: ah, by Christ, what a talent she has for it!

"Now, my children, we are ready to put this marvelous sex machine into operation. Upon my command, let each of us employ his equipment with all the vigor he can possibly summon. One . . . two . . . three . . . Go!!!"

No sooner had the command been given that I found

myself drowned in an ocean of sensation: from beneath
me came the vicious thrusts of Father Télème's monstrous
member as it rooted about my bowels; from in front,
the lightning-quick jabs of Father Ducrez; from each
side, Flavie and Volmar, licking, lapping, biting and
sucking my swollen breasts; from above, the hot, quivering vulva of Mother Delbéne, who, unwilling to leave
a single appendage idle, had taken also to kneading my
stomach with her gentle, delicate fingers while at the
same time passionately kissing the mouth of Father
Ducrez, who had only to lean slightly forward in order
to reach her.

"By Lucifer!" gasped Father Télème from below.
"What a movement this child has in her hips! I've
barely started humping and already I think I'm going
to come!"

"Me, too," panted Father Ducrez. "I'm getting the
benefit here of both your thrusts and hers. It's taking me
to the brink faster than I dreamed possible at my age."

"Well, fuck away, my friends!" encouraged Mother
Delbéne, at the same time rubbing her snatch with increased vigor into my face. "Yes, I say: fuck! Fuck!
We were born to fuck! It was to be fucked that Nature
created us, and, by God, no matter what anyone says,
that's the way we should spend our days. Never mind
the snivelling moralists and grovelling hypocrites: they
have their own reasons for condemning these delicious
heats, these joyous frenzies which confer so much
pleasure upon us: yes, ignore anyone who tells you otherwise: we were born to fuck. Indeed, if the birds and
beasts could talk — if the fish in the sea and the fowl in
the air and the lion in the jungle could speak to us —
we need only put the question to them, and myriad
voices would be exhorted by Nature's own creatures to
fuck, because it is the will of Nature that we fuck and
it is a crime against nature to not fuck: so join with me,
my friends; grind your hips and let your loins smoke;
fuck, I say; fuck, my friends, fuck: I repeat it: fuck!"

The sound of this word, burning more intensely into

my brain each time it was pronounced, served only to
heighten the passions which had been raging inside me.
Soon my limbs went numb and my body quaked under
sensation's furious assault. "Fuck!" I heard myself gasp
in immitation of Mother Delbéne. "Fuck, I say. Fuck!
FUCK!" And with each repetition of the marvelous word
my passions spiralled higher until, suddenly, the dam
broke! . . . the avalanche inundated me! . . . and I
surrendered to the long, slow, warm waves of orgasm.

Now, once we had disentangled ourselves, Mother
Delbéne pulled a cord and three serving-girls appeared
from the depths of the cave. Each carried a tray of
,restoratives — smoked sausages, cheeses and hunks of
bread — and a jug of wine. We of the libertine assembly
leaped hungrily upon the platters, wiping them clean
before the serving-girls even had a chance to set them
on the table. Then, taking the jugs of wine, we separated
into groups of two — Father Ducrez and I, Father
Télème and Flavie, Mother Delbéne and Volmar
(Laurete was left alone in a corner) and slowly proceeded to empty them, swallow by swallow.

As the wine was depleted, the assembly's spirit of
fellowship increased. Soon the six of us were in a circle
again, our bodies flush against each other, a knee in a
crotch here, a hand on a tit there, et cetera. Mother
Delbéne took advantage of the occasion to deliver one of
her thrilling dissertations.

"My friends," she declared, " the education given to
our girls today is unspeakable. It instills prejudices
which contradict all the natural impulses. It turns poor
children away from an appreciation of natural beauty
and makes them slaves to shame, to bashfulness, to sup-
pression of natural desire."

"By God's cock and balls," chortled Father Ducrez,
wine dribbling down his chin; "she speaks the truth."

"I ask you: what good is a 'prudent' and 'well-behaved'
woman in our society?" the abbess went on. "She is but
a female eunuch: nothing more. Did not Nature create

every human being to give aid to his fellows? Well, what better way to aid one another than by sharing bodies which were built to be shared?"

"By Jesus, that's beautiful logic, Mother," cheered Father Télème half-drunkenly. "Perhaps you'd be so kind as to expand upon the thought a bit."

"Very well," replied the abbess. "Let us consider the cock: note its shape: cylindrical, smooth on top, rigid when aroused, et cetera. Now consider the various orifices: the cunt, the asshole, the mouth, et cetera. Do we not see that each of them is shaped in such a manner as to receive the cock? Does that not indicate Nature's wishes to us? Think, momentarily, of the ear: its shape is such, and its location, that fucking it would be all but impossible; indeed, I would venture to say that there isn't a single libertine in France who could stand before us and honestly say that he has fucked an ear. Well, on the basis of this evidence, I think it's rather plain that Nature doesn't particularly wish to encourage ear-fucking, for, if She did, She'd have made it a lot more convenient. Now, by the same token, if Nature did not wish to encourage ass-fucking, cunt-fucking and mouth-fucking, don't you think that she'd make these orifices as impenetrable by the cock as the ear is? Of course She would, my friends, for Nature is all wise; thus, of one thing you may be sure: the ass, the mouth, the cunt — yes, and any other orifice whose shape and location permits such use — are made to be fucked. Period."

"Capital, Mother! Capital!" applauded Father Ducrez, all but reeling from his copious intake of wine. "I wish I was in a fucking church now. I'd repeat your speech verbatim right from the Goddamn pulpit.

"But, Mother," I interrupted, not quite so ready to accept her philosophy completely, "is it not folly for a girl to put these principles into practice? What will happen to her reputation?"

"Her reputation?" she replied, spitting the word out distastefully. "My child, a reputation is like an empty suitcase: it may have its uses, but carrying it around with you constantly may prove to be more trouble than the effort is worth."

"Yes, Mother," put in Flavie, "but convention—"

"Oh, fuck convention!" hissed the abbess impatiently. "Listen, my pet: if convention doesn't further the individual's happiness — if it doesn't gratify his innermost desires — then it is useless. I say, long live the girl who submits to her pure instincts! Long live she who surrenders to every impulse! The more she gives of herself, the more loveable she is; the more happiness she distributes; the more she contributes to a happy, stable society. Let promiscuity became an everyday affair: you'll observe that Virtue soon will become a Vice. Allow adultery the same license as gluttony: chastity will soon be no more highly esteemed than starvation!"

"By Jeremaiah's joint!" bellowed Father Télème. "Who can refute her?! What a shame old Thomas Aquinas isn't here; he'd learn a thing or two.

"Yes, by Christ," cackled Father Ducrez, "he would but he couldn't rebut you because there's no rebutting these Goddamn sentiments. Tell us more, Mother; your lovely rhetoric is getting me excited again."

Mother Delbéne, beaming proudly, continued: "What is the bold lie, this horrendous joke of idealism which insists that we suppress our strongest desires? Why should we suppress them? What wrong do I commit, what injury do I inflict, when upon seeing a beautiful human I say: 'Pray, dear friend, give me that part of your body which is capable of giving so much satisfaction, and, if you desire, take whatever part of me which appeals to you.'?"

"Oh, Sweet Savior's Sanctified Sperm!" cried Father Ducrez, doubling over and clutching his sides. "Mother, your logic is going to make me come. Tell me more, I say; tell me more."

"We speak of brotherhood," the abbess went on. "We speak of doing good and avoiding evil. But there is no brotherhood between people who are hostile or in-different to the needs of others. If the libertine attitude does not soon pervade society we will be doomed — nay, not just us, but the entire world will die, each individual locked in the prison of his own unexamined prejudices, his back broken by the weight of imagined guilt, his vitality withered by disuse."

"Bravo! Bravo, Mother!" chanted Father Ducrez and Father Télème in unison. "Tell us more! Tell us more!"

"My friends," continued the beautiful nun, "I shall make but one more point, then we should resume this evening's festivities, for to preach without practicing is like building a boat and leaving it on the shore. My point is this: throughout history, monarchs and despots have always opposed sexual freedom, for they have always known that it is never easier to oppress than when a people are repressed. We need only turn to the history books for proof of this contention. Emperor Constantine, for example, prescribed the same punish-ment for adultery as for parricide: the guilty party was burned alive, or, as an alternative, sewn into a sack and cast into the sea: well, we know all too well how this same tyrant oppressed the people not only of Italy, but also of France, Greece, Spain, Egypt and the rest of what was then the Roman Empire. Now, what of the ancient Danes? Among them, homicide was punished by the mere payment of a fine, but adultery was punished by death. Is there any among you who requires proof of this civilization's corresponding political savagery? No, let us look to the East: the Mongols today cleave an adulteress in two with a sword; in the Kingdom of Tonkin, she is trampled by an elephant; in Siam, they are slightly more lenient — she is delivered unto the elephant after having been strapped into a specially-made contraption which permits the elephant to enjoy her as if she were a female elephant. This is how adultery is regarded presently in the East; the three countries involved, needless to say are all monarchies. Do you require further examples? The Gauls — our noble ancestors — used to smother an adulteress in excrement. Among the Jews, it was the husbands's personal prerogative to condemn his wife to death. Among the Goths, a husband could personally strangle his wife and, if he testified merely that he suspected her adultery, he was as good as free. Three civilizations, all tyrannical monarchies or oligarchies; the same three civilizations, all practitioners of sexual oppression of the masses. Need I say more, my friends? Need I say more?"

"By Aphrodite's Immaculate Eyes!" thundered Father Ducrez. "Oh, how I wish I was in a pulpit now! I'd tell those bastards a thing or two!"

"So, in conclusion, my friends," Mother Delbéne went on, raising her voice to make herself heard above the drunken vicar's bellowing; "in conclusion, my advice is this: enjoy yourselves to the hilt; refuse your favors to no one; do not be intimidated by the ugly epithet, 'whore,' for an imbecile fails to see that there is real beauty in the title: the world loves a whore in its secret heart because a whore is less interested in her own welfare than in the happiness of others. A whore is Nature's child; the chaste girl is Nature's freak: what can insult Nature more than a girl who clings fitfully and arrogantly to the delusion that her continence is the hallmark of goodness? No, my children, we have no respect in this company for virginity or for the philosophy that excellence and chasity walk hand in hand. I spit on such thoughts. I condemn them."

Having so spoken, Mother Delbéne suddenly fell silent and, for a moment, the entire company sat motionless, each person absorbed in the marvelous ideas which the splendid abbess had set forth so lucidly. Then, kissing her lightly on the cheek, I whispered: "My beloved nun you were magnificent."

"Yes," she replied softly; "I shan't be modest about it, because the magnificence is not my own; it belongs to the thoughts upon which I have expounded: voicing such sentiments, anyone would speak magnificently. But enough talk," she said sharply. "Now the time has come

to abandon the word for the deed." Looking toward
Laurette, who had been sitting in a corner quivering
throughout the whole conversation, she smiled wickedly
and told me: "This wench is yours, Juliette. I've promised her, and now I shall deliver her. Shall I instruct
her to strip, or would you like the pleasure of denuding
her with your own hands?"

I did not answer immediately, but looked into Laurette's eyes, hoping to find there some sort of indication
that the darling little child was as eager to be had by
me as I was eager to have her. There was no indication:
indeed, the only emotion which the lovely brown eyes
registered was fear. Much to my surprise, I found that
this fear excited me ten times as much as any expression
of shared love ever could excite me.

"I'll denude her with my own hands, Mother," I said
gruffly, thrilled beyond measure as I saw the poor girl's
fear intensify; "and I intend to be rough about it."

Laurette, no longer able to contain herself, looked
quickly to each side of her, then turned and tried to run.
But Father Télème had her path blocked before she
could take two steps. "No, my little chit," he chuckled,
delivering her to me; "there's no escape here; the crime
will be committed and the only thing you can do is
submit to it; it's as simple as that."

The small, fragile-boned child now was literally
quaking with fear. Beside myself with glee, I covered
her pale little mouth with mine and thrust my tongue
deeply into her throat. Her body went taut for a moment,
then, unable to resist the pleasurable sensation to which
all humans are subject, she slowly began to relax.

"Please don't hurt me, Juliette," she whispered softly,
bringing her tender lips to my ear. "I'll do whatever you
tell me."

"Indeed you shall, my chit," I chuckled, very much
taken up with the wicked role in which I had been cast.
"Indeed you shall." And, so saying, I viciously ripped her
lily-white, virgin's robe from her shoulders.

The lovely child's trembling, milk-white body was

beautiful beyond belief. Strapping around my waist the huge dildo with which Mother Delbéne had equipped me for the defloration, I smiled lustfully and advanced on my waiting victim.

"Ah, Justine, such impatience," scolded Father Ducrez, touching a restraining hand to my shoulder. "You'll deny yourself nine-tenths of the pleasure if you plunge into things that hastily."

"What would you suggest, Father?" I replied, knowing all too well that the jaded old ecclesiastic must have some monstrous feat of lubricity in store.

"Perhaps," he cackled, "it would improve the taste of your little chicken if we were to baste her first in wine."

Now, no sooner had he voiced this idea than Father Télème and Mother Delbéne — veterans, one trusts, of many a basting — seized the pretty child by the shoulders and ankles and stretched her out on the table. Next, after binding her wrists and ankles to the four table-legs, they drenched her body with gallons of the stuff. Then, one by one, the entire company began to lick the wonderful juice from her body. Tongues inflamed with lust lapped at her toes, probed hungrily along her thighs, flicked at her tiny navel and made damp with hot, dripping saliva the lovely moss which nestled about her sacred vulva. Feverishly, each of the girls present feasted momentarily on the most luscious part, and, as we bent over to lick it, the two libertine priests took turns thrusting their monstrous cocks into our exposed buttocks. When the priests finally were stimulated sufficiently to discharge, Volmar, holding a punchbowl beneath their quivering members, caught up the scalding love-juices; then the bowl-bearing hermaphrodite asked me to contribute my piss to the brew: next, mixing in a drop or two of wine, she stirred the concoction and passed it around; each of us, starting with Mother Delbene, took a small, tart swallow.

As the acrid balm trickled down my throat, I found myself overcome with the desire to put my plans with Laurette into immediate execution. "By Christ's cock,"

I shouted in imitation of my blasphemous priestly companions, "let's delay these proceedings no longer! Spread open those virginal thighs! I'm going to drive this dildo home!"

Instantly the two clerics leaped to my aid, gripping the beautiful Laurette at each knee and spreading her lovely legs with force all but sufficient to split the poor child in half. Then I, delirious with desire, jumped atop the table and furiously buried the enormous dildo in her gaping cunt.

A tortured scream leaped from the poor child's throat and rivers of blood cascaded down her thighs. Then there was another scream — a high-pitched, horrendous screech . . . . and it was not from Laurette! I froze in mid-stroke, terrified.

"Good Heavens!" I gasped. "What's amiss here?"

In reply, I got only another screech — this one louder and more dreadful than the first. Then, in an instant, all the torches were snuffed out and the room was plunged into terrifying darkness: a sudden dizziness took hold of me and my limbs went limp; the table swirled out from under me and the cold, hard floor of the cave crashed into my helpless body.

VI

When I recovered my wits, I was lying in bed and Mother Delbéne was reclining in an armchair alongside me. It was afternoon of the next day.

"Well, my child," she smiled warmly, "it would appear that you've had quite a scare."

"Indeed I have, Mother," I confessed weakly. "I thought for a moment last night that the judgement of an angry god was being visited upon me."

Ah, yes," the beautiful abbess chuckled softly. "That's how this god-fellow has managed to acquire such a following; whenever there's a supernatural phenomenon, people look to him as its author; thus, a splendidly plastic myth has been shaped to explain in one breath

both earthquakes and volcanoes, both fires and floods —
and not only to explain the start of each such phenomenon, mind you, but also to explain its end. Ah, the
illogic of man! But, Juliette: mark my words well: there
is no supernatural effect which is not, upon investigation,
traceable to some natural cause.

"The horrors of last night are an example. The screech
which we heard was that of a large wood owl, hidden
away in the catacombs: apparently he had been startled
by the sounds of our enterprises or by the light from our
torches: in any event, he took flight, and the draft
created by the beating of his enormous wings snuffed
out our torch-flames. Perfectly simple, is it not? Perfectly
natural."

"It certainly is," I replied, "and I deserve to be critici-
zed for doubting your principles. I can see now that it
was quite stupid of me to faint as I did."

"Well," she smiled, "don't feel too badly about it;
Father Ducrez fainted too: like you, he thought that
this god-person was cursing us for our lasciviousness."
Then, leaning forward and kissing me on the lips, she
said: "But let's think no more of the matter; supper will
be served in a few hours and I'd like to rest until then."
So saying, she tucked my blanket up around my neck,
kissed me again and vanished through the door; I fell
into a deep, comfortable sleep.

When I awoke, the supper hour had arrived; but with
it had also arrived news of personal tragedy: a servant,
sent by my mother, reported that my father was gravely
ill; my sister, Justine, and I were instructed to return
home immediately.

Before I left, Mother Delbéne gave me a jar of ointment which she promised would restore my virginity;
then, entrusting Justine and me to the servant who had
come to fetch us, she bade us sad goodbye; with tears
copiously shed, I promised to return as soon as possible.

Alas, dear reader, through the pages of Justine's book
you have learned already the events which transpired
upon our return home: my father died; my mother died

a month later; Justine and I found ourselves destitute. Now we returned to Panthémont: while Justine waited outside in the hall, I went into Mother Delbène's office: but the news of our misfortunes had preceeded us; Mother Delbène received me coldly; instead of offering us food and lodging, she gave me a hundred crowns — money placed into an account years earlier by my father — and told me to go my way. When I reminded her of my love for her, she all but laughed in my face. "My child," she said, "the carnal appetite cannot endure separation. You have been replaced in my affections by another. Now forget me as I have forgotten you."

"But what shall my sister and I do?" I pleaded. "How shall we live?"

"I have prepared you well for libertinage, Juliette," the wicked abbess replied. "You've demonstrated quite a talent for whoring; now go forth and exercise it." So saying, she slammed the door in my face.

Crestfallen, weak of limb and all but broken of spirit, I paused in Mother Delbène's waiting room long enough to dab from my eyes the bitter tears of dejection. Then, fixing my jaw resolutely, I set my course for the years ahead. I said to myself:

I shall follow your advice, Mother Delbène, cruel bitch that you are. I shall be rich and impudent and a more devastating whore than you dared imagine. I shall beware of virtuousness, for I know now that it can lead only to disaster; in its place I shall pursue vice, for vice is always triumphant. I shall evermore stop at nothing — even murder — to avoid penury, for the poor man is the object of universal scorn; and I shall hitherto direct my every step along the path of crime, surrendering completely to every impulse, sacrificing victim upon victim to my slightest caprice. I shall, in short, be the wickedest woman in the world.

Fortified by these reflections — bold ones, you will

concede, for a girl not yet having reached her fifteenth year — I rejoined my sister, Justine. When she failed to be swayed by my arguments, I bade her farewell. Then I headed straight for the whorehouse of Madame Duvergier, to which I had been recommended months earlier by my dear friend, Euphrosine. My first steps along the path of vice were thus officially taken.

BOOK TWO

I

The whorehouse of Madame Duvergier was a monument to elegance and good taste. Magnificent furnishings, lavishly-appointed boudoirs, fastidiously-groomed open gardens, scented Roman baths and the kitchen masterworks of France's most skillful chefs conspired to thrill the senses of even the most jaded debauchees. And then there were the whores: six queen-whores, goddesses one and all, succulent creatures whose keen minds, luscious bodies and fantastic sexual talents could not be surpassed anywhere in the civilized world; thirty-six princess-whores, no less admirably endowed physically but not yet sufficiently quick of mind or skilled in movement to satisfy fully the stern demands of Madame Duvergier's extraordinarily sophisticated clientelle; three hundred and sixty novices, all of comparable beauty but none clever or experienced enough to merit inclusion in the more select group; eight studs, strapping specimens one and all, none under six feet and all blessed with bull-like members, and, finally, four little grooms aged fourteen and fifteen, all pretty of face, delicate of physique and, most important, well-shaped in the buttocks.

This, I say, was the staff of that marvelous place, and

there was not a libertine throughout the whole of the
Continent who could ever say he walked away dissatis-
fied. As a newcomer to whoredom's ranks, I had quite a
tradition to uphold; the reader may soon evaluate for
himself the manner in which I upheld it.

Madame Duvergier started me off, naturally, as a
novice: for six weeks in a row the old whore sold my
virginity to twenty or thirty buyers per day: then, each
evening, she treated me with a pommade similar to that
with which I had been gifted by the heartless Mother
Delbéne; in this manner was the tensity of my vagina
restored for the next day's siege.

When the six-week apprenticeship period had trans-
spired, Duvergier informed me that she was more than
pleased with my work. Thereupon she appointed me to
the rank of princess-whore and I acquired a share in the
profits of the business. "Continue at your present rate
of progress my dear," she told me, "and you'll be a
queen-whore before the year is out; then, after several
years in that capacity, you'll be rich enough to retire
and spend the rest of your life as a gentlewoman." The
wizened old madame's words pleased me: I was resolved,
however, that I would improve upon her time schedule;
as events will show, my improvement was greater than
anyone might have imagined.

My first customer after the promotion to princess-
whore was the Duke of Stern, as infirm, phlegmy,
doddering old man who, as a result of his frequent
campaigns to rid Paris of vice, had acquired a city-wide
reputation as a leading Catholic layman. Naturally, his
position would not permit him to take his pleasures inside the whorehouse itself; thus, he sent his valet, a
slender and terribly attractive young man named Lubin,
to fetch me.

Wishing to make the best possible impression on this,
my first major assignment, I had taken the trouble to
outfit myself with a dress and accessories of unmatched
elegance. The valet, Lubin, took one look at this costume
and shuddered. Then he instructed me to change into

clothes of a tattered street-urchin and to do my best thenceforth to act the part.

I complied with these mystifying instructions and, when Lubin presented me to the duke, that withered old crusader's eyes lighted up like a pair of Christmas candles.

"Ah, my child!" he cackled lecherously. "Lubin tells me that your family is starving and that your mother is selling you to me because it's the only way she can get money for firewood. Is that correct?"

"Yes, alas," I replied in a rehearsed voice of sorrow.

"Well, by fuck, that's what I call enterprise," he said, pinching my breast with his gnarled old fingers. "If more mothers felt that way, there'd be less poverty in this city and a damned sight fewer horny old men. Right, Lubin?"

"Yessir," replied the handsome valet dutifully.

"A nice ass you've got there, too, my chit," the duke went on, lifting my skirt over my hips. "Fine form, good line; yes, by Christ, a nice ass. Wouldn't you say so, Lubin?"

"Marvelous, sire," answered the valet.

"Well don't just stand there looking at it, you stupid prick," the duke snapped impatiently. "Get on your knees and put your tongue in there."

The valet stoically complied with this order and I felt a hot surge of passion as his long, moist tongue snaked into my entrails.

"My poor child, my poor dear child," clucked the duke as Lubin continued to lick my quivering orifice. "Has anyone ever subjected you to this type of lewd behavior in the past?"

"No, sir," I replied, sticking to the script.

"Is she telling the truth, Lubin?"

"Indeed she is, sire," replied the valet, momentarily removing himself from the project at hand. "As far as my supersensory nose and tongue can detect, this child's rectum contains no evidence of recent or past sodomy."

"Like a bird dog, this boy" said the duke, patting

Lubin's head. "Check out her cunt now, Lubin."

The valet promptly lowered me to the floor, urged open my thighs and inserted his tongue experimentally into my much-used vagina.

"Nobody fools this boy, dearie," the duke went on proudly. "He's got a talent second to none. Keep at it, Lubin. Don't let me down, boy."

My splendid examiner thrust his talented tongue in to the very hilt, then withdrew it, stood and make his report: "No evidence of fornication, sire."

"Well, by fuck, that's good to hear," said the depraved old duke with an expression of relief. "It's nice to know that morality hasn't been trampled completely in this sin-infested city." Then, clutching me at the waist, he said: "Come here, my child; sit on my lap. Ah, by Christ, you're a lovely morsel. If the truth were known, I'd like to throw a good fuck into you: unfortunately, due to my advanced years, that's quite out of the question; if you were Venus herself you wouldn't be able to get a — heh, heh — rise out of me. But—" here he grinned lasciviously "—I still have something of a taste for spectacles which please the eye and ear, so you'll find that you haven't been paid just for prancing around here this afternoon."

No sooner had he said this than the evil old man threw me to the floor, ripped off my rags and commanded Lubin to whip me. Obediently the handsome valet seized a huge, black strap from atop the mantle and brought it into play against my bare back and thighs. Waves of pain coarsed through my tender body and I cried out in agony; the duke, beside himself with glee, wrung his hands delightedly and fell into his arm-chair chortling, "Lay it on harder, boy; sting the ass off this little waif."

Before long my back was a latticework of ugly red welts. The duke, kneeling over me and inspecting it care-fully, commanded Lubin to stop. "But," he added, be-ginning to laugh maniacally once again, "we're by no means through with her, are we, my vigorous cohort? By

Christ, I should say not."

"What would you like me to do now, sire?"

"Why, give her some action, boy," replied the duke. "Give her some action."

Lubin promptly undid his trousers and produced a swollen member of immense length — all of twelve or thirteen inches, I would judge. His stoic face expressionless as always, he then knelt over me and thrust the terrifying tool into my mouth.

"Now take a little ride for yourself," ordered the duke. Whereupon Lubin, spurring my ribs with his heels, began to move back and forth on top of me as if he were astride as horse.

Soon the motions of the virile valet — not, I confess, unaided by a flick or two from my most appreciative tongue — brought him to the point of no return. His face still expressionless, the knave flooded my tonsils with jets of scalding semen.

"Well, child, it was nice to see you," said the depraved old duke as Lubin, the deed done, helped me into my rags. "I can't have you back again, for, as you no doubt surmised, I confine my pleasures to virgins. But go in peace, and take with you the knowledge that you've brought a measure of joy this afternoon to an aging man's heart."

Thereupon he ushered Lubin and me to the foyer and watched with the expression of a kindly old uncle as the handsome valet guided me into the carriage for the trip back home.

II

When I returned to my quarters that evening, I related the details of my adventure to Fatima, another of Madame Duvergier's princess-whores. This pretty child, who likewise had been a plaything of the lascivious duke during her earlier days in the house laughed merrily at my apparent consternation.

"Lovely Juliette," she told me, "before too many months have passed, you'll meet characters who'll make that depraved old fart seem comparatively sane. My advice is not to let any of it bother you. After all, what does it matter to a whore which way she's abused; isn't it really six of one, half dozen of the other? Besides, the depraved ones are the best ones to steal from."

"Steal?" I asked incredulously. "Do you steal from your customers?"

"Of course," answered Fatima, obviously shocked at my naiveté. "All whores steal. It's the only way to get ahead in this business. Besides, it's fun — and it's perfectly safe; after all, what nobleman would be willing to sully his reputation by taking a whore to court?"

"But," I argued, "isn't stealing . . . dishonest? Isn't it . . . wrong?"

"Ah, my darling little Juliette," she replied, smothering me with kisses. "Sometimes you entertain the most old-fashioned notions. What you need is to have a little chat with Dorval; he's one of Madame Duvergier's regular customers: in fact, I'm scheduled to entertain him tomorrow night at his home in La Villette; I'll ask Duvergier to include you in the party, and we'll see if your views aren't altered somewhat by his reasoned arguments."

Fatima was as good as her word: early the next afternoon a carriage came for us and we were driven to a large, secluded house in a dense wood on the outskirts of the city. En route, Fatima proceeded to orient me on my future client's ways.

"Dorval is a thief," she said; "one of the most accomplished in all France: he steals as a means of earning a living, naturally, but there's more to it than just that: you see, he's totally incapable of getting an erection unless he first has stimulated himself by robbing someone; furthermore, his whores must be involved in the theft also, or else he is not sexually attracted to them; and, finally, after he has enjoyed a sex act, he must have his whores steal from him."

"What an extraordinary man," I said. "But isn't it risky for him to go about robbing people all the time? Doesn't he fear that eventually he'll be caught?"

"Ah, child," laughed Fatima softly, "you seem to forget that the law exists only for poor people; the rich and the famous disobey it at will — and do so with impunity, because there isn't a judge in the world whom money can't buy. But Dorval usually doesn't even have to worry about paying off judges because his crimes are so well executed that his victims never complain."

"Never complain, you say? How could that be?"

"Well, as I've told you before, few men are willing to undergo the publicity involved in taking a whore to court. Duval realizes this and stages his thefts accordingly. Right at this moment, while you and I are riding toward his house, he has hundreds of spies swarming about Paris; they report to him regularly on the arrival of wealthy foreigners, dignitaries, et cetera; Dorval then offers these visiting simpletons his services as a procurer, arranging liaisons with Madame Duvergier's whores; we, in turn, filch the gentlemen's purses while they're in bed with us."

"Where do these trysts take place?" I asked, becoming more interested by the minute in the workings of this methodical man's mind.

"Dorval owns more than thirty houses like the one which we will visit today," Fatima explained. "They're located all over the countryside surrounding Paris. All are large, well-furnished and, of course, isolated."

"And we're expected to steal as part of our work tonight you say?"

"Yes: Dorval will bring two or three foreigners to the house for dinner. We will dine with them, then adjourn to separate chambers. Once in bed, our mates will drop straight to sleep — thanks to a potion slipped into their drinks during the meal. Then it will be our task to go through the fools' purses and bring everything of worth to Dorval. We'll be rewarded with a fourth of the total which we bring in, plus, of course, our regular salary for a night's work."

Now, scarcely had this discussion ended than the
carriage pulled to a halt in front of the house which was
to serve as a stage for the evening's mischief. On the
porch of the house was a tall, handsome man of perhaps
forty years, lean-faced and quite distinguished looking.
Fatima identified him as none other than our hero,
Dorval.

"Ah, Fatima, I see that you bring me a very handsome
prize," he smiled warmly, helping me from the carriage.
Then, as soon as both my feet were on the ground, he
took to inspecting his prize with great vigor — patting
a buttock here, squeezing a breast there, kissing a cheek
somewhere else, and so forth. "Yes," he said finally, "I
think she'll do quite nicely; quite nicely indeed."

The inspection thus concluded, our host led us into
an immense, high-ceilinged living room with great, oak
beams and an enormous stone fireplace. Here, pouring
brandy for three, he addressed himself immediately to
the business of the day.

"We're running a bit late today, child," he told me,
"so I won't bother to repeat the instruction which I
assume Fatima gave you on the way over here. Let me
just say that I have two elderly, hot-crotched Germans in
the next room and they're dying to meet some attractive
women. One of them, a pig named Conrad, has diamonds on him worth twenty-thousand *écus;* his colleague, a sow named Scheffner, has at least forty-thou-
sands *francs* in his purse. Fatima, as the senior member
of the team, will have Mr. Diamonds Conrad; you, child,
as the novice, will have Mr. Francs Scheffner. I trust
that everything will go smoothly and that there will be
no need later for disciplinary action of any sort; but
remember, my lovely little newcomer, that I'll be
watching your every action through a knothole in the
bedroom wall, so, if you're planning to hold out on me
when accounting-time comes around, you'd be well
advised to alter those plans immediately. Now, if there
are no questions, let us proceed to the dining room

where our two, charming, hot-loined bastards are waiting with their pricks in their hands."

I thought the warning about holding out a bit strange, especially in view of Fatima's earlier assertion that our employer required his whores to steal from him after he had engaged them sexually; however, not wishing to delay proceedings any further, I refrained from raising any question on the matter, promising myself that I would discuss it with Fatima when an opportunity arose; my mind having thus been put to temporary rest on this score, I followed our host into the dining room.

Our two German beaux lived up to their race's reputation for grossness, ugliness and stupidity. My mate, Scheffner, a genuine baron some forty-odd years of age, was toothless, pock-marked and filthy beyond belief; his comrade, Conrad competed with him for honors in each of these categories and had the added distinction of being one of the fattest men who every walked. It required consummate self control on my part not to wince visibly at the mere sight of them.

During the meal, our two animals slobbered over their dishes like swine over a trough, lifting their savage mouths from their dishes only long enough to regale each other and Dorval with coarse jests. Scheffner, for his part, also took to fingering my twat underneath the table, an enterprise which, I confess, wholly ruined what little enjoyment I otherwise might have taken from the meal.

Finally, after what seemed like years, the dessert dishes were taken away and Dorval withdrew discretely to the sitting room, thus clearing the way for our lovers to carry us off to bed. Scheffner wasted no time at all: "hoisting me over his shoulder, he charged into the bedroom and hurled me onto the bed like a stevedore hurling a sack of grain: his clothes were off in a trice and he was on top of me, kissing, biting, hugging, tearing at my garments: I couldn't help but wonder if perhaps things had gone awry in the wine cellar; my mate certainly wasn't acting like a man whose drink had been drugged: yet, the urgency of his assault was such that I had little time for speculation; every ounce of my concentration was required to deal with the situation at hand. Deciding to pacify my panting German pig with the sort of succor he sought, I slipped off my dress and slid into place beneath him: then I guided his tiny, stick-stiff member into port; interestingly enough, my Rhineland Romeo was so short that, while thusly engaged, his face came only up to my breasts; thus he gnawed with toothless gums at my nipples while at the same time hammering away at me with vigorous thrusts of his flabby hips. Soon his movements took on a new urgency and, with as horrendous a barrage of grunts and groans as ever were issued from the throat of any man, the swine ejaculated; then, suddenly, his body went slack and landed in a heap on the bed alongside me; the sleep-potion took effect exactly five minutes too late.

Now that the knave was immobile, I climbed out of bed and rummaged through his clothes. The billfold was there as Dorval had said it would be. I riffled through the bills; there were forty-thousand *francs* exactly; stuffing them into my stocking, I went back to the bed and lay down to await my employer's further instructions.

I did not have to wait long. Scarcely a moment after my head touched the pillow, Dorval bounded into the room. He was naked, pike aloft — and a considerable pike it was, all of ten inches in length and a good two hands' worth in circumference.

"Ah, my darling child!" he cried, embracing me. "You were magnificent! Expert! An artist! I saw everything, and — as the evidence shows — it thrilled me to the core." So saying, he tossed me onto the bed alongside the immobile Scheffner, jerked my legs apart and, while the unconscious old kraut's juice seeped from my love-nest, buried his face in the moist crevice, sucking, licking and lapping with the energy of ten men.

After satisfying himself in this manner, the depraved Dorval took the purse from me. Then he led me down a narrow corridor, halting in front of a pair of side-by-side peepholes. "Look through that one," he said, "you'll get to see how an old pro at this game does business."

The old pro, of course, turned out to be Fatima, who, as chance would have it, was just getting into bed with her beau. I watched as she positioned herself beneath him and received his assault.

"You will observe," commented Dorval, "that the German's clothes, containing his purseful of diamonds, are on a chair alongside the bed. You will also note that, as Fatima establishes coitus with him, she positions herself in such a manner that this chair is within her reach. Now watch: as soon as they begin their coital thrusting, she'll begin to go through the clothes in search of the purse — and she'll not miss a stroke while she does it."

"But I thought," I replied, "that the Germans were to be knocked unconscious by a potion mixed with their wine."

"Yes, I told Fatima to tell you that," said Dorval, not taking his eyes from the peephole. "I thought you might refuse to cooperate otherwise. But the fact of the matter is that the potion is designed to work at the moment of orgasm, not before. You see, I get my jollies watching the act of theft being carried out concurrently with the act of coitus — just as, if you'll observe your friend Fatima, you'll see happen right here in a few moments."

Sure enough, that is exactly what happened. As the monstrous Conrad's panting and puffing testified that the magic moment was approaching, Fatima put her hand on the purse. Then, at precisely the moment of his discharge, lo! — she lifted it from his pocket. He fell unconscious at her side.

"And this," I asked Dorval, "is the spectacle which you desire so much to observe?"

But my host did not answer. Jaw clenched, eyes ablaze, he tore himself away from his peephole and stormed into Fatima's bedroom. Then, as I watched through my peephole, he dashed open her legs and buried his face in her crotch just as he had with me.

When he finally had had his fill of this enterprise, Dorval summoned me from the corridor. Then, arranging Fatima and me on the bed alongside the unconscious German, he launched a dissertation on the subject of theft.

"My lovely comrades," he said, "when society was in its infancy, men distinguished themselves by the amount of brute strength which they possessed. Today, at what we fondly refer to as the height of civilization, we do likewise — only less directly. A case in point is theft: our ancestors went about from place to place taking what they wanted; there was no artifice employed; they simply came, saw and conquered, or, were themselves conquered, as the case might be: we, on the other hand, are master at artifice; we devise thousands upon thousands of different ploys by which we may separate the rightful owner from a piece of property which we want for ourselves; then, having acquired it, we congratulate ourselves on our business acumen, our shrewdness, et cetera; but, in the last analysis, we have done nothing more than our thieving ancestors.

"Take the case of the magistrate who charges a fee for the performance of an act of justice which by rights should be rendered free of charge. Is he not a thief? What of the merchant who sells a sack of potatoes at a price one-third above its intrinsic value? Is he not likewise? What of kings who impose inordinate taxes, dues and tithes upon their subjects? What of noblemen whose income is from rents? All these plunderings have now been given the name of 'business' and thus have been made respectable; but, in essence, are they any less a matter of theft than the direct thefts of our ancestors?

"This, my lovely whores, is why I am a thief: I seek to strip theft of the dishonest trappings with which it has been burdened by civilization: I seek to restore it to its natural state."

Having spoken thusly, he lay down between Fatima and me and began frigging us, one with each hand.

"Do you see?" he went on. "Theft is the greatest erotic stimulant in the entire world. Just the thought of it has charged up my motor once again. I've often wondered what the physiology of this process might be; perhaps there is some impact upon the nervous system. Ah, well, these are matters for latter-day scientists to decide. For the moment I must concern myself with the disposal of the bodies of our two German friends." And, so saying, he left off his frigging and ambled out of the room.

"A strange duck, that fellow," I commented to Fatima after he left.

"Ah, yes," she replied. "That's one of the things which makes whoring such a fascinating occupation: you meet characters of such diversity . . . But, Juliette: look: isn't that a wallet on the floor?"

My gaze followed her finger; indeed on a small throwrug just inside the door lay one of the thickest billfolds I had ever seen.

"Dorval must have dropped it on his way out," she suggested, scampering across the room to pick it up. "Careless of him, wouldn't you say? . . . And, Good Heavens, look what's in it! Juliette, there must be all of a hundred-thousand *francs* here!"

"My word," I gasped. "That's more money than I've ever seen at one time."

"Well, here," she said, taking a fistful of notes and stuffing them into my hands; "hide some in your brassiere, your panties, anywhere; we won't get another opportunity for a haul like this as long as we live; quickly, now, or he's liable to notice that the wallet is missing and come back here looking for it."

"But," I protested, "don't you think we ought to return the money to him?"

"Why of course not," she snapped. "Don't be so naive. Besides, didn't he just give us a very inspiring lecture on what a noble thing theft is — the true state of nature and all that business? Well, the principles apply just as well when you're on the receiving end as when you're dishing it out, don't they?"

"I suppose so," I said hesitantly. Then, thinking for a moment of all the dresses and shoes and lingerie and gowns which a one-half share of one-hundred-thousand *francs* could buy, I began stuffing the notes away with a fury which all but surpassed that of my eager friend. In less than a minute we had managed to dress fully and to hide the whole fortune somewhere or other about our persons. Then, hearts racing with excitement, we stepped gingerly into the corridor and headed for the door.

I had taken only two steps when a pair of hands clutched me from behind. They belonged to a monstrous Negro, all of seven feet tall. His companion, equally monstrous, seized Fatima.

"What is this?" my spunky colleague demanded. We're here as guests of M. Dorval! Unhand us!"

"You are under arrest, ladies," replied her captor emotionlessly. "The crime with which you are charged is theft. You will now be brought to trial."

So saying, the swarthy fellow threw her over his shoulder and started down a stairway into a deep cellar. My assailant did likewise with me. Two stairways later, the four of us were in a dank, dirt-walled subcellar lighted only by a pair of small candles. At one end of the room was a scaffold with two gibbets; from each gibbet hung a rope with an expertly-fashioned noose. At the opposite end of the room was a high judge's bench; behind it, decked out in a powdered white wig and black robe, was Dorval.

"Strip them," he commanded in a voice wholly devoid of tonality.

The two Negro giants complied: our clothes were torn away and the one-hundred-thousand *francs* fluttered around us like leaves in a brisk autumnal wind.

"Well, the evidence is plain enough," said Dorval dryly. "A shroud for each of them, my fine black aides, and see to it that the coffins are ready."

I fell to my knees and began pleading, but Fatima clutched me sharply at the shoulder and told me to be silent. One of the Negroes promptly jerked me to my feet.

"Now, then," Dorval went on. "Do you have anything to say in your defense?"

"Nothing, my lord," replied Fatima in a voice as toneless as his. "We are guilty; punish us as you see fit."

"And you, Juliette?" he asked me.

I was dumb with terror. A small pool of urine materialized on the floor beneath my feet.

"Well?" he said impatiently. "Are you guilty or not?"

"Guilty, your honor," I gasped, horrified beyond imagination.

"Kneel then," he commanded, rising from the bench. "I am about to pronounce sentence."

As I lowered myself into place, Douval climbed from his perch and stood in front of me. Then he unbuttoned his trousers, pulling out a member which was swollen to the bursting point. Stepping forward, he thrust it into my mouth.

"You are going to be hanged," he declared tonelessly, at the same time guiding my jaws back and forth across his throbbing pike. "The whores, Rose Fatima and Claudine Juliette, having been found guilty of theft as charged, are going to be hanged by their Goddamn necks and choked absolutely to ass-fucking death for having deliberately taken and concealed about their persons one-hundred-thousand francs belonging to Mister Dorval. The sentence will be executed immediately."

At precisely this moment the jaded scoundrel sprayed a boiling shower of semen into my trembling mouth. Then, disengaging himself, he returned to the judge's bench. Immediately the Negroes bound our hands behind our backs and carried us off to the scaffold.

Fatima went first. She was hoisted into place and a noose was tied around her neck. Then I was positioned beside her and a rope was likewise tightened about my throat. The feel of the rope triggered within me an explosion of horror; suddenly my sphincter went slack and my feces flooded the scaffold.

"She shits!" shouted Dorval from the judges's bench. "The bitch has the insolence to shit!" Then, leaping from his perch, he dashed across the room. "How dare you shit on my scaffold?!" he cried, picking up handfuls of the foul matter and smearing it all over my body. "The insolence, I say! The insolence of it all!"

Fatima was still as a statue: her eyes stared straight ahead and her body was motionless. I, for my part, could not manage similar self-control; as Dorval stood there before me, my sphincter once more rebelled and the scaffold was inundated with a deluge more than twice the volume of the first.

"Ahhhhhh!!!!" screamed Dorval madly picking up great gobs of the matter and pelting me in the face. "Ahhhhhhhh!!!!"

Finally the fit lifted and he returned to the judge's bench. "Carry out the sentence," he commanded; his voice again was emotionless.

Now the trapdoor suddenly sprung open beneath me. I braced myself for the sharp tug of the rope on my neck. But, lo! — nothing happened. After hanging suspended in air for just an instant, I dropped harmlessly onto a mattress beneath the scaffold. Fatima, equally unscathed, landed beside me. "Don't move," she whispered through clenched teeth; "don't move a muscle."

Eyes shut, jaws snapped closed, I lay silently in place. For a moment there was no sound save that of my breathing. Then I heard footsteps coming across the floor. Opening one eye just a crack, I made out the outlines of Dorval and one of the Negroes peering over the top of the trapdoor.

"Are the bitches still alive?" asked Dorval.

"No, sir," replied the Negro. "They're both dead."

Dorval nodded solemnly. Then, without warning he leaped through the trapdoor and fell upon Fatima; furiously tugging at his trousers, he unsheathed his mammoth member and drove it between her legs; at the moment of penetration she abandoned her lifeless pose and, clutching his waist with her legs, began pumping furiously in rhythm with him; a moment later his gasps and grunts heralded his discharge.

Next the depraved creature—still fully erect—turned to me. Following my companion's example, I remained motionless until he had maneuvered me into position and invaded me. Then I unleashed an assault which bespoke the torrents of fear which had coursed through me since the dreadful moment of our capture by the Negroes; it succeeded in triggering his orgasm almost instantly.

The deeds now done, Dorval climbed out of the trap-door and his footsteps retraced their path across the floor. Then one of the Negroes very gently helped Fatima and me to our feet and brought us to a bedroom. Hot baths awaited us, along with two complete new costumes each. As soon as we had washed and dressed, we were ushered to the waiting carriage and returned to the whorehouse.

"I'm sorry that I was unable to give you more details before we entered his house," Fatima apologized as we rode through the night; "but Dorval insists that every-thing come as a surprise to his newcomer whores, and, occasionally, to make sure that I keep my silence, he hires a girl like you to spy on me."

"Well, it's of no matter now," I replied, more than content just to be out of the accursed madman's reach. "We've managed to make a nice sum of money, even if the earning of it did entail a few hair-raising experi-ences."

"We've made more money than you realize," she said, handing me an envelope chock-full of *franc* notes. "This is your bonus for having played your part so well; Dorval was delighted with you, and he's always a generous man with those who please them."

On that happy note, my episode with the depraved bandit came to close.

III

My next venture in debauchery involved another incredible libertine — a man by the name of Noirceuil.
Charming, exceedingly witty and depraved beyond belief, this rake was obsessed with making his wife, a
lovely girl of perhaps twenty years, witness his libertinage: indeed, not only did he demand that she be
present during his many episodes, but he even forced
forced her to collaborate in each offense.

When I arrived at the darling knave's house, husband and wife were in the bedroom with two strongly-
proportioned lads of perhaps seventeen or eighteen
years of age; Mme. Noirceuil stood by with coffee and
cake while M. Noirceuil lay on the bed, flanked
by his two boys, whom he frigged simultaneously; the
frigging was not suspended to herald my entry; indeed,
my jaded host acknowledged his butler's announcement of me, invited me to sit down and delivered a
brief speech of welcome, all without breaking the
rhythm of his wrist movements. Finally the youths
ejaculated, whereupon Noirceuil ordered his wife to
wipe them clean. Then he turned his attention to me.

"My child," he said, "Madame Duvergier tells me that
you possess the world's most beautiful ass. Would you
have the kindness to display it for my friends and me?"

"Whatever you say, sir," I replied, obediently un-
loosening the clasps on my dress.

"No so fast, my child," he interrupted. "There's no
need to tire yourself undressing when my lovely young
wife is around to do the job." Then, turning to that
much-abused women, he said: "Madame, unveil this
marvel for me, and be gentle about it if you don't want
a shoe up your cunt."

"Sir," the poor creature begged, "please do not subject me to this humiliation."

"But you are my wife," he answered in a tone of
genuine puzzlement. "Wives are meant to be humili-

ated. Didn't anyone ever tell you that?"

Realizing the futility of arguing the point, Mme. Noirceuil silently began to undress me. Her husband watched
with interest throughout. Finally when I was nude except for an undershift of gauze-like material he said:
"All right my dear, I'll carry on from this point; meanwhile take off your own clothes; my two young studs
here look like they might like to have a go at you."

While his wife obediently undressed, Noirceuil wrapped his arms around my knees and buried his face in
my crotch. Then, taking the hem of my slip in his teeth,
he very slowly urged it over my hips and down to my
ankles. This accomplished, he kneaded my buttocks
for awhile, then abandoned the enterprise and turned
again to his wife.

"This lovely spouse of mine," he announced grandly
to the two boys and me, "is the coldest woman this side
of the Arctic Ocean. Indeed, it has been said that no
force on earth or in heaven could ever warm her up.
Well, I, personally, don't believe this; I believe that
beneath that cold exterior lies a spark which needs only to
be fanned into flame. But the question is: how does
one go about it? I ask you, my friends: do any of you
think you can arouse her? Well, I'll offer a prize of two
louis to whoever does."

Taking the cue, all three of us fell instantly upon
the woman; the two boys taking turns biting and pinching her delicate cleft, while I, more gentle, licked her
fright-shriveled nipples as sweetly as I could: alas,
none of these acts budged her an inch. Next the boys
spread open her thighs and launched an assault on her
double citadels, one from the top of her, the other
from beneath; she screamed in pain as the lads' abund-
ant members tore furiously into her helpless entrails.
I, more from a spirit of competition than from compassion, pushed the animals away and began to kiss and
lick her injured parts: still she remained insensitive
to pleasure's proddings. Finally the two boys assaulted
her again, this time with canes and broomhandles; her

back and chest, her arms and legs were covered with
bruises before Nature cloaked her aching body with
a shroud of merciful unconsciousness.

"Well, my friends," said Noirceuil, "it looks like nobody wins the two *louis*. Ah, well; tomorrow I may
give you another chance: as for now, suppose you boys
carry this worthless slut to your bedroom and dress
her wounds with salt; and don't come back until I ring
for you; I'm going to amuse myself for awhile with
friend Juliette and I'd rather be left alone."

Dutifully the two youths picked up the lovely, bruised
body of Mme. Noirceuil and carried it out of the room.
When they were gone, M. Noirceuil lifted me onto
the bed and brought my hand to his throbbing member — which was still as erect as it had been when I
entered the room half an hour before.

"Well," he said, guiding my hand in a brisk frigging
rhythm, "what is your opinion of the punishment meted out tonight to my darling wife?"

"I think it is regrettable," I replied, guessing the role
he wanted me to play, "that she fell unconscious before she suffered the full impact of the pain. I have
seen some women beaten in that manner who stayed
awake for hours, suffering blow after blow after blow
until their skin was completely covered with black and
blue marks and their bones were all but broken. It's a
pity we couldn't have enjoyed a similar spectacle at
Mme. Noirceuil's expenses."

"By Christ," gasped Noirceuil, thrilled beyond belief, "I think I've found a kindred spirit. Tell me, child,
have you always felt this way about other people's sufferings?"

"No," I answered, marvelling at the accuracy with
which I had gauged his temper; "it is an acquired taste;
one which, sad to say, I developed only recently."

"Well, fuck my eyes! Yes, child, I do believe that
I've encountered a fellow libertine; a true lover of evil.
These boys who beat my wife — oh, I suppose they get
some pleasure from it. But violence is not a passion

with them. No, it's a means to an end. They do what I say because I reward them handsomely. But you, my dear; you, my sweet, sweet child; you and I are cut from the same bolt of cloth: I can see it in your eyes."

"Yes, sir, it is true; I cannot hide it from you," I said. And, much to my surprise, I suddenly found myself experiencing a great longing for this man; a carnal love so intense that I wished fervently that the evil sentiments which I had pretended could be genuinely felt, so that he would have all the more reason to love me in return.

"Well, stay with me, child," he smiled; "I'll go to work on that evil base of yours like a sculptor going to work on a chunk of marble; I'll mould your soul; I'll guide your destiny; with me, you'll go very far, very far."

Unable to contain any longer the incredible passion I felt or him, I threw myself upon the wicked man and urgently covered his mouth with mine. "Oh, darling," I gasped, "please love me; love me and kiss me and hold me and thrill me; I've waited all my life to meet someone like you."

"Not so fast, child; emotions hastily expressed are emotions briefly felt; let us hope that there is more to your recognition of our common satanic bond that merely the desire to copulate. Besides, I have heard a few things about you which I would like to confirm before I permit our relationship to develop any farther: for example, is your name not Claudine Juliette and were you not once a *pensionnaire* at Panthemont."

"Indeed, sir, you are right on both counts," I replied, amazed that he was so well acquainted with my background. (I had not breathed a word about Panthemont, dear reader, to anyone I had met since leaving there.)

"And do you not have a younger sister named Justine?"

"Indeed, I do."

"And are you not the daughter of M. and Mme. X —, who died recently within six months of each other?"

"Merciful Satan!" I gasped. "How could you know

these things?"

"Because," he grinned evilly, "I am the man who ruined your father. It was I who gained control of his fortunes and brought about the destruction of his business.
I suppose that now that you know these things you won't
want to see me again."

"Nooooooo," I replied hesistantly, wishing to do everything in my power to prolong the moment (this, dear
reader, shows how strongly I was attracted to this
scoundrel!); "after all, business is business . . . ."

"Ah yes, Juliette, so it is: however, I didn't ruin him
for business reasons; I did so deliberately, and for no
other motive than pure evil. He trusted me, the fool; he
had put all his confidence in me: to have honored that
confidence would have been to have performed a virtuous act, and, since I am dedicated wholly to evil, my
conscience wouldn't permit it."

"I understand your point completely," I said, burying
my face in the warm, thick hairs of his chest. "Moreover, I approve of what you did; if my father was stupid
enough to trust you, then he reaped his just desserts
when you turned on him. My motto is: never trust a soul."

"Well spoken, child," said Noirceuil; "but that is not
my only evil against your household. You see, your
father did not commit suicide to avoid the shame of
bankruptcy. I . . . poisoned him!"

"You fiend," I sighed, rubbing my body deliciously
against his; "I am the victim of your vices, yet I adore
them: your wicked principles drive me mad with desire."

"Juliette, I haven't told you everything yet . . ."

"Then tell me; the more I hear, the more I love you."

"The reason that I poisoned your father was because
he had found out that I was having an affair with your
mother."

"Foolish man; he should have minded his own affairs."

"Juliette, . . . I repeat: I was having an affair with your
mother."

"Then have one with her daughter as well, sir! I implore you! I beseech you! Can't you see that I am mad

about you?"

"Wait, there's more. I poisoned your mother also . . . because she was becoming a nuisance."

"I would have done likewise under the circumstances."

"Then you don't hate me for it?"

"You devil! I love you! I love you! How many times must you be told?"

"You love *me*, the murderer of your parents?"

"Madly. Madly and passionately."

"How could you?"

"I am a creature of the senses. Neither parent has ever stimulated me a fraction as much as has the news that you killed them. I can't understand these strange feelings, but neither can I deny them. I love you. I want you to love me. It is as simple as that."

Noirceuil sighed deeply and, for the first time all night, hugged me to him in a gesture suggesting warmth. "Juliette," he said, "the candid purity of your soul forces me to keep you here with me. You shall not go back to Duvergier. You shall become my mistress. I'll send a carriage tomorrow for your clothes."

"But your wife . . ." I started to say.

"She shall be your slave. You shall be her mistress. Your wish will be her command."

"Ah, Satan! Who could ask for anything more?"

"Oh, darling Juliette," he went on, maneuvering my body in such a manner that his face addressed my navel, and my face addressed his; "darling, darling Juliette; you have the soul of a succubus and I cannot resist you."

"Nor can I resist you," I moaned. "Isn't it obvious, my darling? I love you."

"Libertines don't love, my darling," he corrected me, tenderly kissing me as he spoke. "Libertines hate. Thus, you don't express your attraction to me by saying 'I love you;' you say the reverse."

"I hate you?" I replied, matching the tenderness of his tones.

"Precisely, my dear. Now say it with feeling."

'I hate you, Noirceuil," I declared, passionately touch- ing my mouth to his. "I hate you more than I have ever hated anyone."

"And I hate you, my little whore," he gasped, biting viciously into by lips. "I hate you with all my heart."

IV.

The next day I was installed as mistress of Noirceuil's house, given full charge of all the servants (including his wife) and awarded a pension of one-hundred-thousand *louis* a month to run the place. Thus, less than a year after my turning to a life of vice, I found myself wallow- ing in opulence and wealth. (Can the reader help but contrast this situation with that of my sister Justine a year after she had started her lonely walk along the path of Virtue?) Yes, in every sense of the term, I was a happy woman, and so great was my happiness that I could not resist seizing the first opportunity to visit my former employer and tell her about it.

"Darling Juliette!" cried Duvergier delightedly. "How nice of you to remember me! And your timing could not be better, because I am in a position today to demon- strate to you a phenomenon which will no doubt give you frequent occasion in the future to pause and count the blessings of your relationship with Noirceuil."

So saying she ushered me into her private office and waved to a pair of chairs which were placed alongside each other facing two peepholes in a wall. "It has been said that all women who choose the wanton life are lewd, ignoble whores," she went on; "sit down here with me and I'll show you how false that notion is."

I sat down beside her and glanced through my peep- hole. I found myself looking into a room filled with hand- some, stately, magnificently-robed women.

"In that congregation," Duvergier continued, "are fif- teen wives and daughters whose reputations are — heh, heh — unimpeachable. Well, I happen to know otherwise.

"Do you see that superb blonde? She is the Duchess of Saint-Fal. Married and the mother of three children; believed by everyone to be of spotless virtue. Today she will entertain four men at once in a secluded country-house.

"The tall woman next to her — the one with the saintly face? Well, she's an extremely loving wife, a treasure of domestic devotion. Her one flaw is that she cannot resist priests; she must have at least one per week. I recruit them for her.

"That other girl, the brunette, is engaged to be married next week. She's simply mad over her fiance — so he thinks. Five years ago I sold her virginity; today I'm selling her as a whipping partner; this will be about her five-hundredth assignment from me. Stunning creature, isn't she?

"Now, the tall woman next to her; the one with the gray hair. Such sophistication! Butter wouldn't melt in her mouth! She was educated in England, you know, and speaks their dreadful language like a native. She also shares what I am told is the Britishwoman's natural penchant for cocks. She just can't keep away from them. It is rumored that her devoted husband once caught her frigging a bull. However, one can't believe all one hears these days, can one?

"Now, the one standing to her right is terribly interest-ing. Her father is a famous lawyer and her uncle is an archbishop. She is absolutely mad over ten-year-old boys. I have two little darlings contracted to meet her today.

"See that other one; the slender-waisted looking one? She didn't come by that jaded look by accident. She's one of the most energetic whores ever to spread her legs. And she'll do anything for a *louis:* I won't tell you what she did last week for fifty *francs,* and this despite the fact that her husband has more money than a god and gives her anything she asks him for.

"Now, that little enchantress over there; thirteen or

fourteen years old; do you see her? She works as part of a team. Her accomplice is her mother. They could find other work, of course; but they just love libertinage.

"The girl next to her? The plump beauty? She works with her husband, who serves as her procurer. They don't need the money, but he loves passionately to watch her copulate with other men. She likes being watched, too, so, all in all, they're rather well mated, wouldn't you say?

"Now, how about that sweet one over there? She goes wild at the sight of another naked woman — especially a woman who's having a period. Fancy that!

"And lastly, the redhead near the door; one of the city's most celebrated prudes; in society it is said that she ignores men completely; in reality she'll take on anything that walks. Her insatiable thirst caused two of my best men to faint away from over-exhaustion just last week. I'd venture to say that she gets laid fifty or sixty times per month on the whole — please forgive the pun — and perhaps an additional hundred times or more during her summer vacations .

"Well, there you have them: a collection of some of Paris' most distinguished, ahem, ladies. I show them to you in the event that during your travels as Noirceuil's mistress you find yourself being scorned by them or by any of their ilk. Take the advice of an old madame, my child: regard yourself as inferior to no one: beneath the surface, all women are whores; the only difference is that some are more honest about it than others."

The beloved creature's words warmed my heart. "Dearest friend," I replied, "I am indebted to you more than I can say. If ever I can be of service to you, don't hesistate to ask."

Taking my hand in hers, Duvergier smiled hesitantly. "Well," she said, "now that you mention it, it so happens that occasionally I get calls from clients who would like an extra-special girl, one such as yourself; if such a summons comes, and if you find yourself without something more interesting to occupy your time, would you consent to take the job?"

"Eagerly, madame," I replied. "I state only one require-
ment: a fee of fifty *louis*. In exchange for this amount,
I'll go anywhere at anytime with anyone and do anything."

"Ah, darling Juliette," said the loveable old crone, hugging me to her breast. "You shall be buried in mountains
of money. I'll have men arranged in lines three and four
blocks long just waiting to bid for your services."

"Go to it, madame," I answered her. "Let the world be
made to realize that Juliette-the-pretty-whore wants to
become rich, rich, rich. And, by Lucifer, I won't stop at
anything until my wish is realized."

V.

My greatest desire during the weeks which followed this
visit was to put to the test a theory of evil which lately
had been gnawing at my mind. Dorval, the reader may
remember, had insisted that physically pleasurable sensations resulted from the perpetration of a theft. Meanwhile, I had experienced such sensations as a result of
listening to Noirceuil's accounts of his crimes against my
parents. Could it be, I wondered, that my sensitivity to
such stimuli was so much greater than Dorval's that I
could enjoy vicariously what he could not enjoy except
in actual realization? And, if this were so, did it not
follow that my enjoyment of real crime would, because
of my hypersensitivity, be proportionately greater than
his? If so — zounds, what pleasures lay in store!

The only problem was how to put the theories to the
test. It would be easy enough to steal something from
Noirceuil, of course; but, since everything he owned was
mine for the asking, any such theft would in effect simply
be stealing from myself: besides, since he was a kindred
evil spirit, I doubted that any offense against him would
have the same effect on my passions as would a crime
against someone less corrupt than either of us.

Yet, if not from Noirceuil, from whom should I steal?

I trafficked with no one else; I had no friends or enemies; and the thought of exposing myself to arrest and prosecution as a result of stealing from a stranger was too frightening to contemplate. But then, how was I to commit my crimes? Where would I find a victim?

For days I contemplated these perplexities. Then, one afternoon, in the midst of my musings, I received a call from Duvergier. She had arranged, she said, for me to be one of six whores scheduled to entertain that evening at the home of a millionaire who was renowned for the gracious charity which he bestowed on women of low station — as long as they catered to his often-bizarre whims. The assignment could not have come at a more opportune time: here, in one stroke, was the chance both to put my theory to the test and to do so with impunity, for, as Fatima had long ago pointed out, no millionaire would jeopardize his reputation by hauling a whore to court. "I'll take the job," I told Duvergier; "you can count on me to more than satisfy the requirements."

That evening a carriage bearing five other whores from Duvergier's called for me at Noirceuil's house. Our troupe was then speeded to the millionaire's mansion, where, immediately upon arrival, we were brought to a dark cellar chamber the walls of which were covered entirely with brown satin.

"This is the house of Mondor, the shit-lover," intoned a deep-voiced servant by way of greeting us. "You, as his guests, will obey every instruction carefully. Do as you are told and no harm will come to you; do otherwise and you will long have reason to regret it."

The speech having been delivered, the servant clapped his hands and six young eunuchs appeared. One by one, these gentle gazelles paired off with the six whores. Then the servant clapped his hands again and each eunuch fell busily to undressing his assigned companion. Once undressed, we were given filmy black-and-silver costumes to wear. Then we were instructed to arrange ourselves in a circular formation, like the petals of a sunflower, on a huge, round divan which stood in the center of the floor.

When all this had been accomplished, the shit-loving Mondor entered. He was a tall, well-muscled man, perhaps seventy years of age, but well-preserved and apparently full of sensual appreciation. Completely naked, he showed a member which hung all of eight inches, limp.

Cackling appreciatively, the old roué circled the divan, pinching a breast here, tweaking a buttock there, et cetera. He sniffed our buttocks,' inspected each girl's rectum, ran his fingers through each one's fleece and finally, with a fanatical gleam in his eye, decided that I was the girl who best suited him.

"By fuck!" he shouted, leaping upon me with great vigor. "This little chit has an ass and a half! Quickly now, you others: take those rods and do your stuff."

Lying on top of me, the libertine pantomimed copulation without actually achieving intromission. Meanwhile, the eunuchs, who were standing by in attendance, distributed the rods of which he spoke — slender, brass ones, perhaps two and a half feet in length — to the other five girls in the troupe. Then the rods were put into play, raining blows all over Mondor's back and thighs. He groaned; he sweated; he bled; he called for a rod to be jammed up his ass and for another to be poked into each ear; still he failed to achieve an erection and, finally, he called the proceedings to a halt.

Now, dismissing the other five girls, he brought me to a secluded room. There lying on his stomach while a servant applied ointment to his wounds, he said:

"My child, as you can see, I remain unaroused. What I am going to ask now is that you perform an action which will remedy this fault. Will you consent?"

"Whatever you desire, sir I will gladly do," I replied.

Thereupon he instructed me to squat over his face while he lay on his back. When the position was assumed, he brought his mouth to within inches of my rectum. "Now, child," he whispered urgently; "shit!" I grunted and strained, but without success. "Try harder!" he hissed. "You must try harder! I've never before seen an ass as lovely as yours and I won't be satisfied until it has inundated me completely. Now shit I say; shit!"

Again I strained, then a third time and a fourth, but without success. Then, lo— on the fifth effort the dam broke and a flood of feces hit him full force in the face.

"Ah, by fuck!" he gasped appreciatively, stuffing great lumps of the foul matter into his mouth. "What a taste! I'll bet you eaten nothing but the finest grade of beef all week! I'm beside myself with glee! By fuck, I love this shit!"

I listened with one ear to his ecstatic ravings, but my mind was elewhere: namely, on the dresser next to the bed, where there lay unprotected and indeed all but forgotten a roll of *franc* notes thick enough to choke a cow. Glancing quickly about to see that we were unobserved, I reached for the bundle and, without moving my still-shitting ass an inch, began stuffing the notes into the folds of my hair, which, fortunately, was done up in a large chignon. Mondor was still splashing about joyfully in my feces and all the notes had been stuffed away minutes later when one of the eunuchs entered, paid me generously and saw me to the waiting carriage. The theft went completely unnoticed.

That night, lying in bed with Noirceuil, I related the details of my extravagant adventure. My satanic lover, nodding approvingly, helped me count the money; there were sixty-thousand *francs* in all, each signed and requiring no endorsement. "And the best part of it all," I told him, concluding my tale, "is that I cannot be prosecuted; Mondor wouldn't dare bring charges against me and risk exposure."

"Don't be too sure of that, my chit," Noirceuil replied. "If he suspected you, and if he wanted to punish you, he wouldn't have to risk a thing; he'd need only pass the word discreetly to one judge or another that there was a certain little whore whom he would like to see chastised; he wouldn't even have to say why; a few days later, you'd find yourself on the scaffold."

"But how could that be?" I asked.

"Ah, chit," Noirceuil sighed wearily; "sometimes you're naive beyond belief. Do you think judges are any less corrupt than the rest of us? Why, they're the evilest men on the face of the earth! But don't worry about it; as long as you keep that lovely ass of yours in fine trim and as long as you continue to employ it with your customary skill, you need never worry about the scaffold." Then, laughing darkly, he added: "Besides, once one has realized that we all must die sooner or later, does it make any real difference whether it be on a scaffold or in a bed?"

Warmed by this profound thought, I fell into a deep and viscous sleep.

VI

A year passed, then another. My wealth increased by leaps and bounds. In addition to my pension as Noirceuil's mistress there were my earnings from the liaisons which Duvergier managed to arrange for me four and five times per week. Then there were the proceeds of my thefts; these surpassed all other income by double or treble. On the last day of the second year, I took complete inventory; including my investments and hidden valuables, I was worth more than twelve-million *louis*. Now there could be no doubt about it: I had really arrived.

In the days which followed I made fewer and fewer appointments and began devoting more and more time to the arts. I read all the great books, viewed all the great operas and scrutinized every picture in the Palais Luxembourg. Unfortunately, however, one afternoon I made the mistake in that museum of spending far too long admiring a Titian; it was a mistake which almost cost me my life.

How could this happen? What peril could there be in

examining a painting? Do you wonder, dear reader? Alas, the peril was not in examining the marvelous artwork but in being recognized while I was doing so. The man who recognized me was none other than — (the reader will surely recall him) — Lubin, the handsome valet of the Duke of Stern, my first customer after Madame Duvergier promoted me to the rank of princess-whore.

"Ah, lovely child!" Lubin sighed when I acknowledged his recognition of me; "I am indeed fortunate to have crosed paths with you, for I am in dire need of a friend. No doubt you remember my employer, the duke. Well, as he's got along in years, he's grown more and more ornery. Things reached such a state the other day that he almost decapitated a little girl just because she wouldn't do what he wanted her to. After seeing this I could work or him no longer; gathering my few belongings together, I left his employ.

"But, dear girl, believe it or not, the scoundrel refuses to leave me alone. He has hired some professional thugs to follow me around and harass me. The other day one of them beat me so viciously that I could barely walk, then threw me off a bridge into the Seine; fortunately a group of youngsters were passing by in a rowboat, or I surely would have drowned.

"And that's not the worst of it: the duke has done all he can to prevent me from earning a living; every time I apply for a position, I'm promptly told that it's already been taken (the duke, you see, has passed the word among his friends that I'm not to be hired); I can't work, I've been reduced to begging on the streets, my life is constantly in peril, three days have passed since I've had a morsel to eat . . . by heaven, dear Juliette, that's what I've come to. Can you help me? Can you find in your heart the goodness to offer a bit of succor to this lowly creature who once so lovingly reamed your ass? Have mercy on me, child; mercy . . . ."

I was moved by this tearful plea; yes, and I won't deny it, I also was moved by desires to scissors once again the handsome face of Lubin between my throbbing thighs. Summoning a carriage, I brought the poor creature to Noirceuil's house; there, after seeing to it that he had a full meal and a good, hot bath, I dragged him off to bed; sure enough, he hadn't lost an iota of his talent.

Our love bout over, I gave Lubin two of Noirceuil's suits and ten *louis* pocket money. Then I sent the talented young man on his way, very happy with myself for having brightened his life while at the same time drawing upon his resources to brighten my own. Little did I realize at the time how poorly I really had fared in the bargain.

Two days later, while taking an evening stroll, I was set upon by six brutes with pistols who bound my wrists and ankles, blindfolded me and forced me into a carriage "To the dungeon!" they shouted to the driver.

"Sirs," I begged, "have you not made an error?"

"Yes, we are making an error," replied a voice which I recognized instantly as that of the depraved Duke of Stern. "We should be taking you to the scaffold to wring your dirty neck. But I trust that the police will do the job for us before too much time passes." Whereupon a blow was struck, my eyes saw stars and my limp body fell unconscious to the floor. When I awoke, I was in a dirty, insect-ridden dungeon. For thirty-six hours I was alone. I received neither food nor drink.

Throughout my period of captivity, one thought ran constantly through my mind: never again would I surrender to compassion; having had the poor judgement to give succor, to perform a virtuous deed, I had been snatched away from the splendid life which theretofore was mine, and had been reduced to the lowest of states; now, if the duke's threat was carried out and I was hanged, I would die like a street urchin. Such, I told myself, are the perils of virtue.

But, suddenly, I was summoned from these contemplations by the rattle of a key in the door. Lo! — who should walk into my cell by Noirceuil.

"Ah, Juliette," he sighed wearily. "Now you can see the dangers of surrendering to a virtuous impulse. I've arranged for your release, but it wasn't easy; the duke was so furious that, were it not for the intercession of certain friends of mine, he would have strangled you with his bare hands."

"Oh, thank you, my darling," I sobbed, throwing myself at his feet. "Thank you for saving my life."

"No, don't thank me with tears," he said coldly; "in fact, don't thank me at all; if my prick were to get one ace stiffer from seeing you hang than from delivering you, you'd be on the scaffold this very minute and I'd be out there watching it happen."

Still, I could not refrain from hugging and kissing him in gratitude.

"No, damn you, no!" he shouted, kicking me away from him. "Let there be no demonstrations! I abhor mundane gestures!" Then, jerking me to my feet, he continued: "You must realize that what I have done for you was done in my own interests, not yours. You owe me absolutely nothing." He stroked my head gently. "But you owe it to yourself henceforth never to succumb to the temptations of virtue again; you must never permit yourself to perform an act which is beneficial to your fellow man. Do you understand?"

"Yes, dearest," I replied meekly.

"Then," he snapped, "let us be off!"

When we arrived at his home, Noirceuil elaborated upon the procedure of gaining my release. "It all came about," he said, "through the manipulations of my friend, Saint-Fond, Minister of State for this diseased country of ours. Yes, he is your liberator. I described your ass to him and he decided that the possibilities of amusing himself with it were sufficiently worth the effort of having you spared."

"I shall be forever in his debt," I replied.

"Indeed you shall," said Noirceuil. "He'll see to it that you don't forget it, either. Presently he is very anxious to meet you; in fact, I've arranged for you to entertain him at a dinner-party tonight. He's a great libertine and a devotee of the most monstrous vices and passions; I recommend total submissiveness."

"I shall follow your recommendations, my love," I said. "Henceforth, my soul shall be but an imitation of yours; my will shall be entirely thine."

"Ah, Juliette," he sighed. "You have the instincts of a wolf and the heart of a tiger — if only you don't let yourself fall back into foolish virtue. Now heed my words well: Saint-Fond is as powerful as any man alive; if he chooses, he can arrange for you to receive a sizeable pension for the rest of your life; you can become a woman of leisure and wealth, a whore-lady comparable to any in history. This is your big chance, my little succubus; don't jeopardize it."

"I shan't my darling," I promised, kissing him good-bye. "I promise that I shan't."

Once he was gone, I knelt upon the hard floor. Turning my eyes skyward, I said aloud:

"Fortune, Fate, Providence; whoever Thou art, hear me: if this is how you treat those who embrace evil and wickedness, how can one help but follow such a career? You leave me no choice, whoever-you-are: I must become a queen: a queen of sin an depravity . . ."

BOOK THREE

I

Handsome, articulate, athletic — this was Saint-Fond, a man of some fifty-five years, the last of which were spent in total debauchery. The Minister of State since the last Coronation, he was known throughout the world as a traitor and a thief; he boasted that he had, for motives of personal gain, deliberately sabotaged France's best interests in no fewer than eighteen different foreign treaties: and, on the home front, he was no less

perfidious; he carried on his person at all times no fewer
than ten death letters*, and more than twenty-thousand people had at one time or another been cast into
prison on his orders ("none of whom," he confided
to friends proudly, "ever had committed a single crime").

"My lovely Juliette!" he beamed delightedly as Noirceuil introduced us. "You're more beautiful than I'd even
dared imagine! Our blackguard friend here told me that
you had a praiseworthy ass, but, by Satan, these buns" —
he clutched them — "merit a place in history!"

"And, my friend," put in Noirceuil, "she's as evil-
hearted as she is beautiful. Overlook that tiny lapse into
virtue which resulted in her recent incarceration; other
than that she hasn't performed a virtuous deed since she
left the convent at Panthémont."

"Splendid, splendid, splendid," cheered the depraved
Minister. "Evildoers always delight in the recognition
of fellow evildoers; take it from me — I've done more
evil than any ten men."

"Well, sir," I replied, "I can only say that I hope I give
you reason tonight to believe that you have found in me
a kindred spirit."

"By Christ, Noirceuil, she's clever as well as beautiful!"
raved Saint-Fond. "I think I'm going to like her! a
lot! . . . But, enough talk for the nonce; I've invited you
here for dinner; let's stop chattering and start eating."

So saying, Saint-Fond led the way through an immense, arched corridor into a banquet hall of unbelievable splendor. Great, gold-scalloped pillars rose to
meet a ceiling covered with frescoes of cavorting Cupids
and Dianas; the windows were draped with the finest
brocades; the floors were pure Carrara, and the statues
which ornamented every nook and cranny would have
done Michelangelo proud.

* *lettres de cachet:* literally, "sealed letters;" the term presently
is used to describe any order issued by a sovereign: however, in
Eighteenth Century France, the sovereign's *lettres* almost invariably
were arrest orders, and, without trial, the designated victim was
imprisoned for as long as the sovereign wished, or he was executed; hence, our translation, "death letters."

"Isn't it exquisite?" said the Minister, taking in the whole room with a tremendous sweep of his hand. "I don't think there's another hall like it in all of Europe. All of which goes to prove that evil can be profitable as well as amusing."

Now he led the way to the head table, which groaned under the weight of dozens of roasts, stuffed game, enormous platters of fresh vegetables and huge jugs of wine. "There is the Chief of Staff of the Army," he said, pointing out a uniformed man at a table across the way. "There is the Minister of the Treasury." "There is d'Albert, the Chief Justice of the High Court; be especially kind to him, my little bird; it was he who saved your life twelve hours ago, and you can rest assured that he will expect you to repay his magnanimity."

We took our seats and Saint-Fond pointed out some other guests — this time persons whose distinctions were sexual rather than political. "This is Eglée," he said, indicating a child as pretty and as graceful as any whom I ever have seen; "she's thirteen and simply an enchantress." "Henriette; she has the largest tits in Paris; did you ever in your life see a pair of melons like that?" "Raoul; he's sixteen years old and has fourteen inches of cock; splendid fellow." "David; he's twenty and has been known to stay in the saddle for two and three hours without coming; have you ever heard of such endurance?"

A quick head-count by me revealed that there were exactly four children for each libertine present. I asked Saint-Fond if there was any reason for this precise proportion.

"Ah, yes, chit," he replied; "around here we like to do things systematically; I've arranged for each of my friends to be entertained by two boys and two girls, and the individual foursomes are further subdivided so that a skilled representative of each of the four major passions — ass-fucking, cunt-fucking, mouth-fucking and whipping — is present in each."

Now we dug into the food. It was succulent beyond

belief: the roasts fell apart at the touch of a fork, the sauces were exquisite and the vegetables were as crisp as if they just had been plucked from the ground. As we ate, I reached beneath the table and began frigging Saint-Fond — a spontaneous gesture which was greatly appreciated. Soon he became so aroused that he could contain himself no longer. Tearing me from the table, he shoved me into a linen closet and there, on a blanket of soiled tablecloths, bisected the buttocks he loved so much with a member whose immense size threatened to rip apart my intestines. Then, our delight having been taken, we returned to the table and resumed eating.

After the dessert dishes had been carted away, Noirceuil appeared at my side with Chief Justice d' Albert on his arm. "This is the lovely wench, your honor," said my satanic friend proudly; "she is willing to lie at your feet as payment for your magnificent gesture in saving her life today."

"It would be an unpardonable sin to kill a flower of such rare and elegant quality as this," replied d'Albert, lightly caressing my left breast. "Agreed, Saint-Fond?"

In reply, the Minister stood and took my trembling hands in his, saying a bit drunkenly: "My dear, by the power bestowed in me, I grant you life long impunity for any crime you may have cause to commit."

"Let me add to that," said the Chief Justice; "tomorrow there will be delivered to her a letter from the Chief Minister, nullifying in advance any action which any court in the country eventually might be induced to take against her." And kissing the exposed halves of each of my breasts, he added: "This is a sacred promise, my beloved Juliette."

Saint-Fond giggled at our show of chivalry and groped d'Albert smartly between the buttocks.

"Furthermore," he told the Chief Justice, "I am going to have her rewarded for all the misdeeds which I expect she will commit henceforth. Her prize will be bonuses in the form of pensions running from, let us say, two-thousand to twenty-five-thousand *francs* a year, depending upon the feats."

"It seems to me, Juliette," said Noirceuil, "that your slightest whim has now become the law of the land." Turning to the two politicians, he continued: "You certainly have put to marvelous purpose the authority vested in you by the laws and monarch of this beloved country."

Saint-Fond laughed. "One always labors best in one's own behalf," he said. "Our office is to safeguard and promote the welfare of the king's subjects; in ensuring our own safety and that of this engaging child, are we not carrying out our duties?" Then without even a polite nod to his companions, he seized me between the legs and speedily propelled me to a nearby boudoir..

"Here, take this!" he said, pulling an immense stone from his pocket. "It is a diamond worth ten-thousand *louis,* payment in advance for the pleasures which you are going to afford me this evening." When I hesitated, he added: "Take it my dear, it cost me nothing. It comes from the State funds, not from my pocket."

"Indeed, my lord, your generosity stuns me—"

"My generosity will not stop tonight, Juliette. I want a woman like you in my household; a woman who will stop at nothing to insure my satisfaction.

"I am such a woman, sir."

"Are you sure? Would you, for example, poison someone for me?"

"Do you poison people?"

"Yes, when I have exhausted all other paths of appeal. You are not adverse to such technical problems, are you?"

"Not at all," I assured him. "Every crime I have committed thus far has delighted me. It is merely that at poison I am still a novice."

"Adorable creature," Saint-Fond murmured, "I shall teach you all you need to know."

"When shall the deed be done?"

"Tonight. When we return to the banquet room for liqueurs and small talk, I shall seat one of our lady-guests next to you. Ingratiate yourself with her; deceive her as artfully as you can: then, at a propitious moment, cast this powder" — he handed me an envelope — "into her drink. It's effect will be swift. Succeed, and the post in my household is yours."

"My lord, I am your servant," I replied.

"Good, splendid. Then serve me in another manner. Your vicious nature excites my prick to prodigious dimensions. Offer me a receptacle for it."

"My ass, sir?" I asked, proffering the receptacle to his vision. "Or would you prefer another orifice?"

"Juliette, Juliette," he laughed, advancing upon me with pike aloft. "To fuck you other than in the ass would be like going to Rome and ignoring the Colosseum." And, so saying, he pushed me onto the bed, rolled me onto my stomach and hammered his huge tool into my intestines. As before, it was over quickly: indeed, scarcely had we started than I felt his seed burst warmly into my bowels and his heavy body slide off my much-abused back.

"Well, my dear," said the fast-discharging Minister, now ushering me toward the door, "we have been intimate twice in as many hours; a rather good average, I would say; but don't get the idea, as less bright girls might, that you share anything more than my member; there's no love involved here, no emotional attachment of any sort; it's purely and simply sex. Also, let me warn you never to try to take advantage of the privilege which just was bestowed upon you: I demand respect: apart from the eminent position which I occupy, it so happens that my birth is illustrious, my fortune enormous and my credit rating superior even to the king's; keep that in mind in case you're ever tempted to regard me as your equal."

"I assure you, my lord, that the thought never entered my mind."

"Splendid; let's keep things that way. You see, Juliette, this business about Christian equality is a lot of nonsense. In my view, Nature put the great on earth as she put stars in the sky; they are to shed light upon the

world, never to descend to its level. Such is my pride;
I am unique and powerful and I expect to be treated so.
Is that clear?"

"Completely, sir," I said.

"Fine; then let's return to our guests."

In a moment we were back in the midst of our friends,
joining the party just as d'Albert was repairing to the
boudoir with Henriette and two boys. I took my place
at the table and helped myself to a glass of sherry. Then
I turned to Saint-Fond — but, lo!, he had gone. I looked
about the room; he was nowhere in sight.

Now came the awful surprise — indeed, the most in-
sidious and ugly surprise imaginable. As I stared at them
wide-eyed, Saint-Fond, Noirceuil and a lovely young
woman came through the front door, crossed the room
and seated themselves at the table alongside me. And the
woman — she, apparently, who was to receive my dose of
poison — was none other than . . . Noirceuil's wife!

"My lord," I whispered to the Minister incredulously;
"do my eyes deceive me? Is this the woman you have
designated to be my victim?"

"She is," replied he; "does this change your mind about
doing it?"

"N-n-no," I stammered. "It is just that I am surprised."

"Well, don't let anything surprise you, my dear; and,
above all, don't let anything sway you from executing
your mission, because, if you fail . . . . But let us not talk
about what will happen if you fail; I don't want you
acting under a threat; I want your sole motive in this
deed to be submission to my will, regardless of the consequences."

"As you like it, my lord."

"Fine," said the Minister. And, with that, he turned
to Noirceuil. "Would you believe it, my blackguard
friend?" he said, his overly-loud tone of voice obviously
intended to frighten Mme. Noirceuil. "Tomorrow I am
supposed to prepare and dispatch a death-letter for a
man; a man who, like you, Noirceuil, adores giving his

wife to other men. It seems that this fellow's wife went along with his wishes for a while, but then she complained to her family; now I am supposed to have the man imprisoned."

"Excessively severe punishment," replied Noirceuil dryly.

"Severe, you say?" put in d'Albert, returning from his little orgy. "Why there are dozens of countries where they put such fellows to death."

"Ah, you pawns of the law are all alike," said Noirceuil, not concealing his disgust. "You're a bunch of bloodthirsty bastards. I was told once that there are a great many of you gentlemen of the robe whose pricks rise up indignantly every time you pronounce the sentence of death; I never used to believe it; then it occurred to me that, for no other apparent reason, judges invariably sit behind a bench which comes all the way up to their necks!"

"Don't be bitter, Noirceuil," chuckled Saint-Fond. "After all, one man's meat is another man's poison."

"Yes," added d'Albert; "and why shouldn't one select an occupation which gives him pleasure — as pronouncing death sentences does to me?"

"Exactly; that's the whole answer in a nutshell," said Saint-Fond. "But, gentlemen, we are straying from the point under discussion. What I was about to say was that I think it's a shame the way most wives —" here, winking at d'Albert, he nodded toward Mme. Noirceuil "—are behaving these days. They're undermining the very foundations of libertinage."

"Precisely what do you mean, my friend?" replied d'Albert, grinning wickedly as he came to understand fully the character of the game being played.

"Why, look at them; look at the way they act," said Noirceuil, taking up the argument. "To their 'honor' these bitches sacrifice every sensual delight. They use their shoddy virtue as a whip, slashing and maiming every creature who has the kindness to try to assist them in

the discovery of sensual pleasure. Ah, the vixens; in my
opinion, these cuntless prigs should be isolated from
society; virtue, honor, chastity and modesty should mater-
ialize as massive stone cocks, and each of these vicious
bitches should be impaled upon them as a spider is impaled upon a pin."

"But why this violent invective, my friend?" cried
d'Albert, casting a look of feigned surprise at Mme. Noirceuil. "Surely no one in the present company fits that
description."

"He is referring to me, sir," said Mme. Noirceuil sadly.
"I have appealed to the Pope to dissolve our marriage."

"How horrible!" cried Saint-Fond "Marriage is the
cornerstone of society."

"Yes," said Noirceuil, pretending glumness; "but my
dearest beloved and I have had all we can take of it;
we must call the affair off; *la commedia é finita.*"

"Then she shall be mine," said Saint-Fond, putting an
arm about Mme. Noirceuil's shoulder. "I'll love the bitch.
She's always had a great talent for calling my weapon
to battle." So saying, he tugged the unfortunate woman's
gown over her shoulder and began nibbling at her soft,
white breast. "It's sheer murder," he said, "to give up a
wife as lovely as this."

"I think," chuckled d'Albert evilly, "that murder is
exactly what Noirceuil has in mind."

"Jesus Christ!" gasped Saint-Fond, still gnawing at the
fright-shriveled breast. "You can't mean it!"

"What alternative do I have?" asked Noirceuil impassively.

"Well," replied Saint-Fond, "now that you put it that
way, I suppose your choice is rather limited. So, murder
it must be. But be cautious, my friend; let's not perform
the dastardly deed in an haphazard fashion; we must be
systematic."

"Indeed we must," said d'Albert gravely. "It is my
suggestion that we torture her a bit first so as to put
her in a frame of mind where she will welcome her demise quite readily."

"By Christ, yes!" cheered Saint-Fond. "You're a genius, you old scoundrel. A sheer genius." And, so saying, he seized up a candle from the table and thrust it into Mme. Noirceuil's eyes. "By burning the lashes," he explained, "we make sure that she has no choice but to watch the tortures which will be meted out subsequently."

"Capital! Capital!" boomed d'Albert.

Now, suddenly inspired by this violence, I grabbed a bottle of brandy and poured its contents over the poor woman's head. "Let's light her up, boys!" I called. "Let's cook ourselves a human crepe suzette."

Following my example the depraved threesome ventured forth with brandy bottles of their own. Hands ripped off Mme. Noirceuil's dress; corks popped; her body was saturated with liquor; a candle was thrust against her matted, liquor-soaked mound. Immediately a soft blue flame took form at her pretty pubus, flickered for an instant, then blazed to life; her whole body became one beautiful, blue-and-yellow torch.

"Aiiiiiiieeeeeeeeeeeeeee!!!!!!" gasped the hapless creature falling to the floor and rolling around to snuff out the flames. "Aiiiiiiiiiiieeeeeeeeeeeeeeeeeeee!!!!!!"

Finally the last flame died out. As the three debauchees — along with a crowd of onlookers who had gathered to cheer us on — laughed merrily, the suffering Mme. Noirceuil lifted herself painfully to her feet. Her body looked like a freshly steamed lobster.

"Ah, my poor, dear woman," I sighed with feigned pity. "It must hurt terribly. Here; drink this" — I handed her the glass containing the poison — "it should ease your pain."

With a slight hesitancy which suggested that she doubted my motives yet realized the futility of resistance, she touched the glass to her lips and slowly swallowed the fatal mixture.

Noirceuil waited until the liquid had vanished; then, cackling savagely, he told her: "You are going to meet your friend, Mr. Christ, my darling; he is waiting in heaven for you and you soon will be at his right hand;

the poison which you have drunk should take effect in seconds; a thousand fangs will rip into your chaste bowels and shred them to pieces; your pious ass will disintegrate into a cloud of pain and your sanctimonious tongue will shrivel up into an unrecognizeable lump of charred tissue. Well, die, you bitch, die; you've had a taste of hell on earth; now escape to your cool, ice-pricked God in his fireless heaven."

As if on cue, Mme. Noirceuil suddenly doubled over, her hands clutching her stomach. An expression of absolute horror froze across her lobster-pink face. She fell to the floor, dead.

After a moment of silence, Saint-Fond raised his bowed head and clapped his hand to Noirceuil's shoulder in the manner of a mourner. "My dear friend," he said, "you have sacrificed your wife to the principles which we all hold dear; it is only fair that you be given another to replace her. My daughter, Alexandrine, is fourteen years old and as beautiful as I am wicked. Take her; marry her; enjoy her in any manner which pleases you — my son." Tears welling up in his eyes as he mouthed the word, "son," the solemn-faced Minister now turned to me. "Since Noirceuil is about to marry, Juliette," he said, "I propose that you come and live with me. The money and comfort which I shall shower on you will prove ample compensation for the losses you may incur by leaving your old habitation."

"Does this meet with your approval, darling Noirceuil?" I asked ceremoniously.

"So be it, child; since Saint-Fond and I are both notorious adulterers, there's no doubt that you and I will share the same bed often enough in the future."

"Then it is done," intoned d'Albert. "And now, gentlemen, shall we bury this lovely body?"

Thereupon Mme. Noirceuil's remains were carried into the garden, where they were interred under a rose bush. Thus ended the supper at the home of France's distinguished Minister of State.

II

Two weeks later, there having been completed the exchange agreement under which Noirceuil was to acquire Saint-Fond's daughter as a wife and Saint-Fond was to acquire me as a mistress, I moved into the Minister's magnificent mansion on the Rue du Faubourg Saint-Honoré.

"Madame," said my new lover, greeting me in the foyer, "you see me in the hour of my glory; the king has dealt generously with me — I dare say, in accordance with my just dues — and I have profited accordingly. Today my position is untouchable, my fortune immense and my future assured. And you, my little bird, have been placed in the center of my circle of confidence."

Now, leading me up an enormous, thickly-carpeted, spiral stairway to a marble-walled, second-story sitting room, he continued: "Such a position is not one to be taken lightly, as I'm sure you well realize. And, just to make sure that you appreciate fully the gravity of your responsibilities, I am going show you two keys which I keep on my ring at all times: the first here — look at it closely — is made of pure gold and opens the vault in which all my treasures are stored; do my bidding and you can be certain that I will employ it often in your behalf: the second — examine it, if you will — is of steel and fits the lock of a vacant cell high in the Second Tower at the Bastille; the cell shall be yours if you fail to serve me well."

Replacing the keyring in his pocket, he poured two glasses of brandy and handed one to me. "Now," he went on, let us let proceed to more specific business. As my mistress, dear Juliette, you shall have two functions, one political, the other social. As you might well imagine, in my position it often becomes necessary to kill people, either for the purpose of eliminating their opposition to my programs or simply to divert attention from one or another of my misdeeds; thus, as your first function, you will dispose of all the victims to whom I am unable to attend personally. Now, as regards the second function, let me remind you of the libertine supper at which we first met a fortnight ago. It shall be your duty to stage two such suppers per week. I shall give you a million *francs* per week with which to work, but remember: I require absolute splendor: exquisite meats, rare wines, succulent fowl, spicy soups, exotic fruits; whores of the highest quality, and in quantity; music, spectacle, extravagance: in short, I want magnificence which would make Nero and Caligula look like a pair of beggars."

"You are the Zeus of pleasure, my lord," I replied, thrilled to my fingertips at the thought of such libertine excesses. "I shall most enthusiastically do your bidding."

"Excellent," he said, stroking my buttocks. "The question is: how soon do you think you can arrange for the first such affair?"

I must have at least a month to ready the organization," I answered.

"A month is fine; take exactly that long; I'll expect the first banquet to be staged a month from today." Draining his glass of brandy, he sat behind his desk and tugged open a drawer. "Now, then," he went on, "here is the patent of impunity which d'Albert promised you two weeks ago. I received it from the Chief Minister today. Take it and steal to your heart's desire; you've now been given carte blanche to do so."

"And the death-letters which you promised?" I reminded him.

"Come in here," he said leading me into an adjacent room. "My clerk" he addressed a young man sitting behind a desk "remember this young lady's face. Whenever she requests a death-letter from you deliver it at once. Give her as many as she wishes." The clerk acknowledged the order, whereupon Saint-Fond led me back into the sitting room. "And now, my little bird," he continued, "all the realm is your plaything: destroy it, if you wish, for it is yours to do as you please; all this by courtesy of His Majesty, the King who acts in accordance with that Divine Right which our stooges, the

bishops and priests of the Roman Catholic Church,
proclaim so often and so eloquently before the idiotic
assholes who lack the perspicacity to see through their
lies. Now, tell me that this doesn't tickle your sweet little
pubic hairs!"

"I am overcome, my lord," I said.

"There's one thing more," the Minister smiled. "Here
is a little gift to seal the bargain." So saying, he took
from under his desk a gold-covered casket filled almost
to overflowing with gleaming coins. "There are five-thou-
sand *louis* there, Juliette," he told me. "Take them and
use them as you see fit."

"I am flabbergasted, my lord. Your generosity leaves
me speechless."

"Well there's no need to talk. As a matter of fact,
the enterprise in which I now desire your participation
is one in which speech would be something of a hindr-
ance."

"What do you have in mind, sir?"

"A bit of lubricity, my little bird," he cackled. "A bit
of lubricity to cap off this enchanting morning. Come
with me, please." Now he led me into an oak-panelled
den, the floor of which was covered entirely with mattresses. "This is my sex-room," he explained; "it is the
one room in the house where you are not a queen: here
you assume the rank of common whore; you become a
passion toy, nothing more. Now undress."

Obediently I peeled off my dress, slip and brassiere.
Then, as I slipped the last bit of scanty silk over one
ankle, the Minister suddenly lashed out with his foot.
The blow caught me in the side of the head, knocking me
to the floor.

"Ah, fuck!" he said. "There's nothing like taking them
by surprise." Then, sitting on my stomach, he spread my
thighs and with a small, silver tweezers began plucking
at my pubic hairs.

Sharp pains darted through my body — pleasurable
pinpricks of sensation which aroused my passions to
fever-pitch. However, no sooner had he stoked this heat

than he tired of his project. Putting the tweezers back into his pocket, he took from his vest a gleaming gold medallion attached to a velvet ribbon. "This,' he said, "is the highest award which our nation can bestow upon its servants. I command you to kiss it." I did so. "And now," he said, "piss on it."

As I complied with the strange request, I could not conceal the puzzlement which found expression in my furrowed forehead.

"This profanity may strike you as odd," said Saint-Fond, anticipating my question, "but the fact is that, while I pride myself on what these trinkets represent, I take even greater pride in being free to profane them." Then, smelling the just pissed-upon decoration, he stuffed it back into his vest. "Very well, Juliette," he said; "this has been sufficient mischief for now; put your clothes back on and we'll return to the sitting room."

Once back in that opulent salon, my host showed me a portrait of his daughter, Alexandrine. "You've probably wondered what she looked like — this tender morsel whose services are being exchanged for yours. Tell me, who do you think is getting the better of the bargain, Noirceuil or me?"

"Oh, she's beautiful!" I gasped, totally enchanted by the lovely, long-haired child whose comeliness the portraitist had captured so well. Then, evading the Minister's question by asking one of my own, I said: "Are you going to favor me with a personal look at her before she leaves to join her new master? Perhaps you could arrange an orgy involving the three of us — you, me and her."

"I'm sorry, my little bird; he replied, "that's quite out of the question."

"But surely you're not sending her to Noirceuil without first enjoying her yourself."

"Certainly not. I plucked the fruit from her sweet young vine more than a year ago."

"And now you've ceased to love her?" I asked coquettishly.

"Juliette, Juliette, Juliette," he replied unaware of my

frivolous intent; "oh, my little fool when will you ever learn? I am a libertine! Libertines have no energy to waste on foolishness such as love. Everything must be sacrificed to pleasure. All persons — wives, daughters, mothers, fathers, everyone — all are expendable. I wanted you; my daughter was the price I had to pay. It's as uncomplicated as that."

"But when Noirceuil tires of her? . . ." I teased him. "She'll undergo the usual fate of his wives, I suppose."

"And you don't care?"

"Who knows? Perhaps I'll even participate in the ceremony."

"Ah, my lord!" I exclaimed, suddenly aroused too much to keep up my naive facade. "Your wickedness excites me so. Quick: give me a murder assignment! I want to massacre some innocents! I'm enflamed with the lust to destroy!"

"Marvelous!" he cried, wringing his hands. "There's nothing quite as pleasurable as watching someone who does her work with relish!" Then, opening his desk drawer again, he handed me a slip of paper. "This is a death-letter for a pretty young girl who presently is in prison. I fucked her the other morning while I was making an inspection there and now I'm afraid she might talk to the wrong pepole. Take this and have her executed."

"Ah, I'm ecstatic!" I beamed. "I can just see the ax fall!"

Saint-Fond patted me on the shoulder. "Yes, Juliette," he said, "I think you've got what it takes. You're going to go a long way."

III

I shall interrupt the narrative at this point, dear reader, to describe briefly the style in which I lived as a result of being transferred from Noirceuil to Saint-Fond. To begin with, I was assigned a private apartment in one wing of that magnificent mansion on Rue du Faubourg

Saint-Honoré; then I was given two charming carriages
and four horses; next I hired three lackeys, all huge fellows and very handsome; then I engaged a cook, a
reader, three chambermaids, a hairdresser and a pair
of coachmen, all exciting sexual specimens as well as
capable servants. The contents of my wardrobe was
worth well above one-hundred-thousand *francs*, and
my jewelry was valued at more than a quarter-million
louis d'or . . . and all this, it will be remembered, accru-
ing to me when I was still a few days short of my seven-
teenth year. One can only marvel at the fortunes of Vice.
But now, back to the narrative:

Having been installed as Saint-Fond's mistress, I
set myself promptly to work. In exactly one month, as
I had promised, I was able to provide the first of his suppers. The guest of honor was Chief Justice d'Albert,
and Saint-Ford was most eager to please him; I saw to
it that he was pleased beyond his fondest expectations.

The fête was staged in Saint-Fond's garden. Tables
and chairs were arranged in the form of giant mush-
rooms and were set on a bed of golden daffodils, surrounded by thick, waist-high lilac bushes. For a roof,
I used a bower of roses, and as a table centerpiece a
mountain of gardenias, lilies, gladioli and chrysanthy-
mums. The plates and serving dishes were jade and porcelain; the tablecloth was pure, hand-woven silk.

As soon as the last dessert dish had been cleared away,
I clapped my hands. Immediately the bower of roses
opened overhead and there descended before the startled eyes of the guests a fiery, silver-trimmed chariot. On
it were six girls whom I had spirited away from a convent at Meaux — all virgins aged twelve through fourteen years and one more beautiful than the next: three,
naked except for billowy, cloud-like puffs of gauze about
their arms and legs, represented the three Furies; the
other three, completely nude, represented the Furies'
victims and were imprisoned in chains covered with
the skin of serpents. When the chariot came to a halt

at the foot of the dais, the three Furies alighted and bowed to the guests. Instantly they were greeted with a thunderous ovation.

"Brilliant, my dear!" Saint-Fond cried. "Aboslutely spellbinding!" Then, to d'Albert: "I trust that your grace is pleased with my directress' first offering?"

"Stunned," answered the Chief Justice. "Juliette, you are a goddess; a demon; I never have clapped eyes on a fairer maid."

"Nor have I," the Minister said. "But let us concern ourselves now with these Furies, who, if my eyes do not deceive me, are superbly fleshed also."

"Indeed!" said d'Albert, as if noticing their physical charms for the first time. "By Christ, they're marvelous!" And, so saying, he tore off his pants and began to pursue the prettiest of the three. When he caught her, he took a diamond-studded spyglass from his coat-pocked and began studying her carefully. Then he took her in his arms and said: "Put your tongue in my mouth."

The child complied with this request; whereupon the jaded jurist commanded: "Belch or be bitten."

The poor girl evidently lacked the ability to provide him with that which he sought; but, being quick-witted, she pulled her tongue out of his mouth before he could execute his threat. This cleverness threw the aging justice into a rage. Beating her with the spyglass, he finally succeeded in knocking her to the ground. Then, forcing open her thighs, he shoved the instrument up her anus.

"Aiiiiieeeee!!" screamed the Fury as intromission was complete. But d'Albert, not in the slightest moved toward mercy, only kicked her in the face, then walked away. Her unconscious form was left lying prostrate beneath a lilac bush.

"My good Saint-Fond," the depraved old man now said, "that enterprise excited me more than I can tell you. For an encore, what do you say we have ourselves flogged by the two Furies who remain?"

"Yes — with rose branches!" proposed my hero, going

his guest one better.

No sooner was it said than done: garlands of thorny branches were wrapped around bamboo chutes and the two men were lashed from neck to knee. Then, spurred by their pain to new heights of libertine fancy, the depraved duo called for the three young victims who remained chained in the chariot. D'Albert grabbed a candle in one hand and a fistful of rose petals in the other; next, throwing the youngest virgin onto the ground, he proceeded to cover her untouched mound with rose petals; then, grinning lasciviously, he let dripping wax from his candle seal the petals in place until he had created a lovely rose bouquet between the girl's thighs. This accomplished, the jaded jurist raced toward the lilac bushes with a small glass in his hand; returning, he began to stuff freshly captured bees into the young virgin's sweet hive: piercing screams shattered the air of our idyllic nocturnal setting as the bees feasted on the lovely creature's pure vaginal nectar; all the while, d'Albert stood above her, frigging himself assiduously; finally, when it appeared that the poor child would all but die from her pain, the lecherous old man thrust his hips above her body, held his tool aloft and ejaculated all over his artificial bouquet. "By Christ," he gasped; "that was simply beautiful." Then he collapsed in his chair, completely exhausted.

"Juliette," said the Minister, dismounting from one of the Furies whom he had been embuggering while d'Albert stage his horticultural experiment, "you are a charming and able creature; a master; nay, a genius. Let us leave these unsubtle characters here; in the silence of the arbor — in the secret shadows of eveningtide — we can follow the whims of our fancy without fear of interruption. Come, my child: together we shall shatter all thresholds of human experience; we shall transport ourselves to ecstasies yet undreamed by finite minds."

So saying, he took my hand in his and led me away from the scene of my triumphant debut as the Minister of State's hostess.

IV

Two weeks passed. Each of my suppers was received more enthusiastically than the one before it — and each of my whims, thanks to the generosities of Saint-Fond, was gratified in full measure. I could not ask for a happier situation.

One afternoon, when the necessity to sign certain papers pertinent to his forthcoming wedding brought Noirceuil to the Minister's house, I told him of my new-found contentment. "Out of respect for your principles, my friend, I refrain from thanking you," I said; "however, I did want you to know how much joy your maneuverings have brought me."

"I'm glad to hear it," he replied; "not for your sake, of course, since I couldn't care less what happens to you but for my own, since one can never tell when he may need a favor or two. Anyway, you seem to have Saint-Fond under your thumb; continue to conduct yourself intelligently and you'll soon be one of the wealthiest women in Europe."

"I shall, my love; I swear it. But, tell me, my good mentor: don't you suppose that eventually my libertine looseness will incur Saint-Fond's jealousy."

Noirceuil laughed heartily. "Not a chance, my child," he said. "He realizes that you cannot attain self-expression save through much wrongdoing. Furthermore, your excesses tickle his sense of the absurd, so rest easy: you have nothing to fear on this count." Then, a pensive expression crossing his darkly handsome face, he went on: "But, Juliette, examine briefly the nature of this stupid trait of jealousy: you should realize, my pet, that the jealously of a man for his mistress does not, as many people believe, speak very highly of his regard for her; after all, it is not fondness for the woman which makes her lover jealous, it is dread of the public humiliation which he would suffer were she to have a change of heart about him. Consider this: there is no lover in the world who would not prefer to see his mistress dead rather than unfaithful; hence, it is less the loss of her which moves the jealous man than it is the opprobrium attached to her desertion of him."

"Wise thoughts, my dear," I replied, enchanted at the cool logic of this man; "I didn't realize until now how I have come to miss your instructive discourses."

"Yes," he said; "I've thought of that, Juliette, and I've taken it upon myself to find you someone to replace me. In fact,telling you about her is one of the reasons behind my visit today. I know a widow — a lovely woman with a brilliant criminal mind. Her name is Clairwil, and from now on she will take my place as your tutor. She is a millionairess and knows everybody worth knowing. You can't fail to profit from studying under her."

And thus it happened, dear reader, that I came to meet this magnificent woman who would contribute so much to the shaping of my thoughts in years to come — Clarissa de Clairwil, instructress extraordinaire . . .

V

Clairwil was tall, brunette and marvelously proportioned; her eyes were black, and burned darkly in her pale face; her lips were thick and sensuous; an air of majesty pervaded her entire being. To these regal physical qualities, she added an intellect without peer: her command of English and Italian was on a par with her French; she was an accomplished actress and dancer; she could speak expertly and at great length on any number of academic disciplines, from science to philosophy; she was a poet, a singer, a marvelous pianist and a very capable politician.

Clairwil had been a widow for five years — her husband having met his demise at her hand. She had no children; indeed, she had a hatred for the little creatures which surpassed that of any woman I have ever known. As for the rest of her attitudes toward humanity, they can be summed up in one word: indifference. As she, herself, put it: "My soul is callous, child; it is impassive; I am an entirely self-centered creature; my mind is my prime mover and my heart is encased in stone; I cherish vices, despise virtues and seek above all else that which makes me happy or eases my pains; I would bomb a hospital if so doing would merely alleviate my headache."

With such a splendid personality, one would think, Clairwil should be besieged by adulators of every shape and description; but the truth of the matter is that she had very few friends; indeed, she was as sceptical of friendship as she was of virtue. As she told me on the occasion of our first meeting: "I despise friendship, my dear; a friend is someone you count on when you are too weak to do a job yourself; before I'd admit that I needed help like that, I'd let the job go undone."

Hearing this, I fell into a deep sadness. "But I had hoped so much that you and I could be friends," I told her; "Noirceuil had said so much about you that it became my main ambition to ingratiate myself in your favor."

"Softly, child, softly," replied she. "I said that I despise friendship; but while you and I will not be friends, we'll definitely be collaborators. There's an important difference between the two types of relationship, a difference which, I am sure, I have no need to spell out . . . Ah, and what collaborators we can be! Noirceuil has told me much about you also. We have similar minds, similar vices; we belong together; if we join forces, there's no limit to what we can do: together the two of us can seduce the world!"

So saying, the marvelous woman led the way to her dining room where we were served a repast befitting the first meeting of France's two most notorious female sensualists. Throughout the splendid meal we exchanged thoughts and philosophies, releasing to each other all our innermost secrets, all our unspoken dreams. Then, the meal over, we retired to a sitting room and reclined on velvet-covered pillows; soft candlelight and sparkling wine made the scene complete, and soon I felt the summons of hot desire.

"My dearest Clairwil," I whispered, "we have shared intimacies this afternoon which create a bond all but unbreakable. Yet, the ultimate intimacy remains unapproached. I do not wish to offend you, Madame, or to presume upon our relationship: however, I submit to you that no true voluptuary would refrain any longer from the carnal pleasures. Your body inflames me, Madame. Does mine displease you? If not, avail yourself of it as I avail myself of yours."

"Ah, Christ, Juliette, it's good to hear you talk like that! I was waiting to see if you would," said she, immediately burying her head in my crotch. "My fucking loins are smoking! Quick: undress me: we'll do whatever you like!"

Wtihout delay I went to work at the cincture which held her gown in place. She, no less quickly, brought expert hands into play against the fasteners of my dress. In a trice we were naked as two jaybirds.

Clairwil's body was nothing short of a dream. Smooth, white skin, supple and soft to the touch; gentle, graceful limbs; a trim, flat abdomen which eased upward into the most magnificent breasts — never had I seen a pair quite as lovely!—and beautiful buttocks the likes of which I had never dared imagine.

Instantly we fell upon each other, hugging, kissing, licking, sucking, gnawing, nibbling, biting, lapping. I felt Clairwil's delicate tongue slip between my inflamed thighs and spiral wetly upward, not coming to rest until it had slashed through my throbbing sphincter; meanwhile, her searching fingers played wild, sweet music on my buttocks. I reciprocated with vigor, and in seconds, her tender moans informed me that my efforts were more than up to the task. Orgasm crashed down upon both of us at once, its explosive violence leaving our bodies weary and trembling.

"My dearest dear," I sighed, lying comfortably in her strong arms now that the zenith of pleasure had been reached. "I am transported beyond this world. You are the most exquisite lapper I ever have met."

She chuckled softly. "I adore women," she said; "is it any wonder that I am expert in giving them pleasure? And, just for the record, let me say that you wield a pretty wicked tongue yourself; I take it that you're no newcomer to the rites of Lesbos."

"No; most definitely not; I've worshipped at her altar since I was but a little girl."

"As have I. We are depraved, dear heart; wholly depraved. But let us remind ourselves that it is not our fault that Nature gave us tastes different from the ordinary; we are as we are, and there's nothing that we can do about it; furthermore, I personally am quite happy with my differences: after all, what man could ever know the secrets which we know about giving a woman true sexual delight? Only one of our kind can play upon the strings of another woman; men are gross, vulgar, clumsy idiots in this department: all of which goes to prove that there is nothing more unjust than those laws which prescribe a certain order to the mingling of the sexes; in a sane society we would be permitted to mingle as we please, and those who didn't like it could lump it."

"Ah, dearest instructress, I agree with you fully. But tell me: do I infer from your comments that you actually dislike men?"

"Of course not; I neither like nor dislike them; men are instruments, and, as such, they are to be used — not liked or disliked. Does the carpenter like or dislike his saw; the woodsman his adze; the tailor his needle? Well, no more passionately than this should you or I feel about any man." A lewd brightness lighting up her eyes, she continued: "But women — women, dear Juliette — are another matter. Christ, how they inflame me. I especially admire those foul-mouthed, immodest, vigorous serving-creatures one finds on the streets. They make me feverish with desire. Do you, perchance, have any such in your employ?"

"I have only four women in my permanent hire," I replied, "and I doubt that any of these would meet your criteria."

"My dear, you ought to employ at least twenty. It is clear that I am going to have to teach you how to use your enormous sums of money . . . Well, no matter; for now, we'll use my sluts; I have forty of them — my appetites being stronger than most dykes — and I'm rather sure you'll find the ones I choose delightful."

Reaching over her head, she now tugged a velvet cord; in the distance a bell tinkled softly, and, minutes later, a tall, swarthy servant materialized at our feet.

"Bring me any four of my playmates," commanded Clairwil, "and find me some switches while you're at it."

"As you say, Madame," he replied, bowing.

"Do you whip, my dear?" I asked after the servant had vanished.

"Dear heart, I whip and am whipped in return. There is no surer way to arouse my passions than with a good lashing. Indeed, flagellation is a perfect remedy for exhausted loins; an invigorating stimulant for enfeebled desires: nothing is more exciting than to see a love-object writhing under the savage blows of a switch: blood, sweat, groans, screams, tears, cries, all contribute to an experience of supreme ecstasy . . . Christ, I hope he hurries with those four; discoursing on the subject has filled my bucket to overflowing."

No sooner had she finished speaking than the door creaked open and the servant reappeared. With him were four lovely creatures; all were naked and all were filthy-looking, but their dirt-streaked bodies were superbly built; each carried a bundle of switches.

"Well," mused Clairwil whimsically, "let us begin by order of age. You — the youngest one, with the blonde hair — come here and prostrate yourself at my feet — Now, humbly beg pardon for your clumsy behavior yesterday."

"But, Madame," said the frightened girl, "I never saw you until now."

"She's new here, Juliette," my instructress explained; "she hasn't yet caught onto the rules of the game." Turning back to the girl, she swung out with her fist; the blow sent a fountain of blood gushing from the child's mouth. "I tell you that you are a clumsy whore, fuckface! Now kneel and ask my forgiveness!"

Obediently the girl fell to her knees. "Forgive me, Madame, for whatever it is I may have done," she said contritely.

Clairwil next swung a switch, leaving three gleaming red tracks across the child's breast. "You must be punished, you filthy slut," she screamed savagely. "Look at your body — dirty, filthy, unclean . . . By fuck, you stink! You're rank, I say! The smell of you fills the room! You must be made to pay for this insult you offer my nose!"

Now she tore into the child with unbelievable fury, knocking her to the floor! and whipping her until both sides of the poor youngster's body were covered with wounds. Then, spreading open the welt-ribboned thighs, she plunged her closed fist into the poor creature's womb. The girl's screams of pain were choked off by the merciful intervention of unconsciousness.

Her eyes sparkling, her lips foam-flecked, her forehead studded with beads of perspiration, Clairwil staggered to her feet and addressed herself to the remaining three.

"Next," she said. No one moved.

"Next, I say."

Still there was no movement.

"By fuck, I said NEXT!"

So saying, the enraged instructress seized by the hair the girl in the center of the line and dragged her to her knees.

"Now, Miss Bitch," she snapped, "you will kiss my knees."

As the child leaned forward and touched her lips to the haughty imperieuse's kneecap, Clairwil's leg swung upward. The poor girl took the full force of the blow in her mouth; several teeth were snapped in half; bleeding profusely, the victim was led away.

Clairwil now took a third girl. This hapless creature was forced to lie upon her back while her mistress, slipping on a pair of spiked-heel shoes, jumped madly upon her breasts and stomach. When the suffering child's whole torso was but a grillwork of red wounds, the attack ceased; but now Clairwil dropped suddenly to a squatting position and, without warning, bit into ' one of the girl's breasts with such force that the nipple was completely severed. "Fuck!" screamed my depraved collaborator, sucking madly at the gushing blood. "Fuck! Fuck! *Fuck!!!*"

Finally! the third girl was carried away and the fourth was brought forward. Dumb with terror, the child took one look at Clairwil and beshit herself right on the spot.

"Impudent, impudent creature!" screamed my instructress. "Bloody, indecent bitch!" Kicking and punching with a force scarcely believable, she knocked her victim to the floor, the poor child's body coming to rest directly in the center of the mustard-colored pool of feces which she had discharged. Then, taking a stone bust from its pedestal, the merciless woman dropped it onto the child's head; there was a sickening crunch as the skull cracked open; then, like albumen oozing from an egg, the girl's grey brains spilled out of her head and mingled with the feces.

"By Christ, that was quite a workout," sighed Clairwil wearily as the servant carried off the girl's body. Then, leading me to an adjacent chamber, she tugged another bell-cord. "Bring us a buffet," she told the petite, pretty maid who answered the summons. Then, turning to me, she said: "Violence makes me so hungry! And today was an especially good day; why, I think I could eat a whole cow!"

"Ah, Clairwil," I replied. "I cannot fail to be astonished at the extent of your libertinage. But I must confess, dear collaborator, that I am somewhat disappointed that you didn't permit me to collaborate on this afternoon's undertakings."

"Well, Juliette," she said, "there are times when one wants help with a job and there are times when she'd rather work alone. Today was one of the latter — and, since I'm a creature who gives herself over totally to her whims, I never once thought of letting you join the party, even though I knew full well how badly you must have wanted to. But, don't despair: some other time I surely will feel inclined to include you in the festivities and you'll more than make up for this afternoon's loss. Moreover, now that I have seen that you are not the type of woman who blanches when confronted with some of libertinage's more *outre* endeavors, I shall make plans to have you admitted into a society to which I belong — a society whose membership specializes in obscenities of a much superior dimension to this afternoon's mischief. Indeed, the society's rules are such that members must wreak the greatest infamies upon each other — under pain of expulsion. To our meetings fathers bring daughters, brothers bring sisters, husbands bring wives; there are exchanges of partners, after which each person takes his pleasure in whichever way pleases him most, up to and including murder. Cash prizes are awarded to those who distinguish themselves in infamy or who invent new ways of procuring pleasure."

"Oh, dearest collaborator," I gasped, "you simply must admit me to this charmed circle."

"My precious novice," she replied, "you will be admitted and you will be welcomed with open arms . . . But now the hour grows late; I have an orgy to attend tonight and I must excuse myself from your charming company. My carriage will return you to the Minister's house. Meanwhile, you must promise to visit me again at the earliest opportunity."

"I promise," I said eagerly. "I promise from the bottom of my black little heart . . . ."

VI

That night, after a quick round of buggery with Saint-

Fond, I withdrew to my apartment. But I couldn't sleep:
so stirred up was I by Clairwil's violent words and
actions, I had to commit a crime of my own!

My heart beating wildly at the evil thoughts racing
through my brain, I leaped out of bed and dashed to the
servants' quarters. There I stole a butler's clothes and a
guard's pistol. Then, looking very much like a gentleman
of fashion, I slipped out into the night.

At the first streetcorner to which I came, I stationed
myself inside a doorway and waited for someone to pass.
The prospect of the crime which I was about to commit
thrilled me like nothing I had ever experienced. My
body glistened with sweat. My insides churned with the
turmoil which precedes sexual congress — a fundamental
excitement which honed all my senses to a fine cutting
edge. I was aflame; ablaze; now, for a victim . . .

Suddenly, as if in response to my devil's-prayer, I
heard groans — a woman's voice, soft, low-pitched and
mournful. Racing in the direction from which the sounds
came, I found a tattered, feeble-looking creature hud-
dled upon a doorstep.

"Who are you?" I demanded, drawing closer.

"One cursed by fate," she replied; "if you are the
harbinger of death, I will embrace you gladly."

"What are your difficulties?" I asked, noticing that,
in spite of her grief, she was a rather comely creature.

"My husband has been put in jail; my babies are
starving; now, this house on whose steps I sit, this house
which once was mine, has been taken away from me.
I am a poor, helpless waif tossed by life's storms onto
the shoals of despair."

"By fuck!" I cheered. "You've got quite the talent for
metaphor. I wonder what other talents you have." The
sexual heat welling up inside my body had become almost unbearable; nudging her crushed form with my
toe, I continued: "Come on, now; let me put your talents
to the test; you've quite the little body there; do you
refuse its use to a fellow creature of the nights?"

"Oh please, sir," she moaned; "I have taken all I can

take; spare me this final degradation."

"By Christ's crotch!" I boomed in reply. "Reduced to penury and still you persist in your silly virtuous notions. Well, you must be taught a lesson."

So saying, I seized her by the hair and jerked her to her feet. Then, in an alley alongside the house, I lifted her skirt. Her charms were both very fair and very firm; my passions, already egged on past the limits of normal endurance, all but exploded.

"Good sir," she continued to beg; "please leave me alone; please don't humiliate me; I have been abused enough as it is." Then, when she realized that I could not possibly be persuaded to relent, she attempted to break away.

"Oh no you don't," I cried. Wrapping one arm around her waist and urging her hips forward, I jammed the pistol barrel into her vagina, "Goodbye, bitch," I said softly; "here's a fucking you'll never forget." Whereupon, pulling the trigger, I sent her spinning off into eternity.

Hearing the pistol shots, neighbors dashed open their windows. Cries of "Police! Police!" went up on all sides. I was hailed by an uniformed patrolman and ordered to halt; the discovery of my weapon eliminated all doubt; I was asked my name.

"You'll be informed at the home of the Minister of State," I said boldly, realizing instantly that I finally had the opportunity to put to the test the impunity which had been promised me. "Take me to the Hôtel de Saint-Fond."

We were there in an instant. Saint-Fond, clutching a bathrobe about him, took me by the hand and led me inside.

"You may go now, officer," he told the policeman. "Consider that you have done your job well; a personal commendation will soon find its way to your records." Nodding obediently, the lawman departed.

Now alone with my lover, I related all which had passed. As I told the story I could see the depraved

Minister's member rising to attention. Appropriately, at the very moment when I related my pulling of the trigger, there appeared on the front of his robe a dark, wet stain. When the narration finally was over, he took me on his lap and began stroking my buttocks.

"It is best, my little bird, that you leave Paris immediately," he said. "Order three carriages at once; then proceed to my estate at Sceaux; take with you only four domestics, a cook, a butler and three of the virgins scheduled for immolation at your next supper; then await further instruction from me."

Very content with the success of my crime, I departed from Paris at once.

VII

I had hardly situated myself in the Sceaux estate when one of my servants informed me that a stranger had arrived requesting an audience with me. He had brought with him a sealed message from Saint-Fond.

Taking the message from the servant, I broke the seal and withdrew a small piece of parchment covered with the meticulous calligraphy which I recognized instantly as that of the Minister. It read as follows:

> *Have your domestics seize the bearer of this note and confine him to one of the dungeons in your cellar. His wife and daughter will appear also before long; you will deal with them in the same manner. As ever, S-F.*

Folding the parchment and tucking it back into its envelope, I instructed my servant to prepare the dungeon. Then, proceeding to the foyer, I greeted the unsuspecting soon-to-be-prisoner.

"You are doubtless a friend of his lordship?" I asked.

"Both my family and I have been the happy recipients of his gracious generosities," he replied.

"No doubt you were," I smiled evilly. Then, turning

to a husky servant who stood in waiting, I ordered the man seized and dragged off to the waiting dungeon.

"Madame! I protest!" screamed the astonished gentleman. "There must be some mistake!"

"If so," I chuckled dryly, "you're the one who made it. I only know what I read on the paper." And, so saying, I watched mirthfully as he was dragged off.

Now, no sooner was I back in the drawing room than I heard carriage wheels in the drive. Out of the lavishly-upholstered conveyance stepped the stranger's wife and daughter — both very pretty pieces of flesh, who carried themselves as if fully aware of their charms. I answered the door personally and accepted their letters of introduction — exact replicas of that carried by their unforunate husband and father. Then I motioned to a servant to take them away. They moaned, they pleaded and they screamed, but none of their pitiful entreaties could persuade me to spare them the incarceration which my master had decreed.

The orders now having been carried out, I sat on a couch speculating as to the fate of these hapless individuals. Were they to be robbed? Slain? Made victims of some monstrous feat of lubricity? While I pondered these questions, a fourth visitor arrived; he was one of Saint-Fond's serving boys, a splendid hunk of youth with sinewy shoulders, rippling biceps and a bulge in his trousers large enough to choke a horse; he carried a note which read as follows:

Greet this man warmly and entertain him well. He is to take the leading part in the drama which will be enacted tomorrow: he will be the executioner who, upon my order, will put to death the three persons you now hold prisoner.

Expect me tomorrow morning. Meanwhile, treat the prisoners very cruelly: bread only, a little water and no daylight.—S-F

Tucking the note into a pocket, I led the executioner

into the sitting room and poured each of us a glass of brandy. Merely looking at him created within me the sexual stirrings the awakening of which of late required more and more depraved indulgences. "Tell me your name, sir," I said, almost breathlessly; "and tell me if it's not true that you've left many a young girl in the throes of delirium as a result of an encounter with that marvelous hunk of cock which you've got hanging there."

"My name, Madame," he replied, "is Delcour. As to young girls, I've encountered a great many — but none has ever complained of unpleasant after-effects."

"Well, you're quite a witty fellow," I said, my heart now beating double-time. "Perhaps you would amuse me with some philosophy. Tell me, for instance, how you, as a professional executioner, can take the life of a person who never has wronged you in any way."

"Madame," he replied, "the rationalization which I employ in the performance of my task does not lend itself to facile articulation in terms of a single, easily-understandable principle."

"But, my dear," I insisted, my silk underslip by now thoroughly damp, "you must possess a vast store of information and experience; be so kind as to discourse upon the mechanics of the thing at least."

"What, precisely, do you wish to know, Madame?"

"The sight of blood . . . the screams of agony . . . the sound of bone crushing against bone . . . do these things bring you any pleasure?"

"Well, of course; a man would not be an executioner were the conditions of the job not conducive to enjoyment."

"Then would you say that every sexual passion can be increased and nourished by crime?"

"Unquestionably. Crime is to the passions what nervous fluid is to life: it sustains them, it supplies their strength."

By this point I had grown very hot indeed. "Come, now," I said; "we have the whole night to entertain ourselves with such discussion: first let us give vent to some of these lusts which we so learnedly discuss. Can I count on your cooperation?"

"What would you have me do?"

"Beat me, lap me, bugger me, suck me, fuck me, eat me — that will do for a start. You have a job to perform tomorrow; start preparing for it today. Now I wildly tore my clothes off. "Here is my body!" I panted. "It is completely yours!"

Delcour, taking the commission all too literally, threw me violently over his knees and, withdrawing a pocket knife from his coat, began to put his brand on me . . . by carving his initials in my buttocks!

Screaming, laughing, moaning in pain, I urged him onward. "Carve your address too, my lover!" I screamed. "Carve your sister's name, your brother's, the name of the town in which you were born and the name of the priest who baptized you. Carve the date of your devirgination! Carve the name of every whorehouse in Paris!" Out of my mind with the pleasure-pain sensations, I rolled onto my back. Delcour's eyes, looking down upon me, were afire with lust. "Devour my peach!" I screamed, thrusting open my legs. "Suck out its pit! Plunder me! Pillage me! Suck every pubic hair off my mound! Blast my ovaries to bits! Eat me, fuck me, suck me! Chew off my clitoris! Ravage my womb! Explode my entrails! Jesus Christ, I'm on fire; I'm burning alive; by God's cock and balls, my asshole is smoking!"

Delcour drove on, filling me to overflowing with sensations which threatened to unstring my very nerve endings. He wept with exhaustion as I drove him madly, insanely, mercilessly on from one sexual infamy to another. Finally, unable to sustain the siege any longer, the poor youth collapsed on the floor. I lay alongside him and fell into a deep, untroubled sleep.

Saint-Fond arrived the next day around noon. Uncertain as to what his reaction might be to the sport I had played with his emissary, I decided to tell him everything — lest he hear the story first from someone else.

"My little bird," he sighed wearily, "I cannot repeat

often enough that I couldn't care less about your caprices
— as long as they don't interfere with your duties to
me. You say he carved his initials on your ass — and that
you asked for his address and place of birth also? Well,
fine; it wouldn't bother me if he carved thereon the
whole of Rousseau's writings. You were fucked, you
say? Sucked? Reamed? Splendid: what a shame that
there were not several more orifices through which he
might have brought you pleasure.

"But so much for that. We've business to attend to
here. Let me tell you something of our captives:

"First, the father: by name, M. de Cloris: of all the
men in France, he probably has contributed the most
to my advancement. It was through his intercession with
the king that I obtained the position I now hold; furthermore, his power at court was immense and he used
it in my behalf time and time again. Yet, for an offense
which I won't bother to describe at this time, I've come
to loathe him; and, to make matters worse, he had the
temerity to marry my cousin: well, for that, he must
die."

"Your cousin, my Lord?" I asked. "You say that the
woman downstairs — his wife — is your cousin?"

"Yes, Juliette, I'm afraid she is. And I hate her more
than I hate her husband. You see, I had designs on her
once, but she always resisted my overtures: then I grew
enamored of her daughter; here I met with even
more stubborn resistance. Well, my rage finally reached
the boiling point. I turned the queen against Cloris and
his entire family by leading her to believe that the knave
had sold his daughter to the king; Her Majesty promptly
set a bounty of three-million *francs* upon each of their
heads; thus, not only do I gain my revenge here tomorrow, but also I fatten my purse. What better proof could
there be that the evil inherit the earth? But now, on to
specifics: have you any ideas for the death drama?"

"A great many," I replied, having given the matter
much thought that morning. "The weather is warm these
days, therefore let us costume ourselves provocatively.

I can wear a flimsy veil which covers every part of my
body except the breasts and buttocks, exposing these
in all their naked splendor by means of trapdoor-like
cuts in the cloth. As to the executioner, Delcour, let
us dress him in a black loincloth and with a black band
around his head, but otherwise completely naked; those
gleaming, bronze, rippling muscles of his should add
much to the spectacle. As to yourself, wear more elaborate savage attire: leave your arms and thighs bare, and
wear a headdress resembling a dragon or a Patagonian
serpent; smear red grease paint — there's bound to
be some around the house — all over your face, and we'll
outfit you with a broad baldrick, girding on it all the
instruments necessary for the tortures which you plan to
inflict. Indeed, the costume alone should be enough to
scare them to death."

"Ah, my dear directress!" sighed Saint-Fond. "Your
imagination knows no bounds. Make arrangements for
the costumes at once — and implement whatever other
ideas you may have for the rest of the proceedings.
Tomorrow, by Lucifer, will be an eventful day!"

VIII

The day dawned bright and clear. Wishing to take
advantage of the sunlight, I selected as a stage for the
obscene drama a high-windowed salon in the east wing
of the house. As acolytes, assigned the task of assisting
Saint-Fond, Delcour and me as we went about our
tortures, I appointed the three virgins from my retinue.
By noon everything was in order and I sat down to lunch
with Saint-Fond; then, the meal over, our day's festivities began.

When the Minister entered the salon, his eyes were
captured immediately by the three virgins standing in
a group to the right of the door All were dressed in the
thinnest of gauze, which revealed more than it concealed; their tableau was astonishingly beautiful. The

youngest of the three girls was Louise; she had a slender waist and delightfully firm buttocks: the next was Hélène; her body was rival to that of Venus and her long black hair fell gracefully to her knees: Fulvia was third; she looked like one sired by Cupid, himself; her magnificent mound and breasts would inspire the envy of Minerva.

To the left of this group I had situated the doomed family, naked except for drapings of black crepe. The father and mother knelt, hand in hand, watching each other fearfully; at their feet lay the charming daughter, Julie. Heavy irons had rubbed raw these unfortunate creatures' bare skins; the nipple of Julie's breast peeked incongruously through a link of chain; another length was visible between the thighs of Mme. Cloris; the father's penis had been bound tightly with wet leather, which, now that it had begun to dry, grew tighter and tighter and tighter.

To the left of this tableau stood Delcour, outfitted in the black loincloth described earlier. In one hand he held a huge Saracean blade; in the other, the end of the chain which was wrapped around the victims — which end, whenever he chose to tug it, had dreadful effect upon those whom it bound. To his left, completing the semi-circular trillium of groupings-of-three, were two strapping lads, six feet in height, naked and awesomely membered; their function in the proceedings would be to cart away bodies and to assist if necessary, in the subduing of stubborn victims; lacking something to do at the present time, they stood face to face exchanging tender kisses.

"Charming," said Saint-Fond; "a delight to the eye; I shall stand here for one minute in worshipful contemplation." Then, the minute having elapsed, he said: "Have the guilty ones brought hither." Delcour obediently marched the damned family forward.

"The three of you have been accused of enormous crimes," the depraved Minister intoned ominously. "How do you plead?"

"You know perfectly well that we are innocent," Cloris replied, his face a study in rage. "Besides, this is no law court and you are not a judge. If there has been a crime, and if we are thought guilty of it, bring us before a legally-constituted bench."

"You have broken the law," intoned Saint-Fond, soberly; "you do not merit its protection now: you deserve only the severest punishment. Don't you know the principle of your Church: error has no rights?"

"Coward!" spat Cloris. "If I were set free from these chains, you'd run off in panic."

"Quite right," agreed Saint-Fond amicably. "But, unfortunately for you, that is not the situation; you are in my power — and there is no captor more fiendish than a confirmed coward who has been reproached with his cowardice."

"Everything you have you owe to me," Cloris said, trying again to sway Saint-Fond. "Kill me, if you must; but spare my family. If you act otherwise, your conscience will one day cause you to regret it."

"Remorse," chuckled the Minister, "is not a sentiment with which I have ever had acquaintance." Then, turning to Delcour, he said ceremoniously: "Proceed with the execution."

First to be unbound was Mme Cloris. Limp and bleeding, she was dragged before her fiendishly-costumed judge.

"Ah, whore," said he; "dear cousin, precious cousin. esteemed relative: I shall spread your legs today." Whereupon, his eyes flashing to life, he suddenly knocked her to the floor and proceeded to stamp his feet on her head: ten, twelve, fifteen, twenty times his heavily-booted heels crashed into her until her face and head were hardly distinguishable as a unit of the human anatomy. Next, the half-dead woman was hoisted to her feet and bent over until her head almost touched the floor; then her legs were spread apart, her rectum was held open and her daughter, Julie, was forced to tongue the gaping orifice: while this transpired, Saint-Fond stood behind the girl, beating at her buttocks with his immense member, which he wielded like a club: throughout, the helpless father madly cursed and damned Saint-Fond, but the jaded Minister only laughed at the screaming man's invectives and continued to wage his assault.

Finally tiring of this sport, Saint-Fond now put his penis back into his costume and commanded Julie to lay off her mother's ass. Then he forced the father to em-bugger the daughter while he, himself, embuggered the father. Mme. Cloris, meanwhile, was stretched across a table on her back; Delcour soaked her mound with brandy and set it on fire; then, as the executioner stood urinating on the flames, the two naked youths were given permission to enjoy the ravaged woman's fast-fading charms: one entered her from the front, the other from the rear, and both punched at her bloodied face and head as they thrust their swollen members in and out of her battered and bruised body.

"Enough!" barked Saint-Fond finally, emerging with a jerk from Cloris' anus. Then, as the father pulled his rigid member from Julie's pained buttocks, Delcour, with expert swiftness, lopped off the entire appendage — testicles and all; Saint-Fond, meanwhile, drove a sharp spear into the poor man's throat; a geyser of blood spurted upward and poor Cloris fell to the floor, dead.

Saint-Fond, all but out of his senses with passion, now picked up the still-rigid, amputated penis from the floor and thrust it violently into Julie's vagina, frigging her wildly with it. Enraged, the poor girl tried to scratch the Minister's eyes out, but here, once again, Delcour exhibited his professional talent, reaching out with his huge Saracen blade and slicing off the unfortunate child's buttocks with a single stroke.

Now the minister went completely overboard. His eyes distorted with frenzy, his lips flecked with foam, he seized the two pieces of flesh and sandwiched his own penis between them, thereby embuggering a bodiless ass; meanwhile I flayed with the amputated

penis at Delcour, who had proceeded to encunt poor
Julie and now was fucking her while she bled to death.

By the time this enterprise was dissolved, Mme. Cloris
had almost given up the ghost. Saint-Fond, surveying
her wracked form with an appreciative smile, found a
bottle of brandy; then, spreading the poor woman's vagina wide open, he poured the contents of the entire bottle inside her, soaking her womb and ovaries; this accomplished, he jammed a lighted candle down the yawning
crevice. I watched, awe-struck, as a red glow took form
beneath the woman's navel and slowly began to spread;
in an instant, a flame flickered to life below her breast;
then other flames broke through the skin's surface: with
a great whooshing sound, the body was suddenly ablaze
like a bonfire: the room was silent except for the crackling of the flames until, finally, there was nothing left
of Mme. Cloris but her skeleton.

The three victims now disposed of, Saint-Fond turned
his attention to the three virgins: with a steel-tipped
martinet he meted out one hundred strokes to each
victim; then, starting again with the first, he administered two-hundred strokes each with a cat-o'-nine-tails:
finally, his strength leaving him, the peerless libertine
fell to the floor, exhausted. "Carry me," he gasped to
Delcour and me; "carry me to my bed."

Already half-conscious when we reached the bedroom,
Saint-Fond insisted that I pass the night at his side.
Then, resting one hand on my back and the other in
the cleavage of my buttocks, the unmitigated scoundrel
enjoyed ten hours of undisturbed sleep. When he awoke,
he asked me if it were not true that he was the vilest man
in the world.

"You have no equal, my lord," I replied; "not on earth
or in hell."

"Yes, I believe it's true," he said proudly. "You see,
my pretty one, Nature instilled in me the most irresis-
tible taste for vice, and I've always tried to serve her
as well as do those in whom she instilled an excess of
virtue." Now, smiling seductively, he added: "You, too,

are a paragon of vice, my Juliette, so indulge yourself without fear; yes, surrender eagerly to the baseness of your nature, to the blazing ardor of your passions. Be bold, I say: acknowledge no ruler save your own wantonness; never submit to moral constraint and always seek your own pleasure above everything else, no matter who is made to suffer in consequence."

Deeply moved by this lucid dessertation, I confesed to him that my sole fear was the possibility that his kindness to me might come to an end.

"Juliette," he said, "never fear falling from my graces. I have set you so high in my esteem that such a descent would defy the very laws of logic. If I am the King of Vice, you, sitting at my side, must be my Queen."

"Oh, master," I replied, thrilled to the core, "be ever sure that were I suddenly appointed queen of the entire world my first act would be to bring it to its knees in homage to you."

BOOK FOUR

I

My friends, it is time to tell you a little about myself, and, more important, to describe my enormous wealth so that you may be able to contrast my situation with that in which my sister, who had chosen virtue above all, was at this stage in our lives wallowing. Your own philosophical system will suggest what conclusion to draw from these comparisons.

As to my station, I can only say that I lived on a grand scale; I had to myself an immense townhouse in Paris, a cottage at Sceaux and a small private whorehouse at Barrière-Blanche. A dozen lesbians were permanently in my train, along with four charming chambermaids, a reader, a night nurse, three carriages, ten horses, four virile valets and two gardeners. (None of the males in my employ had a prick smaller than ten inches.)

After salaries and upkeep had been deducted from my pension, I was left with a monthly balance of two-million *louis* to spend on pretty dresses of one kind or another. And, almost needless to say, if ever I found myself a bit short, I needed only turn to Sain-Fond for an extra hundred-thousand or so.

I rose every day at ten. From then until eleven I had myself fucked by my valets. Then, until one, I was at toilette, assisted by my entire retinue. Promptly at one, I gave a private audience to individuals who had come to solicit my favors, or to Saint-Fond when he happened to be in Paris. Then, at two, I hastened to my Barrière-Blanche whorehouse where every day I would find awaiting me four new women and four new men with whom to indulge in the most wanton caprices.

At four I would return to the city and dine with friends. Then, after these truly royal repasts (whose splendors I shall, out of mercy, leave to the reader's imagination), I would either go to the theatre or entertain the Minister. Following this, I would return to my townhouse for supper. Then, after an orgy with selected members of my staff, I would retire for the evening.

Regarding the worth of my wardrobe, my gems, my savings, et cetera, I believe that four-million *louis* would be an accurate estimate. In addition, I had about half that sum in ready cash.

You may wonder, dear reader, in what state were my morals as a result of the enormous power which I enjoyed. Well, of this I am reluctant to speak. And yet I must. The constant libertinage in which I indulged had so deadened the workings of my conscience that I existed for pleasure and pleasure alone; nothing — I repeat, nothing — was of value to me unless it offered a maximum of carnal criminal delights. By way of example, let me relate several incidents surrounding the great famine which broke out in Paris at that time. I recall horrible scenes — girls selling their bodies in the gutter, waifs abandoned, the aged left to rot. Bnt, though hundreds lined up at my door beggings for crumbs, I turned them away. "How can one possibly bestow alms," I would tell them insolently, "when one needs the money for the improvement of her lawns and shrubbery, for the beautification of this path with a stone Cupid, for the decoration of that one with a sculptured Aphrodite?" Yes, weeping mothers, starving infants and begging husbands all failed to penetrate the iron shield surrounding my heart; I simply smiled, shook my head and walked proudly away from the suffering creatures. Moreover, after each incident in which I displayed such heartlessness, I found myself assailed with the most exquisitely pleasurable sensation; indifference to the suffering of others, it seemed, was almost as much fun as sex.

This last discovery led to some fascinating musings. I asked myself: if it is pleasurable merely to deny the destitute the wherewithal to gain respite, how much more pleasurable would it be to be the direct and sole cause of their destitution; in other words, if it is glorious to refuse the good, it must be divine to do the evil!

For days these thoughts spun around my brain like moths around a glowing lamp. Finally I decided to share them with Clairwil. My friend was beside herself with glee.

"Juliette, sweet Juliette," she said; "there can be no doubt in my mind that you're ready now for admitance to the Sodality of the Friends of Crime. I'd like to submit you to the Board of Governors at the next meeting. What do you think: would you like to join at this time?"

"Oh, darling," I replied delightedly; "I can think of nothing I'd like better."

"Splendid, dearest girl; splendid! Then you need only acquaint yourselves with these statutes — I just so happen to have a copy of them here in my purse — and you are as good as in."

So saying, Clairwil withdrew from her purse a well-worn, leather-covered book. I opened it and read as follows:

THE SODALITY OF THE FRIENDS OF CRIME:
ITS STATUTES

Know all men by these presents that, deferring to the common usage, the Sodality shall admit to the service-ability of the word, "crime;" but let it be made plain at the onset that in the employment of the term with reference to any kind of act of whatever sort of color, no pejorative sense is ever intended.

The Sodality is founded on the firm conviction that man is not free, and that, bound absolutely by the laws of Nature, all men have no choice but to obey their impulses, even if these impulses lead to acts which are commonly referred to as criminal.

The following principles shall govern the membership:

1. No distinction shall be drawn between the individuals who compose the Sodality; not that It holds all men equal — a vulgar notion deriving from faulty logic and fanciful philosophy — but because It is persuaded that distinctions of any kind may have a detrimental influence upon members' pleasures.

2. The Sodality dissolves all marital ties and ignores those of blood; under Its roof one should carry on as indiscriminately with the wife of one's neighbor as with one's own, and equally indiscriminately with one's brother, sister, children, nephews, etc.; any refusal to comply with these rules shall constitute grounds for exclusion.

3. A husband is required to sacrifice his wife to the membership; a father, his sons and daughters; a brother, his sister; an uncle, his niece or nephew, etc.

4. Membership is restricted to those persons able to prove a minimum yearly income of twenty-five-thousand livres; dues of membership are ten-thousand francs per annum.

5. *Twenty artists and literary figures shall be admitted upon remittance of the modest fee of a thousand livres per annum; this special consideration is part of the Sodality's policy of patronizing the arts; It regrets that its means do not permit it to welcome at this insignificant price an even larger number of these gifted persons.*

6. *The Members of the Sodality, united through it into one great family, share all their hardships as they do their joys; they aid each other mutually in all of life's various situations; but alms, charities, help extended to widows, orphans or persons in distress are in all cases forbidden.*

7. *An emergency fund of thirty-thousand livres is kept in constant reserve, and is at the disposition of any Member who by accident or ill fate finds himself in difficulties of any sort.*

8. *During the hours devoted to communal indulgences, all Members, male and female, are naked; they must intermingle in the mêlée; partners are chosen indiscriminately, and there is no valid refusal of any request made by a brother Sodalist. Once called upon, each individual must cooperate instantly, unreservedly, gladly; should an individual attempt to shirk his obligations, he will be forced to fulfill them, then driven out of the Sodality.*

9. *Gluttony and drunkenness are encouraged; every member is assured of assistance while indulging in these as in other excesses; all possible measures are taken to facilitate them.*

10. *Men over forty years of age, women over thirty-five are not received by the Sodality; once admitted, however, no member may be expelled on the grounds of old age.*

11. *Oaths, vulgar language and blasphemies in particular are encouraged; they may be employed upon all occassions. Between Members the familar pronoun is compulsory.* *

12. *Repulsive deformities or diseases will not be to-*

lerated. Someone so afflicted, if he presents himself for membership, will be rejected. If an already admitted Member falls prey to such misfortunes, he will be asked to resign.

13. A Member who contracts venereal disease will be obliged to retire until completely restored, his recovery being vouched for by the House Physician.

14. No foreigner will be admitted; provincials are likewise debarred. The Sodality exists only for persons resident in Paris and its environs.

15. High birth will in no wise facilitate admission; the essential is to prove one has the necessary wealth. However pretty a woman may be, she shall not be admitted unless she also be rich; the same will apply to any young man, however handsome.

16. Under no circumstances will the Sodality intrude or interfere in government affairs, nor may any Member. Political speeches are expressly forbidden.

17. Among the facilities offered Sodality members are two seraglios; they are located in the two wings of the main building. One is composed of three-hundred boys ranging in age from seven to twenty-five years of age; the other of a like number of girls, from five to twenty-one. These creatures are constantly replaced; not a week goes by but that at least thirty are winnowed out of each seraglio to make room for fresh accessions; new lots are always in training to fill gaps in the ranks. Sixty procuresses take care of recruitment; there is a Warden for each seraglio.

18. The seraglios are pleasant places, comfortably furnished. In them one does exactly what one likes; the most ferocious passions may be exercised, and all Sodality Members are admitted free of charge; however, a tax

---

* In French, *tu* is the familiar and *vous* the polite form of the pronoun, "you." The polite form is generally used among all persons except family members and other very intimate acquaintances.

—P.J.G.

of one-hundred louis is levied for each murder.

19. *Members who choose to sup in a seraglio are at liberty to do so; entrance tickets are distributed by the President, who cannot refuse them to Members in good standing.*

20. *Total subordination on the part of the inmates prevails in the seraglios; complaints relative to lack of submissiveness or of cooperation will be taken at once to the Warden of the seraglio, or to the President, and no time will be lost chastising the miscreant according to the plantiff's specification; the complainant may inflict the penalty personally if such things amuse him. Although each seraglio contains creatures of only one sex, they may be mixed at will and to taste, males being fetched into the midst of females or females into the midst of males. But inmates of the seraglios may not be removed to the pleasure hall or to a Member's personal residence.*

21. *The lateral pavillions housing the seraglios also contain menageries, where animals of every species await the Member given to bestiality; (this simple passion is altogether natural and must hence be respected like all the rest). Three complaints brought against any one animal are sufficient to have it removed; three requests that it be put to death suffice to have it dispatched without further ado.*

22. *In each seraglio there are four executioners, four jailors, eight whippers, four flayers, four midwives and four surgeons, all at the orders of Members who, in the heat of passion, may have need of such personages: it is understood, of course, that the midwives and surgeons are present not to render humanitarian aids but to assist in tortures; as soon as a seraglio inmate manifests the slightest symptom of illness, he is dismissed and never again permitted to return to the house.*

23. *Each seraglio is surrounded on three sides by high walls. All windows are barred and inmates remain indoors constantly.*

24. Between each building and the wall shielding it lies a space ten feet wide forming an alley bordered by cypress trees; Sodality Members may take seraglio inmates for walks along this secluded pathway to indulge in pleasures most somber and often still more frightening. At the foot of a number of these trees are pits into which victims' bodies may be stuffed.

26. No candidate will be admitted to the Sodality without first signing in blood an oath that he will observe all rules and regulations as set forth herein, or as set forth in bylaws to be promulgated from time to time by the President or by the Board of Governors; further, no Member, upon the revocation of membership, shall reveal any of the secrets of the society, nor shall any candidate or any person offered candidacy reveal any secrets of which he has gained knowledge, said unlawful revelations to result in the issuance by the Sodality of a death warrant, with a reward of extremely generous proportions for whosoever shall execute it.

No sooner had I read the last of these statutes than I found myself filled with an almost boundless excitement. Throwing my arms around Clairwil, I said: "Oh, my friend, my darling friend, you simply must sponsor me; I want to join that sodality more than I've ever wanted anything in my life."

"I'll submit you at the very next general membership meeting," she promised. "And don't worry, my love: with a heart as black as yours, you're bound to be accepted."

II

Now the great day dawned. Clairwil, decked out in a gown of exquisite styling, came calling for me in her carriage. Then for nearly an hour we rode up one street, down another until we found ourselves outside an immense mansion in one of the most bleak and least populous sections of the city.

My heart beat excitedly as the carriage pulled into a dark courtyard virtually enfenced by tall, black trees. Once we were inside, a pair of heavy, iron gates swung behind us and a handsome young lackey opened our door. Then we were led through carpeted corridors to a immense, marble-floored reception room where Clairwil was instructed to undress; I was told to keep my garments on until after my interrogation ceremony.

From the reception room we proceeded to the main ballroom. It was an immense place with walls covered entirely by mirrors and a floor of the finest polished hardwood. At one end of the room was a platform: in the center of the platform was a throne, on which sat an exceedingly handsome — and completely naked — woman of perhaps thirty-five years; Clairwil identified her as the President: to her left and right, also completely naked, were two men and two women, the Board of Governors. In clusters at the foot of the platform and scattered elsewhere about the room were more than three-hundred other men and women; four or five, like me, were candidates and therefore had remained clothed; the rest were naked; some strolled about in pairs, others in trios and quartets; many were poking and prodding each other's bodies experimentally, as if trying to decide who would be best suited for what during the afternoon's subsequent exercises in lubricity.

After a few minutes the President rose and asked in a quiet voice for the attention of the assembly. Immediately the room fell silent. Then she addressed the names of the afternoon's candidates. My name was first on the list.

"My dear," she said, helping me onto the dais, "you have by now acquainted yourself with the Sodality's rules and have become familiar with what is entailed in being submitted as candidate. It is your prerogative before the ceremony goes any farther to withdraw if, for any reason, you feel that you will be unable to discharge the obligations which accrue with candidacy or membership. Would you like to exercise that prerogative at this time?"

"No, ma'am," I replied respectfully.

"Very well, then; let us begin."

Immediately two servants materialized alongside me and, in less time than it takes to tell of it, divested me of every stitch of clothing. For a moment I stood silent and — yes, I admit it — a shade embarrassed as my nude body was scrutinized by the eyes of those several hundred spectators. But my embarrassment was short lived, for, almost immediately, the room rang out with a thunderous burst of applause.

The President then smiled and began the prescribed questioning:

"Do you promise to pass your entire life in libertinage of the lowest order?"

"I do."

"Do you esteem all lewd acts, whatsoever they may be?"

"I do and I always have."

"Do you regard even the most odious impulse as perfectly natural."

"If by 'odious' you mean contrary to the taste of society, I shall answer yes, I do consider all such impulses perfectly natural. But I hasten to point out that I personally consider no natural impulse nor any act resulting therefrom to be odious."

(Applause.)

"Is there any law in the French Criminal Code at the present time which you would not break?"

"There is no such law."

"How many of them have you broken thus far?"

"Since I hold all law in such low regard I never have taken the trouble to find out which acts are proscribed and which are not; therefore I cannot answer the question."

(Applause.)

"Do you believe in God?"

"In whom?"

"In God."

"I don't know what you're talking about."

"Do you believe in a supreme being?"

"I believe only in Nature, Whose gentle voice prompts our every act and Who prohibits nothing which makes Her creatures happy."

(Applause.)

"Do you declare at this time your intention to adhere strictly to Sodality's statutes as they have been read to you by your sponsor?"

"I do."

"And are you prepared to accept the penalties prescribed therein should you prove refractory?"

"I am."

"Swear it."

"I swear."

"Are you married?"

"No."

"Have you ever been whipped?"

"Upon occasion."

"What is your age?"

"I am eighteen."

"Have you had affairs with women?"

"Many times."

"Have you committed crimes?"

"A few."

"Stolen?"

"Yes."

"Taken the life of a human being?"

"I have."

"Do you promise never to swerve from the path which you have followed until now?"

"I do swear it."

(Here a new burst of applause.)

"Will you bring into the Sodality all those related to you by bonds or kinship?"

"I shall."

"Do you agree never to reveal the secrets of the Sodality?"

"I shall never reveal them, I swear it."

"Do you promise to exhibit the most complete indulgence toward all the caprices and all the lewd whims of all Sodality members?"

"I promise it."

"Whom do you prefer, men or women?"

"I am very fond of women; I have a passion for men."

(This display of naiveté brought forth a wave of laughter from the corporation.)

"What do you think of the lash?"

"I like to use it and to have it used upon me."

(This reply was much appreciated also.)

"And your attitude toward cocksucking?"

"I adore it."

"Have you had offspring?"

"No, none."

"Do you intend to refrain from having them?"

"I shall do everything in my power to avoid them."

"You therefore dislike children?"

"I detest them."

"Has your sponsor with her the sum constituting your entrance fee?"

"Yes."

"Are you wealthy?"

"I am; exceedingly."

"And have you ever devoted any of your money to charity?"

"Of course not."

"Then welcome to the Sodality, my child, and may your days among us be extremely happy ones."

Now the other candidates were brought to the dais and were subjected to similar interrogation. Two — a girl my age and a boy several years older — were found acceptable. All the others were dismissed. .

This business having been accomplished, the girl, the boy and I were turned loose for the pleasure of the Members. I had been on the floor barely a minute when an elderly man presented himself; he carried a fistful of switches which he brandished menacingly several inches from my bare buttocks.

"A pity you weren't admitted months ago, my dear,"

he said. "I've been dying to administer a vile switching to a luscious ass like yours. Assume the appropriate position, please."

I bent over and the switches tore painfully into my buttocks. "Ah, sweet are the uses of adversity," I thought as the delicious lashes played their lovely music upon me But alas, the concert was to be short-lived.

"My pretty one!" exclaimed the old man. "You're the one they brought in tonight as a new member, aren't you?" he began.

"Yes, I am."

"What a shame I haven't met you until now," he said, "but, I've been busy in the seraglio." And he proceeded to whip my buttocks with the fistful of switches he held.

Next, a charming young man approached and dealt with me in the same manner, though he whipped me much more vigorously.

"I want some cocks!" I screamed. "Juliette wants some mighty pricks!"

Immediately, my body, like a pin cushion, was pierced with all sizes and shapes of the species — one, two, three, four, five, six, then finally I lost count. The assault was unrelenting; bucket after bucket of scalding sperm came pouring into me; member upon member upon member was thrust into my mouth, my ass, my cunt. Finally after who-knows-how-long, I begged to be allowed to repair to the public lavatory. I was assisted to my feet and escorted to its portals by two-hundred men.

When I entered the lavatory, a young man was bending over the body of a middle-aged woman. She lay on her back on the floor, writhing in pleasure as he stuck red hot needles into each of her breasts. Transfixed, I stood watching this mad scene. At each thrust of the needle the woman screamed out ecstatically; soon blood appeared and the boy fell to sucking the rosy nipples and spitting great mouthfuls of blood into her open mouth. Finally, the two noticed me; both beckoned me to join their festivities.

"I'm sorry, but friends are waiting for me outside," I replied, sad to have to bypass this amusing bit of mischief.

"Well, another time," said the boy. "This is my sister; and you have an invitation to frolic with either of us whenever you like."

I thanked them both and, when I had finished my business, returned to the main ballroom. Activity had increased in my absence and the over all spectacle now was one which outdistanced anything the most lascivious imagination possibly could conceive. Everywhere my eye moved, it fell upon a new monument to varied sexual expression.

There was no sound except sharp exclamations of pleasure and a great deal of blasphemy, often very loud. But, everywhere, order was visible; the most virtuous activities could not have taken place amidst any greater calm.

In another corner of the room, twelve girls leaned against a wall, their alabaster buttocks raised high in the air, while two men walked down the line embuggering them with dildos; each girl discharged, or defecated, or urinated, one of the men caught the product in a small silver bucket and gave it to the next girl in line to eat while she was awaiting servicing.

Next to this charming display stood three barrels with plug holes in them. Inside each barrel was a young boy who pressed his mouth against the open hole and received the member of whoever sought to be serviced. There was a small opening on the top of one barrel, and, while I watched, a young girl squatted over it and dropped three slimy turds onto the head of the barrel's laboring occupant; another man spit into the opening and still another frigging himself released his load of come in it.

The most bizarre and stimulating spectacle, however,

was taking place in the middle of the floor As a small donkey straddled a narrow cot, a woman crawled beneath him. Then two men tried to shove the animal's massive grey member into the woman's cunt. Arching her body upward, the woman managed just barely to engulf the organ's throbbing head. Then her screams of pleasure were changed to screams of horror and pain as her two collaborators over her protests continued to force the animal's bulging prick deeper and deeper into her.

Soon the animal became uncontrollably aroused and began thrusting fiercely at the narrow canal which sought vainly to contain him. Finally, as a throng of onlookers cheered, the sexually-enraged beast split the woman nearly in half; blood poured from her torn and ripped vagina; her intestines were split and great globs of feces spilled over the cot; the donkey pushed harder, drove deeper, his great cock slamming into her until finally a jagged gash split her body up to her navel and her entire stomach spilled out onto the floor. Her lips issued forth a small, feeble cry, then she fell to the floor — dead.

"Bravo! Bravo!" cried the spectators; the donkey had become the hero of the day. A woman now grabbed the animal's bloody cock and sucked it until the beast's scalding come spalttered all over her face and mouth. Meanwhile, a man licked the animal's beshitted ass, and another libertine began fucking the great wound in the dead woman's stomach. I was in a fiery state of sexual insanity as a result of this display and would have joined the madcap group myself had not the President just then grabbed me by the breast and led me to a couch in a secluded corner of the room.

Lying on the couch, enjoying the sensation of her hungry tongue lapping over all my parts, I discovered to my surprise that one of the President's arms was simply a stump; her hand had been cut off at the wrist. I will not burden you, dear reader, with a description of an experience which defies articulation; I am sure you can imagine to what exquisite use that stump of arm was put.

After a time, sweet chimes rang out signifying the dinner hour. With the President, I followed the crowd into an immense dining hall. The decor of the hall simulated a forest; between majestic trees were little glades, within each of which was a table set for twelve; garlands of flowers hung in festoons from the trees and thousands of candles shed a soft light; two servants delegated to each table served it promptly in silence. The meal was sumptuous: hummingbird tongues, little slivers of nightingale wings, fried African antelope soup, roasted elephantballs and luscious Indian cherry pit pudding for dessert. (We libertines may not have had morals, dear reader, but we certainly had style.)

After liqueurs had been served, we returned to the main ballroom. Rare wines and succulent viands made the evening orgies even more luxurious than those of the afternoon. I sustained at least one hundred mad assaults; individuals of every sexual inclination passed through my hands; not a spot on my body was left unsullied. When day finally dawned, I was so everwhelmed by fatigue, so cunt-dry from delicious exertion that I had to adjourn to the countryside for a rest.

III

My month-long novitiate in the Sodality finally came to a close. Now I enjoyed the hot-coveted right to penetrate the seraglios. It was a right which, almost needless to say, I promptly exercised — and Clairwil, eager to acquaint me with all aspects of the operation, volunteered to served as my guide. Each seraglio was divided into four rooms. Each room was reserved for a particular passion; the first, to the simple passions; the second room, to a theatre of flagellation and other perversities; the third, to criminal proceedings and the fourth, to murder.

Clairwil, wanting me to start at the bottom, took me first to the room devoted to the simple passions. There, throwing aside a series of velvet curtains, she revealed an assembly of some of the prettiest boys and girls ever gathered under one roof. My breath caught in my throat as I beheld these lovely creatures; the girls were dressed in gauze shifts and wore garlands of freshly-picked flowers in their hair; all sat in readiness to do our bidding.

My notice was captured instantly by a delightful little peach of a girl with flaming red hair, small, delicate breasts and deliciously-curved hips. I took the lovely child in my arms and began toying with her charming nipples. Clairwil promptly scolded me for employing undue decency.

"That is not the way you treat this trash," said she; "command; they will obey."

My personal appetites were for the gentle approach, but I yielded to my mentor's more mature judgement. "Suck my cunt," I said to the sweet-faced little girl. She immediately fell to her knees, lifted my dress and obeyed the command.

Pointing to another comely girl, Clairwil said: "You eat her ass." The girl's tongue was between my buttocks within a matter of seconds.

"Fart, Juliette," Clairwil now commanded. I complied and my charming reamer, not the slightest bit disturbed continued to ream away.

"Well, Juliette," Clairwil said after a time, "we could dally like this all day, but I'm in the mood for a little change of pace. These creatures here are acceptable enough with respect to merely sensual pursuits, but this afternoon I feel a need for some mental stimulation as well. What do you say we repair to the university? After all, it is there that the greatest minds of France are assembled; I know one such, by name Dean Claude, and he has three balls to boot! Come along, now; I'm sure you'll enjoy meeting him."

Abandoning for the nonce all those lovely children of the seraglio, we hailed a carriage. In an hour we were on the grounds of the most celebrated institution of learning in all Europe. A porter greeted us at the gate and conducted us promptly to the office of Clairwil's friend.

The dean was a thin, hawk-nosed little man of some fifty years. His eyes burned with the feverish energy of the ascetic; an air of mystic melancholia shrouded his countenance. I was irresistibly attracted to him.

"By Plato's prick, Clairwil," boomed this man of letters by way of greeting; "it has been an eternity since I last played Paticus to you. Indeed, the only passion in which I have been engaged since that memorable time is the awesome passion of wrestling some sense out of Aquinas. Ah, my mind has been inflamed, dear Clairwil, but my loins are cold and rusted from lack of use."

"We have come to remedy that situation, dear Claude," she replied. "Little Juliette, here, is without a doubt the most desirable young fuck in the kingdom.

"Well, splendid, splendid," said the learned creature. "But let us not waste another moment. There is a grove not far from here and I've always found it far more conducive to such exercises than the sterile atmosphere of my office. Let's be off, shall we? Time flies!"

So saying, the dean led us out a back door and into the university courtyard. In minutes we found ourselves in a wood. Claude smoothed an area of leaf-littered ground and gestured for us to be seated.

"By Aristotle's ass!" he beamed. "By Socrates' scrotum! My children, you'll never know how madly I've yearned lately for pleasures of the flesh. Perhaps I shall recite a poem or two, after which we can lend ourselves fully to indulgences of the most depraved sort — assuming, of course, that you both find yourselves so inclined."

"Ah, my dear professor," sighed Clairwil. "No poems; just lust. My pants here are wet from anticipation and young Juliette is actually leaking with desire. So let's be on with it: no words, no metaphysics; just actions." And, tossing up her skirts, she grinned: "There, is not this hairy cage a fit lodging place for your bird?"

"By Demosthenes' driving dork!" boomed he. "Fit it is, and I'm not going to waste another moment contemplating it!" Whereupon he seized her at the crotch, tossed her onto the ground, and, tearing open his academic robes, launched a furious assault. But the battle lasted only seconds; Dean Claude, his energies damned up after so long a period of abstinence, no sooner had advanced ere he retreated.

"Well," he said, lifting himself from the ground, "I won't make any apologies. In but a trice this member of mine will again be stiff as Nicomedes' scepter and you can be certain that it won't give up so easily then."

Now he stood, and, in the faded grey light of the afternoon sun, the dean's marvelous member for the first time was visible to me. Dear reader, it was incredible. In terms of length and breadth this splendid scholastic's tool would have given the Sodality's donkey a run for its *louis*; and, dangling beneath the staff, looking very much like a cluster of bagged grapefruits, were not one, not two, but three round, smooth, succulent-looking testicles!

"My good man," I said respectfully, "would you allow me the privillege of frigging that overwhelming organ of yours?"

"My pleasure, child" he said, proferring the immense appendage. "But I warn you that, once aroused, it won't content itself to be merely frigged. Are you prepared to envelop it in your lovely ass?"

"Prepared to attempt, sir," I said, not in the least bit unjustified in my caution.

"Then frig away, chit," said he, "and let the devil take the hindmost!"

Awe-struck, I took the member in my hand. Claude was as good as his word: instantly the organ sprung to life, snaking upwards past his navel and not stopping until its massive head came to rest directly between his breasts.

"By Satan!" I gasped. "Take me, sir! I'm prepared to give my life in your service — and I'm not at all sure that I might not have to."

But, before I could spread my thighs, Clairwil wrested him away from me, flung him to the ground and proceeded to stuff his great organ into her yawning vulva.

"Shove, shove, shove that gargantuan pillar into my sex pot," shrieked she. And, as I watched in fascination, Claude's mightly member slashed, drilled, hammered and pounded its way further and further into her.

"Oh, Christ, I can feel it up to my lungs," she cried. "Jam your balls in there too! Fill my bottomless cunt with your treasures! Fuck me, you mad genius! Shove it through the top of my head!"

I could stand it no longer. I had to have a share of this enterprise. Maneuvering into position between them, I pushed my cunt into Clairwil's mouth. Her pretty teeth had hardly started to nibble my throbbing pink clitoris when I suddenly discharged all over her face.

"I shall come in your mouth too, Clairwil," said Claude, instantly decunting. "Retain my come and replenish me with it when I have finished."

Obediently, Clairwil opened her mouth as wide as she could. Still, she was able to accommodate only half of that enormous organ. Then came the eruption; the force and volume of his ejaculation were such that half of the precious fluid spurted wastefully down her chin and came to rest in a small pool between her breasts. Now Claude put his mouth on top of Clairwil's and recovered from her his just-spilled juices. Meanwhile, I grasping the still dripping dork in my mouth, milked it dry. By this time, I was nearly blind with desire.

Seizing the giant member, I stuffed it — limp though it was — into my vagina. So powerful was the initial sensation that I momentarily passed out.

When I regained my senses, I was lying in Clairwil's arms; Claude sat pensively on the ground between us.

"In Society, my dear Claude, you could make a million *louis* a day with that monstrosity," Clairwil said admiringly.

"Madame," he replied, "I could never abandon my intellectual life. The passions, you see, acquire force beneath the ascetic; the monastic life nurtures the seeds; Paris would only dissipate my energies and eventually taint the strength and purity of my desires."

"You could command the silence of your colleagues whenever you wanted to meditate," I argued. "Your slightest whim would be obeyed as quickly as a king's command."

"No, my lovely child," he said sadly; "my nature is such that I would never be happy except here behind these ivy-laden walls. The vocation of mind takes precedence over the avocation of cock."

Now, no sooner had he said this than Clairwil, suddenly and without warning, seized up a dead branch and brought it crashing against the unsuspecting professor's bald pate. He was motionless for a second, his delicate frame posed like a fragile statue; then, slowly, the poor man's body collapsed into a small pile. He was unconscious.

"By Satan, Clairwil!" I gasped. "Whatever on earth possessed you to do that?"

"A momentary whim," she replied. "As you know, I've always been a slave of my passions." Then, taking a small knife from the fold of her dress, she proceeded to carve her initials into his chest. "What a joke that will be on the old bastard when he wakes up," Clairwil said. Then she led the way out of the wood. Thus ended my experience in the groves of academe.

IV

Scarcely two weeks after the meeting with Claude, dear reader, I made the acquaintance of a man thanks to whom I enjoyed one of the most extraordinarily libertine episodes in my life. I shall devote the major portion of what remains of this chapter to a description of that episode.

One afternoon, while, per custom, I was receiving visitors, one of my servants brought to me a slight, shriveled-looking middle-aged man who requested a private audience. More out of curiosity than anything else, I agreed to interview the shabby, intense-faced little creature. Dismissing everyone else from the room, I motioned him to a chair, seated myself on a couch opposite him and bade him state his business.

"My name," the stranger began, "is Bernole — a name with which I am sure, you are unacquainted. Your mother, however, would recognize it well, and, if she were alive, dear Juliette, she would insist that you grant the favor which I ask."

"Sir," I replied, "your tone does not strike me as fitting for a beggar."

"It is quite possible that I have the right to employ this tone with you, dear child. Kindly look at these papers: a glance will inform you of both my need for this favor and your duty to grant it."

I had but to scan the folio of letters and documents to realize full well the nature of his mission. "By Lucifer!" I gasped. "My mother is guilty of adultery . . . with you!"

"Precisely, Juliette: I am your father. And I can prove it: the girl who was born to your mother and me had a birthmark — a brownish spot the size of a small coin — directly below her right breast. Do you have such a mark?"

"I do, sir."

"Then recognize your father, dearest child!" said he,

rising from the couch and approaching me with extended arms.

"Not so fast, my good man," I replied, fending him off with gentle but firm shoves. "What makes you think that you are welcome after all these years?"

"Oh, cold, unfeeling soul! Oh cruel woman! They told me that you would be like this, but I had refused to believe them . . . Listen to me, Juliette: I have lost all that I had; when your mother died, it was as if a piece had been cut from my heart; since that time my misfortunes have multiplied and I have had to turn to public charity to subsist. Please change this all, darling daughter; help your poor father to restore order to his life."

Dear reader, knowing me as you now do, you will have little difficulty realizing the distaste which this insolent beggar aroused within me. To be sure, he was my father; the proof was there and I accepted it: however, no filial blood warmed my heart toward him; all I felt was indifference to his predicament and disgust at his lack of style.

"Sir," I told him, "you have announced yourself many years too late; I presently neither need a father nor desire one: if you require that my feelings be articulated more precisely than that, please be advised that, unless you relieve me instantly of your loathsome presence, I shall be compelled to have your beggarly ass thrown out that window."

"Ungrateful child!" he hissed. "Have you no mercy?"

"No, sir; nor have I any more patience. Now, get out before I have you cast into a dungeon."

Hearing this, Bernole was seized with a fit of madness; employing new imprecations, new pleas, new invectives, new expressions of endearment, he strove diligently to change my mind: finally, he started to beat his head against the floor, opening a gash over one brow and splattering his blood all over my white rug. The sight of the blood — my blood! blood which coarsed through my veins! — choked me with happiness. Ignoring the damage to the rug (which, after all, could easily be replaced), I watched his fountain spurt forth. Then, after several exquisite minutes, I rang for a servant.

"Expel this clown from my house," I said; "but, before he leaves, find out his address for me."

That evening, as chance would have it, I was scheduled to dine with both Noirceuil and the Minister. I took advantage of the opportunity to ask these libertine gentlemen if either of them ever had heard of my afternoon caller.

"Yes, I once knew a man named Bernole," said Noirceuil. "He had money invested with your father when I robbed him blind. And, as I remember, he was very fond of your mother. He fairly greived when she died. In fact, it was this same Bernole who attempted to have me hanged as the murderer of your father. If this fellow is still around, it is high time that he be put properly out of the way."

"He's around," I said. Then I related the circumstances of the afternoon audience. The narration over, I asked my friends: "What do you think of that?"

"He sounds to me," replied Noirceuil, "like a dirty, thieving, low-down, self-serving, conscienceless son of a bitch — all of which, ordinarily, should make him quite welcome in our company. But his lack of style is distressing; this groveling, this imploring, this begging; it is just too contemptible for words. I think he should be put out of circulation immediately."

"We can lodge him in the Bastille before the day is out," said Saint-Fond.

"No," replied Noirceuil; "this whole situation has great theatrical possibilities; I see in his predicament — and in our resolution of it — pathos, drama, tragedy . . . indeed, all the ingredients for a great show."

"Yes! Yes!" I cried, excited by my former tutor's approach to the matter; "and I can think of a splendid way to stage the production."

"What do you have in mind, Juliette?" panted Saint-Fond, his member stiffening and becoming visible in his pants as he looked into my evil-glinting eyes.

"Patricide!" I whispered wickedly. Then, spelling out my plan: "I'll meet Bernole and tell him that I am dreadfully sorry about what happened today; I'll declare that it was all a misunderstanding: then I'll make overtures to him, provocative sexual overtures; soon I'll have him kissing and fondling me, and before long we'll be making love. Now, no sooner will intromission have been established than you, Saint-Fond, in the role of my lover, will come bursting into the room and, holding a dagger to my breast, enjoin me to kill him or perish myself. Naturally, I'll kill him."

"Bravo, Juliette, bravo!" applauded my two friends. "You are libertinage's most outstanding dramatist!!" continued Saint-Fond. "Count on my complete support."

"And mine," added Noirceuil. "I'm with you all the way."

The next day I sent Bernole a letter begging his forgiveness and assuring him that filial sentiment, though tardily, had finally visited my soul; I asked him to join me that evening for supper. Not in the least bit suspicious, he arrived promptly at eight, full of endearing sentiments — and even bearing a gift of a dozen freshly-picked flowers (stolen, no doubt, from one of the parks).

"Dearest Bernole," I said as we supped, "I am so happy that we have resolved our differences, and I must confess that my affection for you goes much deeper than a daughter's mere filial respect."

"I am quite deeply fond of you, too, dear child," the foolish man said softly.

"Bernole," I went on, "you loved my mother; I want you to love me also: I simply cannot resist the beauty of your body, the sensitivity of your hands, the sobriety of your eyes; I must know you not only as a daughter but also as a mistress, a lover, a concubine . . . Bernole, fuck me!"

The upright man visibly shuddered at hearing these blunt words. "My daughter," he replied shakily, "I seek to reawaken your sense of filial love only. Tax me not with immorality. What you propose is abhorrent to Nature."

Undaunted, I let my straying hands wander hotly up his paternal legs, unbutton his paternal pantaloons and begin caressing his paternal prick.

"Good God, stop this assault!" he cried, brushing my hand away and attempting to replace his rather hefty member inside the drawers whence it had emerged. "How can I be expected to spurn the living image of her whom I worshipped until the very end?"

"Spurn no longer, Bernole," I replied. "Today your beloved is restored to you. Behold in me she whom you loved in the past: she breathes. By mouth is her mouth, my breasts are her breasts, my legs are her legs. Come, my dear father; come fuck us both in sacred union."

Bernole, no longer able to contain himself, swept the dinnerware from the table and, tearing off my clothes with his own, lowered me into place on the table-top. "Oh, dear Juliette," he gasped, launching his invasion; "oh, dearest, dearest Juliette."

I ached with pleasure as his large tool bore strongly into me. Wrapping my legs around his strong, masculine body, I shifted gracefully into his expert rhythm. Our battle was one of strong contrasts: gently he poked me; savagely he rammed me; tenderly he stroked me; violently he rode me.

"Oh, daddy!" I screamed. "Oh, daddy, what a superb prick you have! Oh, daddy, what a beautiful lover you are! I'm coming, daddy! Your baby is on fire! Fuck me, father! Fuck me, fuck me, fuck me!"

At the height of my ravings, the door burst open and in burst Saint-Fond, his face — splendid actor that he was! — a portrait of rage. With him were Noirceuil and Clairwil. Bernole was dragged off my back and bound hand and foot.

"Wench!" Saint-Fond screamed at me. "You have betrayed the trust of your lover! You deserve to be butchered along with this monster! By Christ —" here he brandished a pistol "—I think I'll send you off together at once!"

"Oh, mercy, dearest darling!" I replied. "Spare the sweet Juliette who, in a moment of passion, so foolishly turned away from you. Spare me! Spare me!"

"You wish to live, eh?" he cackled wickedly. "Then you have no choice: there are three balls in this pistol; take it and blow this traitor's brains out."

"This is my father, sir!" I sobbed, tears gushing from my eyes. "I cannot kill him."

"Your father, you say? Do you tell me that I've been cuckolded by an incestuous father? Well, by Christ, you'll kill him immediately or you'll perish yourself!"

Dabbing dry the corners of my eyes, I took the pistol in my hand. Then, my expression of horror changing to one of exquisite pleasure, I faced Bernole. "Beloved father," I said, "will you pardon this act? I am under constraint. I must kill you."

"Vile creature," he answered softly. "Do you think your charade is lost upon me? Do you think I fail to realize what is happening? Well, shoot me, if that's what you have in mind; but spare me having to listen to your feeble theatrics."

"Ah, daddy," I said, feeling for a moment a genuine sadness; "it is only when you stare death in the face that you begin to talk like a man. What a pity; what a shame." Then, the corners of my mouth almost automatically lifting themselves in a small smile, I said: "Fuck you, daddy." And I pulled the trigger.

The ball neatly entered the center of my father's forehead, leaving a small, red hole no larger than a cherry; then it crashed out through the top of his skull, taking with it huge hunks of bone and flesh. Bernole died with his grey, jelly-like brains dribbling down his face — and with Saint-Fond, unbelievably aroused, standing over the body quietly masturbating.

V

Nothing very out of the ordinary befell me during the next two years: I lived with complete abandon as always, never reducing my daily intake of sex, food and drink, and I was intensely happy — until damnable Virtue, that bitch, once again invaded my garden of pleasure and with Her soft, pleading voice tempted me to rebel against a suggestion of my beloved arch-villain Saint-Fond.

I had just attained my twenty-second year at the time and was serving as hostess at one of the Minister's semi-weekly libertine suppers. Once the dishes had been cleared away, my lover got to his feet, commanded the attention of the assemblage and spoke as follows:

"My friends," he said proudly, "I have just conceived the most monstrous feat of lubricity of all time — a plan to depopulate all of France. The first stage involves a program of enforced universal infanticide, whereunder every child who has the misfortune to be conceived will, upon birth, immediately be slain. By continuing this policy for twenty-five years, we soon will have achieved a nation the population of which is wholly middle-aged. Thereupon we need only cut off the food supply and let them all starve to death; this should take no more than five years. Thus, in thirty years, this beloved country of ours can be completely void of human life."

Now, as I envisioned the bodies of these thousands upon thousands of infants being slaughtered; the bodies of hundreds of thousands of adults being withered away by starvation; the beautiful countryside slowly becoming more and more barren until nothing remained but vegetable matter and the cold earth — as I envisioned these things, I say, I found myself unexplainably overcome not with voluptuous excitement but with a wave of nausea. I wanted to tell Saint-Fond that, evil though I might be, I considered his plan far too evil even to be discussed, let alone implemented.

As these thoughts tormented me, the Minister continued to outline one atrocity after the other. Then finally, having spelled out the last ignominious detail, he took me by the hand and asked: "Juliette, my dear, how do you feel about your lover's masterpiece."

The eyes of the entire company were upon me. I tried to reply, but words froze in my throat. My face went livid; my lips began to tremble. "I—, I—, I—" I began; but I could not continue.

"What's this?" cried Saint-Fond incredulously. "Do I detect a glimmer of horror in your eyes? Are you weakening, you vile bitch? Are you? Answer me, my cunt: do you agree with my masterpiece?"

"I do, my lord," I finally managed to spit out; but I had been unable to conceal the grief in my voice; no one was fooled — least of all the dinner guests.

For a moment, Saint-Fond merely stared at me. Then, his jaws clenched in anger, he turned on his heel and marched out of the room. I watched him go and, when the sound of his footsteps died away, I ran straight to my apartment. There I flung myself upon my bed and finally fell into a deeply-troubled sleep.

The dream which haunted this sleep was horrible: I saw a fearful figure putting a torch to all I owned — to my money, to my clothes, to my house, to everything; as all blazed about me, a young girl appeared through the flames, stretching forth her arms to save me; in the attempt, she was burned to a cinder.

"When vice shall cease, woe shall betide!" Thus had predicted a scorceress some years earlier near the whorehouse of Madame Duvergier. Now the prediction came back to me. And, fully awake, I suddenly realized who was the girl in my dream: none other than tender Justine, my unfortunate sister.

I was terrified. What could I do? Where could I go? What would become of me?

As I asked myself these questions, I was startled by a knock on the door. Fearfully opening it, I found my-

self face to face with an ominously-dressed stranger.
He handed me a note. I recognized Noirceuil's hand-
writing. It read as follows:

> *You are ruined. Your virtuous impulse betrayed
> you. Leave Paris now. Saint-Fond is preparing to
> kill you. Fly, and say nothing to your friends. Sin-
> cerely, N . . . P.S. Take with you everything you can
> carry.*

Without wasting a moment, I gathered together my
jewels and *louis* and stuffed them into a chest with a
few of my favorite gowns. Then I jumped into the first
public carriage I found. It was a mail coach for Angers.
This lovely resort town now became my home.

VI

The money which I had taken with me proved to be
quite a bit more than I realized. After buying a comfortable house and equipping it with a small staff, I found
I had enough left to open a gambling casino. I was a
shrewd operator, and, before long, my spot had become
the favorite of businessmen, wealthy travelers and the
nobility. Within a matter of months, I had regained my
former status: little Juliette was once again a successful
woman of the world.

It was at this stage in my life, dear reader, that I met
and eventually decided to marry an old gentleman who
had been pestering me since the first day I opened my
casino. His was Count de Lorsange, of whom mention
has been made in Justine's book. The count was aged
fifty, a bachelor, a banal and stupid pig of a man and
impotent; however, marriage to him conferred upon me
the title of Countess and, under the circumstance, I
thought it best (in gambler's parlance) to hedge my
bets in every way I could: so, we were married, and,
on my wedding night, I spent all my time in bed listening

to him discourse on the advantages of the Christian life. Well, it may have been quite a comedown; but it still was a far sight better than suffering Saint-Fond's wrath.

But two years of Count de Lorsange was all I could take. On the verge of going out of my mind with dullness, mediocrity and sexual abstinence (the swine never let me out of his sight), I one night dropped an envelope of poison into his after-dinner cordial. After three days my beloved husband died peacefully in his bed, surrounded by fifteen priests who chanted him sweetly out of this life and into the next.

With my very chaste husband interred, I went officially into mourning; but it was quite difficult to be genuinely mournful while contemplating my delicious inheritance of four estates valued at fifty-thousand *livres* per year in rents. Deciding to invest this fortune in some physical pleasures long overdue, I headed immediately for Italy. After journeying through Turin, Pisa, Bologna, Florence (wonderful Florence!) and a half dozen more of that marvelous country's splendid towns—during which journeys I cavorted with everyone from street urchins to Hapsburg princes (and princesses!)—I finally came to the capital of the world. . . . the seat of the ancient empire . . . the center of the universe . . . Rome!

* * *

BOOK FIVE

I

Ah, Rome! The city of famous ghosts — Cato, Seneca, Plautus, Caligula, Mark Antony, Lepidus, Octavius, Ovid!

The land of fabled genius! *La bella citta!*

The beginning of my stay in this marvelous place was distinguished by the conquest of a noblewoman — none other than the Princess Borghese. Thirty years of age, bright, charming, evil-minded and wonderfully cruel, this darling person met me at an official dinner given by the French ambassador. We fell in love with each other instantly, and, a week later, I received an invitation to her home. "We shall be alone," she wrote; "everything about you excites me, Countess de Lorsange, and I am determined to explore you." I, no less determined, arrived with heart aflutter.

The weather that afternoon was hot and sultry, like the breath of a hungry lover. Following a succulent repast served by five charming girls in a garden where the scent of roses and jasmine blended provocatively with the splashing murmur of a fountain, the pretty princess drew me off to a lonely summerhouse lost in a glade of sheltering oaks. We entered a circular room; around the wall, which was covered entirely with mirrors, ran a long sofa the seat of which was but six inches off a floor strewn with pillows and cushions. We reclined on some pillows.

"Do call me Olympia instead of princess; dear, and I shall call you Juliette," she said, tenderly kissing my lips.

"Dear Olympia," I replied, "I shall worship the shrine of that name by repeating it a thousand times."

Ah, Juliette," she said; "you are beautiful beyond belief. I'm ravaged by lust for you. Not love, dear flower; pure inflammable lust."

"Is it possible," I replied softly, "that in two different countries Nature has created two so-similar souls?"

"What, Juliette? Are you a libertine too? Dearest, how wonderful! Now we can mingle without the responsibility of love! Ah, you divine gift of Cupid! Let me swallow you in passion!"

So saying, she reached for the cincture on my gown; I, leaning into her outstretched arms, likewise began undressing her: when we were completely naked, we came to grips. Leaping to action, I rolled the marvelously-fleshed beauty on the floor and sprawled between her lovely legs. Her charming vulva tasted of sweet fruit: moist, fleshy, pink with animal innocence. Her cool white legs curled over my shoulders and her milk-white body undulated fiercely with each touch of my tongue. I chewed at the tiny, fine-spun hairs surrounding her holy mound; then, gently tickling her hard, peppermint clitoris with my starved tongue-tip, I bathed my entire face in the sweet nectar of her discharge.

"Ah, darling," she sighed, matching me measure for measure, "my stomach is aflame. I'm whirling, swirling, sinking, spinning off the edge of the world! I'm crumbling into infinity! I'm floating toward the moon! You've imprisoned the very sun in my womb!"

Finally the last delicious tingle of sensation ebbed and we lay exhausted in each other's arms. Olympia did not move; she did not speak; she hardly breathed. Holding her to me, I thought excitedly: now I shall conquer Rome; I shall become one of its legendary ghosts; I shall sup in the halls of Myth with Cicero and the Borgias!

Rolling over in my arms, the princess purred lovingly. "Oh, Juliette," she said, "you inflame me so. One touch from your gentle fingers and I want to be a whore — a foul, dirt-caked, shit-pantsed whore. I want to fuck barons and beggars, bishops and beasts. I want to feel the lash, the knife, the whip, the switch, the belt smash across my buttocks and open my veins; I want to feel the warm stickiness of my own blood gushing out to bathe my body in its pure flow; I want to swim in the stinking, fetid slime of crime and gorge myself with the rotten, worm-infested fruit of total perversion. I want to take the whole world into my bed! Help me, dearest heart; help me, my dear, corrupt Juliette."

"I shall help you, my goddess," I whispered softly, rocking her gently to sleep. " I shall help you."

II

A week later, true to my expectations, I received through Olympia's social secretary an invitation to visit with Cardinal Albani and Cardinal Bernis at the former's summer villa. As an elegantly-garbed butler let me into the plushly-foliaged courtyard, I found myself face to face with none other than Cardinal Bernis himself. With him was Olympia, who while the Cardinal very charmingly kissed my hand, made an obscene gesture with her finger behind his back.

"Welcome, my dear, to the Villa Albani," said the Cardinal ceremoniously, totally unaware of the irreverent gesture and my amused reaction to it. "If you will forgive me for but a moment, I will be back with my friend, Cardinal Albani."

Smiling politely at this poor joke, I watched him pad out of the room on slippered feet. When he was gone, I took my beloved princess' hand in mine.

"I'm certainly pleased to see you here, darling," I told her; "but I'm also surprised: I was under the impression that I was to visit these two distinguished churchmen alone."

"I wanted to surprise you, dearest," she replied. "After that glorious afternoon we spent together, I decided to introduce you personally to these two most important men of Rome. Are you pleased?"

"I adore you," I replied, brushing my lips against her cheek.

"We shall conquer the world, Juliette," she whispered rapturously in return. "What Caesar did with his legions, we shall do with our bodies.

At this point, Cardinal Bernis returned with Cardinal Albani and formal introductions were made all around. This accomplished, we engaged in a lively discussion about the nature of existence, life and death. All four of us agreed that religion is but a sham and that the only rational rule of life was to gratify one's every whim, no matter what the cost or to whom.   .

"Furthermore," Cardinal Albani declared, "it is a sign of grave weakness to change one's mind as one approaches death. Life is long, is it not? Fifty, sixty, seventy years are more than ample time in which to taste of all the pleasures. A man should spend the years of his youth exploring the world in search of a set of principles by which to live and his later years in living as closely as possible to these principles. If he has done so, there is no need for a change of heart as death approaches."

"Quite true," I replied, "and this is one of the many consolations of the happy atheism which I embrace. 'Dust,' to quote that fellow you clerics are so fond of, 'shall return to dust;' I shall submit to bodily disintegration just as calmly, just as passively, as when, out of 'dust,' I took being in my mother's womb."

"Bravo!" applauded Cardinal Bernis. "It's nice to see that our priests haven't poisoned everyone's mind yet . . . Juliette, heed my words: the human animal is just that: an animal. His greatest attribute is his ability to endure, to face calmly the terrible cleavage of life from its root — as happens in death. I have always believed that one should die with a sad smile of resignation; it would be most piquant; man is born, he lives, he dies; the 'parentheses' — birth and death — are important as milestones, as points of reference, but it is what lies between them — life — which counts."

"Yes," said Cardinal Albani. "But let us not get too wrapped up in our contemplations here; after all, philosophy can dull the edge of life's most important weapon: one's prick! Enough philosophy for the nonce — eh, Bernis? Let us cease to discuss life and start once again living it. I would suggest an orgy: one of our mystical communions, understood by few, appreciated by even fewer, but extremely dear to the hearts of those are souls who have 'eaten the bread.' Yes, my children, let us communicate; let us, in the vernacular, go a-fucking; let us fuck and suck!"

So saying, the lecherous cardinal led us into a heavily-curtained room which was lighted by only a few, scattered candles. Olympia and I were instructed to lie on our stomachs on the floor. Then, spreading our legs, the two men of the church invaded our recta with hot pokers which had been warming themselves in the glowing embers of a small fire. Our bodies were wrung by a stinging, unbearable pain; the sickly odor of our burnt flesh filled the room: yet we would not cry out; a million sharp-bladed knives lanced through our bowels, a hundred claws tore at our entrails; sour vomit choked our throats, tears burned our cheeks, pain chewed at us like a mad animal; yet we would not capitulate; we said nothing; we refused to move a muscle. Finally the pokers were removed and the pain ever so slowly began to recede.

"Yes," Cardinal Albani nodded solemnly, "you are consistent, my dear friends; you practice the happy stoicism which you preach. It is indeed a pleasure to welcome you to our circle. Now, one or two more tests of your mettle and we will announce whether or not we find you deserving of the supreme honor which can be bestowed upon a woman."

"Supreme honor?" I replied. "And what, may I ask, is that?"

But the cardinals, hiding behind amused, inscrutable smiles, refused to reply. Instead, Cardinal Bernis rolled me on my back and invaded my vagina with a dildo the size of a small walking cane. The weapon was shoved into me so far that it felt like it would impale one of my lungs, but I refused to show any sign of pain; instead, I stared impassively at the small, round, rubber ball which hung from the end of the instrument.

"No doubt, you are wondering what this small globe contains," said Cardinal Albani, following my gaze. "Well, I'll tell you; it contains hot water; you see, I plan to give you a little douche."

So saying, he squeezed the ball, sending scalding pain shattering through me. White-hot hammers pounded

against my organs, a million nails were being driven into
my womb, I was being roasted alive from inside — and
I was enjoying it, finding immense pleasure in it, surrendering both mind and body to a sensation which over-
powered any I had ever experienced.

Next came Olympia's turn, and she could not contain
her elation as pain's prodigious prick probed her innards. "Shove your swords into my cunt!" she screamed
hysterically. "Dynamite my ass! Blow my womb to pieces!
Rip my breasts from my body, pour molten lead into me,
stuff steaming pitch up my ass, fuck me with a cannon,
I love it, I love it, I love it !!!"

"Well," said Cardinal Bernis, returning the dildo to a
drawer, "they've proved themselves beyond a doubt."
Then, taking Olympia and me in his arms, he announced:
"My dears, you are worthy both in mind and in body.
The supreme honor shall be yours."

Thereupon a cord was tugged, a bell rang and a servant materialized. "See to it that these young women
are returned to their quarters," commanded Cardinal
Bernis. Then, to us he said: "We will be in touch with
you, my dears. It will be only a matter of time."

Now, once on the road back to the city, I asked
Olympia what had been meant by these strange words
about a "supreme honor."

"My dear," she smiled proudly, "we have just been
selected for an audience with the Holy Father — or, as
he is called by some, the Holy Fucker."

"You mean . . .?"

"Yes, my dear, Pius VI, the Pope of Rome! Prepare
yourself, Juliette: we shall soon have the honor of a
very personal audience with that old Papal bull!"

III

A week later the Swiss Guardsman came knocking on my
door. In his hand was a letter — an engraved invitation
to the chamber of Pope Pius the Sixth! I was flabber-

gasted. I, a simple, cunning, beautiful, lewd, criminal whore, was being summoned to the apartment of the most powerful man on earth!

For days before the day of the visit, I was filled with fear and trembling. Then the magic hour came and I arrived with Olympia at the entrance to His Holiness' magnificent chambers. We stepped across the gold-gilded threshold and walked stiffly across the red-carpeted floor toward the majestic throne directly in the center of the room. Sitting on the throne, his features highlighted by flashes of gold light from the immense dome over his head, the Bishop of Rome stared compassionately down upon us.

"My children," he intoned; "my brothers and sisters in the United Christian Family, welcome to the sepulchre and womb of Our Holy Mother the Church. You are three waifs tossed to my shores by the stormy seas of life, and it is I, your Holy Father, yea, the Holy Father of the entire world, who has heard your cries and shall answer them with forgiveness."

I could not tell whether our esteemed host actually took himself seriously or whether he was testing us in the manner of the Cardinals Albani and Bernis; but, deciding that no intelligent man could possibly be so deluded as to believe all that claptrap, and, at the same time, realizing that it would take great intelligence to scale the summit of the papal throne, I decided to take a chance on the theory that we were being tested — that His Holiness wanted nothing more than to try our spunk. I acted accordingly.

"Horseshit, Mr Braschi," I said, addressing him by his civilian name. "You're a fraud and a cheat and you know it."

"But, my child—" he began.

"Fuck you, you old ape," I replied. "I spit upon your Church and I spit upon you."

Immediately his expression turned from one of majesty to one of amusement. Leaning forward, he took me by the hand and chuckled:

"Allright, darling, you're right; but don't ruin my act;
each of us has his own peculiarities and pomposity is
mine." Then, rubbing my head with his hands, he smiled
seductively and said: "My I proceed?"

"By all means," I smiled back. "I like a good caper as
much as anyone."

Sobriety once again draping his countenance, he looked
into the distance and intoned ceremoniously: "I love
you, my children; I love you with a love that is even
greater than the love of Christ, for He loved you only
spiritually and I love you both spiritually and materially.
Yes, my children; I go Christ one better; such are the
labors of His Vicar here on Earth.

"You are gathered here before me, two scummy whores
whose beshitted asses must be reamed of all vestiges
of sin and corruption by my holy pontifical prick *Dominus vobiscum. Et cum spiritu tuo.* My children; yes,
my sisters in this great fiasco which we call existence, my
vulnerable little lambs who are prey to all the vulturous
evils of the world, let me, your mediator to the great
afterlife, bestow a plenary indulgence on each of your
poor, embuggered asses. *Dominus vobiscum. Et cum
spirtu tuo. Gloria in Excelsis Deo.* Ah, by the Lord's
crotch, I love those stupid words . . . To our knees,
whores! To your knees for my papal blessing!"

We fell to our knees. Despite my dislike for his position, I could not fail to feel an evil kinship with this
strangely-unstable, wizened old figure perched on his
throne like an insane hawk. Raising my eyes, I noticed a
bulge surreptitiously beginning to take form beneath the
Holy Father's robe.

"My children," he went on, the bulge becoming bigger
by the second, "I want you to make a general confession
to me. I want you to unburden yourselves of the millstone
of sins which weighs your souls down in the muck of
guilt. Release to me, your spiritual scapegoat, the evil
crimes of your past. I shall bear them away on my own
shoulders and place them at the feet of our King in
Heaven — the Father of us all — he who, only one step

above me, looks over each of us with his all-seeing eyes.

"Juliette, you are a notorious cock-sucker and lesbian; repent! Olympia, you are a notorious cuntlapper and you fuck everything that walks; repent!"

In unison, Olympia and I repeated the word, "repent." For atmosphere, we gnashed our teeth and screamed out for forgiveness. The Pope smiled benignly down on us, tears in his eyes, his right hand vigorously stroking the bulge in his robe.

"And now, my children," he said, "for your penance, you shall accompany me to the chapel and assist me in the performance of our most loving duty as Christians, our most precious and consummante experience with our Divine Leader, the Holy Sacrifice of the Mass."

The Holy Father stepped from his throne and led the way to the Chapel. I could not fail to be astonished at the beauty of the place: the gorgeously-furnished room was thick with the mist of incense; its altar was covered with hundreds of candles which cut through the grey gloom like a hazy winter sun: four naked women stood by the altar, each holding a bottle of wine; meanwhile, three crotchety cardinals knelt at the communion rail.

As the Pope entered the vestry to prepare his vestments, Olympia and I knelt in the front pew. Directly before us, over the altar, was a crucifix — hanging upside down. Behind us, on raised platforms, were a dozen naked choirboys. Scattered throughout the chapel were various and sundry male and female supplicants.

Suddenly a bell chimed and the Pope emerged from the vestry. He wore a cincture and purple stole, which crossed at his chest and hung to his hips, but, other than this, he was naked; accompanying him were two nuns, wearing only their starched white headpieces. Kneeling at the foot of the altar, His Holiness began intoning in a sharp nasal voice his own version of the Prayers at the Foot of the Altar.

"Oh, Master of Slanders," he said; "oh, Dispenser of the benefits of crime; thou marvelous Administrator of sumptuous sins and great and wonderous vices; yes, you Satan, not the other fellow — it is you who we adrore. Oh, thou dark and reasonable light . . ."

Replied the nuns: "We adore thee."

"Oh master of our cocks and cunts . . ."

"*Te adoremus.*"

"Oh flaming prick of the universe . . ."

"*Laus tibi, Satanus.*"

"*Dominus* go-fuck-em . . ."

"*Et cum* fuck-a-you too."

"*Oremus.* Oh thou who savest the honor in families by aborting wombs impregnated with the forgetfulnes coming out of the good orgasm; oh thou mainstay of the poor, thou sultan of the downtrodden; only thou dost fertilize the brain of man whom injustice has crushed; only thou breathest into his soul the spirit of vengeance whereby he can regain his just desserts; to thee we humbly pray. It is thee, oh divine hope of virility, who is supreme; thou dost not demand the bootless offering of chaste lions; thou dost not sing the praises of lenten follies; thou dost not ask that which is unnatural, that which is ridiculous, that which is absurd. Thou art divine, oh Satan; Thou and only Thou . . ."

"Amen," replied the nuns.

Climbing the altar stairs, His Holiness now turned toward the pews, his face reddening, his lips ringed with white. Looking at him, I could feel the force of his passion. His voice seemed to cry out personally to me.

"Oh, master Satan," he sung; "see thy faithful servants? Wouldst thou deliver them from virtue and goodness, in Lucifer we pray, amen."

At this point one of the cardinals rose from the communion rail and, with arms outstretched, made his way up the altar steps. The penis of the pope was rigid and thrust straight out; that of the cardinal, finding its way

"Art thou ready, brother, to piss upon the ring?" asked the Pope.

through the robes, squirmed about as if in search of its

peer.

"Aye, your Holiness."

Thereupon the Pope lowered his papal ring to a point just beneath the tip of the cardinal's penis. When the ceremony was complete, he offered his hand to be kissed by each of the nuns. Then the mass was resumed.

"And now, Satan," continued Pius, forgive us momentarily while we address ourselves to the other fellow . . . Yes, you, Christ: you, you artisan of hoaxes, you bandit of homage, you robber of affection! Hear us, you son of a bitch! Since the day when thou didst emerge from the bowels of a whore, thou hast failed in all thine engagements, thou has belied all thy promises. Centuries have wept awaiting thee, thou fugitive fraud, thou faceless and mute god; thou wast to redeem man and thou hast not; thou wast to appear in glory and thou hast not; thou sleepest, thou impostor; thou knowest that the angels, disgusted at thy inertness, have abandoned thee. Oh, fuck you, Jesus — fuck you up the ass for all the strife you have visited upon us!

"You who were to be the interpreter of our pains but who let us down . . ."

"Go fuck your self," chanted the nuns.

"You who were to be the chamberlain of our tears . . ."

"Go fuck yourself."

"You who defrauded the masses . . ."

"Go fuck yourself."

"You who served as the tool for tyrants and the pawn of despots . . ."

"Go fuck yourself."

"*Oremus.* Tell us, Jesus Christ, where is the Father to who you were supposed to convey our wishes? Don't say it; we know; it would disturb his eternal sleep to give us a sign of his existence at this time. Well, we know you better, you fraud; we, who have seen women disemboweled for a loaf of bread, we who have heard the death rattle of the timid being oppressed by the monarchs whom we, your minions, invariably protected, we know you for what you are and we condemn you for it."

The voice was like a crescendo of vituperation. Listening to it, I found myself overtaken by a great dizziness. The choirboys now sung a hymn and I watched, aflame with desire, as the Pope moved back and forth about the altar, sprinkling everything in sight with holy water. Finally, His Holiness abandoned his ladle and bucket and faced the congregation with arms raised.

"*Ite missa est,*" he chanted. "Go, mass is finished."

And the nuns replied:

"*Statno gratias, allelulia, allelulia.*"

By this time the chapel was thick with incense. I found myself becoming flustered and foggy from the smoke gushing forth from the censers which the three cardinals were waving toward the congregation. Then, through the haze, I watched as they set down the golden, flask-like objects and headed for the nuns.

Now nothing was visible in the smoke-filled room but dim flickers of candlelight and occasional flashes of white, bare flesh. The sounds of mouths sucking, bodies bumping, fingers frigging, pricks plunging — these sounds welled up through the room. Then, from what seemed to be a great distance, there rose the voice of His Holiness.

"Where is my woman?" he cried plaintively. "Where oh where is my consecrated cunt, Juliette?"

My voice went out to him in reply:

"I am coming, beloved."

And it was true — I was telling no lie — for, as I said it, I was running over the damp and writhing bodies which choked the aisles, on through the phalanx of cardiunals and nuns mobbing the altar. Olympia was beside me, competing with me for the great prize, but I fought her off; I was consumed with fervor; I was determined that I — and only I — would have this splendid Lamb of Darkness, the Vicar of Lucifer in the robes of the enemy army.

Now I was almost upon him. His arms stretched out to me. "Oh, Juliette," he called; "you have come, dear heart; oh, thank the ass-fucking, blackpitted gods, you have come."

I wasted not a second of precious time. Taking his splendid member in my hand, I led him to the altar; then, lying on my back on the holy stone, I pulled him into place on top of me, thrust open my legs and guided the pulsating penis into position between my buttocks. His strokes matched mine and, with each of them, the organ grew larger until I thought it would split inside me. Still he drove on, passionately, madly, wildly, crazily.

"Ah, fuck, Juliette," he gasped. "Your boundless fuckability fills my tired old bones with life. He who fucks today will live to fuck another day. Never fear, dear heart, what may befall us, for we are united at last in the spirit of Satan our father, and if we die it is to his bosom that we will fly. Ah, my child I discharge! Lo, I come! Ahhhh, FUCK!!!"

* * *

IV

And so, dear reader, my story comes to a close. Months later, Saint-Fond, having heard of my successful debut in the Papal Palace, would lose his old animosity for me and seek to reingratiate himself in my favor; I would be reunited with Noirceuil and Clairwil, and in their company would pass many a debauched hour; I would be honored by the Sodality of the Friends of Crime and my name would be emblazoned on banners all over the Continent — but all these triumphs, all these joys, pale in comparison with my Great Moment in the arms of *Il Papa, Pio Sesto,* Vicar of Christ on Earth, the Pope of Rome. Thus I end my tome here, and hope that you carry away from it a measure of the happiness which I experienced as a result of the events herein related.

No doubt you have read in Justine's book that, after seeing that poor dear child struck by lightning, I repented and became a Carmelite nun. This, as you can readily imagine after hearing my tale, is a patent lie, promulgated with no other reason but that of discrediting me. Know this, dear reader: I have lived as I have chosen; I face death unashamed and unafraid: I leave you with these thoughts, and with my best wishes for a happy life of your own.

THE END

DONATIEN FRANCOIS ALPHONSE DE SADE
PARIS: 1797

ONE HUNDRED AND TWENTY DAYS OF SODOM, or THE ROMANCE OF THE SCHOOL OF LIBERTINAGE

AUTHOR'S PREFACE: AN INTRODUCTION TO THE SCHOOL OF LIBERTINAGE

The extensive wars which characterized the reign of Louis XIV proved to be a hardship only to the common man; to the bloodsuckers who hovered close to the crown, ready to profit from every disaster, they were no less than a blessing. Ah, the parasites! How they drained France dry! Lapping up the last drop of blood which fell from the nation's battered flesh! Yes, then gnawing and nibbling at the skin and bones in case there hovered within a drop or two more which had escaped notice! The jackals! The knaves!

But the joyride couldn't last forever; eventually there came the day of reckoning, and the villains were brought to justice. Well, not quite all the villains. Four, who had had the foresight to escape before justice's final trumpet sounded, went free as a bird. And these four, being well along in years and now having more money than they could possibly spend in ten lifetimes, resolved to abandon all commercial pursuits and to band together to seek the ultimate excesses of libertinage and sensuality.

The leader of the group was the Duke of Blangis, a monstrous scoundrel who, at age fifty, had indulged at least once in every vice and every crime known to man. Ah, what a libertine! He was a drunk, a liar, a thief, a sodomite, a gourmand and a mother-fucker (having qualified in this last category at age sixteen, when he raped his mother on the way home from his father's funeral). Moreover, he was a devotee of arson, theft, calumny, blasphemy and murder. Indeed, not only did he never so much as dream of a virtue, he actually regarded the whole lot of them with horror, much as the virtuous are prone to regard vice (and, no doubt, for the same reason: lack of exposure).

Physically, Blangis was as splendid as morally he was corrupt. He stood exactly six feet tall and weighed one hundred and eighty pounds. His arms and legs were of enormous strength; his shoulders, broad and powerful; his chest, heavy and wide; his waist, slim; his buttocks, meaty. His face was proud and masculine, with great, dark eyes; handsome, black eyelashes; a straight, stately nose; strong, porcelain-white teeth, and a rugged, well-formed jaw.

These many splendors, however, paled in comparison with his crowning glory — his enormous prick. Ah, what a shaft that was! What a monument! It measured an exact eight inches in circumference and a full fourteen in length, and, when in an erect state, which was more often than not, shot out like a flagpole, not curving one way or the other but extending straight forward, majestic and true. Oh, what a prick! And it enjoyed in functionability the same excellence which characterized its dimensions. The duke could ejaculate as many as eighteen times a day without being any more fatigued after the last than after the first ejaculation; moreover, his splendid ass, when he saw fit to put it to buggery's purposes (which was frequently), could receive as many as fifty-five pricks a day without being any worse for the wear.

This, I say, was the Duke of Blangis, and, if a blacker heart ever beat, it had to be the heart of Satan himself. Indeed, the duke's chief complaint was — and how much more diabolic can one get? — that far too many people misbehaved with impure motives, which is to say that they misbehaved not for evil's sake but simply because of the pleasures attached to certain modes of misbehavior, this motivation, in his view, was deplorable. "It is simple enough," he was wont to observe, "to do this or that when passion spurs one to the task. But the life of such a person must indeed be tortuous, for, since his indulgence was brought about by weakness, how can he fail to regret in the morning that which he enjoyed the evening before. He, on the other hand, who pursues evil for evil's own sake indulges not from weakness but from strength; thus each morning he does not bemoan his excesses of the night before, but rather congratulates himself for having perpetrated them. It is in this direction, surely, that happiness lies."

Sharing this philosophy with the duke, although lacking the physical equipment with which to practice fully what he preached, was the duke's brother, the Bishop of X_____. He had the same black soul as Blangis, the same penchant for crime and the same contempt for religion; yes, and a slyness, a natural cunning which, if anything, outshone that of his brother. But he was an ugly little wart of a man, the bishop was: in years, forty-five; in appearance, disgusting; his features were delicate and slightly effeminate his mouth, foul-looking; his teeth, rotting and misshapen his eyes, small and beady; his body, soft, flabby and hairless: and lo! his member, an insult to the species; no more than five inches in circumference, no more than six in length: perhaps the only redeeming feature about the man was his ass, which though small, had the virtue of being well-rounded and firm to the touch.

As for sexual preference, His Excellency was a devout sodomite, enjoying equally both the active and passive roles. However, his passion for asses was all-consuming: unlike the duke, who could give vent to his energies in any orifice offered him, the bishop confined himself to

asses and nothing but asses: of cunts, he had an abhor-
rence which bordered the maniacal; not only could he
never fuck one, but if, while fucking a female ass, he happened to recall that there was a cunt on the other side,
the recollection all but ruined his pleasure completely.

These faults notwithstanding, the bishop possessed an
immense fortune; moreover, through the many priests
among whom he was influential, he was able to recruit
numerous girls for exercises in debauchery (learning
from his priests which girls had, during confession, admitted to licentious behavior), and thus he was the first
person invited by the duke to become a member of the
group.

The second person invited was Judge Curval. A pillar
of society, he was sixty years of age; tall; thin; dry-
skinned; blue-eyed; white-haired, and all but worn off
his legs by a life of unmitigated depravity. Unwholesome
of mouth and long of nose, the judge resembled nothing
more than a sun-dried string bean; his back was hunched,
his shoulders stooped; his buttocks were so deadened
and desensitized by whipstrokes that you could squeeze
a handful of flesh without his knowing that you did it. In
the center of these sagging, leathery cheeks — you didn't
even have to spread them to see it — was an immense orifice whose unholy diameter, color and odor brought to
mind the asshole of a mare; moreover, the slovenly judge
always left this part of himself in such a state of uncleanliness that it was forever encrusted with a layer of shit
at least half an inch thick.

On the side of the body opposite this monument to
filth hung a prick which, when erect, might have measured eight inches in length and seven in circumference;
however, the erectile state of late had become for Curval increasingly difficult to attain, with the result that he
no longer ever tried to participate in a sexual act wherein
erection was necessary unless he had first made arrangements for the many whippings, beatings, blood-lettings
and so forth which he knew would be necessary to raise

him to the task. As for preferences, he liked men; all the same, he was not wont to reject girls, especially if their cunts and asses gave forth with odors which approximated in strength his own stench. He had a special passion for eating shit, and took advantage of every opportunity to do so, regardless of the source; this act, perhaps more effectively than any other, aroused his passions to the boiling point and often spurred him to ejaculate, even if his prick did not happen to be erect at the time: significantly, while ejaculating, he experienced a sort of lubricious rage which drove him to perform unspeakable acts of cruelty; however, it might be noted that his cruelty was not confined to those times when the jismy juices flowed; indeed, he acquired his fortune by murdering people, then seizing their lands, and often commited murders even when there was no profit to be gained thereby.

The final member of the group was a banker, Durcet, aged forty-three years, a great friend of the Blangis and his one-time schoolmate. Short, squat and chubby, this depraved financier had both the face and figure of a woman and all a woman's tastes: in short, he was a total nance. His prick was unbelievably small — no more than two inches around and less than four inches long — but the deficiency was of no concern to him since he has no desire to employ the member for functions other than excretory; on the other hand, his ass was so often engaged in sexual pursuits that he barely had opportunity to shit; he also was rather fond of oral pleasure, since this enterprise was the only one in which he was capable of playing the aggressive role.

Like his three friends, Durcet worshipped only at the altar of the gods of pleasure; he had committed a profusion of crimes, murder among them, and was accused of having poisoned both his mother and his wife; crimes which he not only refused to deny but about which he actually boasted.

Now, once the group was organized, the four libertines created a common fund. Next they purchased a house on the outskirts of Paris and engaged eight procurers of established reputation — four to recruit girls and four to recruit boys. They they set up a schedule of orgies designed to pamper the tastes, no matter how diverse, of every member of the organization. Four different fetes were conducted each week under the format which follows:

The first evening — called the Eve of Masculinity — was devoted to sodomy, and only men were present. Procurers would bring to the castle a compliment of sixteen healthy young studs, aged twenty to thirty and selected on the basis of prick-size. Then our four heroes, dressed in feminine clothing, would swoop down upon them. Cocks would be sucked, bitten, blown upon, clutched, kneaded, stroked, petted and kissed; they would be taken up asses, squeezed between thighs, imprisoned in armpits and kneepits; songs would be sung in their praise, poems recited, orations delivered. Then, so that our foursome would have ample opportunity to play the male as well as the female role, the procurers would bring on a second compliment of sixteen boys, much younger and predisposed to fulfill the offices of women; the lads, aged twelve to eighteen, were selected on the basis of delicacy of face and body, appearance of innocence, freshness of wit and keenness of intellect; there would be embuggerings and rapes, ass-fuckings and mouth-fuckings, and fuckings between the thighs and behind the balls; before the evening had come to a close, there would have transpired every delight ever known in Sodom and Gomorrah and a great many other delights of which no one in either of those esteemed cities had ever dreamed.

The second evening, given over entirely to girls, was called the Eve of Humiliation. The procurer would bring to the castle twelve young ladies of superior social station, haughty bitches one and all. Our champions then would proceed to teach the lasses some manners. The girls were forced to submit to everything — fingering, kneading, tweaking, pinching, biting, punching, kicking, ear-pulling, the banging of heads against the wall or against other heads), tit-pulling, encunting, embuggering . . . in short, any extravagance the perpetration of which was not prohibited by reason of anatomy or physiology.

The third evening — the Eve of Blackness — also was given over entirely to girls, but to those of a different stripe. Only whores were present, and, in company with them, our libertines wallowed in total debauchery. Shit was eaten, piss drunk, saliva exchanged, farts smelled, vomit swallowed; there were multiple liaisons, and violence abounded; of one hundred whores in attendance at the beginning of each week's festivities, rarely, if ever, did more than fifty or sixty live through the night; there were fustigations, grandings, turnings at the wheel, stabbings, shootings, burnings, whippings, crucifixions . . . the full spectrum of cruelties.

The fourth evening, given over to mixed company, was called the Eve of Defloration. Assembled were only youngsters whose virginity could be certified. Maidenheads then were stolen, cherries busted, pucelages depucelated; when our heroes no longer had the strength to do the deed by prick, they employed candlesticks, dildos and other devices. No one left with an orifice uninvaded in some way or another.

Thus were spent four per week of our libertines' evenings, and the other three were passed in private debauch. However, after several months, Blangis decided that a change was in order. Summoning his colleagues to a meeting, he addressed them as follows:

"Gentlemen, our excesses to date have been gratifying, but, if we would think of ourselves as true scoundrels, we must go much farther in our quest for pleasure; we must go, indeed, to such extremes the very thought of which should strike terror into the hearts of ordinary, mortal men."

"Bravo!" cried his audience of three. "Capital! Superb!"

"But," added Judge Curval after a moment, "what would you suggest we do? What is there, after all, which we have not already done?"

"I don't know," conceded the duke. "I can think of no specific desire which we have failed to satisfy, no specific thirst which we have failed to slake; yet, I cannot help but feel that, if we were to isolate ourselves under circumstances most conducive to lewdness, if we were to extend our every effort to the expansion of lubricity's horizons — if we were to do such, I say, then I have no doubt that we would acquire these new thirsts, recognize these new desires . . . What I propose, therefore, gentlemen, is the establishment of a School of Libertinage. Envision this: a castle high in the Alps, inaccessible save by foot; gathered therein, a complement of the most provocative creatures one can find, splendid specimens of sexuality whose very presence is sufficient to stir the blood of the most jaded rake; eight little girls, with virginal cunts to be fucked, virginal asses to be reamed, virginal tits to be kneaded and mashed and beat to a pulp; also eight little boys, equally virginal, ready to lend themselves to every lubricity which the voluptuous mind can conceive; next, eight fuckers, monsters one and all, with throbbing pricks to probe's one's bowels and rock-hard buttocks to receive their masters' fuck in return; then, four madames — yea, the four most experienced madames in Paris — to advise the company on this passion or that (after all, who would be in a better position to offer advice on the ways of libertinage than those whose lives have been devoted to trafficking in it?); next, four wives, one for each of us, to satisfy wants not satisfiable elsewhere; then four old hags to serve as chaperones for the kiddies, and also to lend themselves to the more perverse varieties of debauch with which from time to time we may choose to amuse ourselves, and, finally, a smattering of lackeys and servants to keep the ship afloat. Envision yourselves, I say, locked up in a castle with a coterie like that; devoting not just an occasional evening to debauch, but — gad, what a prospect! — every waking hour: add to the picture a full schedule of meal's fit for the King, himself; add wines of every vintage, liquers imported from every corner of the globe: by God's gronch, who could ask for anything more?"

"Ah, fuck!" cried the bishop. "What an inventive mind this brother of mine has! I dare say, I could think of nothing to improve the picture. You have my vote, sir."

"Yes, and mine," added Curval. "Moreover, I own the very castle you describe. It's located in Silling, in the Black Forest, far out of the reach of meddlesome authorities; surrounded on four sides by cliffs one-thousand feet high; protected by walls and moats; completely safe and completely comfortable. We need only take possession of it, gentlemen, and it's ours to do with as we wish."

"Splendid," said Durcet. "As to the voting, I shall make it unanimous. I am ready to go whenever the rest of you are. But, duke; may I be permitted a question? You speak of our bringing wives? Don't you think they'd be something of a bother?"

"Ah, my fine nance," smiled Blangis. "Never having had a taste for women, you fail to realize their many uses . . ."

"Hold, duke!" interrupted Curval. "Hold, I say. There's offence in your speech. Durcet may be a nance, but I'm sure that he's as much a libertine as the rest of us; wager some money on it and I'm sure that he can match any of us, depravity for depravity . . ."

"Patience, you jaded jurist," replied Blangis; "I don't question the man's libertinage: but neither of you understands my views on marriage; do you think I want a wife so as to have a legal mistress? By God's cock! I want her, you withered old cunt — I want her for the purpose of serving my whims; for the purpose of veiling an infinite number of secret debauches which can be concealed only by the cloak of marriage. Ah, great fucking-john! We libertines don't marry for morality, Curval; we marry to hold slaves; we marry because women, as wives, are rendered more submissive than mistresses."

"Bravo, duke," shouted Durcet, applauding. "I withdraw my question and I am sure that the good Judge Curval withdraws his objection. Your having explained it thusly now makes the whole matter crystal-clear to me."

"Aye," contributed the bishop. "But there is another question which occurs to me, brother. Since I am unmarried and since you three are widowed, from where will the wives come?"

The duke smiled mischievously, about to reveal the best prize, which had been saved for last. "We shall marry each others' daughters, gentlemen," he grinned. "We shall bring them with us to Silling Castle, and there, in a specially constructed chapel, you, my dear ecclesiastic brother, may perform the ceremonies."

A reverent hush fell over the room. All looked at the duke with undisguised admiration. There was muted, respectful applause. Then, after a minute had passed, Curval spoke as follows:

"Duke, I intend no further disrespect and I should like to preface my remarks with the statement that your plan, as outlined this afternoon, leaves me awe-struck. However, will you permit me another question? I know that you have a daughter — a lovely girl named Julie, if my memory serves me correctly. I have a daughter, Adelaide. But what of our gay friend, Durcet? And what of your holy brother? Whence come their progeny?"

"Sir," said Durcet, "much as it might surprise you, it so happens that during my younger days I planted a seed here and there; not that I ever liked women — I'm a full-blown queer and proud of it — but one experiments in youth, and the result of one of my experiments was my beautiful daughter, Constance."

"And I," added the bishop, "have a daughter, Aline.

It's not that I've ever been any less hateful of cunts — no, I'm an ass-man through and through, and I've always been — but, while a young seminarian, wishing to offend the ass-fucking Almighty in Heaven in as many ways as possible, I undertook the combination of incest, fornication, adultery and sacrilege in a single act by placing a consecrated Host on the tip of my prick and fucking my married sister. Aline is the product of that quadruply-sinful union."

"Well, then, gentlemen," said the duke, restoring order to the proceedings, "are we agreed that we shall marry each others' daughters?"

"Agreed!" cried the chorus, and the meeting came to a close.

Now, in the months which followed, procurers and procuresses were sent scouring the countryside for the most splendid specimens of boyhood, girlhood and fuckerhood, from whom were to be chosen the eight of each group which our heroes would bring with them to the castle. Likewise, there were recruited the four most experienced madames in Paris, the four hag-chaperones and a full crew of cooks, servants, et cetera. Finally, after a year's time, the entire company was ready. Its membership was as follows:

THE FOUR WIVES

JULIE: the daughter of the duke of Blangis, now the wife of Judge Curval, would have given any beautiful woman a run for her money were it not for one capital defect (one which, it is understood, is most responsible for the judge's interest in her): she was fat (gad, was she fat!)—; she was one immense pig of a woman; her breasts were huge and pendulous, her buttocks like a pair of overripe melons, her arms and legs like two sets of stuffed sausage-skins. Yet, this fault to one side, she was not, as the saying goes, a bad head; her nose was pretty and her smile bright; her fine brown eyes and long chestnut hair would have flattered a queen; her cunt was hot and straight, and it yielded as agreeable a sensation as such a locale ever may.

Moreover, she was a true voluptuary. When she was twelve, she had both fucked the duke and tried to seduce the bishop —(unfortunately, he was on boys that year)— and had established carnal connections of one sort or another with virtually every man for miles around. Too, she was a great glutton, eating and drinking on a scale befitting her father's daughter, and had never suffered the learning of even a single principle or religion. Lastly, she was unbelievably filthy, having had effected from childhood a total divorce from water and soap, and having developed in recent years a set of teeth so rotten that they defied credibility. It can be understood all too well, in view of the fact that likes attract, why the judge, himself a staunch enemy of hygiene, found her so desireable.

ADELAIDE: the daughter of Judge Curval and the wife of Durcet, was a true beauty, aged twenty-five, small and slender, extremely delicate in build with slight breasts and slim buttocks, of classic loveliness and the possessor of the finest blonde hair ever to be seen. An extremely intelligent and tender-hearted woman, she was as much a tribute to cleanliness as her father, to filth. Likewise, she was very devout, and, as the reader shall see, performed her Christian duties secretly while imprisoned at Silling Castle, even though doing so imperiled her life.

ALINE: the bishop's daughter and, for the purposes of this enterprise, also his wife, was the most youthful of the four, having just turned eighteen, and was very agreeable in countenance and physique. She had brown eyes, an upturned nose and a mischievous air. Her principal fault was that she was profoundly indolent and lazy. Having been left in crass ignorance by her father—(he blessed her ass when she was ten, then left her to fare for herself)—she knew neither how to read nor write. She abhored the bishop and greatly feared the duke.

CONSTANCE: the daughter of Durcet and the wife of Blangis, was the genuine charmer of the group. She was tall, elegant and the possessor of beauty beyond belief. Her eyes were large, black and full of fire; her mouth extremely small and ornamented by the finest teeth imaginable; her breasts were full and very round, fair as alabaster and as firm; her back was turned in a most enchanting way, its lines sweeping deliciously down until they culminated in the most artistically and most precisely cleft ass which Nature every created — ah! what a monument! perfectly round, not very large but firm, white, dimpled and, when it was opened, sanctuary of the cleanest, cutest, pinkest, most delicate little hole! She was not without brains or wit, and only too well realized the horror of the fate to which she was being committed; like Adelaide, she was exceedingly devout, and could look upon the proceedings at the castle with naught but horror.

THE FOUR MADAMES

MADAME DUCLOS: it was to her that our libertines entrusted the task of relating the one hundred and fifty simple passions. She was forty-eight years old and still rather good-looking; her eyes were handsome, her skin exceedingly fair and her ass was one of the roundest and plumpest that could ever favor a man's gaze; her mouth was fresh and clean, her breasts superb and her hair silky-brown; yet, at first glance, it was obvious from her bearing and manner that this, indeed, was a whore — and one who had passed her life in circumstances the voluptouousness of which most men never even conceive.

MADAME CHAMPVILLE: it was she to whom was entrusted
the task of relating the one hundred and fifty complex
passions. She was fifty years old, slender, handsome. A
lesbian, she had ruined herself financially in order to
support her tastes for girls, and had suffered accordingly.
Her eyes were blue and exceedingly attractive; her
mouth was lovely, still fresh and missing no teeth; she
was flat-chested, but had a belly which was good — although, in all candor, it never aroused envy — and had a
rather prominent mound, through which her clitoris pro-
truded a good three inches when well-warmed. Her ass
was flabby and worn from use.

MADAME MARTAINE: it was she who was responsible
for the narration of the one hundred and fifty criminal
passions. A portly matron of fifty-two, she was well-preserved, very healthy and blessed with the biggest and
most spherical ass one could ever hope to see. She had
devoted her life to sodomized debauch and was so ad-
dicted thereto that she tasted absolutely no joy except
therefrom. The most monstrous pricks struck not one
jot of fear in her heart — yea, she'd suck them in and spit
them out contemptuously, the most intrepid of bugg-
eresses — and she took her delights with equal enthusiasm with persons of either sex.

MADAME DESGRANGES: it was to her that was assigned
the task of narrating the one hundred and fifty murderous passions. A tall, thin woman of fifty-six, this old
whore was vice and lust personified. Ghostly pale and
emaciated, with dead lips and dull eyes, she appeared
about to perish for lack of strength. She once had been a
brunette, but her hair — what there was left of it —
now was snow white. Her body was skeletal. Her ass
was perhaps the most telling indictment of the life of
debauch which she had led: it was withered, torn, worn,
marked and mauled until it more resembled parchment

than flesh, and its hole was so gaping and desensitized that the most enormous prick, unlubricated, could invade her without her realizing it. Moreover, she was missing one breast, three fingers, six teeth an eye and a toe, and, while we do not know the nature of the combats in which the generous Cytherean athlete sustained her injuries, this much is certain: nothing which she had suffered persuaded her to turn from vice's path: as her body was the personification of ugliness, her soul was the repository of the most monstrously lubric sentiments; she was an arsonist, a poisoner, a thief, a sodomite and a procuress; she was guilty of rape, incest, parricide, robbery, abortion, sacrilege, calumny, mutilation and murder. Her assignment as narrator for the murderous passions could not have been more pertinent, for no creature on earth could possibly have known them more intimately than she.

THE EIGHT LITTLE GIRLS

AUGUSTINE: she was fifteen, the daughter of a Languedoc baron; she had a very pretty face, a keen mind and a lovely ass; she had been kidnapped from a convent in Montpellier.

FANNY: she was fourteen and the daughter of a Breton counselor; her face was angelic, her figure delightful and her air both sweet and tender; she had been abducted from her father's own chateau.

ZELMIRE: she was fifteen, the only child of Count de Terville, signeur in Beauce; she was pleasantly plump, pretty and the possessor of a noble soul; she had been scheduled to marry a wealthy noleman, but her abduction (in the woods where she had been hunting game with her father) cut short these plans.

SOPHIE: she was fourteen and the daughter of a businessman from Berry; tall and sensuous-looking, she had been seized while on a promenade with her mother, who, seeking to defend her, was thrown into a river, where she had drowned before her daughter's horrified eyes.

COLOMBE: she was thirteen, a Parisienne and daughter of a counselor to Parlement; her body was succulent, with tiny round breasts and the cutest dimpled buttocks; she had been seized while returning from church with her governess; the governess was stabbed to death.

HEBE: she was twelve and the daughter of a cavalry captain from Orléans; despite her young age, she had an extraordinarily seductive air and seemed to possess a great potential for voluptuity; she had been abducted from a convent after two nuns, bribed by our heroes' emissaries, left the dormitory unguarded.

ROSETTE: she was thirteen and the daughter of a magistrate in Chalon-sur-Saône; her eyes were lovely, her skin more so, and her ass just begged to be reamed; her father had recently died and she was with her mother in the countryside when seized within sight of her relatives by agents disguised as robbers.

MIMI, also called MICHETTE: she was twelve and the daughter of the Marquis de Sénanges; her face and figure were exquisite, her ass beautiful beyond description; she was captured while on a carriage drive with two women from her father's chateau in Bourbon; both women were murdered.

THE EIGHT LITTLE BOYS

ZELAMIR: he was thirteen years old and the only son of a Poitou businessman; handsome, well-muscled and pretty-assed; he had been kidnapped outside his father's house when our rogues ambushed and killed his valet, then made off with the child.

CUPIDON: he was thirteen and the son of a nobleman from La Flèche; tall, athletic and quite attractive, with a prick more than ample for his age; he had been abducted at school after our knaves had bribed his teacher.

NARCISSE: was twelve and a Knight of Malta; his father was a Rouen nobleman who cut quite a dashing figure, and the son carried on in the same tradition; he had been seized on the grounds of the College de Louis-le-Grand at Paris, but only after putting up the most rugged resistance.

ZEPHYR: he was fifteen and unquestionably the most delicious of the entire eight (if their excessive beauty permits the choice of one super-specimen); his father was a Parisian general, and he had been studying at a famous *pension* in that capital city when he was turned over to our scoundrels by the master of the *pension* himself, in exchange for a modest reward.

CELADON: he was fourteen and the son of a magistrate of Nancy; hefty, clear of eye, firm of jaw — in all, a rather stunning creature; he was taken at Lunéville, where he had been visiting an aunt; his capture was facilitated through the offices of a girl his own age, hired by our procurers to draw him into a trap by feigning love for him; the stroke was successful.

ADONIS: he was fifteen and the son of a judge; his appearance was a tribute to the Greek god whose name he bore; he had been kidnapped at the behest of Curval, who had fallen in love with him two years earlier in a meeting at the boy's father's house; he was abducted from the school at Plessis where he was studying.

HYACINTHE: he was fourteen and the son of a retired officer living in Champagne; his face was pretty as a picture, his ass prettier still; he was conscripted while hunting with his father, who had been so imprudent as to permit the boy to stray alone some several score meters from the hunting camp.

GITON: he was thirteen and the son of a Nivernais nobleman; his bearing was slightly effeminate, but his prick most assuredly masculine (the bishop fell in love with him on sight); he had been kidnapped from amidst the pageboys at the King's stable at Versailles, and came along without a fight.

THE EIGHT FUCKERS

HERCULE: he was twenty-six years of age and had a body hewn in the image of the god from whom he took his name; he was endowned with a member nine inches in circumference and thirteen long, and, with only eight discharges, could fill a pint jar to the very brim; yet, he was both gentle and sweet in manner, and had a very tender face.

ANTINOUS: he was thirty and, like the emperor Hadrian's favorite acolyte, after whom he was named, he combined a pretty prick with a marvelous ass, a combination which is (as any libertine can testify) exceedingly rare; he wielded a weapon eight inches around and twelve long, and had a face worthy of his other features.

TOWERCOCK: he was thirty-four and acquired his nickname by the fact that his member was always erect, shooting straight up in the manner of a tower; the member measured eight inches around and eleven long in the erect state; no one had ever seen it otherwise; his face was ugly as sin, but his skill in buggery more than compensated for this minor flaw.

THE GRONCH: he was twenty-nine and the largest man in the troupe, measuring twelve inches around and nineteen on the rod; unfortunately, he was capable of only three discharges a day, each coming after no more than four or five minutes of action; however this flaw was offset by his enormity.

ASSCHOPPER: he was twenty-eight and lugged a club so wide at its head that he could not sodomize without ripping open the portals through which he entered; the fantastic organ measured nine inches in circumference and only eight in length, an unusual disproportion but one regarded with much amusement (and not a little appreciation) by the present company.

VOLCANO: he was twenty-three and acquired his name as a result of his ability to ejaculate endless streams of fuck with barely the slighest provocation; his tool measured nine inches long and seven around, but his endurance was remarkable; once he was observed to have discharged thirty times in a single day.

BIG BLUDGEON: he was thirty, and wielded a tool almost comparable to that of The Gronch, measuring eighteen inches in length and eleven and one half in circumference; his endurance was considerably superior to that of his better-membered competitor, and he was therefore highly esteemed by all who crossed his path.

THE FOUR CHAPERONES

MARIE: she was fifty-eight and had almost no hair left; her eyes were dull, rheumy and stood askew; her nose was broken in three places; her teeth were yellow as sulphur; her belly rippled like waves in the ocean, and one of her buttocks was eaten away by an abcess.

LOUISON: she was sixty, stunted, blind in one eye, lame, hunchbacked and nasty as the devil; her ass was rather good for her age and her skin was still fairly well-kept, but she was ugly as the plague.

THERESE: she was sixty-two and looked like a skeleton; there was not a hair on her head, not a tooth in her mouth and her breath was enough to suffocate a cow; her buttocks were so prodigiously slack that one could have wrapped the flesh around a beanpole; her immense asshole resembled a volcano in width and for aroma a cesspool (some said that she never once in her life had wiped her ass, and that if an observer could force himself to get close enough, he could dig his way through to the shit of infancy); as to her vagina, it was even more horrible — yea, a sepulchre whose fetidity all but made one fade away.

FANCHON: she was sixty-nine, flat-nosed, short and heavy; there was not a crime in the world which she hadn't committed; her mouth as vile, containing but two teeth, and a frightful chancre had almost entirely consumed her cunt; her ass was a monument to filth, coated with scabs and sporting fist-sized hemorrhoids hanging from the hole; she had spent three-quarters of every year of her life in a drunken stupor, as a result of which her stomach heaved up its contents at the slightest provocation — a talent of which our champions took not merely occasional advantage.

*   *   *

Now, when all the above, along with the lackeys and servants, had been assembled at Silling, the gates were sealed and the entire company was marched into the auditorium, where Blangis addressed them as follows:

"My feeble, enfettered creatures, hear me well: you are our prisoners; no expense has been spared to gather you under this roof, and you can rest assured that my libertine colleagues and I will not hesitate at murder to keep you in line now that we have you here.

"First and foremost in your minds as these months unfold should be one thought: you exist solely for our pleasure. Do not delude yourselves into supposing that the ascendancy given you in the outside world will be accorded you here; a thousand times more subjugated than slaves, you must expect nothing but humiliation. The one virtue whose use I recommend to you is obedience; it and no other befits your present state. You are all equal to each other, but you are all wholly subservient to the four of us; you shall address us not by name, but by the title, 'Lord;' when you are called by one of us, you bow; when you pass one of us, you genuflect; in short, we are everything and you are nothing.

"I will not conceal from you the fact that your service will be painful and rigorous; our demands will be great, and the slightest delinquencies will be redressed immediately with corporal and afflicting punishments. Presently you will be read a list of statutes; you are to obey them unfailingly: as concerns matters which may not be covered therein, I can advise only that you use your imagination to figure out what we might desire in a given instance: in short, let our desires be your laws; fly to their bidding, anticipate them, help in giving them birth; not that you have much to gain by doing so, but simply because, by not doing so, you have a great deal to lose.

"Give thought, momentarily, to your circumstances, and may these reflections make you quake: you are beyond the borders of France, in the depths of an uninhabited forest and high among naked mountains; the paths on which you were brought here were destroyed behind you; you are enclosed in an impregnable fortress; no one on earth knows that you are here; you are beyond the reach of friends and relatives; and far as the outside world is concerned, you are already dead; thus, if you breathe, it is only by the leave of your Lords.

"And who are we to whom you find yourselves subordinated? Beings of profound wickedness, one and all; villains who have no god but their lust, no laws but the limits of their endurance, no cares but for their pleasures; unprincipled, debauched, profligate, atheistic. There will, no doubt, be very few imaginable excesses to which we will not be carried. If, unhappily, some of your lives are sacrificed to our intemperance, adjust bravely to the situation, if it is of any consolation to you, remember that none of us is going to live forever, and the best thing which can happen to a woman is to die young.

"Lastly, let me say to you that the one insolence above all for which we simply will not stand is begging for pity in the name of your so-called God. To those of you who still believe in him, let me point out that, while he may have your souls, it is your Lords — my three libertine friends and I — who have your bodies. And if, as the activities of the next four months progress, you are tempted to think about this god of yours, ask yourselves these questions: if there were a God and he were to have any power, would he permit the virtue which honors him, and which you profess, to be sacrificed at the altar of libertinage; would he permit four scoundrels like us to take you prisoner and to subject you to the most monstrous caprices, and all with total impunity; would he allow a feeble creature like me, who would, face-to-face with him, as a flyspeck on a mountain, would he, I say, allow such a creature to ridicule him, to degrade him, to make sport of him, as I do every instant of the day?

"No, my friends, there is no god within the Castle of Silling save your four Lords; remember that and, though all may not go well for you, you shall at least have the satisfaction of knowing that you go to your grave without illusions."

This sermon having been given, the duke descended from his perch; thereupon everyone present, except the four madames and eight fuckers, who knew very well that they were there as priestesses and acolytes rather than as victims, everyone, I say, burst into tears. Our four champions, untouched by the spectacle, retired to their chambers and went soundly to sleep, knowing that on the morrow, at the stroke of ten, the curtain would rise on a saga of libertinage which was to continue, uninterrupted for four entire months.

* * *

And now, dear reader, prepare yourself for the most impure tale ever told — a book the likes of which you are not likely to encounter either among the ancients or among the moderns. All pleasure-taking which is sanctioned by manners or by that foolish god of yours will be excluded; what is left will be naught but infamy.

Many of the extravagances which you are about to witness will no doubt displease you; but there are a few among them which will warm you to the point of shooting your nut, and that, dear reader, is all we seek. We do not fancy ourselves mindreaders; we cannot guess what suits you best: it is up to you to take what pleases you and to leave the rest alone; another reader will do likewise, and another reader still, and so forth until everyone is satisfied.

As for the diversity of the six hundred different passions, you may be sure that it is genuine, even if occasionally several passions resemble another; I ask that you study whichever passion you first believe to be repititious and you will see that a difference indeed exists between it and its mate, and that, however slight it may be, the difference is precisely that refinement, that touch, which distinguishes the character of the libertinage with which we are here involved.

Thus, I give you one-hundred-and-twenty days of Sodom. It is the story of a magnificent banquet—six hundred different plates offering themselves to your appetite. Are you going to eat them all? Of course not. But the prodigious variety enlarges the limits of your choice. Choose what you like and leave the rest — but without declaiming against your leavings simply because they lack the ability to please you. Be a philosopher: take your own and permit the next man his choice of passions.

STATUTES OF THE SCHOOL OF LIBERTINAGE

The company will rise each morning at ten oclock. At this hour, the four fuckers who have not been on night duty will pay the Lords a visit, each fucker bringing with him a little boy. Passing from one bedchamber to another successively, each of the fuckers and each of the boys will perform as bid by the Lords, subject only to restrictions set forth elsewhere in these regulations.

At eleven o'clock, the Lords will repair to the little girls' dormitories. Here will be served breakfast, consisting of chocolate, or of toast dipped in Spanish wine, or of other restoratives. The meal will be served by the eight girls, who will be nude. Supervising the serving will be the chaperones, Marie and Louison. If the Lords are disposed to commit impudicities with the little girls, either before, during or after the service, the latter will lend themselves thereunto with full cooperation; failure to do so will result in severe punishment: however, the Lords will at this time indulge in no private excesses; all acts will be performed before the eyes of the entire assemblage.

Before leaving the girls' quarters, the Lord who has been appointed Overseer of the Month shall conduct an inspection. Girls found to have violated one or another regulation shall be scheduled for punishment on the following orgy-day.

Toilets having been established in the chapel, it shall be illegal for anyone to relieve himself anywhere else in the castle. Furthermore, use of the chapel toilets shall be only by special permission of the Overseer of the Month. Persons found during the morning examinations to have relieved themselves under unauthorized circumstances shall be condemned to death.

All boys and girls having arrived at the castle as virgins, defloration shall take place on the following schedule: during the month of November, mouth-fucking, frigging, et cetera shall be permitted, but there shall be no cunt-fucking or ass-fucking; during December, the girls may be cunt-fucked and, this having been accomplished, the newly-opened orifices will be added to the list of acceptable outlets; during January, the girls and the boys may be ass-fucked, after which the newly-opened orifices likewise will be added to the list of acceptable outlets; during February, anything goes. (This schedule is established for the express purpose of permitting voluptuousness to become irritated by the augmentation of a desire incessantly inflamed and never satisfied, a state which necessarily leads to the lascivious fury which is one of lubricity's most highly delectable feelings.

After leaving the girls' apartments, the Lords will inspect the boys' apartments. The four boys who were not among the morning reception party will receive the Lords as they enter the chamber and will immediately depants themselves; the other four, who have accompanied the inspection party, will stand at the ready: the Lords may indulge in lewd byplay with the four newly-depantsed, but all commerce, as in the girls' dormitories must be public.

At one o'clock, the Lords will proceed to the chapel. It will be at this time that permissions are granted for toileting. Those granted permission will shit or piss as the fancy strikes them. The Lords will observe and may partake of the excrement; however, no lubricity beyond piss-drinking and shit-eating will be permitted.

From two to three, the first two tables will be served — one in the girls' dormitory, the other in the boys'. The service will be by the three kitchen workers. At the first table will sit the eight little girls and the four chaperones;

at the second, the eight little boys, the four wives and the
four storytellers. While this is taking place, the Lords
will gather in the living room to chat and to amuse themselves with the eight fuckers.

At three shall be served the Lords' dinner; the honor
of dining with them shall be afforded only the eight
fuckers, no one else. The meal will be served by the
four wives, who will be entirely naked; they will be assisted by the four chaperones, clad as scorceresses. The
eight fuckers will be at liberty throughout the meal to
handle, fondle, touch or otherwise employ the nude
bodies of the wives in any manner they wish, and the
wives will be permitted neither to refuse nor to defend
themselves.

The meal shall end at five. Thereupon the fuckers shall
retire to their quarters until the hour of general assembly. The Lords, meanwhile, will pass into the salon,
where two little boys and two little girls, who will be
changed daily, will serve coffee and liqueurs. The servants will be nude, but the Lords will not be permitted
to engage in lewdness beyond the point of simple tweaking and fondling.

Shortly before six o'clock, the four serving-children
will withdraw to their dormitories to dress for the evening. At exactly six, the Lords will pass into the auditorium and repair to their assigned alcoves. The following
distribution shall be observed by the others: upon the
throne will be the storyteller; on the tiers below, the
sixteen children, arranged in four quatrains, with two
girls and two boys in front of each Lord's niche; each
quatrain shall be allocated to the niche before which it
stands, lateral niches being excluded from making claims
upon it, and the quatrains will change from day to day;
each child in each quatrain shall have one end of a chain

of artificial flowers secured to his arm so that when the niche's occupant wants this child or that, he need only draw the garland and the child will come running: above each quatrain will be situated a chaperone, assigned to the quatrain and responsive to the orders of the Lord in the quatrain's niche.

The three idle storytellers shall be seated on a bench at the foot of the active storyteller, or, as she shall be called, Narrator of the Month. The three shall be assigned to no one in particular, but will be responsible to do any Lord's bidding.

The four fuckers who are scheduled to spend the night with the Lords will be excused from the assembly so that they may prepare themselves in their chambers for the work ahead. The other four will be divided, one to each Lord's niche; the position of each fucker shall be on the floor at the feet of his Lord.

The four wives will be on the four Lords' couches — but, of course, not necessarily with their own husbands.

Costuming for the assembly shall be as follows: the wives shall be at all times stark naked; the fuckers shall be attired only in close-fitting singlets and shorts of pink taffetta; the Narrator of the Month shall be attired as an elegant courtesan; the idle storytellers shall be attired in similar costumes, but ones not quite as elegant; the little boys and little girls of the quatrains shall always be garbed splendidly, those of each niche in a manner different from those of the other niches, pursuing a variety of themes: costumes will be such that the underparts are constantly exposed and that the rest of the body can be exposed instantly by the pulling out of a pin; chaperones will be costumed in harmony with the attire of the boys and girls in the quatrain to which each is assigned.

At precisely six o'clock, the Narrator of the Month will begin her story. The Lords may interrupt at any point and as frequently as they please. This narration shall last until ten o'clock in the evening, during which time (since the purpose of the assembly is to inflame the imagination), every lubricity will be permitted save those prejudicial to the assigned schedule of deflowerings. The narration shall be suspended for as long as is desired by him who has interrupted and will be resumed only upon his instructions.

The evening meal shall be served at precisely ten o'clock. Wives, storytellers and little girls will dine by themselves in the girls' apartments; the Lords will sup with the four fuckers not scheduled for night duty and with four of the little boys; the other four boys will serve.

Upon conclusion of the meal, the Lords will proceed to the salon for the orgies. The entire company will be present save the four fuckers assigned night duty. The salon will be illuminated by chandeliers and heated to unusually high temperatures. All present will be naked: storytellers, wives, little girls, little boys, chaperones, fuckers, Lords, everyone will sprawl on the floor in the manner of animals; all will commingle, intertwine, couple incestuously, change positions and partners, giving vent to every excess and to every debauch save those prejudicial to the defloration schedule. (During the months when deflowering shall take place, they shall be done with great pomp and ceremony.)

The orgies will cease at precisely two a.m. Thereupon the four night-duty fuckers will lead their assigned Lords to the bedchamber. Each Lord shall retire with his fucker and with a woman, either a wife, a deflowered subject, a storyteller or a chaperone. There shall be no restrictions on what may be done in the bedchamber.

The four chaperones will be held responsible for the behavior of their assigned children and shall report all violations to the Overseer of the Month.

If a storyteller is guilty of misbehavior, her punishment shall be exactly half that due a child for the same act; the reason for this leniency is due to respect for the tellers' narrative talents. Punishment for wives will be double that due children for the same acts.

Any subject who refuses to comply with the request of a Lord, even if such refusal is prompted by physical incapacity, will be punished most severely.

Any person caught in *flagrante delicto* with another person except under circumstances authorized by the Lords will be punished with loss of a limb.

The performance of any act even slightly religious — whatever the act — whoever the subject — shall be punished by death.

The name of God shall never be uttered save blasphemously, or when accompanied by invectives or imprecations; thus qualified, it will be repeated as often as possible.

Any Lord who goes to bed sober will be fined ten-thousand francs.

The four wives will not enjoy prerogatives of any kind over the other women: to the contrary, they shall be treated with a maximum of cruelty and inhumanity; they will be employed in the vilest and most painful enterprises, such as the cleaning of the common and private toilets established in the chapel, and they will, in short, be degraded at every possible opportunity.

A DAY IN THE SCHOOL OF LIBERTINAGE

The company rose at 10 a.m., as had been prescribed.

The four fuckers who had gone unoccupied the previous evening then brought Zéphyr to Blangis, Adonis to Curval, Narcisse to Durcet and Zélamir to the bishop. All four children were both timid and awkward, but, encouraged by the libertines, they carried out very nicely their assigned tasks. Zéphyr gave Bangis a shot up the ass, after which the lusty duke paid him in kind; meanwhile, Curval, Durcet and the bishop, not wishing to risk the depletion of their energies this early in the day, contented themselves to receive without giving back.

At 11 a.m., the bawdy quartet proceeded to the women's quarters where they were served chocolate by the eight nude young girls. Marie and Louison directed these proceedings. The festivities were characterized by a great deal of fondling and kneading, by the grabbing of a breast here, the pinching of a buttock there, and the poor children, hitherto unexposed to such doings, were embarrassed beyond description.

No sooner had the chocolate been served than Blangis got a monstrous erection. On a whim, he decided to measure the circumference of his prick against that of little Michette's waist; there was a difference of only three inches.

Durcet, the month's overseer, conducted the prescribed searches and examinations. The bodies of Hébé and Colombe were found to be insufficiently appetizing, whereupon a punishment of twenty-five lashes each was decreed; they wept, but in vain: Durcet set the day of execution as the following Sunday, at orgy-hour.

Next our heroes went to the boys' apartments. The four boys who had not participated in the 10 a.m. revelry, namely Cupidon, Céladon, Hyacinthe and Giton, bared their asses as prescribed. There followed a period of sport, with Curval kissing each boy on the mouth, Blangis frigging the foursome's pricks and Durcet and the bishop reaming two asses apiece. The inspectors then were completed; no charges of misconduct were decreed. This accomplished, the libertines withdrew to their personal chambers to rest before lunch.

At one o'clock, the four bawds went to the chapel where, as the reader may recall, the sanitary facilities were installed. Of the entire company, only Constance, Duclos, Augustine, Sophie, Zélamir, Cupidon and Louison were present; the rest, assigned roles in the evening's festivities, had been excused to store up their energies.

While the seven aforementioned assisted, our four champions betook themselves to the four special toilets in front of the altar and shit. Then, their asses having been wiped with altar cloths by the attendants, they washed and retired to the salon for lunch.

Pursuant to the statutes barring women from the table, each of the libertines dined in the company of two fuckers. The meals, served by the libertines' wives, were succulent beyond measure. Since the midday fare was to be lighter than the evening meal, only four courses were served, each composed of a scant twelve plates; Burgundy accompanied the hors d'oeuvres; Bordeaux, the entrees; Champagne, the roasts; Hermitage, the entremets and Tokay and Madeira, the dessert.

As the lunch hours passed, spirits rose little by little. The fuckers, being granted full liberty with the bawd's wives, knocked the women about somewhat; Blangis' wife, Constance, having spilled a drop of gravy while serving the roast, was kicked viciously in the ass by one of the two fuckers at her husband's table; Blangis was greatly amused by this. The wife of Curval, too, was a bit clumsy in serving, spilling a small quantity of Champagne as she opened the bottle; the judge, angered, threw his plate at her, and, had she not ducked, she might have been wounded seriously.

By dessert, all four libertines were in lusty humor. Durcet, noticing that the prick of one of the fuckers had stiffened, without further ado, despite the fact that they were at the table, unbuttoned his trousers and presented

his ass; the fucker, knowing full well his station, promptly drove the massive weapon home; then, the operation
having been concluded, both returned to their drinking
and eating as if nothing had happened.

Blangis, amused at this bit of infamy, announced to
the assemblage that, enormous as Towercock's member
might be, he himself would calmly drink three bottles of
wine while being embuggered by that splendid appendage. When the bishop and Durcet expressed doubts that
the feat could be accomplished, Blangis wagered each
one-hundred *louis* that it could. Then, the money having
been handed over to Curval for safekeeping, the duke
proceeded to make good his boast.

When finally the last morsel of food had been eaten
and the last drop of wine had been drunk, our four
lascivious scoundrels adjourned to an anteroom where
coffee and liqueurs were served by a naked quartet of
boys and girls, Adonis, Hyacinthe, Zelmire and Fanny.
Our libertines, half-drunk and ablaze with mischievous
desires, nonetheless were determined to honor their own
laws; thus they contented themselves with kisses, frigging, squeezing, pinching, et cetera (of course, their
capacity for voluptuity was such that they were able to
season these mild endeavors with all the refinements of
debauch and lubricity).

Presently the bishop acquired a vigorous hard-on and
all but ejaculated as the result of Zelmire's skillful frigging: his nerves were jangling and the tingles of orgasmic sensation had begun to take hold of him: yet —
judicious man — he restrained himself and disengaged
the sweet hand of his charming frigger. No sooner had
he done this than the clock sounded the hour for the
libertines' afternoon nap; all four withdrew to their private chambers.

After the nap, our friends moved into the auditorium
and took their places upon the couch. The Duke of
Blangis had his beloved Hercule at his feet and, along-

side him, the nude Adelaide (Durcet's wife and, as the reader may recall, the judge's daughter); stretched out in front of him, costumed as shepherds but with holes cut into the costumes to explose their sexual organs, were Zéphyr, Giton, Augustine and Sophie; they were chaperoned by Louison, dressed as an old peasant woman. At Curval's feet was Towercock; upon his couch lay Constance (Blangis' wife and Durcet's daughter); cavorting on the floor before him, dressed in Spanish costumes and exhibiting their sexual organs, were Adonis, Celadon, Fanny and Zelmire, chaperoned by Fanchon. At the feet of the bishop was Antinous; on his couch was his niece, Julie; before him, costumed as savages (with loincloths which concealed nothing) were the boys, Cupidon and Narcisse, and the girls, Hébé and Rosette; their chaperon was Thérése, who dressed as an old Amazon. Durcet had at his feet Asschopper and, on his couch, Aline, the bishop's daughter; in front of him, dressed as Arab girls (again, costumed in such a manner as to display their sexual organs) were the boys, Zélamir and Hyacinthe, and dressed likewise, the girls, Columbe and Michette; Marie, dressed as an old Arab slave, presided over the quatrain.

Seated below the throne, magnificently dressed in the gowns of Parisienne coutesans, but with their tits and cunts protruding through holes in the cloth, were the three idle storytellers, the Mesdames Champville, Martaine and Desgranges. On the throne, attired in a costume of similar character but considerably greater elegance, was the Narrator of the Month, Madame Duclos.

When all had positioned themselves according to plan, Durcet clapped his hands as a signal for order. "My friends," he announced, "by the power vested in me as Overseer for the Month of November, I declare this meeting underway. The task of narrator having befallen Madame Duclos, she is required to begin on this first evening a recitation of her life's story into which account she is to insert, with pertinent details, descriptions of the one-hundred-and-fifty simple passions. If there be no questions from the floor, I shall request her to begin."

There were no questions; whereupon Duclos began as follows:

It is no slight undertaking, gentlemen, for a humble and uneducated creature like me to attempt to express herself in such esteemed company: but your indulgence reassures me; you ask for nothing but the truth, and I dare say that I am as well equipped as anyone to tell it — especially as concerns matters of libertinage.

My mother was an only child, and, had dwelled with her parents near the Recollets' monastery in Paris. When she one day found herself an orphan, abandoned and without any resources, she obtained permission from these good fathers to beg outside their church. But ever an attractive girl, she soon attracted the notice of this priest, then that one, and eventually she was graduated from the church steps to the rooms, above, when she soon descended pregnant. It was as a consequence of one such adventure that my oldest sister was born and it is more than likely that my own birth came about under like circumstances.

Thus born, so to speak, into the church, I dwelled thereafter more in the House of God than in any other. I helped the maids arrange chairs, I seconded the sacristans in their various operations and I would even have said mass had it been necessary, although I was not yet five years old.

Now, one day, while I was returning to my mother's room, I encountered my sister, who asked me if I had seen Father Laurent. I said I had not.

"Well, look out," said she; "he's on the watch for

*you; he wants to show you what he showed me.
Don't run away, look him straight in the face without
being afraid; he won't touch you, but he'll show you
something very funny, and if you let him do what
he wants, he'll pay you."*

*You may well imagine, sirs, that I not only did not
flee Father Laurent, but actually sought him out;
at that age the voice of modesty is a whisper at best,
and its silence until the time one has left the tute-
lage of Nature is certain proof, is it not, that this
facetious sentiment is far less the product of the
original mother's training than it is the fruit of faulty
education? Well, as I was saying, I flew instantly to
the church and, as I was crossing a little court between the entrance of the churchyard and the convent, into whom should I bump but Father Laurent,
himself. He stopped me.*

Where are you going, Françon?" he asked?

"To arrange the chairs, Father," I replied.

*"Never fear, never fear, your mother will attend
to them," said he. Come along with me." Thereupon
he drew me inside a sequestered chamber. "Well
Françon," said he now pulling a monstrous prick
from his drawers (an instrument the sight of which
nearly toppled me with fright) and beginning to frig
himself industriously, "have you ever seen anything
to equal this muscle? It's what they call a prick, my
little one. It's used for fucking, and that which you
are about to see, that which is going to flow in a
moment or two, is the seed wherefrom all creation
sprang. I've shown it to your sister; I've shown it to
all the little girls of your age. Come, now; lend a
hand; help it along; do as your sister does (she's got
it out of me twenty times and more). Yes, chit, I
show girls my prick and then what do you suppose
I do? I squirt the fuck in their face . . . That's my
passion, child; I have no other . . . and you're going*

to see it."

Instantly I found myself drenched in a white spray; it soaked me from head to foot; some drops of it leapt even into my eyes, because my little head came just to the height of his fly. "Ah! the pretty fuck, the dear fuck I am losing," the man of God cried; "and look at you! You're covered with it."

Gradually regaining control of himself, Father Laurent calmly put his prick away; then he suggested that I bring to him any little companions I might have.

As you may readily fancy, I could not have been more eager to run and tell everything to my sister; she wiped me dry, taking the greatest care to overlook none of the spots; then she demanded half of my wages. Instructed by this example I hastened to round up as many little girls for Father Laurent as I could find. If a girl was familiar to him, he turned her away, explaining to me, "I never see the same one twice, my child." Then he gave me three coins for encouragement and told me to go out and look some more. In the three months which followed, I introduced the perverse priest to more than twenty girls, with whom he employed the identical proceedings which he had employed with me. Together with the stipulation that all the girls be strangers to him, there was another relative to age: he had no use for any girl younger than four or older than seven.

Now, when I, myself, reached age seven, Father Laurent lost interest in my services as a procuress. It was then that I met a newcomer to the convents, Father Louis. He was older than Laurent and had a much more libertine appearance. I liked him immediately.

One day, as I was entering church, Father Louis sidled up to me and asked me to come up to his

room. Scarcely were we in his cell when he bolted
the door and, having poured some elixir into a gob-
let, bade me swallow it. This preparatory step taken,
the reverend, more affectionate than his confrère,
fell to kissing me and fondling my ass. Then, raising
my skirt to my bodice, he asked me whether I did
not desire to piss. Singularly driven to this need by
the strong dose which he had given me to drink, I
assured him the urge to do so was powerful, but that
I did not want to satisfy it in front of him. "Oh, my
goodness, do!" cried the bawdy fellow, "by God, yes;
piss in my presence and, what's worse, piss upon
me! Here it is," he went on, plucking his prick from
his breeches, "here's the tool you're going to moisten;
piss on it now."

Thereupon he lifted me up and set me between
two chairs, then invited me to squat. Holding me in
this posture, he placed a container beneath me and
held his prick between the container and my cunt.
"Off you go, my little one, piss," urged he; "flood my
prick with that enchanting liquid whose hot descent
exerts such a sway over my senses. Piss, my heart,
and inundate my fuck."

The jaded ecclesiastic now began to beat at his
prick with insane vigor. It was easy to see that this
unusual pissing operation was the one which all his
senses most cherished; the sweetest, gentlest ecstasy
crowned his face as the liquids with which he had
swollen my stomach flowed most abundantly out of
me and we simultaneously filled the same pot, he
with fuck, I with piss. The exercise concluded, Louis
delivered roughly the same speech to me which I
had heard from Laurent: he wished to make a procuress of me. Motivated by his generous payment, I
boldly guided every child I knew to him. He had
every one of them do the same thing, and, since he
experienced no compunctions about seeing any one

*of them a second or third time, I found myself with
a tidy little sum of money.*

"Duclos," Judge Curval interrupted at this point, "we
have, I believe, advised you that your narrations must be
decorated with the most numerous and searching details;
how else may we judge the relationship between the passion you describe and human manners unless you are
completely frank and disguise no circumstance? What is
more, the least circumstance is apt to have an immense
influence upon the sensory irritation we expect from
your stories."

"Yes, my Lord," Duclos replied, "I have been advised
to omit no detail and to enter into the most minute par-
ticulars whenever they serve to shed light upon the human personality or upon the species of passion; have I
neglected something?"

"You have," said Curval, "I have not the faintest notion
of your second monk's prick, nor any idea of its discharge.
In addition, did he frig your cunt, pray tell, and did he
have you dandle his device? You see what I mean by
neglected details."

"Your pardon, my Lord," said Duclos, "I shall repair
these present mistakes and avoid them in the future.
Father Louis possessed a very ordinary member, reasonably long but rather thin and in general of a most common shape and turn; he stiffened rather poorly and it
was not until the crisis arrived that he took on a little
consistency. He did not frig my cunt; he was content to
enlarge it with his fingers so as to give free issue to the
urine. His discharge was rapid and intense and brief;
through it he said "Ah fuck! Piss, my dearie, piss this
pretty fountain, piss, piss away.' while saying which he
intermittently sprinkled kisses on my mouth; they were
not excessively libertine."

"That's it, Duclos," said Durcet, "the Judge was right;
I could not visualize a thing on the basis of your first telling, but now I have your man well in view."

"One moment, Duclos," said the bishop upon seeing that she was about to proceed. "I have on my own account a need rather more pressing than to piss."

So saying he drew Narcisse to his alcove; fire leapt from his eyes, his prick was glued to his belly, foam flecked his lips. Everything came to a pause; a discharge was regarded by our heroes as something far too portentous not to suspend everything the moment someone was about to produce one. But upon this occasion Nature's wishes did not correspond with the Bishop's and, several minutes after having retired, he emerged, furious, in the same state of erection. Addressing himself to Durcet, as overseer for November, he said, "Put that little fellow down for some exercise on Saturday and make it strenuous, if you please."

"Be at ease, my dear bishop," replied Durcet, "I promise he'll get what he deserves; meanwhile exercise your throbbing dick on something else; have yourself fucked."

"Sir," spoke up Martaine, "I feel myself greatly disposed to satisfy you, were your Excellency to wish it . . ."

"No, Christ, no!" the Bishop cried. "I don't want a woman's asshole! I'll wait, I'll wait . . . let Duclos continue."

The friends having laughed heartily at the bishop's libertine frankness, the story-teller resumed in these terms:

One day, while bringing one of my little comrades to Father Louis, I found another monk with my perverse priest in his cell. Fearful of having compromised Father Louis, I began to move away, but the cleric reassured me, whereupon my little friend and I went in.

"Well there, Geoffrey, "Father Louis said to his companion, at the same time pushing me towards him, "did I not tell you that she was nice?"

"Why yes indeed, she is," said Geoffrey taking me upon his knee and giving me a kiss. "How old are

you, my little one?"

"Seven, Father."

"Just fifty years younger than I," said he, kissing me anew. "How nice; how nice. Now tell me: are you going to piss for me this afternon?"

"If you like," I replied.

"Then, come into my cell," said he; "we'll leave Father Louis with your little friend and we'll return when all our little needs are satisfied."

Father Geoffrey's cell was not far from Father Louis', and we reached it without being seen. No sooner were we inside than Father Geoffrey, having barricaded the door, told me to get rid of my skirt. I obeyed, whereupon he himself pulled my slip above my navel and, seating me on the edge of his bed, spread my thighs as wide as possible. Scrutinizing me for a moment in this attitude, he with one hand separated the lips of my cunt and with the other unbuttoned his breeches. Then, with quick and energetic movements he began to shake a dark, stunted little prick which seemed not too much inclined to respond. Finally he sealed his lips to those of my cunt and I flooded him with a stream of urine, which he swallowed just as fast as I could piss it out. At this juncture, up shot his member, stiff as a stick, and a load of jism sprayed against my thighs.

Trembling in every limb, Father Geoffrey got to his feet. But I observed, much to my surprise, that, now that his lusts were extinguished, he no longer entertained for my little body the same ardor which had characterized his period of earlier delerium: he rather abruptly gave me some coins, then opened the door and, pointing to his friend's cell, told me to go there. He then shut his door without affording me the opportunity even to bid him good day.

"Ah, yes indeed!" observed Blangis. "Many are the men who cannot bear the moment when illusion is shattered. It is as if one's pride suffers because one has let a woman see him in such a state of feebleness. That's why there's such a feeling of disgust after fucking."

"No, I don't think so, duke," commented Judge Curval, whom Adonis, on his knees, was frigging, and whose hands simultaneously probed the underparts of Zelmire. "It isn't pride; it's disillusionment. Before one gets one's rocks off, the object of one's desires is endowed by his lust with false values. Subsequently, when the veils of illusion fall along with his fuck, perspective is regained. Hence: disgust."

"Well, perhaps you are right," interjected the bishop; "but this woman's tale is just getting interesting: let us permit her to continue."

Thereupon, Duclos resumed her story as follows:

Not long after my episode with Father Geoffrey, I became aware of the overtures of another occupant of that pious retreat, this one a priest of about sixty years, by name, Father Henry. For months he invented every kind of ruse to persuade me to come to his room, but I, not liking him very much, always refused to go. Then, one Sunday morning, I made the mistake of walking past his door. Suddenly a pair of arms shot out and gripped me at the shoulders. The next thing I knew I was in the cell, the door was locked and the depraved old cleric was embracing me with all his heart.

"Ah, my mischievous little snot!" he cried, transported with ecstasy. "I've got you now and you can't escape! Well, fuckatoo — there'll be some sport this fine morning."

Now, the weather was extremely cold at that time and it so happened that my nose was running, as children's usually do in the winter. I drew out a handkerchief to wipe the dribbling mucus, but

Father Henry immediately seized my wrists and prevented the operation.

"What's this? What's this?" he cried. "Be careful there. Let's not waste any of that delicious substance."

Then, stretching me out on his bed, he raised my head upon his knees. "Oh, what a pretty little snot-face," he said, beginning to pant, "how I'm going to suck you."

Therewith, bending over my head and taking my nose in his mouth, he devoured not only all the mucus between my nose anl lips, but even took to darting his tongue into my nostrils — and with such dexterity that he provoked two or three sneezes, which redoubled the flow he desired.

Ask me for no further details bearing upon this fellow, gentlemen; I have nothing to tell; I do not know if he ejaculated, for his prick remained within his cassock throughout the entire operation; likewise, all my clothes were left in place, and he did not even bother to caress my tits or underparts through the garments which covered them. Yes, I give you my word that this old libertine's assault might have been performed upon the most respectable girl in the world without her being given reason to suppose that there was any lewdness involved.

"An interesting tale, Duclos," applauded the judge. "I imagine that that was quite the monastery."

"Shit," noted the bishop dryly, "they're all like that. Why do you think so few priests ever abandon the priesthood?"

"Well, Duclos," said Blangis, ignoring this exchange, "tell us more. Did you ever see Father Henry again?"

Duclos contnued thusly:

I saw the depraved old snot-sucker several times after that, but since he did not pay me any money, I never again made myself available to him.

The next priest with whom I had relations was Father Stephen, a robust and handsome man of about forty. One day I accidentally bumped into him in a corner of the church, near the sacristy, and he invited me to his cell. We were no sooner alone there than he asked me if I knew how to frig a prick.

"God in Heaven!" I cried, blushing to the ears, "I don't even know what you're talking about."

"Well, then, I'll explain it, my chit," said he, bestowing tender kisses upon my mouth and eyes. "It so happens that my unique pleasure in this world is to educate little girls, and the lessons which I give are so excellent that they prove unforgettable. Let me now make you the beneficiary of my wisdom and experience.

"We shall begin by removing your skirts, for, if I am to teach you how to go about giving me pleasure, it's no more than fair that I teach you how to receive pleasure yourself. Now, then: look where my hand is; what you behold is called a cunt, and this is what you must do to awaken felicitous sensations in it: with one finger — (one is all you need) — lightly rub this little protuberance here; it is called, by the way, the clitoris; rub it now and tell me what you feel."

I rubbed and immediately felt a tingle of sensation. I did my best to describe the feeling for him.

"There, you see! he beamed approvingly. "I told you that you wouldn't regret doing this. Now, while your one hand tickles away at that darling little clit, take the other and gradually work it into this delicious crack . . . ah, by fuck, what a lovely ass! . . . that's the way; yes, you're doing it right; now, tell me what you feel."

The sensation was strange and delicious. I was excited beyond belief. I told him so.

"Excellent," replied the lusty ecclesiastic. *"And now it is my turn. Here: take this!"* Whereupon he thrust into my lap a prick the size of a sausage; it was so immense that my two little hands were scarcely able to close around it. *"The marvelous tool which you are holding,"* he explained, *"is called a prick. This movement here"* — he guided my wrist in rapid strokes — *"is called frigging. Now, go to it; put all your strength into it; the more rapid and persistent your movements, the more you will hasten the moment I seek.*

"But," he added, all the while continuing to direct my flying hands, *"bear one essential thing in mind: never allow this skin, which we call prepuce, to cover the prick's head; if you did that all my pleasure would vanish . . . Ahhh! That's it! You're doing well, and you'll soon see the result of your efforts . . ."*

Now pressing himself against my chest, he placed his hands so adroitly and wriggled his fingers with such high art that the pleasures of orgasm rose at last to grip me. My head reeling, I abandoned his prick and wallowed in the marvelous sensations which filled every cell of my body.

Father Stephen waited until the feeling had ebbed; then he reminded me that my work was unfinished; guiding my hand with his, he obliged me to resume the labors which my ecstasy had caused me to interrupt. He very expressly enjoined me to keep my mind strictly on the business at hand, and I did so with all my soul. Going merrily to work, I pumped with such vigor that almost immediately his splendid snake spewed forth all its rage and covered me with its venom. Thereupon Father Stephen acted as if he were going out of his mind with joy; he shouted and profaned, he kissed my mouth, he frigged my cunt.

When finally his fires were dampened, he told me that I was charming and that he greatly hoped I would come back again to see him. Then, pressing a

*silver crown piece into my hand, he conducted me
back to the place from which he had brought me.*

*I was wonderstruck; thrilled; enchanted. What a
difference, I thought, between Father Stephen and
the abrupt Father Geoffrey! What a difference from
snot-sucking Father Henry! I decided to return often
in the future — and, gentlemen, I did; believe me
I did.*

This fifth tale having been concluded, Duclos bowed to
the assemblage. Thereupon Durcet, the overseer, led a
round of applause. This over, a bell was rung and our
four libertines proceeded to the salon for supper.

The meal was served by the eight little girls, all dressed only in that costume with which they were outfitted by
Mother Nature. The diners numbered twenty: the libertine quadrille, the eight fuckers and the eight boys. The
wives and the story-tellers, in great haste so as to be
ready for the orgies, dined apart.

Upon Durcet's signal, the magnificent repast was begun. The first course was a shellfish soup accompanied
by an array of twenty dishes of hors d'oeuvres. Fish entrees came next, followed by entrees of chicken breasts,
followed by an assortment of game prepared in every
possible manner. Next arrived the roasts, rare beyond
belief and indescribably delicious. These were followed
by cold pastry, then by twenty-six entremets of every
description and form. Next came a host of hot and cold
sugared cookies; then bowls of fruit; then ices, chocolate
and table-liqueurs.

The wines, as for lunch, varied with each service; with
the first course, Burgundy; with the second, Italian Chi-
anti; with the third, Italian zinfandel; with the fourth,
Rhine wine; with the fifth, Rhone wine; with the sixth,
Champagne; with the seventh and eighth, two Greek
wines. These were followed by apertifs.

Now, when the last of the glasses and dishes finally had been cleared away, Blangis, half-drunk, said that he would not touch another drop of wine or spirits until he had drunk some of the "nectar of the gods"—by which he meant piss. Selected as his supplier was young Zelmire, who was made to stand on the table and squat over his mouth. He promptly drained her.

"Well, duke, you may drink young piss if you like,'" said Judge Curval at this point, "but, as for me, I like mine to have something of a sting to it — a sting which comes only with age . . . Fanchon, you old fart, come here," he yelled to one of the chaperones. "I'd like to slake my thirsts at the rankest fountain in the universe." So saying, he thrust his head between the old witch's leg and greedily sucked up a flood of her impure urine.

This exercise having ended — and Durcet and the bishop not being disposed to do likewise — the company fell to discussing philosophical matters. The duke, undertaking an exordium in praise of libertinage, argued that licentiousness was inspired by Nature herself and, therefore, that the more numerous one's extravagances, the better they suited the creator of us all. His opinions having been duly applauded, the group headed for the orgy-room to put into practice the principles just expounded.

Everything was in readiness for them when they arrived. The women, already naked, were lying upon pillows strewn about the floor. About them lay, also naked, the fuckers, the boys and the girls. As our heroes reeled in, two of the chaperones began undressing them; the men then leaped upon the women like wolves assailing a sheepfold.

The bishop, whose passions had been cruelly irritated by the failures of the afternoon, fell immediately upon Antinous' sublime ass; simultaneously, Hercule skewered him; vanquished by this dual-fronted assault, the jaded ecclesastic spat out streams of jism so forceful and pungent that he almost fainted in ecstasy; then, numbed from luxury, he fell into a sleep so deep that he had to be carried to his bed.

Curval, inspired by the bishop's example, seized Martaine and embuggered her while simultaneously his own ass was being corked by Zéphyr. Durcet, meanwhile, took Towercock's monstrous tool up his ass while simultaneously sucking the prick of Volcano and, with his free hands, jerking off Big Bludgeon and The Gronch. Blangis, for his part, was more interested in girls, and proceeded to cunt-fuck four of them, discharging inside each, while at the same time he frigged the cunts and kneaded the breasts of half a dozen others.

A thousand other infamies accompanied these before our three valorous athletes — the bishop having already given up the ghost — decided that they had had enough. Then the four fuckers of the night-watch were sent to fetch the wives who had shared our indomitable champions' couches during story-time. With his wife-of-the-moment, each of the libertines adjourned to his private chamber.

Thus were the morning and evening of the first day . . .

BOOK ONE: THE SIMPLE PASSIONS

During the month of November, the narrator is Madame Duclos, who describes the one hundred and fifty simple passions. They are as follows:

1. A priest entices a four-year-old girl into the sacristy and exhibits his prick; then he jerks off, squirting the jism all over her head.

2. Another priest has a little girl piss on his prick.

3. A third priest has a girl piss in his mouth while his lips are fastened to her cunt.

4. A fourth priest lures a child to his room and sucks the snot from her nose.

5. A fifth priest teaches a girl, aged eight, to jerk him off while he frigs her in return.

6. A monsignor kneels on a girl's shoulders while she lies on her back. Jerking off, he innundates her face with his jism, all the while shouting: "Ah, by the sweet fuck of Jehovah, I'll soak this pretty little whore-face."

7. An impotent old man frigs his prick against the outer labia of a nine-year-old girl and, after prolonged efforts of this sort, manages finally to ejaculate.

8. A man jerks off only after having wrapped his prick in the hairs of a whore's head; he comes all over her scalp.

9. A man hires a whore to scratch his ass with her fingernails.

10. A man, after tonguing the asshole of a girl who is crouched on hands and knees, sits behind her on a stool

and jerks off, directing his jism upon her spit-soaked buttocks.

11. A young man jerks off while sucking a woman's tits and comes all over her thighs while he gorges himself on her milk.

12. A man instructs a madame to arrange one of her whores on a bed in such a fashion that the whore's ass is exposed but the rest of her body is covered with sheets and blankets. When this has been accomplished, the man enters the whore's room and jerks off while contemplating the ass, saying all the while: "Ah, what a beautiful ass! How delighted I will be to drown it in fuck!" Eventually he comes, shooting his jism all over the exposed ass. Then he leaves the room without taking one look at the girl with whom he had been involved.

13. A man stretches a girl between two chairs, then sits beneath her. With his mouth, he licks her cunt; with one hand, he fondles her ass; with the other hand, he jerks off.

14. A man hires a whore only to spit in his mouth; he engages her in no other way.

15. An elderly priest jerks off while reaming the ass of a twelve-year-old girl.

16. A priest prides himself on his ability in talking girls into leading lives of sin; but, though he has in thirty years persuaded no fewer than ten thousand of them to abandon virtue, he never fucked (or otherwise enjoyed) a single one of them.

17. A man caresses a girl's ass and frigs himself while watching through a knothole as another man in an adjacent room reams a young whore's asshole.

18. A man who is an exhibitionist arranges at a whore-house to put on a display with a young whore while a voyeur watches from an adjacent room. The voyeur does not know that the exhibitionist is aware of his presence.

19. A man hires a girl to frig him while he sits on a park bench in the middle of Paris.

20. A man hires two whores. Then, pretending to be their pimp, obtains two lovers for them. He watches while the four take their pleasures of each other. His sole pleasure is in pretending pimpery.

21. A man watches through a knothole as a girl jerks off another man, directing his sperm into a porcelain dish. Once the operation has been completed, the voyeur rushes into the room and laps up the sperm, all the while jerking himself off with furious strokes.

22. A man hires a girl to run and jump about until she has begun to perspire profusely. Then he jerks off while smelling her armpits.

23. A man instructs his hired whore to neither wash herself or wipe her ass for six weeks. Then, placing her atop a bidet filled with sparkling Champagne, he bathes her with a sponge. The Champagne in the bidet, of course, becomes united with her filth; whereupon, he drinks it.

24. Another man instructs a hired whore to go three months without washing her feet. Then he jerks himself off while eating the scum which has accumulated between her toes.

25. A general of the army will have commerce only with women who are damaged either by Nature, by libertinage or by the effects of the law; for example, the one-eyed, the lame, the hump-backed, the legless, the

toothless, the mutilated, et cetera. While rubbing his prick against such a woman's deformity, he reams her ass and thereby gains his satisfaction.

26. A man covers a girl's mouth with his and sucks the gas from her belches.

27. A man hires a whore to frig him while she vomits in his mouth.

28. A man vomits into a girl's mouth, then swallows what she spews back to him.

29. A monk has dinner in a whorehouse, eating his food only after he has taken each morsel and swilled it around inside a whore's cunt.

30. A man gives a girl a quart of anise water to drink, then glues his mouth to her ass and swallows her farts.

31. A man hires a sixty-five-year-old whore to blow farts up his nose.
32. A man's tastes are such that his only pleasure is to eat out the cunt of a girl who is menstruating, swallowing the blood and fuck as one.

33. A man's only pleasure is to eat the foeti which have been expelled by pregnant women who miscarry.

34. A man constructs a special floor two feet above the regular floor in one room of a whorehouse. Then, lying below this special floor, he has a whore jerk him off while, above, a second whore jerks off a second man over a knothole. The first man eats the second's man's jism as it falls through.

35. A man has a woman chew slices of bread, then takes them, saliva-soaked, from her mouth and eats them himself.

36. A man hires a whore to sit on a chair with her mouth open while he, standing across the room, jerks off and tries to shoot his jism into this oral target.

37. A man stretches a whore, supine, between two chairs, then lies on top of her and reams her cunt while she sucks his cock.

38. A man hires only whores over sixty years of age who are toothless. Their task is to suck his cock and balls while he reams their asses.

39. A man who has not washed his cock and balls for six months holds a girl by the ears and forces her to suck him off.

40. A man who is impotent takes pleasure from girls pissing in his mouth while reaming their cunts.

41. A man goes to a whorehouse, opens his fly, compels each whore to drop a turd into his trousers, pays his bill and walks away with his load of shit. He never once discharges in the process.

42. A man hires a whore to shit in her pants at noon, then come to his home at six p.m., after having walked about the city all day with the full load. When she arrives, he frigs himself and shoots on her beshitted buttocks.

43. An old farmer jerks off while annointing his prick with shit and piss from a chamberpot into which all the girls at a whorehouse have relieved themselves.

44. A man has 12 plates of meat brought in, then has a whore frig him and shoots on the one he selects.

45. A man places a girl atop a step-ladder, gives her an enema, then instructs her to shit upon his cock. He ejaculates without touching himself as the watery shit falls.

46. A priest gives a girl a milk enema, then drinks the product — milk mixed with shit — as it emerges from her ass.

47. A priest arranges a special chamberpot on a ladder. He frigs himself while smelling and touching shit which a girl, seated above, drops into it.

48. A man hires a whore to shit on a plate and place it under his nose while he sits in his library, reading a book. He upbraids her for her "insolence" when she delivers it, but ejaculates nonetheless.

49. A man frigs himself while women aged seventy and older mount him on a sofa and shit on his belly.

50. A man constructs a portable toilet seat and, placing his head beneath it, he has a girl suck his cock while a working-man shits on his face.

51. A monk jerks off while reaming a girl's ass which is smeared with a two-inch thick coating of shit.

52. A man hires a whore to rub his entire body, including his face, with a vasefull of shit which has been collected from public lavoratories all over Paris.

53. A man takes a potful of shit and shoves the turds up his own ass.

54. A man takes a girl's turd, chews it and swishes it around in his mouth for an hour, then spits out the resulting brown liquid (which is her shit and his saliva combined).

55. A man does something with the shit from four different prostitutes, but no one can discover what he does with them, as he is left alone with them.

56. A libertine sucks a girl's ass, extracting turds the size of pigeon eggs, and eats them, one by one, in an operation which consumes all of two hours before he ejaculates.

57. Another libertine pays a girl to let him belch into her mouth.

58. An old parlimientarian pays a prostitute to shit upon a porcelain dish. He then rubs his nose in the shit while she sucks his cock.

59. A man hires a whore to kiss his ass. As soon as her face is within range, he lets loose with an enormous turd. She is innundated in shit.

60. An abbot jerks himself off while sucking shit from the ass of a boy. Later he also sucks shit from the asses of two grown men, but will not touch a girl.

61. An octogenarian and a prostitute sit, back to back, on a chamberpot and shit in concert. Then, while the prostitute sucks his limp dick, the octogenarian stirs the shit into a batter and eats it.

62. A priest climbs into a barrel filled with shit and pokes his prick through a specially-constructed knothole. Then, while a prostitute jerks him off, he rubs shit in his hair.

63. A man pays a prostitute to shit and piss in a chamberpot and preserve the excrement for a week. When the week is over, he eats the mixture — savoring especially the mould — while simultaneously contemplating the bare ass whence it emerged.

64. An elderly doctor gives an old woman an enema of liquor, then jerks off as she shits it back into his mouth.

65. An Army officer pays a prostitute to shit on a plate, then feed it to him while he lies wrapped in a baby's blanket and simulates an infant's cries.

66. An old rake arranges through his sister, who is abbess of a convent, to acquire the shit of several dozen young nuns. He then hires a prostitute to frig him while he eats first this one's shit, then that one's shit, and so forth.

67. A monk mixes in a pot the shit of ten boys and girls, then eats it while a prostitute sucks his cock.

68. A man shits in a prostitute's mouth, then has her spit it out. Next, while lapping it up from the floor, he jerks off, squirting his come all over her tits.

69. An old magistrate feeds a prostitute a laxative, then lies in a bathtub while she shits upon him.

70. A man shits on a plate, while a second man watches. Next, a prostitute frigs him, directing his come on the turd. Then the second man eats the whole mess.

71. A man shits into a girl's cunt.

72. A man hires a prostitute to spread his buttocks while he shits, then to ream his ass clean with her tongue.

74. Another man — this one a lawyer — gets his thrills by dipping girls into a barrel of shit, then pulling them out and licking them clean.

75. A man pays a whore to shit in his mouth, then kiss him — during the process of which kissing she regains her own turd. (She must swallow it, else he refuses to pay her.)

76. A man hires a prostitute to shit on the floor. Next, he lays a turd of his own alongside hers. Then he instructs her to get down on her hands and knees and eat both turds, during the course of which he reams her asshole.

77. A man hires a twelve-year-old girl to lie on the floor while he squats over her face and lets fly into her mouth the contents from five enemas. Simultaneously, he jerks off with one hand and fingers her twat with the other.

78. A man pays a woman with extremely flabby tits to let him wipe his ass with them.

79. A man whose skin is covered with sores forces a girl to suck every inch of his body — lapping the scabs with her tongue, drinking his pus, et cetera.

80. A monk hires a girl to knead, pinch, scratch and otherwise maltreat his ass. After half an hour's activity, he ejaculates — unaided by frigging or other stimulation.

81. A Benedictine prior pays a girl to whip his cock and balls. He discharges immediately upon application of the lash, even though his prick remains limp.

82. A man hires a girl to whip him on the ass. He discharges on the one hundredth stroke.

83. An elderly tax collector hires a madame to flagellate him with a whip the lashes of which have been soaked for a week in a mixture of shit and piss.

84. A man induces a girl to shove a whip-handle up

his ass. When it is in to the hilt, he ejaculates. His prick is curved in such a fashion that his jism catches him straight in the face.

85. A man hires a prostitute to whip him about the ass and thighs while she shits. The lashes tear into the feces, splattering them about the room. The spectacle thrills him immeasurably.

86. A man pays a prostitute to whip him from his shoulders to knees on both sides of the body. Then he tells her to lie on the floor in a prone position, whereupon he squats over her buttocks and shits on them.

87. A man pays a prostitute to whip him until his body is covered with raw welts, then to piss in a cup and rub the urine into his wounds.

88. A man has himself whipped by another man who is dressed as a girl.

89. A man has a whore slap his face until he gets a hard-on, then jerks him off.

90. A man can ejaculate only after a girl tweaks his nose, pulls his ears, bites his buttocks until they bleed, chews his prick and nips his balls. Aroused thusly, he becomes stiff as a stallion and shoots all over the girl's face.

91. A man hires a whore to tie him to a step-ladder and beat him ferociously with whips and martinets. The beating causes him to ejaculate; there is no frigging or other stimulation involved.

92. A man has his cock and balls assaulted with a golden needle. Not until he is covered with blood does he discharge.

93. A man has himself flailed with nettles until his body is reduced to a scarlet shambles. Then, looking in a mirror, he ejaculates.

94. An old courtier, weary of homages paid him as a result of his high political office, hires whores to humiate him. They, acting under his instructions, "force" him to kneel; then they hit his knuckles with a hickory stick, whip his buttocks with a cane, et cetera. He has orgasm as a result.

95. A young abbot hires a whore to whip him while he eats one of his own turds. He discharges at the moment when the last piece of shit is consumed.

96. A doctor hires a prostitute to whip him and shout blasphemies at while he eats a piece of her shit from a plate.

97. Another doctor has himself whipped while eating a turd produced by a leprous old woman of seventy-three years. "The more repulsive the source of the shit, the tastier the yield," he proclaims to all who will listen.

98. A man has himself beaten with red-hot tongs while he eats the shit of an eighty-year-old valet.

99. Another man has his buttocks, belly, balls and prick stabbed with a heavy cobbler's awl while he eats a turd from a chamberpot.

100. A man hires a whore to suck his cock while simultaneously beating him on the back with a cane. (This is accomplished by her reaching through his legs as he and she lay side-by-side.) He eats a bowl of shit while the act takes place.

101. A man ejaculates while a woman, who is his captive, is forced to kiss the ass of her daughter, a whore.

102. A man pays handsomely the madame of a whore-house to stage the following scene: (a) the man arrives, dressed as a garbage collector, and announces: "I am here, madame, to clean out your toilet;" (b) the madame then leads him to a one-hole chair, the chamberpot of which is filled with a week's accumulation of shit; (c) he takes the pot outside the house and licks it clean, eating every morsel; (d) he returns the clean pot to the madame and asks to be paid for performing the service; (e) she sets after him with a broom, beating him about the shoulders and head — (this is part of the plan!) — and shouting: "Your payment, villain? This is what you deserve!"

103. A man has a girl plunge a knotty stick three inches into his urethral canal, rattle it with the utmost vigor, then frig him while the object is still in place. At the moment of his orgasm, he tells her to pull out the stick, whereupon he discharges upon her pubic hair.

104. An abbot has a girl splash his cock and balls with the molten tallow from a burning candle. The ceremony is sufficient to bring about ejaculation; no frigging, et cetera, is required.

105. A man has a girl stick his buttocks full of pins. Then he sits down on them and jerks off.

106. A man has himself embuggered with a dildo which is filled with warm milk. At the moment of his ejaculation, the liquid is pumped into his intestines.

107. Another man does likewise, except with dildos of progressively larger size, until, finally, he is impaled by one the dimensions of a wine bottle. The milk with which he is innundated in this final enterprise measures approximately one gallon in volume.

108. A man has himself sodomized with a dildo, then whipped while the object is held in place. During this

activity, he eats a girl's shit.

109. A man has all his joints bound with strings. Thus constricted, he jerks off, shooting his fuck at the asshole of a girl who has been situated on all fours, ass toward him, several feet away.

110. A man ties a long cord around his prick; then he gives the free end to a girl, who holds it against her cunt, steps over it and begins walking away. While contemplating her ass as she walks, the man ejaculates; by this time, the cord has been pulled quite taut.

111. A man hires a prostitute to stage the following scene: (a) she lies on a bed, fully clothed save that her cunt is exposed, and begins to frig herself; (b) he enters the room and "surprises" her; (c) she shouts: "How dare you interrupt me, villain?"; (d) he begs forgiveness; (e) she drives him from the room with a series of swift kicks in the ass.

112. Another man stages the same scene, except that on his way out of the room, he "accidentally" unhooks his trousers, which fall to his ankles, and the whore beats him on his bare buttocks with a broomhandle.

113. A third pays a madame to arrange matters thusly: (a) he enters a whore's room and begins ass-fucking her; (b) two men enter the room after him and begin quarreling; (c) both men turn upon our hero and beat him with canes, then walk out, leaving him lying battered on the floor; (d) the girl whom he had been ass-fucking takes him in her arms and consoles him.

114. A fourth stages the same scene as above, except that when the men begin beating him, he starts jerking off. When he gives signs of approaching ejaculation, both men pick him up and throw him out a window. He lands in a pile of horseshit, which has been placed there ex-

pressly for the purpose of breaking his fall.

115. A fifth stages a scene in which he "surprises" another man who is kissing a girl's ass. Our champion begins to upbraid the ass-kisser, calling him a son of a bitch, a tit-licker, a cock-knocker and so forth. The ass-kisser then punches our champion in the mouth, knocking him to the floor; then he "forces" him to suck his cock, which the latter most enthusiastically does.

116. A sixth stages scene in which: (a) he enters a room in a whorehouse; (b) the whore announces that he is her prisoner and orders him to undress; (c) she beats him with a red-hot poker until his body is a latticework of burns and welts; (d) she frees him on the condition that he lick her toes.

117. A seventh stages a scene in which: (a) he is lying in a coffin in the center of a room; (b) a whore enters, bares her ass and requests a good-bye kiss; (c) he reams her asshole; (d) the coffin lid is closed.

118. A man hires a whore to sew up his asshole with heavy cobbler's thread.

119. A man hires a whore to soak with brandy all the hair on his body, then set him afire. He jerks off as he burns, all the while contemplating the whore's belly and cunt.

120. An attorney outfits himself in a horse's halter and has a girl lead him about the room, mount astride him, spur him, whip him, et cetera. He frigs himself and bucks off his rider as he discharges.

121. A man hires a whore to sear his thighs, bake his balls and roast his asshole with the flame of burning candles. He then discharges while reaming her asshole.

122. A man induces a girl to give him a rub-down with a metal curry-comb of the sort which is used on horses.

Next, when his body is but one open wound, he has her rub him with alcohol. The pain from this treatment causes him to discharge instantly.

123. A man induces a girl to pluck out every hair on his ass, blade by blade. While this transpires, he jerks off over a warm turd with which she has just furnished him.

124. A man pays a whore to lacerate his prick with her teeth while at the same time ripping apart his buttocks with an iron comb the teeth of which have been filed to fine points.

125. A judge hires a prostitute to bind him to a St. Andrew's cross and pretend to break his arms and legs with an iron bar.

126. A man induces a girl to jerk him off while both stand naked beneath an open window. Unbeknownst to the girl, the man's colleague is waiting outside the window with a tub of boiling water. When ejaculation approaches, the man gives a signal and his colleague lets fly with the tub, scalding both the man and the girl.

127. A man induces a girl to shower him with a potful of boiling sand; his body is so injured in the enterprise that it appears to be covered with leather rather than skin; he enjoys the suffering.

128. A man hires a whore to accompany him to funeral parlors where the recently dead are being mourned by their families and friends. Standing in front of the coffin, but crouched in such a fashion that no one can see what he is going, the man opens his fly and unlimbers his prick. The the girl jerks him off. He directs his jism into the coffin. Soon, of course, the family and friends realize that the dear departed has been desecrated, but there is nothing that they can do, for the deed already has been done and the frigger and his

accomplice are in flight.

129. A man keeps spies at a cemetery to report every
time a young girl is buried. He then digs up the corpse,
frigs himself over it and handles its buttocks.

130. A man pays a whore to fuck herself simultaneously up the ass and up the cunt with a pair of immense
dildos. He sits across the room and directs the operation.

131. A whore is led naked into a pitch-dark room
where a man pinches her breasts and her buttocks and
finally discharges, all the while emitting blood-curdling
screams and threatening to kill the whore.

132. A man induces a girl with big tits to lie supine on
a couch; then, placing his prick between her tits, he
rotates those massive mammaries until they bring him to
orgasm, all the while, spitting on her face.

133. A man opens a gambling casino, then wanders
about the tables picking the pockets of his customers.
Every time he picks a pocket, he discharges in his pants.

134. A judge rents an apartment overlooking the
square where criminals are executed. Then, on execution days, he sits at his window and, as the victim is be-
headed, jerks off.

135. Another judge goes to the cells of women about to
be executed and offers them a pardon in exchange for
their shitting in his mouth. To those who oblige, he replies: "You shall die anyway. Never trust a judge."

136. A man offers a madame ten louis for the services
of the most pretty young whore to be found. Finally he
is brought an eighteen year old girl who is a veritable
goddess. When she undresses, he begins unbraiding her,

calling her ass flabby, her tits disgusting, her face ugly, and so forth. He then tells her that he would never fuck someone so unattractive. The child, given no reason to suspect his intentions — and being vain, as most extraordinarily pretty girls are apt to be — begins to cry. When he sees this, the man ejaculates.

137. A man goes to the home of a newly-married woman shortly after her husband has left for work, identifies himself as the husband's employer and says that the husband was just killed in a dreadful accident. When the woman faints, our hero pulls up her skirts, then frigs himself, directing his discharge upon her ass.

138. A man kidnaps a woman who is in the ninth month of pregnancy. When her labor pains begin, he starts fondling himself. Then, when the new-born babe's head emerges, he directs his fuck upon it.

139. A man kidnaps a woman who is in the seventh month of pregnancy and forces her to balance herself upon a pedestal fifteen feet high. While watching her, he jerks off.

140. A man kidnaps a mother and her three-year-old child; the mother is then forced to spank the child; when the child begins to scream, the man begins whipping off most vigorously; his discharge is directed upon the screaming child's face.

141. A Benedictine prior hires a prostitute who has incredibly thick patches of hair under her arms and on her cunt. He then shaves these areas clean and jerks off, discharging upon the newly-shorn skin.

142. A libertine sends his valet to hire a whore to lie naked, smeared with chicken blood, in a room, which is outfitted like a funeral parlor. When the girl is in place, our champion enters the room and pretends that he has

just found a corpse. Feeling and fondling the lovely body, he praises the "assassin" on his choice of a victim, expresses wonder that the body is still warm and soliloquizes about how much he would have liked to been the man who "killed" her. Then he reams her asshole and leaves the room, all the while muttering to himself that it's a shame that he couldn't have seen her before she died.

143 A man hires a whore without describing the nature of the services he wants her to perform. When she arrives at his home, she is made to undress and get on her hands and knees. Then two great danes are brought out and the woman is forced to eat with them from a trough. While she eats, her employer frigs himself assiduously, all the while saying: "Oh, the buggeress! Look at her, gorging herself with the dogs! That's how one should treat all women — like dogs. If they were handled thusly, we'd get no more sauciness from them, you could bet your ass on that!"

144. A man sends his valet to hire a whore; she is given no indication of the nature of the services she is to perform. When she arrives at her employer's house, the man pretends that he thinks she is a thief; he calls for his valet to bind her in a sack and throw her into the Seine. The valet places her in the sack per instructions; while this is being done, the man jerks off, then the valet carries the girl out of the room, releases her from the sack, pays her and sends her on her way.

145. A man hires a whore, then leaves her in his library while he steps outside. At this point his valet enters and gives the girl a "gift" of several silver bracelets. When the valet leaves, the employer returns, "finds" the bracelets and accuses the whore of theft. He then summons a colleague who is dressed as a policeman and demands the girl's arrest. The "gendarme" dutifully

hauls the girl away, but, as soon as they are out of the employer's sight, releases her; she goes her way paid as agreed upon and keeping the bracelets as an extra reward.

146. A man goes to great lengths to have women — married and unmarried — seduced. He provides men for them and lets them use his bedroom. Meanwhile, he goes into the next room and, unknown to them, watches through a peephole.

147. A judge hires a whore to cower naked in a corner while he menacingly waves a switch at her. His excitement comes not from striking her, but from merely observing her fright. He ejaculates upon her breasts without any direct stimulation.

148. A man has a woman sit in a children's swing and begins moving back and forth in vigorous arcs. Each time she passes him, she is to fart; if she fails, he slaps her ass. After this ceremony has continued for perhaps an hour, he releases her. There is nothing more to his peculiar passion than what has been described; no friggings, fondlings, et cetera.

149. A man recruits a libertine to shit upon the breasts of the man's wife while he watches.

150. A man hires a whore, then brutally strips her clothes from her back and throws them into a fireplace. "Very well, slut," he says; "now you're going to follow these garments and, by the Lord's fuck, I'm going to have the pleasure of smelling the aroma of your burning flesh." So saying, he falls into a chair and jerks himself off. The whore is released unharmed and given a costume twice as fine as that which was burned. -

BOOK TWO: THE COMPLEX PASSIONS

During the month of December, the narrator's task falls upon Madame Champville, who describes the following one-hundred-and-fifty passions:

1. A man fucks only girls aged three to seven, and limits himself exclusively to the cunt.

2. A man binds a nine-year-old girl's arms and legs in such a manner that her body assumes the position of a crab; then he ass-fucks her.

3. A man seeks to seduce a girl aged thirteen and is refused. Then, holding a pistol to her heart, he rapes her.

4. A man rubs the prick of a colleague against a virgin's labia until the colleague ejaculates; then, using the expelled semen as a lubricating agent, he fucks the virgin himself while the other man holds her.

5. A man devirginates three girls in succession: the first aged seven; the second, five, and the third, still in the cradle.

6. A man fucks only girls aged nine to thirteen. His prick is so immense that four women are required to hold the victim in place while she receives him.

7. A man has his valet fuck a ten-year old maid while he himself fondles both the girl's and the valet's buttocks. When the valet ejaculates inside the girl, the man simultaneously ejaculates upon the valet's buttocks.

8. A man's sexual tastes are such that he will fuck no one except a girl destined to be married on the following day.

9. Another man entertains like tastes, except that he wants to fuck the bride sometime between the hour of the wedding mass and the time she and her husband retire to the bridal bed.

10. A man hires a valet who is extraordinarily handsome and personable. The valet then goes about the business of marrying hundreds of girls. On each wedding night, the girl is brought to the valet's master, who fucks her, then sells her into whoredom.

11. A man's tastes are such that he cannot rest until he has devirginated two sisters in the presence of each other.

12. A man proposes marriage to a girl. They go to his home town, where a ceremony is performed; then they go to bed and he devirginates her. After the devirgination, he reveals that the wedding ceremony was a sham. "I have fucked you and there is nothing you can do about it," he says. Then he leaves her.

13. A man chooses to fornicate only with girls who have just been devirginated before his eyes.

14. A man uses a very large dildo to devirginate a girl; then he jerks off, discharging his semen in the path which he has just plowed. He is not content until the vaginal opening is covered with sperm.

15. A certain Duke fucks only virgins of distinction, who he also beats and abuses in direct proportion to

their father's wealth. He claims to have devirginated more than 1,500 girls over a period of thirty years.

16. A man forces a brother and sister to fuck while he watches; then he, himself, fucks the girl, after which he commands both her and her brother to shit.

17. A man forces a father to fuck his own daughter after the man himself, has devirginated the girl.

18. A man brings his nine-year-old daughter to a brothel, and, while she is held by a prostitute, he fucks her. (The man has a total of twelve daughters, all of whom he has devirginated in this manner.)

19. A man fucks only virgins aged thirty to forty. It is a costly caprice, as they are quite rare.

20. A man fucks only nuns and spends large sums of money to recruit them. His brother, a duke, seizes a nun named Sister Carmel and, while she is held in place by four governesses, the first man devirginates her. The duke then fucks her twice more in a row; when she faints during the second encounter, he continues to fuck her unconscious body.

21. A man can enjoy only adulterous acts. He sends scouts to discover wives who are virtuous and loyal, then kidnaps them and rapes them.

23. A man seduces his friend's wife, then persuades her to prostitute herself. Now, acting as her procurer, he sells her to her husband.

24. A man fucks a married woman on a bed while her daughter, suspended above, offers her clitoris to be licked. Then he reverses the siutation, fucking the daughter while kissing the mother's ass. When he finishes licking the daughter, he forces her to piss; when he finishes kissing the mother, he forces her to shit.

25. Mr. X., a man with four wedded daughters, fucks all and conceives by each. He then looks forward to the further incestuous pleasure of having sexual relations with the children he has incestuously sired. His friend, Mr. Y., meanwhile, has three children whom he sired by his own mother. A daughter of this incestuous union is then married to a son, so that when Y, himself, fucks her, he is fucking his sister, his daughter and his daughter-in-law all in one; the son, likewise, fucks not only his wife but also his sister and his mother-in-law.

26. A man has a girl fondle his prick at the same time that she is being frigged by a second man. The man being fondled ejaculates upon the buttocks of the man frigging the girl.

27. A man licks the ass of Girl A while Girl B kisses his ass and Girl C sucks his cock. Then they exchange positions so that all parties enjoy the same pleasures. Each person is expected to fart frequently during the proceedings.

28. A man eats out the cunt of Girl A while Girl B licks his prick and Girl C reams his ass. The girls discharge their sexual juices, which the man swallows. Then positions are exchanged and the labors resumed.

29. A man licks a girl's ass immediately after she has defecated and before the remains have been wiped away. Simultaneously his own ass, in a similar state of uncleanliness, is licked by a second girl, and, throughout the process, he sodomizes a third girl. Positions are then exchanged until each girl has been enjoyed once in each fashion.

30. A man has two girls frig each other while he watches. When one reports that she is approaching orgasm, he cunt-fucks her, but from the rear, while she continues to frig the other.

31. A man hires an older girl to introduce a younger girl to libertinage. While he watches, the older girl performs acts of cunnilingus and anilingus. Then he himself launches an invasion with his prick of the channels which have thusly been lubricated for him.

32. A man hires five women to amuse him in the following manner: two alternate in receiving him orally, two others in receiving him vaginally; the fifth follows him, and, as he takes his pleasures of the others, sodomizes him with a dildo.

33. Another man hires twelve women to amuse him in random acts. He sucks their clitorises, their asses and their mouths, ingesting much piss, shit and saliva in the process.

34. Still another man enjoys eight women at the same time, each in a different position about his body.*

* This must be illustrated with a drawing—D.A.F.S.

35. A man watches while three men and women fuck in various postures.

36. A man arranges twelve groups of two girls each, their bodies intertwined in such a manner that only their buttocks are visible and the rest of the bodies concealed. While contemplating this mountain of buttocks, he jerks off.

37. A man equips six female couples with dildos and sets them loose in a room paneled with mirrors. While they encunt each other, he runs around the room, kissing them on their buttocks.

38. Another man hires four prostitutes. After getting them drunk, he has one after the other vomit into his mouth.

39. A man hires two girls, one to shit into his mouth, the other to suck his prick and frig his ass. When he discharges, he simultaneously shits into the hand of the girl who is frigging him.

40. A man engages a little boy to ass-fuck him while a second man shits into his mouth. He eats the shit, then has the boy and man exchange positions.

41. A man enjoys three girls in the following fashion: he shits into girl A's mouth and then fucks her; meanwhile, girl B lies between them and Girl C shits in her face; the man then licks C's shit off B's face without

missing a stroke with A. The girls exchange roles so that all three participate in each posture.

42. A man of seventy, for fifty years had thirty girls a day shit into his mouth. Operating thusly five times per week, he has seen a total of 7800 girls for each of the fifty years.

43. Another man, not quite so ambitious, did likewise, but with only twelve girls per day.

44. A man derives pleasure from sitting in a bathtub filled with the piss and shit of thirty women.

45. A man hires four women sixty years of age and older to watch him shit. Then, he divides the feces equally and forces them to eat it. Next the women shit, whereupon he mixes the product of all of them and eats it himself.

46. A man makes two girls shit and forces them to eat each other's product. Then he has them shit a second time and he himself eats the product.

47. Another man employs a mother and her three daughters, eating the girls' feces on the mother's buttocks and the mother's feces on one of the girl's buttocks.

48. A man makes a daughter shit into her mother's mouth, then wipes the girl's ass on the mother's breasts. Next he eats the feces from the mother's mouth. After this he has the mother shit into the daughter's mouth and likewise eats the product.

49. A man makes a father eat his own son's shit; then

the man eats the father's shit.

50. A man eats the shit which a brother has deposited into his sister's cunt, then that which the sister has deposited into her brother's mouth.

51. A man likes to be sworn at by a whore while she is frigging him. He, in turn, blasphemes while kissing her ass.

52. A man likes to fondle a girl in church at the time when the Holy Sacrament is being administered. When possible, he sits near the altar and frigs the girl while she frigs him.

53. A man goes to confession specifically to arouse his confessor's prick by confessing a long list of infamous acts. He jerks off during the recital.

54. A man fucks a girl in the mouth at the moment she merges from the confessional.

55. A man fucks a prostitute throughout a mass in his private chapel and discharges at the moment of Consecration.

56. A man bribes a priest to let him replace him in the confessional. Listening to the young parishioners' confessions he "pardons" them and gives them the worst possible advice.

57. A man brings his daughter to confess to a monk whom he previously has bribed. The father then places himself near the confession box so that he can hear everything she says.

58. A man has mass celebrated in his private chapel. Only naked prostitutes attend. Throughout the ceremony he wanders about, rubbing his prick on each girl's ass.

59. A man bribes a monk to seduce his wife during her confession while the hidden husband watches. If the wife refuses, the husband appears to help the monk subdue her; then the monk fucks her, while the man watches.

60. A man fucks a prostitute in his private chapel while resting both his and her naked parts on the sacred altar stone.

61. A man fucks a naked girl from behind while she bends over a large crucifix and rubs the head of Christ against her clitoris.

62. Another man farts, shits, pisses and finally ejaculates into a chalice which contains consecrated wine.

63. A third man forces a small boy to shit on a paten; then he eats the feces while the boy sucks his penis.

64. A fourth man has two girls shit on a cross, then he himself does likewise. Next he masturbates.

65. A man breaks up a cross, then shits on the debris and burns the entire pile. Later he takes a prostitute to hear a sermon and fucks her while listening to it.

66. A man receives Communion, then has four prostitutes shit into his mouth while the sacred wafer is on his tongue.

67. A man sends a whore to Communion, then fucks her in her mouth when she returns.

68. A man interrupts a priest who is saying mass in a private chapel and ejaculates into the chalice. He then has a prostitute frig the priest into the chalice. Subsequently he forces the priest to drink from the chalice.

69. A man interrupts mass just as soon as the Host has been consecrated and forces the priest to shove it up a prostitute's cunt.

70. A man induces a whore to fart upon the Host; next he does likewise. Then he swallows the Host while fucking the girl.

71. Another man shits upon the Host, forces a prostitute to do the same and then tosses the whole business into a privy hole.

72. A man tickles a prostitute's clitoris with the Host, and, after she has discharged upon it, slips it into her vagina, then tamps it to the womb with his penis.

72. A man cuts up a Host with a knife and shoves the crumbs up his ass.

74. A man ejaculates upon the Host, then feeds both the biscuit and his semen to a dog.

75. A girl sucks a man's cock during mass. He ejaculates. The host is elevated.

76. A man hires two women to whip his ass. After each woman has given him ten strokes, she frigs his asshole.

77. A man has two girls whip him while two others fart into his mouth; they rotate so that each girl performs each act.

78. A man is whipped by his wife while fucking his daughter, then vice versa.

79. A man fucks one girl while being whipped by another; then the girls exchange roles.

80. A man is whipped while kissing a boy's ass and simultaneously fucking a girl in the mouth.

81. A libertine is whipped by an old woman while he fucks her husband in the mouth. Meanwhile, the couple's daughter shits into the libertine's mouth.

82. A man is whipped while frigging himself; he ejaculates upon a crucifix wedged between a girl's buttocks.

83. A man is whipped while fucking a prostitute; he shoves a Host up her cunt before inserting his penis.

84. A man is whipped by each prostitute in a brothel while kissing the madame' ass and having her fart, piss and shit into his mouth.

85. A man employs twelve cab-drivers each morning

to amuse him, two at a time, one whipping him while the other farts in his mouth.

86. Another man likes to be whipped and ridden while being held on his hands and knees by three girls and while being mounted and flogged by a fourth. Each girl takes her turn at riding and lashing.

87. A naked man asks 'forgiveness' of five girls and throws himself down on his knees before them. Each girl then is allowed to demand a penance, and the man is whipped one hundred times for each penance he refuses to do. One girl demands that he licks up her spittle from the floor; another wishes to shit into his mouth; a third, who is menstruating, demands that he eat out her cunt; a fourth makes him lick between her dirty toes, and the fifth asks him to lick the discharge from her nose.

88. A man engages a procuress to provide him with fifteen girls six times a week; the girls, in teams of three, whip him, suck him and shit on him, taking turns at each act as directed by the procuress. The man is made deliriously happy by such activity and finally achieves orgasm.

89. A man has his ass slapped and squeezed by twenty-five prostitutes.

90. A man sets up a mock court and has himself tried by six prostitutes, who know that he wishes to be sentenced to hanging. He is hanged but does not die; the cord breaks, at which moment he ejaculates.

91. A man stands before a semi-circle of six old women, who spit in his face while three young prosti-

tutes whip him.

92. A man is sodomized with the handle of a whip administered by one naked girl while another whips him across his thighs and penis. He ejaculates over the body of the whipper.

93. Two women whip a man with a bull's dismembered prick while a third woman, kneeling before him, jerks him off until he discharges on her breasts.

94. A man engages in a mock fight with six whip-wielding women. He pretends to avoid their lashes and pretends to atempt grabbing the whip from them, but in reality, he revels in their abuse.

95. A man runs up and down between two rows of twelve girls who flagellate him with a variety of different style whips. He ejaculates on the ninth time he runs the gauntlet.

96. A man has first the soles of his feet, then his prick and then his thighs whipped, while three women successively mount him and shit into his mouth.

97. A man is whipped by three girls, wielding alternately a martinet, a bull's prick and a cat o' nine tails. A fourth girl kneels beneath him sucking his cock and reaming his ass while she is being sodomized by the man's valet.

98. A man hires six girls to prick him with a needle, pinch him, burn him, bite him, scratch him and flagellate him until he ejaculates.

99. A man is ass-fucked by his valet while a girl, who is naked, balances on a very small pedestal. She is required to remain motionless, without falling, as he ejaculates all over her bare body.

100. A man fingers a girl's ass while he, himself, is masturbated by a colleague. The girl is forced to hold a very short candle which she may not drop until the man has ejaculated. By forcing himself to think of nonsexual matters, he refrains from ejaculating until the girl's fingers have been singed by the candle flame.

101. A man stages a banquet where the only light is that provided by candles shoved up the asses of six girls lying prone around the table.

102. During the supper, this man forces a girl to kneel on sharp pebbles while two tilted candles above her drip hot wax on her naked breasts and back. She is warned that if she makes the slightest movement during the course of the meal, she will be dismissed instantly.

103. A man locks a girl for four days in a narrow cage where she can neither lie down nor sit.

104. A girl is wrapped up in a large blanket with a cat and is forced to leap and dance about while the cat bites and scratches her. She must not fall and must continue her antics until the man watching discharges.

105. A man rubs a certain itching powder into the skin of a woman, causing her to scratch herself until she bleeds. While he watches, the man masturbates.

106. A man forces a woman to drink something which causes her menstruation cycle to stop. Eventually she may be choked by the unexpelled blood.

107. A woman is given a medicine intended for horses. It causes vomiting and diarrhea. Her captor enjoys watching her suffer.

108. A nude girl is rubbed with honey and tied to a column; there a swarm of large flies attack her.

109. A girl is bound, naked, to a fast-revolving pivot. Her captor watches her until he ejaculates.

110. A man hangs a naked girl upside down and watches her until he discharges.

111. A girl is forced to swallow a heavy dose of castor oil and is persuaded that it is poison. Her captor masturbates while watching her suffer.

112. A man beats and paws a girl's breasts until they are bruised and blackened.

113. A man beats and mauls a girl's ass for three hours, ejaculating only after he has drawn blood.

114. A man forces a girl to climb a tall ladder. When she reaches the height of twenty feet, a rung, previously tampered with, breaks. She falls onto mattresses below, where the man pounces upon her and fucks her.

115. A man sits in an easy chair and forces a girl to kneel naked before him. Then he slaps her face hard as he can until he ejaculates.

116. A man beats a girl's knuckles with hickory branches.

117. A man slaps a girl's buttocks until they are red and raw.

118. A man shoves a bellows up a girl's ass and inflates her.

119. A girl is given an enema of boiling water. Her captor watches her writhe in pain, then jerks off, ejaculating upon her buttocks.

120. A depraved man recruits six pious women under false pretenses. He then beats them with a crucifix and with rosaries and forces each to pose as a statue of the Virgin upon an alter during a mass. At the consecration, the women are required to shit upon the Host.

121. A man forces a woman to run naked through a garden on a winter night. Cords are stretched across her path to make her fall.

122. A man strips a woman and throws her into a vat of almost boiling water. She is not allowed to emerge until he has ejaculated over her body.

123. A girl is bound naked to a post in a garden on a winter day. There she is forced to recite five "Our Fathers" and five "Hail Marys." Her captor watches while being jerked off by a second girl.

124. A man puts a strong glue on the rim of a toilet seat and sends a girl to use it. She is stuck to the seat. Meanwhile a small charcoal burner has been placed in-

side the toilet bowl. It scorches her, and when she leaps
up in pain, she leaves a circle of skin behind.

125. A man gets a girl so drunk that she passes out.
She is then placed on a bed, which is raised with pulleys.
In the middle of the night, when she reaches out for the
customary chamber pot, she tumbles out of the bed and
falls, groping, onto a mattress below. The man is waiting
there and promptly fucks her.

126. The same man has a girl run naked through a
garden, following her and threatening her with a large
walking stick. When finally she falls down with exhaustion, he leaps upon her and fucks her.

127. A man whips a girl one hundred times, in series
of ten blows each. Between whippings he kisses the girl
passionately about the ass.

128. A man flogs a girl with a whip the thongs of which
have been dipped in brandy. When the girl is bleeding
satisfactorily, the man ejaculates upon her buttocks.

129. A man's tastes are such that he whips only little
girls between five and seven years of age, and always
under such circumstances as to make the whipping appear to be legitimate punishment.

130. A woman confesses to a priest, who gives her five
hundred lashes as a penance.

131. A man gives four women six hundred lashes each.

132. The same ceremony is repeated with twenty

women, each of whom is given six hundred lashes by the man's two valets, who relieve each other in the task while their master masturbates.

133. A man beats several boys aged fourteen to sixteen years. When he is finished, he sucks their cocks.

134. A naked girl is forced to enter a room where two men fall upon her and whip each of her buttocks until it is raw. The girl is then bound, and a third man frigs both himself and the two others. The jism of all three is directed upon the girl's bleeding parts.

135. A girl is bound hand and foot, facing a wall. Between her and the wall is placed a blade of sharp steel adjusted to the heighth of her stomach. Then she is beaten. When she leans forward to avoid the lash, she is cut.

136. A man whips a girl in the following manner: one hundred lashes on the first day, two hundred on the second, three hundred on the third, and so forth, not ceasing until the ninth day.

137. A man has a prostitute crouch on all fours and mounts her back facing her rear — tightening his legs about her ribs. Then he flogs her with a martinet in such a manner that the thongs cut into her cunt.

138. A man has a pregnant woman bent backwards over a cylinder with her head tied to the seat of a chair. Next her legs are stretched as far apart as possible so that her full belly is taut and her vagina is wide open. He then beats a rhythm with a whip on her swollen belly until she bleeds.

. This accomplished, he ejaculates on her face.

139. A man kidnaps several fifteen-year old girls and whips them with sting-nettle until they are torn and raw.

140. A man uses a bull's dismembered prick to beat the buttocks of four women until they are torn and raw.

141. A man whips six women with steel-tipped martinets. He ejaculates only after the blood of all six is flowing freely.

142. A man kidnaps several pregnant women and flogs them until pieces of flesh fall from their buttocks.

143. A girl is given a piece of bread which has been dipped in wax and lighted. She is then required to light a candle which has been placed high above her head. She must accomplish this feat in a hurry or burn herself. While she is leaping for the candle, a man flogs her with a leather-thonged whip. When she succeeds in lighting the candle, the game is ended.

144. A man whips his wife and his daughter, then places them both in a brothel and has them flogged while he watches.

145. A bound girl is whipped from the nape of the neck to the calves of her legs. Her tormenter doesn't stop until she is raw.

146. A certain man whips only women's breasts, insisting that they be very large. He pays double for a pregnant woman.

147. A man whips the faces of pretty girls with a

bundle of dry switches.

148. A man whips women over their entire body with dry switches, completely devastating their faces, genitalia, buttocks and breasts.

149. A man whips boys aged sixteen to twenty years with a bull's prick.

150. A man is whipped in one room by four girls until he is about to ejaculate. Then he rushes into another room where a fifth girl waits for him, nude. He beats her with a bull's prick and ejaculates all over her.

BOOK THREE: THE CRIMINAL PASSIONS

During the month of January, Madame Martaine assumes the role of narrator. She describes the one hundred and fifty criminal passions, which are as follows:

1. A man likes nothing better than to be fucked up the ass. He can never find a prick too big for him..

2. A man delights in the anal devirgination of girls aged three to seven. His daily regimen involves fucking two girls per day; one vaginally, in the morning, the other anally, in the afternoon. His orgasm last six minutes, and he bellows like a bull while it is in progress.

3. A mother sells the anal virginity of her son, aged seven, to a man who specializes in sodomizing boys of this age only.

4. When Martaine was thirteen years old and her brother fifteen, they went to the home of a man who paid them to conduct the following act: the brother fucked the sister in the cunt, while the employer alternately ass-fucked one, then the other.

5. A man, while sodomizing a brother and sister, enlists the aid of another man to sodomize him.

6. A man has four girls fart in his mouth while he ass-fucks a fifth. The girls then rotate: all fart; all are ass-fucked; the man does not ejaculate until he has finished with the entire five.

7. A man ass-fucks three small boys; after each act, the boy involved is made to shit; while one boy is shitting, the man jerks off the boy next in line.

8. A man fucks a sister in the mouth while her brother shits in the man's mouth; the siblings' roles are then reversed. Throughout the process, a second man fucks the first man up the ass.

9. A man will fuck only fifteen-year-old girls, and only up the ass, and only after they have been whipped strenuously.

10. A man pinches and pounds a girl's buttocks for one hour, then ass-fucks her while a second man flogs her with great violence.   ----

11. A man fucks only during mass, he comes at the moment the Host is elevated.

12. Another man ass-fucks girls while at the same

time he rubs his feet on a crucifix. He requires that the girl treat the crucifix with like contempt.

13. A monk forces a girl to shit. Then he wipes her ass. This accomplished, he shoves a consecrated Host up her ass, then forces it into her intestines by embuggering her with his enormous prick.

14. A man sodomizes one boy while he himself is sodomized by a second; in each case, a Host is used as a shield — which is to say, it precedes the fucker's prick into the appropriate ass. On the nape of the neck of the boy whom the man is sodomizing there rests another Host; at the man's command, a third boy shits on it. These activities transpire until the man ejaculates; horrendous blasphemies are shouted throughout.

z15. A man sodomizes a priest while the latter is saying mass. During the consecreation, the fucker withdraws his prick long enough for the priest who is being fucked to shove the newly-consecrated Host up his ass, then the act of sodomy is resumed.

16. A man fucks only very old women, and only while they are being whipped.

17. Another man sodomizes only very old men, while a colleague fucks him.

18. A man embuggers his son.

19. A man sodomizes only Negroes, freaks or deform-

ed persons.

20. A man, wishing to combine incest, adultery, sodomy and sacrilege, fucks his married daughter up the ass while using a Host as a shield.

21. A man has two men alternately ass-fuck and flagellate him while he, himself, sodomizes a young boy, and while an old man shits into his mouth. At the moment when he ejaculates, he also swallows the shit.

22. A man hires two men to take turns fucking him, one up the ass, the other in the mouth, for two hours.

23. A man stages an orgy with ten men, whom he pays according to each man's number of ejaculations. In a given day, this man can withstand as many as twenty-four pricks up his ass without achieving orgasm.

24. In order to finance his tastes for embuggering boys, a man prostitutes his wife, his daughter and his sister; he watches while they entertain their customers.

25. A man employs eight men at one time in the following manner: Number One fucks him in the mouth; Number Two, up the ass; Number Three, behind the left ball; Number Four, behind the right ball; Number Five and Six, with their pricks in his hands; Number Seven, between his thighs, and Number Eight, rubbing his prick against the man's face.

26. A young bawd has an elderly man ass-fucked by a hired lackey while he watches. Several times the lackey's prick is removed from the old man's ass and placed in the mouth of the bawd, who sucks it; then the bawd

sucks the old man's prick and ass directly. Finally, a chain is set up, the bawd ass-fucking the old man, the lackey ass-fucking the bawd and the lacky being whipped on the back by the bawd's governess.

27. While he ass-fucks a fifteen year old girl, a man strangles her, thereby causing her ass to constrict and increasing his pleasure. Throughout the act he is flogged by a colleague, who wields a whip made from a bull's prick.

28. A man derives great ecstasy for two full hours by shoving up his ass two large balls of quicksilver, then gyrating his torso, forcing the balls to rise and descend in cadence. During this enterprise, he also sucks pricks, swallows jism and eats shit.

29. A man is ass-fucked by a father while he, himself ass-fucks the father's son and daughter.

30. A man places a girl prone on a bed, with a turkey's head squeezed between her legs. Then he fucks the turkey, but it appears as if he is fucking the girl. At the same time, he is ass-fucked from above. Both the man and his ass-fucker discharge at the same time, whereupon the girl, as prearranged, cuts the turkey's throat.

31. A man fucks a goat from behind while at the same time being flogged. The goat conceives and gives birth to a monster, half-man and half-goat. The man then fucks this creature up the ass.

32. A man fucks only bucks, and only up the ass.

33. A man has a woman's cunt lapped by a trained dog. At the moment of the woman's orgasm, the man shoots the dog; the woman is not harmed.

34. A man shoves a Host up a swan's ass then fucks the animal. He strangles the bird at the moment he attains orgasm.

35. A special wicker basket is built with an opening at one end. A man then places himself inside the basket, with his ass at the opening. Next, the whole basket is covered with horsehide, to resemble a mare, and the man's ass is covered with mare's fuck. This accomplished a genuine horse is led to the contraption; mistaking it for a mare, he fucks it — his prick going up the man's ass. Concurrently the man ass-fucks a small white dog, which he has brought into the basket with him.

36. In a similar basket, decked in cowhide, a man places a woman. He then watches as she is fucked by a bull.

37. A man fucks a cow. The cow conceives and gives birth to a monster. The man then fucks the monster.

38. A man is ass-fucked by a tamed serpent while he himself ass-fucks a cat in a basket.

39. A man fucks a she-donkey while he himself is ass-fucked by a male donkey.*

*An elaborate machine is necessary to this enterprise. We will describe it elsewhere.—D.A.F.S.

40. The same man fucks a goat up the nostrils while the goat licks his balls. Concurrently, his ass is reamed by a second man and his back is flogged by a third.

41. The same man ass-fucks a sheep while a dog reams his ass.

42. The same man ass-fucks a dog, cutting off the head at the moment of orgasm.

43. The same man hires a prostitute to jerk off a donkey. He has a colleague fuck him up the ass while he observes this spectacle.

44. The same man encloses a monkey in a basket and fucks it up the ass.

45. A man engages a procuress to locate girls who are wanted by the police. Fearing that he will turn them over to the authorities, the girls then have no choice but to allow him to whip them violently.

46. A woman with beautiful hair is brought to this man. Pretending to admire the hair, he cuts it off. She cries and her tears so excite him that he ejaculates without even touching his prick.

47. A second of his lovely captives is led into a dark room where the man and several colleagues, pretending to be police officers, talk about different punishments they plan to inflict upon her once she is caught. Finally, the man reaches out and grabs her. Her scream brings him to orgasm — again without any tactile stimulus.

48. A third of his captives is led into an underground vault lit by only one flickering oil lamp, the orange flame of which serves to heighten the gloom. After a moment, the lamp is extinguished; horrible cries and screams and the rattling of chains—all prearranged—are heard. The woman faints, whereupon the man jumps upon her unconscious form and fucks her up the ass.

49. A fourth captive is brought to the same chamber, is stripped and is thrust into a coffin. While a colleague nails the coffin lid in place, the man jerks off to the rhythm of the hammer.

50. A certain duke buys the corpses of recently murdered girls. These he places on a bed covered with black satin sheets, then fondles each body, exploring every crack and crevass of it. Finally, he ass-fucks each dead woman, after which each body is carted away.

51. Another man buys the corpses of a boy and a girl; he sodomizes the former while reaming the ass of the latter.

52. A man brings a young girl into a room filled with wax dummies which look very much like real corpses. Each dummy is "wounded" in some way — one with a knife, the other with a noose, et cetera. The man asks the girl to select one of the depicted means by which she would like to be killed.

53. A man ties a girl face to face with a corpse and whips her until her back is covered with blood.

54. A girl who is menstruating is brought to a cellar where a mischievous libertine waits hidden near a pool of icy water twelve feet across and eight feet deep. The girl is pushed into the water and, when he hears the splash the libertine ejaculates.

55. The same libertine lowers a naked girl into a deep well and shouts down that he is going to bombard her with large stones. He throws in a few chunks of sod to frighten her, then jerks off, dripping his semen onto her head.

56. A pregnant woman is so frightened by threats, curses and floggings that she either aborts on the spot, or does so shortly after she returns home.

57. A girl is locked in a black dungeon, surrounded by cats, rats and mice, and is given to understand that she will remain there for the rest of her life. The libertine responsible for her incarceration then goes to her door every day and masturbates while chatting with her.

58. A man shoves sheafs of straw up a girl's ass, ignites them and watches her buttocks sizzle as the straw burns.

59. A girl is tied to a cross which is suspended from a ceiling; next, she is whipped until her back is raw. Then her captor unties her and throws her out a window. A mattress had been placed beneath the window to break her fall; thus she lands uninjured. When her captor hears her hit the mattress, he ejaculates.

60. A girl is forced to swallow a drug which disorders her imagination and causes her to experience horrible hallucinations. She thinks the room is being flooded, sees water rise, jumps on a chair to avoid being drowned and, at her captor's command, dives head-first into the "water." She is badly injured in her fall to the stone floor, upon seeing which her captor ejaculates.

61. A libertine suspends a girl outside a tower by a rope running through a pulley on the roof. Then he stands at the window outside which the girl is hanging and masturbates while threatening to cut the rope.

62. A man places a charcoal brazier beneath a trapdoor. Then he suspends a girl over the door, holding her in place with cords tied to each arm and each leg. Next he opens the trapdoor, and the girl is scorched with the heat. Then, while fondling his prick, the man begins tugging at one cord, then another; the girl realizes that if any of them break she will fall into the fire. Having sufficiently terrorized her in this manner, the man now puts a large weight on her stomach. Then he jerks off, squirting his jism all over her. This accomplished, he tugs hard at the free ends of all four cords, lifting the girl away from the fire but rupturing her stomach in the process.

63. A girl is bound to a low stool. Then a dagger is suspended from the ceiling by a hair. Its position is such that the blade is directly over her skull; if the

hair breaks, she will be killed instantly. While watching the poor child's anxious contortions, her captor frigs himself. After he comes, he unties her. Then he beats her buttocks with the dagger until they are red with blood and he jerks off again, this time ejaculating on the bloody buttocks.

64. A man kidnaps a novice from a convent and ass-fucks her. When he ejaculates, he fires two pistols so close to her ears that the powder burns her hair.

65. A girl is placed in a torture-chair which is balanced on springs; when she sits, a number of springs release iron rings which bind her tightly in place. Levers and gears then shoot out twenty daggers whose points graze her skin. Her captor, while watching, masturbates, discharging his semen all over her.

66. A girl is carried by an elevator into a small crypt which is hung in black and furnished with a coffin and an assortment of skulls. Six wax dummies, armed with clubs, swords, pistols, sabres, poiniards and lances, seem ready to leap on her. When she faints from her terror, her captor flogs her until she is revived, then ass-fucks her.

67. A girl is led into a room in a tower, where she finds poison and a small dagger on a table. She is told to choose the manner of her death. She selects the poison, which is actually a heavy opiate. During her subsequent incapacitation, her captor ass-fucks her.

68. A girl is laid upon a decapitation block and embuggered. Then, the decapitation procedure commences.

But, as the blade falls, a rope suddenly snatches the girl's body from under it. Her captor ejaculates as the blade sinks three inches into the woodblock.

69. A woman is forced to stand on a stool with a noose around her neck. Her captor sits in an armchair and has the woman's daughter frig him. When he discharges he pulls a string which dislodges the stool from beneath the mother, leaving her hanging. Valets cut the woman down and bleed her with a leech to revive her, unbeknownst to her daughter, who is taken off to bed with the libertine and ass-fucked all night, thinking that her mother has been killed.

70. A libertine holds a girl by her ears and parades her around a room. He ejaculates during the promenade.

71. A man pinches a girl's body, turning her flesh black and blue. However, he spares her breasts.

72. A man pinches and kneads a woman's breasts until they are completely bruised.

73. Another man writes letters and words upon a woman's breasts with a poisoned needle. When her breasts become infected, she suffers considerably.

74. A man drives two thousand pins into the breasts of a woman, ejaculating upon insertion of the two-thousandth.

75. A libertine drives hat-pins into a girl's breasts and buttocks. He ejaculates after the last pin is driven home.

76. A girl is given a great quantity of liquor to drink. While she is drunk, her captor sews up her cunt and asshole. The knave then takes pleasure in watching her nearly collapse with the need to piss and shit, which she cannot do. Finally she breaks the threads with the pressure of the urine and feces.

77. Four men jerk off one another while cuffing and kicking a girl about a room like a football. They discharge after she is felled by their blows.

78. A girl is placed in a pneumatic machine and is alternately deprived of air, then given it. Finally she is released, whereupon her captor brings her to his dining table and eats food only after she has chewed it.

79. The same libertine binds a girl, belly-down, on a dining table and eats a piping hot omelette served upon her buttocks.

80. The same libertine ties a girl's head over a very hot grill and roasts her until she is unconscious.

81. Another man gently and very gradually toasts the skin of a girl's breasts and buttocks, using sulphur-tipped matches.

82. The same man enjoys snuffing out candles over and over again in a girl's ass and cunt.

83. Another man singes a girl's eyelashes. Unable to close her eyes, she no longer can sleep at night.

84. Clapping a pistol to a girl's heart, a libertine forces her to chew and swallow a live coal. He then douches her cunt with alcohol.

85. Four girls are made to dance naked around four pillars, on a path studded with broken glass, sharp metal, pointed tacks, and nails. A man at each pillar lashes each girl as she dances past.

86. A man beats the face of a girl until her nose bleeds; he then continues to punch her until he ejaculates, mixing his semen with the blood on her face.

87. A man pinches a girl with highly heated tongs, shredding her buttocks, vulva and breasts.

88. A man places little mounds of gunpowder between the breasts of a nude girl and sets fire to the mounds.

89. A man inserts a cylinder of gunpowder in a girl's cunt and ignites it. When she explodes he ejaculates.

90. A man pours brandy all over a girl's body and lights it. He ejaculates while watching her burn.

91. The same man gives a girl an enema with boiling oil.

92. After thoroughly whipping a girl's vulva a man thrusts red-hot irons up her cunt and ass.

93. After whipping a pregnant woman, a man tramples upon her until she aborts.

94. A man feigns caresses with a girl while fucking her; but, at the moment of orgasm, he slams the unsuspecting creature's head against a wall. She falls unconscious.

95. Four libertines conduct a "trial" for a girl and "sentence" her to one hundred strokes, twenty-five from each. The first flogs her from the back to the loins, the second from the loins to the calves, the third from the neck to the navel and the fourth from the belly to the shins.

96. Using a pin, a man pricks a girl's eyes, nipples and clitoris.

97. A man pours molten sealing-wax between a girl's buttocks, into her cunt and between her breasts.

98. A man opens the veins of a girl's arm and bleeds her until she faints.

99. A libertine forces a girl to shit for him, then bleeds both her arms. Now and again he stops the operation and flogs her, then reopens the wounds. When she collapses, he experiences his orgasm.

100. A libertine bleeds a girl from all four of her limbs and from her jugular vein. He jerks off while

watching the five fountains of blood.

101. A libertine scratches his initials all over a girl's buttocks and breasts.

102. A man scratches a girl vigorously with a nail, cutting deep wounds into her breasts. He next cauterizes the wounds with a red-hot iron.

103. A man who enjoys girls only with his mouth is bound hand and foot and dressed in a tiger's skin, as if he were a wild animal. He then is frigged, kissed, sucked and reamed — but not permitted to ejaculate. Next a young girl is tied, nude, opposite him. The man's captors then set him free and he leaps on the girl, biting her everywhere, especially on her nipples and on her clitoris. He roars and cries ferociously and ejaculates while shrieking. The girl is then forced to shit and he eats her excrement from the floor.

104. A libertine pulls out a girl's teeth and scratches her gums with heated needles.

105. The same man takes one of the girl's fingers in his hands and snaps it in half.

106. He then flattens one of her feet with a hammer.

107. He then saws off one of her hands at the wrist.

108. While jerking off, a man batters in a girl's front teeth with a hammer.

109. He then amputates one foot with a rusty knife.

110. He then breaks one of her arms while sodomizing her.

111. With a crowbar, he breaks a bone in another woman's leg. He sodomizes her afterwards.

112. He ties a woman atop a step-ladder, her arms bound to her feet. Then he kicks over the ladder, breaking her bones.

113. After other odious acts, the same libertine cuts off one of the girl's ears.

114. He slits her lips and her nostrils.

115. After having sucked and bitten the girl's tongue, he pierces it with a hot iron.

116. He tears the nails from her fingers and toes.

117. He cuts off one of her fingers at the last joint.

118. Fifteen or twenty drops of molten lead are dropped into a girl's mouth and her gums are burned with alcohol.

119. After having a girl lick the shit from his ass with her tongue, a libertine snips off the end of the tongue. Then, he sodomizes the girl.

120. A man uses a corkscrew to bore holes in a girl's flesh: when removed, the device takes with it chunks of flesh as thick as they are deep.

121. The same man transforms a ten-year-old boy

into a eunuch by carving out the youth's genitals.

122. With a pair of scissors, a man cuts off a woman's nipples.

123. A libertine sucks the mouth and tongue of a girl, then he breaks a bottle against her face.

124. A man tears off both of a girl's legs, ties one of her hands behind her back, then gives her a little stick with which to defend herself as he attacks her with a sword, wounding her in many places. He finally ejaculates on her wounds.

125. A man stretches a girl on a cross and breaks her arms and legs.

126. A man uses a pistol to shoot off a girl's nipples.

127. A man has a girl crouch down twenty feet away with her buttocks facing him; he then fires a shot up her ass.

128. Another man whips a pregnant woman's belly until she miscarries.

129. A man ass-fucks a boy of seventeen, then very neatly castrates the youth.

130. A man uses a razor to cut off the clitoris of a young virgin, then fucks her with a hot, iron poker.

131. This same libertine with his bare hands pulls the foetus from the womb of a woman eight months

pregnant.

132. The same knave bores through a pregnant woman's ass to her womb, causing the child to be born anally.

133. Another libertine cuts off a girl's both hands at the wrist, then cauterizes the wounds with a hot iron.

134. The same man pulls out a second girl's tongue by the roots, cauterizing the wound with a hot iron.

135. The same man ass-fucks a third girl while a colleague cuts off one of her legs.

136. A man extracts all of a woman's teeth, replacing them with red-hot nails, which he secures in place with a hammer. This is done after he makes her suck his cock.

137. The same man gouges out a victim's eyes. Then he pricks all her fingers with a needle while his friend, a bishop, ass-fucks her.

138. The same man blinds a victim by pouring molten sealing-wax into her eyes.

139. A libertine slices off a woman's breast, then cooks it on a griddle and eats it.

140. The same man beats and sodomizes another girl, then amputates her buttocks and eats them.

141. He shaves off a third girl's ears.

142. He cuts off a fourth girl's extremities—ten fingers, ten toes, two nipples, her clitoris and the tip of her tongue.

143. A libertine carves away several chunks of a girl's flesh, then roasts them on a spit and invites her to share them with him.

144. The same depraved man amputates the four limbs of a boy, then sodomizes his trunk. Treating the wounds immediately thereafter, he keeps the youth alive for a year during which he sodomizes him continually.

145. A man chains one of a girl's hands to a wall and leaves her without food. Two days later he gives her a large knife and places just out of her reach a heaping array of delicacies. If she wishes to eat, she must cut off her forearm; otherwise she will die of starvation. Her torturer watches her through a window.

146. A man manacles in like fashion a mother and a daughter, so that, in order for both to survive, one must sacrifice a hand. He amuses himself listening to them discuss their situation.

147. A man soundly whips a girl, then plucks out her eyes and places her in a locked room. He tells her that food is in the room if she searches for it. However, he has placed a heated iron plate between the girl and the food. He amuses himself watching her decide whether

to burn herself or perish.

148. A man ties a girl's four limbs to ropes, then, raising and dropping the ropes one at a time, he dislocates all four limbs. The victim never touches the ground throughout the proceedings.

149. A man with a spear inflicts deep wounds on a girl, then pours hot molten lead and boiling pitch into them.

150. The moment a mother gives birth to a child, her libertine captor binds her, hand-and-foot, and ties her child not far away. She must thus watch the child die without being able to help it. Afterwards the libertine flogs the mother, aiming particularly at her cunt, so that his whip strokes slice right into it.

BOOK FOUR: THE MURDEROUS PASSIONS

During the month of February, the narrator is Madame Desranges. She describes one-hundred-and-fifty murderous passions, as follows:

1. A man locks a beggarwoman in a dungeon and leaves her to starve to death. He keeps a close watch on her and frigs himself while observing her torment; however, he does not experience orgasm until the moment of her death.

2. A man keeps a woman in a prison cell, daily diminishing her ration of food until she starves to death. During the period of imprisonment, he collects her feces and has it served to him on a platter each night.

3. A man whose prime pleasure used to be the sucking of saliva from a woman's mouth more recently has developed a taste for imprisoning a woman in a dungeon without food for thirty days, on the last one of which he enters the dungeon and masturbates, ejaculating upon her corpse.

4. A man kills women by forcing them to urinate after days of having been given nothing to drink; eventually blood is called upon to replace urine, and it is in this manner that they expire.

5. The same man flogs a woman, then kills her by refusing to let her go to sleep. At the height of her anguish, he hangs her by her heels from the ceiling; then one of his colleagues probes her throat until she is forced to vomit; the man, meanwhile, lies on the floor beneath her, jerking off and at the same time eating the vomit which falls upon him from above.

6. A man who used to enjoy eating a woman's shit as it emerged from her ass now grows tired of the practice. Blaming the woman for his antipathy, he feeds

her for one month on a diet of only stale bread and cheap wine, as a result of which she dies.

7. A man who is very skillful at fucking and, therefore, in great demand among certain women, invents a deadly poison which he applies to the tip of his prick prior to each session. Generally his partners die at precisely the moment he experiences orgasm.

8. A man who used to enjoy eating a woman's vomit grows tired of the practice and, blaming her, murders her with poison.

9. A man who used to collect shit as it emerged from its owner's ass feels shame as a result of this former behavior. To purge his guilt he injects his former contributors with an enema containing toxic ingredients dissolved in boiling water. They die.

10. A man binds a woman to a revolving stake on which she pivots uninterruptedly until she dies.

11. A man murders a prostitute, then breaks her neck and twists her head around so that he may contemplate her face and her ass.

12. A man abducts women and has them fucked by a stallion. Ordinarily they die.

13. A former sodomite, forced into retirement by impotence, delights in burying girls in mud up to the waist and maintaining them thus until the lower half of the body rots.

14. A man takes such delight in watching a certain

woman's reaction as her clitoris is fondled that he hires
an alternate to continue the work when he tires of it.
The woman is frigged continuously until she dies.

15. A flogger perfects his art to such an extent that
he soon is able to cover every part of a woman's body
with his lashes. On his most skillful days, the woman
dies at the precise moment when the last unmarked
part of her is covered.

16. A man ties a hungry girl by the neck, then places
a sumptous meal before her. If she reaches for the
food, she will strangle; if not she will die of hunger.

17. A man whips a whore about the breast and buttocks so ferociously that she dies.

18. A man poses as a surgeon so that he may recruit
female patients. When he has ten of them, he bleeds
them to death.

19. A man shuts a woman in a steaming bath-house
and watches through a window as she dies of asphyxiation.

20. A man hires a young girl to pretend to be his
mother, wrapping him in a baby blanket and feeding
him horseshit on a spoon. After the meal, he wraps her
in the blanket and smothers her to death.

21. A man binds a girl inside a donkey's untanned
skin in such a manner that only her head is emergent.
Then he feeds her and cares for her until the skin

shrinks, crushing her to death.

22. A man hangs a girl by the feet until she stifles and dies.

23. A man hires a whore, inserts a funnel into her mouth and floods her with liquids until her skin explodes from the pressure.

24. A man buckles a pair of small "Dutch ovens" over a girl's breasts, then lowers her over a stove. She dies as the heat causes her blood literally to boil, clogging the pasages around the heart.

25. A man hangs a girl by the feet over a pond. Then he lowers her, head first, into the water, not pulling her out until she is on the verge of drowning. The dunking is repeated again and again until, finally, the woman swallows enough water to kill her.

26. A man imprisons a girl between two iron slabs. Fires are then lit on opposite sides of the slabs. One fire cooks the girl from the front, the other from behind; she remains in capitvity until the fat on her body melts, at which time, dead, she is "freed."

27. A man imprisons a girl between four mattresses. She suffocates.

28. A man hires a whore. While fucking her up the ass, he touches a pistol to her head. Then, at the moment of his ejaculations, he blows her brains out.

29. A man flings a woman from the top of a high

tower. When she lands with a thud on the sharp gravel below, he ejaculates.

30. A man hires a whore and ties a black silk cord around her neck as he ass-fucks her. He then strangles her at his moment of orgasm.

31. A man used to have a penchant for fucking girls while they slept. He now improves upon this taste: killing them with a large dose of opium, he fucks them during their death-sleep.

32. A man ties a stone around a girl's neck, then throws her into a lake. She drowns.

33. A man pours molten lead into a sleeping girl's ear.

34. A man kills a girl by beating in her temples with a hammer.

35. A man shoves a lightning rod up a woman's ass, then ties her to his roof during a thunderstorm. At a propitious moment, lightning strikes, she is lit up brilliantly for an instant, then her cindered corpse lies black and horrible-looking on the shingles.

36. A man tricks a woman into standing, bent over, in front of a cannon. He then pulls the laniard and the cannonball blows off her ass.

37. A man ties virgins to a wheel and tortures them until they consent to being fucked by him. Then he chokes them to death.

38. A man places a woman in a guillotine. As he frigs himself, he commands his valet to let the blade fall. When her head drops into the basket, he ejaculates.

39. A man kills women on consigning them to a dungeon.

40. A man ties a pregnant woman supine on a stone floor. Then he drops an immense iron weight on her stomach, crushing both her and her foetus in one stroke.

41. A man inserts a long pin into the neck of a girl he is cunt-fucking. She dies at his moment of his orgasm.

42. A man singes the bodies of captive women with the flame from a candle. When they have been tortured sufficiently in this manner, he completes the job by throwing them into a glowing furnace.

43. A man conceals a dagger under his pillow. While fucking a woman, he suddenly unsheathes it and sinks it into her heart. She dies at the moment he ejaculates.

44. A man imbeds a rocket, nose-first, into a girl's cunt. The fuse then is ignited. The rocket ascends, flies around and finally crashes to the earth, all with the girl still attached. She does not die until the moment of impact.

45. The same man stuffs cartridges into each orifice of

a woman's body — the asshole, the cunt, the nostrils,
the ears, the eyes, the mouth, between the breasts, the
armpits, the kneepits, et cetera. Then he lowers her on
pulleys into a fire. All cartridges explode simultaneously. The effect is devastating.

46. A man mixes poison with bathpowder. Girls who
sniff it immediately fall dead.

47. A man flogs a girl's neck and breasts. He then
plunges a crowbar into her throat. It nails her to the
table beneath her, her blood shoots up in a guyser and
she dies writhing on the improvised stake.

48. A man hires a whore, takes her to his barn and
demands that she shit while he watches. When the
enterprise is complete, he complains that her feces was
of insufficient quantity. Then he begins chasing her
about the building with a pitchfork. Hoping to escape,
the naked girl runs up a ladder which appears to lead
to a loft; instead, it leads to a vat of boiling water, into
which she tumbles; her death is the result not only of
scalding but of drowning and asphyxiation as well. Her
tormentor's joy is beyond measure.

49. A man kills his wives — twenty-two, all told — by
poisoning them. He only likes to fuck them in the ass.

50. A man invites thirty girls to a ten-course banquet.
His cooks have been instructed to poison three dishes
in each course, thereby killing the entire assemblage
by the time the meal is finished.

51. A man pretends to be the benefactor of the poor, distributing large quantities of meats and vegetables to them every holiday. No one realizes that the foods are poisoned, killing all who eat them within a week.

52. A man devises a drug which, sprinkled on the ground, will kill whoever walks over it bare-footed. He then goes to the sea and sprinkles wide areas of beach. No one ever learns how the deaths were caused.

53. Another man invents a drug which takes two weeks to kill a person, causing indescribable tortures during the interim. No doctor can diagnose the ailment. The evil alchemist takes keenest pleasure in visiting his victims while they are in the death throes.

54. A third man invents a powder which renders its takers immobile, but very much alive. Deemed dead, the hapless creatures are buried. They do not regain consciousness until they are securely locked in their coffins. After internment, the murderer endeavors to find the exact spot where his victim is buried; there he puts his ear to the ground and listens for screams; if he hears anything, he is ecstatic.

55. A man, highly esteemed because of his political influence, carries with him from banquet to banquet a tube of poisoned powder. With it he murders the hosts, who do not die until they have suffered an intense, two-day-long agony.

56. A man injects poison into nurses' breasts, thereby killing both the nurses and the infants to whom they give suck.

57. A man who used to enjoy receiving in his mouth milk enemas which he had administered to young girls now devises a new passion: he administers enemas of toxic substances which kill by eating away the walls of the intestines, causing horrible pains and spasms.

58. A man delights in setting fire to poorhouses, then watching the inhabitants try — usually unsuccessfully — to escape the flames.

59. A man visits pregnant women, bringing with him a perfume the inhalation of which causes them to abort.

60. A man pretends to be an obstetrician. In this disguise he delivers women's babies, then murders the infants before their mothers' very eyes.

61. An abbot and two laymen kidnap a woman whose pregnancy has entered the ninth month. Then they open her belly, snatch out the child, burn it before its mother's eyes, replace it in the womb with a package of sulphur and quicksilver, set the package afire, restitch the belly, then wait until the mother explodes. While waiting, they jerk each other off.

62. A man hires twenty women to bear him children. Then he ass-fucks each child on his or her fifth birthday, after which he throws the victim into a fire.

63. A man hides some of his jewelry in a servant's

wardrobe, then accuses her of theft. When she is hanged, he stands in the prison courtyard frigging himself beneath his coat while watching the spectacle.

64. A notorious shit-lover designs a special toilet, which he installs in his home. Then he induces guests to sit upon it. Once the intended victim is seated, the seat buckles, give way and drops the sitter into a deep ditch filled with shit, where she is left to die.

65. A man places a girl who cannot swim on a narrow plank which spans a deep vat of boiling water. Then he lights a fire at one end of the plank. As the fire approaches her, she has little choice but to try to crawl to the other side. If, however, she succeeds in crossing the plank without falling into the vat, she is by no means safe, for, unbeknownst to her, the far end of the plank, once her weight is upon it, will collapse, precipitating her into a hole containing a bed of live coals. Watching her struggle futilely to save herself, the man frigs himself industriously.

66. A man kidnaps the most beautiful sixteen-year-old girl he can find. Then, after fastening her head to a spring, he ass-fucks her. When his orgasm approaches, he touches a switch and the spring pulls the girl's head into a machine furnished with steel teeth. The machine then goes into motion and the teeth grind up her head while the man discharges his hot jism into her writhing, twitching ass.

67. A man who is a great connoisseur of asses lures a pretty girl into a canoe into the bottom of which has been drilled a hole. Then he abandons the canoe, which sinks. The girl drowns.

68. A man entices a girl into a specially prepared

room where a trapdoor yields beneath her step, plunging her into a cellar. Here he pounces upon her, plunging a dagger into her breasts, her cunt, her belly, her asshole and so forth. Prior to this, he both ass-fucks and flogs her.

69. A man jams a girl on an untamed and unbroken horse. The horse is then loosened, dragging the girl along a rocky terrain and finally, throwing her over a cliff.

70. A man invents a special bed. Once tucked into it, a girl finds herself catapulted into a brazier of hot coals. When she climbs out of the brazier, the man is standing by with a pitchfork and drives her back onto the coals.

71. On the pretext of bestowing kindness, a man lures a beggarwoman into his home. There he ass-fucks her, then breaks her back and leaves her to die in a dungeon.

72. A man drugs a girl who is asleep in her own bedroom, the window of which is but a few feet above the ground. He then takes her to another room, identical to her own in every respect except that is in a tower some several score feet above ground. Next, the diabolical libertine sets fire to some rubbish outside the door. Awakened, the girl leaps out the window — which she believes is safe — and lands in a blooded heap upon the murderous rocks far below. His sole satisfaction is derived from watching her die; he does not molest her sexually in any manner.

73. A man daily removes a pea-sized morsel of flesh

from a girl's body. The wounds are not dressed, and so she dies, figuratively speaking, over a low fire.

74. A man bleeds women one ounce per day until they expire.

75. A man jabs a woman's buttocks with daggers, leaving the weapons in her flesh like pins in a pincushion. Then he amputates her arms and legs and watches her as she bleeds to death.

76. A man hires a giant to hold little girls (all virgins) over a charcoal brazier, head-first, until the poor children expire from the heat.

77. A man singes the breasts and buttocks of a girl wtih a match. Then he coats her body with sulphur-coated slivers, lights them and watches her suffer. The patient lives six hours, during all of which the man is in ecstasy.

78. A man inserts a funnel into a woman's mouth and pours molten lead down her throat.

79. A man twists a woman's fingers and toes, breaking them; then he snaps all her limbs, rips out her tongue and gouges out her eyes. This accomplished, he abandons her to die.

80. A man ties a naked boy to a cross, binding him with cords, and leaves him as food for ravens.

81. A man fastens a woman to a wall, then pricks her flesh with pins. The blood attracts flies; it takes perhaps a week.

82. A man who is a passionate admirer of asses brings a girl to an underground cave and leaves her food for three days. He spends a week embracing her ass before leaving her to her destruction.

83. A physician cuts out a living girl's heart, then fucks the warm hole which that organ occupied. This enterprise complete, he replaces the heart and sews up the wound.

84. A second physician chops off a girl's hand, sucks the marrow from her bone, fills the bone with molten leads and sews the hand back on,

85. A man uses an ingenious machine to chop a girl into small pieces. This is a Chinese torture.

86. A man impales a girl's cunt with the point of a pick, then wedges the pick handle in a vise so that she sits on her perch as if astride a horse. Next he ties a cannonball to each of her ankles; when the cannonballs are dropped to the floor, the pick tears into the girl's intestines and stomach, killing her.

87. A man flogs the skin off a girl, then soaks her in a strong lye solution.

88. A man first severs a girl's fingers; then he plucks

off gobs of her flesh with a pair of red-hot tongs. All told, he whittles away piecemeal at the poor child's body for five days before she dies.

89. A man slices off a girl's breasts and buttocks and eats them. Then he dresses the wounds with alcohol, which burns the flesh so violently that there soon is little left to her but her bones.

90. A man cooks a little girl in a double boiler.

91. A man roasts alive a girl on a spit. Before this enterprise, he ass-fucks her.

92. A man fastens a little girl to a wall by shoving a spear through her ass, out the opposite side just below her tits, then into the wall. Then he leaves her to die while he studies her contortions.

93. A man attaches a woman to a wheel, sets it in motion and watches while she is stretched to death.

94. A man ties a girl's arms and legs to four saplings which have been bent toward the center of a circle. Then he releases the trees, which, when they spring erect, neatly quarter the girl.

95. A man suspends a girl from a machine which repeatedly lowers her into and lifts her out of a fire. The enterprise is continued until she dies.

96. A man covers a girl with several pounds of sul-

phur, then uses her for a torch.

97. A man, by reaching bare-handed into their ass-holes, rips out the intestines of a boy and a girl. Next he shoves the boy's intestines up the girl's ass and the girl's intestines up the boy's ass. This accomplished, he ties them back to back and watches them perish.

98. A man roasts several girls upon a grill, turning them over and over again with a giant spatula until they are well done.

99. A man suspends a woman in the air by means of four strings tied one to each of her limbs. Then, directly beneath her asshole, he places a sharp pike. Next he cuts the strings and she falls. The pike goes in all the way to her lungs.

100. A man cuts steaks from a girl's buttocks and eats them. When he runs out of edible flesh, he has her sandwiched between two heavy planks and sawed in two.

101. A man kidnaps a brother and sister. Then he tells the brother than the only way the youth can save his own life is by fucking his sister and immediately there-after strangling her. The boy agrees and begins to do so. While brother and sister cunt-fuck, their captor ass-fucks both of them, then withdraws. Next the broth-er strangles the sister as planned. However, he is not spared; rather, his captor pulls a string, releasing a trapdoor through which both the brother and the dead sister fall into an immense charcoal brazier, where their bodies are promptly burned to ashes.

102. A man forces a father to cunt-fuck the father's

daughter while their captor watches. Then the captor ass-fucks her while the father holds her. Next, the captor informs the father that the girl must perish in one of two ways: (a) the father may strangle her, in which event her death may be quick and merciful, or (b) the captor will strangle her, but only after forcing her to undergo the most ignominious atrocities, all of which the father will be made to witness. Rather than submit his daughter to these frightful tortures, the father agrees to strangle her with a noose of black silk; but, while he is preparing the noose, he is seized by the captor and bound to a stake; then, before his eyes, his daughter is flayed alive, rolled upon burning iron nails and cast into a brazier. This accomplished, the captor strangles the father and dumps him into the brazier also.

103. An enthusiastic ass-lover kidnaps a mother and daughter. He then tells the daughter that the only way the mother's life may be spared is if the daughter consents to the amputation of both her own hands. The little girl agrees, whereupon both are severed at the wrists. Next, the kidnapper places her on a stool and ties a noose around her neck. Then he brings the other end of the noose to the mother, who is in an adjacent room, and orders her to pull. The mother, in pulling, unwittingly chokes her hand-less daughter to death. The kidnapper then brings the mother to view the daughter's corpse. As she looks at it in horror, the mother is killed by a blow from an axe, which is sunk into the back of her skull.

104. A man kidnaps a mother and her son. Then he tells the mother that the only way she may spare her own life is to kill the boy. If she refuses, he kills the boy before her eyes. If she consents, she is tied to her son's corpse and left to die.

105. A man ass-fucks two sisters. Then he binds them to a machine which consists of two gears which turn into each other. Next he fastens a dagger to each girl's chest. When the machine is put into operation, the girls — fastened to the gears — turn into one another, each imbedding her dagger into her sister's heart.

106. A man locks a mother and her four daughters in a room with five daggers. Then he gives them nothing to eat for five days. On the fifth day they finally surrender to temptation and begin carving each other up for food. The mother is the last to die.

107. A man kidnaps two pregnant girls and ties them, facing each other, to steel plates. Great pressure is then brought to bear on the opposite sides of the plates, squeezing them together like the jaws of a vice. The two girls and their unborn children are crushed to a pulp.

108. Mr. X persuades Mr. Y that the latter's mistress has been fucking Mr. Z. Then he brings Y to an obscurely lit room where someone lies asleep on a bed. The sleeper, says X, is none other than Z — after saying which he immediately vanishes. Whereupon Y, infuriated, plunges the dagger into the sleeping person's heart. The room then is flooded with light and Y recognizes his victim not as Z but as . . . his mistress! No sooner has recognition dawned upon him than X shoots him with a pistol.

109. After embuggering a boy, a man shoves the barrel of a shotgun up the lad's ass and pulls the trigger. The gun and the villain's prick discharge simultaneously.

110. A libertine forces a young husband to watch the

latter's wife being mutilated. Next he compels the hapless spouse to eat her buttocks, tits and heart. When this demand has been satisfied, the libertine fastens the husband to a wall with a spear.

111. A man cuts off a boy's balls, then serves them to him in a ragout. After the youth has eaten them, the man stuffs his emptied scrotum with sulphur, causing insufferable pain. Then he ass-fucks him until he dies.

112. A man drives a spear through a girl's asshole and out the top of her head.

113. While ass-fucking a girl, a man slices open the top of her head and fills the cavity with molten lead.

114. A man ties a young boy to a revolving wheel in such a manner as to expose the youth's buttocks to a mechanical whip. Then he has his table set beneath the wheel and observes the spectacle of mechanized flogging at dinner time every day for a week until the youth dies.

115. A man flogs a young boy, smears his body with honey, then watches as flies gather.

116. A man nails a boy's feet to one post and his hands to another. Then he slices off the youth's prick.

117. The same man arms another boy with only a light stick, then thrusts him into a lion's cage. The animal immediately pounces upon the youth and devours

him. The libertine discharges as the last of the boy's body vanishes in the lion's mouth.

118. Clothed in a mare's skin, his asshole smeared with mare's-jism, a small boy is surrendered to a horse. The enterprise kills him.

119. A young boy is placed in a machine which stretches his limbs, dislocating each joint. Then his ribs are broken individually; next, his pelvis and spine. When finally all bones are broken, he dies.

120. A man hires a pretty girl to suck the cock of a young boy until he has been drained completely dry. Given no nourishment, the lad eventually dies.

121. A surgeon performs four operations in a single day. He intentionally botches them all, causing his patients to die.

122. A man shaves off a boy's cock and balls, then, with a red hot iron, hollows out a cunt where the genitals had been. While fucking this newly-manufactured orifice, he strangles the boy.

123. A man scratches a boy with an iron comb, then rubs him with alcohol. He repeats this over and over until the boy dies.

124. A man ass-fucks a father while the father's two children are forced to watch. When the man achieves orgasm, he simultaneously kills both children, stabbing the first with one hand while strangling the second with the other.

125. A man assembles six women who are in the

eighth month of pregnancy and ties them in a circle, back to back, with their bellies prominently thrust forward. Then he splits the belly of A with a dagger; pierces B's with a lance; kicks C's one hundred times; deflates D's with a club; smashes E's with a sledgehammer, and destroys F's with a crowbar.

126. A diabolical libertine kidnaps two women and locks them in a dungeon. Then he says: "Deny God and religion if you want to live." Now, both women have already been cautioned by the libertine's valet that they would be threatened in this manner and have been told that the way to save themselves is by refusing to give in to the blasphemous demands. Therefore, Woman A, hearing the order, remains mute — whereupon the libertine touches a pistol to her temple, pulls the trigger and blows her brains out, declaring solemnly: "There's one for God." Next, Woman B., struck by the example of the first, assents to the proposal and renounces both God and religion in the strongest terms — whereupon the libertine likewise blows her brains out, declaring: "And there's one for the Devil."

127. A man stages a dance in a large ballroom. As the couples move about on the floor, he releases a cord which causes the ceiling to collapse, killing them all.

128. A libertine locks three pregnant women in a dungeon without food. When they give birth, he ties their children around their necks and says: "There's your food."

129. A libertine ass-fucks a young man while the latter's mistress is forced to watch, then ass-fucks the mistress while the young man is forced to watch. This

accomplished, he compels them to cunt-fuck, during the course of which he drives a spear through bodies, fastening them to the floor, where they are left to die.

130. A man amputates an arm or a leg from each of six prostitutes, then throws the dismembered whores into a pond. As they thrash about, he offers them an iron pike, but it is heated red-hot. They cannot hold on to it, so they drown.

131. A man invents a poison which, mixed with water in a reservoir, wipes out an entire city of people.

132. A man locks three women and their children in an iron cage. Next he lights a fire beneath the cage. As the floor heats, the captives dance about in pain, and take their children in their arms, but finally all die.

133. A man seals a pregnant woman inside a barrel the walls of which are studded with sharp spikes. Then he rolls the barrel down a hill, killing her.

134. A libertine studs the ground around a tower with sharp steel rods. Then he and his asociates pitch out the window several children whom the libertine already has ass-fucked. The children are killed when impaled. The libertine's biggest thrill comes when he is splashed with their blood.

135. A man builds a huge bonfire. Then he ties bundles of straw around the bodies of six naked, pregnant women and throws them into it. As the women run out of the fire trying to save themselves, he drives them

back in with a pitchfork. Finally, when all six are half-roasted, he pulls a cord and the floor on which the fire has been built gives way; the women tumble into a large vat of boiling water, wherein they eventually die.

.136. A cruel libertine assembles a family of beggars over a mine and watches as they are blown to bits.

137. A man wishes to combine the sins of sodomy, murder, incest, rape, sacrilege and adultery, so he has himself ass-fucked by his bastard son (who uses a Host as a shield) while simultaneously he himself rapes his married niece, whom he later kills.

138. A man strangles a mother while ass-fucking her, then turns over the corpse and cunt-fucks it. Next he murders her daughter with a knife, slashing off both breasts and ass-fucking the corpse. Finally, he hurls both cadavers into a fire and jerks off while watching them burn.

139. A man lines up a circle of nine women and sets off fireworks in each one's ass. Then he ties two pregnant women together in the shape of a ball and fires them from a cannon.

140. A man locks two naked pregnant women in a room, equips them with knives, then trains a rifle on them and commands that they fight, promising to shoot them dead if they dally. When one finally is killed, he rushes into the room and attacks the other with a sword, disembowelling her and burning her entrails with alcohol.

141. A man binds a pregnant woman to a torture wheel beneath which is bound the girl's mother, her

head flung back, her mouth forced open and ready to receive whatever blood, excretions, et cetera, flow from the daughter's corpse.

142. A man cunt-fucks a girl on a bed of short-stemmed nails, then flips her over and ass-fucks her. Next he sandwiches her between two planks studded with longer nails and she is stabbed in a multitude of places. The procedure is carried out slowly, giving her ample opportunity to experience pain before she dies.

143. A man nails a pregnant woman to a table, driving one spike into each eye, one through the mouth, two others through the breasts and a last one through her cunt. Then he burns her nipples and her clitoris with a taper, after which he breaks both her legs and drives pins into each of her knees. Finally he hammers an enormous spike through her navel, killing both mother and child.

144. A man binds two beautiful girls mouth-to-mouth and places by their side an excellent meal. Since neither can reach the food, they began to bite and eat at each other when the pangs of hunger are felt. Eventually one collapses of starvation and their captor kills the second.

145. A man binds two pregnant women to the ends of a pair of long tilting poles. Then, inserting the opposite ends of the poles into a cleverly-designed machine, he has the women pounded against each other until both die.

146. A man binds six pregnant women into a cage constructed of iron hoops. Little by little the hoops contract until the six women and their children are crushed. While this enterprise goes on, their captor

slices off the women's buttocks.

147. A man suspends three girls over three holes: A hangs by her tongue over a very deep well; B by her tits over a charcoal brazier, and C, whose scalp has been loosened, by her hair over a pit studded with iron rods. Eventually the weight of their bodies cause the girls to fall free; thus, A's tongue is torn from her mouth, B's tits from her chest and C's scalp from her head.   .

148. By means of a hollow tube, a mouse is introduced into a girl's cunt. The tube is then withdrawn, the cunt sewn up and the mouse, unable to escape, devours the girl's insides.

149. A girl is forced to swallow a snake, which feeds upon her entrails.

150. This, the last passion, shall be termed The Devil's Passion, or The Passion of Hell. It merits description at some length:

A certain nobleman, aged forty is so wealthy that he has no business concerns and thus spends all his time gratifying his passions. He has the prick of a stallion — twelve inches long (when erect) and nine inches in circumference — and he exercises it at debauches staged every fortnight in a stone house on the outskirts of Paris. There are no walls inside the house: the whole is but one spacious room, the floor of which is covered entirely with mattresses. Upon entering the room, one sees a single window — a large, casement type which opens to a cellar thirty feet below. There is also an attic, access to which is gained through a trapdoor.

For each of his fortnightly orgies, the nobleman requires fifteen virgins who have passed their fourteenth

birthday but have not yet reached their eighteenth. In
the interest of obtaining such, he employs a fleet of six
procurers, who roam about the country, sparing neither
effort nor expense in recruiting victims. Those abducted
are imprisoned in a convent near Paris. (The convent
is completely under the nobleman's control.)

On the evening before each orgy, the nobleman goes
to the convent and examines personally the current
stock. The girls must be absolutely perfect; the slightest flaw means rejection, and rejected girls are killed
instantly. When finally fifteen have been found acceptable, they are brought to the stone house. All are stripped naked. Then the nobleman conducts a preliminary
screening: he touches, fondles, feels, probes, prods and
experiments with the luscious bare bodies; he scrutin-
izes every crack and crevass; he sucks mouths, licks
cunts, reams assholes and has each girl shit into his
mouth. Finally, as a result of this inspection, he decides
the order in which he would like the fifteen to entertain him on the following night. The girls then are assigned numbers from one to fifteen and the nobleman
brands the number of each upon her bare left tit, just
below the shoulder.

The following night finds the girls waiting in the attic. The nobleman summons girl number one and she
is dropped through the trapdoor into his lair. He catches
her in his arms, bounces her about on the mattress-
covered floor several times, then takes up a switch and
begins to beat her delicious buttocks. When the buttocks are red, he embuggers her; however, he does not
ejaculate; rather, he withdraws his prick, still rock-hard,
and moves on to the next phase of activity — cunt-
fucking her. While he cunt-fucks, the nobleman beats
at her back with a cane; then, as during the sodomi-
zation, he withdraws before ejaculating. Now the girl,
having been devirginated in both holes, is whipped
thoroughly, not only upon the back, but about the
thighs, belly, breasts, shoulders and face. Finally the

nobleman picks up a spear and stabs her six times with it, once in each buttock, once in each tit and once in each side of the belly. Now weakened from loss of blood, the girl stands dizzily in the center of the room while the nobleman ties a ribbon around her neck; this ribbon is to advise his colleagues in the cellar below which of fifteen supplementary tortures for which to prepare her. Once the ribbon has been affixed, the nobleman places the girl before the casement window and gives her a vicious kick in the ass, sending her tumbling through the window and into the cellar.

The same licentiousness is wreaked upon each of the remaining girls, who are summoned from the attic one by one. Thus the nobleman acquires a total of thirty cherries — fifteen ass-cherries and fifteen cunt-cherries —and his real fun is yet to begin.

The cellar into which the girls tumble from the casement window is equipped with fifteen ingenious torture machines, each of which is presided over by a swarthy executioner; all executioners are dressed in black and wear masks and demonic insignia. As each girl falls in, she is seized by the appropriate executioner, who recognizes her by the ribbon tied about her neck, and is fastened to the appropriate torture machine. However, the machines are not put into action until the nobleman arrives after his inspection of the fifteenth girl.

The nobleman, almost needless to say, enters the cellar in a state of indescribable excitation; his prick is virtually glued against his belly, so hot is it from having plowed thirty theretofore virginal canals; he is foaming at the mouth.

Taking a look about the cellar and seeing that everything is in order, he gives the signal. Then all the torture machines are set in motion at once, and the executions proceed simultaneously with a great clatter and horrendous screams.

The torture machines are as follows:

(1) A girl is strapped to a wheel which rotates uninterruptedly against an outer circle studded with razors and nails. These sharp devices scratch, tear and slice the unfortunate girl everywhere, but since the wounds are not deep, she lives for at least two hours before bleeding to death.

(2) A girl is stretched taut by pulleys attached to her arms and legs, then lowered to a position two inches above a red-hot iron plate; she slowly melts.

(3) A girl is attached by the waist to a burning iron rod; her limbs are clamped in manacles which are twisted and turned, thereby dislocating her joints.

(4) A girl is suspended over a charcoal brazier by cords attached to her arms and legs. The cords are pulled tighter and tighter until these limbs are amputated, at which time her trunk falls into the brazier.

(5) A cast-iron pot, cooked until it is red hot, is fitted over a girl's head. It is large enough that it does not touch her skin; thus the skull slowly melts and the head is grilled, but she retains consciousness to the very end.

(6) A girl is chained inside a vat of oil. Then a fire is lit beneath the vat, bringing the liquid to a slow boil.

(7) A girl is strapped before a mechanical bow which six times a minute shoots small arrows into her body. The arrows are treated chemically in such a fashion that none will go into the back of another, but rather each will seek out a fresh patch of skin; thus, the process continues until she is completely and flawlessly feathered.

(8) A girl is very slowly lowered, feet-first, into a vat of molten ʼead.

(9) A girl is suspended over a charcoal brazier by

four pulleys attached to her arms and legs. Then her executioner pricks every inch of her body with a red-hot iron goad.

(10) A girl is chained to a pillar under a large glass bell. Then twenty hungry reptiles are set free; they devour her alive.

(11) A girl is chained by one hand to a rafter, then a heavy cannonball is attached to each of her feet. Eventually the weight of the cannonballs causes her hand to be severed, at which time she falls into a furnace.

(12) A girl is hung from a rafter by a hook driven through her mouth and out the back of her neck. Then a deluge of burning pitch is poured down her throat.

(13) A girl's flesh is opened; her nerves are plucked out and tied into knots; then nails are driven into her bones.

(14) A girl is alternately torn with red-hot tongs and whipped upon her ass and cunt with martinets whose steel tips have been dipped in alcohol. Intermittently she is also scratched with burning iron-pronged rakes.

(15) A girl is poisoned by a drug which eats away, acid-like, her entrails, hurling her into frightful convulsions. Death does not come for hours, and throughout she is tortured with iron rods, hot lead, nails, rakes, et cetera.

Once the torture machines have been set into motion, the nobleman strides around the cellar, first looking in on this enterprise, then looking in on that, and so on. As he strides about, he shouts the most outrageous blasphemies — for example, "May the leprous prick of Lazarus squirt come all over your mother's face." With each moment, his passion increases until finally he can no longer contain himself (or his jism). Dropping into an armchair, he summons two lackeys who suck him off, one on each ball while his cock rests between their faces. This causes him to have the most tremendous orgasm, which is accompanied by shouts like the bellows of a bull and by blasphemies the peers of which have never been heard on earth, in heaven or in hell; the volume of his cries is such that he drowns out the clamoring of the fifteen girls being tortured. When his orgasm is complete, the nobleman leisurely contemplates the torture machines again. He does this until the last of the girls has died and been buried. Then he leaves the stone house for another fortnight, returning to Paris a happy and a tired man.

* * *

AFTERWORD

And now, dear reader, you have concluded our tales of the school of libertinage. It is your author's hope that you found gratification therein and that you will put the book down having learned a not inconsiderable lesson.

Would you scorn our libertines for practicing this or that vice? Well, they likewise scorn you for practicing this or that virtue. In the last analysis, it matters not a jot to anyone — least of all to Nature, who, in supplying us with our tastes, could not fail to realize that we would act upon them.

Does this shock you, oh virtuous people?! Does this burn those ears of yours which, from infancy, have been assailed with the fables of the Church? Well, go in peace: if those absurdities which you have been taught are true; if, as you have been told, there is a hell wherein shall be punished the perpetrators of vice, then, no doubt, we shall burn there; but, as Blangis might have put it, a hell inhabited by those of our stripe is, all its tortures notwithstanding, infinitely preferable to a heaven occupied by the monotonous creatures whom we find held up to us as examples of virtue.

Therefore, ye virtuous, go your way in comfort; hark unto the words of your crucified leader, who said, if the message has been transmitted to me accurately, "Virtue is its own reward." As for we of voluptuous bent, we find our rewards in vice, and if there be future punishments due, they shall be readily accepted by all libertines, not the least of whom is your humble servant,

— DONATIEN ALPHONSE FRANCOIS DE SADE
Bastille, 1785

THE END

DIALOGUE BETWEEN
A PRIEST AND A DYING MAN

PRIEST: In the name of the Father, and of the Son, and of the Holy Ghost, amen. The fatal hour now has come when at last the scales of delusion must fall from the eyes of man; when at last the errors and vices of a lifetime must be recognized. Tell me, my son: Do you repent the ignominious sins into which weakness and human frailty have led you?

DYING MAN: Yes, my friend, I do indeed repent.

PRIEST: Then I rejoice for you. Your repentance will provide you with the key to Heaven — once, of course, your sins are absolved through the most holy sacrament of pennance.

DYING MAN: I'm afraid I don't understand you, my friend — not any more than you understand me.

PRIEST: I understand you completely.

DYING MAN: To the contrary; you understand me not at all. You see, I believe I was created — by Nature; by a Force; by "God," if that's the term you prefer — with strong passions; with sharp tastes. And I believe that the sole reason for which I was placed upon this earth was to satisfy these passions and tastes. Therefore, what I repent is not my sins but the fact that I made only modest use of the "sinful" faculties with which I was provided; had I been truly devout, I would have satisfied them to the fullest, and this I did not do: misled by your absurd dogmas, confused by your inane sophistries, I picked only an occasional apple when I might have harvested an entire orchard. This is what I regret, my friend, and this is my only regret.

PRIEST: But your reasoning is fallacious. You attribute to Nature what are merely the products of your corrupted flesh. God did not create you for these things . . .

DYING MAN: Please, my friend; I am a dying man: do not add to my miseries with sophistical rhetoric. If you must talk to me, at least have the kindness to observe the fundamental principles of logic. For example, define your terms: what do you mean by "god," and what by "corrupted flesh?"

PRIEST: Why, God is the Master of the universe, of course. The Author of all being. He who created everything, and without Whom there is nothing. He Who maintains all existence through the mere fact of His existence . . .

DYING MAN: He sounds like quite a man. Strange, isn't it, that someone so powerful would make the mistake of creating a corrupted flesh?

PRIEST: But, don't you see, that's part of His Divine Love for us! What glory would men have — what good would they deserve — if they didn't earn it by the use of their free will? Could a man earn the right to Heaven if there were not the possibility of doing Good and avoiding Evil?

DYING MAN: In other words, your creator made his mistakes deliberately — in order to test his creations?

PRIEST: He didn't make mistakes, my son. He merely gave man the right — the privilege — of making a choice.

DYING MAN: But why bother? If this "god" is as almighty as you say, and if he wanted man to be good, why didn't he just create him good? Why go through all the other machinations?

PRIEST: Ah, my son: who is there among us mortals to fathom the Mind of God? How can we, with our finite intelligence, grasp the Infinite Intelligence behind the Scheme of Things?

DYING MAN: Stop, my friend, before I vomit. You are multiplying causes and confusing effects; creating a second problem because you can't solve the first. All the wonders which you attribute to your "god" may merely be the result of accident; the result of physical laws which your logic and your mathematics are not sufficiently sophisticated to define. Perfect your reasoning processes, advance your mathematics; you'll soon have no need for your god.

PRIEST: You are a wretch. You are blind. I took you for merely a sinner, but you are worse: you have shut your heart to Truth. I have nothing more to say to you; there is no restoring hearing to the deaf and sight to the blind.

DYING MAN: Hold, my friend: you speak of deafness, of blindness; how so? It is you who magnifies; you who complicates; you who piles errors one atop the other. I merely shift; examine; dissect. Now tell me: who is blind and deaf?

PRIEST: *Satan! Satan! Satan!* The Word of God defiled in such a manner. *Oh, Father, forgive this wretch; let me suffer in his stead, that he might be saved.* Tell me, my son: do you not believe in God at all?

DYING MAN: No — and for a very good reason: it is impossible to believe in what one cannot understand. And you, preacher: I defy you to profess faith in this "god" the ways of whom you admit your finite intelligence cannot grasp, if you cannot understand him, you cannot prove his existence; and if you cannot prove his existence, you are either a fool or a madman to believe in him.

PRIEST: But I *can* prove his existence. Surely you are familiar with St. Thomas Aquinas' argument from casuality: every effect must have a cause, and the first cause must be supreme . . .

DYING MAN: Oh, yes, I've heard that tired old argument many times — but it is predicated on the fallacy that certain "truths" are self-evident. Rubbish, my friend. Nothing is self-evident. *Prove* to me that matter is inert and I'll concede that there must have been a "prime mover." *Prove* that Nature is not self-sufficient and I'll grant that she is ruled by a higher force. But, unless you can prove these things, expect no belief on my part.

PRIEST: But what of the order in the universe? You observe the well-regulated movements of the sun. Surely you don't think this came about by accident.

DYING MAN: I observe the sun, yes — and I accept its existence, but its movements do not amaze me; the operation is entirely mechanical. True, I do not know the specific mechanics. However, this does not mean that they cannot be known. As I have said, perfect your reasoning processes, advance your mathematics. Therein lies the understanding of this mystery; not in your "god" — he is merely a glorification of the mystery, not an explanation of it.

PRIEST: Then what of the other mysteries of life? Surely you don't regard them all as problems in mathematics.

DYING MAN: Mysteries? At this time, my friend, when my soul stands in need of calm enlightenment, please refrain from torturing me with dogmatic riddles. They only irritate me.

PRIEST: You speak of your soul, my son. Do you realize what will happen to your soul after you die?

DYING MAN: I am not afraid. My soul and I have always been the best of friends.

PRIEST: Then do what is right for your soul: atone for your sins.

DYING MAN: Sins? What are sins? At times I am moved to perform good actions, at times evil ones. Nature has a need for both. It is not up to me to question my own passions, but merely to respond as best I can to Nature's varying and occasionally contradictory needs.

PRIEST: And so you conclude that whatever exists is therefore necessary.

DYING MAN: That is correct.

PRIEST: But if everything is necessary, it must be regulated.

DYING MAN: Perhaps. Let us say that I accept your premise for the sake of argument.

PRIEST: Well, if it must be regulated, what can regulate it but the omnipotent and omniscient hand of God?

DYING MAN: I disagree. Would you say that gunpowder must ignite when you touch a flame to it?

PRIEST: Of course.

DYING MAN: And is that flame omnipotent and omniscient?

PRIEST: Certainly not.

DYING MAN: Then, is it not possible that events came about by themselves — without any assistance from your "god" — and that therefore behind all things is a "primary cause" which acts with no reason whatsoever?

PRIEST: What are you trying to prove?

DYING MAN: Simply that if natural effects have natural causes, there is no need of this "god" whom you have invented to explain them. As I have shown you, he cannot be described by the senses. Therefore he is quite useless to the working of Nature, and I must conclude that, being superfluous, he is nothing but a product of your imagination.

PRIEST: Well, I can see that you insist upon renouncing the road to salvation. Since I can be of no further service, I shall leave you to contemplate the Hell which awaits you.

DYING MAN: Hold, my friend. I've waited all my life for the opportunity to discuss my thoughts on these matters without the fear of your inquisitors' torments. Do not be so heartless as to deny me that opportunity now that it has finally come.

PRIEST: What is there to discuss once you have refused to accept the basic premises upon which philosophy is based?

DYING MAN: I have a question to ask you. Let us suppose that I were weak and foolish enough to accept the existence of this being you call "god." How would you suggest I worship him? Should I accept the reveries of Confucius or the follies of Brahma? Should I prostrate myself before the great snake of the Africans, or should I join the Peruvians in their adoration of the sun? Or would you recommend one of the so-called "heresies" — perhaps that of Luther, or of Calvin, or of Huss?

PRIEST: Don't you know my answer?

DYING MAN: If I can guess it, you are being quite egotistical.

PRIEST: Egotistical, my son? No, altruistic: it is out of love for you that I want you to share my beliefs.

DYING MAN: You could not love either of us if you would foist upon him such patent nonsense.

PRIEST: You call it nonsense. But what of Jesus Christ? Can you deny the miracles which He had performed?

DYING MAN: My friend, Jesus Christ was nothing more than a vulgar sleight-of-hand artist, an arrant fraud.

PRIEST: *Oh, Merciful Heaven!* I can only marvel that we have not yet been struck down by a bolt of lightning.

DYING MAN: There will be no lightning, my friend. All around us will remain peaceful and quiet. We are free to continue our discussion.

PRIEST: I will not be a party to any discussion in which Our Lord and Redeemer, Jesus Christ, is blasphemed.

DYING MAN: Then I shall bow to your idiosyncrasies and blaspheme no more. But let me say this: if your "god" really existed, as you are gullible enough to believe, he could not have selected a less persuasive ambassador than the man from Nazareth.

PRIEST: But what of the prophecies? The miracles? The martyrs? Don't they persuade you?

DYING MAN: They persuade me only that your entire creed is but a mammoth hoax. You ask me to accept the prophecies as proof. What could be less convincing a proof than that which has not yet been proved itself?! Before I could accept a prophecy as valid proof, I would have to be sure that the prophet had actually pronounced it; but the only testimony to this is that of certain witnesses — namely your Synoptics — whose objectivity is certainly open to question. Furthermore, what evidence is there that these prophecies preceded the events to which they pertained? No evidence whatsover. Perhaps the prophecies persuade *you* that Christ is divine; to me they merely suggest that certain writers had a convenient lapse of memory on the matter of dates.

PRIEST: And the mircales?

DYING MAN: Bah! Charlatans have always performed them and imbeciles have always been duped by them. No doubt the first shipbuilder was accepted by some as a miracle-worker; likewise the inventor of gunpowder and, if we care to go back that far, his ancestor who discovered fire. You define a miracle as a phenomenon which overcomes the laws of Nature, but who can say where Nature ends and miraculousness begins? Like the fire and gunpowder and the ship, today's miracle is tomorrow's routine convenience.

PRIEST: And the martyrs? Do they likewise fail to move you?

DYING MAN: Surely this is the weakest of your arguments. To manufacture martyrs all you need is revolution on one side and resistance on the other. Stir men up; pit them against each other; then, when the corpses have piled up, call those in your ranks martyrs and those in the enemy ranks infidels.

PRIEST: I can see that there is no way to move you. You remain obstinate to the very end. I pity you.

DYING MAN: Ah, my friend. Don't pity me. Pity yourself, for it is you who suffers the clouded vision, you who needs to fabricate mysterious divinities to explain away your insecurities. Be honest with yourself: if your "god" really did exist, would he need miracles, martyrs and prophecies to champion his cause? Of course not. He would write his laws across the heart of every man, and all would be moved to love and serve him in the same manner; they would be as incapable of resisting his graces as they are now incapable of going without food and sleep.

PRIEST: But you reason this way with only *finite* intelligence. Who can fathom the Divine Will?

DYING MAN: Bah, preacher. Bah. Is this the only defense you can offer? You insult your "god" more with your insipid arguments than I insult him with my blasphemies. I merely fail to believe; but you have the impudence to identify yourself as one of his missionaries, then to argue his existence on the basis of myths which would be transparent to an alert ten-year-old. You boast that you have the One, True Faith, and yet you know as well as I that nine-tenths of the world's peoples have never even heard of it. Be rational: your Jesus is no better than the Jew's Moses, and Moses is no better than the Arab's Mohammed, and all three of them are no better than the Chinaman's Confucious — who at least had the merit of being amusing while all the others were interminable bores. Religious leaders, they called themselves. But philosophers scoffed at them, thinking men spurned them and the law — if there were law, and not merely legislation — should have exterminated them.

PRIEST: If you accept the traditional histories, you'll agree that the law exterminated at least one.

DYING MAN: Yes, and he got what he deserved — but not soon enough. If the leaders of Jerusalem were wise and just they would have done away with Christ long before he was able to cause all that trouble.

PRIEST: You speak of justice. Don't you think that justice demands an afterlife where good will be rewarded and evil punished? And don't you fear the treatment which justice will demand in your case?

DYING MAN: There is nothing to fear, for the worst that can possibly happen to me is the end of my conscious existence — and, while this is an unpleasant prospect to contemplate, it certainly is no cause for fear. Oh, I know your theories of Heaven and Hell; but these are the fabrications of pride, not reason; a rational man can see that there is neither creation nor annihilation, but merely transformation: today I am a man, tomorrow a tree, the next day a stone — and what does it matter to anyone?

PRIEST: Then you feel no remorse?

DYING MAN: Of course not. If there are no punishments or rewards, what joy is there the absence of which to regret, what suffering the presence of which to bemoan?   .

PRIEST: There is nothing more to say. As long as you persist in these thoughts, I cannot help you.

DYING MAN: No, my friend, but you can help many others. Go out into the world and preach not your tired old sophistries but the only law of morality worth observing, the Natural law: "Treat all men as you would have them treat you, and never cause more pain than you yourself would want to suffer." This is the only principle worth preaching, preacher. Renounce your "gods" and your religions; none of them has ever accomplished anything but the stirring of hatred in mankind and the butchery of billions of human beings in the name of one or another "true faith." Forget, too, your idea of another world; this is the only world there is, and if you seek happiness you must find it here.

PRIEST: Happiness? Here? Have you found it here, my son?

DYING MAN: On occasion, yes.

PRIEST: Where?

DYING MAN: In what you would call the "lustful" pleasures. I have idolized them from the moment I knew what they were, and I now hold them dearer than all else.

PRIEST: What a shame, then, that, believing as you do, you wasted your last hours in dialogue with me instead of in the embrace of one of your voluptuaries.

DYING MAN: You are too quick to dismiss me, my friend. The fact of the matter is that there are presently waiting in the next room six girls whose loveliness is a tribute to the splendid Nature who created them. I have reserved them for this, my last moment — and because, despite our differences, you have remained my lifelong friend, I want you to share them with me. I have given you ample opportunity to convince me of your beliefs; now grant me equal opportunity to convince you of mine. Condemn not my "corrupt nature," but instead give Nature the chance to "corrupt" you. If you are unshakeably convinced of the goodness and mercy of your "god," you have nothing to lose — for, after sinning today, you may repent tomorrow. On the other hand, if you entertain any doubts about the principles which you so enthusiastically proclaim, put yourself to the test now; do not wait until you find yourself, like me, on death's threshold, for then it will be too late. Now, let me call the girls ...

NOTE: At this point the dying man rang and the six girls entered. Their attire was provocative, their manner more so; before long the priest surrendered completely to his feelings and for the first time experienced the exquisite pleasures he theretofore had always railed against. Thus ended the dialogue of the priest and the dying man.

—DONATIEN ALPHONSE FRANÇOIS DE SADE
   Vincennes, 1782

THE END

LAST WILL AND TESTAMENT

For the execution of clauses hereinafter set forth, I rely upon the filial piety of my children, wishing that their own children may subsequently be as reliable to them as they have been to me.

Clause I: Wishing to give evidence, as far as my poor powers permit, of my extreme gratitude for the care bestowed upon me and loving friendship afforded me by Marie-Constance Reinelle, I hereby bequeath to her eighty thousand *livres,* said sum to be deducted from the freest and most unattached portion of my legacy.

Clause II: I further bequeath to the aforementioned Madame Reinelle all the furniture, effects, linen, clothing, books or papers which are in my quarters at the time of my demise, with the exception of my father's papers, which shall be handed over to my children.

Clause III: It is expressedly understood that the above bequests do not in any way deprive Madame Reinelle of any rights, claims or levies she may wish to make upon my estate, whatever her reasons may be.

Clause IV: In consideration for the trouble which the execution of this will shall have occasioned him, I bequeath to Mr. Finot, notary at Charenton-Saint-Maurice, a ring valued at twelve hundred *livres.*

Clause V. Finally I forbid the dissection of my body under any pretext whatsoever and desire most stringently that it shall remain in the room in which I died for forty-eight hours in a wooden coffin which shall be nailed shut only after said forty-eight hours have elapsed. The timber merchant, LeNormand, in Versailles, shall be requested to come with his wagon and bring my body to the forest on my property at Malmaison, where without ceremony of any kind it should be buried in the first thicket he sees upon entering the forest. The grave should be dug by the present tenant at Malmaison under the direction of LeNormand, who shall not leave until the burial is complete. He may, if he so desires, permit to accompany him whichever of my friends and/relatives, if any, wish to accord me this final proof of their attachment — he may permit them, I say provided only that the enterprise be conducted without any pomp or ceremony of any sort. Once the grave has been covered over, the ground should be sprinkled with acorns so that all traces of the grave shall disappear from the face of the earth as quickly as I expect all memory of me shall fade out of the minds of all men but those very few who in their goodness have loved me until these last moments of my existence (and memory of whom I carry with me to the very end).

Executed at Charenton-Saint-Maurice in sound mind and sound body this thirtieth day of January in the year one thousand eight hundred and six.

—DONATIEN ALPHONSE FRANÇOIS DE SADE

THE END

BIBLIOGRAPHY

Astorg, Bertrand d', *Introduction au monde de la terreur.* Paris: Editions du Seuil, 1945.

Beauvoir, Simone de, *Must we Burn de Sade?* Translated by Annette Michelson, London: P. Nevill, 1953.

Bessmertny, Alexander, *Der Marquis de Sade.* Berlin: Querschnitt, 1925.

Blanchot, Maurice, *Lautrémont et Sade.* Paris: Editions de Minuit, 1949

Bloch, Iwan, *Marquis de Sade: his life and works,* Translated by James Bruce, New York: Brittany Press, 1948.

Desbordes, Jean, *Le vrai visage du marquis de Sade.* Paris: Editions de la Nouvelle Revue Critique, 1939.

Drummond, Walter, *Philosopher of Evil.* Evanston, Illinois: Regency Books, 1926.

Eulenburg, Albert, *Der Marquis de Sade.* Berlin: Die Zukunft, 1899.

Ginisty, Paul, *Lettres inédites de la Marquise de Sade.* Paris: La Grande Revue, 1899.

Heine, Maurice, *Le Marquis de Sade; texte établis et préfacé par Gilbert Lély.* Paris: Gallimard, 1950.

Klossowski, Pierre, "Le mal et la négation d'autrui dans la philosophie de D.A.F. de Sade," *Recherches philosophiques.* Paris, 1936; Annee 4, pages 268-293.

— *Sade, mon prochain.* Paris: Editions du Seuil, 1947.

Lély, Gilbert, *The Marquis de Sade: a biography.* Translated by Alec Brown. New York: Grove Press, Inc. 1962.

— *Vie du Marquis de Sade; écrite sur les données nouvelles et accompagnée de nombreux documents le plus souvents inédits.* Paris: Gallimard, 1952 & 1957.

Librairie Jean Jacques Pauvert, *L'affaire Sade; compte rendu exact du proces intenté par le Ministre public. Contient notamments les témoignages de Georges Bataille, André Breton, Jean Cocteau, Jean Paulhan et le texte intégral de la plaidorie prononcée par Maitre Maurice Garçon.* Paris: J. J. Pauvert, 1957.

Manganella, Diego, "Ombre nel tempo: la Marchesa di Sade," *Nuova antologia.* Roma: 1922; Ser. 6, V. 218, pages 205-216.

Rickword, Edgell, "Notes for a Study of Sade," *Calendar of Modern Letters.* London, 1926; V. 2, pages 421-431.

Sade, Donatien-Alphonse-François, Marquis de, *Addresse d'un citoyen de Paris, au Roi des Français.* Paris: Girouard, n.d.

— *L'Aigle, Mademoiselle, Lettres publiées pour la première fois sur les manuscrits autographes inédits, avec une préface et un commentaire par Gilbert Lély,* Paris: G. Artigues, 1949.

— *Aline et Valcour, ou le roman philosophique.* Paris: Vve. Girouard, 1795.

— *Amis du Crime, Les.* Paris: Date and Publisher unknown.

— *Bordel de Venise. Nouvelle édition, ornée d'aquarelles scandaleuses de Couperyn.* Venezia: Publisher and date unknown.
Cahiers personnels (1803-1804). *Publiées pour la première fois sur les manuscrits autographes inédits avec une préface et des notes par Gilbert Lély.* Paris: Correa, 1953.

— *120 Journées de Sodome, Les, ou l'Ecole du Libertinage. Edition critique, établier sur le manuscrit original autographe par Maurice Heine.* Paris: Publisher unknown, 1931-1935.

— *Complete Justine, Philosophy in the Bedroom, and Other Writings, The. Compiled and translated by*

*Richard Seaver and Austryn Wainhouse, with intro-
ductions by Jean Paulhan and Maurice Blanchot.* New
York: Grove Press, 1965.

—*Correspondance inédites du M. de Sade; de ses
proches familiers, publiée avec une introduction, des
annales, et des notes par Paul Bourdin.* Paris: Librairie
de France, 1929.

—*Crimes de L'Amour, Les; nouvelles héroiques et tra-
giques, precédé d'une Idée sur les romans.* Paris:
Massé, 1800. (Contient: I: Juliette et Raunai ou la
conspiration d'Amboise; La Double Epreuve, II: Miss
Henriette Stralson ou les Effets de désespoir; Faxe-
lange ou les torts de l'ambition, III: Rodrigue ou la
Tour enchantée; Laurence et Antonio; Ernestine, IV:
Dorgeville ou le Criminel par Vertu; La Comtesse de
Sancerre ou La Rivale de sa fille; Eugenie de Franval.)

—*Crimes de l'Amour, Les.* Brussels: Gay et Douce. 1881.

—*Dialogue entre un pretre et un moribond, publié pour
la premiere fois sur le manuscrit autographe inédit,
avec un avant-propos et des notes par Maurice Heine.*
Paris: Stendhal et Compagnie, 1926.

—*Dialogue between a priest and a dying man, edited
with an introduction and notes by Maurice Heine.*
Translated by Samuel Putnam. Chicago: P. Covici,
1927.

—*Dialogue entre un pretre et un moribund, précédé
d'une étude sur la vie et l'oeuvre de l'auteur par Jean
Bossu.* Herblay (Sein-et-oise: Editions de Mdee
Libre, 195-?

—*Dorci, ou la Bizerrie du Sort, avec une notice sur
l'auteur par Anatole France.* Paris: Charavay Freres,
1881.

—*Ecrits politiques, suivis de, Oxtiern, ou les Malheurs
du Libertinage, drame en trois actes et en prose,* Paris:
J. J. Pauvert, 1957.

—*Emilie de Tourville, ou, La Cruaté Fraternelle.* Paris: J. Fort, 1926.

—*Ernestine, avec dix eaux-fortes de Sylvain Sauvage.* Paris: J. Fort, 1926.

—*Geschicte der Juliette, oder die Wonnen des Lasters, eingeleitet durch eine Biographie des Verfassers.* Bucharest: Cesareano, 1892.

—*Histoire de Juliette, ou les Prosperités du Vice.* Brussels: Publisher Unknown, 1870.

—*Histoire de Justine, ou les Malheurs de la Vertu.* Brussels: Publisher unknown, 1870.

—*Historiettes, Contes et Fabliaux, publiés sur le texte authentique de la Société du roman philosophique, avec un avant-propos par Maurice Heine.* Paris: S. Kra, 1927.

—*Idée sur les Romans, publiée avec préface, notes et documents inédits par Octave Uzanne.* Paris: E. Rouveyre, 1878.

—*Immortalité, Francais!, A l'encore un effort si vous voulez etre républicains et libres de vos opinions.* Paris: Au Chef-lieu de Globe, 1948.

—*Infortunes de la Vertu, Les, avec une introduction par Maurice Heine.* Paris: Fourcade, 1930.

—*Infortunes de la Vertu, Les, avec un notice de Maurice Heine, une bibliographie de Robert Valencay et une introduction par Jean Paulhan.* Paris: Les Editions du Point du Jour, 1946.

—*Justine, ou Les Malheurs de la Vertu, En Hollande, chez les Libraires Associes.* Paris: Girouard, 1791.

—*Justine, ou les Malheurs de la Vertu, A Londres.* Paris: Cazin, 1792.

—*Justine, ou les Malheurs re la Vertu, Troisieme edi-*

tion corrigée et augmentée; Philadelphie. Paris: Publisher unknown, 1794.

—*Justine, ou les Malheurs de la Vertu.* Paris: I. Liseux, 1884.

—*Justine: the Misfortunes of Virtue.* New York: Castle Books, 1964.

—*Leonore et Clementine ou les Tartufes de l'Inquisition, avec une notice bibliographique par Louis Perceau.* Paris: Le Cabinet du Livre, 1930.

—*Morceaux choisis, publiés avec une prologue, une introduction et une poeme, un aid-mémoire biographique, une bibliographique, treize documents hors-texte et deux lettres inédites du marquis, par Gilbert Lely.* Paris: O. Seghers, 1949.

—*Nouvelle Justine, La, ou les Malheurs de la Vertu, suivie de l'Histoire de Juliette sa soeur.* En Hollande. Probably Paris: Publisher unknown, 1797.

—*Oeuvre de M. de Sade, L':* Zoloe, Justine, Juliette, la Philosophie dans le Boudoir, Oxtiern ou les Malheurs du Libertinage. *Pages choisies, introduction, essail bibliographique et notes par Guillaume Apollinaire.* Paris: Bibliotheque des Curieux, 1909.

—*Oeuvres choisies et pages magnistrales de M. de Sade, publiées, commentées et annotées par Maurice Heine.* Paris: Edition du Trianon, 1933.

—*Opus Sadicum, a philosophical romance translated for the first time from the original French, by Isidore Liseux.* Paris: I. Liseux, 1889.

—*Oxtiern, ou les Malheurs du Libertinage.* Sceux: Palimugre, 1948.

—*Pages Curieuses, receullies et préfacées par Balkis. Illustration de Maurice L'Hoir.* Paris: Les Bibliophiles Libertins, 1929.

—*Petition de la Section des Piques aux représentans du peuple francais*. Paris: L'Imprimerie de la Section des Piques, 1793.

—*Petition des sections de Paris a la Convention nationale*. Paris: L'Imprimerie de la Section des Piques, 179-?

—*Philosophie dans le Boudoir, La, ouvrage posthume de l'auteur de Justine*. London: Publisher unknown. 1795.

—*Philosophie dans le Boudoir, La, ou les Instituteurs libertins, dialogues destinés a l'éducation des jeunes demoiselles*. London: Publisher unknown, 1795.

—*Philosophie dans le Boudoir, La, edition intégrale, précedée d'une étude sur le M. de Sade et le sadisme, par Helpey. Edition privée, aux dépens de la Sociéte des etudes sadiques*. Paris: Publisher and date unknown.

—*Projet de petition des Sections de Paris a la Convention nationale*. Paris: L'Imprimerie de la Sections des Piques, date unknown.

—*Sade Quartet, De, four stories from Contes et Fabliaux*, translated from the French by Margaret Crosland. London: Owen, 1963.

—*Section des Piques a ses Freres et amis de la Société de la Liberté et de l'Egalité, a Saintes, département de la Charente-Inférieure*. Paris: L'Imprimerie de la Section des Piques, 1793.

—*Section des Piques; Discours prononcé a la fete decernée par la Section des Piques aux manes de Marat et de la Pelletier*. Paris: L'Imprimerie de la Section des Piques, 1793.

—*Section des Piques; Extraits des Registres des deliberations de l'Assemblée generale et permanente de la Section des Piques*, Paris: L'Imprimerie de la Section des Piques, 1793.

—*Section des piques. Ideé sur le mode de la sanction des Loix, par un citoyen de cette Section*, Paris: L'Imprimerie de la rue Saint-Fiacre no. 2, 1792.

— *Textos escogidos y precedidos por un ensayo el libertino y la revolucion por Jorge Gaitan Duran.* Bogota: Ediciones Mito, 1960.

— *Zoloé.* Paris: Bibliotheque des Curieus, 1926.

— *Zoloé et ses deux acolythes, ou Quelques décades de la vie des trois jolies femmes, histoire veritable du siécle dernier, par un contemporain.* Paris: Publisher and date unknown.

— *Zoloé, précéde d' une etude bio-bigliographique de Fernand · Mitton.* Paris: Librairie Intermediairie du Bibliophile, 1928.

Sarfati, Salvador, *Essai medico-psychologique sur le Marquis de Sade.* Lyon: Bosc Freres & Riou, 1930.

Serra, Dante, *L'avventurosa vita del marchesa de Sade.* Milan: Ceschina, 1950.

Utopistes et le question sexuelle, les; le symbolisme sexuelle; de Sade, non conformiste et libre penseur. (Author unknown) Paris: Edtitions de "L'En Dehors," 1935.

Vincentis, Gioacchino de "Vite in margine. Il marchesa de Sade." *Eloquenza.* Rome: 1934; Sept.-Oct., pages 314-325.

Wilson, Edmund, *Eight essays.* Garden City: Doubleday, 1954. "The Vogue of the Marquis de Sade."

Waldemar, Charles, *Hollenfahrt des Marquis de Sade.* Schmiden: F. Decker, 1963.

THE END